VARSITY Series

by USA TODAY bestselling author

GINGER SCOTT

VARSITY

SERIES

GINGER SCOTT

VARSITY HEARTBREAKER

VARSITY
Heartbreaker

Cover Design by Ginger Scott, Little Miss Write LLC

Photograph by Wander Aguiar Photography

For Autumn.
You so get me.

ONE

It's quite a thing for a girl to watch her future go up in smoke. I suppose I'm being a little melodramatic, given that it's my mom who lost her job, not me. And honestly, I hate how dependent my dreams are on her hard work. I've never found it fair, but there are a lot of things in my life that I consider unjust but nonetheless are sewn into my fabric. What's one more?

My mom worked at Tiny Prints Studio in the mall at the edge of Allensville, our town that's like a pimple on Indianapolis's forehead. We're a nice zit, but economically? Full-on parasite. Most of the department stores closed when the huge outlet mall opened off the turnpike a year ago, and the empty spaces taken up by a charter school, pawn shop and thrift store. Other than the few remaining fast food joints, the photography studio was the only original business still operating in the plaza . . . until Tuesday.

Rent on the studio was too much for the couple who owned the business, and retirement was far more inviting than negotiating. They gave a few of the oldest pieces of equipment to my mom, sold the rest, then rode off for warmer temps in some retirement burb near Phoenix. Meanwhile, Kristen Mabee is once again working the wedding circuit, shooting weddings all over the tri-state area so we can stay in this shitty house full of shitty memories of how my shitty dad decided to walk out on us.

And me?

Well, no more Montessori school, for starters. It's not posh private-school expensive, but it does cost, and public school is nice and free. And anything beyond community college is out of the blueprint too, unless the bowling alley gives me a hundred-dollar-an-hour raise. Not likely. In my immediate future, though, I wish like hell there's a way I could borrow my mom's photo tech to touch up the photo on my ID before my first day back at Public. I seriously miss the warm cocoon of the tiny Montessori school I got to go to for junior year.

"June, it's fine!" My best friend Abby rips the card from my hand and tosses it into her back seat. It's a mess back there so I'll be lucky to find it before school starts on Monday.

"I'm cross-eyed." I sigh, pulling the visor down and flipping on the light for the mirror. Am I always that way or just for this one picture?

"Nobody will ever see it. I promise," she says.

I flip the visor back up, not convinced that I don't actually look that way in real life, and flop back into my seat. Six people have already seen it, and the school photocopied it twice for registration. At this rate, my high school ID photo is in line for billboard placement any day now.

"You promise I'm going to know people at this party?" I'm not great with socializing. It was part of the appeal of going to a small school for the last year. The closer we get to the D'Angelo house, the more ill-fitting my T-shirt feels. I swear it shrank in the wash. I don't buy belly shirts, but I see my flesh when I raise my arms up halfway. And the top of my jeans is folding in on itself. It makes the zipper part bulge like I'm some jock with a huge cup. I squirm in my seat and shimmy the tight black pants down my hips while simultaneously tugging the black and white striped T-shirt toward my waist.

Abby glances at me and laughs.

"You're being nuts. You look great. And it's everyone you remember from sophomore year. It'll be like you never left." She pulls into a free space at the side of the road about four houses down from the twins' house. Cars line up both sides of the street, and we can hear the music thumping the moment Abby opens the driver's side door.

"I don't really *like* everyone from sophomore year. And I did leave for a reason." Perspiration builds at my neck despite the coolness of the late summer air.

"You left because you thought people didn't like you." She actually rolls her eyes when she says it, which pisses me off a little. She makes it seem so insignificant. She's always thought most of it was in my head, but a few things were plainly undeniable. The dog poop left on the hood of my car about a dozen times when it was parked at school was just the tip of the iceberg.

"Abby, someone literally picked my car up and moved it into the middle of the drainage area by the school. Being a dick like that takes a coordinated effort. That's a bit of a sign."

"Yeah, I know. But people at this school are just dicks, like, unilaterally. To everyone." She nods in halfhearted acknowledgement, flipping her own mirror down to touch up the red on her lips. She turns to me and holds out the gloss. I recoil and she shrugs. Abby is pin-up beautiful. Her hair is this caramel color that lightens every summer, and her skin is a rich, cocoa brown. She got curves in eighth grade, and her skin is expensive and flawless. Her mom got her into modeling when she was young, and she's been landing some big print ads lately. At a thousand dollars a gig, the money in her college account has grown to Ivy League proportions over the years. I've always been her alt-friend with near-black hair that I sometimes wear in braids on either side of my head because it's literally the only hair style I know how to do. My friend has always said she'd trade me her hair and curves in a heartbeat for my green eyes. I wish trades like that were a thing. Done deal. Enjoy the lanky body with knobby knees and size A cups.

"Look, everyone has gotten older," she begins, flipping her mirror closed and flicking her long-nailed fingertips toward my door handle in a gesture that urges me to get out. My hand grips the handle, but I can't seem to bring myself to open the door. "You're living in the past too much. People don't care about pranks and childish things like grudges or whatever."

"You mean bullying," I correct. A grudge would mean I did something wrong, and I would know *who* I wronged. I've never known any of it. It's just these little things that always came out of nowhere and built up. And yeah, maybe Abby is right—our school is full of immature pranksters. I've seen others get hit with the fallout, too. But for me, it wore me down.

"Fine, *bullying*. All I'm saying, June, is we're going to be eighteen this year—all of us. This is it, the last moments of unabandoned freedom and youth! We're supposed to party and stay out late and maybe even—*gasp!*—fail a class that doesn't count on our transcripts. And there are so many boys we need to kiss! I *know* you wanna kiss boys at parties, June."

I hate that I blush when she teases me. I get out of the car just to escape her conversation, but it only delays the inevitable. She's going to bring this all back to Lucas Fuller. It always comes back to him.

I've been in love with my neighbor since the day he moved in at the start of our sixth-grade year. We were instant friends, though admittedly, my attraction to him was heavily dimples and blue-eye driven at first. Our moms took turns with school carpool duties. We swam together in the same summer league. We wasted away afternoons licking sticky grape-flavored popsicle juice from our arms while we sat in the sun on the roof of the old Buick my dad stored in our back yard. Technically, Lucas Fuller was my first kiss—it was an eighth grade dare in the back of a field trip bus. Our lips were puckered, there was zero tongue, and our eyes were wide open. Even after that awkward kiss, not a single day passed without us either hanging out or texting each other good night. I made my mom drive me two hours away once to watch his freshman football game, and I was always the one yelling the loudest for his home ones.

Mostly—more than anything—Lucas Fuller was my person. I'm shy, painfully so, but never around him. We had a pact that we would never lie, and there would be zero secrets.

Now, that's all that's left.

The summer after our freshman year, it all just stopped. Everything—no rides, no glances in my direction, no acknowledgement of my existence. I called and texted and left so many unanswered messages. When I went to his house, nobody opened the door, even when I knew they all were home. My parents divorced around then, and my grandmother moved in because she got too sick to live on her own. My mom worked and took care of her, and when she couldn't, I did. Hospice came and went, my grandmother's belongings were set out in our driveway for people to pick through so we could collect quarters and dimes to piece together enough to cover her last few expenses. My world was falling apart, and my best friend, the one person who swore we would never keep secrets from each other, was both right next door and a million miles away. That's when Abby and I got closer. She'd been through a lot of the same things I was going through, and she's the kind of person who insists on helping.

Dragging me out to this party, though? It doesn't feel much like help. It's more of the torture variety.

"And would you look at that. It's a black Nissan pickup truck with . . . oh! FULLER1 license plates!" Abby points in the direction of an oversized tire as if I don't know it's Lucas's truck she's talking about.

"He's at every party, Abs. And no, I'm not going to talk to him. It's not like he doesn't know where to find me. If he wanted to talk, we would have by now." I look down at my feet while I push my fists into my pockets and shuffle along the blacktop. After a few steps, I run into my friend's waiting palms as she grips me by the shoulders and shakes me until I meet her gaze.

"Maybe you should just finally move on and spend tonight talking to someone—hell, *anyone*—else." Abby's eyes plead with mine for a non-verbal agreement that I'll try to be a normal high school senior for just one night.

"You're someone else. I talk to you," I quip. I'm only partly teasing.

Abby shoves off me and walks backward a few steps, giving me a challenging stare before spinning on her heel.

"I meant someone with a penis. And no, before you make another joke, I do not have a secret dick tucked away in my pants." Her pace picks up, bringing us closer to the front door of the party house. I laugh a little, silently, because her penis joke was funny, but by the time her hand is firmly on the D'Angelos' doorknob, my amusement has shifted to a need to vomit.

"Ready?" she asks.

"No." Her mouth twists to say "tough shit," and with one push, we're inside.

Competing music blasts from two separate rooms, the hard thump of indie punk trying to drown out rib-shaking hip hop beats. Faces I don't really recognize nod at Abby then me as we walk through the crowded living room toward the kitchen area. Two girls face each other over a coffee table littered with beer cans and vape pens, yelling about who is disrespecting whom. The overwhelming cacophony ratchets up my urge to run. Abby must sense it because she grabs my hand and tugs me close, keeping me right at her side until we get to the open doorway that leads to the back yard.

"Why is this fun again?" I say close to her ear. I'm still not sure she can hear me.

She bends down and flips open a red cooler filled with freezing water and melting ice. She fishes her hand around, coming up with two beers.

"Here. You're drinking one," she says, pulling back the tab then pressing the lip of the can to my mouth as if I'm a baby needing to be fed. I shake my head and step back, taking the can from her hand.

"I don't like beer."

"You've never tried beer," she retorts.

Our mini staring competition lasts about two seconds before I give in and take a small sip. Her mouth ticks up with satisfaction, but when she tips her head back to take a drink from her own beer, I spill a little of mine on the rocks and let my mouth sour. Beer is gross.

"Oh, my God, is that—? No. It couldn't be!" I recognize Tory D'Angelo's voice without having to turn and face him. His presence motivates me to take another drink of my beer; I suddenly regret pouring so much out.

"June Mabee!" He snakes his hands around my hips as he steps in behind me. I spit out what's left in my mouth and move away from him with a jerk of my elbow. We aren't close. In fact, the only real interaction he and I have had was when I let him copy my science quiz answers during freshman science. I hate myself for letting peer pressure work on me. I should have let the asshole fail.

"Aww, maybe Mabee, what's wrong?" He's drunk, which amps up his assholeness a little. He's been teasing me about my last name since junior high. So clever, saying it twice.

"You were right, Abby. Everyone's grown up so much," I say, giving my friend an icy glare. Her dry smile puckers on one side but she doesn't argue with my reasoning. Kinda hard with Tory still hovering around us, breaking all kinds of personal space rules. Most girls let him get away with it because, in terms of good looks? He's damn near perfection. While he's smug about it, his twin brother Hayden is nearly oblivious to the power he could have at his fingertips. Bronzed skin, chiseled jawlines, light brown hair that somehow makes them both look like they just got in from a jog along the beach—the D'Angelo boys are Calvin Klein models in the making.

"Don't you have some freshman to hit on?" Bless Abby's confidence. One of the best perks of our friendship is her ability to say those things I wish I could.

"Still sore that I wouldn't let you suck my dick this summer, Abs?" He actually pushes his tongue in his cheek to accentuate his crass reply. What a fool. She's going to burn him to the ground.

"Isn't it more like . . ." My friend takes a thin pretzel stick from a bowl on the patio table nearby and pinches it between her thumb and finger, holding it a few inches away from Tory's face. His eyes haze and his jaw twitches. Even though it's only the three of us here to witness her rip on him, the joke breaks through and embarrasses him. I wish I could trade her my green eyes for *that skill* right there.

"Come on, June. Looks like the cool kids are all over there," my friend says. She purposely ignores the raging bull she leaves standing alone and weaves our hands together to drag me along the deck.

"He's probably going to remember tonight all wrong and think I'm the one who said all that, you know." I step on a wooden beam and lift myself to sit on the deck's guardrail. Abby does the same, but swings one leg over so she straddles it facing me.

"Good. Then you'll have a reputation of not putting up with shit from douchebags," she says, pulling her phone from the small purse she's wearing across her body. She holds it up before I can protest and snaps my photo.

"Why? Why do you always do that? You must have an endless collection of me making dumb-as-hell faces," I protest. I start to laugh a little, too.

"If it didn't work on your foul moods so well, I wouldn't do it." She takes one more shot before tucking the phone into the zipper pouch of her bag.

That she has hundreds of those pics scratches at me a little. It means I've been in a foul mood hundreds of times. I had to come back to Public because we couldn't afford the Montessori school anymore, so maybe it means I get to reinvent myself a little. Maybe Abby is a little right in saying that we are all getting older—none of us are the same people we were two years ago. *I'm* not the same. At least, I don't have to be.

"I'm sorry." I half shout the words to my friend because the music is still making it hard to hear. I'm probably not going to be able to apologize to her more than this one time, so I have to make sure she hears it.

Her mouth curves slowly and she flits her thick black lashes at me before leaning forward enough to push gently at my shoulder.

"Aww, June. You're getting all mushy."

I squeeze my eyes shut in playful shame.

"Apology accepted. I'm not sure what you're apologizing for, but I'll save it up and cash it in when I feel like it," she says.

"Okay." I laugh, opening my eyes as my friend tips her head back and drinks the rest of her beer. When she's done, she leans forward again, reaching for my can to test the weight. It's still nearly half full, even with the portion I dumped, so I give it to her reluctantly.

Her eyes haze with suspicion.

"One of us is driving home. Let it be me, okay? I'm not a big beer girl anyhow." I hold her stare as we each grasp the cup between us. She hasn't fully committed yet so I don't let go.

"Abby, I promise. I'm going to stay, and I'll have fun, just not with the beer, okay?"

Her eyes squint a little more. She's still not buying it.

"How about this? Whatever they're doing in there, on the sofas"—some stupid game I would normally make fun of—"you take my beer and I'll go play that game." I regret my offer the second the cup leaves my grip. She gulps nearly half of it down before wiping her chin along her forearm and kicking her leg over the beam to stand on the deck.

Shit. We're going to play a party game.

"Well, all right then," she says, threading our fingers together and tugging me forward until I lose the balance battle and fall to my feet.

Not wanting to look as though I'm being dragged into this—even though I am—I loop my arm around my friend's and smile at her. She isn't convinced. She tosses her head back in laughter, but lets me save face while we make our way inside. At the huge sectional sofa , people are tossing dice on a giant trunk-style coffee table and picking small papers out of a bowl depending on the number they roll. Abby and I kneel on the floor behind a few of the others.

"I'm not next. You're next!" One of the many faces I don't know but recognize shoves playfully at another vaguely familiar girl. In their fit of nervous giggling, the one holding the dice glances in my direction.

"New girl! Your turn." Bile shoots up my throat and burns.

"Oh, no." I hold up a palm and shake my head as if refusing hors d'oeurves.

"She's being shy. She'll play. What's the game?" Abby takes the dice and plops them in my palm, which she has to pry open after lifting my fist from the carpet.

I make wide eyes at her while I hold my breath, but she shakes me off.

"You promised," she says, holding up the rest of her beer and tipping it back with an "*ahh.*"

I inhale deeply while the girl who volunteered me explains the rules. "You roll a number and pick out that many dares."

"So, I could have to do twelve dares?" I ask this as though I'm really going to roll these dice.

"Oh, my God, no! You pick them and then the last person who went gets to pick which one you do. Like, Naomi made me walk to the kitchen and back in her bra!"

This game seems incredibly complex for what it really is: Truth or dare, sans the truth part. I'd like to make a motion that we add the truth part back in, but that's because I'm painfully boring.

"So, who gets to pick my dare?" I'm still acting as if I'm really planning to play.

"I do." I recognize the voice without turning around. Of all of the faces I don't recognize here, that voice belongs to one I know I will. For as long as I have loved Lucas Fuller, Ava Pryor has hated me. I'd blame her for all the lame pranks I endured sophomore year, but overt bullying isn't her style. She's more of the "burn you with a glare" kinda girl, and that glare has this amazing power to make a person feel insignificant with a bat of her lashes.

I glance over my shoulder and that stare is ready and waiting to zap my ego—what little there is of it—to shit.

"Lola went last," the girl I've identified as Naomi says.

"That's because I had to refill my beer. Scoot." Ava flits her fingers and the girls slide apart to make space for her on the center of the couch. She steps between Abby and me on her way to sit down.

"I'm not doing this," I mumble to my friend. She's already taken the dice from me, though, and thrown them on the table.

"It's time to stand up and show some balls." I meet her eyes, trying to plead my way out of this, silently begging her to take my turn, but with the slight cock of her chin I can tell she's going to make me walk through this fire.

"Four," Ava says, a tinge of disappointment in her tone that I rolled such a low number.

"Okay, so I just . . ." I reach toward the bowl and Ava taps it toward me with the toe of her white canvas shoe.

I pull it toward me and search the contents, hoping to find clues in the poorly folded strips of paper, but it's no use. It doesn't matter how deep I dig into the plastic snack bowl. I pick out four from the top of the heap and toss them on the table as I sit back on my heels.

"Let's see," Ava says, leaning forward and rubbing her palms. I'm sweating watching her meticulously unfold the first paper and drag her gaze along the scribbled line. She's twirling a lock of her white-blonde hair around her finger while her mouth moves slightly with the words. I stare intently at her face, trying to read her lips. She stops and flits her thick black fake lashes up to stare at me from underneath. Her mouth curves up on one side.

"This one." She tosses it on the table, but before I can grab it, Abby does.

"You didn't read them all yet," my friend says, looking at the paper and chuckling lightly.

"Don't need to. That one's the winner." Ava leans back on the oversized sofa cushion and folds her arms over her chest while crossing her legs.

"You afraid of the dark? Spiders?" Abby flicks the paper toward me with her index finger. I pick it up and read.

SPEND FIVE MINUTES IN THE GARAGE IN THE DARK

"Uh, not really . . . I guess." I feel as if there's probably a trick so I'm not going to boast confidently. There's a catch. I know there is.

"Good, then the time should just fly right by," Ava says, both sides of her mouth curved into an ominous grin. She glances down the darkened hallway behind me, toward what I assume is the garage door.

"Now?" *That sounded stupid. Of course now.*

"Uh huh," she says, flitting her fingers at me with the same nonchalance she had when she forced the girls to give up their seats. Ava is a stereotype. That stereotype is bitch.

"All right," I say through a sigh. I get to my feet and tug up my jeans a little, my shirt now feeling like a goddamn halter.

"Atta girl," Abby says, slapping my ass just before I make my way to the garage. Naomi is quick on my heels, probably to lock the door behind me. Do any of them realize I can hit the button inside?

The escape plan zips through my mind just as I open the door, but then it's quickly replaced with panic and dread so toxic that my knees buckle a little. Naomi pushes me inside and slams the door shut. The lock clicks behind me, and Lucas meets my stare. He's sitting on a folding chair with his phone in his palm.

"Oh, fuck me." Disdain slips from his mouth the moment everything goes black. *This* was the catch. Five minutes in the dark, locked in the garage, but not alone.

With Lucas Fuller.

I spin around and flatten my palms on the wall, feeling in search of a switch or the garage door opener. Something stabs at the side of my palm as I slide it closer to the door.

"Shit!" I mutter under my breath and feel along my skin. It's damp. I cut myself on something. My phone is in my back pocket, so I take it out awkwardly with the opposite hand; it slips from my grip and bounces at my feet. I want to cry. I also want to punch things.

I'm mid-squat when the glow of a phone light brightens the ground a few feet in front of me. I glance up and squint at the flash from Lucas's phone.

"Thanks," I say. I feel humbled, and mortified. My phone is just underneath the front end of one of the cars. Lowering myself, I reach out until my hand lands on it to drag it closer. The garage goes dark again.

Tapping on my phone with the hope it still works, I rest back on my legs, resigned to this pathetic position for the remaining four minutes I'm stuck here. The cracks on my phone screen take up most of the surface, and one of the corners is badly chipped. With my luck, I'm sure I'll find a way to prick my finger on it . . . *again.*

The metal chair Lucas was sitting in screeches along the floor, so I glance up to see whether I can see him. I can make out his form. His long arms stretch upward, and I bet if he jumped just a little, his fingertips would graze the ceiling. He's wearing a light T-shirt and jeans, a flannel tied around his waist. It's too dark with only my phone light to tell whether he's looking at me or not, and I'm not sure which I prefer.

As his feet slide closer, I let my body relax into a sitting position, legs folded around each other like a pretzel. I cup my broken phone in my lap and graze my fingertips along the screen to send shouty-cap swears to Abby. The dome light from the car flickers on at my right, and from my periphery, I see Lucas lean inside. He taps a button near the rearview mirror and the garage door lifts.

I stand to brush dust from my knees and ass, and flip my hair back just in time to come face-to-face with the source of that sharp pain I sometimes feel when I look out my bedroom window. Those blue eyes still glow like sapphires, even in the faintest of light, but the boyish dimples have given way to harsh angles and a set jaw framing emotionless lips. Lucas has always been three or four inches taller than me, but that difference feels even greater as he stares down at me.

"I didn't know you were in here." Fuck, I haven't spoken to him in two years and the first words I say are a pathetic apology for being in a garage at the same time. I roll my shoulders and force myself to stand straighter—taller. His head cocks to the side ever so slightly and he lifts his hand, holding the garage door opener out for me to take. I do, and I hate that I do. This is not how this conversation between us was supposed to go. *He* was supposed to apologize, not me. And he should be giving me flowers, not some taped-together garage clicker from one of his asshole friend's cars.

"Tell Ava she's a dick." He doesn't stick around to wait for my response, turning and taking long strides out of the garage with his hands shoved in his pockets and his pace evident of just how much he wants to get away from me.

There's a little more than a minute left on my time in here, assuming those assholes plan on sticking with their own dumb rule. By the time Lucas disappears around the bushes at the end of the long driveway, I've made up my mind to take his last bit of advice. With the garage remote in my hand, I leave the same way Lucas did and reenter the house through the front door, elbowing through the people gathered in the front room. I toss the opener into the bowl of paper dares, and the gossip fest that's probably going down on the sofa ceases immediately. I feel my best friend's eyes on me without having to look. My focus is set on the ice princess leaning forward and folding her hands on her pushed-together knees like she's some sort of lady.

"You're a dick, Ava." I hold her stare for a breath, just long enough for her to understand that I mean it, and I'm not afraid of her opinion of me anymore. I don't know where the chip on her shoulder came from, but I didn't put it there. If she wants to keep it, that's on her.

I glance down to where my friend is still sitting on the floor, and the approving grin that has spread across her entire face tells me two things: one, I've just entertained the shit out of her; and two, she's giving me a gold star for the night.

"This game is juvenile. Next time, I'll bring the games to the party, ladies, and we'll have some *real* fun." Abby winks at Ava as she gets to her feet and walks right through the middle of the group of girls still huddled around the scene. She reaches into her pocket and hands me her keys, then links our arms together as we turn our backs on only the first dose of drama we're bound to see this year.

I don't say a word and she doesn't ask questions as our feet hit the blacktop and we cut through the rows of cars lining the street. I notice that Lucas's truck is still here about a second before his headlights flick on and the engine roars to life.

"Looks like someone else thought that party was pretty lame, too," my friend says. And because she's my rock, and because I don't lie to her, I tell her everything.

"He was in the garage. And he's a dick, too." I save that last part until we're walking right next to his unrolled window. I glance his way after I say it, and our eyes meet for a brief moment. When Abby and I get another full car length away, his tires peel out as he takes off.

"Well, if this ain't a new June Mabee," she says, swaying her hip into me. I gurgle out a faint laugh and smile with tight lips. My smile falls as soon as our arms part and my friend walks to the passenger side of her car.

Sure, I'm proud of what I did. Doesn't mean I don't wish like hell that none of it happened.

TWO

I guess I made a name for myself, beyond "that girl who lives next to the Fullers." That's what I'm usually called, especially by the girls who had crushes on Lucas in junior high and our freshman year. A few times, his groupies have tried to befriend me just to worm their way into a sleepover so they can stare at him through my window.

Joke's always on them. I don't have sleepovers, except with Abby, and she doesn't count because she's like family. That's my mom's rule. She's funny about having strangers in the house. Even more so since my dad left. I think maybe she's become really distrustful. I guess I have, too.

I wonder how many sleepover requests I'll get now that I'm "the girl who told off Ava Pryor." Maybe it was a deterrent for others. Though, judging by the fact I'm now walking through the halls of Public with not just one, but *three* other people, I can't deny that calling Ava a dick had some sort of quantum effect.

"So, where did you move here from?" Naomi, my first friend from the party, asks.

Abby laughs hard enough to spit out her iced latte. Her mom runs a coffee shop so we start every morning there. Even when I went to a different school, we both got up thirty minutes early to have our coffee talk time.

"You've known each other since fourth grade, when *you* moved here, Naomi," Abby says. She and I glance at each other with crooked smiles while Naomi literally stops in her tracks.

"We had the same homeroom freshman year," I add through a crooked smile. I shrug on the outside, but the truth is I only figured that out last night when I looked them both up in my freshman yearbook.

"I recognized her," Lola brags, tipping her head back as she pours the crumbs from her granola packet into her mouth. It's hard to tell whether she's bluffing or not. Lola has a certain cockiness about her, an appealing kind. I don't know her well enough yet, but when I do, I'll tell her she looks just like the girl from *Clueless*.

"I have to check in with the office," I announce at the sound of the first bell. I accept the awkward side-hug-squeeze from Abby. She's pushing the envelope today on the dress code. It's not so much the length of her shorts, but rather the words on her shirt. I'm pretty sure the asterisk filling in for the U between the F and CK isn't going to slide by.

"We all have first lunch, so I'll grab a table," Naomi shouts over the rush of people between us. She's maybe five-one, but she makes up for her small size with large volume.

Slightly bolstered by the fact I've somehow started my final year of high school with actual lunch plans rather than aimlessly wandering rows of tables with my tray, I push through the door without really noticing the body coming at it from the opposite side. If it weren't a glass door, I might have pushed harder, but seeing the familiar deep blue wool and white leather sleeves of Lucas's letterman jacket is like getting hit with a flashing red stop sign shrouded by flares.

"Sorry." Damn it. Back to apologies.

I step back to let him through, but to my surprise, he does the same. I catch the short twitch his mouth makes in amusement. It wasn't quite a laugh, but it was definitely light years from the scowl I got last night.

Not wanting him to change his mind, I push the glass forward and step through. He reaches to take the door's weight just as my hand lets go, and his fingertips run along the tops of my knuckles. It's nothing more than an accident, and I see the slight recoil in his arm when it happens. The effect on me, though, is exactly the opposite. I glow—flush with the shot of adrenaline and long-lost affection. I would swear he cut me, the leftover feeling along my hand is so strong.

"June!" Maggie Williams went to high school with my mom. Not here, ironically, but in Fort Wayne. Her and Mom are more Facebook friends than *real* friends, but Maggie's always been nice. And it's good to have a familiar face in the front office.

"Lucas! Wait!" she shouts, just before the glass door closes. I turn quickly to see whether he heard, hoping he escapes without her making some sort of embarrassing connection, like reminding him who I am even though we're neighbors. But the good student and well-mannered guy that Lucas is wins the battle and he turns, cracking the doorway open to hear her out.

"Can you take June here to your first hour? She's in your class."

I'm pretty sure Lucas and I both vomit a little. There's definitely a pregnant pause. The air is stagnant long enough for Maggie to blink twice with irritation and shake the paper she holds out for me to take. That little movement triggers my response, and I take my schedule from her hand.

"Sure," Lucas says, flashing his classic tight-lipped smile. I know him well enough to recognize that's the one he gives when he's playing nice. He made that face when Tory D'Angelo won MVP at the eighth grade football banquet, and he made it again when his parents told him they were spending New Year's three years ago camping at Yosemite, just the three of them. Those lips are air-tight right now, and that bend is going to break even the moment we step back into the hallway.

"Let me know if you need anything today, 'kay, hon?" Maggie's already answering the attendance line, pen in hand and phone propped on her shoulder. Not that I could ask her to rewind life a hair or two and not mention the idea of Lucas showing me anywhere, but maybe if she weren't swamped I could make up another question or two to stall and let him get away.

I suppose he's doing a fine job of running away as it is, though. For every step he takes, I have to make two. I'm not that much shorter, so I know he's pushing it. Our first hour is physics, the farthest building on campus, which means "I'll be sweaty and breathless by the time my ass finds a seat in there."

I said that part out loud. *Shit.*

"Not my problem," Lucas says over his shoulder. His arms pump as if he's a speed walker. He pushes open the double doors of the A building and flings them open enough to give me a chance to zip through behind him. He was probably rooting for them to close on my shoulders. All I can focus on are his leather sleeves and that it's a little warm, now that we're outside.

"You know, it's like eighty, and humid," I say, somehow halting my words before tacking on a bit about how stupid his jacket is. I also think he's cute in it, which is fucking up my head right now. I'm both physically and emotionally hot, and I want to take it out on that jacket and the ego it represents. I've never even seen him play in a varsity game.

He doesn't respond, and that's probably for the best. Also, either I'm getting faster or he's slowing down because the gap between us is tightening. Students rush past us, probably taking up all of the seats in our class, which is still a good four hundred yards away. I'm almost in sync with his steps when he turns and stops in the middle of the walkway.

"We don't have to do this, you know." He points at me then to himself. I have no idea what he means, and my expression must say so because he explains. "Pretend we have some bond or shit. You have your life, I have mine that I've built here. Just go to class, hang out with your friend, get your straight A's or whatever."

"Friends," I cut in.

He shrugs and wrinkles his brow, annoyed.

"You said I should hang out with my *friend,* but I have *friends,* Lucas." *You used to be one of them.*

"Sure. Just . . ." He pauses, his jaw stiffening the way it does when he's frustrated. So many of his nuances are etched in my memory bank. With a slight shake to his head, he glances up and takes a deep breath, letting his shoulders quickly lift and fall. His gaze leaves the sky and lands back on me. "I'm just saying, it's not like we really know each other now. That's all."

He turns and continues down the path, but I don't bother to keep up. I let him get several feet ahead, far enough that the doors to the science building close behind him while I have many steps to go. I let him go in case I have to cry, but really, I'm just pissed. The clenched sensation in my gut makes me want to scream. My hand flattens along the bar for the double doors, but I stop before pushing and check my reflection in the tinted glass. I don't want to look the way I feel. While I don't really *know* people here very well, they know enough about me to put together the crush I once had on the guy who just walked into Physics. I'm already chasing him in there. I don't need to look upset about it, too.

With one heavy exhale, I push the right door open and slip quietly inside. The bells have sounded and the classroom doors are closed. I'm holding this golden late pass of a new student's schedule, though, so I can take my time. My steps are measured, a fraction of what they were outside. Might as well also take advantage of this time to cool down. I let Abby talk me into wearing my hair down straight. It feels like a damp warm blanket on my back and shoulders, though, and I'm pretty sure my flat iron work to smooth out the kinks has all been undone. My hair isn't curly, but it's far from perfectly straight. It's more tousled without the supermodel image that word conjures.

The class door flies open easily but I manage to grab the handle before it flings into the wall. My entry still catches most everyone's attention. I focus on the teacher, an older man wearing a shirt like my dad owned—collared and polo-style with a single breast pocket. Today's color is orange. *Vivid* orange. I wonder what the rest of his closet looks like.

"I'm sorry. I'm new, and I had to stop at the office," I explain, diffusing the disgruntled look forming on his face. He wasn't here my freshman year. I knew all the teachers, despite only knowing maybe six students.

"Oh, yes! Miss Mabee." A few snickers are poorly masked by fake coughs. People my age are so amused by alliteration. He takes my paper and tips his glasses forward on his nose. He has a thin comb over, and the gel he used to swipe the hairs from right to left is still fresh. It glistens.

"I hope you're all right with a front-row seat," he says, bending at the edge of his desk to sign my form. He points with the tip of his pen to the only open seat in the classroom. I've already noticed it though, and the six-foot-something pissed-off jock sitting behind it.

"Here you go," the teacher says, handing back my paper. I keep my focus on the teacher's name on the page rather than the desk I'm sliding into. He didn't say it when I walked in, so the pronunciation is still a mystery to me—*Slatvka.*

Situated in my chair, I lean forward, elbows on the small desktop so my hair doesn't tangle itself with anything Lucas-related behind me. I'm so obsessed with that fear that I reach behind my neck and sweep it over my right shoulder, entwining it with my mechanical pencil and flinging it around like a rogue swing set.

"Oh, my God," I whisper just as the pencil falls loose and onto the floor, bouncing backward of course. I run my fingers through my now-tangled hair, flattening it over my shoulder before I lean to the side and slouch in my seat in an attempt to reach my pencil. Our teacher is writing a list of the things we need to purchase for class on the board, and he's about to hand out the syllabus, which means I have about three more seconds before he turns around and spots my contortionist act. The rest of the class is already privy to this spectacular view. I'm nearly flat in my seat, head practically resting on Lucas's desktop behind me while my hand flails about, fingers stretching and pinching desperately at the floor but coming up with nothing but air.

Lucas groans and taps on the top of my head with a flick of his finger.

"Sit up," he says, leaning to his right while I do, and easily picking up my pencil. I twist just enough to glance at him sideways, taking the pencil in my hand. He doesn't let go right away, holding on for an extra two or three seconds to make sure I feel the burn of everyone staring at me. It irritates me, and the *thank you* I was preparing to say gets swapped out for an entirely different response.

"You could have picked it up sooner." I give my best glower, and he lets go of the tip, pulling the eraser out and tossing it back on the floor where it bounces a good four or five feet away. I breathe out a faint laugh then look back at him before turning around for the final time—*ever!*

"Good thing I don't make mistakes," I say, holding his gaze for a beat then turning to greet Mr. Slatvka just in time to take the syllabus from him.

I busy myself copying down the list of items that I plan to get tonight at the office supply store, feeling pleased with myself for how I handled that little interaction. When our teacher makes it to the back of the classroom, Lucas leans forward on his elbows and brings his mouth close enough to my neck that I feel the tickle of his warm breath.

"June," he says, breathing out my name. Both the sound and the feel of it along my skin force me to stop writing and pay attention to the prickle of every hair on my body. I blink at the words typed on my paper. "You are so far from perfect, you have no clue."

His weight shifts against the back of my seat where his desktop touches my chair, and I shake with the blunt force of his shoe on the leg of my chair as he rests it there, pushing me forward an inch or two.

This isn't one of those moments when I don't have a response. I've got one. It just wouldn't put him in his place. I say it in my head instead of giving him the satisfaction.

I know exactly how imperfect I am.

THREE

The day just gets better and better. And by better, I mean complete nosedive into a shit pool.

I had the option of getting out of school early this year. I earned enough credits, and none of the last hour electives appealed to me. I hate cooking, so culinary was out. I've already taken photography—*and* I live with a photographer—and the thought of being in the weight room with half of the football team trying to *bulk up* sounded like torture. But Abby has to be here for the full day, and she begged.

She begged, and I caved.

I figured being a teacher's assistant for the last hour would be a cake walk, and I'd be able to sit in the back of the class and fly through my homework in an hour. I'm assigned to a freshman algebra class, so the only work I'll have to help with is making copies and handing out paper since student grading isn't allowed. It looked promising, until Tory was camped out in Mr. Newsome's chair when I walked in. He's Mr. Newsome's favorite, because Tory D'Angelo and his brother Hayden are the one-two punch on Public's basketball team, and Mr. Newsome is their coach. I could have been assigned to any classroom for this hour, and somehow, I'm doubling up with him.

"Why the glum look, Mabee?" Tory twists side to side in the office chair a few feet away from me. I've been pretending to ignore his existence while I review the stack of class rules and instructions I collected today, and jot down lists of other teachers I can potentially assist.

"No glum look. Just relishing how comfortable this box is, and what a gentleman you are," I say without peeling my eyes from my work. I'm sitting on a large storage bin filled with donated school supplies like note cards, handwipes and tissues. This class is full and there are no extra chairs. Tory hasn't moved from his seat—too busy playing solitaire on the teacher's laptop.

"Oh, I'm a gentleman. I offered to share." He swivels so his knees are square with me then pats his thigh.

"I'm not sitting on your lap," I say, my tone flat and head tilted. I've twisted my hair into a knot and poked two pencils through it to hold it in place. It's slipping a little, so tiny hairs stick out in all directions and tickle my face. I pull the pencils free to retwist.

"You should leave it down," Tory says. Ignoring him, I continue to twist, holding one pencil in my hand and one gripped by my teeth.

"I'm serious," he continues. I give in with a sideways look as I poke one pencil through my attempt at a bun; once I feel it's secure, I take the pencil from my mouth and maneuver it around my head.

"I'm waiting for the misogynistic joke that usually follows everything you've ever said to me." I wiggle the second pencil until everything feels secure then let my hands fall flat to my lap, my focus still on Tory.

A few seconds pass without him saying a word, and while I partly brace myself for a doozy of a comeback, a piece of me also feels guilty for laying into him after a compliment. He eventually shrugs and turns back to the computer, clicking away at card graphics while wearing a flat line on his mouth.

"June, can I get a hand with these?" Mr. Newsome asks. Delighted to leave the close quarters with Tory, I unfurl my legs and stretch to a stand as I take a stack of stapled papers from the teacher. Rather than passing several at a time up the rows, I drop one at every desk, mostly to stretch the activity out a little longer.

There are a few packets left when I get to the last student, so I hold them up to signal I'm done. Mr. Newsome nods for me to leave them on his desk, and I head back to my box-seat only to find it occupied by Tory. The desk chair is turned to the side for easy access, and my papers are stacked in front of the laptop. The asshole makes me grin a little and I glance down at where he's slouched on the box, back against the wall, as I pass by. He looks up from his phone for a hint and our eyes meet.

"Yeah, yeah. Don't say I never gave you nothin'," he says with an uneven smile and shift of his eyes. His thumb scrolls through a series of Instagram images like he's playing roulette, and my mouth forms the shape to utter "thank you" back to him. Before the words come out, though, he stops on a picture of a woman in barely-there lingerie, and I decide to just be smug about this. Might as well let this class period end with his nice gesture rather than open an opportunity for him to show me all of his sordid follows on social media.

The bell is mid-ring by the time Tory is up from the box and headed to the door. He holds out a fist to pound with Mr. Newsome, who suggests he only go half-speed in football practice and save yourself for the sport that really matters.

Tory laughs quietly and nods, leaving the room without looking back to where he left me the comfortable seat. I wait for everyone to clear out so I can pitch an idea to Mr. Newsome, but as the last few students leave, Lucas slips in and I practically sprint back to the chair. Pulling the pencils from my makeshift bun, I let my hair fall to my left side to shade my face and provide camouflage.

"You have a sec? I need help on something, and I'm not sure how to handle it." It's a different tone from Lucas than I've been hearing; this one is more like the boy I grew up with. There's an uncertainty to it, and respect. Our interactions have been far from courteous.

"Sure, you wanna step outside?" I tense at Mr. Newsome's response. Clearly, he means it's not private in here.

"No, it's—" I turn my head and my hair slides apart like a veil, and my eyes hit Lucas's for a breath. He holds his stare on me and responds. "It's fine. It's not anything private."

Emboldened by being allowed to stay, I tuck the hair behind my ear and offer an apologetic smile that's quickly dismissed when Lucas turns his shoulder to me and shoves his hands in his pockets. I blink away and return my focus to my papers, drawing the same doodle of flowers and leaves that I started earlier in the day.

"What's going on?" Mr. Newsome's tone is lowered, but I can still hear every word. *I should leave.*

"It's about Tennessee," Lucas says. I'm guessing it's college. Even though I quit attending Public games when I quit going to school here, it was impossible not to hear about them. Lucas started as a sophomore, and they went to state last year. Plus, he's always been smart, so I imagine his college options are plentiful. A lot bigger than the tiny list I'm left with now that we're surviving on wedding photos. Not that I have any clue what I want to study or become. I just want to go somewhere different; reinvent myself a little.

"I see. You know how I feel about it, but it's up to you, really," Mr. Newsome says. I can't help the eavesdropping, and the exchange has my curious mind buzzing. Tennessee isn't that far from here, maybe a five or six-hour drive. Not that I'll be driving there to visit him or anything. The time I spent on that calculation was wholly unnecessary.

"If it were up to me, I wouldn't be here, would I?" Lucas laughs lightly, but it sounds frustrated. I tilt my head in time to catch him running his hand through his thick hair then rubbing both palms on his face. "Gah! Maybe I should just flip a coin!"

Mr. Newsome laughs at the joke, but Lucas doesn't. I turn my head to the side again to inspect his face, in search of those little tells he's always had that once served as windows into his true feelings. For the briefest moment, his lips twitch, almost as if he's about to be sick. He's angry, maybe trapped, but it washes away in a flash when he catches me looking.

He sniffles and his eyes flit back to Mr. Newsome.

"You know what? I'll figure it out. I gotta get to practice." He lightly pounds his left fist against the door frame as he takes a step back. Our eyes meet one last time, and I can tell he would rather I wasn't here for whatever this conversation is really about.

"Let me make a call, talk to him." Mr. Newsome's plea does little to break through the guards Lucas has already raised.

"Maybe. I'll let ya know. Whatever, right?" A deep raspy laugh comes from his chest as he disappears around the doorway. Mr. Newsome steps out, holding the door open with his foot while he throws a Hail Mary.

"It might help! Lucas?" Mr. Newsome's fingers rap against the door frame, counting down the seconds it probably takes Lucas to walk to the end of the hallway and out the double doors. His chin eventually falls to his chest, and he mouths out "damn it."

I gather my stack of papers and relocate my doodle to the bottom of the pile along with my list of alternate teachers I could help this semester. It doesn't feel like the right time to ask.

I'm pushing in the chair when Mr. Newsome turns his focus back to the inside of his classroom, his eyes flashing quickly with shock as he remembers I'm in here, waiting.

"June, sorry. You know Lucas, right? From your freshman algebra class?" He lets the door shut behind him and moves to one of the desks that face his, leaning back to sit on the desktop. I give him a crooked smile and short laugh.

"Yeah, he's hard to forget," I say, not mentioning all the ways Lucas and I have history. Even if our relationship was drawn from our time in Mr. Newsome's class and nothing else, Lucas would have made an impression. He took our extra credit math games so seriously, leaping with pounding his chest when he scored the most points and earned credit he didn't need. He tested out of geometry and second-year algebra and went right to pre-calc. I'm smart, but I don't enjoy math, not like Lucas did . . . *does.* At least, I guess he still does.

"Kid has a chance to go to MIT." He mutters the words under his breath, but probably louder than he realizes. Lucas is choosing between MIT and Tennessee. He shakes his head out of a semi-trance and palms both his cheeks, clapping them lightly. "Sorry, I was just thinking out loud. What did you need?"

My thumb runs along the edge of my stacked papers, feeling for the staple on the last form, the one I wrote my backup list of teachers on.

"You have two assistants." I'm hemming, hawing, hedging—all of it.

His head falls back with a belly laugh, and I pause with my thumb on the top of the page I need for reference.

"I guess you could say that, but Tory D'Angelo isn't much of an assistant. I just like keeping an eye on that kid, keeps him out of trouble. I was glad they gave me two of you. I promise I won't overburden you." He leans forward and cups the side of his mouth. "I know some of you like to use these gigs to get homework done."

A nervous laugh shakes my chest and shoulders.

"Yeah, umm." I mash my lips together and kick myself inside over what I'm about to do. "No, I was just going to say I hope it's okay that I stay, even though you already have Tory. I . . . I like it in here. It's quiet enough."

He punches out a laugh and pushes off from the table, leaning forward to the stack of papers Tory left behind. He rolls them and slaps them against his other palm.

"If you can find quiet with Tory in the room, then you have Zen secrets I need to learn." He holds up the roll of papers. "The guy had one job today, to make sure he took these things home."

"I can give them to him," I volunteer, clearly having some out-of-body experience.

Mr. Newsome lowers his head and holds the roll out toward me, his head cocked to the side.

"You sure? I don't mind hassling him. It's one of my favorite hobbies," he jokes.

I shake my head and smile. "No, really. I don't mind." *Yes, yes! I do mind. What is this being that has inhabited my body and is making me do things I am loathe to do?*

"Great."

And in less than a minute, I go from fixing the debacle that is my last hour of the day to walking out of Mr. Newsome's class with a sweaty stack of papers from teachers who probably don't expect Tory to follow instructions anyhow.

After I exit the building, I unbend Tory's sheets and stack them with mine, noticing culinary on the top. At least I don't have to cook with him.

"What took you so long?" Abby swings her feet out and leaves the comfort of the short cement wall that weaves between the math building and library.

"Overachiever," I say, handing her the stack of papers. She scrunches up her face and taps on Tory's name with her thumb.

"You are? Or he is?" She's joking, of course. I take the papers back and feel for my keys in my front pocket. Tomorrow, I'll be bogged down with a heavy bag and folders.

"I'm stuck being a TA with him in Newsome." This is actually the first lie I've ever told Abby. I comfort myself with the logic that it's a slight exaggeration. I'm not stuck. I just blew my chance to get *un*stuck.

Abby lets out a slow laugh that starts like a trickle but becomes a fire hose of amusement as she crosses her arms and has to pause to catch her breath.

"Holy shit, you have the worst luck! The only person worse to be stuck with is Ava." I smile into the air while I press the unlock button on my key fob.

"Yeah," I hazily agree. Though that isn't really true. There's one person who would even top her on the list, and I can't seem to get away from him. Even when we both try.

FOUR

This marks the second time I've been to the D'Angelo house in three days. That's a record for me, one I had no intention of setting. I figured coming here now, though, during football practice, would spare me having to see the twins or any of their friends.

Lucas.

I've never prayed harder for my little beater of a car to not break down. It's idling pretty high as I crawl along the D'Angelo's street. My fifteen-year-old Honda may be approaching two-hundred-thousand miles, but it got me through a year of back-and-forth to my other school without fail. It was loyal by me, so I'm loyal by it.

As if I could get a new car.

The white brick home with black trim and fancy shutters comes into view as I slow at the side of the opposite curb. This place looks a lot different in the daylight. I'm pretty sure there were condoms hanging from the huge oak tree in the center of their front yard when I left Saturday night. I wonder whether the twins took care of the mess or if their parents deal with it, chalking it up to the price of having two popular teenagers in the house.

I kill my engine and lean forward to kiss the top of my steering wheel, a superstitious gesture I started a month ago when the pinging sound became louder. I'm busy separating Tory's papers from my own when I notice someone moving toward the back of the wide driveway that winds up the side of the property and to the infamous garage at the back of the twins' house. A bolt flashes from the back of my neck straight to my gut, my heart pounding with a dose of adrenaline. I'm not even sure what I saw, but just being here after what happened in that garage two days ago puts me on edge. Without pause, I sink down below window level, my knees bent as far as they will so I practically rest my shins on the gas and brake pedals.

No matter who it is, I now have to stay here until I'm sure they're gone. I won't be able to climb out gracefully, and I'm not certain I didn't just make a scene. My car sorta sticks out, what with the patch job on the driver's side fender and the two-tone blue paint from years of enduring Indiana winters and salted roads. But from across the street I'm not immediately visible, and I intend to stay that way.

I slow my breathing to hear what's happening outside, but it's no use. I'm basically panting like an overheated golden retriever. And my makeshift bun has fallen to shit yet again, so I'm swimming in a web of my own hair. When I hear what sounds like the rumbling of a nearby vehicle, I brave lifting my body just enough to see out my driver's side window. A small trail of exhaust puffs out from behind the retaining wall. Someone is probably pulling out of the garage, which means if I wait another moment, I can drop these papers at the front door and put a rock on top of them, call it a day.

I swallow and flinch when I see the chrome bumper, but hold steady, feeling pretty well-hidden. A deep gray truck rolls into view then pauses again, no more exhaust to obscure the details. For a moment, I think maybe someone forgot something inside, but even as I rationalize, I know better. I'm glued to the scene, and I don't think I could not follow through, merely to confirm this awful gut feeling. I don't want to be right, mostly because this is something I don't want to be burdened knowing. It's too late, though. Really, I knew it the second I saw the color of the truck. It's too easy to put together.

I *know* that truck.

I see it every night.

In the driveway next door to me.

Still, even in the face of this blatant evidence, I hope there is something else happening, another explanation. The truck continues its path backward, the dark silhouette of the driver just vague enough that it could still be explained, could be anyone.

But the license plate—I know that plate.

The brake lights trigger more panic, and I tuck myself a little lower in the seat, ready to duck out of view, but the truck is idling again. Waiting.

For someone padding down the driveway in bare feet.

Mrs. D'Angelo isn't wearing much. It's mid-afternoon, and I don't know whether she's a stay-at-home mom or if she goes to an office every day, but I do know Lucas's dad does. He works in Indy at a big law firm. And whatever he is doing at the D'Angelos' house right now doesn't look like business. It also doesn't look neighborly. It looks like a secret, the kind I'm certain my dad had. The kind that rips families apart.

Her T-shirt rises up the length of her thigh as she lifts up on her toes and reaches through the driver's side window. They kiss. That much I can infer. She takes his hand and he lets her as she falls back down to her heels, the white sleeve of his dress shirt rolled up to his elbow. I wonder if he even bothered to tuck it in. A sourness coats my taste buds at the image, and whether I want to or not, I superimpose my dad in the same position, of leaving some woman's house who isn't my mom after having . . .

They hold on to each other in the way people in love linger, only this . . . it isn't love. It's a scandal. It's four in the afternoon, and I've seen way too much.

The truck's brake lights go dark again so I duck low in my seat, completely hidden. There's nothing more to see. Now, it's only time to wait. I'm tempted to sit up tall enough to catch Mr. Fuller's face as he drives away, but I don't know what I'd do if he saw me. I'm already sitting in a car he could recognize. If he sees me here, I'll be living with more than knowing this secret, I'll be living with knowing that *he* knows I know.

That's messy.

Messier.

I feel sick.

The truck's engine fades into the distance, the familiar turn up ahead signaled by the change in gears just before I hear nothing. I can't fathom Tory's mom hanging around the front of the house in the thinnest, shortest T-shirt in the world, but maybe she is, so I stay hunkered down for almost a full three minutes. I lift myself up slowly, my legs cramping from the awkward position, and I rub at my knees and thighs as I get up high enough to scan my surroundings.

The street is quiet. The house is quiet. I glance to my right, to the seat where my school papers are splayed out with Tory's on top. He doesn't really care about any of this. And he won't do anything with them if I give them to him. I promised Mr. Newsome, but really, what do I owe that guy?

I might be tipping the scale in the direction I want, but who cares? I crank the engine, thank every god I'm aware of that it starts, and drive home the long way so I don't have to turn around and risk being noticed.

I told Abby I would be over today, but all I want to do is hide and figure out how to emotionally sort this new baggage. I want to donate this baggage; give it away. It's not mine, yet here it is, taking up *my mental space!*

I can't stop diving into my life of two years ago, my dad explaining to me that sometimes people grow apart while my mother sobbed and slammed doors upstairs. His quick departure. His quick engagement. How young the other woman is. How disappointing my father had become. How much it hurt to go through. It would hurt Lucas, learning this. He wouldn't believe me because, well, we don't talk. But eventually, he would have to.

I . . . could hurt him with this.

I shake my head, hating the satisfying feeling that thought leaves etched in my chest. This is not the person I am.

My trip home isn't long enough, and the punk music I turn up loud enough that my nearly dead speakers buzz doesn't do shit to distract me from processing all of this. I'm not stupid—people cheat on other people all the time. My father included. But that was *my* life crisis. I had no choice but to suck it up and push through to the other side. Seeing Lucas's dad having an affair forces a choice on me like a ton of falling bricks. It's this heavy wet blanket that suffocates me. I have a choice: tell Lucas, or keep this to myself and try to simply forget. It's that I know *why* I would be telling him that eats at me. I would be telling him to watch him go through everything I did. And then I'd step back and watch him do it alone.

He and I aren't friends. We don't talk, though I will see him every day for the next several months. If I tell him, he probably won't believe me, and he'll hate me for being the bearer of the news.

Nobody knows what I saw. I'm the only one who has to live with this. If it ever comes out some other way, the fact I kept this secret won't be relevant. Nobody will care, because I am nothing to Lucas Fuller. He said as much. He has his life, and I have mine.

Resolved, I pull into my driveway and put my car in park without even a glance at the house to the left. Kicking the drip pan under my car, I purposely walk sideways, avoiding any temptation to check the other driveway, to inspect the garage, or to change my mind. I move to my passenger side and grab my papers from the seat, taking Tory's too. I'll just buy two of everything and set him up with supplies for the semester. I'll pick up a shift at the bowling alley to cover the cost.

I make it to our garage door, to the keypad, type in my birthday followed by my mom's, and duck to get inside faster. Mom is out with the van, so I halt for a moment in the center of the garage, giving myself one more chance to weigh my options. My gaze lands on the extra remote taped to the wall with Velcro. The higher the garage door rises, the more defined the remote becomes thanks to the light. What are the odds? Me and the D'Angelos have the same goddamn garage opener.

I blink at it once then curl my right hand into a fist, the memory of the one Lucas handed me vivid in my memory—that night, the look on his face, playing in my head like a hi-def movie. I push aside the temptation to retaliate, hurt for hurt, and leave the burden of what I witnessed behind me on the garage floor. Then I march forward and slap my hand on the remote to close it off behind me. I push through the door and head straight to the stairs, not bothering to stop in my room before stripping away my clothes and turning on the hot water for a shower. I'm numb as I step under the falling spray, and don't really want to clean anything. I just want to stand here for a while and think, or rather try *not* to think. It's inevitable, though. As small as my world feels sometimes, right now, the box is closing in. I heave a sob—just one—and press my palms into my eyes. I tilt my head back to let the water wash away any evidence along with the renewed rage I have for my dad. Opening my mouth to let water fill the space, I test my voice in case I need to scream. The urge is gone, so I right my head and spit the warm water out.

Football practice isn't over until 6:30. I could go out for my supplies and be back without ever having to see anyone from that house about a hundred feet to the west of me. My body is listless, though, so with a towel wrapped around my hair and another wrapped around my body, I pad out the door, leaving steamy footprints on the wood floor.

There's this strange pain in my heart that holds me to the bed. I want to see him. Both of them—Lucas *and* his dad. I'm not sure why. Whatever the reason, I don't think it says anything good about me.

She started calling about forty minutes ago, and eighty-one missed calls means I probably slept through a lot of vibrations on my phone. Amazing, since it's stuck to my face. My head aches from the pull of the towel still wrapped around my damp hair. The towel on my body is still loosely held in place. I catch Abby's current call right before she hangs up (no doubt only to try again).

"Yeah, I know. Sorry." I've learned that it's better to head her lectures off at the pass. I sit up and unwrap my hair to relieve the pressure and see what kind of mess I've made.

"You know, I thought you were dead." She's exaggerating—by a lot. She must need something.

"Surprise! I'm not," I say, clutching my towel together at my chest while I drag my body and the discarded wet one from my head back to the bathroom. "I think I figured out how to make beachy waves, though."

Combing through my hair with my fingertips, I wait for the big ask that has to be coming any minute now. After several seconds of silence, I stop noodling with my head and hold my phone out to see if Abby hung up.

"You there?"

"Yeah, I'm waiting. Beachy waves," she says, annoyed I haven't told her yet.

I cough out a short laugh and go back to pushing around loose hairs. My head is still super wet, but maybe an entire night in the towel would do the trick.

"I was kidding, sort of. I slept in a towel," I say.

"Oh. Well that's not a very big breakthrough. Look, I need you to do me a favor." And there it is.

"Sure," I agree. This is a mistake.

"Awesome. So Friday, after the game, we're going to this place off the Interstate about fifteen miles or so. The road is dirt, so if your mom will let you take the van—"

"Hold up," I break in, snapping out of the beachy waves trance to realize the details of what she's signing me up for. "No more parties. I did a party."

"June, you *barely* did a party. And senior year is not a single-item checklist," she says.

"Yes, it is." I'm quick. "And that last party was pretty close to a low point."

"Ha, no way," she says. "I refuse to let you diminish what you achieved."

My friend is moving around while she talks, and sometimes her face muffles her words, but I get the gist of her argument from a few keywords —"stood up to her" and "made friends."

"I made some enemies too," I argue. I'm being contrary, but I also just woke up and everything from a few hours ago is resurfacing in my thought pool.

"You already had those enemies, so nothing new. Now, Friday. Do you want to pick me up and drive us to the game? Naomi and Lola are in too, and there's a lot of room in the van. That way we can go right to the creek—"

"Abby!" As if shouting her name has ever gotten her to give up a fight.

The line is silent for a few seconds. I finally accept that she is not going to give in and I am going to another party.

"You know minivans aren't off-road vehicles, right?" I wait through more silence from her, finally giving in with a sigh. "Yeah . . . I'll pick you up before the game."

"Stellar. Okay, see you in the morning." She ends the call without giving me a chance to reverse course.

The smell of burnt tomato is carrying upstairs, which means my mom must be home and attempting to cook. My dad was a griller. He still is, I guess, for another woman and kid in Florida. When he left, he took everything remotely culinary with him, which was fine because mom and I really only know how to make sandwiches and heat things up. Over the last year, though, Mom has been ambitious, with little to no improvement on her cooking skills.

I drop my towel and slide into my favorite sweats and long-sleeved T-shirt, then stop in my room to put on some flipflops and grab my keys and wallet. I have my supplies list memorized, so I leave the papers behind and rush down the stairs in time to move the pot from the burner before marinara sauce bubbles through the lid.

"Mom! You ruined dinner . . . again!" It's not a mean thing to say. It's a common thing to say.

"Damn it! Sorry!" My mom's voice is faint through the garage door.

I turn the burner off and note the still water in the pot she never turned on, curling my lips on the right side in amusement as I shake my head. A thud against the garage door pulls my attention away, so I leave the burnt sauce to cool and open the door for my mom, her arms weighed down with two cases of water. I take one from her and plop it on the counter just inside.

"Thanks. They had a two-for-one so I stocked up. I booked two shoots this weekend! One wedding and one family session." Her grin is so high it lifts her eyebrows. She's proud, and so am I.

"That was fast!" I say.

She nods after dropping the second case on the counter near the other one. Hands on her hips, she blows up at the dark brown cut of bangs that's grown long enough to hide her eyes. They part with her breath and she turns her focus to the stove, sighing.

"I'll order in," she says.

"Actually"—I touch her shoulder just before she moves to the drawer that holds our takeout menus—"I have to run out for school supplies. I'll pick up. Pizza?"

"Perfect." She looks relieved, and tired. She's spent the last few days calling every client she ever had at the studio and putting cards and flyers in every coffee shop within a ten-mile radius. My mom is incredibly talented at portrait photography, but the hustle part of the business doesn't come naturally. Hustle ranks right up there with cooking. Two jobs in one weekend—that's huge for her, and vital for us.

I leave my mom as she's pulling the smoldering pot away from the stove, slipping out the door before guilt tricks me into offering to clean that, too. I hate wet food, even crusty sauce bits singed onto metal.

Not paying much attention on my trip out the garage to my car, I press the unlock button on the key fob, triggering the honking sound and scaring the father-son duo playing hoops in the driveway just a strip of grass away from ours. The ball bounces away from their game, through the grass and toward me while they both stare. I stop it with my foot and glance up to meet their uneasy eyes.

I'm one-hundred percent certain this is weirder for me than for either of them. I was never really close to Lucas's dad, Todd, mostly because of his work schedule and how little he's home. But I would wave, he would wave, we'd pass pleasantries and make jokes and say hi. That little bit of banter ceased when Lucas pulled away. They're like a team, but I don't get the game we're playing. Every accidental interaction has been strange over the last two years, but now, I have the advantage of knowing what a scumbag Mr. Fuller is. And Lucas is blissfully ignorant.

I could crush them right now if I wanted to.

Without weighing the post part of my actions, I bend my knee and kick the ball back at them, punting it with the top of my bare foot hard enough that I'm pretty sure a bruise is forming. The airborne ball sails about two dozen feet to the right, up the property line and down the slope of our back yards into the thick weeds that Mom and I need to pull someday. It gets lodged under the crooked bumper of the old Buick my dad left behind, and it's rough arrival sends a flight of birds flurrying out of the yard.

Fuck. That was dramatic.

"Oops," I say, my eyes off in the distance, still watching the last few birds flap their wings and leave the premises. I can't believe I did that. I wonder if this is what my mom means when she utters "hormones" under her breath at me.

Following up my rash decision with another one, I decide the only thing that could make this worse is apologizing, so I continue my trip around the front of my car, get in, and turn the key.

It clicks.

Several clicks in a row.

The same clicks that the van made when we got the news that we needed a new alternator.

I lean forward—still not buckled in—and kiss my steering wheel, sure that the Fuller men are watching and wondering what the fuck I'm on.

"Please," I whisper, turning the key and pumping the gas once like my dad used to tell me. The ignition catches, the vibration of hope rattling my fingers where they grip the switch and key. I press the pedal down just a little more, and the sweet sound of a dozen-plus-year-old Honda firing up fills my ears.

I shift into reverse and peel out backward with my eyes glued to the rearview mirror. The car dips from the driveway and into the road and I crank the wheel with every intention of hauling ass out of this place and not coming home until I'm sure Lucas and his dad are inside. But whatever it is that's growing inside me, this thing that makes me speak up, act out, and be . . . abrasive and bold—it boils to the top. With my car tenuously idling at the curb in front of Lucas's driveway, I turn to my right, drawn to this gut feeling that he would be there. He was.

While his dad was wading through the knee-high crab grass and dandelion, Lucas had walked to the end of his driveway, probably on the off chance he'd get the last silent word. I meet his stare and promise myself not to blink, and not to drive away until he gives first. My nostrils flare, and the evening air chills the breath puffing from his barely parted lips. My window fogs, but I can still see him clearly under the glow of the streetlight—the same streetlight he and I used to beat with spoons to usher in the new year at midnight every January first. Maybe I imagine it, but the longer we hold on to this, the harder his chest heaves with what looks like anger and pain. The more time that passes, the more determined I am to win.

Without interruption of headlights and the heavy blaring of a car horn, I think maybe Lucas and I would have remained here in this dumb power play until the sun came up and my car ran out of gas. But we both blink and jerk our gazes away to the white Chevy Tahoe violently flashing its brights at me. I shade my eyes as if I have to visually confirm that it's Lucas's mom, but my buzzing pulse kicks in my sense of autopilot, and I reverse several feet to clear the Fuller driveway. Shannon Fuller doesn't glance my way once as she pulls into her home, driving straight into the family garage and closing the door the second the Tahoe's bumper clears the line. When I look back to where Lucas was standing, he's gone. I scan the driveway and the deepest part of our properties where our yards meet without a glint of him or his dad.

They've gone inside. Mom came home and the game is over. I'm still here, so I guess that means I won. I look back to the road ahead, the street empty through the next several stop signs, and I drive off for school supplies, pizza, and a handle on my pride.

FIVE

Abby can't fathom why I would go out of my way to do something nice for Tory D'Angelo. It's fair to call it into question, and I can't quite find the right words to explain that I'm not really doing anything to be nice to him; I'm doing it to make a show of being nice to him in front of Lucas.

I accepted the truth last night sometime around the checkout counter at the office supply store when I slid my credit card for seventy-four bucks' worth of binders, paper, labels, and pens. That's a chunk of money and two hours of my time spent on a guy I've never really liked. Yeah, it all sank in right at that moment.

"Your new boyfriend is coming. Go woo him with the protractor and pencil bag," Abby says, making a joke and pointing to the side parking lot where Lucas and the twins just pulled in beside each other.

"You're a bitch sometimes," I say, pushing off from my front bumper, where we've been leaning and waiting for the last ten minutes.

"Yeah, I know. But at least I don't buy presents for assholes," she shouts at me. It draws a few stares from people hanging out in the lot, but I ignore them. My eyes are focused on Lucas, sitting with one leg out of his truck and his hand resting on his steering wheel. He's wearing a hat today, all black with deep blue AP embroidered on the front for Allensville Public. He's not strutting his peacock feather of a varsity jacket today either. Just a plain black T-shirt that hugs his biceps. No matter the argument I make in my head, the twins just don't fill out their shirts quite the same way Lucas does.

I fight the urge to lower my gaze to my feet when I get closer, and I'm rewarded by catching the moment Lucas notices me and shifts his position in his truck, his arm sliding from the wheel and his body sitting taller as I approach. He's talking to the twins, who stand right beside his truck. He nods out his front window, silently telling them to look my direction, and when Hayden and Tory see me, I put on the performance of my life.

My eyes leave Lucas and greet Tory, all my effort going into an effortless smile I hope breezes across my face.

"Mabee, what's up," the arrogant twin says. He holds out a palm and moves a few steps toward me.

Everything in my body buzzes with caution. This could be a trick. I always assume there's a trick waiting. Nasty words written about me in bathroom stalls, dicks drawn in the dust of my car window, late-night hang-ups from blocked numbers—it's hard to take Abby's word that juvenile shit is behind us, especially after the immature prank I fell victim to at the party.

I take Tory's hand, half waiting for him to pull it away at the last second and laugh like a third-grader. He doesn't. Instead, he tugs me toward his chest and wraps his other arm around me briefly in a hug. It's an odd feeling, being swallowed up by his masculine sent, the coolness of his freshly showered body under a T-shirt, his muscles hard, and his height about the same as Lucas. In a brief lapse of judgement, I indulge and understand why so many girls date him. This . . . it feels nice.

"Hey," I utter out nervously. I swallow down the dry feeling in my throat as we pull apart and glance to the right, to Lucas. It's as if he's watching a television show, concentration and suspicion denting his brow, his chin propped up on the back of his palm as he leans into the center console of his truck. His bewilderment sparks a joy in my chest that paints the richest sinister smile on my lips. I flit my eyes back to Tory and lift the bag. "I come bearing gifts."

Tory's eyes widen and he bares his teeth in a genuine grin mixed with laughter, like a boy being given a toy from Santa. For once, I don't even think he'll make something dirty out of this. He takes the bag from me, a plastic strap in each hand, and opens it wide to look inside. His mouth sours a little and he looks in deeper, exaggerating before popping his view back to me.

"School shit?" His neck shrinks into his shoulders in playful repulsion so I laugh to keep the mood light, shoving at him playfully. Flirtatiously.

"Yes, but you left your list in class yesterday. You left all of your papers, actually. They're in there too." I make eyes toward the bag dangling from his hands, but his gaze seems stuck on me. I think I've stumped him . . . or he's afraid I'm falling in love with him. Whatever the cause, I think he's going to be kind to me right now.

"Thanks, Mabee. I mean, I probably won't use half of this shit, but . . . yeah. Hey, that was nice," he says, lightly laughing out his words. He opens his arms, welcoming me in for another hug, so I accept, resting my cheek on his hard chest and wrapping my arms around his body as far as they'll go. I look right at Lucas while I'm there, eyes hazed and smile daring him to do his worst.

"You're welcome," I say, letting my hands run along his sides while I let go. Tory tilts his head and looks at me sideways, and that little motion sends a chill through my chest. I'm flirting with fire now, and mixed signals aren't really part of who I am. I ball my hands into fists, shove them in my pockets, and take in my surroundings one last time. Both Tory and his brother watch me with puzzled expressions, Lucas, with his mouth a hard, flat line and eyes frozen cold.

I lift my hand to wave good-bye and turn to head back to Abby, focusing on the pattern her feet make as they kick back and forth from where she sits on the hood of my car. I imagine laughter behind me, partly because I expect it, but it's not real. When I focus, I hear nothing, not even the sound of people walking close behind. My body feels hot and my pulse is pounding in all parts of my body—fingertips, throat, ears, legs. I'm nearly jelly when I reach my friend, and she slides from my car and hands me my black and white checkered backpack, fully stocked with my "school shit."

"That went well," she says, an eyebrow raised. I can't feel my feet.

"I don't know if I have a barometer to measure how that went," I say.

"I don't know what that means." She shrugs. I twist my head to meet her eyes as we walk toward the main doors of the front building. The longer I look at her, the harder it becomes to hold in my laughter. When it breaks free, Abby joins in, and I'm pretty sure she thinks we're laughing because she doesn't know what a barometer is, but that's not what's funny at all. Nothing's funny, really. Things are nuts, way out of my comfort ballpark, but funny? Certainly not. Nervous, tenuous, doubtful, sad—that's what things are. And they're that way because of Lucas Fuller and what he is and was to me.

I part ways with my friend after the first building and begin my trek to the science area, the burning hole in my chest growing hotter the closer I get. My pace is quick enough that I get settled in my seat before Lucas arrives. I'm well into my act of being distracted by reading when I feel him shove his large body into the seat behind me. I jerk forward when his desk bangs into my chair, but grit my teeth instead of engaging him.

"Oops, sorry." His tone is flat and purposely cold.

I put the end of my pencil in my mouth, my teeth squeezing at the eraser with light pressure that takes all of my attention. Most of my attention. Not nearly enough of my attention.

"My dad says you're unhinged." His face is close to the back of my head. My hair is pulled back into a messy bun today, which means every bit of his breath slithers around my bare neck.

"Your dad's a real good judge of character, I bet," I say just loud enough that I'm sure he hears me. I chomp down on my pencil hard enough to bend the metal band around the eraser and stare toward the door. Our teacher stands outside waiting for stragglers to rush in before he closes it. Being early was the wrong choice. It would have been better to just come face-to-face with him once than having to sit here in this cone of silence where I swear I can hear every breath he takes. I wonder if he can hear my heart thundering.

My chair shifts with the weight of his foot, which is now balanced on the back leg. He taps his toe against the metal a few times, and I refuse to believe he's unaware of how annoying that is. The door finally closing behind our teacher, I bend to my side and unzip my backpack, pulling out my new pack of folders and a notebook.

"You get Tory pink ones too?" Lucas chuckles out his lame tease as he leans forward, his hands gripped around the front of his desk to pull his body close. Rather than respond, I smile with my lips pressed together tightly and meet his glare blink for blink. He eventually leans back in his seat, laughing quietly while stretching his arms over his head, fingers woven together. I wait for him to look away before turning around.

Lucas's little digs stop as soon as our teacher's lecture begins, and the next hour is a blissful lesson on velocity. I'm almost free, the minutes nearing the top of the hour signaling the end of class, when Mr. Slatvka drops a bomb in the form of a giant Ziploc filled with Hot Wheels track and a few cars on my desktop.

"Mabee and Fuller, partners," he says, waggling his finger in a motion to nonverbally link us together. He moves down the line to the next pair before I register what just happened.

"Fuck," Lucas breathes out in a whisper behind me. I turn to match his groan with one of my own.

"I don't like it either," I say, lifting my hand to request to work with *anybody* else. Before our teacher turns to notice me, though, the bell sounds and the classroom erupts into chaos. The final bag in his hand is given to a group of three, the benefit of being near the end in a world of odd numbers. I lower my hand slowly and wonder why all of this is happening to me.

"It's fine. Just give me the bag and I'll do everything for us," Lucas says, pulling his backpack from the side of his desk and slinging it over his shoulder as he stands. His T-shirt lifts up a little when he weaves his other arm through his shoulder straps, and my eyes zero in on the tanned line where his dark jeans rest low on his hips, a red band from his boxer briefs showing above the waistband. At least, I imagine they're briefs. Shit, I'm imagining him in briefs.

"No, I'll do it. Screw you," I say, tossing the bag into my backpack and zipping it inside before standing and sliding my bag over my shoulder.

"Fine, whatever," he says, looking off to the side as he brushes by me and moves out the door. I let the rest of the class filter out to form a human wall of space between us, but my eyes still lock on his position the minute I leave the room. He pushes through the double doors, and the tinted glass does little to dissuade me from stalking him with my eyes until I'm outside, too. I follow in his steps around the media center, toward the gym where I expect he'll peel off and duck inside for weights or some other stupid jock thing, but instead, he fishes out his keys from his pocket and continues toward the front of the school.

He's leaving. And judging by the way he scans to his right and left, he's timing his steps perfectly to catch the front gate before it locks and forces him to exit through the office. He slips out undetected and jogs into the sea of student parking spots, stopping at a red sports car about four rows deep where he ducks inside the passenger door and fades in with the rest of the mundane background.

We're seniors now. Almost eighteen. Adults.

Different people than we were.

I wonder who Lucas has become.

SIX

I'm two days back at my old school and already doing a boy's homework for him. Granted, this is technically my homework, too, but still, there's some tragic irony in this.

It's taken me an hour to rig the tracks in a way that this experiment will work with only one person. By the time my mom walks through the door from a quick grocery run, I'm sweaty and trigger-happy irritable. In case she couldn't tell by the cold shoulder I gave her when she walked in, I drop a big fat F-bomb when the tape gives way under the weight of the cars I carefully balanced on the makeshift bridge from the wall to the table. The only car to make the full trip before the bridge collapses is sailing off the end of the table as my mom steps into the kitchen. It ricochets off of her shin.

"Playing with your old toys, I see?" She rubs at the spot where a tiny Pontiac Firebird nailed her about six inches below her knee.

"I fucking hate this school!" I rip the intact tracks apart in my mini tantrum. I snap out of it quickly and am met by my mom's disappointed stare. "Ducking, sorry," I correct.

Her straight-lined lips curl up on one side as her eyes squint in tepid forgiveness. Our swearing arrangement is we can auto-correct swear in front of each other. *Ducking* gets used a lot.

"Coffee break?" She's still giving me her sideways look as she sets a plastic bag on the counter and pulls out a roll of towels and a package of our favorite brew. It's her silent acknowledgement of my bad mood met with her own warning that I've used my free pass. I breathe in and hold my chest full for a few seconds, then relax my shoulders with a heavy exhale.

"Coffee break, yeah," I relent. I got hooked on coffee after dad left. Mom sometimes got up really early in the morning for no reason, and I'd find her down here before the sun came up sipping on straight black coffee. I acquired the taste after six or seven cups, and now coffee breaks have become our thing.

She fills the pot at the sink and holds up her fingers, switching between one and two.

"Two," I say, answering how many cups I want. "Always two." A pathetic, tired laugh falls from my lips and I rest my head on my arms on our kitchen table. I roll one of the cars back and forth in front of my face while I consider finding this stupid experiment on YouTube so I can copy someone else's results.

Once the coffeemaker starts brewing, my mom leans against the counter with her hands gripping the edge on either side of her.

"So, what is this mini Daytona thing all about?" she says, nodding at the few pieces of track that ended up on the floor. I bend down and pick them up, slapping them on the pile on the table.

"Physics experiment on velocity," I say.

"Ah," she says, the brewer gurgling behind her. She turns to watch it finish. We both like our coffee piping hot, even in the heat of summer. "Seems like a lot of moving parts to do on your own."

"Yeah, well my partner sucks," I let out, not really thinking.

"Already? On day one?" she asks.

"Uh huh," I mutter, hoping that now that she's busy pulling the pot from the warmer and pouring our cups she'll move on to something else. She slides my cup to me and leaves what's left in the pot to keep it warm. When she joins me at the table, cradling her World's Best Mom mug in both hands as she blows steam from the rim, I know she's going to keep fishing.

"Most people met right after school or during study hall, but my partner plays football." I lift one brow and tilt my head to the left, toward the Fuller's house. She studies me a for a few moments then slowly nods, a faint frown at her lips.

"I see. Hence why you couldn't meet up after school. Convenient you live right next door to each other though, so maybe . . ." She leans her head to the right and glances toward the Fuller house. It's been a while since she suggested I do anything with Lucas. I guess after the dozens of excuses I gave her, she got the point.

I laugh, probably harder than she expects. Instead of getting into it, I take a long sip of my dark night coffee. It's acidic and delicious in a way that has the power to burn away a bad day. I will it to work on this one. My mom takes the same kind of sip, which softens me a little. I forget how hard all of this is on her. I know how tight our bills are. And I know how small the support checks are from my father. He's a con-man. Not literally, but enough of one that he got the judge to believe his salary was a third of what it really is. I think if I weren't so close to graduating, Mom would sell this house and move us into something cheaper. Maybe I should bring it up so we could move into a different school district.

"You and I have never really talked about it, you know," my mom says. I'm not sure which *it* she's talking about. There are many—their marriage troubles, the miscarriage I know she had when I was eight, the new woman in Dad's life.

She means Lucas.

"What's to talk about?" I say, testing the temperature of the coffee against my lips. It's no longer scalding so I take a bigger drink.

"You guys were so close." She's inching into the topic so I start to rebuild the track for my project.

"Yep." I'm short. Probably overstepping my free pass to be a bitch but I really, truly, do not want to get into the saga of me and Lucas Fuller.

After a few breaths of quiet, my mom snaps together pieces of track with me, putting them in pairs and passing them my way until I again have one long, twelve-foot strip. We admire our work, finishing our coffee in silence. My mom twirls the worksheet around on the table so she can read the instructions, and I gauge her reaction in her eyes. She's exaggerating a little, grimacing at the calculations and the number of trials I'm supposed to conduct to find averages and means. I know better than to ask her for help. She long ago made the point that she would never enable me from having to face challenges, especially when the adversity was something as solvable as being strong enough to stand up for myself.

It's weird how effective her silence is. The shadows cast across our ceiling are familiar, the same ones I've memorized during football season for the last two years. Lucas's practice is over, the glare of his headlights through our windows lining up right where it should when he parks. The brightness dims, followed by the heavy clunk of a truck door. I glance from the window to my mom, and find her eyes waiting on me. She doesn't say a word, instead reaches for my empty cup, her tight smile holding so much inside.

It's hard not to imagine how different things could be. Like right now, my mom's back turned to me as she rinses out our coffee mugs. In some other dimension, maybe I'm not sitting at this table alone. Maybe my father kept his promise to stay through thick and thin. Or maybe . . . maybe the one soul I trusted all of my secrets with didn't pull away. I half imagine Lucas knocking at our side door and turn my head, wishing to see his shadow at the window.

"So, I have some bad news." My least favorite sentence pulls me back to reality. Just hearing it makes me want to rip my track apart again.

"Hit me with it." I sit back in my chair and brace myself for something heavy. She does the same against the counter. Her eyes are tired, the dark circles a shade of purple now that they're not hidden by makeup. She cut her hair super short a few weeks ago, buzzing the back and sides. She said she wanted something easy to do, but I think she liked the idea of something inexpensive. It looks nice on her, though she keeps mentioning how much she hates how it brings out her grays. I'll be gray too one day, just like her. Our natural hair color is exactly the same.

"It's more of a good news, bad news thing," she begins, and I relax a little. The last bad news thing was when she lost her job. "You know how I said I booked two shoots?"

I nod, my mind racing with possibilities. *Is it someone famous? It's for a magazine! Maybe a royal wedding?*

"It's in Dayton. The wedding?" I blink a few times, slowly, mentally working through what she's saying.

"We're going to Dayton?" The divot between my brows is so deep I can actually feel it on my face without using my hands.

My mom laughs lightly.

"*I'm* going to Dayton. I have to leave tomorrow, which I know . . . You don't love staying alone. But the family hired me when their original photographer backed out and they want to capture the rehearsal dinner along with a few other things, and the amount they are paying is . . ." She trails off, holding her palms out in front of her to indicate a massive amount.

I smile and reassuringly tilt my head to the side.

"I don't mind staying here alone. I'm really proud of you," I say. Her eyes twitch and gloss quickly, which naturally forces my tough-as-nails mom to busy herself by running a paper towel around the counter to distract me from the emotion creeping up on her face.

"Just four days, four and a half max." Her voice wavers, but she coughs the clue away.

"Piece of cake," I say, stealing a glance out the window to the dark house just two driveways away.

"And I'll still leave you the van for the game Friday," she says. I was hoping she would forget that I asked to use it. My mom and Abby must be in cahoots to force me into some semblance of a normal senior year.

"Well, I need to get everything ready. I'm going to run out to Clicks and see if I can rent an extra light kit for the weekend." Our eyes meet briefly and a silent thank-you passes between us.

I stare out the window while my mom gathers her things and heads out the side door to her van. I stand while she backs out so I can watch her go, and let my gaze get lost on the space she leaves behind. I'm not sure how much time passes, but it's enough that I'm lulled into a deep trance that only the thumping beat of the Fuller's backyard audio system can snap me from. Always with the Kanye. Lucas Fuller listens to Kanye more than *Kanye* listens to Kanye.

The house is dark, which means he's probably just sitting in his back yard drinking one of his father's beers and watching dumb fucking Tik Tok videos while I do our assignment by myself. All because of some childish caste system that we fell into in high school.

By the time I realize I've got a chokehold on the section of track in my palm, the plastic siding cuts into my hand. I relax my hold to assess the damage, a deep red line broken through the skin right along my life line. So appropriate.

Without pulling my focus from the glowing haze of lights in Lucas's back yard, I yank the track into a few manageable pieces, gather the cars and worksheet, and stuff it all into the bag it came home in. I pull the Notre Dame sweatshirt I found at Goodwill over my head and down over my hips, and stuff my feet in a pair of Vans. I leave the same way my mom did, my long strides carrying me across my driveway, the strip of grass between our homes, and up the side of Lucas's house. The music is so loud the bass vibrates in my chest, which only fuels my courage. What a fucking asshole!

With one deep breath to ensure I get the words all out in one go, I round the corner of his home and step onto the brick walkway that leads to the patio. The pool light is on, casting an aqua glow around the yard, but the lounge chairs and hammock I expect to see him in are all empty. My steps slow, a twitch of caution flicking against the side of my neck. The large window that looks out from the Fuller kitchen is just to my left, but the only light glowing inside is the small panel light that illuminates the floor near the pantry. Not that I'd be able to hear anything other than the music, but there is a stillness that eats up my surroundings; it feels as though I'm here all alone.

I hug the project bag to my chest and scan every possible nook as I inch deeper into the covered patio and up the steps to the deck. The fire pit Lucas and I used to roast marshmallows sits in the center, and it looks unused since the last time he and I made treats in the flames. The chairs around the deck are covered. The Fullers don't have big parties like they used to. I run my finger along one of the tarps, drawing a line in the dust, then stop to lean against the railing and blow the particles away in the breeze.

That's when I spot him, and he isn't alone.

Lucas and Ava are lying in the center of the trampoline, barely visible if it weren't for the pool light. My throat burns with fire from my stomach, and the fuming rage that carried me to this house has shifted into dread and panic over being caught. My hands shake and my legs have very little feeling. Despite the near stroke I might be having, I can't look away. Her body is arched, her flannel shirt open to expose her white lacey bra that Lucas is slowly peeling away with his teeth as he holds himself over her from the side. His left hand is sunk inside her unbuttoned jeans, and Ava is writhing with his touch. He's wearing his gray football T-shirt and black joggers that are low on his hips, and is probably seconds from losing his shirt and letting her touch him just as intimately. He moves like a predator, slow and stealthy, and where his shirt rises up, the side of a cut V that traces hard-earned abs dives lower. The scene is so erotic and private yet I'm glued to it, trembling with the threat of tears. I'm so fucking jealous, and I hate that I am because this is not *my* Lucas anymore. This feels like a betrayal, though I know it's not. That should be me lying there. It was supposed to be me.

In a different life.

The music fades between songs and a deep, masculine moan cuts through the quiet. I swallow hard at the familiar voice making that sound, lock my jaw and hold my breath. I slowly back away, just as Ava's hips rise and her hands help Lucas slide down her jeans. I turn quickly when I'm sure I'm out of view, but in my rush, I kick one of the chairs, the metal leg screeching against the wood deck so loudly it's impossible it wasn't heard.

"Shit," I breathe out silently, breaking into a run that turns into a full sprint across our driveways and back to my house. I slam the side door closed behind me, lock it, and fly up the stairs two at a time until I'm in the safety of my room. I close my door behind me and toss the bag to the corner, burying myself under my comforter without bothering to turn on the lights.

A million futures play out in my mind, and none of them are easy. They all come with pain.

I hate this fucking school.

And I hate my fucking neighbor.

I hate that I loved him so much even more.

SEVEN

I wake up early to see my mom off and to bullshit my way through the project I never finished last night. I went the YouTube video route, changing all of the numbers by the same percentage so the results weren't an exact copy.

All of the extra things added to my morning leave no time for a shower though, so I braid my hair into one long weave that runs from one side to the other. I have to lay down to finish because my arms are getting tired. I wrap a band around the end of my braid then let my arms flop to my sides. Staring at my ceiling, I replay what I saw last night in my head, dragging my own hand slowly up my side and over my shirt to my right breast. I look nothing like Ava, all flat in the places where she is round. I touch the soft peak of my breast and run my thumb over my own nipple until it hardens under my long-sleeved T-shirt and cotton bra. I let my hand fall away, trailing it down the length of my body, stopping just above my waistband, too embarrassed to touch myself anywhere else.

I'm a girl playing woman.

It's tempting to call myself out sick today. My voice and my mother's sound eerily similar, and nobody would think I was ditching. Running away isn't supposed to be my thing now, though. Senior year—parties, freedom, courage and kissing. I laugh out once for nobody to hear.

"What a load of crap," I say.

I sit up and drag my backpack toward me, zipping it up after I make sure my fake project worksheet is inside. I tuck my phone in my back pocket and double knot the laces on my boots, then grab a flannel from the hook behind my door before heading downstairs. While the days still feel very much like summer, the mornings and late afternoons are fall and I hate being cold. I poke my arms through the unbuttoned shirt and pause as I look down at the plaid pattern. It's too much like Ava's. Newly committed to being chilly instead, I pull my arms free again and roll the shirt up, tossing it into a deep corner in the laundry-slash-mud room. I really want to throw it away but mom only bought it for me last month.

With my backpack slung over one shoulder, I snag a granola bar from the cabinet and a strawberry milk from the fridge, holding the bar in my teeth while I lock the side door behind me. I'm almost looking forward to my lazy drive to school with my favorite breakfast. I know Mom picked up the strawberry milks so I won't miss her so much. I smile as I twist the cap loose.

As I approach my car, I notice something resting on the windshield. It's mostly white, and almost looks like a scrunchie wrapped around my wiper blade. I unlock my door and toss my bag across to the passenger seat, then reach for the twisted piece of cloth. I realize what it is right before my hand makes contact and I pause, breathing out hard, short puffs through my nose to the familiar beat of the last Kanye song I heard. I pull my keys from my pocket and poke the long one meant for my ignition through the lacey item that's barely within my reach. I drag the material toward me and pinch it to hold up for inspection.

The panties are mostly white with little black hearts sewn everywhere, and the coverage they would provide is minimal. It's the bottom part that matches the bra I got a glimpse of; at least, I'm pretty sure it is. Last night's hurt and fury stirs in my belly. I twist to take in the still house behind me, the garage closed and the downstairs as quiet as it was last night. Lucas's truck is gone, which probably means I am not being watched. I carry the thong—held by my thumb and middle finger—into my car and unzip my backpack to tuck it inside. I back down the driveway, squealing my tires a little when I hit the road.

I buckle up while moving, then reach to zip my bag closed again. There's a chance I missed one of the four-way stops leaving my neighborhood, and I'm not sure how I got to where I am, a block from school. All I can think about are the underwear; it's basically tunnel vision for my thoughts.

Ava's panties are in my backpack. What the ever-loving fuck?

Abby is waiting for me in her car, her music loud enough that I can hear it through both of our closed windows and with my engine on. She's happy. That's her personality. Very little to find fault with in the world according to my best friend, even though she's getting hauled into court again next week as part of her parents' constant and bitter custody battle. Her dad, who has seen her maybe twice since she and I have been best friends, lives in Miami now. He wants custody because he wants the money she earns modeling, and she's not eighteen for six more months. Her mom recently put it all into an S-Corp, Abigail Cortez LLC. My friend is an LLC. Her father wants it dissolved. It's a Netflix documentary-worthy mess.

Maybe having some chick's underpants in my backpack isn't so bad.

I glance at the zipper and give one last thought to what's hidden behind it, then pull the bag into my lap, kill my engine, and get out to wait for Abby to finish crimping her eyelashes. She's still singing the last few lines of the song when she gets out and joins me on the hood of her car to stare at other people and make judgements about them we would never say to their faces. That's a lie. *She* would say it. Me, never. Except maybe . . .

"Ava Pryor looks like she had a boob job," my friend says, both of our necks craned to the left, watching the platinum blonde mean girl hop out of Lucas's truck. I wonder if she slept at his house or if he picked her up this morning.

"I have her panties in my backpack," I say, all monotone as I zone out watching my apparent arch nemesis shimmy down her barely existent corduroy skirt. I wait for them to kiss, ignoring my friend's elbow that has now nudged me twice. But from the moment they exit the truck it's as if they aren't even acquainted. Lucas peels off and joins the twins and this guy Cannon who came here junior year when I was gone. Abby is obsessed with him, but he never *ever* does anything social, or dates, or smiles. He clearly talks, because I'm watching that happen, but talking to Abby is another thing. I have the distinct feeling he is the reason I'm driving out to the creek Friday night.

"Panties. Spill it." She pushes me hard enough that I lose my balance and stumble a few steps to my right. I smirk, though, and bring my bag to the front of my chest, unzipping the top for her to peer inside. I don't expect her to reach in and grab them. Stupid of me.

"Get out!"

I blush a little because her volume draws attention, and she's unfurled a thong to display in front of us.

"Abs, those ain't washed," I warn, and she tosses them back in my bag, immediately digging in her purse for her orange-scented hand sanitizer.

"How did you end up with those?"

I'm not completely sure, but I have a pretty good idea. I tell my friend only the facts so I don't have to delve into the intricacies of me walking in on her and Lucas, which would undoubtedly lead to me doing our assignment on my own, and him taking advantage of me, and me pining . . .

"I found them on my car this morning." I meet her wide stare with a solid one of my own, my mouth a hard line touched with a hint of a smile that says, *"I can't make this shit up."*

Abby nods slowly and the first bell sounds from the school speakers.

"Guess that's better than dog shit," she says.

We kick off from her car and head toward the main doors, Lucas and the twins a few paces in front of us. This time, though, I don't bother walking slow. I let it all play out so my steps are only a few behind his, and when he glances back enough that I see his jaw and the flick of his lashes, I let a slow, deep grin take over my face.

When we arrive at the science building, I'm close enough behind Lucas that, if he were a gentleman, he'd hold the double doors open for me. I'm not surprised when they slam shut behind him; it only strengthens my resolve for how I'm going to handle this—*handle him.*

I slow my stride enough that he gets into our classroom and his seat before me. I want him sitting for this, and I want other people around to witness. His big frame is stuffed into the desk when I enter the classroom, his black bag on the floor next to one foot, his right leg stretched out into the aisle next to my seat. His notebook is out and he's slowly spinning a pen in his right hand, his eyes red from what I imagine was a late night. His focus on the whiteboard seems forced, reluctant. His concentration breaks only for a breath, and that's when his gaze flits to me. His pen never stops turning, but his eyes follow my movement, his expression almost hostile. He's wearing the same clothes I saw him in last night, and I force myself to soothe the burn and scorn eating at my insides with this newfound hatred that I've decided to nurture.

Pausing right in front of my seat, I dump my heavy bag on my chair, then unzip the top and look my former friend right in the face. His eyes move from my hands to my gaze in one blink. The blue is muddied by alcohol, lack of sleep, Ava—*whatever.* It's not as effective on me as it once was. What was once so beautiful has become ugly. I wait for him to believe this is it, I'm just going to glare. Finally, he shakes his head and shrugs.

"What?"

My smile spreads a little wider. I reach in my bag and grab his girlfriend's panties, then toss them on his desk.

"Pretty sure these are yours," I say, waiting to capture a mental picture of his agape mouth, lost for words. His jaw works side to side while he stares at the undies, and a sharp laugh leaves his chest.

Satisfied, I take my seat and pull out my project and notes. I'm still undecided on dropping the fact that I did the project alone, not that it will matter to our teacher. There's an unwritten rule that football players get a free pass around here.

"Hey, June." Lucas's voice is steady and calm. I didn't think the bullet I fired would sting for long, but I know it stung. I saw it on his face, and that's enough.

I turn my head to the left enough that I can view him in my periphery. He leans forward and tugs lightly on my braid, an almost flirtatious tease that maybe would have sent my heart into butterfly Olympics before last night. Now, though, I see it for what it is. It's bait.

"Thanks," he says, his hand swallowing up Ava's panties in a slow sweeping movement along his desktop. He leans to his left and pushes the thin, lacey garment into his right pocket, his eyes never leaving mine. I can feel my body growing hot, but I don't let him see how affected I am.

"You're welcome," I manage to say. I'm stronger than I think I am. "Don't mention it," I add, then turn around, never letting my focus stray from the front of the room for the rest of the hour. And when our teacher collects our projects, I wait for most of the class—for Lucas—to clear out, and write a note on the top of my assignment.

Lucas Fuller had nothing to do with this project. If you want to know why, ask Ava Pryor.

I hand it in and leave without commenting out loud. It will be what it will be. And it is going to feel like forever.

EIGHT

I'd forgotten what Friday nights are like around here. For the last two years, I spent them watching back-to-back sit-coms while binge eating excessively-buttered popcorn and peanut M&Ms. Sophomore year, I was busy helping my mom care for my grandmother, and last year, I wasn't an Allensville Public Fighting Eagle so no need to expose myself to all of the rah-rah pep shit.

I'm in the thick of pompoms and shirtless teenage boys painted orange and blue now, though. Public is a decent team. Lucas is a more than decent quarterback. There's buzz about this season, but the entire school shows up for the first home game regardless. It's the perfect storm of panic-inducing high school chaos.

It's also easy to get caught up in.

I pick the girls up in my mom's van and we blare power-chick music all the way here. I almost forget how small I am by the time we walk through the gates to the field. Ava Pryor is sure to remind me.

"I'm pretty sure she gets in as a child," she shouts when I walk up to the ticket window with my five bucks and my ugly ID. As tough as I've trained my skin over the last week, her words still cut, almost as much as the laughter it spawns from people nearby. Even still, I walk on. But she catches up, shoving the blue jersey she's wearing in my face—Lucas's away jersey.

I've been staring at her back—the bold number 1 centered under his last name—and I can't shake how much mental space I am giving to such an awful person.

"She hates you, you know?" Lola rests her chin on my shoulder so she can talk into my ear above the sound of the drumline sitting a section to our right.

"I'm well aware," I say with a wry smile.

My new friend puts her arm around me and squeezes, an awkward hug, but mostly because I don't know how to do those kinds of things. I exhale and let my body accept her affection. Lola holds her popcorn bag out to the side, tipping it for me to grab a handful. Might as well have my favorite Friday-night food since I'm enduring being here. I scoop some kernels from the bag and lick at the salty bits one at a time, trying like hell to ignore the girl I hate as much as she hates me.

There's a camera crew on the field—a *real* one, not our student-run Internet show. They've positioned camera guys on either side of the banner being stretched out by a tower of cheerleaders. When the team trickles out, everyone in the student section—which has basically grown to be two-thirds of the stands—gets on their feet to scream. Abby is standing in front of me and she turns, catches me not doing my part, and points in that threatening way she has.

"Fine," I mouth, cupping my hands around my lips and shouting, "Go Eagles!" as loud as I can. The sheer volume of my own voice, the togetherness of this moment, all of it—it infects me. My smile quits being pretend, and I get caught up in my role. I have a part to play, albeit probably not as important as everyone thinks, but for the next three hours, I will be a superfan. For the next three hours, nothing matters more than winning this game and destroying some school from South Bend.

The young men on the field shout in unison, growling with testosterone and pounding into each other, smacking helmets to helmets and gripping at facemasks to amp up their game faces. They explode through the banner, confetti covering the corner of the field as it's fired from a few cannons held by some of our cheerleaders. Lucas is the first to break through, holding an American flag as he sprints straight down the center of the field, his co-captains running behind him with two Eagles flags.

My All-American boy.

He was so much younger the last time I saw him run like this. He was a leader that seemed too small to lead, but now—now he's the guy with the V that cuts down his abs and whose arms completely fill out the sleeves of his jersey; whose neck doesn't seem so pencil-thin anymore. His sweaty hair is swept to either side, and the black lines swiped under his eyes somehow make him seem like this superhero.

A hero who abandoned me when he got popular and when my life fell to shit, I remind myself.

The team captains are met by one of the coaches at the fifty-yard line. He takes their flags to fold them while the boys huddle up to pray. It's such a blatant disregard for the separation of church and state, yet it seems nothing could be more important than this bonding happening in front of us all. More than the quiet power of the moment, though, is that Lucas is the one leading the prayer. Arms over shoulders, circles standing within circles, these boys who I've seen do the most unchristian-like things give respect to his words. I wish I could hear him or be close enough to read his lips. Some of the boys look up to the sky, a few of them holding their helmets high while their heads lower. Lucas's eyes are closed, and there's an innocence in his features, that much I can see from here. They all start clapping and an echoing "Amen" accompanies their formation of a tighter circle until the clapping becomes thunder and soon . . . fuel.

Lucas is the last to walk away from this private spot on the field. His head down, I recognize the familiar invisible weight on his shoulders. Even as kids, he always felt so damn responsible for everything and everyone. Especially for me. He rode his bike through rain to sneak me my favorite candy bar when my parents were fighting downstairs. And he insisted we fall asleep still on our phone call to each other if I felt scared or off. He sensed things when I didn't share. He took burdens from me, whether I wanted him to or not, and shouldered them until he was sure my smile was real again.

I miss him. I miss him so fucking much.

I press my palms into my eyes while my friends aren't looking, and manage to stop myself from feeling all of this somewhere so public. In less than a minute, the game takes over and distracts me from anything other than the anticipation and hope that brews in my belly every time Lucas throws the ball. He's gotten better. I understand why his opportunity window is so big. There's an easiness to the way he moves, and it's more than instinct. He has plenty of that, though, after throwing the ball down our street to his dad every night—a million which ways and for hours on end. They haven't thrown since freshman year, but that's probably because Lucas has outgrown what his dad can give him. Either that, or his dad is too busy at his best friends' house.

It suddenly becomes impossible to turn off my thoughts. I wonder if Lucas knows. Maybe that's what changed him. I scan the crowd off to our left, to the sections where parents sit to gloat and brag which number their kid wears on the field. Lucas's dad is the only one standing the entire time, not giving a rat's ass about the dozens behind him who can't see. A week ago, I would have seen a proud father in this scene, but now, I see a man who wants the credit, a man who maybe wants to live through and off of his son's achievements. His expression after every amazing feat Lucas accomplishes is less one of pride and more one of validation. A check mark that moves him up a scale even though really . . . he hasn't done jack shit.

His wife sits next to him, her purse tucked close to her hip, her hands folded in her lap, knuckles near white as they squeeze in fear every time someone threatens to knock her son out. Still proud, she is also the exact opposite of the growing ego standing next to her.

I wonder if she knows where her husband goes during the day?

The more I study his parents, the more every inch Lucas fights for on the field is colored with resentment in my eyes. Balls are thrown with extra zip. I think the newspaper called him stronger than your normal high school senior, but maybe what they see is hatred playing out like a game. But his dad and him, they don't hate each other. They were just playing basketball together, laughing. *Until I kicked their ball into the weed oblivion of my yard.*

The truth about what I see and what this family really is muddies more every time I think I understand. I quit focusing so much on Lucas and pay attention to the other players, the ones I know even though I never thought I'd want to. Like the twins. Or that Cannon guy, who Abby has been straining her neck all night to stare at. I don't think she even knows the score of the game.

We're on our feet for most of the first half, and I can barely feel the bottoms of my feet by the time the buzzer calls halftime and our boys run to the locker rooms with a 14-0 lead. Lucas's mom joins his father, both standing to arch their backs and shake feeling back into their legs. I look away when Mrs. Fuller turns her attention in my direction. But I miscalculate and my gaze lands on Ava, who has turned around to stare straight up at me, despite every single minion around her facing the other way. Her eyes haze, so I jack up the right side of my mouth and lift my hand in a wave I'm sure makes her blood boil, then I get my friends' attention.

"Hey, did Abby tell you guys about Ava's underwear?" I'm not being quiet, but I'm not loud enough that anyone other than my friends hear. The way they all jerk their focus to me and then to Ava, though, makes her squirm.

"Why?" Naomi asks, turning to look at me again. Ava's glare grows heated, and my smile inches up into my eyes.

"Someone left them on my car. I'm guessing she did." I shrug and shift my gaze to my friend. Naomi busts out a hard laugh.

"Well, no shit. Girl hates you," she says, echoing the same thing Lola said when the game started.

"Why?" I shake my head, amused and a bit baffled at the concept. In terms of having your shit together, Ava's got me beat hands down—she has her hooks in Lucas, as far as I know her family isn't diced up by a nasty divorce, and, despite how much I like to poke fun of her glossy style, she's actually kind of pretty. *Really* pretty. Sexy for sure.

Naomi's cheek falls to her shoulder and Lola laughs at some inside joke I clearly don't get. The longer I don't laugh with them or nod or agree, the more amused they get until finally, Lola explains.

"You had him. Lucas! You guys were . . . " She twists her fingers together to show how tight Lucas and I once were. I nod like it all makes sense, but the part I hold on to is the moment her fingers pull apart and never come back to meet as they once did. I never really had him like she does. I can't imagine him looking at me the way he did her on the trampoline.

Hungry.

Despite wanting to break the rule I made for myself after the first half, I don't give Ava another ounce of my physical attention for the rest of the game. Mentally, though, she swims all over my insides. I replay walking in on them, measuring up her cruel glances over the years, the slight shoves against my shoulder when we pass in the hall, and how those things line up with Lucas and me, and our friendship. No matter how hard I try to see it, high-fives and late-night burger runs don't match up with the kind of relationship they have now.

I would trade twenty football games for one of these parties. Hell, I'd trade a dozen house parties for whatever the fuck this is that my friends and I are walking into.

I know my attitude is a little tainted from having to process more Ava business. Still, I don't think getting mud caked on the sides of my white Vans just to get pot smoke blown in my face is anywhere close to my recipe for the perfect night. On my way to the beer truck, I walk by some asshat carrying all the beer, which I won't drink. Maybe I'm the one with something wrong, though, because everyone else here seems happy—perfectly, miserably happy.

Almost everyone here is well on their way to becoming drunk. I've run into one other sober person, and I counted sixteen cars, which means a lot of these people better be camping here tonight. I'm sure they're not. I'd love to call every one of them out on it, but you don't win high school popularity points by stopping dumbasses from committing involuntary manslaughter.

"Miss Mabee!" The familiar D'Angelo lilt actually makes me smile.

"My second favorite D'Angelo twin," I tease back, turning to find my unlikely friend sitting on the tailgate of someone's truck, covering his heart with both palms, feigning his untimely death by insult.

I nod to the rest of my friends to head to the beer truck without me and pull myself up to sit next to Tory. His hair is wet, combed straight back minus the stray section that squiggles over his left eye. He smells like men's body wash, and he's wearing his away jersey, his home one muddied from tonight's game.

"So tell me, you come to the party looking for me?" He winks over his crooked smile. I bat at him playfully.

"You know it," I say. His laugh in response is genuine.

"Abby dragged me here," I clear up, nodding toward my friend who has already found a spot near this mysterious Cannon guy.

"That's two parties, back-to-back weekends! Dare I say it, you're well on your way to a streak," Tory jokes.

I glance to my side with a tight-lipped smile, feeling a little prudish because he's right, I am a bit of a hermit. For good reason, though.

"I'm kidding with you. You know that, right?" His eyes soften and he dips his head, meeting my stare.

I nod. "I do."

Tory tilts his head back and takes a long swig from his bottle of beer. I take this moment to survey the rest of the crowd. I haven't seen Lucas's truck yet, or Ava, and I hate that I'm looking for them. Even more, though, I hate that Tory catches me in the act.

"He's always late to shit. Some things never change," he says, nudging my arm with his elbow as he scoots a little closer. I chuckle at his commentary, remembering all the things Lucas was late for with me.

"You know that jerk was late to our summer swim relay when we were eleven?" I say. "He showed up just in time to swim anchor." Tory laughs hard enough that he spits out some of his beer.

"Serious?" he questions.

I nod and hold up the scouts honor sign.

"He still a jerk?" he asks, laughing lightly through the words. His expression falls into a less spirited one though the longer it takes me to answer. I never do.

Jerk or not, he isn't late this time. He's right on time, pulling his truck up right next to the one Tory and I are sitting in. At least seven people are in the back, and four more lined up next to him in the cab. The scent of alcohol is strong, and bottles clank as people climb out of the truck. I kick my feet out and hop to the ground, dusting off the back of my jeans and twisting in place to find my friends, any of them. My attention comes screaming back to Tory after a second, when his hand grabs my fingers. At first, my eyes sear the place where he's holding my hand hostage, then my gaze flits up to Tory's cocky smirk.

"Don't let him run you off," he says, rushing the words out before Lucas rounds the back of his truck and stops a few feet away from us with a sour look on his face. The trapped feeling makes it hard to breathe.

"Hey, man. Can you help me with this keg?" Lucas's eyes bounce from where Tory's hand is on mine to Tory's eyes, and that little victory from seeing it bother him helps me slow my pulse and stay where I am a moment or two longer.

"Yeah, bro. Where we takin' it?" Tory runs his thumb over the top of my knuckles, and I react on auto, pulling my hand away and stuffing both of them in the front pocket of my hoodie. I don't leave yet, though. I'm not sure whether what Tory did there was for me, or for Lucas, but it was a weird line nonetheless.

"Uh, Jake's truck, I guess. Isn't that where the rest of the shit is?" Lucas shifts on his feet, glancing at me a few times, but never stopping to actually *look* at me. He's agitated and keeps pulling his black Public hat from his head to smooth out his long hair underneath before putting it back on backward.

Tory hops down from the truck, his feet crunching into the earth less than a foot from me. He leans in, the sweet scent from a wax pen on his breath. "Wait here. I'll be right back."

I'm not sure why I obey his request. I stay put, though, while he climbs into the back of Lucas's truck and the two of them haul the keg to the tailgate, then call Hayden over to help lift it out. I stick by the back of Tory's truck for several minutes while he lingers by the drinks, laughing and joking with his friends. Maybe he forgot about me. But before I give in to the urge to search out my friends, he jogs over from across the large open area we're all parked around.

He hands me a Coke, not fully letting go when I grip it, instead tapping the top a few times. "I ran with it. Don't want it to explode on you," he explains. I wonder if my face is as quizzical as it feels.

"You're being nice to me." I didn't mean that to come out with sound.

Tory stops tapping my drink as he shakes with a hard laugh and looks down at the ground, nodding and biting at his bottom lip that eventually slips into an amused smile. I pop the tab and take a long drink, thirstier than I realize.

"You were nice to me first, you know," he says, holding his beer up to toast against my can. I smile all crooked and tap my Coke into his Bud.

"Technically . . ." I nod my head side-to-side and look up to the right.

"Fine, I gave you a chair. *Oh, look what a gentleman I am*," he mocks.

We both ease back into leaning against the tailgate and laugh together, maybe admitting we had each other a little wrong.

"So, tell me, Mabee. I thought your parents were super strict. How did you get them to let you drive the mom van out here for such a sordid affair?" He eyes me over his bottle as he tilts it back for another long drink. He'll be drunk within the hour at this pace.

"Well," I begin, pausing as I shift my position, letting my free arm hug my waist. I don't talk about my family, but maybe that's another thing I should change. I lean my head to the side and let out a short nervous laugh. He reaches forward, lightly touching my arm.

"Go on," he urges.

I look up at him, a part of me maybe making sure he's earnestly interested. His eyes don't move from mine, so I take a deep breath. "It's just *parent*, really. They split up, freshman year."

He nods, and it's a little bit like he's familiar with this part, but maybe I'm just reading into that.

"And my mom, she would prefer me to be a little, no . . . *a lot* more social than I am." He snickers at that, taking yet one more drink. I let my arm fall free of my stomach and hold my Coke in both palms, swishing it a little to hear the fizz.

"She workin' tonight?" He cocks a brow, and I respond with a sideways look. If he's looking to take me home—*alone*—that's a hard no.

"Yes," I say tentatively. "But she knows I'm here. We switched cars so I could drive."

He licks his lips, the slightest appearance of his tongue, and my trust fortress rearms itself. He backs off though, shifting his posture and putting a little more distance between us. He holds his now-empty bottle up for me to salute again. He's getting buzzed, but I indulge him.

"Cheers to the designated drivers!" he says.

"Cheers!" a few people nearby echo, because he's getting kind of loud.

"You need another?" He taps on the top of my can. It's still half full.

"I'm good." I nod. He tips his head back and takes the last remaining droplets of his beer, then tosses the bottle into a pile forming at the center of this gathering.

"Well, I'm empty. I'll be back in a bit!" His stride has gotten looser, but for whatever reason, he's still a little engaged in talking to me. It's better than me wandering around lost. My girlfriends have all found circles to join, all of them drinking at about the same pace as Tory. I'm going to keep the windows down on the way home in case anybody vomits.

A heavy clunk to my right jerks my attention around. Lucas is pushing the tailgate of his truck up, missing the catch the first few times and shoving it three more times before it holds. He claps his hands together to remove the dirt—his truck's been through some mud, it seems—but remains behind his vehicle for a few long seconds, his eyes focused on the ground. His jaw works back and forth in thought before his gaze finally lifts to meet mine. It doesn't stick. He and I, we can't seem to look at each other for long.

"Be smart with that," he says, signaling with a short wave to where Tory is talking with my friends. I stare at the scene for a beat to decipher his message. I glance back his way to find the top of his hat, the brim turned forward again so he can hide. Coward.

"You jealous or something?"

I can't believe that was out loud.

His shoulders quake with a quiet laugh and he shakes his head, eyes looking back at the ground. He lifts his head to meet my stare and to raise the right side of his mouth in a mocking laugh.

"Sure, June." His gaze lingers a little longer this time, a flatness to his eyes that insults me without words. That look is meant to call me stupid. But I know that look wouldn't be necessary if what I said didn't hurt him a little.

I had him. Once. In my own way. And that's why Ava hates me.

Lucas walks in the opposite direction from me, heading into a thick outcropping of trees that sinks down a ravine. It's where Ava is, and a few of the others I saw smoking joints by the beer. Maybe he'll get high and find some sort of peace. None of that will do anything to solve how he's going to feel when his parents' marriage falls apart. Of course, there's always the chance that his dad gets away with it forever.

Whatever.

I sit on the back of Tory's truck, waiting for him to come back, uneasy again when half an hour passes. I busy myself playing dumb games on my phone, eventually texting Abby to come rescue me. She doesn't show up for ten more minutes, and when she does, the other girls are with her. We all crawl into the bed of the truck and pull our knees up to gossip and talk shit about other people who are probably having the same conversations about us. For the first time since freshman year, I feel I belong. An hour of easy jokes passes, girl time and camaraderie. Tory and his brother eventually join us and we censor our jokes from including them, but the easiness continues.

Tory doesn't start next to me, but eventually he winds up there, sitting on the side of the truck bed, his leg against my shoulder, keeping me close. A few times, he even reaches down and squeezes my shoulders gently while telling a story. I look up at him, both nervous but kind of glad to be the object of anyone's anything. I should have known none of that would last.

"Careful there, Tory. Little virgin girl might just be a cock tease," Ava says, her voice carrying up and over our conversation from the end of the tailgate. It takes me a second to understand what's happening, how those words are meant to hurt me, but when I do, I scramble to my feet and walk to the edge of the truck. I might not have curves, but I do have muscle. And I have rage. I could pound Ava Pryor into the dirt if I wanted to.

"At least I'm not the one who throws her panties around people's cars," I say, drawing exaggerated *ooo's* from my friends and a few who pretend they know what I'm talking about.

Ava lets out a short laugh and puts her hand on her hip, her makeup smudged from being drunk and her hair tangled from whatever it is she probably just did with Lucas. I hop down and land a few feet in front of her, my act tough enough to make her flinch back a step or two. Her reaction emboldens me. I step closer, but this time she holds her ground. Pretty soon, we're close enough to kiss.

"Mommy out working the streets tonight? That why they let you come out to play?" she says, her voice low but the words loud enough that the people around us hear.

My mouth waters with instant rage, and without thinking it through, I step back and fling my right open palm against her face hard enough that her body staggers a few steps to my left. Her squeal gets even more attention, and my hand throbs from the contact. *That fucking hurt!* She's totally going to have a black eye.

I'm glowing off this power trip, energized by the shouts from my friends behind me. Ava finds her balance and spits at the ground, then shifts her weight to come back at me. I lift my right arm again, figuring I might as well keep all the hurt in one place. Before I can take a good swing though, this time with a fist, a strong hand wraps around my wrist and pulls it to the side before another hand holds at the center of Ava's chest.

"You!" Lucas is staring Ava down, a warning in his wide eyes. She argues a few times but he talks over her, pointing to his truck. "Get your ass in there. That's enough!"

I've started to laugh, but Lucas's attention focuses on me next. His eyes lock on mine, a million words passing behind them all at once. Disappointment, regret . . . apology maybe?

"Just . . . fucking stop, June," he says, exasperation in his voice. My clenched muscles weaken, and my arm grows limp and falls from his hold. My eyes peer over his shoulder to Ava, slowly walking backward. *Why her?*

"Your mom's a fucking whore, you know!" she shouts, her words stunning me where I stand. Lucas took away my weapons. He left me defenseless.

"I said get your ass in my truck!" He points at her more forcefully, a redness coloring his neck, the lines showing how tense he is, how angry.

His eyes come back to me and the expression isn't soft. There is no pity in his gaze. He's holding back. There are things he wants to say, and I wish he just would. What else could be said that would hurt me now? He doesn't speak though, instead falling back a step or two as he shakes his head, a silent way to say "don't."

I shake my head in response, a shudder kicking my chest with a short cry that I wipe away in an instant with my forearm.

"Is she your girlfriend? That?" I let out a judgmental laugh and point at the cruel person crawling into his passenger side. I bite my lip through more sad laughter, then look into his eyes, the blue now roiling with fire. "Or is she just some girl you fuck? No matter what, you know she's part of your story now. That . . . that is what you are—*who you are.*"

Everything around us has become quiet. Lucas doesn't flinch. The burn settles into my cheeks the longer he stares at me. I'm being foolish.

Foolish, foolish girl with some unrequited crush.

Goddamn, what have I done?

Lucas spits at the ground in front of him and looks to Tory who holds up two open palms, claiming his innocence. He is innocent. This scene, it's all me.

I remain still until Lucas walks completely away, rounding his truck and getting inside. His engine roars, but I don't move until Abby's hand gently runs down my shoulder and arm. She squeezes me to her side and I tremble a little, still coming down from the high of being so damn mad and letting it out.

"Can we be done now?" I ask, wondering how in the hell I'm going to calm down enough to drive.

"Yeah, we can be done," she says, moving her hand down my arm even more until her hand grasps a strong hold of mine. "I know it doesn't feel like it right now, but you did something good right there."

"It feels the exact opposite of good," I admit, nervous pulse-laden words falling from my numb lips.

"I know. Doesn't mean it's not, though," she says, guiding me to our van. I get in and wait while the others take their spot. They don't talk until I'm ready, and they never make me say anything more. They repeat the scenario over and over, praising me for being strong. All I can see, though, are those damn blue, disappointed eyes that went home with someone else.

For a while, I haven't come out here at night. Living next door to Lucas means our old shared hiding places are off limits. But eventually, I realize he doesn't care about the abandoned treehouse falling apart near the back of my yard, or the rusted-out shell of the Forty-eight Buick that my dad left behind for my mom to deal with when he decided he didn't love her anymore. I don't come out here often because I can still see Lucas's window, the view into his room all too clear when his light is on. He paces a lot when he's on the phone. He also likes to leave the lights on when he brings girls upstairs late at night. I've seen too much from this front seat of the tire-less car that will never run. But the burn on my cheeks from the very public words said by his on-again, off-again girlfriend in front of virtually everyone in our senior class is too hot for me to care about any of that. I need a place to hide where even Abby can't find me for a while—a place to cry it out.

Goddamn him for deciding now, *of all the nows*, is the one he chooses to finally show up again in the dark corner where our yards meet. It's well after midnight, and I'd planned on staying here until sunrise, away from my phone that I'm sure Abby is blowing up, and away from my house where maybe my new friends might come knocking, worried. At least my mom isn't home; I'm not sure I could hide my state from her.

I close my eyes and sniffle hard while he's still a good four or five strides away from the passenger door. It creaks open, popping when the hinge catches, and I jerk my head to the right and open my eyes. He slides in next to me and yanks the door closed behind him. It's filthy in here, and his weight on the ripped fabric sends a poof of dust into the closed cabin.

"You didn't have to come check on me. I'll survive." I cough through my last few words and inwardly chide myself for liking that he showed up. He quickly dashes the fantasy that he came here because he cared.

He starts with a heavy sigh, his hands cupping his jean-covered knees and irritably scratching at them.

"I'm not here for you, June. I'm here to tell you—no, to *beg* you—to please keep your nosey ass out of my life."

My mouth falls open, and my chest is hammered with a mix of hurt and anger. Before I can react with words, Lucas shifts in his seat, bringing his right knee up to lean to the side and palm the rotted out dashboard. His large hand pats down, leaving a dustless print in its wake. I suddenly feel small.

His head shakes, and his face wears a soured expression.

"You judge—" he begins.

"No, I don't." I interrupt in protest, but his hand pats down again with his forced laugh.

"You do, and it's so . . . hypocritical. What I do with Ava, whether she's my girlfriend, whether we break up, whomever I decide to be with and however far that goes? None. Of. Your. Business." He leans back against the door and gives me the full heat of his stare. My pulse races to keep up with the arguments forming in my mind—all the things I know—that could devastate him. I was only defending myself. None of this was about him, not completely. And how can I be a hypocrite when I'm still a virgin?

"You missed most of everything I said, Lucas. I wasn't talking about you. That rant—it was about me." His face is stone cold and still. I don't know why I expect my childhood friend to break through this hard exterior that's swallowed him whole.

"I heard you. And you're right, every person you fuck becomes a part of your story."

I swallow at how bluntly he sums up my point.

"But people write themselves into our stories lots of ways, June." He shakes his head and lowers his gaze to his lap as his hand slides down the dash with a heavy exhale. The last evidence of his boyish youth is dusted along his cheeks and eyelashes in golden freckles and highlights picked up by the moonlight. Even those are seemingly disappearing before my eyes.

The crack of the door opening behind him breaks my hard stare, and in one smooth movement he steps from the passenger side and bends down to level me with his cerulean eyes. I wrote to Crayola once when we were younger because I wanted them to make a crayon I could use to do his eyes justice. What a foolish crush I've had.

"We've never fucked, but you sure are part of my story." I wince because that's not a compliment. "I can't delete you, but I sure don't need you taking up any more chapters. Stay the fuck out of my business, and go find yourself a boyfriend who can be all of these things you think are real."

He pauses for a brief moment, long enough to grin with half his mouth and puff out the smallest laugh at my expense. He slams the door as he backs away, and I don't bother to shift my position to watch where he goes. Like he said, he's none of my business.

Except as far as stories go, he's always been a major plot line in mine. Not sure life gets a rewrite the way fiction does. At the very least, I don't think I'll be hiding my feelings in the Buick again for a while.

NINE

I'm not sure I've slept since the party Friday night. Maybe my brain has shut down a little here and there, but I'm pretty sure my eyes focused on various points in my empty house for every single second of the last forty-eight hours. My head is pounding, deep dark circles look like charcoal under my eyes, and my mom should be home any minute.

I'm going to have to play sick.

I'm going to need my strength to get through Monday morning, sitting in front of Lucas without falling into the temptation to engage. Maybe it's delirium, but the more I think about everything he said, the harder it is to reconcile his arguments with his behavior. He pushes me as much as I push him. The fact we have to share proximity at home— At school? That's neither of our faults. But when he opens his mouth to speak to me, he makes a choice, and he chooses every word he says. I need to become the bigger person and ignore the temptation to participate in this tug-of-war we've entered into. Even if I have the power to win by dropping a bomb on his happy home life.

I hear the familiar whirl of my car engine in the driveway, so I get into position, wrapping myself in my favorite quilt and turning the TV low on the home improvement channel while I bundle myself on the couch for my mom to discover. It takes her a few minutes to get her things together and make her way through the side door, but when it opens, I call out to let her know where I am.

Time to perform.

"I'm on the couch," I yell, coughing at the end of my sentence. I saw a movie like this once where a kid faked sick so he could ditch school and run amuck all over Chicago. I only want to avoid prying questions over my emotional state.

"Hey!" She sounds beat, her bags banging into the wall as she rounds the corner to where I am. She stops just behind the couch, dropping her bags. "Oh, someone not feeling so hot?"

"Cold, I think. Started not feeling well after the party." This lie has to have some truth to it. I'm not good at lying to my mom. I don't do it, ever . . . much. Fuck, I'm doing it now.

"Fever?" She reaches over the back of the couch and presses her cool hand to my forehead. I don't have one, but that feels good. Lack of sleep might feel a lot like a fever.

I glance up as she pulls her hand away, and I must look rougher than I imagine because my mom flinches at the sight of me.

"I haven't slept very well," I say, adding to the hard sell.

Her gaze lingers on me for a few long seconds, and I sense she's running her bullshit meter. I might not be passing.

We both startle when the front bell rings. I sit up and run my fingers through my tangled nest of hair while my mom rushes over to look through the side window. I've been wearing the same sweatpants and unicorn shirt since I left the Buick, but anyone who comes to our door wouldn't care, so I get to my feet in case it's something my mom needs help with.

"It's a . . . boy?" She says that as if she's not sure, so I move a little closer.

"Like, one we know?" My response sounds amused.

"Well, the only one I know lives next door, and this isn't him, but he looks like Lucas. Maybe one of his friends?"

Shit.

I glance down at my unicorn shirt with a new perspective. There's a chocolate ice cream stain right where the horn is, like magic popping out of the magic unicorn tip. I don't have to peek through the window to know, but I do anyway, just as Tory cups his eyes and peeks inside. He laughs when our eyes meet, then waves.

"Friend of yours?" My mom lifts a brow, teasingly. I don't get male visitors. I've had one boyfriend, and he was from my Montessori school and lived more than twenty miles away. We either met in the middle at the mall, or my mom dropped me off at his house.

"He's in my fifth hour," I say, moving past my mom to answer the door.

"I'll get rid of him," I add, opening the door and hoping Tory didn't hear me dismiss him like that. I'm not out to purposely hurt feelings—at least, not *everyone's* feelings.

Only a few people's feelings.

"Getting rid of me, huh?"

"Sorry." I wince. "I didn't want my mom to get all . . . nosy?"

He smirks at my response.

"No, no, I'm not flirting." I stop any ideas he might have about a me and him, expecting him to laugh it off with me. When he doesn't, I shrink my chin into my chest and back up toward the door, a little freaked out.

"Why would that be so bad?" He leans into the post of our front porch, thumbs hooked in his front pockets, hair combed to the side and one eyebrow raised. Basically, he's a character from Grease the way he stands in his letter jacket.

"Tory . . ." A nervous giggle is the only thing I can seem to get out after his name.

He stares at me long enough for my anxious laughter to subside, then moves down a step and sits, gesturing for me to sit with him. I do, resting with my back against the guardrail so I'm as far from him as I can be while sharing a step. He laughs at my invisible wall, mocking me a little by moving close enough to his side of the wooden stair to cling to the post. I relax a little when he does it and shrug off my overreaction.

"Look, I'm not saying date me. I don't date," he begins. I puff out a laugh.

"How romantic."

He glares at me with straight-lined lips.

"I can be very romantic. I promise you, romance is all over this body," he says, running his hand around his chest. I laugh genuinely at his expense.

"Fuck off," he says, standing and walking down my walkway.

"Tory, I'm sorry," I say, feeling guilty. He stops and turns a few yards away, facing me as he exhales.

"I like your company. And honestly? I could use a friend who isn't . . . your jackass neighbor. Or my twin. Or some other jock who thinks and acts like I do."

I wait him out for a beat, surveying the nuances of his expression, but they never betray his words. I think he honestly just wants to spend time with me.

I look down at my shirt and pull the unicorn out from my chest. "Even if I decide to go somewhere with you while wearing this?"

His eyes dip down and his mouth hangs open.

"No, on second thought, forget it. I mean, I was digging your vibe and all, but then I noticed that little chocolate stain and—" He pauses, stepping closer and pointing at my shirt. I look down and he flicks his finger up at my nose, a joke my mom's brother, my uncle John, does every single freaking time he sees me. I roll my eyes and stand to face off with him.

"Come on, let's go get burgers. Drive-thru, clearly," he says, waving an arm up and down at my appearance. I laugh, but I also want to go. I want to get out of here, out of my funk.

"All right, let me get some shoes and tell my mom," I say, padding up the step and back to the door.

"Meet you in my car," Tory says over his shoulder.

I wave in acknowledgement as I step inside. My mom is waiting right where I left her, probably overtly watching out the window.

"Don't stare like that," I say, walking by her and toward the sofa, where my flip flops have lived for two days. I'm doing my best to combat her gooey, mushy boy-crush eyes. My mom has long had hopes for some normalcy in my coming-of-age story. It's never been about being a busybody, or a matchmaker, but more that she's afraid her story has changed the course of mine. I'd never tell her this, but I think maybe it has.

I toss my hoodie on over my makeshift pajamas, my phone and wallet tucked in the pocket, and slide back toward the door in my flipflops. My mom halts me with a stiff arm, though, before I get to the door.

"So, we're not feeling sick now, huh?" Her brow arches . . . again. It's been doing that a lot.

"I haven't been out of the house in two days, and someone wants to buy me a burger. It's a free burger," I say, shaking my head.

She turns her head just a fraction, side-eying me, and says "Uh huh." "Midnight," she adds, with a stern nod.

I nod back, though it is weird for her to give me a curfew. She's never given me one before, but that's probably because I literally don't go anywhere. At least, I haven't gone anywhere during these risk-laden teenage years. My hunch is that Tory's slick look has something to do with this. He does put off a bit of an "I'm gonna head to some drag-races with your daughter in tow" kind of face.

The front door doesn't close behind me until I'm almost to Tory's car, and the only reason I know it finally does is because of the hysterical laughter Tory bursts into as he rolls down the passenger window of his Toyota.

"I'm sorry. My mom—"

"Is being a mom," he interrupts. "Mine is just as embarrassing."

I laugh lightly as I slide into the seat and buckle up, but when I turn my head away, I'm sure the scowl is harsh on my face. His mom. Lucas's dad. Best friends with this secret I know happening behind their backs. I swallow and turn back to nod that I'm ready while clutching my phone and wallet in my lap.

"Two-fers?" he asks, shifting into drive and flipping around in front of Lucas's house.

"Sounds good," I say, a little rush of nerves tickling my chest. Two-fers is pretty much *the* place for high schoolers in our community. They sponsor every Public football game. But they also have the best crinkle fries in the county, so having to sit in the D'Angelo car in my jammies in front of people who have always intimidated the hell out of me is maybe worth it. Plus, the drive is short.

I glance to Tory's phone screen, his cell sitting in the cup holder while it streams to his speakers. He's listening to old-school R&B, and I don't know why that surprises me, but it does.

"What? I don't strike you as a Wilson Pickett fan?" He turns the volume up and mouths the words along with the song. It takes me a few lines of the song to notice he's making his version up.

"You're such a bullshitter!" I take his phone into my palm and sift through the songs, all of them as choice as this one. Then I note the name on the playlist.

HAYDEN'S SHIT

I smack at Tory's leg and set his phone back in the cup holder.

"You like this stuff?"

I nod, singing along with the correct words. My voice, however, is terrible. This song in particular occupies space within me. Lucas and I sang this in a talent show at his parents' house, along with a few of his cousins and my parents and some other family friends. That was back when those backyard chairs that now collect dust had people in them.

We pull into the crowded Two-fer's parking lot and into a scene that looks a whole lot like the party I endured Friday night. Tory must sense my unease because he turns the music down and nudges my arm with his fist.

"We'll stay in the car, do the drive-thru and park out of the way," he says.

I smile and breathe a sigh of relief.

The drive-thru line is surprisingly short given the crowd around the joint, but most people go to the walk-up window then hang out. Two cop cars sit facing each other near the last two parking spaces. There tend to be a lot of fights at Two-fers, so the police have started filling out their reports here. I'm pretty sure they get free food.

"So, are you a dog or burger kinda girl?" Tory asks, leaning his arm out his window, waiting to give our order.

"Dog, all the way," I say, catching the instant snicker on his lips.

"Please don't make a dick joke," I sigh out.

"Doggy style?" He shoots me a crooked smile but quickly apologizes. He orders two double-dog deals with Cokes and pulls around to the window. We're a few cars back from the front, and a new quiet has settled in.

"I'm not a prude," I say. Not sure why *that's* the word I choose, but I don't want him thinking I'm someone I'm not, or that I'm actually offended by his lame jokes. I just sometimes need a break from them.

"I'm not sure how to respond to that," he says through a nervous laugh.

I blush.

"I don't mean, like, well—" I stammer.

"I know what you mean. I talk a lot of shit and I'm loud and obnoxious, and fuck, can I get lit at a party!" Guilty laughter tumbles out of him. "I guess it's a little bit my crutch, if that makes sense? Like, that's my part that I play. I'm the douchebag." He swings his fist from right to left to accentuate his sarcasm.

"You're not a douchebag," I reassure as we move up another space.

He turns his head and tilts it to rest against his seat, a wry smile playing at his lips.

"Come on, be honest. You wouldn't have said that a week ago."

I fess up quickly and nod.

"Oh, absolutely not. You were a douchebag then, but that's only because I didn't really know the other identities of Salvatore D'Angelo." He cringes as I use his whole name.

"And what are those other identities?" he asks.

I twist my lips and look up, blowing at the loose hairs that have fallen loose from the messy bun I twisted my hair into while he was ordering.

"I think maybe . . . yeah . . . damn, I'm about to say this." I level him with a serious look. "You're part gentleman."

He stares at me, unflinching, dead serious—for about three seconds.

"Get outta here!" He shoves at me playfully and waves a hand, brushing off the compliment. I let it go there because that's his way of saying thanks. It was a rather back-handed way to say something nice to him anyhow, and that's because I'm uncomfortable. That trust thing with me, it's a tough nut to crack.

I flip through a few more songs on his brother's playlist until we get to the window for our food. I notice he gives me the box with more fries, and I almost point out how that's one of his gentlemanly qualities, but a black Nissan cuts off our path, pulling into one of the spaces to our right. It's Lucas.

And Ava.

"We can leave," Tory offers.

"No," I hum, my gaze stuck on Lucas's form as he maneuvers his truck in backward. Tory hovers near the exit for a second but lets me make this call, pulling his car into a spot almost directly across from them.

I do my best to focus on my fries after that, searching for the perfect one with slightly burnt tips and golden grooves. I lick the salt from my fingers and mumble out, "This is good" as I take a bite that clears out nearly a third of one of my dogs. I go in for a second bite, and Tory halts me, handing me a packet of ketchup. I look at it with my mouth agape and flit my eyes to him.

"Nobody, I mean *nobody,* puts ketchup on a hot dog," I say, putting on the best raspy voice I've got. I play serious for a few more seconds, waiting for Tory to laugh, but he just shrugs and goes on drenching his food in that tomato shit.

Lucas would have gotten that joke. One summer, we watched every Dirty Harry movie Eastwood made. His dad had the collection on Blu-ray. He probably still does, last relevant Blu-ray collection in America, I bet. We liked the swearing and the violence—me, mostly because my parents didn't let me watch that stuff at home, and him, I think, because he was the one sneaking it for me. We couldn't eat hotdogs without laughing, but we never said the line out loud in front of our parents for fear they put it together.

That memory hangs heavy in my chest, and my eyes glance out the front window for the first time in a while. Across the way, Ava is talking out the passenger window to a few other girls, and Lucas is eating his fries one at a time, looking anywhere but at her.

I bet he's bored. That's me, wishing.

"Hey, don't you work at Eight Lanes?"

"Huh?" I stir out of my trance and turn to find Tory's eyes, his mouth full from his last bite. He glances out the window to Lucas then back at me with a muffled laugh from cheeks filled with bready bun bits.

"Sorry, I can't help it," I admit.

"You got a crush or something?" He takes another big bite, but stares at me through his chewing, as if that's an easy question to answer. Besides, I'm pretty sure he knows the history there. I've known him as long as I've known Lucas, longer maybe.

"It's complicated," I say.

"Yeah, I figured. He does this same weird shit you do when I'm with him," he says, finishing the last bite of his second dog. Meanwhile, I have one and a half left. He takes a long drink of his soda while I stare at him, waiting for him to elaborate.

"What?" he asks, when he finally looks at me again.

"What same weird shit?" I ask.

I'm jittery all of a sudden.

"You know, he stares at you to make sure you're not having too much fun over here while he's over there, pretending he's not *really* looking at you, or if he is then it's because you irritate him or whatever." He sours his mouth and rolls his eyes. "I don't get you guys."

"I was gone for a full year. I wasn't around to stare at." I brush him off. I pick at my hotdog, pretty sure I won't be able to eat the second one.

"Yeah, but like at your house on weekends, or if you were somewhere we were, his attention wandered off a little. He hated me calling him on it, which of course, ya know, means I basically watch him like a hawk so I can needle him about any glance he gives your way." He breathes out a laugh, lifting a shoulder in a braggart kind of way.

"What a friend," I deadpan.

"A real gentleman," he corrects, with a wink. He reaches toward my lap and points at the still-wrapped dog. "You gonna eat that?"

I lift both hands and puff out my cheeks. He grabs it and devours it in four bites.

"So, Eight Lanes," he says. "That's what I was asking you about before, when you were off in your *la la fairy crush land*."

I close my eyes and shake my head, dismissing that term.

"I know, I know . . . it's complicated," he says, reaching over to my box and stealing a few fries.

"Yes, I work at Eight Lanes," I say, pivoting the topic away from Lucas.

"Think you can get me a job there?" His hand creeps over to swipe a few more of my fries, but this time I swat his knuckles.

"Ow!" He plays it up a little, shaking his hand.

I try to imagine my work shift with Tory hanging around, and even though I think the bosses would hate him, he would be fun to have around, and we *are* hiring.

"I'll see what I can do," I say, not making promises.

Tory brushes salt from his hands and gathers up the trash into the Two-fers bag, tossing it out his window and into the trash about twenty feet away. I clutch my container of fries to my chest and continue to pick at them as he shifts gears and slowly pulls out. Always my own worst enemy, I spend these moments studying Lucas, half hoping to catch him in the act of looking back. I don't really expect to, but then, just before I look away, our eyes meet. I don't know why I care so much. And I can't believe he really does. But there's a visceral pain that comes with this brief exchange. I taste it. And for whatever reason, it hurts like hell.

TEN

Somehow, I manage to get through one Friday with no game and no party. My best friend has the flu. Even dog tired and burning up, she still tries to rally. But when she can't get through a sentence without hacking up a lung, her mom puts her foot down. Abby has a pretty big commercial to film in a couple weeks. Right now, she sounds like a chain smoker.

Lola and Naomi don't have the same pull over me that Abby does. Besides that, I picked up the Friday shift since I hadn't worked at the bowling alley during my first week of school. I need the cash. I'm going to need to save about two thousand dollars to pay for the first year at County College, which at this point is pretty much my dream school.

I thought I would enjoy my old routine—ear pods in, *Best of Bowie* on repeat, all the free popcorn I want. Yet, all I can think about is the score, where Lola and Naomi are sitting without me, and whether or not Lucas's dad is standing for the entire game. I give in about midway through my shift and follow the score on the high school sports app on my phone.

That's a lie. I don't care about the score. I care about Lucas's performance. I find myself rooting for him, waiting for small updates on passing yards and completions when we have the ball.

We win, and Lucas threw for almost three hundred fifty yards. I'm satisfied. I catch myself smiling as I wipe down the shoe rental counter at the end of my shift. I drive home in a roundabout way, finally giving in and driving by the damn field. The lights are still on, and the forty-two to ten score is still up on the board to show off our blowout. The stands are completely empty.

But not the parking lot.

One black Nissan truck. I turn off my lights and pull to the side of the road for a minute, maybe two. Lucas's lights are on, and his truck faces to the side, so I have a decent view of the cab. He's alone. No glow of a phone light, no Ava. He's merely a profile from this distance, but there are nuances to his movements.

He's slouched down enough that his head rests on his headrest, his eyes looking up, or maybe closed in thought. His palm runs down his face a few times, seconds apart. I leave just after he leans forward and presses his forehead to the steering wheel. I recognize when someone feels defeated and lost. Even as we stand now, I can't sit here and watch it. I think about it though, all the way until I can't keep my eyes open at 4 a.m.

I wake up this morning and pledge to clear my mind of all things Lucas. I blow that promise when all the seniors on the football team come barreling into the alley. I run to fix stray pins and clean the ball return gears, a job I really don't need to do; I run back there to hide. And now . . . I'm stuck.

It's amazing the clout people give to seventeen and eighteen-year-old dudes simply because they can throw balls and run into people while wearing pads. Morty, the guy who owns this joint, just brought their table a pitcher of beer and a full pizza. I bet he doesn't bring that when the marching band kids come in for the midnight bowl.

Hypocrite.

It's a bit of a tight squeeze back here, so I find a spot between lanes five and six, wedged between the pinsetters. A few of us eat our lunches back here because the Wi-Fi is pretty good in this area and you can stream Netflix on your phone without buffering. I finished the first season of *The Office* back here during my first month on the job.

I'm not streaming anything now, though. I'm too caught up in the show happening at the other end of the lanes. They're loud, typical jockheads making crass jokes and picking each other up just to prove they can. We're a little slow this morning, but a few of the families have moved to lanes on the other end just to gain some space. Morty should probably turn the music up, too.

While most of the guys pace around racks looking for balls, Lucas and Tory enter names on the screen. Lucas is wearing his hoodie pulled over his head, his mouth a hard line and face full of shadows. I wonder if it's leftover frustration from whatever feelings he was trying to process last night after the game. I read the highlights when I got home, thinking maybe I missed something when I was following on my phone, but no—his game was impeccable. Maybe his father didn't think so.

His father.

I keep coming back to it.

My phone buzzes in my back pocket, so I stand to pull it out, balancing carefully in the small space so I don't bump into any of the machinery. It's a text from a number I don't recognize.

We can see you, FYI

I scrunch my face and glance to either side. Nobody is back here, which means whoever is texting me is out there.

Tory?

It takes less than a breath for my phone to buzz in my palm.

No shit.

I laugh silently and lean out to peek through the back of the pinsetter to where the boys are, about three alleys over. I hold my palm out close to my body when I spot him standing behind Lucas, who is still focused on the screen. He holds his hand out the same way then looks at his phone and begins typing again.

There's a mirror.

Brow drawn in, I blink at his text a few times, now settled back in my safe spot. My eyes scan to both sides again while I mentally draw the schematics of this place and think about the sound pads on the walls, the bright lights and disco colors. And then it hits me. I lean my head back slowly, lifting my chin until my gaze finds itself reflected right back at me, upside down.

Motherfuck.

I punch out a laugh and contemplate how many times I've sat back here, oblivious to the fact anyone with a little curiosity could watch the flip-side version of me doing lord knows what. I'm pretty sure I've picked my nose once or twice, just a little. I *know* I've pulled out a wedgie or adjusted bras. The more I study my reflection, the more I realize all of the details you can see—like the way even a modest shirt like my Eight Lanes uniform is unbuttoned just enough for a view. I think about the senior league made up of mostly sixty-five-plus men who comes in on Sundays and always tries to "tip" me, and cringe.

Are you hiding or on break?

I consider going with the harmless little lie, then I fall into my usual pattern.

I'm hiding. Don't laugh.

It's too late, though, because I already hear him bellowing. I twist to look around the pinsetter again and this time, I'm met with four sets of eyes—both D'Angelo twins, some big guy who I think is named Kade, and Lucas. Three smiles and one mouth that is completely void of being human.

My body is hot, and I'm pretty sure a bead of sweat just dripped down my spine. My neck is hot; even with my hair pulled back into a knot, I'm cooking. They keep this place freezing, so I know it's just me.

Tory invites me to join them with a huge gesture, as if I'm somewhere on the other side of a field. I swallow and Lucas turns to look at his friend; his shoulders visibly slumping. I type a quick message to Tory.

Pretty sure I'm only half invited.

I stare at him while he reads, noting the way his body shakes in amusement. He doesn't bother to text back this time, instead cupping his mouth with one hand. I brace myself for it about a half-second before the sound comes out.

"Maybe Mabee would like to come say hi to her friends!" His hand slowly falls away, and a smug-ass grin covers his face. My joints turn to Jell-O.

Friends.

I'm pretty sure I only have one friend over there. I definitely have one enemy.

I can't stay here, though. Even faking work on one of the ball returns would look like an excuse. Plus, now that I know everyone can see me, I might not ever break back here again. I shove my phone into the back pocket of my jeans and relent, ducking under one of the frames and stepping onto the space between the far lanes. I know better than to look away from my feet, but my ego gets the best of me and I glance up, just for a second, to see whether Lucas is watching me. That's when I fall.

Bowling lane wax is not to be trifled with. One misstep sends my left foot two feet to the left, my arms flailing to find balance while my right foot struggles to hold on. It's useless to fight it, but I decide to give in too late. My legs jut out too far in front of my body and I'm airborne for what feels like a full minute, though I'm sure it's only a blink. The wind leaves my lungs as soon as I slam to the wood, but that's not what hurts the most. My head falls back onto the sharp corner of the gutter, and actual stars form around my vision like bright fireworks flashing in front of my face.

"June!"

My name sounds as if it's being shouted through a tunnel. I'm not sure whether the echo is in my head or in the room. The gasping sounds coming from my own mouth seem so foreign, and my head is ringing. The thunderous sound of running feet rushes my way, and in my daze, I expect to see ten guys rushing to my aid. My head falls to the right and my eyes struggle to stay open.

I have a fucking concussion. I know I do.

My vision is super fuzzy, and fading in and out. What appears to be three pair of legs sliding my direction settles into one pair by the time the person they belong to is at my side.

"June, careful. Don't move."

Ignoring the advice, I roll to my side, but only because I think I might vomit.

"You can't carry her on that. You'll slip, too!"

That voice is distinct. It's Morty, worried about all of the damn accident claim forms he'll have to fill out. Whomever he's yelling at doesn't seem to be listening because hands slide under my ribs and my right hip . On instinct, I reach up with my right arm and grab on to the shoulder of my life raft. It's only when my face is flat against the soft cotton of the hoodie that I recognize who is lifting me against his chest.

I breathe in Lucas's scent, the mix of his mom's lavender fabric softener and the wood and cinnamon of his cologne. He shifts his arms as he moves his legs under his body to stand, and I cling harder, not wanting to fall again. We rise easily, his arms and chest muscles flexing to maintain balance and hold me up.

"I can walk," I utter.

"Shhh," he responds quickly.

My view is of his jawline, the tendon on his neck defined from stress. His feet give way with his tiny steps, and he pauses.

"This shit is slippery," he shouts to his friends.

We have a carpet we roll out when things like this happen, not that they happen often. It's happened twice since I've worked here, and both times were drunk league bowlers who rushed the lane, pissed off about the ten pin not falling. I'm sure Morty is rushing to get the rug now, but Lucas keeps moving us forward.

I stare at his chin, not wanting to look because things around the room are spinning. His chin is my true north. It's the only thing not fucking moving.

"Almost there," he says, reassuring me.

I flinch when his body lunges forward with two massive steps. His balance steadies, though. He tucks his chin to look down, and our gazes meet for a second. That void expression I've seen lately has been replaced with a more stoic one, and his eyes have a concerned tilt to them.

"Tory, someone needs to drive her home, man. Get your car."

Lucas bends down and sets me in one of the plastic seats by the computer and ball return. My hand grips his sweatshirt as he slides me from his hold, and I end up tugging on the material at his waist. I think maybe he's going to step away, put some distance between us. But when I tug, he crouches down next to me and keeps his hand at the base of my neck.

"She's your neighbor, Lucas. Get over yourself and drive her home," Tory says. Lucas twists his head to look up at his friend, but I keep my focus on his chin and jaw. It's firm, and I sense he's not thrilled about getting a lecture.

While their stare-off stretches into long seconds, a new wave of vertigo tackles my brain and I have to close my eyes to will it away. With his attention divided, Lucas's help with my balance slips and as the stomach acid crawls up my throat, I lurch toward the floor. I fall from his grip and catch myself with my palms on the floor, but not before I throw up a little on my Eight Lanes shirt.

Keys jingle as they soar through the air over my head, and Tory takes off in a sprint. Finn, the college dude who's my assistant manager, has already rushed over with a bucket and mop, and the scent of Pine Sol assaults my nose. I cup my face as Lucas sweeps me back into his cradled arms and carries me through the front area and out the doors. I'd be mortified by all of this but I am in so much pain and so sick and dizzy that I don't have room to consider anything else.

Lucas's truck rumbles to the curb, and we pause as Tory rushes from the driver's side and opens the door so Lucas can set me inside. I fumble with the seat belt once he gets me into a sitting position, but his hand covers mine to stop me.

"You're not even close," he says, taking over until I hear the click.

He gently closes the passenger door, and I rest my head on the window as soon as it's secure. I'm not totally sure when Lucas gets into the driver's side, or when he pulls away from the bowling alley, but we're suddenly about halfway between my work and my home, and I'm kinda freaked because I missed some stuff.

"Hey, the tracks are coming up. I'll try to take them slow, but you might wanna pull your head from the window," he says. His voice is soft. I guess all our relationship required was a freaking traumatic brain injury for us to not be dicks to one another.

I sit up just before his tires crawl over the rough road, but the slow rocking sensation makes my world spin again and I moan.

"I think we need to get you looked at," Lucas says, reaching across the seats and palming my shoulder to help center me. I roll my head and look at him with sleepy eyes. When he pulls up to the last stop sign before my house, he glances to his right and studies my gaze for a few long seconds. For the slightest moment, I feel fine.

"You wait in the truck. I'll run in and get your mom," he says, gaze turning back to the road as he moves through the intersection. I reach up and press my palm against my own head, trying to work the thought inside to my mouth.

"She's not home." I finally get the basics out for him.

"Okay, well, I need your phone then so I can call her."

I nod slowly and reach around my body, feeling for my phone. My grip on it is poor when I get it out of my pocket, and I end up flinging it onto the floor in front of me.

"I'm so sorry," I say. I start to bend forward to get it, but Lucas pulls to the side of the road and touches my shoulder again to get me to stop. Once near the curb a few houses away from where we live, he scoots to the center of the seat and bends down, his body basically covering my entire lap. Despite my whirling environment, I'm acutely aware of his nearness and touch. Somehow, I don't fall over his back in a desperate hug. I want to, though, so my head must not be that far gone.

He lifts himself upright with my phone in his palm, and taps my screen to bring up the keypad. I open my mouth, prepared to utter my password, but he just types it in—04080901. I stare at him until he presses the phone to his ear and looks my way.

"Your birthday and your mom's birthday, same as the garage," he says, blinking once. I can't look away, even when he drops his gaze to his lap as he waits through a few rings before my mom answers.

"Mrs. Mabee, it's Lucas . . . Fuller," he says.

My mom's voice is muted, but her concern comes through in her tone and pitch.

"It's all right, but June slipped at work. I was there with some of the guys, and I didn't want her driving. Yeah . . . of course." He leans forward on his fist, resting his weight on his steering wheel like he did in the parking lot after the game last night.

"Sure, I can wait here. I kinda think she needs to go to the ER though?" He rolls his head to give me a sideways glance. I lift the right side of my mouth in a half grimace. I don't love doctors. Since my grandmother stayed with us and passed away, I've become a little wary of medical stuff.

"Yeah, she threw up once." He keeps his gaze on me but his focus roams around my face, his expression a little scientific, as though he's playing doctor and trying to diagnose something.

"I can do that. Yes. No, not a problem." There's a pause while she talks and he shifts the truck into drive and glances up into the rearview mirror. "I will call you the second we're there."

The call ends and Lucas sets my phone in the small cubbyhole above his stereo buttons. He isn't pulling forward; instead, he makes a wide U-turn, so I know we're not going home. We're going to the hospital. I'm a little panicked about it.

"Your mom said she's at the market or something? Is she like a cashier?" I can barely focus on his question, and my answer comes to me slowly.

"What? No, ummm," I stammer, scowling while I try to organize my thoughts. We are going to the ER but he also asked a question, two things. "She's selling her photography. She's shooting on her own now, and it's a farmer's market up north. Good for business."

He nods.

"Am I going to die?"

Lucas spits out a laugh and turns to see whether I'm joking. I'm not joking. Even though I know I'm not going to die, I'm not joking. This is how my brain works when hospitals get involved.

"No, June," he assures, looking back to the road. He reaches over and pats my knee, almost a fatherly gesture. I'm not sure how I feel about it, but I do feel less like I'm going to die.

My phone rings so I reach for it at the same time Lucas does.

"You're driving," I chastise.

He chuckles. "Yeah, well, you thought you were dying so I thought I should maybe answer."

I'd roll my eyes but I'm pretty sure that would send me tumbling out of the truck, so I look at my phone screen and palm the device between both hands. The caller ID says my mom, so I answer and put her on speaker.

"Mom?" I do a lousy job of hiding my panic.

"June? It's gonna be fine. We just want to make sure it's only a concussion, okay? Lucas? Are you there?" My mom has flipped into management mode. She's good in a crisis, which is probably a good thing because I seem to find a lot of those.

"Yes, ma'am," he says, moving into the left turn lane for the main road out of our neighborhood.

"I called the advanced urgent care on Seventy-Fifth. She's on the waiting list so hopefully you can walk right in and get through. They have my card and insurance on file. If you don't mind taking her home after? I would never make it there in time." I think she feels like a bad parent for leaving my care in the hands of a seventeen-year-old boy who bullied me only a week ago. She doesn't know that last part though, so maybe she just feels bad about the first thing.

"Got it. I'll make sure I call you when we get out of the doc," he says.

"Thanks," my mom says, pausing on the line. I pull the phone into my lap and take her off speaker, lifting the phone to my ear.

"I'm a little freaked out," I admit to her.

She expects this from me. I can tell because she has a speech prepared; I'm sure they're all the right words. It turns out I don't need any of those right now, though, because while I listen to her, Lucas reaches over and grabs my left hand. I don't think he's letting go, either.

I know I'm not.

ELEVEN

My head will be just fine. That was the consensus after an MRI.

My heart, however—it's fucked.

We wait for almost two hours before they call me in, which means it's dark by the time Lucas brings me home. We didn't talk much in the waiting room, mostly because my head was killing me and the TV mounted to the wall was playing *Friends* reruns so it was pretty easy to space out. It was never awkward, though. The quiet? It was natural, as were the few times he leaned forward to make sure my eyes were open as I sat slumped in the chair next to him, or when he made sure the air wasn't hitting me too hard during the drive home.

I start to think—hope—that maybe we're turning some kind of corner, that my clumsy fall and head injury might result in a little bit of good. Then Lucas turns his headlights off about four houses from ours and slows his truck as he leans close to the windshield, searching for something mysterious up ahead.

I ask if he sees something, like an animal or a person. My heart jumps, imagining maybe there's a burglar at my house.

"Get out." His voice is quiet but urgent. I sit up, attentive, and cling to the seat.

"Is something wrong?" My skin tingles with the rush of adrenaline.

"June, just fucking get out!"

I listen. I goddamn listen and obey and get out of the truck, medical papers in my hand along with a list of concussion symptoms to watch out for. I barely get the passenger door closed and he turns around and speeds off, leaving me under a canopy of trees casting creepy-ass shadows on the road, about four hundred yards from my house. When my mom asks a half-dozen times on Sunday to call Lucas for her so she can thank him—walk next door and ring their bell, buy him stupid cookies—I lie and say Tory ended up bringing me home.

"Lucas had somewhere he needed to go," I say. "He basically handed me off. He said he wouldn't be home all day."

She knows I'm lying by about 3 p.m. when the thump of that blasted basketball pounds on the driveway next door. She quits asking after that.

Thing is, not once do I think about that my car is still parked at Eight Lanes. Not when my mom took off early this morning for some school photo sessions she booked at the elementary school. Not a single time when she and I discuss that I'm not allowed to drive for twenty-four to forty-eight hours. And not when I talk to my best friend over breakfast, swapping stories about our weekends and how much shittier mine was than hers.

I don't think about it until right now as I look out upon my very empty driveway.

"Shit."

I pull my phone from my back pocket and redial Abby, hoping to catch her before she gets to school. I have a glint of hope when she answers right away.

"Dude, I need a ride!" I'm pacing while I talk, and as I move up the driveway, the Fuller garage opening clanks behind me. I shade my eyes from the morning sun as I glance over my shoulder to see whose car it is. It's Lucas's mom, and his dad's car is already gone.

"I'm at school. I have to meet with my counsellor about taking off most of November for that short film I was telling you about." Damn. I forgot.

"It's okay," I say, feeling very much *not* okay. I'm going to be late, and to me, being late is maybe one of the most painful things in life. I'd rather go through another MRI.

"Maybe you can get the bus?" She knows better, but I let her off the hook with a casual "Yeah, good idea" before I let her go. The bus left several minutes ago. I'd be better off running to school, but I'm not a runner. Two-plus miles might get me there by lunch. Fine, by second hour.

I'm staring at Lucas's truck. He's definitely leaving soon. It only makes sense for me to ask him for a ride, yet I still mull over the idea of a taxi or an Uber. He rounds the back of his house before I have a chance to duck out of sight, and stops about ten feet away from me, our eyes locked in a state of awkward panic. He's slowly chewing a bite from a protein bar, and his hand is frozen, holding it near his lips.

"I need a ride." I blurt out my request fast and loud. I wish I could write it off as a side-effect of my injury but no, that was just nerves playing out.

"Why?" he asks through a full mouth. He finishes chewing his bite and swallows hard while glancing over my shoulder as if there's some invisible van ready to take me to school.

"My car is still at work and my mom had a job," I say. I swallow, though not because I'm eating a protein bar. I'm choking down pride.

Lucas shifts his feet and glances to his truck, then to the closed garage behind him.

"Your mom just left," I say, filling in what I suspect he's trying to discern. Maybe he's hiding me from her. It stings a little.

His teeth grip his bottom lip and his jaw tightens as his eyes flit a few times between me and his truck. I start to feel really uncomfortable. I'm also dwelling on the dark walk home I had Saturday night, when he told me to get the fuck out of his truck.

I walk toward his passenger door without permission, and when he utters the word "Wait," I cut him off.

"You fucking owe me," I say, turning and pointing at him harshly.

His tongue pushes at the inside of his cheek but I hold my position, my glare full of fire and determination. He exhales and looks down, his expression frustrated but also yielding. I tug open the door the second he pushes the key fob and releases the lock, and I'm buckled and ready with my bag nestled between my knees before he even opens his door.

He drops his bag in the back of the truck then sighs, staring at the open space between us. He climbs in and reaches for the folding console on his way inside, knocking it down so we have a barrier. It's childish, and I don't care that he helped me after my accident; he's treating me as though I have the plague.

I wait until he gets in, his stupid letterman jacket sleeves crinkling as his arms bend, and I slam the center console back up to create a bench seat, leaving the path between us wide open. His head falls to the side and he stares at the space, an annoyed smile playing at his lips. Eventually, he shakes his head and turns on the truck, looking up to adjust his mirror.

"You and Tory friends now?" He slides through his phone and starts a playlist, some rap song playing loud enough to drown out my reply, so I decide I just won't answer.

A short laugh passes through my lips before I can trap it, but it's masked by the vibrations rattling the truck so Lucas doesn't notice. I lean my head on the passenger window but the buzzing is too much to take. My head still hurts a little, but thankfully my vision has been fine.

We zip backward down the driveway and Lucas jerks the wheel, taking off with enough force that my body jostles and my head slams into the headrest. A momentary heartbeat must fool him into caring because he glances to his right to check on me, and I happen to look just in time to see his widened eyes. The concern quickly switches off, though, and he's back to staring straight ahead, rolling through the various stop signs out of our neighborhood.

I'm sick of this hot and cold thing he does. I know I'm guilty of sometimes provoking it a little. Honestly, I'm not sure what drives me to needle him so much, other than no matter how hard I will this feeling away, there's a constant broadcast running through my head, telling me that the Lucas and me from a few years ago is still salvageable.

"Why did you make me walk?" I speak that loud enough that there is no doubt he heard. His eyes flinch a little, his lashes quaking at the sound of my voice. He pretends he didn't hear a word, and maybe it's because he doesn't want to answer. Or maybe he doesn't know the answer. Or maybe he's continuing this push-pull routine because he's as desperate as I am to cling to some sort of connection between us.

I let my glare burn into the side of his face until the heat of it is so intense that he has to deal with it.

"June, just drop it," he says.

Damn it. I'm going to engage. I punch the power button on his stereo system with my thumb, stuffing the cab with silence while we still have at least a mile or more in our trip to school. When he reaches forward, I slap his hand away, my fingertips stinging his wrist. He bunches his face and turns to give me an angry stare, but in the midst our childish feud, a car turns into our lane, nearly sideswiping his truck right outside my door. Lucas swerves and his arm juts out to hold me in place, a stiff arm across my chest that I grab like a child on their first roller coaster. The entire incident lasts maybe three seconds, but in its wake, Lucas is protecting me and I'm holding on for dear life. I unfurl my fingers and release my hold when our eyes meet, and he retracts his arm, putting his hand back on the wheel. His expression goes blank, and I hate how practiced he's become at erasing moments.

My breathing is hard, the in and out keeping pace with the pounding in my chest. Meanwhile, Mr. Stoic-faced letterman-jacket wearer rushes through the last light before school, clearing the intersection on yellow.

"You trying to get into another near accident?" I scold. The look on his face remains impressively unfazed.

We're running a few minutes behind, but the twins are still waiting around their parking spot, the space next to them open and waiting for Lucas to pull in. No Ava around, or Abby, or my new group of friends. Nobody to witness the shocking display of the two of us pulling into the school lot in the same vehicle. But having to face Tory and Hayden with me in tow must be enough to make Lucas overreact because he cruises right past his usual spot, opting instead for one in the far corner, near the football field. We'll have to haul ass to make it to class on time from here, and my ankle isn't in sprinting shape.

I pull my bag to my chest and get out before Lucas fully shifts into park, and manage to get a few yards ahead of him before he reaches into the back of his truck for his things. I notice when glancing over my shoulder that he's ditched his jacket, leaving it in his truck. He's wearing all black, a thin long-sleeved T-shirt that hugs his body and black jeans that ride low on his hips. I hate how attracted I am to him, even still.

It takes every ounce of determination in my body to maintain my speed to make sure Lucas doesn't somehow sprint past me, and when I find my legs working into a near jog, I laugh inwardly at how ridiculous all of this is. But that doesn't stop me from taking things up one more notch.

"And yeah, Tory and I are friends now. *For now.* I mean, who knows," I say as he moves into the space next to me just outside our first period doorway. I glide into the room first, taking my seat a breath before he falls into his, the now familiar kick of his foot against the leg of my chair jostling me. In my unreasonable state, I dig my feet into the floor and push back in my chair with just as much force, my seat back clanking into his desktop with a snap. Momentarily, I actually wanted his fingers to be caught in there, like a trap. My emotions are cooled by the puzzled look on our teacher's face, so I lift a hand and apologize, making an excuse.

"Sorry, bag strap was caught on something," I say, fussing with my backpack at the side of my chair.

Lucas's heavy foot hammers at the leg again, but this time I'm levelheaded enough to ignore it. And as the pattern continues for the next hour, I grow smug, because I pissed him off with that Tory thing, and more than that, that I've stopped playing along.

Game. Set. Match.

TWELVE

Abby is able to drive me to Eight Lanes after school. A lot of good that does, though; my car refuses to start. The sweet girl gave me her last rev over the weekend. I wish I had known, maybe I would have savored the sound. I call my mom while Abby drives me home and tell her the bad news; she arranges for a tow truck to haul my car home. My Uncle John knows his way around an engine, and he promises to come up from Fort Wayne to give it a look next weekend. In the meantime, my trips to school are going to be pieced together with rides from Abby, Lola, and Naomi, because my mom's photography venture is taking off and she's looking to rent studio space for portraits. It's good news, and I'm willing to wake up early and walk to school just to keep her busy and our bills paid.

"Do you think your mom would be down with doing my new headshots?" Abby's been posing in front of the mirror on the back of my closet door for about ten minutes.

"For sure," I answer, tugging out my laptop and logging in to my student portal. My friend flops down on my bed next to me and pushes my laptop closed.

"I was working on that, you know," I groan. She pulls it from my reach.

"You work too hard on that. Senior year, remember the plan? Coast a little." She lays back and tugs at the back of my T-shirt, coaxing me to rest next to her.

"I'm pretty sure the plan has been blown." I blow out hard enough to move the few stray hairs that fall across my lips.

"Nah, plan is in full motion," my friend says, pulling her phone from her back pocket and holding it above her face. She scrolls through a few social media apps in search of something and stops on some comment left by a person tagged RedTedFred.

June and Tory totally dating.

My eyes blink quickly and I push the phone away from my face. I'd call it meaningless, but even a wallflower like me knows that high school gossip carries a little bit of weight.

"We're not dating," I clarify.

"I know. You'd tell me." There's a lilt in her tone that tells me she's not one-hundred percent sure that I would. And since I'm sitting on so many things I haven't told her, I can't honestly agree and say "Of course I would," so I say nothing.

"Rumors are stupid. And I'm not dating Tory D'Angelo." Of course, I totally used that very same suspicion to piss off the boy next door and let him wonder what's up between Tory and me. I'm such a fucking hypocrite.

"The fact you've stirred curiosity is a good thing," Abby says. She rolls to her side to face me and begins twisting pieces of my hair.

"How is that?" I don't know why I'm asking. I guess maybe there's a little part of me that's hooked on the drama. That's painful to admit to myself, so I tuck that thought somewhere deep and pretend I never had it.

"People like a good story." She shrugs her top shoulder and lets go of the twist of my hair she's been holding. It unravels like silk.

"I don't like being the story." I glance at her sideways and she gives me a crooked smile.

"Yeah, you do. Just a little." My friend tucks in her knees and rocks herself back to a sitting position. I stay where I'm at, pondering her words and feeling a little guilty about the dash of truth to them.

"I miss Lucas," I admit. It's strange how light my chest feels after saying that out loud.

My friend swings her backpack over her arms and stands from my bed.

"You should try really talking to him, and then tell him that," she says with her back to me.

"Probably," I agree. I do a sit up on the center of my bed, then scoot my feet to the floor to hug my friend good-bye at the waist. Maybe next time I'll tell her about the affair I witnessed and she can help me figure out how that secret fits in with me and Lucas having a real conversation.

I follow Abby downstairs, answering a call from my mom as I wave bye to my friend.

"The tow should be there in an hour. Can you hang around the house to sign for it? They have my card on file." There's chatter in the background.

"Sure. Where are you?" My eyes tail my friend's car as it rolls down the street, switching focus to an unfamiliar red sports car that passes her on the way and slows at Lucas's driveway. There's a blonde woman driving, her hair cropped bluntly at her shoulders and oversized black sunglasses shading her eyes.

"I think I found a space!" My mom's excitement draws me back in, but from the side door of our house I spy on the stranger pulling slowly up the Fuller driveway. The garage opens, unveiling Lucas's mom's car, and his mother guides the red car into the space where her husband usually parks.

Divorce attorney? This is how rumors start.

"That's awesome, Mom. Are you gonna get it?" My attention is split in half.

"Negotiating now," my mom says. She mentions a few other things, and I hear the words dinner and order, but I don't retain much else. I end the call with her and close the side door most of the way so I can spy the proper way.

My mind spins with these clues, rearranging them to make sense, and then the roar of Lucas's truck grinds up the driveway. I slam the door closed, eliminating the slight crack I was peeking through and move to the kitchen window, slitting the shutters enough to hide my profile.

Lucas should be at practice right now. He pulls his truck in close to the house, slipping out the driver's side and rushing around the back of the house as if he forgot something. He's wearing his gray practice shirt and his football pants, halfway dressed out for a practice, so I wonder if he did forget something at home. The longer he remains inside, though, the less likely that theory holds.

Almost thirty minutes pass with me staring at Lucas's truck and the closed garage door hiding some strange visitor's car. I have to pee, but I'm so afraid I'll miss something and waste this time I've invested. My persistence pays off a few minutes later when the garage door opens and the red car's reverse lights glow bright. Lucas walks out through the open garage along with his mom, and they both wave to the blonde woman backing out. I'm too far away to discern whether they're scowling or smiling, but they don't linger. Lucas jogs backward to his truck and his mom gets in her own vehicle, and they both disappear in less than a minute.

An hour of my life is gone.

It's almost seven at night by the time the tow truck driver rings our bell. My mom's words are starting to make more sense now, since it's dinner time and she isn't home. I ordered a pizza from Rudy's twenty minutes ago, and the delivery man shows up while I'm guiding the tow up my driveway. I pay for the pizza and hold the box at my hip while the tow driver disconnects my car from his bed.

As the tow truck leaves, I plop a seat on the trunk of my car and open up the piping hot box of pizza next to me to let it cool. I should call Abby or text the other girls to see if they want to come over and share. I pull out my phone to do just that, but stop short when Tory pulls up at the end of my driveway. I tuck my phone in my pocket and lean back against my rear window while he walks up my driveway.

I'm fanning the rumors.

"What's up, Mabee?" His gray shirt is drenched with sweat and his hair is damp and twisted in various directions from wearing his helmet.

"To what do I owe the honor?" I gesture to the pizza at my side, offering him a slice. He doesn't hesitate, pulling a piece free, the stringy cheese threading through the air.

"I'm starving, thanks," he says, blowing on the end for a few seconds before taking an impatient bite. He waves his hand at his mouth and chews with it open.

"It just got here. Might be hot," I say, wincing with guilt.

"Ya think?" He laughs while he chews, but goes in for more, not deterred by the burn I'm sure that left on the roof of his mouth.

"You waiting on Lucas?" I glance to my right, to the driveway still empty after all the activity it held earlier.

"I came to check on you," he says, moving the pizza box closer to me and taking a seat on the back of my car. It dips with his weight.

"Really?" There's a twist in my chest from his answer. I'm not sure I want him checking on me because that lends credibility to the rumor, and we aren't dating. It makes me think maybe he thinks we are, though.

He leans back on the rear window and holds the slice at an angle, guiding the rest of it in his mouth.

"You ate that in three bites," I observe.

He chortles with his cheeks puffed out, full of crust.

"Like I said"—he muffles out the words—"I'm starving."

He pulls out another slice and hands it to me. I test the temperature with my palm. It's cool enough to nibble. Tory doesn't waste time with small bites, devouring a second piece in the time it takes me to get through an eighth of my first one.

"So. Abby . . ."

I'm chewing when he hits me with the awkward transition. That's probably for the best because the little pause I'm forced to make helps me put things together. He has a thing for my friend.

"What about her?" I smirk to myself.

"You think she really hates me?" he asks.

We're both leaning back on the car window, staring up at the dimming sky and eating pizza. I can tell he's trying to keep this casual, to not assign it too much meaning. Somehow, in the first two weeks of school, this obnoxious twin has become one of my best friends. I breathe out a little laugh at that thought.

"Sometimes it seems she hates all of us," I say, rolling my head to the side and squinting at him with one eye.

He pulls out another slice, this time folding it in half and biting from the crust end. He nods slowly and glances at me sideways while chewing.

"Sometimes isn't *all* the time, so that means there's a shot." He winks and his coyness sparks a warm feeling in my chest, making me grin.

"There is always a shot," I say.

He turns his head to face upward and nods, smiling through another bite.

"Speaking of . . ."

The rumble of a truck breaks up our quiet. I will myself to not glance to the right, even as the driver's side door opens and slams shut.

"Hey, Princess!" Tory teases, holding up his hand in a wave as he lies next to me. I eye him from the side and notice he's not looking Lucas's way. He's taunting him, maybe for sport . . . maybe for me.

I let him.

There's no immediate response from Lucas, only the slow shuffling of his feet drawing closer. Nerves make me want to fill the silence, but I'll only say something I'll regret, or something that will push this game between us to a new level. I can't judge Lucas for being hurtful and taunting if I do the exact same things.

"You got your car back," he says.

Yeah, guess you don't have to worry about me begging for rides anymore. I let that thought pass through, discarding it. It's not the right thing to say.

"I did." I pat my hand against the metal and roll my head to the side until my gaze lands on him. He's trying not to say the wrong things, too. I can tell by the tightness in his neck, the way his shoulders are high despite the bag of gear dangling from his right arm and heavy backpack pulling down the left.

"That's good." He takes a few steps closer, stopping just short of the place where his driveway blends into the shared grass between our yards. My gaze flits down to his feet, his socks rolled down to expose the difference between the clean skin on his legs and the dirty. He's wearing the same Nike slides he's had since junior high.

"Your feet never grew after that big burst, huh?" I nod toward his shoes and he lifts his right toes. This natural conversation feels so strange but so nice. I'm a little sad Tory is here to witness it, because his presence keeps things from getting too deep.

"Yeah, well, it took me a few years to grow into my size thirteens." His laugh is raspy. It's real. I trace his body up to his face, catching a glimpse of his mouth before he raises his head to look at me. He's biting his lip like a child, amused by his own giant feet. When his eyes meet mine, there's a softness there that's been so fleeting. It's the same face he wore in the truck on the way to the hospital and when he sat next to me in the ER.

Such sweetness ruined in a blink by the sound of his father's truck pulling in the driveway behind him. Lucas looks down and to the side, his muscles automatically growing harder and his attention shifting. He takes a few steps back as his dad stops just short of pulling into the garage.

"Lucas?" He slams the door closed behind him and takes a few long strides in our direction. I swear Lucas swallows hard.

"I was just talking with Tory," he says, leaving me out of the picture. Tory's elbow moves into my side in acknowledgement and I swallow down the hurt feelings.

"Mind telling me why Coach called me tonight?" His dad couldn't care less that Tory and I are feet away from them.

"Well, I wasn't on that call, you were, so . . ." There's an edge to Lucas's voice.

Sucking in my lips, I make myself quietly invisible as I look to my left and meet Tory's heavy stare. He shakes his head slightly, a hardness to his jaw and sadness in his eyes. This is something we aren't supposed to see, a moment Lucas would rather keep from my view.

"Tory, do you know why my son skipped out on an hour of practice today?"

Tory's eyes don't immediately shift from mine, and I keep my head turned to face him, not wanting to be questioned next or see the look on

Mr. Fuller's face that matches his tone. Tory blinks his gaze up a notch and casually shrugs his shoulder.

The quiet brews thicker, so much so that there's almost a smell to it—a choking thickness with the scent of iron.

"Thanks, Tor. You're a real fuckin' help," Mr. Fuller says.

Tory's eyes dim and a heavy grimace glues his lips shut.

"Let's just go inside," Lucas says, his shoes rubbing along the pavement with belabored steps that scratch and pull, as though he's trying to drag every ounce of this topic and conversation somewhere private along with him.

"This a joke to you, Luc?" The sound of his steps halts with his dad's accusation.

I shouldn't get involved.

"Maybe Mrs. D'Angelo knows." The words come out without a plan or a filter. My voice is loud, and my eyes scan the stars above my head in an effort to seem indifferent. Tory snorts a laugh at my side, because he thinks I'm saying random snarky shit to help Lucas out. There's nothing random about the words I chose.

With a deep inhale, I sit up and slide from the back of my car, my stare finding the one I knew would be waiting for me. Todd Fuller has always had a heavy brow. It's a little gray, a peppering that matches his short, well-trimmed beard. He wears a suit well—the look of a boss with expensive ties, his gold watch exposed when he raises his arm. His glare is purposeful, meant to intimidate me, but it also hides some major fucking fear. I shot close to home, and he knows there's no coincidence in anything I said.

A menacing grin flashes across his face, wicked like his eyes, and then he resumes his act, shaking his head and waving his hand at me, dismissing my words as garbage.

"Get inside," he finally huffs, marching past his only child, his golden boy who I'm starting to think only ever played football to make his old man happy. Pity they're both so miserable.

Lucas stays put until his dad climbs back into his truck and hits the button to raise the garage door. His mom's car is already parked inside, and I can't help but believe Mr. Fuller is taking this inside because he doesn't want her overhearing.

"I gotta go, Mabee." Tory squeezes my shoulder from behind, then leans to grab one more slice of pizza as he heads back to his car. "Call if you need me, Luc." He holds up a peace sign and Lucas does the same. His gaze follows his friend's path until he pulls away in his car, then it flits back to me, a deep crease cut between his brows.

A few wordless seconds pass, and my need to fill silence gets the best of me.

"I'm sorry," I croak out. I feel a heavy coat of shame, and I don't know whether it's my empathy for Lucas or for what I know but don't fully disclose.

"Don't be," he says, no bite or warning in his tone. His mouth forms a tight line, a forced smile meant to cover serious hurt and pain. He glances to the side of me and nods. "Glad you got your car back."

I nod, keeping the details of the blown engine and my lack of transportation to myself for now. This isn't the time for favors, and my ride is covered. Plus, I can tell Lucas wants to get whatever is waiting for him in the garage over with; I'd rather not have to look him in the eye.

This is a good place to leave things.

THIRTEEN

It was an impulsive decision. Almost as knee-jerk as when I blurted out Mrs. D'Angelo's name in front of Lucas's dad. Whatever it was that made me go through with it, when I walked into school on Tuesday morning after Abby drove me in, I went straight to the office and begged my counselor to put me in an independent study for my physics credit. As much as I want to have forced interactions with Lucas every day, I haven't wanted them for the right reasons. Starting every morning like that, so negative and contentious, won't get either of us anywhere healthy. I might not see much of him anymore, but I'd rather have rare, meaningful interactions that he chooses to be present for than ones where we show up for attendance.

I easily got my mom to buy off on the plan. I'm good at physics, and I did most of the work my junior year in other ways. I just need the official credit. I took advantage of my mom being busy and distracted, trying to get out of the house with arms full of gear and her phone on speaker while she spoke with her broker about the studio space she's renting in Old Town.

I miss our angsty morning battles—little pushes and shoves and biting comments—but the void is the kind a druggie has when going through withdrawal. Maybe that's why I agreed to the game tonight—a little taste of Lucas from a safe distance.

Controlled abuse.

As the fourth quarter ticks down, I don't feel any giddiness at all over the sight of him. We're down by two touchdowns. I'm not much of an optimist, but the small fraction of me that is knows that even the great Lucas Fuller can't close that gap against Pinewood Crest in less than two minutes. Their defense is rabid, borderline on sportsmanship, and twice the size of our offensive line. Lucas has been sacked three times this half, two the first half. His dad left at the end of the third, forcing his mom to leave her spot in the away stands so he could drive them home. He didn't even stand during the game like he normally does. He was disappointed, and he wanted to make sure anyone looking knew he was not proud of his son's performance.

As if anyone gives two shits what middle-aged Todd Fuller thinks.

"Hey guys, the party got moved to Sammy's garage. I'm still in if you are," Abby says, glancing over her shoulder at me with puppy eyes. I sigh and picture my evening, sitting on some metal chair in a garage while people drink and play beer pong.

"I'm down."

"Me, too."

Lola and Naomi sell me out quickly. I laugh under my breath and close my eyes as I lift my shoulders.

"Fine," I say in one long breath.

"You don't have to," Abby says, and I open my gaze on her, expecting to see the opposite message in her expression. She seems genuine.

"Are you sure?" I tilt my head, waiting for her to smack my leg and tell me to get my ass to the party.

"Yeah, I mean it's Sammy's garage. It's not an epic moment." I'm not sure whether she classifies it that way to let me off the hook or she's strategically saving up my party attendance requirements for better, bigger blowouts ahead. Regardless, I'm thankful for the break.

"Ohhhh!" The collective moan in the small crowd left on our side sends my attention back to the field, just in time to catch Lucas pulling himself to his knees.

"Line isn't doing their job tonight," some old man commentates behind me.

"Bullshit. QB's head isn't in this one. Sucks to lose to them, too. We might not make playoffs because of this." I recognize the second voice as Mr. D'Angelo. He doesn't make it to many games because his work puts him out of the state a lot. Tory mentioned something about him getting home for this one, though. At least his son looked good tonight, as good as anyone can look losing twenty-one to seven.

The girls stand, straightening their jeans on their hips and putting on their mini backpacks to leave before the rest of the home crowd. I kinda want to see this game to the very end, though. Not because of optimism, but because nobody here is in Lucas's corner. I feel . . . obligated, I guess?

"June, you ready?" Abby is already a few steps down the bleachers. I haven't even stood.

"Can I meet you guys at the car? I want to see the end."

My friend scrunches her face as if I just told her I'd like to eat a cup of ass soup.

"I told Tory I'd stay," I say, playing guilty.

Her eyes narrow.

"That thing still just a rumor, June?" She's only half teasing, I can tell by the slight slant of her head.

"Yes, Abby." My response is stern enough for her to stop prying, and over her shoulder she tells me to hurry while she and the girls leave the sparse away stands.

Lucas won't even get in the game again. The clock is under a minute, and the other team is just burning the seconds. He's alone on the opposite end of the action, helmet off and dangling from a weary right arm, a towel tucked in the back of his pants on the left side. He's staring at the clock instead of his defense, just hoping it all ends. None of this is fun for him; I can tell. I'm starting to wonder if I'm the only one who can.

Both teams crowd the field before all the seconds tick down, and Lucas is last to walk through the Eagles line and shake hands with the other squad. Even his coaches are ahead of him, avoiding him rather than getting angry. Not that the outcome of this game rests squarely on his shoulders, or that the failures were completely his fault. Maybe everyone here has just gotten used to him carrying them. When talent runs thin, Lucas plays harder to make up the difference. He's always been that way. Always can be exhausting.

I wait until our line of players filters toward the end zone before I climb from the stands. I'm the lone person on this side, a standout. I walk around the track on the outside of the fence while the team crosses the field on their way to the bus. When I reach the gate, I have to wait for them to exit, not wanting to dart through the horde of pissed off teenaged boys and grown men who act like them. I catch Tory's eye and he lifts his chin in acknowledgement, the strap of his mouthpiece dangling from his lips as he chews on it. Most of the guys wear the same expression, defeat haunting their eyes, fear draining the color from their cheeks. They're going to get their asses chewed in that bus for the thirty-minute drive home, and that lecture . . . it matters to a lot of them. Not all of them, though.

Clearly not *one* of them.

Lucas wears his helmet balanced atop his head, the face mask not pulled down but resting against his forehead. He's chewing at his plastic mouthpiece with such a vice grip that it's become malformed, the gnawed remnants hanging from his mouth. We're close enough to touch as he approaches the gate.

I form fists with the long sleeves of my Eagles hoodie and hold my breath, hoping it's okay that I'm even here. His gaze flits toward me for a beat as he passes, just long enough for the muddied blue to reach inside my heart and spear it just a little.

I wait for the field crew to zip through with their cart, mostly to buy time and distance between the team and me—between Lucas and me. I spot Abby's car near the exit, pulled up close to the curb, and I jog toward her before she honks and draws attention to me. I lost the front seat to Naomi, so I round the car and climb into the seat behind Abby. I catch her eyes on mine in her rearview mirror while I buckle up, and there's an understanding in them that I should have known would be there. She knows why I stayed, same way she knows why I would never date Tory D'Angelo. My heart is still loyal to Lucas Fuller, no matter how much of an asshole he can be.

Our exchange is wordless, and I'm strategically quiet for the ride home, making sure to sing along with the radio and give my opinion on things when it's easy. I speak up just enough to not make anyone question where my mind is, but my mind is long gone. It's at home, in the front seat of a rusted-out Buick, while I stare up at the window of the boy I once knew so well.

When Abby drops me off at my house, I make her promise to call me for a ride home from the party. My mom is home, which means the van is mine. It would have been the perfect night for me to play designated driver, but I *really* don't want to be at a party. I want to be right here, sitting in this dirty seat that I swore I'd never get in again the last time Lucas found me here.

Maybe I knew deep down he would come. A part of me surely hoped for it. I've been sitting out here for about an hour. I expected it to take time for the team to make the trip home, for him to shower and change, and to get out of going to a party he doesn't want to be at either.

His hair is damp and falling over his eyes as he weaves through the tall weeds and the abandoned tires that will never hold air. Nicolas Mabee's Junkyard, that's what this place is. Fitting that I'm out here, too, among my dad's leftover, forgotten treasures.

The door pops when he opens it, the palm print from the last time he sat here waiting to greet him. He leaves the door open but sits with both legs inside. I roll down the window on my side as far as it will go, which is only inches, but it lets a cross breeze flow through the cab, clearing out some of the mustiness.

I'm stuck on the faintness of his freckles across the bridge of his nose. I get lost in them, admiring quietly while he stares straight ahead into whatever picture his mind is conjuring. We sit like this for long minutes, hiding from expectations, from our past, from our futures—from our parents. I'd be content if this quiet lasted for hours, for it to be all he needs before he leaves the car and goes back to his life inside that house. But the outside world doesn't want anything I do.

His phone blares out the Kanye song he was listening to the night I walked in on him with Ava. He leans to the side to pull his phone from his pocket, checks the screen, and quickly dismisses the call. The alert sounds again the second he tucks his phone away, so this time he powers it off and tosses it on the filthy dashboard. He leans forward and rubs both palms over his face, then into his hair.

Through it all, I don't talk. I'll wait as long as he needs to find his words, and if he never finds them, I'll be his companion for this soothing bit of silence.

His hands clasp in front of him as he leans forward and rests his weight on the dash. His body inflates with a deep breath, spilling out through his nose.

"I want to go to MIT." He nods, acknowledging his wishes out loud.

"That's amazing." I hope that's the answer he wants to hear. His head falls forward, resting on his hands, and he rolls it side to side as he kicks at the ripped-up flooring beneath his feet.

"It is, isn't it?" He rolls his head to the side until our eyes meet. A smile flashes on his lips, a defeated remnant of pride.

His palms flatten and he shifts his weight so his cheek rests on his folded hands and arms, his eyes blinking slowly as he stares at me. I feel this overwhelming pressure to give him some sort of solution.

"I got an offer from Tennessee," he continues.

I nod, remembering the conversation I overheard him have with Mr. Newsome.

"That's awesome, too." This time, my response makes him laugh. He leans back and balls his fists to his eyes, a semi-maniacal laugh slipping into a more desperate one.

"You're right. It is." His hands fall into his lap, and I'm caught on the dirt and tape that still mar his fingers.

"What do you want?" My gaze moves back up to his, and everything behind it is so lost. He shakes his head while he turns to the side, twisting so his body faces me.

"Does that matter?" he says, a quick lift of his shoulders.

"It should," I answer. Another laugh punches through his chest.

I look down to the shifter between us, the marble ball on top of the stick the one thing my dad put new in this car before he took off. I wonder if it's even worth anything. I grab it in my palm and twist until it gives, unscrewing it until it's finally just a stone ball with a screw-hole in it. I toss it in my hand a few times, testing the weight, then I hold it out for Lucas to take.

He squints a little, leaning closer before taking it from me. Our fingers touch slightly, and it's everything to me. Somehow, I steady myself enough to take in the way his lashes shadow his eyes, blinking as he studies my stupid gift.

"Thanks. I always wanted this thing," he says.

"I know," I say, chuckling.

My dad used to yell at him for taking this ornament off the car and throwing it around the yard. Lucas even tossed it in his pool once and made me dive in to get it back.

"It's yours now," I say, though my worst self is waiting in the wings to bite me. "Or you could give it to Ava."

He doesn't glance up at my comment, and I'm glad. I wish I could take it back. I hate that I said it. I know it was her who called. She's probably burning up his phone while it's powered down, leaving angry messages and threats for me. I'm probably giving her dislike for me too much credit; I doubt I take up that much of her headspace.

"Why'd you leave physics?" He still hasn't looked up, instead keeping his focus on the shiny ball in his palm. Oh, how I wish I could look away from him.

"Seemed it was for the best." I give him the truth, and I don't really have to dive into the details. He knows how we've been behaving. We haven't been very good to each other, not for a very long time.

"Yeah," he breathes out.

He tosses the ball in his palm a few times, then lines it up with the screw sticking out of the top of the shifter. He turns it, tightening it back into place.

"I don't really want it," he says, finally glancing in my direction. An amused curve plays at one side of his lips. "I just liked that it pissed your dad off."

We both laugh.

"It did," I recall.

His gaze lingers, but rather than turning mine away, I spend it on his every facial feature—the permanent crease that's etched into the corners of his mouth from his smile, the tiny scar that splits his right eyebrow from where he hit his head on the monkey bars and needed stitches, and the way his right ear sticks out a little more than his left.

"Ava's not my girlfriend, just so you know."

His words slam into my chest, but I mask my reaction, drawing in a long breath through my nose to keep my heart at bay.

"She seems like your girlfriend," I say, not even sure why. Maybe I just need to be sure of some things.

"She's not," he answers quick. "She's just . . ." His chest fills with a heavy breath and guilt taints his eyes, pulling the corners down along with the edges of his mouth. "She's just this mistake I make sometimes."

I shake my head, and his face puzzles.

"She's not a mistake," I say.

"Okay," he says. He doesn't understand, and I don't entirely either, but there's something behind that word that needs fixing.

"I might not like her very much, but no girl deserves to be labeled a mistake. She's a lot of things, but mistake isn't one of them. Your moments with her had purpose, even if they were brief and not love. Your actions can be a mistake, but not the person." My eyes tear at my own words. I don't know that I've ever been this vulnerable, not even with Lucas. I run my arm over my face and sniffle.

"Okay," he says, a gentle laugh seeping through.

"Okay," I repeat.

Every light in his back yard flicks on at once, and we both turn our heads, startled by it. His dad's figure moves from one end of the patio to the other.

"He's probably looking for me," he says.

"Let him," I say, my bravado amusing him.

"I wish I could, but—"

"But he's the reason you can't go to MIT?" I kinda knew in my gut, and when his gaze shifts to mine, he confirms it.

"He went to Tennessee, and me and football—"

"You're living his dream," I fill in. He nods, every bit of joy slipping from his eyes and the lift in his cheeks. His dad is an anchor that is drowning him. I should tell him the truth, set him free. If only there were a way it wouldn't destroy his family like it did mine.

"He'll come around," I say, my words the push he needs to exit the car and abandon our conversation.

"Doubtful," he says, both palms on the roof of the car as he dips his head into my view. I can feel the part of him that wants to stay here screaming from behind his eyes. Those damn expectations, though—the pull is strong.

"Thanks, June." He raps on the top of the car once then backs away, closing the door. I wait until he disappears through the thick brush and weeds, then I roll the window up and leave the driver's side. I can hear his father's voice through the night air. He isn't shouting, but he's also not being a father. He's lecturing, reprograming, willing Lucas to love all the things he wants him to. People don't work like that, though.

If they did, I would have willed Lucas to love me a long time ago.

By the time I get inside, my mom isn't around; she probably went upstairs. I shut off the lights downstairs, and gather up the documents she left scattered on the counter. There are a few printout photos of a storefront, so I carry them over to the faint night light glowing near the stove and picture her space being there. It's the perfect size, with an old-fashioned awning over a huge window and green door. The inside is empty except for the black and white checkered tiles and a single barber's chair in the middle. I'm sure she'll have to redo the inside, but I kind of hope that chair sticks around.

I leave the photos on the stack of forms and round the corner, racing up the stairs two at a time because I don't like the dark. My mom is asleep sideways on her bed, still wearing her jeans and the business blazer she says makes her look professional. I don't want to disturb her, so I turn her light off and close her door so she has quiet. I'll make sure she's up when I leave for work in the morning.

My room glows from the small mood lamp that is never off in the corner of my room. The blue light is just enough to see by, and it calms my active imagination whenever I'm alone. I pull my phone, cash and school ID from my back pocket and toss it on my bed, kicking my shoes off and rolling my socks from my feet with my toes. I move to my window to close my shutters, but I tilt them enough to look into Lucas's yard before I shut them completely.

The lights are off now. I push the slats closed, but a ticking sound rattles against the other side of the glass. I hold my breath to hear it more clearly, and just when I think maybe my mind is playing tricks on me, I hear it again. This time, it's more of a scattering sound—pebbles. I open the slats and look down, my pulse racing. I manage to catch a view of Lucas's next throw. This time, it's a dozen tiny rocks clinking against my metal frame, the vinyl siding, and the glass.

I pull both sides of my shutters open and lift the window open so I can hear him.

"What are you doing? You can't run away to here. I mean, he'll find you," I joke.

"You were never a mistake," he says, not even reacting to my words.

I stare at him with my mouth agape, not sure what to make of this gesture or this big revelation that's so important he has to throw rocks at my window at eleven-thirty at night.

"Okay," I say, grinning with a thumbs up.

"No, June . . ." He holds up a finger then rushes forward. Lucas used to climb up the eaves on our porch to tap on my window all the time. He was like Spiderman, his hands sticky and feet stickier. His body is a lot bulkier now, and the sounds of his shoes on the lower angles of the roof are clunky, but his height makes up for his lack of agility. His hands grip my window ledge within seconds, and he lifts his body up easily as I back away.

The racing in my chest is nonstop, and it's no longer fear of a boogeyman or the dark. I'm afraid of this not being what I think it is—what I hope it is. Lucas pulls his body through my window a leg at a time until he's literally the air I'm breathing. He looks almost lost, standing right inside my window, his hands not sure whether they should relax or move to illustrate his point. His eyes blink rapidly at first, then his gaze locks on mine and his teeth hold the tip of his tongue as he breathes out a nervous laugh.

"When you said those things, about how no girl wants to be a mistake." He shakes his head but his eyes never leave mine. "You meant you. You weren't talking about Ava."

He steps toward me and my hands ball into fists at my hips. I bang them against my skin anxiously as I glance to the side, to my mirror that still has pictures of me and Lucas taped to it.

"I'm sorry, June," he says, and even though I feel him stepping closer, I don't look. I can't look. If my eyes meet his right now, I'll sob, and I don't want to break down in front of Lucas Fuller. That's not how this goes.

"You are not a mistake," he repeats, his body close enough that heat radiates from his chest, blocking the cool breeze streaming in through my open window.

"Got it. Thanks," I say, belittling his honesty. I thought this is what I want, but now that it's happening, it's too hard. There's too much attention on me, too many things stripped away.

His fingertips tickle against my chin and with slight pressure, he coaxes my gaze toward him. Fighting it would be childish, but looking him in the eyes feels deeply impossible. I'm not sure I'll survive it.

He takes away that choice.

With both of his hands cupping my cheeks, Lucas erases the few inches left between us, tilting my chin up so I'm forced to meet his eyes. They're even bluer in my light, blue like the midnight sky.

"You are not a mistake," he says, his eyes holding mine hostage to make sure they see every word formed on his lips.

I nod, a shaky movement on the verge of falling apart in a breath.

"Okay," he says through a crooked smile. I'm too close to see the dimple it forms, but I don't need to, I've memorized it.

His thumb sweeps away the moisture forming under my right eye and I croak out, "Thanks."

"Don't mention it," he says, repeating the touch on my left cheek.

I've held my breath so long, through my words and his, that the sensation makes my head float and my chest burn. I'm afraid of the sound I'll make, but if I don't get air, I'll die here. This would be a good death.

My lips part with a quaver, and the light gasp is the last thing I remember before Lucas's eyes dart to the slight movement. His right thumb traces along my cheek, over my top lip and onto my bottom one, stroking along it slowly until my eyes have no choice but to close. I sense his body moving before his lips touch mine, a feather-light brush of both of his lips along the plumpness of my bottom one.

Another tear is forming, and I have no choice but to accept it. My hands relax at my sides and move forward until I find the softness of his shirt. I grip it, bunching it tightly against his chest.

Lucas's nose brushes the side of mine as he cocks his head the other way, his mouth taking a gentle taste of my upper lip this time. My mouth on autopilot, my lips beg to move with his. I'm not sure whether I'm the one who deepens the kiss or he is, but as my hands let go of his shirt and snake their way up his chest and around his neck, his palms move to the back of my head and draw me close to taste me fully. His tongue teases against mine, the softness meeting the sharp edges of my teeth. I nibble at his top lip as he sucks in my bottom one, running his tongue along the delicate skin. I wait for him to walk me backward, for him to lift me up and force my legs to wrap around him. All of my fantasies over the last two years rush my senses at once, but I let him be the guide. I'm still not certain this is real.

Only when he's out of breath does he release his mouth's hold on mine. I chance opening my eyes when his forehead rests against mine, and I look up to see his eyelids closed tightly as he rocks us back and forth where we stand.

"That was not a mistake," he whispers, his body sending me zero signs that he plans to move from this position any time soon.

"Okay," I whisper back, stepping up on my toes and chastely pressing my lips to his. This time, his are the ones to break and tremble. I hold our kiss still, my teeth grazing against his bottom lip when I finally let go.

"Okay," I repeat the words against him. I say them again, hoping maybe, after enough times, we'll both believe this. "Okay."

FOURTEEN

"You can't tell anyone."

That's the last thing Lucas said to me before he fled out my window, leaping from the eave to rush across the lawn toward his house.

He didn't say why, but his eyes expressed how important it is that this thing, whatever it is, stay between us and nobody else. I think maybe he's worried about Ava or his dad saying something to interrupt whatever we have.

What do we have?

Besides secrets.

I'm going to drown in secrets.

Something has to give, and having my best friend spend her Saturday afternoon with me at work while I dole out shoes for league bowlers is making it incredibly hard not to break my promise to Lucas. There are so many things I haven't told Abby, and she and I don't keep secrets. We don't lie. I'm not supposed to lie to anyone—my mom, Lucas, Abby. I may as well add Tory to that list because I don't like lying to him.

I don't want to stop kissing Lucas, or do something that might risk him ever kissing me again. I can't tell Abby about last night, not yet. Not the kiss. But I can maybe tell her about some things. I need someone to tell.

"I caught Lucas fighting with his dad last night," I spill out while I refill my friend's Dr. Pepper. I swear the only reason she comes to visit me at work is for free sugar.

"Tell me something new," she says, her eyes fluttering with sarcasm. I slide the full cup of soda over to her and she puts her lid back on. Her straw is pink on the end from her lipstick.

"Yeah, I know, but I mean, I heard *a lot* of their argument. I guess Lucas wants to go to MIT?" Her eyes blink wide as her lips let go of her straw.

"Lucas Fuller is smart?" She coughs out a laugh.

I chuckle.

"Yeah, I know, it's a surprise. He's like, maybe fourth or fifth in our class?" I don't know why I'm being vague with details. He's fourth. I know because I checked.

"Huh. Who knew?" she says.

I did.

"That must drive you wild. Your hottie crush also has a brain!" she cackles out and leans back, spinning once on her stool.

"You have no idea," I say, more truth to those words than she realizes.

"So, what's the big deal? The Fuller kid is smart and wants to build rockets or some shit, and they, like . . . don't want him to do that?" She goes back to taking a long suck on her straw. She's already gulped down a third of her refill.

"He got an offer from Tennessee," I add.

This time, she puts the drink down. Abby was a cheerleader our freshman and sophomore years, and she knows football. She quit cheering after she broke her wrist, but she's still a diehard for the game. Notre Dame football used to be a holiday in her house, every Saturday. Her dad played. Her mom cheered. And now that they're divorced, Abby has to sneak-watch the games because her mom can't stand the sight of the blue and gold. All of this to say, she gets how big an offer is to play at Tennessee. She also knows that's where Lucas's dad played—until one game knocked him out of the sport forever.

"Damn!" She shakes her head as her gaze drifts off with thought.

"Yup." I nod.

A few league teams wrap up their games and deliver their shoes to the counter. I hate getting backed up with racking shoes, so I set them all on the floor to spray the insides, coughing from the cloud of fumes. When I stand again, it's no longer my best friend sitting on the other side of the counter from me—it's my best friend, and Lucas Fuller, and both D'Angelo twins.

Shit.

"Maybe Mabee, what's up?" Tory leans over the counter with an arm stretched out to give me a sideways hug. I walk forward, stiff and unsure how to navigate this, reach around and pat him on the back while his arm encircles me. I look to Lucas mid-embrace, and his gaze traps mine, not letting go until Tory's hand is no longer touching my skin. His look is possessive, and if anyone else were looking at him, our secret would be blown.

I'd be fine with that.

"Nice game Friday, Luc." Abby gives me a sideways glance and a short wink, and the moment she starts, I regret not giving her every single detail of every secret I hold. As far as she believes, Lucas still treats me like shit and feels pressure about football from his dad. It's the perfect storm for my best friend to enact a little vengeance on my behalf.

"Fuck off, Abby," Lucas fires back. He takes a seat on the stool farthest from the rest of us and shifts his gaze to me. His face is full of indifference, and it hurts a little to see. I can't tell whether he's acting or changed his mind.

"Can I get a water?" He nods toward the tap.

I saunter toward the ice machine, grab a cup and scoop ice while my eyes hazily study him.

"It's a buck for the cup," I say.

Abby titters and takes a long drink through her straw until her cup is empty enough for her to make the slurping sound.

"Ahh," she says, tapping her cup on the counter. "Some of us get freebies."

A short laugh escapes my nose, and my cheeks burn a little with guilt. From this new perspective, it's funny to watch my friend stick up for me.

Lucas cocks his head to the side and shifts his eyes to glance harshly at my friend, but leans to pull his wallet from the back pocket of his jeans. He mostly wears all black, black jeans, black hoodie, and his black End Zone ball cap pulled low and shading his eyes. It makes his glare more ominous, especially when light finds a way in to illuminate his blue eyes from the shadow. I can't stop staring at his mouth. He's wearing a hard expression, so his lips don't stretch with the fullness of his smile, but it doesn't stop me from imagining it. That smile played out against mine only hours ago. I kissed that smile until I was raw.

Wallet in hand, he slips out his debit card and tosses it so it slides toward me on the counter. I slap my palm down to stop it, and pick it up, checking the name against the person who sent it to me.

"Lucas *A.* Fuller," I accentuate his middle initial, knowing it stands for Andrew. I set the card back on the counter and flick it back toward him with my index finger. He catches it in his lap. "I'm afraid I can only take cash."

I shrug and give him a wry smile, pulling the lid from the cup I just filled so I can threaten to pour out his water. I'm partly playing along and half sincere in pushing him, and the mix of it all makes me drunk on feelings. Why can't we tell people that we've found our way back? Why can't I kiss him again here and now?

His mouth ticks up on one side as the water trickles from the cup. I think he doesn't think I'll go through with this. A cup of water isn't a very big deal, but it's the only deal I've got. If we're playing the part of hatemates, I'm going to make it convincing.

"Ah ah," he says, lifting his palm slightly. He tucks his card back in his wallet and leaves his grinning eyes on me as he feels around for something else. He pulls a folded receipt from one of the compartments, then digs into the next slot to slide out a folded up dollar bill. When it falls on the counter, though, a golden wrapped condom packet slips out with it. My eyes flit to that first, as do his.

I stop pouring, my gaze on the condom that fell out, the condom that is probably tucked in there for those "mistake" times he mentioned in the car last night. I top off his cup and refasten the lid, pulling a wrapped straw from the box under the register.

"Here," I say, walking it over to stand right in front of him, the bar top between us. With my tongue wedged between my back teeth and cheek, I breathe out a snort laugh and smile on the right side of my mouth as I slide my palm across the counter, collecting both the dollar and the condom.

I unfold the bill and slip it in the register, shutting the drawer with my hip. I then pinch the condom packet between my thumb and index finger and hold it up for everyone to see. The twins are holding fists to their mouths to contain their laughter, and Abby is twisting in her seat with nervous excitement. I examine the print on it closely, my stomach swimming with jealousy.

"Ribbed for her pleasure," I read, punctuating the short sentence with a click of the tongue. "Well . . ." I lean forward, resting my elbow on the surface between us, and hold out the package for him to put back where it belongs.

He pinches the other side and we both hold on for a second, his eyes hazing in a warning that I'm taking this too far. I can't help the green monster that beats in my chest, though.

"I hope she enjoys it," I say, finally letting go.

He lets out a breathy laugh and chews at the inside of his cheek as he tucks the condom back in the tight fit of his wallet. He stands to put his wallet back in his pocket, then pulls the water cup in his grip, holding it up to toast me before biting the end of his straw with his teeth.

"She better," he says, a flash to his eyes that sends an electric jolt through my veins that makes me want to crawl over this counter and both choke him and kiss him at the same time.

"Gentlemen?" He turns his focus to his friends and they shake their heads, I'm guessing in awe of how big of an ass he can be. They follow him toward the pool tables anyhow, leaving me with Abby to pick apart the scene I just lived, but with her missing half the story.

"That was intense," she says, holding her lid down on her drink when I reach for it. "I'm good. I think three Dr. Peppers in an hour is my max."

"You want some water?" I want to give her more free shit, and to brag about it loudly.

She shakes her head and stands from her seat, pulling her keys from her purse. I still have two hours on my shift. I guess it's not fair to expect her to hang out here the entire time.

"Think you can manage to not get in any throw-downs before I pick you up at five?" Without warning, she spins around, lifts her phone and snaps a photo of the both of us. I'm sure I look like a raging lunatic or a cross-eyed loser.

"Why? When are you going to stop doing that?" I whine.

"Oh, June." She leans forward and blows a kiss at me over the counter. "You know the answer to that." She winks and I flip her off.

"Have a good day at work, honey," she says, her heels clicking along the polished concrete floor on her way out. I stare over to the pool tables and catch both D'Angelo twins angling their necks to watch every sway of my friend's hips as she leaves. Heels aren't part of her normal wardrobe; she has a shoot in them in a few days and has been wearing them nonstop this weekend to get used to balancing in them. When paired with her short-shorts and tight sweater, though, she looks like a fucking natural.

Rather than take my break under the mirror again, I decide to skip it altogether and just pick at the sandwich I packed. I slip it out of the plastic lunch bag under the counter and unwrap some of the plastic wrap to tear off a piece of the crust covered in peanut butter. We were out of jelly, so I loaded it up thick. Just one bite has my mouth fighting for moisture, so I fill a cup with ice and water.

"Employees don't have to follow that dollar rule I guess, huh?" Lucas walks over alone, the twins still battling over a new game of nine-ball several yards behind him.

"You just missed it. I donated a condom to the register," I say, my tone flat and eyes focused on nothing but the edge of my sandwich.

"June, don't be like that," he says, and I laugh at his pathetic apology.

I tear off another bite and pop it in my mouth, flitting my gaze up to meet his while I chew. I lean my hip into the counter and smirk through my bite, licking peanut butter from my teeth before taking another drink.

"Be like what? Like your dirty little secret?" I narrow one eye and tilt my head as I stare at him.

He props himself up on one of the stools and runs his palms over his face.

"It's complicated, June." He pulls his hat away and weaves a hand through his hair as he glares at me.

Your dad is having an affair.

With your best friend's mom.

The hard truth runs through my brain on a mental teleprompter, over and over. I take another bite and chase it with more water.

"Excuse me," I say, haphazardly wrapping my sandwich and tucking it back in the plastic bag. I wipe my hands on a damp towel and step around the other end of the bar, around the counter to the hallway that leads to the child care room and the bathrooms. I dip inside the women's room and walk into the last stall. Before I can latch the door closed, someone pushes from the other side.

"June, don't do this," Lucas pleads.

I laugh, nervously, because *what the fuck*, we're in the ladies room!

"You need to get out of here," I say in a loud whisper. I push back, my feet sliding with my effort. It's the stupid Vans; these aren't nonstick shoes. Morty is right to lecture me about it every time I'm up for review.

When I realize I can't overpower him, I relent and step back; he falls into my body in the tight space, his hand clutching the top of the stall. Stepping in even closer, he closes the door and locks it.

"What, because the two pair of legs won't be a giveaway?" I grimace then glance down, but he doesn't laugh at my attempt at humor, and just sighs.

"Where should I begin?" His left hand slides down the wall until his forearm rests to the right of my head. I should probably feel trapped but I somehow don't.

"You said I'm not a mistake," I begin. The burn is already crawling up my throat and I won't be able to handle this conversation without getting a little ugly.

Lucas lets out a soft breath that tickles my face. I try to look away and avoid his eyes, but his other hand finds my cheek and he turns me toward him.

"I did, and I meant it," he says, this Lucas so very different from the one who gave that little performance at the bar. I suppose I'm a different June, too. Here, I'm vulnerable. I hid it better before.

Our eyes tangle with near apology, our lips twitching with almost words.

"Out there," I finally muster the beginning, only to be stopped by the hard breath that leaves my chest. I shudder and Lucas's eyes drop just below my gaze. It gives me the excuse to cry, so I do. I blink out a single tear that stops at the corner of my mouth. "I felt like a pretty big mistake out there. And every single second that passed just made me feel more and more like I . . . like me and you? We don't belong."

My breath hitches on the last few words, and I hate how weak my voice sounds. I sniffle and straighten my posture, standing taller with my back flat against the fiberglass wall I'm leaning on. Lucas blinks a few times, his gaze still a fraction below mine, eventually closing his eyes completely and letting his head fall forward to rest against mine. Both of his hands draw in until his thumbs are on my cheeks, not sweeping the damp emotions away but rather feeling that my tears happened and he's to blame.

"June, nobody can know," he hums, and the words come out as if they're covered in razors, cutting him from the inside.

"Is it Ava? So you can still sleep with her?"

"No, June. Fuck Ava," he growls, stepping back, shaking his head and finally meeting my stare.

"Exactly," I laugh out.

His glare dims, and his jaw tightens.

"I ended things with Ava. Completely."

"Mmm." I nod, feeling the last vestiges of my tears cut down my hot cheeks. "That what you held on to the condom for?"

His head falls to the side as he exhales, his mouth a frustrated line and a sag to his shoulders.

"I didn't even know that was in there, June." He swallows and looks to the side, to the tiles on the back wall that are scrawled with insults about girls from now and long ago, and proclamations of love for boys who will probably never know some girl loved them.

I'm being unfair.

I'm overreacting.

We had one kiss, and maybe it doesn't mean anything.

He's keeping me a secret.

So many secrets.

"Your dad is having an affair," I blurt out. I cup my mouth quickly, wishing I could swallow the words before their sound meets his ears.

His eyes flare.

I wait for him to counter my accusation, to explain it away or deny it. He does none of it, though. All he does . . . is leave.

FIFTEEN

That's not how I wanted any of this to happen. I never wanted to hurt Lucas with the things I came to know, but that's exactly what I did. I hurt him. And that hurt us.

There's no more keeping a lid on things when Abby picks me up. I held myself together through the rest of my shift and then fell apart in her car to the point she had to pull over and just stare at me. We've been squatting in this sketchy abandoned convenience store parking lot for the last hour while I blubber through the whole story over and over again. No matter how many times I tell it, the end is always the same.

"Are you sure you saw what you saw?" She's asked me this once already. I wish my answer was different. I could even argue that I didn't get a good look at Mr. Fuller's face pulling out of the D'Angelo garage, but the truck was undeniably his.

"It was him, Abs. And I just ruined Lucas's life." I feel sick because I told him the truth out of spite. Because I was jealous.

"Well then, you should talk," she says, turning to put her seat belt back on and shift her car into drive. I do the same, fumbling with the buckle because my hands are jittery all of a sudden.

"What, like . . . now?" I say.

"No, I was thinking maybe you could wait another two years, then show up at his dorm at MIT or Tennessee or wherever the fuck he ends up going." She's gotten too good at sarcasm.

"That's not fair," I protest.

"Look, I'm driving you home. If you decide to go inside and hide in your room until school on Monday, that's on you. But if you want to see a change, well . . . to quote the inspirational sign in our principal's office—'you must be the change you want to see.'" She's proud of that speech. She lifts her detox juice drink from her center console and puckers her lips on the straw as she sucks up the last few drops.

"One day, you'll need my advice, and I'll be right about something you won't want to do. It's going to feel really good." I slump in the passenger seat and cross my arms, pouting out the window.

"Probably not, but okay," my friend says. I try to hold in the laugh, but I end up spitting it out despite myself. Damn her, so self-assured.

The closer we get to my house, the tighter my chest becomes, my lungs squeezed by the invisible elephant rocking into me. By the time we're a block away, I realize that even avoiding Lucas won't get rid of the massive anxiety knot caught in my throat and making me sick. The only thing that can get you to the other side of the circle of fire is walking through the flames.

Abby pulls into my driveway, stopping near the end. I figure she does it so I have to walk the extra distance and really consider my options, but when I look up, I see that's not why at all.

Lucas is sitting in the bed of his truck with the tailgate down, his back resting against the cab, ankles crossed. He's wearing a cut-off pair of sweats, the ones he usually wears when he goes out for a run, and the same black hoodie he had on earlier. His hair is tousled and sweaty and his cheeks are red from the cool air. He runs when he needs to think. He's been doing that since junior high. I could never keep up.

"I guess that makes my decision easier," I groan, lowering myself in my friend's seat just a little.

Her lights shine on him, but he doesn't bother to shade his eyes. He draws one knee up and pulls a water bottle into his hand, twists the cap off, and gulps most of it down.

"He doesn't really look like he wants to talk," I say. More excuses.

My friend turns her head and I feel her heated stare on my face seconds before I let my head fall to the side to meet the reckoning of her gaze.

"I know," I say, unhooking my seat belt to let the strap slide up and over my shoulder.

"It's not like things between you can get any worse." Damn her for being so on point tonight.

I nod and get out of the car, untucking my Eight Lanes shirt from my skinny jeans as I drag my zipper jacket along the ground at my side. I feel as if I'm in trouble. My heart drums to the rhythm of a death metal band, and to kick things up a notch, my friend beeps her horn as she pulls out of my driveway.

"Shit!" I jump and clutch my chest, glaring at her as she drives away, and hoping like hell Lucas is laughing at me when I turn back around.

He's not.

"What's up, Maybe Mabee?" He uses the nickname Tory has for me on purpose. I guess he gets jealous over things, too.

"I'm sorry." I ran through a dozen different methods for getting into this conversation with him during my trip home. Now that I'm staring into his sad eyes, the light completely dim behind them, I decide direct is best.

He nods. "Okay. Thanks," he says, drawing the bottle to his lips and tipping his head back to drink it dry. He screws the cap on and throws the empty plastic container into the middle of his driveway. I shuffle over in its direction to pick it up.

"Let my dad pick it up. Maybe I'll throw the rest of his shit out here too."

I stop where I stand and evaluate his face, the lethargy of his limbs and the crushed spirit emanating from behind his eyes. I've been that disappointed in someone before, too. Ignoring his wish, I pick up the bottle and walk it over to the recycling bin my mom put near the curb this morning.

His eyes meet mine when I turn around again, and as tempting as making a break for my house is right now, it's less of an option than it was a few minutes ago.

"Can I climb in there with you?"

His eyes remain blank at my question, but when I lean into my steps, attempting to move toward him, he stiffens.

"Can't." His back teeth clamp down hard. "This"—he pauses, pointing at me and then himself—"does not happen in front of people."

Undeterred, I move forward anyhow, because who's going to see besides his dad pulling in late from who knows where? Or his mom, who never leaves the house after she's home. Before my palms touch the back of his truck, he gets to his feet and vaults over the edge to the ground.

"Just get in," he huffs. His keys jingle on their way out of his pocket.

I push up the tailgate and do as he asks, climbing in and buckling up, then studying his every tick and nuanced motion as he revs his engine and backs us away from our homes. We get a comfortable six or seven blocks away, near one of the preserves and out of view of streetlights or passing cars. He pulls to the side of the road and flips on his hazards.

"Tell me how you know," he demands, his hands rolling against the steering wheel with a strong enough grip that his skin squeals against the rubber.

I'm speechless for a few long seconds, working out what order to say things in. There really isn't a way to protect everyone involved, which means Tory will be hurt by this too. I'm instantly thrown back into my own parents' divorce, the way my mom hung up the phone and just stared at my father, knowing that whatever the person on the other end of the line told her was true.

"I hate that I'm the one who knows this, Lucas," I begin.

"I understand." He's strangely calm, and I wonder if he had his suspicions. Drawing in a long breath, I steady myself and simply talk, like a well-rehearsed witness on the stand.

"There are details that are hard—"

He cuts me off mid-breath.

"It's all hard. I know. Just . . . just tell me," he begs, his voice a mix of frustration and maybe suspicion, as if on some level he knows what I'm about to say.

"I was dropping something off at Tory's house while you all were at practice. I'd just put my car in park when I saw their garage open and a truck pull out."

Again, when I pause for a breath, he interjects his own reasoning. "Lots of people have trucks," he says.

"They do," I respond. His body is fully relaxed, but his hands still cling to the steering wheel. "Not ones with license plates framed in gold with *Tennessee Forever* etched on the top and bottom."

His throat moves with the harsh swallow of truth. I twist in my seat to face him more directly as I continue.

"I saw them kiss, Lucas. Your dad and—

"Don't," he interrupts, shaking his head. There's a coldness in his tone, and a definitive essence to his request. I don't know if I expected him to get angry, to cry, or what, but his reaction is almost robotic.

His eyes are still fixed on the empty roadway ahead.

"I don't want to know too much. Details have a way of becoming nightmares and they poison everything." His eyes glance downward, and his hands fall to the sides of the wheel.

I suspect he doesn't want this to become a permanent wedge in his friendship with the twins, Tory especially.

"Just promise me that you are sure."

I let the request linger in the quiet of the cab, my concentration on the perfect syncopation of his clicking hazards and the on and off of the red glow that comes with them.

"I wouldn't have ever said it if I wasn't one-hundred percent sure, Luc." My hand makes a move toward him, but he's still closed off so I leave my palm flat on the seat between us.

Squinting, he leans forward and looks up through the windshield.

"There's supposed to be a meteor shower tonight. They said on the news that the best views are after midnight." His profile glows from the moon and the lights of the car. The quiet on the surface of his face covers a lot of other junk, but peeling masks off takes time. I still wear mine a lot. It took Abby and her push for me to actually enjoy my senior year for me to even try wearing different ones. I still don't think I've found my own yet.

"I don't have anywhere to be," I say, my voice devoid of the unease from a moment ago.

"We need full dark," he says, leaning back and turning his head to face me slowly. Our eyes meet in the glowing red moments of the flashing lights.

"We should keep driving then." My gaze is met with a slow blink before he turns to face the road again, shifting the truck into drive and killing the hazards as he pulls us back onto the roadway.

I count the mile markers on the roadside, though both of us are familiar with the route. We rode our bikes out this way one summer. My tire blew, so Lucas let me sit on his handlebars for the rest of the way. From the thick trees, there's an open field where the abandoned drive-in theater used to stand. One day, it will be bulldozed and turned into fancy houses. That hasn't happened yet, though, and the only question that I'm pretty sure nags in each of our minds is whether the radio boxes are still standing on their posts.

I count five miles before I stop keeping track and dare to push the power on his stereo. I brace myself to be assaulted with heavy bass, but the volume is surprisingly low. The familiar riff of Mustang Sally pushes my smile into my cheeks. What are the odds that I hear the same Wilson Pickett song twice in the same month. I mouth the words out of habit, but when Lucas's voice utters the lyrics along with me, I let my terrible voice go and sing at the top of my lungs. We're both grinning by the time he pulls onto the dirt road and through the unintimidating trespassing warning signs covered in graffiti.

"I heard this song last week with Tory," I say. Lucas drops off from the chorus and glances at me as we rock along with the tires on the rough terrain.

"Oh, yeah?" There's a tinge of jealousy in his voice, and I quickly try to fix it.

"He didn't know the words," I add in, laughing. He just nods, and when he looks away I squeeze my eyes shut, feeling daft because the song has nothing to do with his reaction. It's that I was sharing one of our songs with Tory.

Lucas flips his high beams on so we can tell where we're at and whether we're going to run into remnants of the old screen and the sound box posts. The landscape looks almost exactly the same as it did after that long bike ride, only more of the wood has rotted away and vandals have taken care of other bits. The radios, though, still seem intact.

"They're still here," I say, the delighted voice of a ten-year-old coming out of my mouth. "Stop the car. Let's see if any work," I say, unbuckling quickly.

Lucas skids to a stop and we both jump out, searching with the help of his truck's brights. The first three boxes I find are missing cords, and even though Lucas finds a few that are connected, he can't get power to any of them. Stubborn and unwilling to quit, he and I scour the lot until we're out of the shelter of his truck beams and are now fumbling in the moonlight. When I find one that lights up when my thumb presses the button, I squeal.

"Oh, my God!"

I can barely see Lucas's form, but I hear his steps along the ground nearby.

"Don't let go. I'll find one, too," he says, rummaging through a few more boxes before reaching the final row, closest to where the screen used to be.

The dark surroundings close in on me, and I consider giving up or asking Lucas to pull his truck closer so we have some light. My fears dissolve the second I hear Lucas's voice pipe through the radio in my hand.

"Breaker niner-niner," he jokes. It's the only trucker lingo we know and it's probably not even accurate.

"I cannot believe we found two that work!" We laugh with a mixture of nostalgia and exhaustion.

The twins taught Lucas this trick when we were younger, and he's the one who talked me into riding our bikes all the way out here one day to try it out. For whatever reason, the old radios have a setting that turns them into makeshift walkie talkies. It's more of a channel, like what the police use, my dad explained when we told him. We didn't care what it was. For us, it was like having a cellphone when our parents said we weren't old enough. Of course, we could only talk to each other. And we had to ride our bikes out into the boonies to make the calls.

"It's so dark, I can barely see you," I say into the intercom.

"Mwahaha." He drags out a devilish laugh that crackles through the microphone.

"Don't be a jerk. You know I don't like the dark." I squat down and pull an abandoned crate close enough to sit while we talk.

"I wish someone would reopen this place," I lament.

"Maybe I do that instead of go to MIT or Tennessee. Look, problem solved." A bitter laugh slips out.

"I think you really want to go to MIT," I say.

There's a long pause before he breathes out a "Yeah."

"Your dad has even less of a right dictating now."

He coughs, and I can tell it's forced.

"We can talk about other things." I'm not sure what else there is, so I wait for him to lead.

"I'm sorry I was a jerk," he finally says.

I was one, too, but I'm not ready to admit that to him quite yet.

"I miss us, Lucas." I cup the radio in my palms and stare at it, willing him to say the same words through the microphone.

"What happened?" I wipe away a quick tear and wait again. The only sounds I hear are his occasional breaths from yards away over a barely functioning line. I don't know why it's easier to talk like this. It always was. The first time my parents had a blow-out argument that ended in my dad storming out and staying at a hotel for a week, I confessed it here and only to Lucas. And when he threw all our best glasses to the floor and told my mother she was a tramp . . . we talked about that here too.

"Do you think you could help me with something?" His ask feels heavy, partly because of his tone but also because he purposely avoided the things I asked. I kind of want to force a trade, a favor from me for a truth from him.

"One date," I say.

His silence tells me it's either a *no* or he's confused.

"With me, I mean. I want to go out on a real date, in front of people." I grip my bottom lip with my teeth and brace myself for rejection. I expect it, and if he does say no then at least I'll know what this is and where I stand. I'll know that our kiss was a moment of weakness on his part, and I'll quit trying to break inside his toughest parts.

"One date," he repeats, and I sit up straight, muscles tight at the thought that he's actually considering it.

"Yes. That's my offer. Take it or leave it."

The quiet lasts a little longer this time, and the dead space is filled with the occasional crackling sound of our connection. After a few final pops, the small green light on my device flickers off. Whatever residual electricity I was drawing on is gone.

"Went dead!" I shout, waving my hand.

Lucas drops his box, and it swings from the cord, banging into the post. I wait for him to come back, but he hasn't moved. I can tell he's standing, and his hands are either rubbing at his neck or on his face. The lack of response to my offer is starting to make me feel desperate, and the more seconds that pass without him moving or speaking, the less I want a yes at all.

I'm about to shout "never mind" when his voice cuts through the cool air.

"I get to pick the place," he yells.

His body shifts, the shadow of hands falls to his sides.

"So you can pick somewhere nobody will see you with me?" I let out a guttural laugh after my fair question. I don't want to be a secret. And I refuse to believe that kiss was anything other than real and honest. Whatever he's afraid of in this world, it can't be me. It can't be *us*.

I can tell his head is bending down as he moves closer. He's still too far to hear the crunch of his feet on the dirt, but with every stride he takes, I'm given a new detail. His right thumb is hooked in the pocket of his torn-up sweats. His brow is heavy and his focus is on the ground before him. His mouth is closed, but the usual tightness is gone.

Soon, I hear him. I smell him.

"You ashamed of me, Lucas Fuller? Is that what all of this is about?" I hold out my open palms, the harsh realization that I've been pushing aside for two years finally boiling to the surface.

He lifts his chin and his eyes soften with the slight tilt of his head.

"It's nothing like that, June." He shakes his head as if I'm supposed to understand, but I don't.

"What's it like then, Lucas? Because here's what it's like to me. We're best friends, then we're not. We live a hundred feet apart, and for two years, I see you only in passing, through open shutters and truck windows. I come back to school, and we're enemies. I resent you, but only because you resent me, and I have no idea why. None of it—no clue. But then there are these few tiny moments when I see you. When I *really* see you. My Lucas shows up to take care of me, and he talks and he shares for one night. We kiss, then just . . . like . . . that." I snap my fingers and his eyes flit to my hand. I hold my turned-up palm, thumb against fingers, in front of my eyes.

"You can't tell anyone." I throw his words back at him, the ones he said after the breathtaking night that left my lips raw and my heart even rawer.

His lips shut tight and he draws in a long breath through his nose, slowly shaking his head. I think it means he understands me, but at this point, who knows? Maybe it means he's about to tap out and ditch me here. Wouldn't be the first time in the last month he made me walk home in the dark. Though this is a hell of a lot farther than a block.

"You're right." His scratchy voice breaks through the quiet.

I blink.

"I'm sorry, could you repeat that please?" I say into my broken speaker. He glances up from the ground and wears a brief crooked smile. His gaze holds on, and after a beat, his head falls to the side.

"You . . . are right," he says again.

I'm skeptical, so I turn my head and glance at him sideways.

"So, is that a yes? To the—"

"It's a yes to the date. And a yes that it won't be in a cave. I will take you somewhere that has actual living, breathing humans nearby. There might be food, and there will probably be a movie because this is Indiana and our options are slim."

I let out a short laugh.

"Come here," he says, finger calling me to my feet. He drops both hands in his pockets and cocks his head to the side.

He can make me so damn mad, and then he looks at me like that. My stubborn side stays put because I hate that all it takes is a look.

"Please," he adds, and his sweetness—his attention—pushes me over the edge. I stand and brush off the back of my jeans, then stuff my hands in my pockets, swishing side-to-side while I scoot my feet closer to his. He takes the final few steps toward me and gently grabs my wrists, pulling my hands from their hiding spots. His fingers find the spaces between mine until we're holding hands palm-to-palm like a mirror image of each other.

His bottom lip is heavy with unsaid words, and his eyes dip below my gaze as he struggles to speak.

"I don't want—" He stops short, knitting his brows. Eventually his eyes close. "I don't want my family to fuck it up. I want to keep this ours for a little while."

His eyes reopen on mine and there is a hardness to them, a brewing anger that I want to ask about but somehow know that now is not the time. His father holds him to his own set of expectations yet doesn't live up to them himself.

I step close, bring our elbows together until we stand like extras doing some ballroom dance in a period drama. I lift myself up on my toes so I'm closer to his face, staring hard into his eyes.

The crickets from the surrounding trees are singing, and if I were rich —I mean *really* rich—I would buy this lot of land and build a home for me and Lucas right here. It's a fantasy kind of future, but I haven't indulged in fantasies in a very long time. What's the harm in giving in to one right now?

"What's the favor?" A faint smile paints my lips. We're standing so close that Lucas can only focus on one of my eyes at a time. I shift my gaze in harmony with his until the curves in our mouths match exactly.

"I'm going to interview for MIT. And Coach and my dad . . . they can't know." Uneasiness pulls the corners of his eyes down, and his breathing stills.

"They won't," I assure him, knowing that I can't—and shouldn't—make that promise. But more than that, I can't let him not try for this. It's what's in his heart. He wouldn't have told me about it if it didn't weigh on him so heavily.

"I have a plan. You'll need to take my truck."

I grin and he shakes my hands in his, laughing lightly with his head tilted back.

"I'm gonna want it back in one piece," he says.

I shake my head. "No promises."

He smiles with puckered lips and looks down at me with narrowed eyes.

"Do you need help getting ready for the interview? Is it at school? Or do you go to an office?" I rattle out a few more questions, but stop, letting my voice trail off with breathy whispered words when I realize he's more than just amused by me.

"What?" My cheeks are burning and I'm so grateful that it's dark outside.

Lucas pulls my hands up around his neck, then delicately traces his fingertips down my arms to my waist until we stand like we're dancing without music. I fall back down on my heels and he removes the last few inches between us so he can tower over me. My eyes flit up to his hair, mussy from his run but now dry. I push the locks dipping over his right eye out of the way, the soft curl that the strands form tempting my fingers to stick around and play.

"June?"

It's hard to look him in the eyes right now. He's looking at me with want, which is something I never fully prepared for. I look up briefly but dip my gaze when the pounding in my chest feels unbearable.

I have zero control over my mouth right now. My lips are vibrating, and if he forces me to use words, they will be a scrambled, blubbering mess. Lucas eases my nerves with a soft stroke of his thumb across my bottom lip. Then a tender touch from the back of his fingers along the line of my jaw and my cheek. He lifts my chin until it's hard to not let my gaze follow, meeting his. Wordlessly, he asks for permission, eyes falling to my mouth briefly, then returning to my stare.

I melt quickly, wanting badly to relive the kiss we had in my bedroom. I'm still so full of questions, though. I feel this pull that comes from somewhere else entirely, and I think it's my past self. I owe it to the girl I was a year ago—two years ago—to get answers before I give in to the lure of kissing Lucas Fuller. I spent too many nights wondering what I did to cause my best friend to abandon our relationship. He was too cruel for it to be meaningless hormones, and too committed for it to be high school politics or a dare. My feelings war inside my head until it becomes impossible to hide the trepidation that drags down every last bit of happiness finally blooming on my face. My body stiffens in warning and Lucas steps back just enough to study me, and the reciprocal weight of doom that tugs at his light gives us enough space for me to once again ask the hardest question of my life. This time, I can't give in without getting an answer.

"What happened?" I'm shaking where I stand, terrified of the answer.

Lucas shakes his head, and I think he's begging me not to ask. The mystery is too much, though. I need to know. I need it for there to ever be an *us* again.

"Why did you pull away? Lucas . . . I need to know."

His hands fidget at my sides, his fingers squeezing at my hips with light pressure, as if he's afraid I might run.

"Please don't make me tell you, June. Don't make me say it."

A wave of nausea makes me dizzy, and a light sweat covers my neck. He has to know I'm too far in to go back now. I can't kiss him with this cloud threatening us. I could never accept it as real; it would always be a distraction, his way of once again getting out of the hard truth. He is my weakness, but he used to be my strength. I need to know where that part of him went and why.

He shakes his head harder, like a man trying to banish a bad dream, troublesome thoughts or voices in his head. Through it all, his hands stay on my hips, threatening to slip away but never quite fully letting go.

"June," he pleads, squeezing his eyes shut. He finally breaks his touch on me and grips at his hair, and I am truly scared.

I wait through his labored, heavy breaths and force myself to maintain my hold on his red, tortured eyes. When the fight is finally choked from his body, his hands go limp at his sides. He offers one last breath, one last chance to touch my hand to his mouth and stop the onslaught of words that will change everything.

I don't.

"This isn't my father's first affair."

We're both breathless. I ignore all other sounds; no more crickets or faraway hum of traffic. The darkness has eaten any light that's left, and I hold on as Lucas drags me down a rabbit hole that will change me forever.

"My dad was seeing your mom."

Those were the nights I made my own dinner.

"My mom caught them together."

That's when my dad said she was a hypocrite.

"He begged my mom not to leave."

My dad took advantage of an easy out.

"My mom wanted him to make you and your mom move, but she settled for us never talking to you again."

Us. Lucas. Me.

"She said she would tell everyone how your mom and my dad met."

My mouth waters with anger and all I can muster is a strong shake to my head.

"He hired her, June. She needed money to get away from your dad and still be able to afford . . . things. And my father paid. He paid over and over. And he said he wasn't the only one."

Over and over.

I am numb.

"I didn't want you to know. I didn't want anyone to ever know. I didn't . . ."

My mom slept with Lucas's dad so I could fucking go to college. Those are the *things* she wanted to afford. Me. She wanted to be able to afford me.

Lucas didn't want me to know.

And now I do.

And nothing.

Is.

The same.

SIXTEEN

"We haven't seen the meteors yet," I say, lying back on the roof of Lucas's truck. He's still standing on the ground next to the driver's side door.

About an hour ago, Lucas asked if I wanted him to take me home. That's when I climbed up here. I'm not even sure what home is anymore. I have too many questions, and every single one I ask doesn't seem to have an answer.

None of this makes sense.

Mrs. Fuller caught my mom and her husband together late one night at my mother's photo studio. She hired a private investigator who traced the money, about ten thousand dollars, and who followed my mom for two weeks, documenting a dozen late-night meet-ups with her husband at the photo studio as well as twice at his office downtown. It was all suspicion until she read the six months of text messages between them. Six months is how long my parents were in therapy. When she confronted her husband, phone records in hand, he caved. I keep asking Lucas for details, but he says he doesn't really know. It's more likely he doesn't want to tell me.

What did the messages say?

Did she tell him she loved him?

Did anyone say they were sorry?

"The clouds are rolling in," Lucas says. I think he's said it twice. I'm only half here; the other half is still mining theories and picking apart scant information while feeling incredibly betrayed.

"Sit with me?" I roll my head to the side and stare at him sideways. He wants to take it back. How do I tell him I don't believe it? Am I being naïve?

Lucas exhales, his hands tucked in the pocket of his hoodie, which is now pulled up over his head, weighing down his wild hair in the breeze. It's getting colder out, and he's still wearing shorts.

"You can grab my jacket from the floor of your truck. Use it to cover up?" I offer.

His mouth ticks up in a slight smile before he glances down and nods to himself.

"Okay, June," he says, giving in to my request.

He opens the passenger side to grab my jacket, also flipping off the headlights to save the battery. A second later, music plays from the radio. I flatten the side of my head so my ear is pressed against the roof. The song is familiar, but I can't quite place it. When the truck rocks from the weight of Lucas hoisting himself up on the roof, I turn the other way.

"Here," he says, handing me my jacket as he slides his legs up to sit beside me. I push the jacket back to him.

"You're in shorts. I thought you could use it to cover up," I say.

He shakes his head with a soft laugh.

"I don't get cold." His eyes seem so damn sorry.

"That's not true," I say, wincing at my words. That was unfair.

"I didn't mean it like that," I add.

His head falls to the side.

"Yes, you did," he says, his voice breathy and full of regret.

"I'm sorry."

"Don't be." His eyes move down my body to where my hands are balled up in the bottom of my shirt to stay warm. He unzips my jacket and spreads it over my torso.

"Your mom is probably worried about you," he says out of the side of his mouth. He leans back, palms against the roof of the truck while his long legs drape down the windshield. My legs are falling asleep from being bent in front of me, but I don't want to stop looking at the stars. I haven't seen a single meteor yet. I want to. I want something to make a wish on.

Without asking, I lift myself on my arms enough to shift my body to the side, lying my head in Lucas's lap. I roll so I'm looking up again, and his eyes are waiting for me.

"I'm probably not very soft," he says through a breathy laugh.

"You're softer than you think," I say, one eye squinting a little. Lucas's body shakes with his amusement.

"Okay then," he says, tilting his chin to the sky. The moment he looks up, a flicker of light streaks across the sky, ducking behind one of the thin clouds and reflecting little flickers of light as the meteor burns up.

"Oh, my God!" My grin stretches into my tight cheeks. Joy is such a foreign feeling.

"Wow," Lucas says, his eyes still trained on the space above where a piece of star just died. I should probably close my eyes to make a wish, but I've shut my eyes enough lately. I want to keep them wide open. I want to take the things I want.

I pull my hands free from the cover of my jacket, slide my left palm up Lucas's chest, and lift myself just as his chin drops to look down. My hand travels up his neck and jaw, ducking underneath the cover of his hoodie into the cool thickness of his hair. Without giving myself a chance to think twice, I press my lips to his.

His body hesitates in reaction, a flinch that nips at my lips. There's a sudden stiffness in his chest as it sucks in a quick breath and his muscles become defensive on reflex. I get it. After what he told me—with confusion taking over my head and the mess that is us—kissing is probably not the way to work through any of it. But kissing Lucas Fuller is the only thing that makes sense right now. I let my lips dance along his like a ghost, light tickles of skin on skin until he breaks and brings his hands up to cradle my body and head. I push his hood from his head as both my hands dive into his hair, his mouth now working mine with urgency. His kiss feels desperate, as if he wants to get as much as he can before this all disappears. The sensation spurs me to do the same.

My face cradled in his hands, I slide my palms forward to do the same to him, shifting my body until I'm on my knees. Lucas leans back a little and I slide my right leg over his lap so I'm straddling him. The sensation of my body sitting on the hardness of his reaction causes his breath to hitch against my mouth. His hands break free of my face, falling back to catch his weight on the roof of the truck.

I sit up but leave my hands on him, raking my fingers down the front of his hoodie like claws. His hooded eyes stare at me and his lips are pink from where my teeth held on just a breath ago. He's panting, trying to be good, but his eyes betray his wants as they dip and lower, guiding his thoughts to my mouth, my neck, my breasts. I roll my hips against him and he swallows, biting his fat bottom lip and letting go with a "Fuuuck."

I'm out of my element, guided only by what my body feels and wants. I've kissed boys, made out in dark corners or, when teachers weren't looking, behind the trees surrounding the basketball court at my tiny Montessori school. I don't want to chastely kiss Lucas like a child right now. I want to touch him, taste him, leave my mark on him so anyone who questions us knows we had this—a moment for us.

For me.

My hands wander to the bottom of his hoodie and I lift it until he helps me remove it completely, tossing it over his shoulder and into the back of the truck. He's so very much not the boy I first met when my fingers roam along his bare skin to discover hard muscles that curve and dip. I flatten my palms against his sides and trace the proof that despite what he wants, he is disciplined in the gym and on the field. I paint my fingertips back down toward the light dusting of golden hairs that begin at his belly button and disappear under the band of his cut-off sweats.

I tug at the knotted string, easily sliding it free, but before I can touch inside, Lucas's hands cover mine. He pulls them to his mouth, tethering them together and grazing his teeth against the inside of my left wrist with a gentle bite. He lifts my arms high then glides his hands down the length of my arms over the hard peaks of my breasts to the bottom of my work shirt, quickly rolling it up in his palms and raising it up my midriff and chest. I tilt my head up as he pulls it over my face, then take over and toss it into the truck bed where his sweatshirt now lies.

My arms fall to his shoulders, fingers musing in the soft tufts of hair that curl from his scalp at the base of his neck. I bend my head down enough that our noses touch, my gaze locked on his. His lashes fall shut with the heavy weight of want, and his mouth moves to the right side of my neck. I lean to give him access, his hand sliding the strap of my bra down my shoulder. His mouth follows the trail of his fingertips as they drag the satin, then the lace lower until the hard pink peak of my breast is exposed. His tongue circles it just before his lips leave a soft wet kiss that he dries with his cooling breath. I pucker under his control.

I lean back to expose more of my neck, my body angled so he can easily slide the rest of my bra away. Virgin white lace that has only ever been seen by me loosens around my skin as his hands deftly unclasp the hook in the back. Lucas discards the garment to the side, covering my right breast with his palm while his mouth covers the left. He sucks me to a hard peak, painful pleasure igniting a pool between my legs. I push into his erection to ease my need and he groans against my body.

My hair is twisted in a loose bun at the base of my neck. Lucas hooks a finger in the band and pulls it free, letting my hair blow wildly until he can gather it in his palm. He wraps it around his hand once and tugs it back, coaxing my back to arch so my breasts are high enough for his tongue to taste them raw. I push into him when his teeth graze against the hardened peak of one. I'm begging him to bite, and I know he wants to.

My hands push down the back of his neck to his shoulder blades, and I pull myself into him as I right my head. I need to kiss him. My mouth is hungry. His hands clear the blowing strands of hair from my face as our mouths connect again in a kiss that means to strip us both of oxygen. Our tongues tangle as I pull his lip into my mouth a moment before he does the same to me. Heat boils in my body and I grind into his lap, needing the friction—needing to feel how hard he is for me against how wet I am for him.

The moment I press into him, his hands let go of my face and rush to my hips, tugging me close, fingers gripping at the back pocket of my jeans and rocking me back and forth on his lap. I ride the sensation, knowing I'm going to have an orgasm still in my panties and jeans, but I want more from him—more *for* him. Even if our past fucks up our future, I want to have this moment. I want Lucas to be my first.

I always have.

I feel between us, finding the strings I was forced to abandon a moment ago, once again tugging his pants loose, this time without him slowing me. My fingertips feel along the band of his waist and I pull toward me, making room for my hand to slip inside. Lucas isn't wearing anything underneath, and my hand immediately brushes the searing hot hardness of his cock.

"June." He croaks out my name.

I sit back to make room and lean forward, pressing my forehead into his, both of us breathing as our lips touch with many tiny kisses.

"I want to touch you," I say. He's weak under my spell, nodding and shifting his hips; I lower his shorts enough to completely free his erection.

"Am I doing this right?" I ask, my fingers slowly wrapping around the warm shaft. I squeeze with light pressure and I feel him flex in my hold.

He nods, grabbing the back of my head and bringing my mouth to his.

"Yeah," he pants.

I move my hand up and down in a slow rhythm, letting the soft skin slide under my touch. I pull myself up as tall as I can on my knees. While my head rests on his, I lower my chin to see how he reacts under my touch. It's both exactly and nothing as I imagined this part of him to be. I'd never admit to anyone, not even Abby, but I've fantasized about this too. Along with the romance and kisses and sweetness, I also lay in bed some nights and pretend my hands are on him, and his are on me.

His palms grip the back of my thighs as I stroke him, sliding up centimeters at a time until he finally cups my ass. I grip him harder at the sensation of his fingers clawing into my back pockets, his fingertips rough against the denim of my jeans.

Impatient, I put my hand over his right one, threading my fingers between his knuckles to guide his grip forward and to the front of my jeans. He's more than willing, his hands tugging on the button of my jeans and unfastening it deftly, followed by the zipper. His thumbs hook inside the band of my panties, plain white and cotton that I wish were sexier than they are. I hadn't planned on any of this.

As he tugs my pants down my hips, I shift from above him, helping to pull them down completely. His hands grip my sides and he encourages me to lie on my back. I kick my shoes from my feet and wriggle my legs free, parting my knees as he moves to kneel between my legs. His gaze begins at my breasts then rises until his eyes meet mine. I nod and whisper "Yes." It's just enough for him to reach in his front pocket and pull out his wallet.

I hold my bottom lip between my teeth in anticipation, and giggle when he holds the small black packet up in presentation. It's not the same one I teased him about the other day, which means he got this new, in hopes that maybe he and I would take this step.

I flatten my sweating palms on the surface of the truck, tucking them under my hips to hide my nerves as Lucas rolls the condom on himself. He's somehow bigger in his own hand, though it's probably my perspective. I'm nervous, and a little afraid of the pain.

Lucas lowers himself so he hovers over me, his weight held by his forearms as I lie caged between them. His nose brushes against mine lightly and his lips brush against mine, parting just enough to suckle on my top lip. I lift my chin to give him more of my mouth, shutting my eyes to be brave.

His right arm moves to the space between us so he can guide himself inside me. I feel the tip at my entrance and clench, sucking in air and arching my back so my hips reflexively pull away.

"Okay?" he whispers, his mouth ticking against my ear. A rush of shivers trails down the right side of my body, leaving tiny bumps in its wake.

"Yes," I nod, squeezing my eyes tighter.

I try to breathe and force my body to relax as he pushes himself in more, pausing to let me adapt to the feel of having him there. He rocks his hips in short strokes, never fully leaving me and not fully pushing inside. His tongue traces a cool line from my chin down to the nape of my neck where his mouth sucks at the tender part of my skin. He kisses the spot.

"I left a tiny bruise there so you'll see it in the morning and know this was real." His voice is husky and a little dominant, but not overbearing. It's perfect, and it turns me on.

"Ready?" he asks. I nod again, this time moving my hips lower so his access is straighter. He rests his weight on me, holding himself up on his arms so his hands can brush the sweat-dampened hairs from my face. His thumbs run along my cheeks just under my eyes, luring them open to witness his devilish smile. The faint curl on his lips is proof of how satisfied he is with this, how much he wanted it, too.

His head tilts enough for him to kiss me hard, and with my cries muffled by his mouth, he pushes in deep, breaking any remaining threads of my youth with his thrust. I whimper against his mouth but kiss back harder, holding on to his bottom lip with my teeth, biting through the pain so hard that I may have drawn a little blood.

Lucas pulls back, the slide of his hard-on slow and slick. I feel wet and swollen despite the pain, which lessens with every plunge he takes into me. For minutes, he's methodical and gentle, though his cock sinks in deep. The feel of the tip against my insides teases a sensitive spot that drowns my head in endorphins every single time his hips rock. Soon, I'm meeting his thrusts with pressure of my own, my hands no longer sitting by idle on the roof of the car, but gripping at the material of his sweat shorts that are pulled so low on his hips that his ass is exposed. I pull him into me by the band of his pants, eventually wrapping my legs around him to hold him deep inside while his lower body pumps rhythmically, keeping up with our panting breaths. We chase the sensation and my insides constrict and pulse uncontrollably, forcing a moaning cry from my mouth. I muffle it against the bare skin of his shoulder as he grows tight inside me, filling the condom.

Pulses carry through our cores and he pushes into me a few more times before rolling to the side and pulling out, leaving our sex-covered sweat-strewn bodies exposed to the open air, now fully dark of stars as a thickness of clouds shrouds the sky.

I always imagined this is when I would be shy or embarrassed, when I realize what I did and everything that can be seen, and feel suddenly inadequate. I don't feel any of that. I've pushed aside every part of our story that doesn't fit and that I don't want to yet accept so I can label this moment as purely mine, a greedy piece of our story that I will come back to always.

No longer the girl playing the part of a woman, I roll to my side and trail my fingers down Lucas's chest and stomach, moving lower until I reach the still pulsing tip of his swollen cock. I glance up to catch his eyes shaded by his long, dark lashes as he stares at me with both suspicion and need. My body still teeming with electricity from every firing nerve, I hold his gaze hostage and roll to my knees, once again straddling him. I pleasure myself by pressing his erection into his abdomen, writhing and teasing myself against its length until I come again . . . and again.

SEVENTEEN

The sun is up, barely, as we pull into Lucas's driveway. I'm sure my mom is livid that I didn't reply to any of her calls or texts. I also didn't answer my phone when Abby started calling. I'm a little surprised there isn't a police car in our driveway. I started feeling guilty when we decided it was time to head home. It was selfish to ignore everyone, but I couldn't handle all of the extra noise. My head isn't right to talk with my mom, and I don't know where to begin in explaining all of this to my best friend.

But now, the reality is playing out. I have to let it, and I have no choice but to be present for it. The empty driveways, the quiet homes, the light glowing from my kitchen window where I know my mom is sitting, phone in hand, waiting. I have to face it all. I'm all she has left, besides her brother who we see maybe three times a year. How do I untangle all of the questions I have for her? My gut says one thing, but then Lucas is so resolute about his version of the story. Even if none of it's true, having the theory live in this universe has changed how I see things, how I see people.

How I see her.

I knew we wouldn't be alone in this driveway for long. Lucas's truck lights up the first floor of our house, so it's inevitable that my mom sees it and comes outside, hoping it's me. She looks manic, her hair wild in all directions as she pads out clutching her phone as she tightly hugs her body. She's wearing the same T-shirt and jeans I saw her in yesterday morning.

"How come boys have it so easy? It's so hypocritical," I say. "You're rolling in at the crack of dawn too, but I don't see your mother out in the driveway waiting to rip your head off after she finishes hugging you." I make no attempt to leave this quiet bubble I'm in with Lucas. The moment I open this passenger door, our moment will be over.

"I guess it's a matter of conditioning. My parents are kind of used to me not coming home on weekends." He stretches his hand out on the seat between us and rolls his palm over. I put my hand inside and he squeezes tightly.

"I don't want to do this," I say.

"That's why I never said anything before," he says, his voice full of sorry.

I grimace in the other direction because I wish he had. We could be well past this point if I'd only known. Waiting to get a shot at the doctor is always so much worse than when they put on the Band-Aid.

My mom has stopped about halfway between our house and Lucas's truck, but her face is easy to read from here.

Where the fuck have you been and why didn't you call or text like you always *do?* That's what that expression says.

"Wish me luck," I say, leaning into him, turning his chin to face me and pressing my lips on his one last time. I slide across the seat and pop open my door, but the moment I step outside, I catch his mom's waiting stare, and her expression . . . it's nothing like the worried one my mom wears.

"I'm sorry," I say to my mom, my eyes bouncing between her and Lucas's mom, who stands just inside her side door. She's holding a coffee mug and casually leaning into the frame as she blows on the steam rising from her cup. Her stance suggests she's not amused. Maybe it's the information I'm now privy to, but I can see the subtleties—the disapproving glare and tight grip on the mug. I turn around, mostly out of loyalty to the boy I just gave my most important first to, but he's already backing out of the driveway. I'd fault him for running away, but I had the same idea. He just had the keys.

"I was worried sick." My mom's words come out with vibrato, the result of wanting to cry and being too tired to give in to the urge.

"We lost track of time," I say, taking urgent steps past her, heading inside our house. I don't want to put on a show for Shannon Fuller, especially when I'm not convinced she has her story right.

"Lost track of time? June, it's another entire day!" My mom slams the side door closed behind her. I'd turn to face her but I'm too busy taking in the various open drawers dumped onto the counters and the contents of my backpack spilled out on the kitchen table.

"Were we robbed?" I know we weren't but I can't quite figure out what this mess is all about.

"I was trying to find clues about where you were. Phone numbers, information in your school planner, a ticket stub . . . I don't know!" I turn to catch her hands in the air, phone still clutched in one of them. I wonder who she's dialed. I don't have many friends, and she doesn't know Naomi or Lola.

"I'm sorry. I really am," I say, because—right now—I am. I didn't mean to make my mom worry, but I would spend my night exactly the same way every time I'm given the chance. I move toward the refrigerator, pausing to rummage through a few of the things on the counter from the drawers. I lift up a pizza menu and laugh out a breath, holding it up for my mom to see.

"You checked with the pizza guy?" I'm making a joke of something she doesn't think is funny. It's not funny. I'm just not ready to tell her how unfunny all of it is.

"June, I called every phone number I could find in the goddamn house. You never just disappear. We—me and you—we don't do that to each other!" Her eyes are glossy, and I should probably drop my edge and step into her with a hug right now, but what she just said sticks a little. I cock my head slightly and narrow my eyes on her.

"You sure?" I'm slipping into one of those conversations I can't take back, and I don't like that I am. Nevertheless, I can't stop.

"I'm sorry?" Her voice has elevated into yelling. This is the voice she used with my dad when he came home late.

"I'm just saying, me and you . . . we don't hold things back from each other. Is that what you're saying?"

An intense quiet builds between us for a few seconds before she answers with a booming "Yes!"

I slowly nod and turn to the fridge, pulling out a bottle of water. I'm so thirsty. I pull the lid off and drink nearly half of it before recapping it and holding it to my side as I let the fridge door close and turn back to face my mom.

"Okay, then," I say. "I was out with Lucas. We had sex. I'm going to bed." I march past her, knowing she's stunned by that little bomb, and I take the time it bought me all the way upstairs, where I proceed to lock my bedroom door, set my water on my night stand, close my shutters, and crawl under my velvet blue blanket with my phone.

I don't want to talk to anyone except Lucas, so I shoot my bestie a short text so she knows I'm alive and epic shit went down, but I can't tell her until tomorrow. She responds instantly with about four lines of exclamation points, but she follows it up with two hearts, so I know Abby and I are good.

I toss my phone to the side and pull my blanket up over my head, and for the next two hours I remember every single spot that Lucas touched me. Somewhere in my best daydreams, I fall asleep and don't crack a lid open until early evening, when my phone buzzes at my side with a text from Lucas.

Hi.

EIGHTEEN

In many ways, it's another typical Monday morning. Abby is waiting in my driveway blasting some song she texted me was super hype and dropped late last night. I rush around my room searching for a T-shirt that's not too wrinkled to wear because I traded time to shower and prep a normal look for the day for thirty extra minutes of sleep. I've lived this morning before. It's my normal mode. My Groundhog Day. I'm always a bit disheveled, not great with sticking to a morning routine, and my haphazard style makes my supermodel best friend mental. But this dose of chaos, it works for me. Usually.

Today, my mom is waiting downstairs in the kitchen and there is an invisible brick wall between us that she'll expect me to climb over before I leave. I don't feel much for climbing. At least, not *that* wall. Lucas always made the trip up my porch roof look easy. I'm nowhere near as strong as he is, but down has to be easier than up. The thought struck me before I fell asleep again at about four this morning, mid-text with Lucas as we went over the plan for today. I juggled between messaging him and FaceTiming Abby so I could give her a full deposition of all things drama that is my life. Not surprisingly, most of her questions weren't about the gossip about my mother but instead were centered around my first time and details of Lucas's, umm, parts. I learned two key things from our talk. One, my best friend has seen way more penises than I have. Seven to my one, to be exact. Also, apparently, Lucas stacks up pretty well in terms of size. The entire conversation made me want to die, especially because I was texting him while having it.

I maybe should have taken Lucas up on his offer to drive me to school—he could have helped me scale down the side of my house—but I didn't want to risk running into his mom again. I don't like the way she looks at me, as though I'm guilty. And even though Lucas said he no longer cares what his parents think, deep down he does. He cares that his dad doesn't like his choices, and he cares that his mom has been hurt.

My mom has been hurt, too. And I care about that, which is the reason I don't want to face her just yet, or at least that's what I rationalize. I'm not ready to be civilized, and I don't know how to word my questions. I need to be prepared for her answers, as well—whether my suspicions are right, that she's done nothing wrong, or Lucas's version is true and she's as much to blame as my father. I need to be mentally prepared to embrace and move forward on either path. Right now, I only want to floor it in reverse.

This brings me to where I stand right now, literally, two feet planted on the tacky surface of the A-frame that covers my porch. I've taken myself to the brink of reason, avoiding my mom by roof leaping. The slide down the wall was a longer drop than I thought, and it's left me a bit frozen here. The drop down from the spot where the A-frame ends, where the gutter drips rainwater into my mom's flower garden, is about the same distance. My pocket buzzes from my phone so I lean flat against the wall, my backpack strap wrapped tightly around my right wrist, and pull my phone out with my left hand. It's Abby calling, so I glance up to see her hunched over her steering wheel and staring out her windshield with her mouth agape.

I answer.

"I didn't think this through," I say through nervous giggling.

"What the fuck, June!" It's kinda funny how her mouth moves just a hair before I hear the words in my ear.

"I'm avoiding my mom." I shrug, the movement making me a little off balance for a blip and I bend my knees, gripping to the surface beneath my feet.

"Yeah, well, you're probably gonna have to deal with her when you fall and break something and she has to haul your ass to the emergency room." She leans back in her seat but just a little. My friend is looking from side to side, maybe searching for help. I don't want any, except for hers. The last thing I need is assistance from the problems I'm hiding from.

"I'm coming down," I say, my voice quavering as I cautiously lower myself until I'm on my ass, sitting with legs pointing down the slope. God, how I wish this were really a slide.

"I'm coming out," Abby says.

"No!" I stop her fast. "Don't. If you come out, my mom will see you and then she'll come out, and then—"

"And then your ass climbed out a window for nothing. Yeah, I got it. This is fucked up."

I sigh.

"I know. Just give me a minute. I'm going to scoot." I drag my butt along the grainy shingles about six inches before stretching my legs out like an inch worm to do it again.

"You look ridiculous," my friend says.

"You better not be filming me," I fire back.

"I'm not, but I took a picture. You know, for my collection of June in her moods." She's amused by this, but all I can focus on is not dying. I end our call and slip my phone back into my pocket.

In reality, I'm not that high, but maybe I have a fear of heights I was never fully aware of. Being up here has my heart racing and sweat pouring from every part of my body. I scoot and work my feet in a rhythm, quickening my pace until I finally reach the edge of the eave and am able to slide forward enough that my legs dangle. Our living room windows are just to my right. This is the corner where we usually put our Christmas tree. There's a lamp there now, which helps to mask the view of me. My mom was in the kitchen before I left. I snuck a quick view down the stairs to see her sitting on one of the stools by the counter closest to the side door. If I can be silent with this, I might just make it out without her hearing.

I pull my backpack to my chest and ready my hands on either side to heave it into the middle of the lawn. The grass needs to be mowed, but it's also dry from the cooler weather, which makes it kind of like hay. I count on my decent aim as I shove my bag through the air. It lands on a thicker spot in the lawn and rolls a few times until coming to rest about a dozen feet from my friend's car. I'm next, but there is no hay beneath me, only damp soil and my mother's petunias. That isn't much to break a fall.

Feeling all kinds of ridiculous, I push myself up so my feet are under me, balanced on the edge of the eave, toes on the curve of the gutter. I rock forward and hold on to the edge with my hands, leaning out just enough to spot my landing before gravity takes over and I tumble to the ground. I land with my knees and palms deep in my mom's garden, muddy water squishing up from the ground and staining my jeans and covering my hands. Amped from adrenaline, I bolt to my feet and sprint to my bag, grabbing it and rushing to my friend's car. I shut the door on the strap of my backpack but leave it there, the strap dragging along the ground and my bag locked to the area near my feet.

"Go, go!" I wave my arms emphatically. In my own mind, I just made so much noise. I nervously stare out the windshield as my friend pulls out of my driveway; my house remains still, and the side door stays closed. In about twenty minutes, my mom will discover the open window from my room and skyrocket to a new level of pissed. She'll probably think I'm on drugs. I'm going to have to deal with everything today one way or another. I can't live like this, and if I don't come home for another night, my mom will think I've run away. That's not even on the table. I'd miss her too much, even if the things Lucas told me are true.

Abby finishes poking fun of my lame-ass sneaking-out skills for the first few minutes of our drive, but she becomes quiet as we get closer to school. I haven't asked her point-blank what she thinks the truth is, and I know why I haven't. Abby cuts through bullshit. She's rarely wrong, even if the way she gives advice comes off harsh. She was right when she said I had to break out of my shell and quit worrying what people thought of me. As crazy as all of this shit I'm going through is, at least I'm living. I'm experiencing, growing, falling and picking myself up. I've rebuilt myself into something stronger, into the kind of girl who is on the verge of being an adult and who might be capable of handling the cruel things this world throws at people. Before this, I was balancing on eggshells and sheltering my feelings. Abby was right, I needed to move forward.

Just like I need to now.

"Do you think—"

I stop there, bracing myself for her honest answer before finishing the question. I don't even have to, though, because my friend is so in sync with me that she knows where my words are going.

"I think it doesn't matter," she says. I glance at her to assess her expression. Her face is matter-of-fact as she lifts herself high enough in her seat to check the line of red on her lips.

"How can it not?" I ask.

She shrugs and sits back down as we cross the final intersection before school.

"Well, either your mom did what she had to because she didn't have a choice, or Mr. Fuller is a big fucking liar. And frankly, he's already proven he's the least to be trusted in this cast of characters. I'm pretty sure no matter how this plays out, your mom is the good guy." Abby eases into her favorite spot right by the front of school and turns her car off before facing me with her signature *you-know-I'm-right* smile.

"How come you get to be smart and confident, *and* look like that?" I'm only half joking. For real, it isn't fair.

She purses her lips with sarcasm and leans her head to the side.

"June, honey. Looks and brains are not mutually exclusive."

Her lips briefly curve up on the ends to punctuate her brilliant response just before she opens her door and gets out of her car, leaving me there in wonder. Sometimes I wonder whether she and I would have become such good friends if Lucas and I never had our falling out. Maybe things do happen the way they're supposed to.

Lucas is waiting for me in his truck, the twins hanging out on the bench near where they park. Abby and I walk over to get Lucas's key and go over the plan for the day with him. Tory pops up from the bench to offer her his seat, and I chuckle lightly as I hop into the passenger side to talk to Lucas.

"What's funny?" he asks.

"Tory thinks being a gentleman is going to win Abby over," I say.

"Huh," Lucas responds, leaning back with his wrists balanced on the steering wheel as we both stare at the odd little love triangle forming in front of us. Last night, Abby told me she was thinking about making a move on Hayden, already moving on from the new guy, Cannon. "He's too moody," she said.

I haven't mentioned anything to Abby about Tory because I don't know how serious he is about the little crush he eluded to, and I've got enough balls in the air. I don't need to stir up new drama.

"So, the key?" I bring Lucas's attention back to our mission.

"Oh, yeah. Here," he says, pulling his key from the ignition and handing it to me. The only truck I've ever driven was my uncle's, and it was a piece of shit stick-shift with zero power steering. Lucas's truck is a four-by-four and the engine rumbles in the driveway. There may be more car geek in my genes than I ever realized.

"I see that twinkle in your eyes. Don't get crazy," he jokes. His hand covers mine, which now holds his key. My eyes dip to where we touch. I wonder if he'll hold my hand when the bell rings and we walk into the building.

"Let me go over things one more time, just to make sure I have it down. At lunch, we both slip out the gate and you get in the car with the MIT lady while I go to your truck and drive it to Two-fers."

He nods, but I can tell he's anxious.

"You'll do great," I reassure him.

He quakes with a breathy laugh and turns to the side, resting his head on his seat back as his blue eyes settle on me. There's a trust in his gaze that I've missed so much, but there's a new fondness—a deep tenderness—in his expression now too. I know in my heart that he has never, not once, looked at Ava this way.

"I'm not really worried about the interview," he says.

I twist to face him, mimicking his position. I tuck his keys in my bag by my feet and lean forward, taking his hand in both of mine. His fingers are callused from falls and summers spent taking snaps and gripping the football. These same rough hands felt so soft on my skin. His palm opens and I weave my fingers through his, and his thumb strokes the side of my hand, tracing a line from knuckle to knuckle.

"Lucas, there is no way your dad can't be proud of his son getting into MIT," I say.

He nods half-heartedly. He doesn't believe that's true, and maybe I don't fully either. I'm starting to think his dad might not actually *have* a heart, but rather a cold stone in his chest that serves as a greedy magnet, driving him to take and take with little or no regard for the people he hurts along the way.

The bell sounds, forcing us to break from this quiet moment inside his cab. Still not sure how things stand about Lucas and me in public, I squeeze his hand just before letting go. I reach for my bag to bring it to my lap, but before I fully open the passenger door, Lucas leans across the short distance between us, gliding his hand along my cheek and into my messy twist of hair. He kisses me hard, with a deep sense of urgency as if my kiss will somehow be his lucky charm to survive the day. Any thought that's the case, though, dwindles the moment our lips part and my gaze lands on a steaming Ava Pryor standing a dozen feet away.

"Fuuck," Lucas breathes out, sinking his gaze to his lap, then out his window.

"She'd find out eventually," I say, ignoring the hammering in my chest that warns me bad shit is coming my way.

"Yeah," Lucas hums. His already tight face is now tighter.

"Does she know about MIT?" I ask, and he quickly shakes his head.

"She doesn't know shit," he says, flashing his gaze to mine quickly for reassurance.

I spare a quick glance in her direction to see if she's still lingering, but she already moved on. Her tiny form punches harsh steps into the ground as she marches down the main walkway into school.

"I'll see you at lunch," I say over my shoulder before opening his truck and sliding to the ground. I hoist my bag over my shoulder, giving Lucas one last glance.

"I wish you were still in my first hour," he says before I shut the door, and even though I do, too, I'm also glad he misses me being there.

I smile and ponder how much I want this day to go smoothly for him as I head on my way to the independent study room. Even though he said Ava Pryor doesn't know shit, I can't help but constantly scan my landscape on the lookout for her. That bitch is a sniper, I swear.

The lunch bell blares, and I practically leap from my seat, my legs having primed themselves with nervous bouncing for the last twenty minutes. My stride is so long that I get to the gate at the front of the school well before Lucas shows up, so I walk near the office and check a few texts on my phone to avoid eye contact with any of the teachers or administrators. There's a single text from my mom that I can't get myself to open. I've only seen the preview, and the beginning words make me feel pretty terrible.

June, I am worried sick. Please just tell me . . .

I assume it goes on to say "that you're all right." I am all right. *Ish.* I'm also a lot wrong. And a whole lot confused and angry.

"*Psst,*" a hushed voice sounds from behind me. I turn to see Lucas walking up, his tall, muscular body looking like an elite work of art in black pants and a crisp white shirt with rolled-up sleeves. The gray tie that I can tell he made a few attempts at hangs loose around his neck. He lifts his chin as he approaches, so I drop my bag at my feet and reach up to grab the satin ends.

"These things are tricky," I say through a wide smile. He's so handsome right now, my mind has become complete goo. I'm not sure whether I want to straighten his tie, or lick him.

"I fucking hate ties. They choke me," he complains, swallowing hard and stretching out his collar with the movement of his neck.

"You're a big man," I say, blushing at my words, my focus on the work my hands are doing with the tie. I catch the smirk playing on his lips, so I playfully bat at his chest.

"Shush, or I won't help you," I say.

A gravelly laugh leaves his chest.

I get the knot just right on the first try, which is impressive since I haven't tied one of these since my father left. I tug a few times to get the line of it straight, tucking the back tail into the loop on the back of the front one. I fold his collar down and brush away a tiny bit of lint. He smells like soap and vanilla. I'm almost certain his mom pressed this shirt for him this morning. Her towels always smelled just like this; I remember from the times I went over to swim.

"There," I say, bashfully glancing up at him. He looks down at me with a coy smile, and for the first time maybe ever, I believe in my gut that this boy is truly smitten with me, as much as I am with him.

"Wish me luck," he says.

I shake my head.

"You don't need it. Break a leg," I offer instead. He laughs with a short eye roll and then grabs the open gate as one of the late-start seniors walks through.

"Ready?" he asks. I hold his keys in my palm and jingle them.

"Let's do this," I say. I let him walk out first, his strides long and purposeful toward the middle of the lot, the same direction he went the last time I saw him do this. The red car sticks out, though I think only to me, and because I'm looking for it. I pieced it together when he told me he already met with the representative a few times.

Today's interview is at a nearby restaurant, with two other admissions deans. Our principal knows he's leaving for it, and Lucas said he understands the sensitivity of keeping this a secret from his coach. I'm not sure he knows about me, though, so I don't dawdle. I jog toward Lucas's truck in an effort to get there unnoticed. But I don't make it without at least one person seeing me. I don't see her coming at all, or the fist she sends into my nose like a rocket.

Ava fucking Pryor just punched me, and I'm pretty sure she spit on me too. I'm in a fit of rage, and all I want to do is drive every ounce of my body right through hers, flattening her ass on the pavement. But that would make a scene. Teachers would come running, and people would spot me out here at Lucas's truck, with his keys, while he's on a covert mission to live his best life without interference from the people who want to run it for him. Goddamn, my face hurts, and my pride hurts a shit-ton more, but I have loved Lucas Fuller longer than I've hated Ava Pryor. So for him, I wipe my bloody nose along the sleeve of my sweatshirt and get in his truck, firing it up and peeling out to head to Two-fers, where I hope they have a lot of fucking napkins.

NINETEEN

There really isn't an easy way to mask a black eye. There's also a chance my nose is broken. I'm honestly kind of impressed with Ava's form. She hit me good, a nice shot, square up on the bone, causing my right eye to swell shut.

I spend my entire lunch hour in the Two-fer's bathroom. I know I'm supposed to go through the drive-thru so nobody can tell for sure who's driving, but I'm such a mess. And now, I'm the proud owner of a Two-fers long-sleeve T-shirt. I bought the red one because I might as well be prepared for the next bloody nose.

There isn't a way for me to hide this from Lucas. I have to give him his keys, but the plan is to be super discreet on his way into the locker room. Maybe he'll be in such a hurry he won't have time to ask questions. What I don't count on is Tory.

"Maybe Mabee, wonder what you're hanging around here for," Tory teases as he jogs up the ramp to the locker room entrance. I'm sitting on the middle of the steps that rise up the opposite side, my right eye facing away from view.

Tory isn't shy with me. He moves up the steps and sits with his back resting on the opposite wall, our feet practically touching. He stretches his toes forward, tapping the sole of his shoe into mine. I do my best to look at him sideways, but when he mocks my weird posture and side-eyes, I give in and get it over with.

"Damn! You get in a fight, Mabee?"

I shrug it off, but his eyes linger on the puffy side of my face, and I can only bluff that it's no big deal for so long. When his eyes narrow, I glean that he's probably piecing it together. I don't have more than one enemy. Hell, I only have a handful of friends.

"Ava do that shit to you?" He knows; I can tell by his tone.

I tip my chin just a little.

"Hope you fucked her shit up right back," he says, leaning forward and moving to the step above me to inspect my eye more closely. "You need to get a cold compress on that. I can get something in the training room."

"It's fine," I say, not wanting the attention. Besides, the last thing I need is Lucas seeing this.

"It's not fine. I'll be, like, two minutes, tops. Just sit tight," he says, rushing in the door and cutting off a few guys heading in for practice.

My pulse is jittery, and I keep feeling as if my heart is missing beats. I just want to get Lucas his key and be on my way. But if anyone sees me handing it to him, they'll know I had his truck, and then maybe he wasn't at Two-fers, and instead . . .

"Here," Tory says, making better time than I expect. He hands me a small plastic bag filled with ice, and one of the white towels they use at practices. I put the ice on my face first without wrapping it, but Tory stops me before I press it on my skin too hard. "No, here."

He's wrapping the towel around the bag when a shadow moves over both of us where we're sitting.

"What the fuck happened?" Lucas kneels down next to me, his eyes glaring at Tory as if he had something to do with my face.

"I'm fine," I say, clutching his key in my right palm, wanting to slip it to him and run away.

"Your ex had a field day with her face," Tory says, a hint of accusation in his tone. There's a short standoff between them as they hover on either side of me, the cold ice bag still clutched in Tory's hands.

There was a time when the thought of two varsity football players fighting over my honor seemed like a dream, but now, in the middle of it, I just want them to get over themselves—get over me!

"Gentlemen?" Coach Loma has a very distinct voice. It's effective on a field with a hundred teenaged boys all vying to be hotshots. He barks and they listen. One word brings Tory and Lucas to instant attention, eyes widening before their necks snap up to look him in the eye.

"I had an accident, Coach, and they happened to catch me before I fell all the way. I went end-over-end," I lie, laughing nervously as I rip the ice and towel from Tory's grip and hold it to the side of my face.

Lucas understands why I'm lying, but Tory's reaction is a little less believable, which causes Coach Loma to question things more than I want him to.

"Lemme see what you've got going here," he says, pushing Lucas out of the way. Stress knots my stomach and chest as Lucas hops down a few steps, now too far to pass him his keys. I'm so focused on the mission that I barely respond to Coach as he peels the towel from my face and tips my chin up to have a good look at my shiner.

"You said you got this falling down the stairs?" he asks.

I nod, but it's painfully obvious that didn't happen. This is going horribly wrong.

"Mind if I get our trainer to come give you a look? Just a little concussion protocol, and since it happened on campus, we'll need to fill out an incident form," he says, standing and pulling his khaki pants up by his belt loops.

Shit. An incident report.

"Okay," I croak. As everyone stands, I flutter my eyes closed, wishing like hell I could go back and tell him I got in a fight. I'd still probably be dealing with a trainer and an incident report, though. Goddamn, Ava Pryor!

Lucas's bag is about an arm's length from me, but my aim is shit so I can't toss his keys with certainty that I'll make the shot. I can discern from the heavy silent glares Coach is giving both of the boys that he's dismissing them from my aid and telling them to get their asses to practice. My last chance is to somehow stall Lucas. As he reaches for one strap of his backpack, I reach for the other, pulling hard enough to yank it from his hand and slide it closer to me.

"Oh, dang, sorry. I thought this was mine," I lie. My bag is bright pink. Lucas's is black. I'm so lame it's painful. While everyone puzzles at me, I manage to slip his key into the side pocket before Lucas lifts the bag up and over his shoulder.

"It's fine," he says, brow heavy as he stares down at me. I'm pretty sure he knows I put the key in there. That's not what his frown is about. He's worried about my face, and maybe he feels a little responsible. He doesn't own Ava, though. She's a bitch all on her own.

"Maybe call your mom or dad, Miss . . ."

"June," I finish for Coach. "June Mabee." I add my last name. He has no reason to remember who I am. I am one of hundreds of students he had freshman year for health class.

"Right, okay. Well, call your parents, June," he says.

"It's just my mom," I respond. Not sure why he would care about that detail, but I've become accustomed to making the correction. I don't like my dad getting parental credit. Of course, I'm not exactly thrilled to call my mom right now.

Tory and Lucas reluctantly head in the locker room, and I pull my legs in to make room for the dozens of players now rushing down the steps to go change. Coach Loma is on the phone with who I assume is probably the trainer, and he nods toward my bag and mouths the words, "Call your mom."

I don't want to in the worst way, but explaining would make things so much worse. I'm already neck deep in fibs. I nod and pull my phone from my bag, noting the text message from my mom that I still haven't fully read. I swipe right by it and hit call on my phone to dial her. She answers before I even hear a ring.

"June?" She's frantic, and her voice is raw with exhaustion. I'm an asshole. And a coward. I don't even know for sure if she's a liar, or worse.

"I'm at school, and I fell. They're going to fill out an incident report, but I'm by the gymnasium, and Coach saw me. He thinks maybe I have a concussion?" I'm trying to keep my voice quiet and calm, but I can hear her rapid breathing on the other end quickening with worry.

"I'll be right there," she says.

"Mom, I'm fine. Abby is giving me a ride home anyway."

"June," she interjects. Her voice is stern.

I swallow.

"Okay," I say.

"Tell the coach I will come in through the office. Should I meet you by the gym?" I can already hear the van firing up. The thought of her rushing through campus to meet me at the gym so she can gawk at my black eye has me wanting to throw up. Of course, if I throw up, that's a sign of a concussion, which will only make this rabbit hole deeper because I already had a concussion.

"I'm sure we can meet you at the office." I glance up at Coach and he nods.

"Okay, well, I'm on my way." By the time I end the call with my mom, the trainer is at my side, tilting my head up so he can shine a penlight in my eyes. The man is maybe twenty-two, and his degree is in exercise. He's not really qualified to diagnose head trauma, but I don't have any so I let him do his thing. I trace the movement of his finger as he draws it out then in again, and I promptly answer his series of easy questions, spelling my first and last names, and listing the last three presidents. *I wonder if our football players can pass this part,* I muse to myself.

Once I've satisfied his test, Coach pats my shoulder and helps me to my feet, still eyeing me suspiciously. I only hope he doesn't think Lucas or Tory punched me in the face. I wouldn't want to start that kind of scandal.

Coach sends the trainer along with me to make sure I'm all right during my walk to the office. He carries my backpack for me, but I keep my phone, texting Abby so she knows I won't need a ride home. She writes back instantly.

I'm here with your mom. I heard. You . . . fell?

I sigh, reading her text and typing my response.

Long story.

She shoots back a laughing emoji, but she has no idea what a mess this is.

My mom is standing at the front desk when I walk in through the side doors. She's wearing one of her cotton T-shirt dresses, so at least she changed from what I saw her wearing this morning, and her hair in a twisted knot on top of her head. When I step through the glass doors into the lobby, she rushes to me and holds both sides of my face, smooshing them with her purse and phone still in her hands.

"June Mabee, you have a black eye!" She tilts my head down and steps up on her toes as if looking at it from above makes it seem somehow less of an injury.

"I'm fine." I shake my head, glancing to the side to meet Abby's gaze. My friend's eyes are narrowed, but for a different reason. Abby's taken a punch or two in her life. She's given her fair share of black eyes, too. She's not naïve, so I shake my head slightly once my mom lets go as a signal for her not to question—not right now.

I shift back to meet my mom's waiting stare. She's so broken, and I'm to blame for a lot of that.

"Kristen," Maggie Williams's familiar voice draws our attention to the main desk. My mom hesitates for a moment. In the past, when she's run into Maggie with me, there have been hugs. Right now, though, my mom is embarrassed. Here I am, black eye and all. It's awkward.

"I guess there's a form?" My mom moves around the desk to take the seat Maggie has pulled out for her.

"It's just a formality," Maggie says, sliding the already-prepared document around for my mom to review and sign. She leans into my mom and whispers loudly, "It's so you don't sue the school."

"Should I?" My mom leans back, holding the pen away from the signature line.

"No!" I blurt out.

I cover my face and Abby slides over to stand at my side.

"Well, I don't know," my mom continues. There's a deep wrinkle on her brow as she turns her focus to me. I can no longer tell whether she's serious about suing or using the threat to bait me into spilling my guts.

"Please," I beg. I'm sweating, which probably makes me look even more banged up, but it's because I really just want to be done with this.

My mom studies me for a few seconds then pinches one side of her mouth, clicking the pen in and out a few times before finally leaning forward and signing her name to the line.

"Thanks, Kristen. Hey, we should get together for real sometime, ya know? Like in a place where we can have booze!" Maggie's raspy laugh sparks a brief smile on my mom's lips and she agrees that sounds nice.

I walk out toward the parking lot, ready to bolt for Abby's car, but my mom is one step ahead of me. We barely get through the doors before she catches them behind us.

"June? The van," she says, pointing to where she parked along the curb in front of the office like an ambulance.

I breathe in long and deep but nod. My friend gives me a hug and whispers, "Call me" in my ear. I dump my bag on the back seat before climbing in the front. My mom is already waiting for me, and she eyes my movements like a hawk as I fasten my buckle.

"Do I at least get to know what happened to your face?"

It's hard to look her in the eyes. I tell her everything, basically. It's just that I have this horror that she hasn't been keeping up her end of the bargain. I can't fathom her keeping secrets from me, but a secret that big . . . she would have to.

"No," I answer, finally. Her eyes curse at me just before her mouth snaps shut in shock.

"Okay, then." She flips her gaze to the front, cranking the van and shifting into drive without hesitation. "I guess you can get used to me driving you to and from school for the next month."

Her tone is clipped.

"I guess," I say coolly, lifting my towel-covered icepack to my face and holding it in such a way that I block my mom's view of me.

This has to end. I need to tell her everything Lucas told me so she has the chance to either verify it, or not. Maybe she'll lie, but at least I won't be holding this feeling in anymore. Then I can tell her about my face and what happened with Ava, and about Lucas's interview today. I know she would be proud. My mom loved Lucas, to the point of teasing me when she knew I had developed a crush. Of course, now that I threw the little V-card announcement at her, she might look at him differently.

"I don't know what's going on with you, June, but I won't just sit back and let you fall into yourself. You can be mad. I'll give you time. I'll even give you a break about today. I'm not stupid, and it's pretty clear to everyone that you have a black eye. I just hope you aren't in a situation where someone . . ."

Her voice trails off and I know it's because the thought of me letting a guy hit me touches a raw nerve in her heart. My dad never laid a hand on her directly, but he threw things when he got angry. And from the few things she's told me about her high school boyfriends, I think she's faced worse than my dad's keys being thrown at her face.

"I'm not being unsafe," I finally say, relenting and dropping the ice pack from my eye as we pull into our driveway. My mom stops the van just past the curb, and I expect to find her eyes waiting for me as I face her. But when I look, I find she's not looking at me at all. Her focus is glued straight ahead and her mouth hangs open wide, anger reddening her cheeks and shaking her clinched jaw. I snap my gaze to her sightline, and at first what my eyes take in seems too enormous to be real.

The word WHORE is spray-painted in red across our garage door. The can used to create it is left abandoned in our driveway, its lid a few yards away. On instinct, I crank my neck to the left, searching the Fuller house for spying eyes. The garage is closed, as is the side door and all the shutters. But something this bold isn't Mrs. Fuller's style; she abhors confrontation. Asking her husband and son to ignore our existence seems more like her. The message written on our house, it isn't for my mom. It's for me. And I have an eye that matches it perfectly.

TWENTY

"Someone doesn't like me."

That's all I say as I exit the van, slamming the door closed behind me. I grab some acetone and some of my dad's old rags from the garage, then immediately start scrubbing the word off the garage door. My efforts fade the color, but the word is still there. It is still *very much* there.

My mom helps for a while. She keeps her promise of not prying into more today, though I can tell as she scrubs next to me that she so badly wants to. I can't really mask my tears, but I wear the grit on my face right along with the pain, which makes open, honest conversation less approachable.

That word isn't going away without paint. If I had my way, I would go buy a gallon of whatever's on hand and roll it on. My mom says she'll do it in the morning, after she drops me off at school.

She is still my ride, to and from, until I do something to make it otherwise.

Lucas will see it. I've been sitting in the center of my bed with the lights off for two hours, waiting for his practice to end. I only now locked my bedroom door. I want to make sure my mom won't try coming in, though if she does and is met with a lock, she'll flip her lid even more than she already has. She's worried. I'm worried, too. Somebody hates me, and somebody knows things meant to hurt me.

I can't quite see the full driveway from my window, but I see his lights spill across the ground. They stay on for several long seconds, even as I hear his door open and close. He's looking at the graffiti. It's strange how, even though I am nothing like that word, simply having it on my home makes me somehow feel dirty.

Lucas's lights flick off and his heavy door slams shut again. I don't bother going to the window. I've left it open, anticipating him. I'm not sure whether I want to pound on his chest and curse him for bringing this down on me or if I want him to hold me and make it better. I figure I'll know when I see him.

The skidding of his shoes on the roof shingles draws near, so I scoot to the end of the bed, my feet on the floor and my hands cupping my bare knees. I'm wearing my sleep shirt because it's the only thing that makes me feel comfortable. Now, I feel like that word, even though it's just a large cotton T-shirt.

"June." His voice is urgent as his hands wrap around the sill of the window. He lifts himself up easily, his hair wet from the shower he took after practice, his gray T-shirt sticking to his damp skin.

I ball my fists on top of my thighs, collecting the anger building in my veins, but as I prepare to pound my hands into his chest, he drops to his knees in front of me and gently cups my face. Tender eyes examine the bruising on my face.

"I'm so sorry," he says, repeating it three or four times until finally holding my gaze to his.

My hands relax and my palms grip at his shirt, and I cling to him like a bear cub, pressing the uninjured side of my face against his chest as I let out a silent sob. He lifts himself up to stand, holding me to him, one hand cradling my head while the other holds my weight. He turns to sit on the bed and I rest my weight against him. His palm runs up my back soothingly, and he tucks my face into the nook just under his jaw. He breaths out a soft hush into my ear.

"I know, June. I'm so sorry. I'm so fucking sorry." He rocks me with his words, slowly, lulling me into more normal breathing.

"She painted my house," I cry, my voice muffled against his body.

"I know," he says, his voice quiet and still at my ear.

For almost half an hour, I sit like this, hugged tightly in his arms, my face hot with tears while his fingers delicately tickle along my bare arms until the shaking in my chest calms. My house is silent beyond my door, and I'm not sure whether my mom is in her room or still sitting on the sofa, staring out the front window while she sips at wine and waits for whoever painted our house to show up and do it again. I told her they wouldn't, but she simply shot me a look indicating that if I was allowed to be left alone, so was she.

"How was the interview?" Even my whisper sounds hoarse. Lucas's body shakes under me. He's fallen to his back, but keeps me cradled to him.

"There are more pressing things," he murmurs, finally moving his hand from my arm and up to my hair, combing his fingers through the long, tangled strands as he brushes them from my face.

"Not really," I sigh out. "I mean, if all this happened and you didn't get in, that would suck." I shift to look him in the eyes. He raises his chin to see me better. I do my best to wink out of my black eye but it's fairly swollen; maybe it looks like a tic. Lucas gives out a soft, sympathetic laugh anyhow.

He runs his thumb along my deep purple skin and I can barely feel his touch. His eyes land on mine after tracing the line he draws around my bruising.

"I'm in," he says, mouth closed tightly with an uncertain smile pushing up the sides.

I lift myself and push down on his chest, knocking the wind from him a little. He holds my wrists as I do.

"Shut up!" My shouted whisper breaks the silence and Lucas quickly cups my mouth and holds in his laughter.

"Shhh, I can't go to MIT if your mom shoots me first," he jokes.

I laugh with him then roll to his side, resting my palms on his beautiful strong cheeks.

"Lucas, I am so proud of you," I say, blinking wildly. There's a strong hesitation poorly hidden behind his eyes, the weight of this finally being real.

"He'll come around," I say, predicting that it's his dad he's worried about.

He shakes his head and looks down to where our legs are tangled, mine bare and his covered in his joggers.

"I don't even care. I'm going, and my mom said with the scholarship money I'll get, they can pay the rest."

I'm glad he's not looking me in the eyes right now, because his victory stings a little, and I'm not proud of feeling jealous. Not that I want to go to MIT, but I would love to go to one of the state schools. My grades are good enough to qualify for a few different tuition grants, but there are still so many expenses left to cover. Unless colleges let people camp in tents and eat from their garbage.

"My mom knows you helped," he says, his long lashes blinking up and uncovering his blue eyes as he peers up at me. For a short breath, I'm distracted from all of the sucky things in my life and just stare in wonder at them and the fact I can kiss them closed right now if I want.

"And she'll still let you go?" I joke. My laugh is short-lived, though. The way his mom glared at me flashes in my head.

"My mom doesn't hate you, June. She's just—"

"Hurt," I finish for him.

I get it. It's the same reason I haven't been to visit my father once since he left and moved in with Jamie—Jamie, who is only ten years older than me. Of course, he's only invited me to his condo once, so I guess I haven't had to reject him much.

"Yeah, she's hurt," Lucas says, breaking up my thoughts. "When she found out about the affair, she went through a pretty dark time."

"You haven't told her about the new one, have you? The new affair?" I can't believe this is the discussion we have to have. Statistically, this many adults having affairs or getting divorced is actually not an anomaly. I know, because I checked on Reddit. Still, it seems impossible that this is where our adults all ended up. Weren't they all just drinking together in the Fuller back yard while we swam and lit sparklers on the Fourth of July?

"I haven't told her," Lucas says, moving close enough to touch his nose to mine. His eyes close, heavy with exhaustion. It's been a long stretch of days for both of us.

"Have you told Tory yet?" I ask.

He shakes his head, rubbing his nose softly against mine.

"I'm sorry about . . . the word. On the garage," he says. I let my eyes fall shut to lock out the pain of it.

"You told Ava about my mom and your dad," I whisper. I figure that's how she knew.

He doesn't affirm my question so much as he huffs out a breath and apologizes again. "I'm sorry. I don't even know why I did, but it slipped out once."

"*Shhh*," I hum. I can't hear about her now. I don't care about their intimate secrets. And while I won't let him call her a mistake, I will let him feel as if he made a few. Trusting her was definitely one of them.

"I'm sorry, June. I'm sorry, I'm sorry . . ." His words fade.

I close the distance between us and press my lips to his. It's not a sensual moment, but rather a sweet one. His lips part slightly, as do mine, and we hold a chaste kiss between us for as long as it takes him to fall into slumber.

My window is still open, and the air outside is cold. Our feet are covered by my turned-down blanket, so I gingerly reach to drag it up our bodies. As bad as I want to keep my eyes open, to stay present for this moment, I just can't. It's more than being tired. In the midst of all this awful, I think I'm also a little bit happy.

TWENTY-ONE

I'm not sure when Lucas woke up and snuck out my window, but by the time my eyes open this morning, he's gone. He left behind a little reminder, though, one he had to go back to his truck to get. I spent the first ten minutes of my morning just staring at it hanging from the back of my desk chair.

The sleeves of his letterman jacket make the same stupid crinkling sound they do when he wears it. My smile turns into a laugh as I sink my left arm in, then my right. The lining is cool, but I'll be dying of heat by lunch time, if I even wear this thing all day. Who am I kidding? I'm wearing this jacket for always. I'm probably never giving it back.

In a way, it makes me feel a little stronger for the day that lies ahead. I can't live like this, with secrets between me and my mom. And I won't let someone like Ava Pryor make me feel small. I mean, I am a senior now. I've grown up. I've grown . . . period. This jacket, it makes me feel a little badass—a little bit like Abby.

Embraced in the woodsy scent of the boy I think might really, truly be my boyfriend, I unlock my bedroom door and take in a deep breath. Today, I'm walking down those stairs. Honestly, I may never scale my roof again.

My mom is humming to herself in the kitchen, and I pause halfway down the steps to listen. I don't think she's happy, but maybe she slept a little. Or maybe she found her own symbolic jacket, something to make her feel a little bit badass, too.

"Good morning." I announce myself as I round the corner into the kitchen, and she turns, surprised to hear my voice. Her face is covered with dots of paint, as is her T-shirt. It's one of my dad's old ones she kept for things like gardening. She said it felt nice to ruin them. Well, this one . . . it's toast.

My mom puckers her lips as she leans over the counter and balances herself on her forearms, palms flat, her coffee mug between them.

"Are we talking now?" she asks me, her eyes surveying the jacket I wear.

I suck in my top lip and breathe in through my nose as I slowly nod.

"We're *starting* to talk again," I say. I can't unpack all of the garbage in my head during a short ride to school, but I can open the gates again. For a while after the divorce, my mom had this buzz word she used, something she got from the counselling sessions she tried. I throw it out there now, not to mock her, but to make her laugh.

"We'll . . . *dialogue,*" I say. She breaks into an instant smile and eventually winks at me, turning around to top off her cup before grabbing her keys and purse to drive me to school.

I open the side door first, slinging my bag over my shoulder and glancing up in time to catch Mrs. Fuller's full view as she backs out from her driveway. Her tires screech to a quick stop, the jolt enough to fling her hair forward and force her sunglasses from her face. Rather than run, I maintain my pace and walk right to the passenger door of our van. I refuse to let my relationship with Lucas be shrapnel to our parents' failed relationships. I keep the jacket on even as I get into the seat and strap myself in. The jacket is really smothering and the fit is oversized, but I'm going to make sure I maximize the sightings of me in this garment. One hurdle is down already as Mrs. Fuller finally finishes backing out and pulls away. My next mission is the spray paint artist, Ava Pryor.

My eyes leave the rearview mirror and finally focus on my marred garage door. The pink and red stains of WHORE are gone, which explains the paint dots all over my mother's body. What I don't quite understand, though, is the enormous middle finger she painted in its place. My mouth is still hanging open when she gets in the van.

"You like it?" she asks. I blink once and turn my gaze to hers. There's a proud smile on her mouth, and I know it's partly there because mothers are alphas too. In many ways, they are the alpha-ist of them all. Instead of hiding and taking the abuse, my mom decided to let the world know the Mabee girls don't take shit from anyone.

"I do," I say, returning my focus to our freshly painted garage door. My smile pushes into my eyes, and that nervous thunder that's been abusing my chest for the last few weeks is a calm purr. "I like it a lot."

My cockiness sticks with me as my mom drops me off at the front of the school. Despite the itching desire to hunt down Ava and take a victory lap around her, I don't. I don't run to Lucas, either. Instead, I drag my feet on my way in, smearing a few chalk lines drawn on the front sidewalk to celebrate spirit week. I stop at my best friend's car and lean back, stretching out my arm so she can feel the thick leather of this very hot fucking jacket.

"Boom! Look who's running this shit now," Abby says, tugging on the sleeve then holding a fist out for me. I pound it and call her "bruh" just to mock the guys who usually walk around in these. That includes Lucas, and Tory, but over the last few weeks they've grown accustomed to me taking them down a peg.

"You sure I can't retaliate against her for that shiner?" Abby asks. She pops a piece of gum in her mouth and snaps it aggressively.

I told her the real story last night before Lucas came. She also knows about the garage. She hasn't seen my mom's artwork, though.

"It's fine. I don't even care about Ava Pryor anymore." My eye stings a little when I say it.

"Liar," she says.

"You're right," I admit with a laugh. "But I don't care quite as much."

The bell rings and I push off of the front of my friend's car, walking with a little swagger.

"My mom has to drive me home today, but you should come by and see what she's done with the garage."

She squints at me suspiciously.

"It's a worthy surprise," I add.

"Well, all right then." My friend reaches to the side and grabs my hand for a squeeze, and we part at the office doors.

I stretch to shove them open and suddenly a palm reaches over me and pushes the door open wide. I recognize his arm, the freckles that form the little dipper just above his wrist. I smell the coconut from his shampoo. To be sure, I pause my steps so his large body crashes into me from behind, and when his arms wrap around my midsection and he walks me forward, away from my independent study room, I give in with a teasing guess.

"Earl? Is that you?"

He spins me fast and catches my jaw in his palm, stepping in close as he towers over me with a kiss. It feels as though the whole world is watching, and it makes me smile.

"This public enough for you?" He runs the pad of his thumb over my lip and my body chills.

"It's getting there," I say. He holds on to my hand, but walks backward toward his class—the class I could still be in with him, but damn me and my pride. Maybe this is better, heart growing fonder and all. As he moves away, our fingers slip apart.

"This jacket is really fucking hot," I joke.

"You love it," he teases.

"I love you," I say.

Shit.

He stops moving. Maybe he also stopped breathing. His eyes are huge, mouth open, but maybe that's a smile on his lips? Maybe not. It's definitely an amused expression. I wonder if the whole world just heard that.

My eyes are definitely wide, I can tell by the air stinging them. My mouth waters a little bit too. It does that when I eat olives, because I threw up once on olives. I think maybe I throw up on *I love you's.*

Shit.

I drop a prayer, and it's quickly answered by the ringing bell and rush of students filing through the office doors behind me. My class is ten paces back, his is about a hundred forward. Why isn't he moving?

My black eye is threatening to leak so I blink moisture back into the surface and wave my hand as if it's a powerful eraser that can take back slips of the tongue.

"I'm really tired. I meant the jacket. I love your jacket. Oh, God, umm." I smile exaggeratingly huge, showing my teeth like a first grader waiting for the tooth fairy, and squeeze my eyes shut tight as I shout "Good-bye," then turn and actually run to my independent study room.

That's not how that was supposed to happen. Things like that, though, they seem to keep happening with Lucas.

Drowning in sweat from my embarrassment, I pull off Lucas's jacket as soon as I make it to my seat. I leave it on my lap because I like the security it offers me. I actually do love this stupid jacket.

I also love the boy.

I manage to make it through the entire day without seeing Lucas. I was prepared at lunch to explain away my blurted-out confession. I don't want to scare him. Even though I've known him for years, maybe it seems psycho to come right out with *I love you's* this fast. Or maybe not. Abby is no help because boys tell her they love her on a monthly basis. She's never said it once herself, though. Not once. Except to me and her mom. Lucas never showed up at lunch, though, so I was off the hook. He sent me a text when Abby and I were throwing away our trash and said he got called into the principal's office. My guess is it was something to formalize his scholarship offer.

My mom texted before school was over and warned me she would be twenty minutes late. I, of course, offered to go home with Abby instead, but her response was a cackling emoji face.

The traffic should be cleared out by the time she arrives, so I've been spared from standing near the bus line where chaos breeds more chaos every afternoon at 2:20. And since I don't have to wait in the normal pickup spot, I venture around the back side of the gym to the slope that leads down to the football practice field. The guys aren't doing much yet, just some stretching. Lucas is easy to spot; he's on his back at the sidelines with his right leg in the air. The trainer—the same one who assessed my lovely shiner—is leaning into his leg and holding it straight as he pushes it toward Lucas's body. It's amazing how inflexible these athletes are.

"That's a nice jacket you have there."

I swallow hard. It's been a while since I've heard Mr. Fuller's voice. He's always had this dominant edge. I used to be afraid of it; when we were kids, he was always the parent I didn't want catching us doing anything wrong. Now, though, I recognize those tones and inflections for what they are—crutches to make a small man feel bigger than he is.

"Thanks. I think I'll keep it," I say, twisting to the side and offering him a closed, smug smile.

He chuckles and pauses his steps, sinking his hands into the pockets of his blazer and glancing down to where his boots meet the dry grass of the hillside.

"You know, people who live in glass houses shouldn't throw stones." He smirks, proud of his plagiarized idiom. I let him think he's won for a few seconds, just long enough for his ego to inflate a little bit more.

"That's a very good point, Mr. Fuller. No, they sure shouldn't." As the satisfaction of saying the perfect thing at the perfect moment seeps into my veins, I breathe in deep as this big, scary man shrinks a little before my eyes.

His scowl breaks through the façade he works so hard to maintain, and his mouth chews on his words. He wants to break me, but what he doesn't know is I've already been broken and rebuilt.

"Say hi to Mrs. D'Angelo for me," I say before turning and heading up the hill with the heat of his eyes scalding the back of my head.

I pushed down the first domino, and I know how these things work. The tumbling has begun, and there really isn't a clean way to stop it. The only thing left is to sit back and watch it burn.

I walk through the lot as it clears, and as I get closer to the entrance, I pull my phone out to check my mom's location on our app. She's a block away, so I go ahead and call her.

"I'm almost there," she answers immediately.

"I know, I saw. I'm walking to meet you, so turn in at that parking lot right at the corner. I think I want some ice cream. My treat." I can't see her, but I can imagine the face she's making by the tiny breath she exhales into the phone. It's a grateful laugh, a short one that touches her eyes and makes her shoulders drop with relief.

"That sounds . . . really nice." She's right. It does.

We end up timing things just right, and I step up to my mom's van just as she pulls in. I hold up my palm for her not to lock the door and open the passenger side to peel off my jacket. I'll like this jacket more when it's winter and I'm standing in the bleachers watching one of Lucas's playoff games. It's strange because I don't only hope I'll be there doing that. I know I will. I have this strange, quiet confidence in us.

"So, when do I get to ask about the jacket?" She lifts a brow as I scrunch mine a bit.

"Maybe when I feel less embarrassed about my knee-jerk confession when I stormed past you at six in the morning?" I smile through gritted teeth, suddenly feeling the heat of telling my mother I had sex.

"Right, well . . ." She pulls the keys from the ignition and we meet at the front of the van.

"I won't dwell. I'm not *my* mother, but because I'm not, I need to be direct about a few things. You're being safe?" she asks.

"Yes. Oh, my God," I cover my face. There's an older couple enjoying sundaes at a sidewalk table about four feet away. I want to die.

"And what you did, it was your choice?" she continues.

I nod, eyes still closed tight and hand shading my face.

"And you know that all it takes is once to—"

"Yes!" I cut her off before she has a chance to blurt out the word *pregnant*. I look down at my feet and usher us into the small mom and pop store called Jan's that has served scoops to my mom and me since it opened when

I was six. I guess Jan was one of the owners' moms. I always forget which one, but she passed away shortly after they opened.

My cheeks cool from the freezers, and my nose perks up at the scent of pistachio and vanilla as soon as we step inside. The girl working behind the counter is new. A lot of the sophomores and juniors at Public get their first jobs here because it's so close to school. She's young, probably still fifteen. It's nice when the owners are working because they always know our orders the moment we walk in.

I step up close to the glass and lean in to make sure they have my cherry jubilee flavor. The carton looks loaded enough to give me a double, so that's what I order. My mom gets pistachio, and we both wait while the girl, who's tag says her name is Marylee, scoops our dishes. My mom takes our bowls to a booth in the corner, and I hand the girl my card to pay. She shakes her head no.

"You can have it for free," she says, a shy smile tugging up the corners of her mouth.

"Oh-okay. Thanks," I stammer, putting away my card. I turn to walk away, assuming she must be a relative of the owners or something and maybe recognizes us that way, but I stop on a hunch and turn back around.

"Umm, not to be rude, but . . . why?" I ask.

She shrugs and glances off to the side. "I don't know. Just, aren't you Lucas Fuller's girlfriend?"

An audible laugh flies out of my chest, and I have to apologize immediately because I think it freaked her out a little.

"I'm just not used to that . . . term, I guess?" A giddy laugh bubbles in my throat. "You know, I can still pay."

This free pass for the popular crowd thing is bizarre.

"No, really. I want to, to be nice." I can tell I make her uncomfortable, so I smile and nod.

"Thanks, Marylee. That's really cool of you." I commit her name to memory as I head to the booth to join my mom. I'll find her at school tomorrow and if she has our lunch hour, ask her to join me and Abby and Lucas, if he shows up, and the twins. And I'm going to make sure she feels as special as she made me feel right now. She probably deserves it a whole lot more. All I did was lose my virginity to a quarterback.

I'm still floating on a cloud of kindness when I slip into the seat across from my mom. She hands me a spoon and I immediately scrape away at the melted layer forming at the top of my ice cream. The milky part is always the best.

"So . . ." My mom always starts awkward conversations with me like this. She said the same thing when she told me about the divorce. And that same two-letter transition was how she asked about Lucas and his jacket. I'm guessing the graffiti incident is probably what's coming next.

"You wanna talk about the whole *whore* thing?" I quirk a brow and push a spoonful of ice cream in my mouth.

"I wanna talk about the whole whore thing," my mom reiterates.

I'm not sure there's a way to back into this topic delicately, though I've practiced a few times. I definitely don't want to start by asking her about the money Mr. Fuller gave her, or the affair they may or may not have had. I decide to go with plan C—talking about Mrs. D'Angelo—which was my favorite as of this morning.

"It's kind of a long story," I say.

"I've got time," my mom says, dragging her spoon over the surface of her scoops. The best part about this place is the massive size of the servings. I don't dare explore the calorie count. I much prefer the sound of two scoops to two-million grams of sugar.

"I've been hanging out with Tory D'Angelo a little."

My mom's face lights up as her lips close around her spoon.

"I remember that kid. He's one of the twins, right? Weren't they at your birthday party at the lake?" She's talking around her spoon, and it's nice to see her amused. It's going to make it hard when I have to crush her spirit.

"They were. Tory's the one who went skinny dipping." I grimace and my mom makes a sour face. We were nine at the time, but still old enough to make seeing a naked boy in a crowd feel uncomfortable.

"Right. Yes. So, he's the one you're hanging out with now. Interesting choice." She's teasing me a little, and I'm not sure whether she's trying to relax me or herself. The tension between us over the last couple of days has been strangling her.

"He's actually a lot nicer than I gave him credit for," I admit. A proudness plays out on her face at my words.

I gather my thoughts as I consume a large bite. My mom's gaze lifts to meet mine as she waits, expectantly.

"I was dropping some school things off at his house after the first day, and I saw . . . *something.*" God, why is this so hard to say? Maybe because once I start pulling this thread, the rest will come out fast. So very fast.

My mom stops eating, deep interest in the direction of this story taking hold of her. I'm sure she expects another story about Tory, but I can't drag things out.

"I saw Mr. Fuller there, and they were kissing. It was pretty obvious, and it did not look like it was the first time they'd . . . *kissed*." I add weight to that word so my mom knows it means more. I can tell she understands by the heaviness that pushes down on her brow and pulls in her eyes. She pushes her bowl toward the center of the table, and I hate that I'm ruining her appetite. I'm also terrified that she's upset. Not because finding out something about your friends' parents is hard, but because she's jealous due to her own past with Lucas's dad.

"Did you tell Lucas? Or Tory?" Genuine concern is apparent in her tone.

"Lucas knows," I say, looking down at my spoon. I've started to draw patterns in my ice cream. What a waste of two perfectly good desserts this has become. "I'm not sure how to tell Tory, or even if I should."

My mom nods, seeming to understand. I feel sick wading into this next phase, but I have to do it. I owe it to all of us to hear this one unheard side of the story.

"There's more," I say, licking my suddenly dry lips. I hold my front teeth together and flit my gaze to my mom's a few times, searching for strength to hold it. I can't, and if I look at her again, I'll chicken out. I bring my hands onto the table and weave them together, pressing my thumbs together as a distraction.

"Lucas said that wasn't his dad's first affair." I wait while those words sit in the air between us. I hold my breath and tune my ears for clues, searching for a gasp or some hint in my mom's reaction that what Lucas said is true. The longer her perfect quiet goes on, the easier it is to lift my chin and bring my eyes to meet hers. When I find them waiting with a cluelessness to the words I'm about to level her with, I loudly gulp in air and let my shoulders relax from the place they've been hunched up near my ears.

"Mom, Lucas thinks his father had an affair with you." I let that falsehood marinate for a while, let her mind make sense of it. I can tell by the short tic her face makes and the dent in her forehead that the mere thought of having an affair with Todd Fuller is ludicrous.

"He does," she finally says, a hint of ire in her words.

I nod.

"So does Mrs. Fuller," I add.

My mom lets out a gut-busting laugh that draws the attention of a couple ordering at the counter several feet away.

"Really?" She narrows her eyes, her open mouth caught in a look of disbelief.

"Lucas said she saw you two one night at his office . . . and he gave you money—"

She slaps the table before I can finish filling in the blanks, and tosses her head back in hysterical laughter. I look over my shoulder and give a short wave to the concerned couple, and to Marylee who mouths to me, "Is she okay?"

"That fucking asshole!" My mom slides from the booth and drags her cup with her. She marches up to the counter and I scramble to follow her.

"I'm so sorry, hon, but we have an emergency to tend to. Can we get to-go lids?" Marylee nods nervously and rummages around the bottom cabinets for lids to fit our cups. She hands us two and my mom slaps one on her ice cream. She hands me mine over her shoulder and stomps toward the door.

"Where are we going?" I'm pretty sure I know, but I want verbal confirmation that my mom is about to commit murder.

"We're going to set the record straight. And then, after the dust settles, me and you are going to enjoy our fucking ice cream." She's pointing at me while she spits out her words, and I'm both terrified and inspired by her strength.

TWENTY-TWO

I didn't even know my mom had a lawn chair.

Somewhere, from the depths of our garage, behind that enormous door painted with a huge F-U, she found one. It's lime green and aluminum, and she made sure to drag it across our driveway and into the Fuller's front yard without a single care for the scene it made and the atrocious sound it caused as it scraped along the pavement.

She's been sitting in that chair, legs crossed and venom ready to spew at her enemies, for the last hour. I vacillate between pacing behind her while I bite at my barely-there fingernails and staring at her from our kitchen window while I snack on random shit from our refrigerator. I'm down to pickles now, and not even spears. I've forked out at least a dozen dill chips. I'm nervous eating, which is the only reason I've held off from the ice cream—I want to enjoy it, not just angry-eat it.

I told Lucas to call me the moment he's heading home from practice. I want to be the one to tell him he had things wrong. My mom is going to set the record straight with fire and fury, but Lucas has had enough of that. It's not his fault he wasn't given the right set of facts. He just suffered from the lies. We both did.

The darker it gets outside without my phone buzzing in my palm, the more worried I become that I won't be able to warn him. Thankfully, the first set of headlights to light up the Fuller driveway don't belong to a man.

Without looking, I dial Abby and put my phone on speaker as I stare out at the scene unfolding in front of the Fuller garage.

"What's up? Did it all go down? Did your mom punch him in the face?" Abby loves a good fight. She also loves my mom, sometimes a little more than her own.

"I think maybe you should come over," I say while my mom follows the white Tahoe into the garage, stopping where the door slides closed. Her feet are purposely planted between the beams, making it impossible for Mrs. Fuller to close the door on her.

"I'm so there. Stay on the line; tell me what I miss," my friend says.

"I don't think I can. Just . . . get here," I demand. I end the call before she can protest and pocket my phone so my hands are free. I move to the side door, opening it enough to step into the frame, but I wait here for now. Of all the conversations about to happen, this is the one that has me most on edge.

The Tahoe's tail lights darken and the driver's side door opens. I can't see more than Shannon Fuller's legs. She's wearing black dress pants and black heels. My mom? She's in flip flops and rolled up jeans. Fucking country mouse versus city mouse is about to go down.

Both women stand still, and though I can't see Lucas's mom's face, I can tell by the lack of movement that they are both silent. My mom nods her head, a quick tip of her chin as she folds her arms over her chest. Finally, Mrs. Fuller steps toward my mom, and when the two women are standing in a faceoff, bodies closed to warmth and affection, I move from the doorway. I cross the driveway to insert myself in this conversation on my mom's behalf.

"I don't want them dating."

Those are the first words I hear leaving Lucas's mom's lips. It's a crushing blow to the joy I felt earlier in the day. It's also the least important thing on the table.

"My daughter is an incredible person. He's lucky to have her love, and you do not get to belittle their feelings, especially since you've chosen to believe in lies." My mom's defense of me emboldens my self-esteem, though it still stings from Lucas's mom's words. The bad things always hit harder than the good, even when they aren't true.

"I have never, nor would I ever, sleep with another woman's husband," my mom continues. I take note of the words she's chosen and walk closer, and a bit taller, from hearing them. She's speaking them as a woman who has been hurt by other women.

"Kristen, I don't want to do this. I know what I know. And your daughter is here. She doesn't need to hear the sordid details," Lucas's mom says. I'm now only a few feet from them. My mom glances at me over her shoulder and reaches her hand out, urging me closer. I go, but a little reluctantly.

"You don't get to think she's not good enough for Lucas but too good for the truth. We are clearing this up tonight, and I'm not leaving this spot until we do. All of us. Todd included." My mom's voice is firm, teetering on the edge of angry but never falling off that ledge. It's weird to hear her call Lucas's parents by their first names. It reminds me how close we once were. I realize I'm not the only one who lost a friend in this web of lies Mr. Fuller spun. My mom and Lucas's mom did, too—they lost each other.

"Kristen, go home," Lucas's mom says, a pleading tone in her voice.

"I won't. Not until this is fixed," my mom says, and she weaves her arm through mine, locking me to her side.

Abby's car pulls along the curb in front of my house. I'm tempted to yell for her to stay inside, but that's not my friend's style. I see her moving closer in my periphery, and it doesn't take long for Lucas's mom to react to the growing audience.

"Oh, for Christ's sake, I'm not doing this," she says, her palm waving us away as she turns to head deeper into her garage.

"You sure? Todd just pulled up and Lucas is behind him. And I'm not moving. I'm going to say things that your husband needs to hear, and I am pretty sure you need to witness them!" My mom's words are grittier, and I can feel the rigid muscles in her arms. She's preparing to fight with more than words if she has to.

"Babe? What's going on here?" Mr. Fuller's gaze is locked on me and my mother despite the way he turns his head toward his wife. He looks like a fox sneaking away from the hens, and my mom is the farmer holding a rifle to his head.

"Our neighbors were just leaving," Mrs. Fuller says.

"June?" I twist at the sound of Lucas's voice, but stay where I am. My mom needs me here.

"We weren't leaving, Todd. We were just getting to the bottom of this big fat fucking lie you've concocted. That's what we're doing," my mom says. Most of the eyes in the area double in size, but not Mr. Fuller's. His shift and scan, looking for his next set of smoke and mirrors that enables him to keep having his cake and eating it too.

"Kristen, you don't know what you're saying," he says, but already I can tell from the cracks in his wife's expression that she's no longer sure she was ever given the truth.

"Oh, I know what I'm doing. I'm ruining your day, that's what I'm doing." My mom moves from her spot next to me, taking slow, methodical steps toward Lucas's dad. For a blip, Mrs. Fuller lurches as if she's about to step in front of my mom, in defense of her husband and the delicate story she's believed for two years. But she backs off, a worried scowl souring her expression.

"You never helped me with my divorce out of the kindness of your heart. You were setting up an alibi." My mom pauses a few feet from the witness she is about to badger, just shy of being able to poke his chest.

"Nicolas was going to leave you with pennies, Kristen. Of course I wanted to make sure your ex didn't absolutely ruin your life just because he had a lawyer and you didn't. I'm just sorry that you blurred the lines of my kindness. Babe—" Mr. Fuller turns toward his wife, his body rigid and fists at his sides. This is the posture of a desperate man. "She's twisting reality. And I'm so sorry you have to hear it. What happened was a mistake, but I guess to her . . . it meant more."

Mistake.

He has no idea how much of a trigger that word is.

"Is Mrs. D'Angelo a mistake too?" I expect the words to be coming from my mouth, but they aren't. Lucas has injected himself into this mess, standing up to his father and hitting him at his weakest point.

"The twins' mom?" Mrs. Fuller is catching on. She strides toward her husband and shoves at his shoulder. He desperately grabs at her wrist, catching it to block her swings, but she comes at him with another shove.

"Who told you that? Did she?" Mr. Fuller points at my mother, his finger a searing point right at her nose. It's a marvel my mom doesn't bite it off.

"I did," I step in. My body is trembling, but sometimes dominoes make a big quake when they fall. And the ones toppling now? They're enormous.

"Baby, she's lying. I mean, come on!" Todd Fuller's nervous laughter is paired with a whole lot of sweat. He's literally backed into a corner. The only thing left to do is to put him out of his misery. And the only person who deserves to do that is my mom.

"Tell me everything," Mrs. Fuller says, magic words that are about to change the face of her family forever.

The truth takes almost an hour to piece together between us, both me and Lucas's mom filling in gaps as my mom shares the true side of her story. When all is said and done, the illusion Todd Fuller worked so hard to create is a long-gone mirage, and the carnage left in its wake is irreparable.

As my parents' marriage was rapidly approaching a cliff, Mr. Fuller was just beginning to stray from his wife. It started during football camp our freshman year, when he and Natalia D'Angelo both volunteered as chaperones for the team trip down to Florida. Two weeks at a resort hotel while the boys were busy being molded for the gridiron gave them idle time, and I guess somewhere along the way, their fucking clothes fell off.

Lucas's mom was becoming suspicious, and when his dad caught her checking his phone, he panicked and changed the contact name from NATALIA, to ?MAYBE. His clever ruse sent her searching the wrong rabbit hole, and while the real texts my mother had with Lucas's dad were short, curt and confined to legal business, the fake ones were dirty and disheartening. That's because those texts were with Natalia, whom he has been sleeping with for almost three years now.

Mr. Fuller hooked my mom into his web by taking advantage of her despair. My parents were separated and my father was not going to pay to support me. Of course, he didn't really *want* me either. So when the kind neighbor whose name is on the letterhead for a fancy Indianapolis family law firm offered to help her out, pro bono, my mom leapt at the offer. It meant she sometimes had to drive downtown to meet him, and sit through after-hours negotiations with my dad's lawyer with Todd Fuller at her side. Not wanting to be a complete snake, when he negotiated a settlement of ten grand to cover my mom's legal expenses, Mr. Fuller gave that money to her. He handed it over in a seedy manila envelope, and he did it like that because he knew his wife was watching—or at least the private investigator she'd hired a month before was.

A spiraling drinking habit coupled with a prescription overdose led to a complete breakdown, and that's when Lucas's mom went into the hospital. My parents' divorce finalized that same week, and from her hospital bed, Mrs. Fuller begged her husband to end it with my mom. She played right into his hands, telling him she already knew everything. Of course she did. He made sure she knew what he wanted her to, which was nowhere close to the truth.

His long business trips while his wife struggled to find her mind weren't really about business. While Mr. Fuller snuck off with his son's best friend's mom, Lucas was terrified that his mom would never be the same. He spent every free moment with her in the hospital and then eventually at home when she was released. She didn't go back to work for three months, the demands of her ad agency job too much to handle. Her son held her together. And he made her promises.

He did whatever she asked. And when the ask came to cut me out of his life, he did it. I was already deep in my own shattered family crisis, helping my mom angrily pack up my father's things for donation and acting as the go-between for some of their phone conversations when he refused to pay bills he still owed her for. I didn't exactly reach out, but only because Lucas didn't either. The polarizing effect was a widening divide that made it easy for Lucas to buy into his father's lies. And since I was so used to being tossed away, I assumed Lucas and my dad were alike.

"Get. Out!"

Those two punctuated words, screamed by Lucas's mom, cut off Todd Fuller's litany of reasons and excuses. He stammers out a few more words, his face red and his arms flailing, fingers pointing. His fingers are always pointing—everywhere but to himself.

"Babe, you're not being rational," he says, belittling her in front of all of us. This time, though, instead of falling apart, she doubles in size and strength.

"So help me God, Todd, if you do not run upstairs and grab a bag full of your shit and leave this house right now, I will throw your things out the window and advertise free yard sale goods," Lucas's mom says.

Abby chortles over my shoulder, and I turn with my mouth wide. I almost forgot she's there. I am so rapt by the truth that I haven't looked around at all throughout the shouting. I'm too focused on inserting my facts where I finally discover they fit. Sometime, though, in the middle of it all, Tory walked up. He stays back to let the chaos roll, but he's definitely close enough to hear the heartbreaking facts that pertain to him.

"Tory," I croak. Lucas turns to see his friend. Abby shoots around on her heels. And the adults behaving like children let their shouting simmer into sudden quiet.

Tory's jaw is tense, a brewing anger in his eyes that's so opposite of the good-humored prankster that usually lives there. His glare is set on Lucas's dad as he moves forward, parting our small crowd. He stops at his friend's chest and places his palm flat over Lucas's heart, patting it kindly but firmly, a gesture that says, "I got this one."

It takes him approximately five more steps to square his body with Todd Fuller's, and even though Lucas's dad has about four inches on him, the youth and discipline Tory has in the gym make him no match.

"Leave my family the fuck alone," he says. "Oh, and your son . . . he's going to MIT. And you . . . you were a shitty football player."

The swing is hard and swift, Tory's fist landing in the soft cushion that separates Mr. Fuller's top teeth from his bottom along his cheek. The cracking sound is sharp and timed perfectly with the landing. A broken jaw is probably pretty painful. But even more so is an obliterated ego, which Tory puts the final nail in before walking back to his car and speeding away.

TWENTY-THREE

I've observed that a strange thing sometimes happens when you've gone through a divorce and survived it emotionally. You become a beacon of hope for others looking to do the same.

My mom hasn't called my father in a year. As long as his checks come, there really isn't a reason for them to talk. He sent her a text when he proposed to Jamie. She sent one back saying *OK.* Other than that small exchange, it has been radio silence between them. But when Lucas's mom came to mine, ashamed and humble and afraid for her livelihood, in search of a lawyer to go up against the man she was leaving, my mom knew the only worthy opponent was the slimeball who represented my father.

For two weeks, my mom has been Shannon Fuller's personal divorce route tour guide. Tonight, she talked Shannon into having a little fun down at her new studio. I guess boudoir photoshoots are an empowering thing for newly single women to do. After a shopping marathon at Victoria's Secret, my mom took her to have her hair and makeup professionally done. They've been at the studio shooting for four hours now, but they also took two bottles of wine. I have a feeling they'll be spending the night there.

Fine by me. It means Lucas and I don't have to talk in hushed whispers. Though I like the hushed whispers too, for entirely other reasons.

It's strange how fast time passes when we're together. He's climbed through my window almost every night since the episode we have affectionately labeled BFM for Big Fat Mistake. The only night he missed was the one when he helped me climb down so I could sneak out and drive up to

Chicago with him and Tory and Hayden and Abby. Tory said he wanted to stand by the lake and look up at the skyline, and Lucas wants to erase his father's bad deeds and do right by his best friend. We made the three-hour trip in just over two and rolled back into the driveway just before sunrise. I told my mom about it afterward because I didn't want to start a new collection of secrets. Of course, she doesn't know about the nights Lucas is in my room. I have to have a few things, and as much as I want our bond to rebuild and grow, I also don't want to give up the feeling of having Lucas's arms around me when I fall asleep at night.

Or the feeling of having his fingertips tease along my midriff, as they are right now.

"So, about that date," I say, my eyelids lowered as I look down to where his head rests on my hips. His devilish gaze is focused on the work of his fingers that are slowly inching my shirt up my ribs.

"Yeah?" he hums without glancing up. His eyes close and he rolls his head to press a cool kiss on the skin next to my belly button. He opens them as his tongue takes a quick taste.

"Don't think you can use your typical ploys to distract me," I say, my hips already fighting to squirm because *fuck*, his ploys work.

"Okay," he hums again, this time dragging his tongue up higher, his bottom lip catching on my skin while his hand pushes my T-shirt up further. When his hand pauses at the spot where he should encounter my bra—but doesn't—his eyebrows lift.

"What's this?" His lip curls on one side, and I match with a smirk of my own.

"It's yours if you talk about the date you promised me," I tease.

He breathes out a laugh and inches higher still. I arch on instinct and he shifts so his weight is balanced on both elbows, his hands free to pull my shirt up the rest of the way until my breasts are exposed to the air.

"Ah ah," I say, barely getting the sound out as my breath hitches. I hold up a finger and waggle it in front of his face. "No dessert before dinner."

His lips tighten and curve on the ends, eyes hazing with all kinds of dirty thoughts. He moves his head forward enough to allow his mouth to close around my finger, his teeth gently biting the knuckle as he playfully growls.

"You are all dessert, June," he says, letting go of his hold on my finger.

"One. Date." I stand my ground, though I know all of this is for play. The play is almost as arousing as the other things. Maybe even more.

"All right," he says, tipping his chin and kissing the skin just below my breasts.

I sharply suck in air and push my tits up, wanting more. Lucas ups the ante and kisses closer to the center of my pebbled peaks, a kiss for each curve of my breasts, all the way around, but never fully where I need his lips most.

"Homecoming," he says.

I laugh out because homecoming is *so not* either of us.

"What would I wear?" I question.

He lifts himself forward and flicks his tongue at the tip of my breast. I quake as he blows dry the cool spot he left behind, a tightly puckered smile playing on his lips.

"Black dress," he says, pausing to torture my other breast the same way. "I'll wear my black jeans, and that dark gray sweater over a shirt and tie." His cheek dimples with a tempting smile because he knows that look is my favorite. I asked him about that sweater last week.

"Okay. Black dress, and you . . . sexy as fuck. Got it," I say, knowing he likes it when I talk to him that way. His eyes flutter closed and he growls against my body, dragging his nose along the center of my chest and pausing with his lips brushing lightly atop my right nipple.

"Nothing under your dress," he says, his tongue taking another pass, a longer and harder one this time that bends my back into an arch that opens access for his hands to slide underneath, leaving him in complete control over me.

"That seems risky, me in a black dress at homecoming with nothing on . . . down . . . there." I bring one knee up and lift my hips, wanting to push myself into him and ease the building pressure.

"Those are my demands, June." He licks again and I bend to his will, my eyes barely able to remain open as I stare into him, calling his bluff. He isn't bluffing, though, and the thought of being out with him that way has me curious and hungry.

"I think I can do that," I say, my answer maybe surprising him a little. His right brow lifts higher than the left.

"So, it's a date?" He covers my right breast with his mouth and sucks hard, leaving nothing but the grip of his teeth, and ending with a gentle tug that has me wanting all of him. Now.

"It's a date. Now, please, Lucas. For all that is holy, will you fuck me?" I end my plea with a whimper and it amuses him more than normal. His eyes haze even more than they already are as he rolls my shirt up over my head, taking my arms along with it. He twists the fabric together, tethering my hands loosely above my head then sits up on his knees, my legs parted on either side of him. He's done playing games and teasing me, and his fingers curl around the band of my pink lace panties. I bought them with Abby with this night in mind, and I'm fairly certain they've done the job as the top of Lucas's cock protrudes from the band of his gray joggers. He rarely wears underwear, I've learned. A trait I have come to love for moments like this.

He slides my panties down my lifted hips, and I bend one leg at a time to free them completely. Lucas leans over my body, reaches for his wallet on the night table, and he pulls a condom out, clenching the packet in his teeth. His lips tick up a hint on one side, bringing his dimple back into play. I draw my knees up on either side of him, wanting him to ease the ache I have building desperately.

"You like it when I do dirty things to you, don't you, June?" he mumbles from between teeth gripping the wrapped condom.

I nod because yes, I do.

Lucas tears the packet open with his teeth and one-handedly pulls himself free from the band of his pants. He rolls the condom on slowly with the other. I lift my hips, begging him to stop the torture as he holds himself a fraction of an inch from where I so desperately need him.

He doesn't make me wait long, dragging the tip of his cock down my center twice then pushing inside me in a long, slow thrust. My legs automatically wrap around his waist, and he holds my hips as he works himself in and out of my body. This is the first time we've had sex without muffling our sounds against each other since the abandoned drive-in theater. I let go of some of the inhibitions that come with having to be painfully quiet in my room at night.

Obeying and leaving my hands over my head, I let Lucas drive my body toward climax, my hips holding steady to meet each push of him inside me. I've learned that I can give him pleasure with the smallest movement of my hips, so when I can tell he's starting to lose himself in me, I roll my body to tempt him closer to the fire. I know he's about to come when he falls forward and rests his forehead against mine, one arm holding his weight at the side of my head while the other hand holds my wrists together where I've left them tied in my T-shirt.

Every rock of his hips pushes me closer, his hips working harder and muscles clenching more. I cry out in pleasure against his bare shoulder, biting him lightly and squeezing my eyes closed as the first wave takes me over the cliff and sends me floating in a sea of satisfying riptides, wave after wave as my body clenches around him and I rock my hips up to meet every drive he makes into me. Finally, his body grows so tight, the feel of him so thick inside, that I know he's about to come. I pull his mouth to mine and kiss him harder than I ever have, my tongue probing, teeth tugging on his bottom lip, and soft whimpers falling from my mouth as his breath falls away and his body is nothing but sweat and sex and listless bliss.

He rolls our bodies together so his weight is no longer on me, and I toss my shirt to the side so I can move my fingers through his cool, damp hair, our bodies sticky and moist. I lie like this with him still flexing inside me for several long minutes, content to fall asleep with him there, locked together in a permanence that happens when someone is your first and you give your whole essence to them completely.

"Did I really just agree to homecoming?" He chuckles, and I love the crackling sound it makes in his chest, the slight tremors and vibration of his body under my touch.

"You did," I say, glancing up at him with a tempting smile. "And I agreed to nothing under my dress."

His mouth curls to match mine, a lustfulness touching the corners, drawing them up toward excitable eyes.

"You did," he says, pleased—and possibly aroused—again.

"I better get flowers," I add, knowing that right now, I could get anything I want. But as it stands, I pretty much have it all.

TWENTY-FOUR

Most seniors endure a lot of impromptu photo sessions with their parents when they reach certain milestones. I've never gone to a homecoming dance, or *any* dance for that matter. Freshmen weren't allowed, and my Montessori school was too small to hold anything other than a craft fair. As far as milestones go, this is the first one I've had warranting photographs.

Of course, my mother is a professional photographer, so one session with her may make up for five or ten missed occasions.

The orders were clear, and we all obeyed. Me, Abby, Lola and Naomi arrived early and got dressed and did our hair and makeup upstairs in Lucas's mom's room. It was hard not to look around and notice the stark absence of anything masculine. Only Abby brought it up out loud, and only once. "I'm glad she's divorcing his ass," she said. That summed it up, and that's all we needed to clear the room of the bad energy and make way for magic.

While we dressed upstairs, Lucas, the twins and a few of the other guys from the team get dressed in my house, in my room. I did my best to hide things I thought might be embarrassing, but I feel better knowing Lucas is there. If Tory decides to go rummaging through my drawers, he'll throat punch him.

While we all get ready, my mom sets up a ridiculous amount of equipment—two umbrella lights, four different flashes, and a seamless paper backdrop hanging from some contraption she built out of PVC pipe.

Nobody questions her, especially not me. The only photos I have of me and Lucas together are from before our bodies matured, when holding hands felt super racy and taboo. Oh, the things we've done to each other since then.

The main photos, of course, could only happen in one place. My mom has always been in love with the staircase inside the Fuller home. While our layouts are the same, our interiors are drastically different. My home would be what one might call the "base model," while Lucas's house is filled with the best upgrades. And the best feature, for both my mother and me, is the iron staircase that winds from one end of the house down to the foyer. This is why we had to dress here—to make a *grand* entrance that my mom could capture on film.

My mom bought about two dozen packs of fairy lights for her "vision," and she and Lucas's mom spent almost the entire day weaving the thin wires around the railing for a glittering effect. At one point, when I came by to drop off some clear tape, I overheard Shannon telling my mom that she wishes they had "done this a lot sooner." I didn't pry, and I didn't linger to eavesdrop, but I'm pretty sure she was talking about coming together and living with the truth.

The brash laughter from downstairs now that the boys have all come inside echoes through the high-ceilinged foyer and practically beats down Lucas's mom's door. I've been ready for almost an hour, but in that time, I've doubted every square inch of myself at least twice. Mostly, that I'm wearing a very short dress with nothing underneath. I've kept this secret from Abby; some moments are meant to be special and only shared between Lucas and me. Knowing he can touch me with one flit of my dress is one of those kinds of things.

My hair is pulled up into a loose ponytail that Abby curled into spirals that fall down my shoulders and back. The dress I bought is strapless with a back that scoops clear to the spot where my spine curves inward at my lower back. The amount of fabric that covers my ass is minimal, so my dancing tonight will not be bold and big. It's fine, though, because I intend on remaining in Lucas's arms most of the night.

"Here," Abby says, stepping behind me and dusting my shoulders and chest with a little bit of glitter. I barely recognize myself in the mirror, the gawky alt girl with long, dark hair almost looks like a princess. It's probably the glitter.

"He's going to lose his mind," she says, dropping her chin to my shoulder. I peek at her, looking away from our reflection and toward my friend who has always thought I'm beautiful. She holds her hand out and snaps a photo of the two of us together, and my smile stretches wider.

"For once, you caught a moment of me in a good mood," I say, laughing.

"Well, there was bound to be one," she says, snapping one more photo as I roll my eyes at her lame joke.

"And . . . there she is," she teases.

I reach for her phone in playful retaliation, but before I can catch her, there's a soft knock at the door. Lucas's mom slips in and holds her palms to her face. She shakes her head at the sight of the four of us, all done up as if we're heading to a royal ball.

"So, this is what it's like to have daughters," she says, genuine awe in her expression. I reach for her hand and squeeze it the moment she gives it to me. I still haven't let Lucas read the letter she wrote me after everything went down, but he knows she gave it to me. She spent two pages apologizing for believing I could be anything other than someone special. I cried when I read it, not realizing how much it hurt to have her think poorly of me because of something she believed my mom did. Her list of my best qualities was exhaustive, but it was also deeply personal and purposeful. She wasn't generic about a single thing, and described moments when Lucas and I were together as kids. She credited me for him finally finding his own voice, but I don't know that I did anything other than rip the tape from his mouth. Lucas was already near to breaking free of his father's expectations. All I did was give him a tiny shove.

"The guys are ready, ladies," she says, pausing at the door and lining us up to walk down one at a time. I know my mom's drill, and we will be repeating this sequence about eight more times to make sure she gets the perfect shot. But this first time will be the one that counts the most for me. It will be the first time Lucas looks up and sees me as more than the girl next door. A sexy, mature, driven and confident almost eighteen-year-old is about to walk down the steps and take his hand. I'll know exactly what our immediate future holds by that initial reaction. I'm ready for it.

Abby walks down the steps first, and we all giggle at the cat calls and whistles the boys deliver down below. We decided to go together as a group tonight since Lucas and I are the only *real* couple, but I know for a fact Tory sees Abby with the same colored glasses Lucas does me. He's just not quite ready to grow up and admit it.

Lola and Naomi go next, and I watch through the cracked doorway as they stop to pose on nearly every step. My mom is hysterical with laughter, but deep down, she actually thinks some of the poses they strike might work for commercial purposes. Her business hat is never far away.

My heart beats wildly the farther down the steps the girls go, and when the eyes staring from below all dart up to the doorway I'm hiding behind, my palms begin to sweat.

"I'm nervous," I whisper, giggling for Lucas's mom.

"You're stunning," she says. Without giving me more time to panic, she pushes the door open and steps back so I'm the only thing there for Lucas to see. He came dressed as promised, his straight black pants, dark gray V-neck sweater, crisp white shirt, and black tie. The preppy look may very well only work on him for me. It does work, though. It works without exception, and it works quickly. My insides shift from being anxious to being amorous. I step onto the landing, wrap my hand around the railing, and look down on the blue eyes peering up.

"You are beautiful," Lucas mouths, and my mouth stretches into a smile, the satin feeling of the deep red color on my lips making it easy to shine with happiness. He moves forward, away from the seven other guys here with him, and as I take the stairs one at a time, praying I don't fall in these shoes that are way too high for my novice feet to navigate in, he climbs to meet me.

My mother's cameras click rapidly, and as silly as I thought she was with some of this, I'm glad she's capturing this moment. If Lucas never looks up at me again, I'll always have the way he's looking at me now.

With only three steps left between us, Lucas takes one final stride, clearing them all until we share the same stair. He stands close, his hands bracing my elbows as I hold on to his biceps, not towering over me as he usually does thanks to the stupid amount of height added by my shoes.

"Look who's all grown up," he says through a playful smirk. His eyes are crystal waters against the dark gray of his sweater. I breathe in his scent and instantly am drunk on the warm vanilla and burning wood notes. Lucas takes advantage of my liquid state by tipping up my chin and possessively dropping his mouth on mine. His hand snakes around my back, landing low enough for his fingers to dip inside the fabric that drapes above my ass. He leans me back, and someone in the room whistles. I blush from being the center of attention, but I'm also rushed with heat from his touch.

I lean all of my weight into his strong hand as he holds me perilously over the cascading stairs, tethering us to gravity with his other hand on the banister. When he pulls away, I smile against his lips, happy to etch this moment in stone. One more heartbeat, though, makes it another milestone in my life.

"I love you, too," he says, his lips playfully brushing against the nape of my neck. He raises me and our gazes lock, his serious despite the flirtatious lilt of his lips, which are a little pink from my lip stick.

"I love you," I mouth, knowing nobody below can see me. His cheek indents briefly, a hint of his dimple appearing like a sign to let me know he read my lips . . . just as he heard me slip up and say those words before, way too early.

As I predict, my mom, the consummate professional, makes us repeat every single thing we do three more times, then she spends an hour taking shots of couples and groups on the stairs and in front of her plain backdrop. Before she shuts down her lights, though, I make her do one thing she hates but will thank me for down the road.

I drag my resistant mother outside to stand with me in front of our middle-finger garage door, and we stand together, embracing, her in her ripped jeans and Tommy sweatshirt and me in my two-hundred-dollar cocktail dress that my mom said I deserved despite my argument that it cost too much.

I had prepared Lucas's mom for the job, and from the digital proofs I checked on my mom's laptop, I'd say she came through beautifully. I will take that image of her and me together with me everywhere I go, and no matter how much life changes, my relationship with her will be my one true constant. My rock. That paint will soon be covered up, but the badass who did it? She's forever.

I expect attention when Lucas and I finally walk into the homecoming dance. Not because of the rumors swirling about everything that went down, but because of the epic performance he had on the field last night. His dad still showed up for the game, though his mother sat with us while his dad stood alone down by the fence. He didn't leave, because as broken as his relationship with his son is, he can't give up the high he gets from watching him do things he never could. Lucas is gifted on the field. He also happens to have a gifted mind, and for the boy I love, that's far more inspiring.

A few players stop us as we make our way toward the dance floor, handshakes and bro hugs take place with me at Lucas's side. But when the first slow song begins to play, everything—and everyone else—disappears. I find a home against Lucas's chest, and I intend on staying here until he takes me somewhere to be alone. The sensual touch of his hand on my bare back keeps my nerves firing no matter how slow or soft the song is we dance to, and I know we've been indulged when the DJ announces one more before he turns things up a notch. I don't quite expect this, though.

To most people in the room, this isn't a slow song. In fact, judging by the sneers and jokes, most people don't even know what this song is. But I know. Hayden D'Angelo knows. And now his twin knows, too.

"Did you set this up?" I say, leaning back and quirking a brow as "Midnight Hour" transforms our high school gym into a time machine right back to the nineteen-sixties.

"I thought you did!" Lucas laughs, flattening his hand on his chest and crossing his heart.

I narrow my eyes in thought, and scan the room in search of my suspect, but I don't have to look far. Tory leans proudly with his right elbow on the tower speaker near the DJ booth. He blows on his fingertips then runs them down the length of his lapel like a regular fucking Sinatra. My, I have taught him well.

The dance floor clears for the most part, but Lucas and I stay there for the entire song, singing along with the chorus, showcasing the worst of our vocal talents. When the DJ breaks through the end of the song asking the homecoming royalty court to step forward, I peel back so Lucas can join the other seniors standing near the platform set up under the basketball scoreboard. He instead slides back and out of the way with me, letting the twins and that guy Cannon walk up on their own. It's glaringly obvious he's not where he should be as three guys stand to the right of our principal and four girls stand to his left. Even more obvious is the disdain on Ava's face as she stares across the half court at me. There was a time when that small, insignificant action of hers would make me feel incredibly small, but tonight, it only serves as a source of amusement.

"She could not possibly hate me more," I say. Lucas bends his head down and claps through the reading of the nominees for king, including himself.

"Ava?" he questions.

I punch out a short laugh. "Yeah. She hasn't really bothered me since the whole spray paint and black eye incidents. What's weird, though, is I don't get why she hated me so much when you were dating her."

Lucas's eyes glimmer in his gaze, and a smirk paints his lips.

"Oh, I know why," he says, standing tall and not filling in the details just to torture me.

I clap through the list of queen nominees but keep my skeptical eyes on my boyfriend, my stare penetrating his ability to ignore it.

"Let's get out of here," he says, turning to the side to kiss the top of my head. I look up and meet his smile.

"But you're probably gonna win," I say.

"I don't really give a shit," he responds.

I give him side eyes for a moment, but it's easy to see he's telling the truth. I take his waiting hand and we weave through the crowd, having only stayed for four songs. They announce Ava's name behind us as we let the gym doors fall closed. It's a perfect way to leave her, on top of her completely irrelevant and fake mountain. It doesn't change the question I'm still dying to know the answer to, though. I hold my tongue until we get to Lucas's truck, patient a few minutes longer than I expect because Lucas quickly discovers I followed through with my promise in wearing this dress.

I sit sideways in his passenger seat with him standing between my legs. My body satiated from his touch, I peel away from our kiss and reach up to grab the knot of his tie. I tug it forcefully, and he grins.

"Tell me, Lucas Fuller. Why does Ava Pryor hate me so much?"

I may never be prepared for his answer.

"Because when she told me she was in love with me at her eighth grade birthday party I told her I was in love with you. And deep down, she knows I never stopped."

EPILOGUE

It's strange to contemplate where we all started the year—where Lucas and I started the year. There was a time when I dreaded this day . . . graduation. I was so deep in my own head that I thought the day would come and go without things like parties, or friends. Certainly not boyfriends. And yet somehow, I'm in a world where I have all three.

In six hours, I'll walk across a stage and be handed a ticket to my future. That future isn't as dim as I fear it would be, either. My mom is an inspiration. She believes in her work, and she works hard. That hard work has turned a solo photography business into something that not only pays the bills but also afforded her to tuck away enough for me to go to Indiana East. It's not Notre Dame or Ball State, but it is away from home, and an adventure. And it has a really great liberal arts program, so maybe I'll be able to figure out what the hell I want to be when I grow up.

Grow up.

It's funny to look back and remember those words Abby said to me when the year began: that we've all grown up. She was right. In many ways, we have. But we've also got a lot of growing left to do. I hope somehow we're lucky enough to still be together at the end . . . all of us.

Lucas leaves after summer for MIT. He's going to love it there, and I'm all right with that because I know he loves me too. I might lose him for a little while to that great big world he's going to experience. But his roots will always be here, on some tree-lined street about an hour from a big city, where a pair of driveways brought us together when we were young.

I trust him enough to know he'll always come back to me in one form or another, and we will always be in love, even if it's only first love. I can't help but believe there's a chance that me and him? We might be the real deal. The forever, and the always.

"Are you sure you aren't peeking?" Lucas shouts. He left me here at the bottom of his driveway about ten minutes ago with this stupid tie wrapped around my face. He tied it snug, so not only can I not see, I might actually be blind. He said he has a graduation gift for me that requires a little maneuvering. I'm nervous about what that means.

"I promise!" I shout back.

"Okay, you'll know when to pull off the blindfold," he says. I shake my head because I have no idea what that could possibly mean, but trust . . . I trust *him*. So, here goes nothing.

At first, all I hear is the slamming of a car door. I lose count how many seconds pass before another noise touches my ears, but when it does, yeah . . . he's right. It's time to pull off the blindfold.

"No fucking way!"

My dad's impossible project, the piece of junk I assumed my mom finally had hauled away, is backing out of Lucas Fuller's garage. On its own. Nobody is pushing it. It's being driven.

The rumble is like honey to the ears, and even though the body is in desperate need of a paint job, the form . . . my God, the form of that vehicle is sexy.

"I can't believe you got the Buick running!" I shout so he hears me over the deep growl spilling from the engine.

Lucas hops out, leaving the door open behind him. The seats are still torn, but the dash looks new, and the steering wheel is in the right position with a leather wrap around it. I palm my face and stare in shock as I walk closer, sitting inside briefly so I can touch everything. I step back out, closing the door behind me, and put my hands right back on my cheeks, tears forming in my eyes.

"I figured what good is an MIT degree if I can't get my girl a car to drive to college in," he says with a casual shrug. He acts as if this is no big deal but I know what shape that car was in. It was a shell. A ghost. He brought it back from the dead. And he did it for me.

I leap at him in an instant, arms wrapping around his neck as he catches me at the waist and swings me in a circle, my dress and graduation gown flowing around my body.

"You like it?" He dips his chin as he sets me on my feet and I step up on my toes to kiss him.

"I could not love a single thing more," I say, the smile on my mouth aching as it stabs into my cheeks. This is what happiness is.

"I feel really bad," I say with a soft laugh.

His brow dents.

"Because I didn't get you anything that big," I say, glancing over my shoulder to take in the car still rumbling out its sweet sounding idle behind me. I bite my bottom lip and turn my gaze back to him, a little excited because while I didn't get him a car, I did get him something he'll like.

"That's a fairly sinister grin you've got there, June Mabee." His eyes lower and one brow lifts.

I let him stew with his thoughts and fantasies for a few seconds, then I tug his hands into mine and lead him backward toward the back seat of the car that is now mine. He follows willingly as I open the door and get in. He drops a knee on the seat between my legs and I slide until my back is pressed against the opposite window. He's wearing his dress shirt and dark gray pants, a black tie, and silver cufflinks on his rolled-up sleeves. I'm going to enjoy messing up his look later, but for right now, I feel he might just deserve a preview.

I let the sides of my graduation gown fall open and slowly unbutton the front of my dress one button at a time. My mom and his mom are picking up food. My dad won't show up until the ceremony, and his dad might not show up at all. We have a small moment alone to make a memory, and what I bought for him is meant to make an impression.

As my dress falls open, the thin white lace over my breasts and the matching panties come into view, and Lucas's gaze scorches its way down my body. He leans forward without hesitation, and I open my legs to make room for him to completely crawl inside. When he shuts the heavy door behind him, I decide his pressed shirt doesn't have to be perfect to walk across a stage, and maybe it's all right if he gets a little messy now.

That's what life is. It's messy. It's sexy. It's ugly. It's brutally hard yet joyous all at once. And this life, it's all mine. Just like the boy who is making me feel like the woman I never thought I'd become . . . right . . . now.

THE END

ACKNOWLEDGMENTS

I'm gonna keep this short and sweet. This series is about the ride, about escaping our reality a little right now and living in between some angsty, fun pages, feeling some swoon then holding hands over our hearts. I wanted to write a world of characters to take us all away, and I wanted a dash of sports in the mix because hey…it's me! And I miss sports!

This series was started in the middle of a pandemic. Never in a million years did I think I'd write that statement. And it turns out that leaning on others when writing during the middle of a pandemic is crucial. There is no way I could have jumped feet first into this thing without my support team and without the readers holding out supportive hands ready to catch me after THE END.

This series has lived in my head for about a year, but shaking off the stress of the world today proved a little tricky. Thank you, Autumn, for telling 2020 to take a seat and shut up and let me write and edit. I always need you but this year, I need you a little more. My betas, Jen, Shelley, TeriLyn—I love you. Brenda Letendre and Tina Scott, bless you and your editing genius. And finally, my sweet Tim and Carter, my world, thanks for being the constant in the storm.

If you enjoyed this book, please consider leaving a review. The book market is daunting for us small authors, and getting the word out in this increasingly noisy world is becoming so hard. I am incredibly thankful to my readers and supporters for every boost they give. It's those viral shares, the recommendations to friends, that help get my stories seen, and I don't for one minute take any of that for granted. I get to do this because you give me your time and your passion—you tell others to give my books a try. So thank you all…to the moon!

And hey, don't worry…I'm in my groove now. You guys are going to love Varsity Tiebreaker and Varsity Rulebreaker. Take that, 2020!

VARSITY CAPTAIN

VARSITY
Captain

Cover Design by Ginger Scott, Little Miss Write LLC

For Team Lucas.

ONE

Lucas Fuller

It's hard not having anything to say to the man I've idolized half my life. That's what our rides home from practice have become, though—disciplined silence with momentary flashes of politeness between father and son.

"Is the air on high enough for you?" *There's his contribution.*

"I'm good." *My polite response is now in the can.*

I'm still months away from getting my license. I can't wait until I'm able to drive myself to football workouts. There's already a brand new Nissan pickup truck in the driveway, and it's hard not to think of it as a bribe. I'll take it, though. That's the least I can squeeze out of the shitty situation I fell into simply by being Todd Fuller's kid.

I still can't see how we got to this point. It just seems so . . . I don't know, impossible? I guess that's what every kid thinks before their parents' marriage falls apart. Mine are clinging to the scraps, and Dad seems desperate to repair those tattered threads. Mom, she just seems angry. Maybe a little unwell too. And her rage seems dialed in on the one person I need to talk to—June Mabee.

My best friend and neighbor is the only person who has ever gotten me. She's the only person I can vent to when I'm sick of the pressure from football. Sometimes it feels as though my dad is shaping me into his trophy just so he can brag about me to his friends and colleagues, and June is the only person who doesn't make me feel like a whiny privileged asshole for feeling crushed by it all.

I guess I can understand my mom's fury and wanting to keep "our business in our house," as she frequently says, but June isn't a threat. She's as much an innocent bystander as I am.

Dad pulls into our driveway and I chance a quick glance to June's house. Our driveways nearly connect, and when I stand in just the right place I can see life inside her house—she and her mom moving around the kitchen, or June running up the stairs, the shadow of her passing across the curtains in her room. I wish I could run into that house, into her room, lock myself inside and avoid everything else for a little while. *Forever.*

"Get cleaned up for dinner. Mom made a roast. She'd like us to eat at the table." Dad kills the engine on his truck and climbs out, but I give myself a tiny moment inside alone.

We started eating dinner together as a family when it all unraveled. It's part of my mom's need to hold on. My dad says it's important to her. I don't know. I think they're focusing on a lot of the wrong things to call important. But what do I know: I'm a fifteen-year-old kid.

Dad pauses at the garage door leading into the laundry room, waiting for me. I relent and climb out after him, and the second my feet step over the threshold, my stomach tightens into the impossible knot that seems to live there when I'm in this house.

Dad heads to the right, toward the kitchen, and I veer left, to the stairs. I take them two at a time. I open the door and drop my bag just inside, then close it with a gentle click. My back falls against the woodgrain and I breathe out, my tight shoulders relaxing a tick as I rub my hand over my face.

It doesn't take long for the shouting to start. The rounds of arguing have gotten shorter over the last few days, but they still happen regularly. Dinner seems to be a trigger. Probably because my dad always missed dinner . . . *before*. Now, his mere presence at the meal is an opportunity to remind him of the ones he missed, and the lies he used as excuses.

At least Mom is sober. Still, I'm always on guard, watching over her and looking for signs that she's slipping. I've started a daily practice of sifting through the backs of our cabinets, behind the dry goods and the rarely used cleaning products—her common hiding spots. They've been clear for weeks. Dad cleared out his office liquor cabinet when she came home, but I'm sure that's only temporary. I tell myself I'd be able to tell, that there would be obvious signs she's drinking or taking pills. Would there, though? I missed them the first time. Of course, I wasn't really looking. I was too absorbed in my own shit to notice. Not that it's my job, but if not me, then who?

My pocket buzzes with a message to my phone and I lift my head to stare out my window. I already know who it's from. Summer has always been June and my time. She's been helping me find a part-time job that might work around my football practices. I haven't responded to the last job posting she sent. It's getting harder to be two people—the person I am in this house, and the one I am with her. It feels like a betrayal both ways no matter what I do. But June doesn't need to feel like I do. She has enough happening in her life. Her dad moved out weeks ago. I watched him pack up and go. As bad as things are in this house, my dad stayed.

She must be somewhere else because I don't see her light on in her room, and downstairs seems quiet. I hope she's made a new group of friends. I hope she is out enjoying her summer. I hope she doesn't depend on me to be her person, because I don't know if I can.

Curious, I pull my phone out to read her text.

JUNE: *Hey! Everything ok? Haven't heard from you for a few days, but I know practice already started for summer. Did you check out the job I sent? It's for ice cream. Ice! Cream! Lucas—free ice cream. That's all I'm saying. OK, well, enough of that. I also wanted to see if you wanted to get dive-in movie passes for the pool this year. They're half off if I get them now. Let me know! Ahh! Summer!*

I'm smiling by the time I'm done reading. Spending time with June does that to me, even if it's only time with her words. Tory keeps nudging me to ask her out, like *out* out, as in a date, but it seems wrong. She's like my sister, only . . . very much *not* my sister. I think if I asked, she'd say yes. And that makes it scarier. Things with us would change, and as much as I've thought about the *what ifs*, there's a whole lot of risk involved. I open her message to reply and hover my thumbs over the keyboard, dying to type YES to all of it. Then the yelling grows louder.

"I'm sorry but I don't feel bad about her divorce. That's what that woman gets!"

"Shannon, you're getting carried away . . ."

I wince. My dad always stokes the fire. It's as if he wants her to go back to rehab.

"You are done helping her, you hear me? She can get a new lawyer, Todd. She has a job. No more charity from you. No more *anything* from you or I swear to God, I'm gone! I'm gone and I will make sure everyone knows exactly what that house is all about."

I slip my phone back into my pocket at the sound of someone's heavy feet stomping up the stairs. I'm not sure who I want it to be more—*or less.*

The soft knock on my door spikes up my pulse. I hold my breath and twist where I stand, cracking open the door . My mom's eyes are wild, but I can tell she's trying to calm down. She shuts them and draws in a deep breath through her nose, huffing out once and letting her shoulders drop as I open my door wide and move to my bed.

"I'm sorry," she says, coming in and taking a seat next to me. "I know you can hear that, and that's not right. Not fair to you."

"It's fine." More blanket lies from my mouth. I'm never fine or good, but that's all I can seem to tell people.

"We're gonna be okay, Lucas." My mom's tone is oddly assured. I lift my head and meet her gaze, feeling as if I have to play along. I'm also hopeful, but along with that feeling comes a sense of falling, like walking along a very thin edge.

"Okay," I croak out.

I hate this.

"I bet the Mabees will move. So even that won't be weird after a while. And we'll just go on with our lives, and be stronger as a family. Hey, why don't you invite the D'Angelo boys over, have a sleepover?"

She's excited by the idea, and even though it's the last thing I'm in the mood for, I smile and nod.

"Sure. Sounds fun," I lie.

She gets up from the bed and runs her palms down the front of her slacks, straightening out the wrinkles. She's flawless somehow, even after coming home from work and stepping right into the kitchen. My mom works so hard at holding the façade together. I hope she doesn't do it for me. I'd just as soon deal with crumbles.

"Hey, and Lucas? I know that you and June are close, but maybe . . . maybe give each other some space for a while. She's been told a lot of lies, and I'm not sure she's ready to deal with the truth yet. It seems maybe it's easier if you sort of drift apart. You're getting older anyhow. It happens. And besides that, I'm sure they'll move."

She presses her lips into a forced smile so I do the same.

"Yeah."

She nods at my response, pleased. My phone buzzes in my pocket just before she leaves, though, and her eyes twitch. I know she wants to stick around to see who my message is from. I'm sure she already knows.

"I'll call Tory now, see if they want to come over."

She fixates on my slight grin, studying my face for a full breath. My need to swallow consumes me, but I don't—that would reek of guilt. And I am guilty. June is in my pocket. My mom is in my room. My family is broken.

One more nod, this one tinged with a sour bitterness that injects me with guilt, is all I get before she shuts my door and leaves me alone with my dilemma. I glance at my phone again.

JUNE: ?

It's clear that June doesn't know what's going on. She's in blissful ignorance, and honestly, I hope she stays there. Unfortunately, I can't go back.

We can't go back.

As painful as it is, I let my thumb continue its destructive movement over my phone screen, sliding June's name to the side, revealing the option to block her texts, her calls—her everything. It won't be forever. It's just for now, until things get figured out, until my parents work through their issues and her mom finds them a new place. I'll call her as soon as it's over and explain everything, and maybe we'll still get to have our summer. Maybe she'll understand.

The lies. They just keep on coming.

TWO

Two years later, the night before senior year

"You know those D1 offers can be rescinded."

I wonder how many times this year my dad is going to rattle off that line. I bombed one test last year—*one*—and I didn't even truly bomb it. I got a C. But it was enough to get the *you know those D1 offers* comment from my old man.

Tonight's offense? Acting like a typical eighteen-year-old boy.

It's not that my dad has a thing against me going to parties. It's that he has a thing about me going to parties at the D'Angelo house. Tory and Hayden aren't trouble really, but they do throw big parties that sometimes get out of hand. Their parents are gone a lot, and there's not much to do around here, so when the twins host a party, everyone we know shows up.

Almost everyone.

"I'll probably be home early. Relax," I shout as the door shuts behind me, cutting my dad off from throwing in one more empty warning. I couldn't give a shit about my D1 offers, which, of course, I can never say out loud. I'm pretty sure my dad's head would actually blow off of his neck if I told him that. Me playing ball for a big school has been on his dream list for me since I was born. Making up for his shortcomings, I guess. My old man only got a year in before his arm gave out.

Sometimes, I wonder if mine will, too. A part of me wishes for it.

Tory's waiting in the passenger seat, and the fucker scares the shit out of me when I climb in my truck. I punch his bicep. *Hard.*

"Damn, Fuller!" He rubs the sore spot. I hope it bruises.

"Don't sneak up on me like that. I thought I was picking you up. What'd you do, walk here?" I glance around and check my mirrors, looking for a car that dropped him off.

"Just back out. I'll tell you when we start rolling."

Despite his request, I leave my tires parked right where they are and glare at him. It takes about two seconds for him to break.

"Fine. I had Hayden drop me off. While you were changing and talking to your dad, I snagged some top-shelf shit from his cabinet. We're seniors now. Time to graduate from beer, get a little more *fucked up*."

I roll my eyes and crank the engine.

"I'll stick with the beer, thanks." I sigh.

My friend shakes his head while I reverse. He can peer pressure me all he wants, it's futile. I do what I want, and I'm impervious to the power of adolescent suggestion. I refuse to be a lemming.

"I heard Abby say she's bringing June tonight," Tory pipes in, nodding toward the dark house next door as I shift and race down my street.

"Like Abby would actually talk to you."

"Fuck off. She did. So what if when I asked if she was coming she said 'Yeah, and I'm bringing June so we can both shoot you down at once.'"

I can't help but snort out a massive laugh.

"*Pshh*, whatever. You're gonna have to deal with June is all."

I let my laughter linger, but it quit being real seconds ago. As much as I want to pretend June isn't a problem for me, she very much is. I have forbidden myself from even thinking about her, which came easily when she switched schools for our junior year. I guess she's back now. Her mom lost her job or some shit, so private school was a no-go. She probably deserved it. I'm sure her boss found out about her side gigs. I just don't know how June hasn't figured it out yet. Whatever, though. Not my problem.

"I mean, it's not like you're really *with* Ava anymore, so I don't see why talking to June is such a big deal," Tory continues.

"My issues with June have nothing to do with Ava. Drop it, Tor."

He mocks me, repeating my words in a whiny voice that sounds nothing like me, then turns the stereo up and quits provoking me. Tory knows my story, mostly. He was around when the Mabees drove my mom over the edge. It's hard to hide your mom's alcohol and pill addiction, especially when it ends with her being hauled off to rehab. I needed someone to talk to about it, and Tory is my best friend. He was my support system. And yeah, he's right about Ava, my ex. She hates June more than anyone I've met, besides my mom. If I spend even a second talking to June in front of Ava, she'll probably punch a hole through Tory's wall. I can't do anything to send Mom on another spiral like the one my dad did a couple years ago. No girl is worth doing that.

June was a childhood friend. A crush. People grow apart. It happens, like my mom said.

Cars are already piled up on the street surrounding Tory's house, so I find the closest spot I can. Tory's twin, Hayden, is shooting hoops in the driveway when we show up, and a few girls are outside drinking. I back away to give my friend room to take a pass from his brother and dunk the ball so he can get the applause that follows. He eats it up.

Tory's ten times the athlete I am. He'll be in the NBA one day. No doubt. But I don't think anything gets him going quite like the adoration of females watching him put on a show.

"Come on, Lucas. One quick game. What do you say?" He's taunting me, his shirt already off as he spins the ball on his fingertip. Two of the girls sitting on the back of the twins' car giggle at the sight.

"I'm good. Not much in the mood to get my ass kicked, but thanks." I carry the bottles of liquor he swiped from my dad into the garage and then the house. I think my dad kept booze out of our house for a full month before he quit caring about the temptation it was to my mom. I often wonder if he was trying to lure her off her path again so he could look righteous while she looked weak. At the same time, part of me thinks she refuses to take his bait just to spite him. Maybe I'm giving their mental warfare too much credit. I don't know.

The music is already up to an obscene volume. I don't mind it because it makes it hard to talk to people, and I'm not much in the mood to talk. I nod hello to a few people I recognize on my way in, then bury myself in the kitchen, tucking the whiskey and vodka into a corner before getting myself a cup and filling it with beer from the keg.

I'm mid-sip when the last voice I'm in the mood for crawls around my neck and into my ear.

"I brought your jersey. If you want it."

Why I ever gave Ava my old jersey to wear is beyond me. I was probably drunk, angry, and horny. Three toxic ingredients to combine. It was summer, and I'd just gotten my first D1 offer. My dad was already planning how to turn one offer into a dozen. Most of the guys on our team loved that the school let us keep old jerseys when the program got new ones. I couldn't wait to get rid of it.

I couldn't wait to get inside Ava.

Problem met solution, and I got my dick wet as a result. Seemed like a win-win at the time.

I was desperate to be someone else. *Anyone.* As long as I didn't have to hear about all the ways I was failing to be the man my dad never was. Hearing his bullshit gets harder and harder, especially given his massive flaws. I don't call him on it, though. I play the part of a good son—the Fuller's *perfect* son. I do it for my mom. If I seem happy, she can be happy, or at least continue to pretend she is. Our lives are a fragile house of cards simply waiting for the fan to blow them over.

Downing a third of my beer, I turn slowly, the feel of Ava's long fingernails dragging along my skin from neck to shoulder, then chest as I meet her gaze.

"You have it with you?"

A coy smile plays at her bright red lips. I kinda figured.

"It's in my car. We could go get it now, if you want." She drags her long-ass nail down the center of my chest and tugs on the waist of my jeans. My dick swells, because it's desperate. The rest of me knows better, and I'm not drinking more than the contents of this cup tonight.

I wrap my hand around her wrist and pull it away from my pants. Her lips puff up into her signature pouty face, but that look doesn't work on me sober, and I'm, well, done with the games.

"You keep it. Think of it as a souvenir."

I meet Ava's eyes long enough to see the flinch followed by the simmer of anger. I walk away, leaving her to seethe and plot methods to strike back at me. I'm sure she will. It's what she lives for. She isn't a nice person, not really. She's hot, and for a while, that's what I was into. Or maybe that's what I told myself I needed. Now? I just want to do my own thing. When my dad finds out that thing isn't football? I can kiss my college fund good-bye.

"Hey, why so mopey?" Tory slings his sweaty arm around my neck and pulls me toward him. I shrug it off, feeling trapped. His breath already reeks of tequila, and I've only been away from him for five minutes.

"I'm not mopey, I . . . I don't know. I'm gonna just reset my head. Give me a few, okay?" I tilt my head toward the garage door, thinking maybe I can sit in one of the D'Angelo cars for a while and play some music while Tory's brother plays basketball.

"You mean, you're gonna go mope in the garage alone," he says, a brow quirked.

It's accurate, fine. But it's still irritating.

"Dude, whatever. Go drink some of the top shelf shit you stole from my dad so the ass-beating I'm going to get will be worth it."

My friend winks and tells me he's on top of it, and the moment his back is turned, I duck into the garage. I guess the pickup basketball is done. The garage is closed, leaving me alone under the buzz of fluorescent lights. I maneuver my way through the space. The sedan is parked inside, leaving a gaping hole where their dad usually parks his truck. I head to the far corner and pull one of the folding chairs out from the stack leaning on the wall, flipping it open and straddling the seat. I amuse myself with the non-stop stream of puckered lips on social media. Why every girl in this town has to make the same duck-face in her selfie, I have no clue. I make a game of counting each one, and eventually chuckle out loud at the massive number of images that look exactly the same. Even Tory makes that face in a few. Then one of them stops my laughter. This shot, it's different.

I pause on Abby Cortez's account. It's not her I'm staring at. Abby doesn't post many pics of herself. Probably because her face is already all over the magazine stands and social ads. She's the most famous person in this town, having been in a GAP ad twice. I'm paused on an entirely different person, one with long dark hair wrapped around a heart-shaped face, cheeks speckled with stardust-like freckles, and wide green eyes. June looks as though she's about to swear in the photo, and her hand is half raised in protest, her smile caught somewhere between surprised and irritated.

I've seen her make that face a million times. It's the version of her being playfully teased. I smile without realizing it at first and instantly force it away when I do. I'm not supposed to feel things when I see pictures of June. But for some reason, seeing that picture just now makes me feel lonely. It makes me miss her. Even if we never became something, we would have been friends. She'd know exactly what to tell me about college and football. She'd tell me to talk to my dad.

I laugh softly and close the image app, switching to my email. The admissions portal is still highlighted with my last offer from Northwest State. My dad doesn't even know about this one. He wouldn't want me to go there anyhow. It's too small. Funny, that's the only school that really appeals for football. I like the academics. But I might come out of there with a degree and nothing else, and that's not good enough for Todd Fuller. What would he tell his friends?

The voices pick up on the other side of the door, and the music is thumping more than before. I could probably head inside and get lost in the crowd, maybe even slip away after an hour to go home and just sleep. I'd give anything for a restful night. All I do is toss and turn and think about what I want but can't have. Lately, I've gotten an average of four hours of sleep a night, and those hours are broken up by long rounds of self-doubt and internal debate. My conclusion is always the same: I'll play college football to make my dad happy. What's four years, really? I can handle four years of college football. I'll get a degree out of it. Sure, it will be business and not engineering, but I can turn that into something. Maybe grad school on my own if my grades hold up. I'll do dad's dream to pay for mine.

A squealing laugh draws my eyes up to the garage door and out of my endless mental loop. It's Lola, one of Ava's friends. I recognize the timbre of her exaggerated laugh. She's trying to impress Ava by laughing at one of her jokes, I'm sure. I've seen her do it for the last two years just to keep her coveted place in the Ava Pryor social circle. It must be exhausting.

I'm about to go back to surfing my phone when the garage door pops open and a body thrusts through, almost as if it's being pushed. Long, wild hair tangles over her face, but she pushes the strands from her eyes in time for us to make eye contact.

The lights go out.

The door clicks locked behind her.

"Oh, fuck me." I realize as it's happening that I say those words out loud. I probably sound like a dick. But seriously, locked in a dark garage with June Mabee is the last position I want to be in. What kind of night is this? First Ava, now June. I'm not in the mood for layers of family drama, and June is basically one big family drama bomb. Staring at her face in a social media post is one thing, but being stuck with her in a small space? No. I can't do this. I didn't even want to come to this party. I just didn't want to be at home. And since everyone I know is here, that left few options.

I should have gone bowling by myself.

"Shit!" June's hands are rubbing along the wall near the door. I'm sure she cut herself on one of the broken nail heads while searching for a garage door opener. One hasn't hung there for years. But when it did, it hung on that nail head. She's probably bleeding. I've cut myself on it before. It fucking hurts.

A slight gasp slips from her mouth, followed by the clonking of her phone as it tumbles along the ground. It glows for a second, but shuts off mid-crash. I'm pretty sure she busted the screen.

It's damn near impossible to see in here, but I can make out enough of her profile to tell she's squatting and patting along the concrete, feeling for her phone. I should help instead of just sitting here. Solidifying my reputation as a massive prick, I guess. It's better that way. She'll have less interest in talking to me. With a little luck, we won't have any classes together and life can go on, business as usual, as if she never came back to Public at all.

Guilt grips at my chest, though, the longer she crawls on her hands and knees, probably bleeding from that damn exposed nail. *Tory should hammer that shit. Seriously.*

I flip my phone around and shine the flashlight on her, illuminating the ground.

"Thanks," she says.

My lips part to say "you're welcome," but nothing comes out. I don't remember how to talk to her like a human.

She sits back when she reaches her phone, and I peer over her shoulder long enough to catch a glimpse of the busted-up screen. Giggling echoes from the opposite side of the door, and Ava's devious laugh lingers a little longer than the others. June's in here because of her. One big two-for-one prank, it seems. Ava found a way to get back at both of us, not that June deserves any of her shit. It's my fault June is even on Ava's radar and for that, I have major regrets. I said things to Ava when I was at my lowest, things I didn't fully understand, and I let my anger rule. I let secrets slip.

I step away from the chair, the metal legs screeching along the floor. The racket draws June's attention and she turns her phone brightness in my direction. My eyes dart to the ceiling and I stretch my arms up in order to avoid making eye contact with her again. It's suffocating in here, being alone with her in such a confined space. My belly itches with this need to scream. I don't know what words would come out, though. They probably wouldn't be nice, and that's not fair to her. It's just the way I've trained myself to react. Why couldn't her mom have moved? Why did they have to stay? They flaunt their smiles and carefree attitudes in front of my mom, rubbing what happened in her face. Their presence is a constant reminder, and I'm worried that one small thing will send my mom back down the spiral that almost killed her the first time.

If Ava's going to play games, I'm going to end them. I step around June and tug open the driver's side door, leaning in enough to press the garage door button clipped to the visor. I pull the opener out with me to hand it to June and let her decide her own fate. My breath catches, though, when I find her rising to her feet. The ends of her hair brush against my chest as she flips her head up. I don't think she noticed, but the feather-light tickle brought about a million memories from our past scorching to the front of my mind. Her damn hair was always getting in the way. She somehow hooked it on my braces once in the pool, and the first major haircut she had to get came after my gum got tangled in her ponytail.

My jaw flexes as I stare down at her. I've always been taller, but I swear she fits beneath me now, a perfect fit. Green eyes like emeralds, wide and frantic.

"I didn't know you were in here." The words spill from her lips in a desperate excuse, and there's a sharp pinch at my insides. The epiphany fills my chest all at once—while I've been avoiding June Mabee, she's been avoiding me right back. I drew boundaries, and she respected them. I want to ask her what she knows, to see if she's embarrassed about her mom's behavior, angry about things the way I am. But that would only rekindle our connection, and we're better off severed.

My mom is better off.

I hold the opener up for her to take, and she hesitates at first, eventually uncurling her shaking palm below my hand. I drop the device in, avoiding skin-to-skin contact as if one touch would burn me.

Our eyes meet one last time, hers still wide and uncertain. Her lips part, and I'm terrified she's going to speak again. I don't want to hear apologies on her mom's behalf, and I don't want to explain why I've been distant. I don't want to do any of this in Tory's garage, or anywhere . . . *ever.*

"Tell Ava she's a dick," I say, settling on the one true thing that June and I can agree on. I won't make this moment about us, but instead about the person who used our circumstances for her own amusement.

I leave June with the key to leave when she wants and head down the D'Angelo driveway and to the dark street toward my truck. I never look back, and when I get home, I go right to bed where I don't sleep a damn wink.

THREE

First day, senior year

I always thought I would feel like a king pulling into the school parking lot on the first day of my senior year. The reality is far less gratifying. Everyone is the same. Everything looks the same. Even *I* look the same—the same letterman jacket, my name stitched on the right side, my number on the left.

It's all so typical.

Tory slaps his palm into mine for a shake as I get out of my truck.

"Yo, Lucas! You hear about your girl June last night?"

I bristle.

"Why would I hear about June? And she's not my girl." I look around to make sure nobody is listening. I don't want people starting rumors that aren't rooted in anything other than Tory's big mouth.

"Yeah, whatever you say, man. Anyway, she called out your ex, told her she was a dick then stomped off into the sunset. Fucking epic, yo! It's all everyone's talking about."

I lift my brow and nod, feigning mild interest, but as I lean against the front of my truck and glance out toward the road leading to our school, I full-on grin. June called someone a dick. That's so completely out of her comfort zone, and I'm almost proud of her; maybe more proud of me for giving her the tools to use. I wipe the grin away before turning back to my friends.

For a few minutes, I let myself indulge in the attention. Letter jackets and workout shirts tend to catch girls' eyes. So does a six-foot-plus frame. Other than the twins, I'm probably the tallest guy on campus. And what they have on me in height I make up for in muscle mass. I get a lot of looks, and it doesn't hurt when half the cheer squad insists on giving me welcome hugs on their way from the parking lot into the school. Ava doesn't bother, and I'm relieved that I don't have to replay the scene from last night with her. I've already decided I'm dropping any class I have with her. I don't care if I have to take pottery to make up the credit hours.

That thought reminds me that I haven't picked up my unofficial transcripts from the front office. I'm sending them off to MIT, without my dad's blessing. I have to know whether I'm good enough, and if I manage to get myself in, I'll worry about the next part.

"Hey, I'll catch you at lunch. I've gotta check in with admin." I grip Tory's hand as I peel away and leave them to gossip about who's already hooking up this year.

I push through the glass doors into the office, and three guys are already sitting in a line outside the dean's office, blood on one of their shirts.

"Fighting already on the first day?" I say to Maggie, the front office secretary.

"Oh, my God, right? Freshmen," she jokes, shaking her head. She holds up a finger as she takes a call on her headset. Maggie runs just about everything up here—attendance, records, lost items, delinquents. If you're on her good side, she also takes care of you with special treats, like the Snickers bar she tosses me from the top drawer in her desk.

I unwrap the bite-sized snack and pop it in my mouth whole, spending the next minute amusing myself with the three terrified fourteen-year-olds slowly dragging their feet into the dean's office.

"You here for this?" Maggie says, drawing my attention back to her. She hands me the sealed envelope and I tap it against the counter, feeling the weight of it. It's like gold.

"Thanks," I say, smiling and winking. I can't help but ooze charm when I'm talking to Maggie. She's easy, and the fact she babies me as if I were her own kid doesn't hurt. I crave that kind of parenting, and I'm sure it would break my mom to see me eat it up. I also know the days of getting this kind of attention at home are over.

Maggie reaches forward and pats my cheek and I smile as I back away as she takes another call. I'm riding the high of a good mood as I push into the glass door to head out into the halls. I'm met with resistance—and bright green eyes. The universe has it out for me. After two years of barely catching a glance of June, I'm literally running into her everywhere.

I step to the side, waving a hand to usher her through. She does the exact same thing, then mouths a quick "sorry" when our eyes meet, and for some reason, I'm so fucking entertained a smile takes over my mouth. I correct it, but I can't erase it completely. She's still June.

It's okay to smile. It's not as if I can't be cordial, right? That's how I'll get through senior year. I'll make June an acquaintance; be polite in passing. But no talking.

She takes me up on the invitation and pushes through the door. It's heavy, and if she lets it go it's going to clang loud enough to turn everyone's heads our way, so I reach to grab the edge. Timing is everything, though, and my fingertips pass over her knuckles on the exchange. My hand curls on reflex and I abandon the door, pulling my fist back to my chest as if I've been scorched. My initial worry is that someone saw us touch—*that someone saw the way my eyes dipped and my lips parted.* In that slight millisecond, though, I also catch the blush that colors June's neck and cheeks. As far down as I have buried my instincts to care about this girl, I can't seem to keep them from showing when I least expect it.

"June!" Thank God for Maggie's enthusiasm. She rushes around the counter to hug June and hand her a packet, probably her registration papers. I take advantage of the distraction and duck out, but before the door closes behind me, Maggie calls my name.

I should keep walking. Get out of the situation—free. My feet betray me, though, as do my deeply entrenched manners when it comes to adults. My fingers find their way to the door's gap, slipping in to hold it open, and my eyes flit from June to Maggie in a flash.

"Can you take June here to your first hour? She's in your class."

Fuck.

I think I just blacked out a little. I definitely took too long to respond because Maggie is shaking the papers in her hand at me, as if rousing my attention back to the present. June grabs the papers, her cheeks once again red, probably from being embarrassed.

"Sure," I say, forcing my tight-lipped smile to make an appearance. It keeps me from talking, and I'm not sure what would come out of my mouth right now. I'd either apologize and become too friendly or vomit out the impossible position June is putting me in just by being here.

I turn, assuming June will follow me, and I'm steaming, lost in my mind, and unable to hear whatever Maggie tells her on our way out the door.

Of course June is in my first hour. And of course it's on the opposite end of campus. It's about half a mile from here. I know it is because we run the length of campus during spring football workouts. I'm tempted to start jogging now, to get this little jaunt over without us feeling the need to make small talk.

"I'll be sweaty and breathless by the time my ass finds a seat in there."

Too late. I roll my eyes at first, but I slow a step because I might be speeding a bit. Okay, a lot.

"Not my problem," I level back at her.

My throat tightens and my chest feels heavy. That was a shitty way to react, but seriously, this isn't fun for me either. She has to get it on some level, doesn't she? She should be just as mad at me. Not that what her mom did isn't worse than my father's indiscretion. I'm not even sure how many lives that woman destroyed, all for cash. June doesn't know that part, though, and as angry as I might get, I'm not cold enough to hurt her with it. It would crumble her small life. Her dad's already gone, and her grandma died while she was caring for her. No, June doesn't need a ruined relationship with her mom on top of everything else. She has enough to work through, including finding a new way to pay for college now that her mom's money stream has stopped.

I barrel through the double doors of the A building, pushing them extra wide so June has enough time to slip through. Her body bangs against one of the doors, and I wince at the thought of what that probably looked like. I'm so mad, and I need to calm down. I drill back to what the therapist told me to do when I first saw her two years ago. I close my eyes while I walk because I know the route by heart, and I draw in a deep breath, holding my lungs full for four steps before letting the air slowly stream out through my lips. My pulse doesn't seem to be slowing, so I draw in a breath again, this time opening my eyes.

"You know, it's like eighty, and humid."

June's remark fucks up my mobile meditation session. I do my best to reset but all I hear is her voice, repeating that dumb sentence over and over. I get the subtle dig. I'm wearing my letterman jacket, and she's taking a pot shot at my ego. What's funny, though, is she knows I'm not about ego. Or at least, she did. She hasn't really *known* me in a while, which means I can be whatever guy I need to in order to keep our relationship basically non-existent.

I stop in the middle of the walkway, and a small part of me hopes June is close enough behind that she'll run into my back. I'm not sure whether I want to do it to rattle her or physically touch her, though, and that tangled debate continues to mess with my head. I'm resolved to draw a firm line, regardless. If I don't, we are going to keep going on like this—swiping at each other, glaring, and then wondering what it all means.

I'm going to define it now. It means she and I can't be anything. If I rebuilt the bridge between us, it would kill my mom, maybe even literally.

"We don't have to do this, you know." I point at her, then to my chest. Her eyes draw in, that little wrinkle denting her forehead. God help me if she cries. I could never handle seeing her cry. I press on. "Pretend we have some bond or shit. You have your life, I have mine that I've built here. Just go to class, hang out with your friend, get your straight A's or whatever."

"Friends," she fires back.

Shit. Yeah, I did go there.

I shrug her response off, pretending I have no clue what she's getting at.

"You said I should hang out with my *friend*, but I have *friends*, Lucas."

I used to be one of them.

"Sure. Just . . ." I draw in a sharp breath and press my molars together. I can feel my jaw popping. I forgot how much June could frustrate me, even when we were close. I glance up and remind myself how easy life was when I could pretend she didn't exist, that she wasn't just next door. I drop my chin when I feel strong enough to push on, and I fight through the resistance to say these terrible things when our eyes meet.

"I'm just saying, it's not like we really know each other now. That's all."

I turn and head toward our class building, not bothering to stick around to hear—*or see*—her reaction. I get the gist when her shoes are no longer trotting on the pavement behind me, trying to keep up.

There are a few seats left when I file in, so I take the one in the second row, gambling that June won't want to be in the front row on her first day back. But fate has other ideas, and as the remaining students slip through the door and take up the open spots, I'm left with one empty, the one in front of me. All hopes that June changed her mind and decided to drop out—*like that would ever happen*—fizzle the moment she barrels through the door. She tries to cool her entry by catching the handle before the door slams into the wall, but it's too late. We're all looking at her.

"I'm sorry. I'm new, and I had to stop at the office." She gives her excuse, and her papers, to our teacher and I slink down in my seat and try to become invisible. It's not that June has any other choice but to sit here, but I don't have to react to it. The class giggles when our teacher calls her *Miss Mabee,* and I sneak in a raised lip on the opposite side of my face. Alliteration is funny.

"I hope you're all right with a front-row seat," the teacher says.

I glance her way briefly and avoid making eye contact as she works her way to the desk, sliding in from the side. She's trying to make herself small. I can tell, but in her efforts to wrangle her hair into a twist at her shoulder, she manages to snag her mechanical pencil, flinging it around like a yo-yo. It drops to the floor, right by my shoe.

"Oh, my God," June mutters.

Her chin is tucked into the crook of her shoulder. I'm about to put her out of her misery and bend to get her pencil when I overhear one of the girls in our class behind me.

"They totally hooked up freshman year."

That's a rumor I haven't heard in a while. People around here like to make that claim about a lot of pairings, and the only reason someone is uttering it now is because June is back, and yeah, she and I used to spend a lot of time together when we were freshmen. But it's a lie. And it's a lie I can't have making its way around town and social circles and hitting my mom's ears.

June has contorted herself in her chair, her head practically resting on my desktop at this point, her hair swimming all over the place, sticking to my jeans and my hands. I pull my palms from my desktop as she waves her arm around the floor, fingers stretching to reach her pencil. The giggling picks up steam behind me, so to end it all I tap June on the head.

"Sit up," I bark in a whisper. She does, and I feel a bit like I scolded her. I kind of did. I grab her pencil easily and hold it out for her to take. Both of our hands grip an end as I prep myself to respond with *you're welcome*, but she doesn't say *thank you*, instead hitting me with, "You could have picked it up sooner."

My mouth hangs open and a breathy laugh puffs out my chest as stifled laughter builds behind me. She's turned in her seat enough to meet my gaze, and I lock on this time, glaring at her hard. I tug the eraser from her pencil tip and toss it on the floor to punish her. *There. Take that.*

God, I'm a child.

She shakes her head at me, admonishing me with a quick roll of the eyes as she shifts back to face the front. "Good thing I don't make mistakes," she spits over her shoulder.

I feel the stares from everyone around us, and even if nobody's whispering yet, they will be. I'm irrationally mad now. More than that, I'm embarrassed. I haven't felt this ugliness since people started to talk about my dad having an affair. I tap my own pencil on the cover of my notepad, biding my time and waging war with my own thoughts, hoping I'll make a smart decision.

Be the bigger man, Lucas.

Maybe June was right about my ego. Maybe it has grown, and maybe I like it that way. How dare she take shots at it. I lean forward before I realize, my mouth hovering inches from her neck, which is now exposed thanks to her finally getting her long hair under control. I breathe, just a little, and tiny bumps form on her skin. I like the power I have over her, even when she pretends to hate me.

"June. You are so far from perfect, you have no clue."

I hang where I am for just a breath, leaving her on edge, waiting for me to say more. I won't, though. I don't need to. It's true; she doesn't have a clue. That's what this has always been about. I know our families' snarled, sordid secrets, and June doesn't. Maybe I am being cruel, but I could be so much crueler. All I have to do is let her in on the hard, cold truth.

FOUR

Two days later

"Are you trying to hype me up or melt me down?" I ask Tory as he stares down at me while hanging from the rim in his driveway.

It's not like guys can just go play quick games of pick-up football, and since my best friend is destined to play pro basketball one day, I'm relegated to being embarrassed on the court anytime we play pick-up.

"We can switch to HORSE if you want," he teases, dropping to the ground with the grace of an insect-bitten super hero.

I grimace and march over to the ball that now rests in the gutter of his driveway. It rolled there after he slammed it so hard it literally bounced back high enough to go through the hoop again.

"I should probably just get this over with. Quick and painless, like you said." I toss him the ball and he tucks it against his side, checking something on his phone.

"You know who you really should get advice from?" He flips his phone screen around to flash a photo from social media of him and June, from the class they both assist in, and I tilt my head up and fall back a few steps in sync with my eyeroll.

"Have I told you how awesome it is that you and June are instant friends again for some reason? Because if I haven't, let me now. It's so fucking awesome. Not annoying at all." I pick up my gray T-shirt and slip it on before running my hand through my sweaty hair. I swear I work five times as hard to keep up with him out here in the driveway than I do out on the football field on Friday nights.

"I do believe you're jealous," Tory says. This is not the first time he's made that remark. And *that* is *also* annoying.

"Yes. So jealous," I deadpan.

The tightness in my chest and stomach pisses me off, but I chalk it up to Tory's constant needling.

He follows me to my truck, and we slap hands before I get in.

"In all seriousness, dude, you need to have this conversation with your dad. If you want to go to MIT, then that's what you should do."

I hold his stare for a beat, trying to see myself in his eyes. I bet if Tory were dealing with this dilemma, he would take his own advice. He would do what he wanted, follow his heart. I'm so used to making sure both of my parents are happy with my decisions, though, and for my dad, me playing D1 ball has always been the dream. There are thousands of hours of Pee Wee football, youth leagues, private lessons, and trainers wrapped up in that dream. And he'll fund the incidentals for anywhere I get an offer. MIT, though? That dream is one I have to fund. Not that I don't expect to get a pretty sweet offer. Schools like that don't invite you to apply for special programs if they don't think you can hack it, and they're not willing to cover a chunk of the cost.

"I'll let you know how it goes," I say.

Before I can shut the truck door, Tory gets in one more round of advice. There's something about his expression this time that's more serious. He isn't snickering, or wiggling his eyebrows. His gaze is set and his mouth is a straight line.

"Talk to her. It will help. I know it will."

I let his suggestion fall flat, shutting my door and staring at him through the glass of the closed window. I don't know why he thinks talking to June is so important all of a sudden. I keep kicking around the idea that June secretly *wants* to talk to me, that she's planting the idea of mending bridges in Tory's head during their class. That's the guilt eating at me, though. I recognize it, from those first few weeks two years ago when I stopped taking her calls and quit looking in her direction. I knew it wasn't nice then. It still isn't. But it's necessary, and the separation has kept my mom sober and happy.

Tory isn't wrong about one thing, though. June does give great advice. Even now, with our relationship as fucked up as ever, I truly think she would want the best for me. She would support me. She always had a way of making me feel strong when I felt weak.

The glow from her kitchen window as I pull into my driveway is just another beacon calling out to me. My parents aren't home. They're at a fundraiser for one of the charities my mom volunteers for. It's in the city, so they'll be spending the night. If ever there was a time for me to break the pact I made with my mom, it would be now.

I have a built-in excuse. June's my partner for the physics project, and I would venture to guess she's working on it right now. I can stop by, chalk it up to us needing to act like adults and do a class project together. Small talk can lead to questions about our future, where she's going, and where I am. And if the mood fits, maybe, for a tiny splice in time, I can get my best friend back.

I check the garage to make sure my parents are gone, and double check the house with a quick shout inside to make sure one of them didn't stay behind. Satisfied that the coast is clear, I cross that forbidden line onto the Mabee property, not stopping until I get to the side door that leads into their kitchen. June's back is to me as I peer through the window, and the toy car tracks for our physics project are set up on her dining table. My fist forms and my arm primes to knock, despite the hot lava making its way up my throat thanks to nerves. A fraction before I connect with the door, though, her mom steps into the frame from across the room. Our eyes lock. There's no way she doesn't see me.

Before she can alert June, I turn and sprint. I don't register the distance I cover from their driveway to mine. I don't bother to rush through the garage or the front door, opting instead for the darkness of the back yard. My parents almost always leave the sliding glass door unlocked, and I'm relieved their habits haven't changed as I slide it open barely enough to fit my body through, heaving it shut behind me.

I'm breathing hard, and it's not because I ran. Maybe June's mom didn't notice. *That's absurd. We made eye contact.*

I pace, first around the table and into the kitchen then back to the glass door, my eyes scanning my back yard with a suspicion that I've been followed. I go through the same motions a few more times, my pulse finally calming when enough time has passed to assure me that June, or worse, her mom, isn't marching over to find out what I was doing.

What I was doing was indulging in what felt good. I was remembering home, simpler times when I could talk to June the same way Tory seems able to all of a sudden. It was a dumb idea. What would I have even said?

It's good June's mom caught me. She stopped me from making a huge mistake.

My palms are still sweaty so I tug open the fridge door and grab two beer bottles. I plan on drinking them both. I sync my phone to the speakers outside and put on my favorite Kanye album. I slip back through the glass door and kick my feet up in one of the loungers, popping the cap from the first beer and taking a long sip. It numbs my nerves enough to let me take a full breath.

I pull my phone out to check my messages, finding one from Ava. I stare at it, leaving it unread, as I finish the first beer.

She's bored. We broke up. Well, *I* broke us up. But we've broken up before. I'm not sure we were ever really a thing. It would be so easy to fall into old habits. Ava would listen to me. She just doesn't take in my words. And I won't get any good advice from her about how to deal with my dad. I can't bring up what happened at June's just now either. She'd lose her shit.

Ava has held a grudge against June since her eighth grade birthday party. All her friends bullied her into admitting she was in love with me. I was shocked to hear those words—terrified, actually. I knew Ava wasn't in love with me. We were barely in our teens, and the only thing she knew about me was that I played football and she liked my hair. Rather than laugh at her, I told her I was sorry but I was in love with someone else. When she pressed, I said it was June.

I don't know why I said that. It wasn't a crush I'd been harboring. It's just that when the subject of love came up, June was the only person I could think of.

I thought of June.

I set the empty bottle on a nearby table and pull the cap off number two. I'm rattled at my own thoughts. I've never self-analyzed this before, but now that I am, there has to be more to it. My stomach feels heavy, maybe a little sick, and I know it's not the beer. I can hold my beer. I've had plenty of practice. This uneasiness is something else entirely.

Instead of opening Ava's message, I find myself skimming through my list of contacts, pausing over the one name that is grayed out.

JUNE MABEE

I blocked her to protect us both. I did it to keep me from slipping, to make sure I didn't expose my mom to a message she wouldn't want to see or think I was hiding something behind her back. I knew I would be weak when it came to June.

I hover my thumb over her name, taking one more swig of liquid courage before giving in and unblocking her number. I slide across her name, pausing one more time before selecting *unblock*. The minute I do, her image populates her contact file. It's an old photo, one I took three years ago. It's a portal to our past, and I find myself studying the odd details, like her braces and the small cut on her right cheek where I hit her with a Frisbee. She wasn't looking when I threw it, sure, but June could never catch very well.

Our old messages read like a frozen moment in time, a blip before the world ended. Her question mark, waiting for my response that never came, punches me in the gut. I wonder how many messages she sent that went nowhere. I built a wall that kept it all out, but I never once considered she kept trying to get through. Or worse, *she didn't.*

I lay my phone flat on my chest and nestle into the lounger, rolling my head to the side where all I can see are the overgrown shrubs and tall grass poorly hiding the old Buick in June's yard. Her dad had plans for that thing. June always hoped he would give it to her when she turned sixteen, but that wish was a pipedream. Her mom ruined that. I bet her dad couldn't stand the thought of working on that car anymore after they split. It's probably why he left it here, abandoned.

It's easier to slip into anger. The other option is to miss June. I've been good about keeping those feelings at bay, but fucking Tory had to get all friendly with her. I hate him a little for it. A beer and a half in, I'm willing to admit I'm a tad jealous too. June's off limits, and he should respect that. If I have this massive crush he likes to tell me I do, then he should know better. I down the rest of beer number two and toss my phone on the side table then head into the kitchen to grab myself two more. I come back to a new message notification, and the fact my heart skips with hope pisses me off. As if unblocking June automatically made her text me. She's probably texting Tory.

I open to see it's Ava, and I read her message thread now that she's pinged me again. Her first message was a simple 'what's up' kinda thing, but this new one has my bad instincts tingling.

AVA: *On my way. Friend dropping me off.*

I stare at her last words and calculate the time as I crack open beer number three. I know what her message means. Ava's coming over here to fuck. That's what we do. It's not a relationship, it's an on-again-off-again itch we scratch. It isn't right, and it's not healthy for either of us, but I'm not telling her no.

Raising the music's volume on my phone, I leave it on the lounger and move to the trampoline, taking my beer with me. I kick off my shoes and throw my sweatshirt out toward the patio table then climb up to the center of the trampoline where I bounce on my toes to the rhythm of Kanye. It takes Ava two songs to show up, and by the time she reaches the trampoline, I'm so gone in my head with jealousy, resentment, and a cruel need to smudge out any pure thoughts I've had for June in the last hour.

"How was practice?" She crawls up on the trampoline, her legs parted as she sits on her knees. She couldn't give two shits about my practice. She's already unbuttoning the flannel shirt she's wearing.

I polish off my beer and toss the bottle into the grass, sinking to my knees and moving toward her. I tug on the front of her jeans as soon as they're within reach, and when they open, she gasps.

"Come here," I order.

Her mouth curls on one side and she bats her oversized lashes. Once she's close enough, I sweep my arm under her back and legs and lay her on the center of the trampoline. My mind plays evil tricks, though, and for a flash, I look down and expect to meet green eyes. I'm searching for dark hair, but instead it's waves of blonde around her face.

Ava. This is Ava.

Attempting to drown out this sudden craving for June, I kiss Ava hard, my teeth grazing her lips and neck as I nip and taste her skin. She grabs fistfuls of my gray T-shirt, and usually by this point I'm hard as fuck. Tonight, though? Yeah, I'm aroused, but it's as though my dick is waiting for something else. *Someone else.*

"Fuck," I growl. Ava assumes it's dirty talk for her, but really, I'm angry. I'm confused.

I kiss my way down her shoulder, a curve I've been on before, one I swore I'd give up. I'm so weak. I wish this was June.

What the fuck?

Squeezing my eyes shut, I press my forehead against hers as I lift myself over her body. Holding my weight up with one arm, I trace the curve of her breast down to her stomach with my fingertips. She arches against my soft touch, and I flatten my palm on her stomach.

June. Fucking June.

I bite at her bra strap, gripping it with my teeth and tugging it over the bend of her shoulder. My mouth covers her breast and the hard peak pushes through the lace against my tongue. My teeth act as a vice, clamping down on the raw tip as Ava writhes under me, her hips bucking, wanting my hand to travel lower. Something seems to be stopping me, though, and as much as I'd love to give myself credit for having self-restraint, that's not the case.

My cock is harder now, and I could lose myself if I wanted. My body doesn't care if this is Ava or June or my goddamned pillow. I need release. But it's my head holding me back. Someone *in* my head.

My fingertips push under the band of Ava's panties, and she moans into my mouth. This should be enough. I should take this all the way right now. Why the fuck can't I?

And then she's here. June is fucking here, not in my mind, not in some delusion, but actually fucking here.

Goddamn her mom for telling her I came by. That's why she's here. She's a dozen yards away, and I'm fucking grinding on Ava. I glance across the patio as June steps closer. My chin rubs against Ava's nipple and she whimpers, and the kind part of me wants to tell her to be quiet. I want to hide this from June.

Then there's the evil prick side of me that wants her to witness it. I want her to call Tory and cry about it. I want her to hate me a little more, to tell her mom they have to move. I want her out of my school, out of my fucking head.

My hand slides into Ava's panties, and she's wet and so fucking ready for me. My finger dips inside her and she moves with me. My cock flexes in my joggers. Ava pushes up into me, my hand covering her, and the momentary relief of feeling her hips roll into me draws a growling moan from somewhere deep inside my body.

Ava does the work, lifting her hips again and pushes her jeans over her curves, down her thighs. I pull them all the way from her legs, and as she kicks them away, metal scrapes along the patio about a dozen feet away.

Reality comes crashing in.

Fuck.

Fuck. Fuck. Fuck.

I run my forearm over my brow, trying to work feeling back into my face. Guilt has me in its grip. That was cruel. What I just did? I tried to hurt June, and that makes me no better than her mom and my dad and the damage they did. Squeezing my eyes shut, I lay down at Ava's side, my finger still inside her. Her leg lifts, her knee moving over my thigh, and if I let this go on, I'll be buried inside her in seconds. I won't care what it says about me. I might even pretend it's June the entire time. Ava won't care, and that part . . . that's not okay either. She should care.

"No," I grunt, pushing her leg back down and urging her to lay flat.

"Just you," I say, my eyes meeting hers briefly. She bites her lip, melting into pleasure as I tease her with my thumb and dust her mouth with a feather-light kiss. I force a smile on my face, a heavy one, full of unrelenting physical need and twisted with self-hate. I fight my thoughts, my inner voice on constant replay, calling me out for the piece of shit I am for doing this to both girls. I please Ava, because that's the least I can do. And I hold her against my chest when she's done, tickling her back with my fingertips, pretending it's June the entire fucking time.

FIVE

My head is killing me. I went through five beers last night. Ava had one. I let her sleep on the couch, and I must have fallen asleep in the chair playing that stupid rock crushing game on my phone. I don't remember nodding off, but I do remember everything else. I have to quit making bad decisions. I feel like a massive asshole. Ava's making it even worse, sitting next to me in my truck, trying to hold my hand. I keep flinching and pulling my hand away.

"You're fucking moody." She shuts the passenger door with a little extra zip and leaves me with my thoughts, heading toward her friends.

She's not wrong. I *am* fucking moody.

Tory and Hayden are sitting on the curb near their car with Cannon, the new guy. *Maybe he'd like Ava?* For a few seconds, I consider hooking him up with an intro while my eyes scan the rest of the parking lot. It doesn't take long for my gaze to meet June's. She's leaning against the front of her friend Abby's car with her arms crossed. I get the sense she's been watching me for a while, which means she saw Ava get out of my truck a few seconds ago.

I drop my focus to my door handle and swear off all things June and Ava for the next twenty-four hours as I exit my truck. My plan is foiled the second I join my friends, thanks to Tory and his nosey ass.

"You talk to June?"

I groan at his question, leaning my head back and pushing both fists into my seriously tired eyes.

"No, but I drank a six-pack of Miller and apparently invited Ava over." Tory was bound to find out anyhow. He starts laughing, covering his mouth with one hand and slapping my chest with the other. I flick it away.

"Dude, just . . . *stop*," I say.

The bell rings, so we all head toward the main doors. Cannon peels off first, and Hayden ditches us about midway through our walk. I'm acutely aware of how close June is behind me. Tory must be, too, because he keeps insisting on talking about her in his roundabout way.

"You need to quit Ava, dude. She's bad for you. And frankly, you're bad for her," he says.

"Thanks." My answer is gruff and clipped.

"I just mean—"

"You mean I should say fuck it all and get with June," I cut in.

Tory spits out a hard laugh.

"That's the *last* thing I think." He's still chuckling as I turn and glare at him. I've got a dozen more steps before he leaves me for his weightlifting class. When it becomes clear he doesn't plan on elaborating, I hold out my palms.

"What the fuck does that mean?"

He turns to head toward the weight room, spinning on his heels to walk backward. "It means I'm starting to think she's too good for you." He winks and turns to jog the rest of the way.

I can't tell whether he's joking or being serious. Whatever his intent, it pushes my buttons. I'm hungover, my head's a mess, and I still have the whole MIT conversation hanging in the balance. I practically fall into my seat for physics, and I pull out my notebook and pen so I look prepared. I'm staring at the white board at the front of the class, letting the scribbled notes blur together as my eyes relax when June literally sucks up all air within a five-foot radius. My eyes dash to her, ignoring my mental plea to not engage.

I keep spinning the pen in my hand and ready myself for her inevitable questions. *Why did I come to her house? What's my deal with Ava? Did I see her? Did I know she was there? Was I trying to hurt her?*

Mental screams echo between my ears, my answers all muddled and confused and desperate for her to tell me that none of it matters and I'll be okay. I can't believe I'm sitting here in the same clothes I wore yesterday, my breath a toxic mix of fermented wheat and grain and the milk I chugged this morning straight from the carton. The longer June stands there, just . . . just . . . smirking, the louder my inner debate grows. The bigger the threat of nausea building in my gut and throat. The more I start to see the ways Tory was not joking. Not even a little.

"What?" I finally spit out.

She reaches into her backpack and pulls out a pair of panties then tosses them on my desk.

Fucking hell. Those are Ava's.

"Pretty sure these are yours," she says. Her voice is smug. *Why isn't she hurt by this?* Clearly, Ava did this to mess with her. It's mean. It's *more* than mean. It's female psychological warfare. And yet here she stands, unscathed. Unaffected. Not a speck of jealousy.

I waited too long. June has moved on.

I puff out a laugh to mask my pain and she takes her seat. Leaning to her side, she reaches into her bag again, and I prepare to have one of Ava's bras thrown in my face. Instead, she pulls out the project she spent the night working on alone. Her mom had to have told her. She knows I tried to come by. As seconds turn into minutes, though, I realize she's done. Throwing my dirty deeds, so to speak, in my face was her big finale.

"Hey, June," I find myself saying.

She turns her head, just enough to let me get a good view of the curl of her lashes and her soft jawline marking the space between her ear and lips—perfect lips. Pouty, but not pretend. Soft. *Kissable.* Her hair is in a braid today, one that zigzags from the right side of her head to her left, loosely gathered at the nape of her neck. I lean forward enough to gently tug on it. Her lips part.

Bingo.

"Thanks," I say, letting my hand slowly cover the lacy, heart-patterned panties. Her eyes shift in rapid movements, letting me know she saw it in her periphery. I tuck the garment into my pocket and hold her stare. This time, I'm the one wearing the smug smile on my face.

"You're welcome," she says, her voice a fraction of the confident one she used before. "Don't mention it," she adds, trying to really sell how little she cares.

I know better, though. As much as she and I both have tried to erase old bonds and feelings, there's history there. And it tells me that she's as mixed up and confused about us as I am.

SIX

Friday could not come fast enough. As little as my heart beats for the game, the routine of it is comforting. And it doesn't hurt to lose myself for a little while and play the part of varsity captain. Applying to MIT? That was hard. The inevitable argument coming my way over going there instead of one of the dozen schools offering me starting roster spots will be hard. Running through a paper banner held by cheerleaders and shouting at the people in the bleachers to get up and show their support for this meaningless game is easy. It's a role I play. I'm good at it. *Maybe I should just give in to my fate.*

The emotions come easy. I lead the pack of grunting teenage boys through a guttural countdown until we all shout "Public" and I rush at the banner, breaking through, flag pole clutched in my fists, the red, white, and blue fabric waving over my shoulder as I blaze onto the field. Coach jogs toward us and I hand him my flag before I peel off with the other seniors to gather the team and lead our prayer.

I volunteered for this. It felt like my duty as quarterback. Honestly, the prayer before every game stresses me out more than getting into the end zone. I'm definitely unqualified—a sinner born from the king of sinners. But for some reason I was born with this innate ability to lead, or at least fake it really well.

The weight is heavy on my chest as I stretch my arms out and cup my hands, urging my boys in close. Our collective hot breath mingles with sweet smell of wet grass and the stench of body wrap spray, sweat and unwashed pads.

"Alright, boys. Let's do this," I begin.

Eyes closed and heads bowed, but I keep mine open for a few extra seconds, scanning my teammates for signs that one of them isn't buying into my words. I kept expecting it last season, but nobody ever caved and called me out on my bullshit. So here it goes, recycled words from the year before, rearranged a little so they sound brand new. I shut my eyes.

"Lord, we ask you to give us the strength to perform at our best tonight, to make our parents, our siblings, our fellow students and teachers proud with our actions. Let us have each other's backs, even when it's hard. Let us find the strength to carry one another one more yard when our legs are tired and heavy. Keep us safe so our mothers don't worry. Bless us with good health so we can be our best. And let us play with the same respect and sportsmanship we ask of the men on the other side of the field. In your name, Amen."

"Amen."

"Alright, let's bring it in!" Tory takes over and I finally exhale and open my eyes. I clap loud, contributing to the thunder we create as a unit with our hands while Tory yells so loudly his voice cracks. We grunt and repeat random, violent words—*hit them hard, take them out, they ain't nothin'!* It's all such a contrast to the words I just said, yet the hype easily spills from our mouths.

We break with a final clap and everyone dashes to the sideline but me. I need time alone to fully transform into the man I need to be for the next three hours. I'm going to get knocked around, flattened on my back, and I have to be in the mental state to take it, to *live* for it. Every time I lose my wind tonight, I must fill my lungs up fuller. I will find a way to score. I will be flawless on my feet. I will hit my spots, take care of my receivers and never—ever—drop the ball.

I breathe in one last draw through my nose and lift my gaze, my eyes zeroing in on my dad in the stands. He's just off the fifty, already on his feet with his arms crossed over his chest, evaluating. I don't need to be close enough to detect the details. I have them memorized—the divot in his forehead, the way he gnaws at the inside of his mouth as he formulates his evaluation of everything. No matter how perfect I am, there will be flaws for us to discuss.

This is how he loves me.

I'm realizing this is really more about how he loves himself.

My mind switches off, and for the next two hours, my body carries me through. Easy. Mindless. A golden boy. Beloved. And when the game is over, they're all cheering my name. Everyone but the guy still standing in the cleared-out bleachers, arms crossed over his chest.

I'm not much in the mood to party tonight, but the other option is going home and being held prisoner by my father's mental notes and desire to watch game film just hours after the game finished. Lucky me, my father gets the film link sent to him from the drop box, a request the coaching staff grants because they love how invested he is in the team's success.

It's a nightmare.

Pretty much everyone is going to be blitzed by the end of the night, so I offer to pile most of the offense into my truck, leaving their vehicles at school. It's not that I'm being responsible; the pressure of having to drive people out of here will keep me from getting totally shitfaced, and after drinking *way* too much the other night with Ava, I'm not interested in a repeat.

Shit. *Ava.*

I've been avoiding her the last few days. Nothing too obvious, but making myself busier than necessary to avoid having to talk about what we are and aren't. I've already heard her opinions through the not-so-quiet rumor mill. She's claiming us "back together" and is already plotting how we'll be crowned homecoming king and queen. Maybe it would be easier to go along with her plans. It would definitely keep June away.

My truck weighed down with five linemen in the back, I make one last stop to pick up a few of the cheerleaders. Two of the guys leap from the back to help Katy, the cheer captain, roll a keg down her driveway and hoist it into my truck. Her mom is either the coolest or worst on the planet, depending on perspective. She always supplies us with kegs on game nights. She's single, and behaves a lot like a teenager herself. She's shown up to a few of our parties in the woods, and I'm pretty sure she's hooked up with a senior or two. I'd rather not know the truth, so I don't ask for details when the whispering starts. The gossip doesn't seem to embarrass Katy, and maybe that's because her mom sleeping with a few eighteen-year-olds is nothing compared to what went down between June's mom and my dad, and a whole lot of other men around Allensville.

I'm sure Ava's told Katy about my dad's affair. I'm sure she's told *lots* of people. I managed to keep the truth about what went down to a small circle for two years. Originally, it was out of respect for June and my mom. Now? I just want to graduate and get out of this place without having to rehash my shitty family life. And if June doesn't know the part her mom played by now, that's on her mom. I'm sick of managing the collateral damage, and I'm even more tired of Ava holding my secret over my head as a way to pretend we're close. She doesn't overtly threaten to spill it, but the suggestion is always there. Even the other morning, after I fucked up and spent the night with her, she dropped little hints about how she's always there when I need to deal with my "trauma," and how she'd make sure June left me alone if her presence at school ever became too much for me to handle. Her hate for June has nothing to do with me and I know it. Those emotions are born of petty jealousy.

With everyone piled back into the truck, I peel down the street and out of town. One of the girls passes around an open can of beer while someone blows weed into my fucking face. My jaw is locked tight and I'm half tempted to pull over in the middle of the forest and kick every damn person out of my truck, leaving their asses to walk the rest of the way in for the party. I hold it together, though, because the other option is home, and as fucking annoying as being the bus driver for these idiots is, it still beats game film with Pops.

I press the gas when my tires hit the dirt road and a few bottles clank in the truck bed as I wind through the thick trees toward the clearing. The glow of parked cars, headlights, and the bonfire motivates me to drive faster, and when I see the front of the twins' dad's truck, a sense of relief washes over me. Their car would never make it out here.

Slamming the truck into park, I kill the engine and flop back into my seat while everyone tumbles out. They're already lit. An hour from now, most of them will either be barfing in a ditch or passed out.

When the last passenger slams the door shut, I indulge in a heavy exhale. My truck stinks. I roll down my window so maybe it will air out before I head home then hop out and scan the crowd for Tory. He's not in the mix. Instead, he's right next to me, sitting in the back of his dad's truck, holding June's hand. *What the fuck?*

I force my gaze up to my friend, but I'm not fast enough to not get caught looking. He's doing this to be a dick. It isn't cool, leading June on just to get under my skin.

"Hey, man. Can you help me with this keg?" Even with my inner voice commanding me to keep my focus on my friend's face, my eyes disobey and zero in on the place where Tory's hand is wrapped around June's. *What is she even doing here?* She hates parties. This makes two in a row. Goddamn, do I have anywhere left to hide?

"Yeah, bro. Where we takin' it?" Tory answers, his thumb stroking June's knuckles, a move he makes because he *knows* I'm looking.

Asshole.

June's had enough, thank God, and pulls her hand away, shoving her fists into the front pocket of her hoodie. I turn my attention to the keg and my tailgate.

"Uh, Jake's truck, I guess. Isn't that where the rest of the shit is?" I glance toward June without thinking and she's sucking in her lips. I can't tell whether she's embarrassed I caught her holding Tory's hand or simply uncomfortable around me. I pull my hat off and twist it around backward, studying June the entire time. Her eyes flip up nervously, and I have to admit the power I have over her makes me feel a bit smug.

Tory finally hops down but leans close to June, whispering something. I turn away before he gets the satisfaction of knowing I saw him, and a second later he's helping me hoist the keg out of the back of my truck.

"Hey, Hayden! Come give us a hand!" I shout when I spot the other D'Angelo twin. The three of us carry it over to Jake's truck where nearly everyone is gathered, including June's friend, Abby. *Why the hell was June hanging out away from everyone, alone . . . with Tory?*

Tory pats his hands together when we get the keg situated just right and I pull a cup from the stack nearby and hand it to him. He shakes his head and glances over his shoulder, smirking.

"Nah, I'm good with the shit I brought."

I hold steady until he turns back to face me and our eyes meet.

"You're good, huh?" My mouth in a hard line, I challenge him with my stare. He's fucking with me, and I'm so not in the mood to engage. If he thinks hanging out with June tonight is going to bother me, fine. Let him waste his entire night on that shit.

"Yep. I'm gonna grab a Coke for June." He reaches across my body, pulling a soda from the cooler along with a bottle of Miller, his smile growing into that aching grin of his, the one he gets when he dunks on me. *Fucking show off.*

"How nice of you," I say, rolling my eyes and turning my attention to the keg to fill a cup for myself. By the time I turn back, Tory's already jogged halfway across the clearing toward June. I drink more than I intend to on the first sip while I catch what I'm pretty sure is a genuine smile on her face, and that's the last bit of attention I plan on giving those two for the rest of the night.

"How cute. Tory's showing her pity attention. Or maybe . . . maybe he's into her." Ava's voice snakes over my shoulder just before her hands creep around my sides and slide under my T-shirt, nails clawing at my chest. I tip my cup back and swallow more beer. I should be into this. Any other guy here would kill to be in this position.

"Whatever," I mutter, turning my head and dropping my chin enough to meet her mouth. I kiss her, a move I'll regret but one that temporarily drowns out the noise in my head.

"I heard Katy brought some of the good shit. Wanna smoke?" She lifts up on her toes, bouncing.

I don't want to smoke. I hate the way that shit smells; even the pen crap meant to smell like candy smells like chemical ass. Ava knows I don't do that shit. She caught me looking at June, and she aims to keep close tabs on me.

"Yeah, I'll hang with you. But don't get stupid. I'm not in the mood to play babysitter to your high ass." I shrug her grip from my waist then down the rest of my beer before tossing the cup toward Jake's truck. I walk backward and hold on to Ava's hungry gaze, willing my mind to play along.

Quit thinking about June. Quit thinking about June . . . and Tory.

Ava pulls her mouth into a tight smile, her eyes flirting with me as she folds her hands together and holds her knuckles to her lips.

"Be right there," I say, scolding myself internally for the direction I'm headed.

"Hey, bro!" Tory slaps my back before I spin around. I twist and meet his palm mid-air with my own and we shake.

"I hear Katy brought a blunt!" He points over his shoulder to the thick forest Ava slipped into when I walked away. I nod and my friend shoots me a crooked smile. He doesn't smoke often, but the few times he has have made him a nightmare to deal with. He gets paranoid, and childish—somehow more immature than he is normally. He's left June to sit alone in the back of the truck, and I feel a little twinge in my gut. I'm worried he's going to abandon her there. She'll sit there waiting for him to come back, because that's how she is—trusting. *Gah! Why do I care?*

"You comin'?" He cocks a brow.

I nod.

"Yeah, give me a minute."

His gaze darts over my shoulder, toward June, and an arrogant chuckle escapes his mouth.

"I'm just checking my truck. Relax," I lie.

"Uh huh," he says through a growing smirk. He holds up his empty beer bottle and spins around, so damn sure he caught me.

I keep my eyes on the ground most of the way to my truck, taking a wide route so June can't see me walk up. I left my phone in the center console, so I pop into the driver's side unnoticed and grab my cell before moving toward the back of the truck to lift the tailgate. The latch has been giving me trouble lately, and naturally, it's in rare form tonight. It takes me three tries to get it to catch, and I feel June's eyes boring into me without even looking to confirm she's staring.

I should just walk away. The smart move would be to head in the other direction, to follow the same path I took here. *Do not engage, Lucas Fuller. She and Tory and whatever the hell bond they're forming is none of your business.*

Against my best judgement, I look up. Her eyes are waiting. My chest burns. I look back down and press my molars together, my jaw popping. I breathe out through my nose and shake my head.

"Be smart with that," I say, nodding toward Tory. He's chugging a beer now, and he's about to take a hit. He's going to act like a real asshole soon. June twists to look in his direction and I adjust my hat, spinning it so my brim hides my view of her.

"You jealous or something?"

I can't believe she said that. I chuckle quietly, my eyes on the ground. *Yeah. I am. I'm fucking jealous, and I hate it because I don't want to care about you.* Those feelings? They stop right now.

I pop my head up and give her a crooked smile.

"Sure, June." I force my eyes to remain indifferent, my stare blank. I've got a slight buzz forming from the beer, so I give in to it and let it wash away the tightness in my belly. I can tell it's working by the way her cheeks flush and her eyes shift from side to side. I made her feel uncomfortable, and I feel both guilty and satisfied.

I leave before I say anything else—*before she responds*—and make my way toward Ava and the others who are getting drunk and high by the riverbed. I take a seat on one of the flat rocks near the small trickle of water and Ava plops herself onto my lap, her laughter loud and obnoxious. I'm not sure how many minutes pass before I snap out of my head—an hour perhaps? But after tuning out everyone around me, I'm abruptly brought back to the present as Ava leaps from my thighs, her sudden ire focused on a now-full truck bed. Tory made his way back to June, and half of Ava's old friend circle is sitting with them, laughing.

"I wonder if they know what a social pariah she is." Her words come out in a slur, but she's coherent enough that I sense the dangerous anger in her tone. She's going to make a scene.

"Just leave her alone. Come back. We were having a nice time," I say, reaching my hand out to her and curling my fingers. Her eyes dip to my hand and for a moment, I think she might be giving in. Then another round of laughter echoes across the way, drawing both of our stares in their direction.

Ava punches out a laugh and tosses her hair over her shoulder as she looks me in the eyes.

"Your mind has not left her all night. Don't you fucking lie to me, Lucas Fuller," she seethes.

I sigh, because that's what I'm supposed to do. She isn't wrong, though, and I'm pretty certain she sees through my sad attempt.

"No, she needs to go. She's not welcome here," Ava mutters, her hands forming fists as if she knows how to use them. I don't doubt that drunk and angry, Ava could be a scrappy handful. But she's never really thrown a punch, and she sure as shit isn't athletic. June outweighs her by twenty pounds. Not that June's a fighter either, but I think she'd defend herself if she had to. Ava wouldn't stand a chance.

"Ava, stop," I call after her, pushing myself up from the rock. Nobody around us seems to be paying attention, thank God. But she catches enough eyes during her march across the clearing toward June and the others to make this scene worthwhile.

"Fuck," I breathe out, dropping my hands into my pockets and feeling for my keys. I need to get her out of here.

I'm not sure what Ava said to make June leap from the back of the truck, but the fact she just did has me doubling my strides toward them. And when June hauls off and slaps her, I break into a jog. I reach the two of them just as Ava regains her balance and lunges at June. I thrust an open palm against Ava's clavicle and manage to catch June's oncoming fist in my other hand. June's eyes are red and wild. I'm not sure what Ava said, but I have a feeling it was personal and cruel.

"You!" I stare into Ava's eyes, willing her to peel her crazed gaze from June and onto me. There goes any hope of keeping this incident low-key. Everyone, and I mean *everyone,* has gathered around us to watch.

"Lucas—"

"Get your ass in there. That's enough!" I push her toward my truck, and she pouts but jerks her body away from me, thank God in the right direction.

Behind me, June begins to laugh. This is a game to her. Being at this party, in my business, next to my house—in my life. A fucking game! *Doesn't she get it?*

"Just . . . fucking stop, June," I plead, rolling my head until my eyes land on her. She freezes under my stare, her eyes wide with shock as her shoulders drop and her muscles relax. I let go of my hold on her wrist and shake my head.

"Your mom's a fucking whore, you know!" Ava shouts from behind me.

I spin around and point at her.

"I said get your ass in my truck!" She's drunk. That's what I'll tell June. High and drunk and . . . mean. Everyone knows she's mean.

I turn my attention back to June, and while I figure she'll be hurt, the pure devastation that seems to have colored her cheeks and sunk in her eyes catches me off guard. Ava's a bully. This can't be the first time she's said something like this to June, can it? Or maybe it is. Maybe June doesn't even know how close to the truth Ava's insult is.

Now is not the time to sort this out. I'm not her therapist. I'm nobody's therapist. June's lips part with a hopeless breath, and before she can speak, I shake my head, backing away from the girl I used to run to when I felt the way her eyes tell me she feels right now.

"Is she your girlfriend? That?" June grunts out a laugh and points to the passenger side of my truck. Thank God the door is shut, otherwise I'm sure Ava would come out with her claws ready. *Don't do this, June. Don't make this worse.*

"Or is she just some girl you fuck? No matter what, you know she's part of your story now. That . . . that is what you are."

We are surrounded by silence. I don't even think the people staring at us are bothering to breathe, too afraid they'll miss some of the drama. My teeth clench and I meet June's stare, her eyes glossed with tears she wants to shed but is too angry or stubborn to.

No, June, she is not my girlfriend. And yes, June, she's some girl I fuck. And it's none of your business. See, I'm a piece of shit just like my dad, but at least I don't make promises to people only to break them. I don't wreck marriages and bust up families.

I hold those thoughts in, despite the fire raging in my chest. They aren't the right words to say; they're fueled by hate and anger—reactionary. I would only make things worse, pour gas on smoldering embers. In less than a year, I'll be out of here. Out of June's life and away from my parents. I can keep my mouth shut until then.

I lean forward a tick, eyes still squared with hers, and I spit on the ground, turning my glare toward Tory. I swear he's smirking as he holds up his open palms and plays innocent. Fucking pot-stirrer, that's what he is.

I turn my back to June and climb in my truck, firing it up and pulling away from this nightmare with enough zip that my back tires kick dirt up at the lingering onlookers. That's what they get, nosy fuckers.

Thankfully, Ava doesn't pick a fight with me until we're well on our way toward home. I'd love to lay on the gas and speed our asses home, but my breath is still fresh from that beer and the last thing I need to deal with is getting pulled over and hauled in for my dad to come pick up.

"She started it, you know. She *always* starts it." I figured Ava wouldn't be silent the entire way home.

"She didn't start anything." I sigh.

"You always defend her!"

I glance to my right in time to see her huff in her seat and cross her arms over her chest like a petulant child. I chuckle at it, which pisses her off even more.

"You do!" Ava retorts.

"Sure, whatever," I mutter, rolling my gaze away from her and back to the road. We're back in town, minutes from her house.

Even Ava's silence is obnoxious. She fidgets for attention, sighing and shifting her legs, tucking one leg under the other only to switch them seconds later. She wants me to console her, or to pull over and have it out so we can end up making out. I'm not in the mood. Honestly, all I want in the world is to be alone.

I pull to a hard stop in front of Ava's house and her hands fly forward, slapping against the dashboard.

"Jesus, Lucas!"

I breathe out heavily and tighten my grip on the wheel, preparing myself. *Please, just get out of my truck. Get out of my truck. Get out of my truck. Get out—*

"Are you in love with her?"

Fuck.

Ava grips my arm, tugging it from the steering wheel and toward her chest so she can hold on to it. It's a power play move she does, clinging to me physically to express some weird desperation.

"Tell me, Lucas. Is that why you let her get away with so much?

Because you love her?" Ava has been jealous of June since junior high. Back then, yeah, I had a crush on June, and we were close. Ava always had a thing for me; therefore, June was the enemy. It's been literal years now, and Ava is fully aware of the bad blood between my family and June's. She's looking for attention.

"No, Ava. I'm not in love with her." I shrug the rest of her tirade off as I sink into my seat while she continues to hang on to me. I want her to get out of my truck, to go inside and not call me the second I drive away. I want to take back that night on my patio that should never have happened. Hell, the entire year of off-and-on hookups between us—take those back too!

I run my palms over my face as I groan.

"All I want, Ava. No . . . all I *need,* is for there to be nothing linking me with June Mabee other than our goddamn property line. And when you start shit with her, all you do is force me to acknowledge her, talk to her. I don't want to do any of that. Do you understand?"

"I'm sorry." She hums two words she doesn't mean. She wants me to console her and tell her it's okay, but I'm not that guy. I don't know why she thinks I would be. I've never been that way with her. I'm not sure I'm capable of being conciliatory. Loving. Fuck, I'm barely amicable.

"You drank a lot tonight. Go inside and get some rest. We'll talk tomorrow, when we both have clear heads."

I'm pinching the bridge of my nose so hard I may actually crack the bone. Ava sidles closer to me and raises herself enough to press her lips to my cheek. I shift my eyes as she does, glaring at her. I'm not doing this.

"You're right. I don't know what came over me. I just get so angry at her, seeing her, knowing what she did—"

"What her mom did," I correct. That's the one line I won't let Ava cross. She's intent on ascribing June's mother's misdeeds to June herself, and that's not fair. She can resent June for plenty of other reasons she's cooked up in her head, but that one isn't going to fly, not ever.

"Whatever." She shrugs my response off and pops open the door, slipping out of the seat, her balance a little off. She's playing it up some. She's drunk, but I've seen her knock back several shots of tequila and walk just fine. This little show is for affect.

"Call me," she says, hazing her eyes and blinking slowly as she tugs at the frayed bottom of her cropped T-shirt. A month or two ago and I would say fuck it and tell her to climb back in here with me. Something's changed. *I've* changed. I'm not sure why, but I feel it.

Ava shuts the door, her eyes flaring when I let it latch, and before she can grip the handle and jerk it back open, I drive away. I crank the music up and smack my palms against the steering wheel, keeping time with this new rapper Tory's got me listening to. I like the guy's lyrics, but they hit a little close to home when he repeats the phrase *girls from your past show up like ghosts.* I flip the stereo off and drive the rest of the way home in silence.

I sit in my driveway for several minutes, the motor off and lights out. It's peaceful in this small space. Nobody yelling, zero passive-aggressive digs about fidelity, no game film and coaching tips from a forty-five-year-old has-been. I'm tempted to spend the night in my driver's seat, but when my cab lights up with the glow from a pair of headlights pulling into June's driveway, I slink down and curse myself for not going inside sooner.

June drove her mom's van. I can barely see the top of her head as she climbs out of the driver's seat. I hold my breath, listening for the sound of another door or the sliding one on the side. After a few seconds of silence, I exhale, glad June's come home alone. For some reason, I feel that if Abby were with her she'd be braver, more likely to march over to my truck to inspect the insides or pound on my front door and demand to see me. She's alone, though, so I sit up and spy as she hovers at the edge of her driveway and stares up at the sky. Eventually, she runs the back of her palm over her eyes and slumps her shoulders, heading inside. She leaves her back door slightly ajar, and I'm both curious and cautious. The longer she's inside and the door remains open, the more jacked up my nerves become. I can't let her go to bed with her door beckoning some intruder. I'll have to close it, which puts me way too close to that house. Again.

I'm reaching for my door handle when June suddenly appears from the house. I sink lower in my seat but look on as she shuffles toward the thick weeds and tall grass near the back of her driveway. That brush obscures her dad's old Buick. That relic is the only thing he left behind when he moved out.

The familiar creak of the car's door cuts through the quiet air, penetrating its way into the cab of my truck. The *clunk* of the door closing comes next. It's been awhile since I've seen June wander out there. She and I used that car like a playhouse, and as we got older, we hid in there and watched scary movies on my phone. For a while after her dad left, she would sit in that car late at night. I caught her looking up at my window once, and I'm not sure whether that's why she quit hiding in there or the car just lost its luster. Tonight, though? The Buick called to her.

I pull one leg up and rest my arm on my knee, staring into the darkness for any sign of movement. There's no glow from a phone, so she isn't in there texting Abby or reliving the night on social media. That sort of stuff isn't really June's style anyway. Not that I know *what* her style is anymore. My gut tells me some things haven't changed. She's still the type of girl who would rather spend the night on the fringe of a party than in the mix of things. But I never pegged her as one to drop the kind of words she did tonight. Maybe the June I remember has blurred into something else entirely. It would make sense, given what she's been through. I know how the last few years have changed me—how what our parents did changed me.

I feel trapped in this truck, and part of me wonders if she's sitting in the Buick staring right at me, waiting for me to make a move so she can rush out and pounce, blasting me with more insults. What was that bullshit about my story? *Pffft.* I've never been in control of my narrative. She knows that. Every line of my life is written by my dad's wishes. Any freedom I had was dashed by his mistakes. I'm the way I am because cold and callous doesn't require feeling. I wrote June out of my story because I wanted to keep my mom in it. And if she thinks that makes me an asshole, fine. I'm an asshole. She's an asshole, too.

After twenty minutes of stewing, I decide to put an end to this charade. I thought I'd been distant enough, unfriendly and unwelcoming. Now, I'm going to be mean and direct. I hop out of my truck and ease the door closed. She doesn't need to know I've been watching her this whole time. I cut my way through the brush, and by the time I'm four or five yards away, our eyes meet. My hand knows what to do, operating on memory as it tugs open the piece of shit passenger door, popping loudly when the spring catches. I get in, my weight kicking up a cloud of dust from the old seat.

"You didn't have to come check on me. I'll survive." June's tone is coated with contempt. Unlike Ava, June doesn't fish for affection. She lashes out. She and I are more alike than she realizes.

I sigh as I slap my hands on my knees and curl my fingers, clawing against the denim.

"I'm not here for you, June. I'm here to tell you—no, to *beg* you—to please keep your nosy ass out of my life." There, I did it. No mystery to solve with my request. There is no secret, hidden message, no undercurrent that contradicts what I'm asking.

I glance at June as her mouth falls open, and I can feel it in my bones that she's going to argue with me. I can practically hear her response formulating in her head—*I didn't do anything, Lucas. It was all Ava.* Still, she was there, at a party I damn well *know* she didn't want to be at. She's inserting herself into my life just to needle me with her presence. I don't know whether she thinks it will wear me down or that I'll suddenly cave and decide being friends with her is worth sending my mom down a spiral again right before I leave for college. But it needs to stop. This game between us . . . it's done.

I shake my head, twisting in the seat, taking up space to command this exchange. My palm covers the dash, more dirt and debris puffing into the air.

"You judge—" I begin.

"No, I don't."

I groan inwardly as my eyes flutter shut in frustration. So damn quick to argue with me. I pat down on the dash again, laughing out hard.

"You do, and it's so . . . hypocritical. What I do with Ava, whether she's my girlfriend, whether we break up, whomever I decide to be with and however far that goes? None. Of. Your. Business."

I lean back and level her with an angry stare. My pulse is drumming, and I'm tempted to scream I'm so frustrated that I have to have this conversation right now. I hope like hell my mom isn't seeing this.

"You missed most of everything I said, Lucas. I wasn't talking about you. That rant—it was about me."

Bullshit. I hold her gaze hostage, unwilling to blink.

"I heard you. And you're right, every person you *fuck* becomes a part of your story."

June swallows hard as I throw her words back at her.

"But people write themselves into our stories lots of ways, June." I shake my head and look down at my lap. My fingertips draw lines in the dust as my hand falls from the dash. My throat burns. As hard as I try to close this door, it's still painful being this close to her. Memories of *us*—of my friend and the girl who made me laugh and do stupid things like make snow angels in the winter—break into my armor. I can't let them.

I push the door open, stopping just outside to lean down and level her with one final glare.

"We've never fucked, but you sure are part of my story. I can't delete you, but I sure don't need you taking up any more chapters. Stay the fuck out of my business, and go find yourself a boyfriend who can be all of these things you think are real."

I force out a quick laugh as my mouth ticks up on one side, then slam the door behind me. The urge to turn around and apologize is instant.

That was easily the cruelest I've ever been, and I'm ashamed. I told myself it was necessary, but now that I'm on the other side of it all . . . I'm not so certain. Those are the worst words I have ever uttered, and I said them to the one person I used to consider the most important person in my life.

One foot in front of the other, that's my mantra all the way back to my house. One step after the other, until I'm upstairs. I drop the shade because if I don't, I'll spend the rest of the night trying to catch a glimpse of the girl I just broke into a thousand pieces inside a Buick. And then my heart will beg me to put her back together.

SEVEN

My mom is dragging my dad to church. She does this every few months, and he goes because he knows it makes her happy. I think she likes that everyone there doesn't know the history of their marriage over the last few years. They're this perfect couple, and she can play the professional married to a lawyer who is so busy—too busy to join her every Sunday.

I opt out every time. It's a few hours to myself at home, and it's blissful. Today's stint stretched into the evening, though. My parents were invited out to dinner, and they went. I spent the entire day going through old things in my closet and filling two trash bags with crap that doesn't fit. My dad probably wants to hang on to my old jerseys so he can make a shrine or some shit, but I'm not going to give him the chance. I might regret it, but for now it feels right to shed this old stuff, so I go with it.

My phone buzzes as I drop the stuffed bags into the back of my truck. I pull it out and answer without looking. It's Ava.

"Hey, I'm hungry and the girls are at Two-fers. Come pick me up?"

I stop at my door with one foot inside and pinch the bridge of my nose. My stomach rumbles.

"Yeah, I guess I'm hungry." *You should make a sandwich at home, Lucas. You know you're giving in to her trick. She wants to spend time with you, and you're weak. You feel guilty because you were mean to June. Now you want to cover it up with an Ava-shaped Band-Aid, you fucking loser.*

"Awesome. See you in five." She hangs up before I can back out, not that I would. My conscience puts up a pathetic fight. Besides, it would be nice to be gone by the time my parents do get home, stretch this day of bliss out as long as I can.

I hop in my truck and peel down our street, slowing when I see the twins' car heading my direction. It's Tory, probably on his way to my place. We stop next to each other and roll down our windows.

"Hey, Tor. What's up?" My body is jumpy. I'm literally sneaking out to see a girl I don't want to and if Tory asks, he'll give me shit about it.

"Just . . . out." He shrugs and puckers his lips into his signature smirk. He's up to something.

"I'm headed to Goodwill, dropping off some donations." I tilt my head toward the back, as if I need to show him visual proof. He glances toward the bed of the truck and nods.

"Ah." His smirk lingers.

"You need something?" My eyes squint in consideration, part of my top-notch acting job.

"Nah. I'm good." His answer is quick, and it digs at me a little, my face morphing into a questioning expression with an eyebrow up, head cocked.

"Thought I'd see what June's up to. Maybe ask about working at the bowling alley with her." *And there it is.*

"Oh, yeah? That's a good idea." I force a tight-lipped smile on my face in follow-up, and Tory does the same. Eventually, a laugh slips out his mouth.

"You going out with Ava?" He lifts a brow, so damn proud he caught me.

I shrug.

"I dunno. Maybe. She mentioned something about grabbing dinner at Two-fers with some of her friends. I'm pretty hungry." *Or I was hungry until I ran into Tory and he dropped June's name.*

"Oh, yeah? Maybe I'll swing by. You know . . . after." He looks toward the Mabee house, and I know that mind of his is scheming. I wish he'd drop this fascination with me and June. If he's truly into her, then he should ask her out and they can date. It's fine. Whatever.

"Yeah, well, I should get going." I give him a nod and he reciprocates as we pull away from each other. I leave my window down so the rush of air can hit my face in an attempt to wash away the deep wrinkle I feel between my eyes. I get that line when I'm pissed or anxious. The last thing I need is Ava asking about it, offering to give me a head rub.

My pulse feels less like a death metal drummer living in my chest by the time I pull up to the Goodwill. I toss my bags into the donation bin and head to Ava's house. She's on her phone when I pull up to the curb and she keeps talking to whomever is on the other line as she gets into the truck. I do my best to ignore her conversation, something about dress shopping for the winter formal that's not for a few weeks. She ends her call just as we pull into Two-fers and unbuckles her belt so she can slide closer to me. My arms stiffen, and she huffs audibly.

"This place is really going downhill," she announces, crossing her arms over her chest.

At first, I assume it's some petty reaction to my cold shoulder, but I get what she means the second I look to my left and see Tory's car pulling through the end of the drive-thru lane, June in the passenger seat. *That motherfucker.*

I park near Ava's friends, and thankfully, she gets out of the truck and starts gabbing before she realizes Tory and June stuck around. I'm sure it's no coincidence that he's here with her, after I dropped the info about where I was going. I'm also certain he parked where he did—fifty feet away and staring right at us—on purpose.

I slip out of the truck and glance their direction, glad they aren't looking my way. I stop at the bumper and pat my hand on the hood, getting Ava's attention.

"What do you want?"

She bunches her face as if she's going to get anything other than a chicken wrap and a water. It takes her about five seconds to answer—"chicken wrap and a water."

"Right," I say, turning and laughing quietly at the predictability.

I dash to the walk-up window and place our order, leaning against the wall while I wait. I pull my phone out and drop a text to Tory.

ME: *Classy move, bro.*

I wait a few seconds for him to write back, but he doesn't. He probably won't in front of June. I push my phone into my back pocket when my name is called and grab our bag of food before jogging back to my truck.

I hand Ava her food and she sets it on the passenger seat so she can keep talking about whatever the latest rumor is to travel through her circle of friends. I'm not fully engaged, but I hear someone cheated on someone else, and it sounds as if they're blaming it on the new guy, Cannon. I lean toward the window to get Ava's attention.

"Hey, don't do that." I shake my head, chastising her.

She holds up two open palms.

"What?"

"You know what." My chest deflates. This is the reason I could never fall for her. She's too focused on drama—making it, spreading it, turning it into a forest fire of bullying. "Cannon's a good guy. He just got here, and he's here for baseball and that's it. Don't rope him into your web of immature bullshit." I circle my finger in the air for affect, which earns me a harsh glare.

"You're in a mood," she huffs back, glancing down at her food and drink. She grabs it and makes brief eye contact with me before turning her attention back to her friends. If she wasn't here, they'd be talking about her right now, because that's the sad reality of it. That's who they are.

She's part of your story now. That . . . that is what you are.

June's words haven't left my mind for two days. She was trying to hurt me back, and I know that, but she was also on point. *Who am I? Am I the guy who sits in this parking lot talking shit about people who aren't here to defend themselves?* I glance around, pods of people all doing the same thing Ava and her friends are. Then I shift my gaze back to Tory's car, where he and June are laughing. She punches his arm lightly, which she used to do to me. I rub my bicep instinctually just before catching Tory leaning toward her with what looks like a packet of ketchup.

"You don't put ketchup on hot dogs, you asshole," I mutter to myself. My lip curls into a familiar grin on one side the moment June pushes his hand—and the offending ketchup—away. She and I once spent an entire summer watching Dirty Harry movies, and our big takeaway was that Clint Eastwood hates ketchup on hot dogs. It was our inside joke every time we went to Two-fers.

Laughter booms from outside my side window, catching my attention. Ava and her friends have noticed June, a few of them craning their necks, no doubt making up stories about her hooking up with Tory. She wouldn't give him the time of day like that. And he wouldn't cross that line. At least, I don't think.

I look back to the car, to the lightness in their movements, the way June picks up her soda and sucks at the straw through a smile. I'm a voyeur, and my stomach twists inside itself. I shouldn't care about any of this, but I can't stop indulging in looks inside that car. I want to know what they're saying. I want to know how Tory got her to come here, whether he said I would be here or if he tricked her, as I assume he did.

I pick at my fries, watching the scene before me like a guy alone at a drive-in movie, munching on my snacks and watching the slow, unwinding plot that's narrated by thoughts in my head. *Would I be okay if Tory dated June?* I said I would be—to him, to myself. I really don't think I would.

I'm caught in this inner debate when movement catches my eyes and breaks my stare into nothingness. I'm instantly drawn inside Tory's moving car as he slowly pulls out, and June glances up from her lap in time for our eyes meet. It's brief. No light glares glinting off the windshield or cars driving between us to break the connection or distract us. Everything gets undeniably slow, but it's only that way for the two of us. Her lips part, and even though there's no way I possibly can hear her, I swear I do. There's a gasp. It's painful, filled with our youth, our past, our friendship, and that constant *what if* that was there between us. It's changed. It's become a *why.*

Why are we so broken?

I follow her profile when she turns away, and I watch Tory's taillights fade in the distance. Fighting the urge to dump the rest of my food and ditch Ava so I can follow them home, I pull out my phone to see if my friend has texted me back. His answer is short, and the last thing I need to consider.

TORY: *Jealous?*

EIGHT

I rolled up to school late this morning, leaving myself barely enough time to slip into class. I'm sure Tory spent the morning congratulating himself on making me jealous or admit to feelings for June, thinking that's why I was late. I wish it was. As loathe as I am to deal with that emotional baggage, it would be a million times easier than the shit pile my dad threw on my lap this morning.

"This is Jon Foster, from Tennessee."

I was barely awake when I ambled down the stairs into our kitchen. Apparently, Jon Foster met my dad during their dinner. He's friends of a friend from the church my dad has no honest interest in attending. Never one to miss a chance to network, Todd Fuller was at his very best last night and managed to lure the new head of recruiting for his alma mater over to our house for breakfast. My dad wasn't a stud in his day, which is half the reason he put the effort into making me good. But he was good enough to get a back-up gig at Tennessee, and still be a name people recognize, though they aren't totally sure why.

"Now, this isn't an official visit, you understand, Lucas?" Jon Foster winked as he shook my hand and spoke those words. Of course I understand. This is how my dad has brokered half of these meetings. They've all turned into offers, so it's not that he doesn't know the game. It's that I don't want to participate. He's bringing these people to our home under false pretenses. They're getting sold a bill of goods—*me*. I will never be the player they think they'll get if I commit to their school. My heart isn't in it.

I sat through breakfast and nodded when it seemed I should. My dad did most of the talking, as is the norm, and I managed to skip out of there with mere minutes left to get to school. Dad was ready to call me in sick. Mom ignored the entire situation, gathering her things to head out for work, a scowl on her face because my father was gushing over some stranger he just met more than he ever has for her.

I guess if there's a bonus to any of this, it is that my rushed morning left me zero time to interact with June. Other than the staring contest in the Two-fers parking lot, we haven't made eye contact once since I said those things to her in the Buick. As soon as the guilt begins to ebb, something happens and it comes roaring back to my belly. It creeps up in the weirdest ways, too. Like when I spotted the bottle of ketchup in our refrigerator this morning during breakfast.

"Lucas, I need to see you after class for some recommendations I was asked to submit," our teacher says as I take my seat.

"Sure. Thanks," I answer. My eyes train on June's neck and the small swirls of hair that curl at the base. She doesn't flinch at my voice and I fight the urge to taunt her.

Jealous?

Tory's text hit me square in the face again this morning. I was flipping through my phone, trying to stem my anxiety while my dad talked me up to the rep from one of the country's top colleges. I'm man enough to admit to myself that I am jealous of Tory and June's relationship. I envy him for being able to talk to her so easily, to laugh with her. I bet she gives him great advice. I'm sure she's making him a better person—*not hard, since he's a total douchebag*. Jealous romantically? I didn't think so, yet here I am, wanting to pull her braids and doodle a smiley face on her neck, like a fourth grader with a stupid crush.

I slouch into my seat and set my focus on the front of the classroom. I'm not really listening, but I manage to copy down the notes on the screen. I pick up the sealed envelope from my teacher when she dismisses us. It's not until I'm out the door that I read it and realize it's made out to MIT with room for me to fill in the admissions address.

I stop mid-stride and peel off to the quad, taking a seat atop one of the picnic tables. Holding the envelope up, I study it closely to see what words I can make out. At least four of my teachers had to fill out this form, answering questions about my academic record and character. *My character.* They hold my future in their hands—in this envelope. I could rip it open and read what they wrote, beg Maggie for a new stamped envelope with the school logo and type up the address at home. But what would that say about my character?

My character.

That temptation is quickly dashed as I glance over my shoulder and catch a glimpse of June opening the door to the media center. That's fate telling me to put the envelope away and let it be whatever it will. I've already used up my questionable character free pass with this girl.

I zip my personal Hail Mary for my future into my backpack and sling the strap over my shoulder. That's when my gaze comes square with my father's. He's here. On campus. With his new friend.

I breathe in deeply and try not to let my true feelings make their way into my expression as I stride across the quad toward him.

"Hey, pal." My father reaches out a hand to shake and then pats me on the back with the other. He has never done this. *We* have never done this. It's a performance, and I'm going along with it. I hate myself a little.

"Jon wanted to check out the school, talk with Coach. Ya know." Dad nods and winks, his signal that another offer—his favorite yet—is in the bag.

"Great!" I beam, my smile aching where it presses into my cheeks. I reach an arm around to press my palm on my dad's back. If I look as though I'm playing the part, he's less likely to rope me into lunch or something. "I'm sorry I have to run. I have a lab to finish for chemistry. I look forward to seeing you out there today."

I point toward my dad's new temporary best friend and smile as I skip backward. When I turn my back, I hear my dad mention something about my academic work ethic. I should feel proud, but honestly? I hate that the only reason he brags about my brains is because he thinks it will give me an edge in football recruiting.

I lied about the lab. I finished my work last week, which *thank God!* I spend the rest of the hour sitting on my stool by my clean work station while I research various techniques for seeing through envelopes on my phone. To keep myself from dwelling on the envelope for the rest of the day—and from doing something stupid with it—I jet home during lunch and fill out the address, pop on a stamp from my mom's desk drawer, and drop the documents in the postal box on my way back to school.

The act takes away my temptation, but it does little to stop me from thinking about my future and MIT. In fact, the second I mail that last piece of admissions content off, my brain goes into overdrive with panic. I'm not sure which has me freaked out more—failing and not getting into the special program or getting the call that I'm in and having to make a choice.

I obsess over that quandary through my last two hours of the day. Usually, in a situation like this, I would race to practice, ready to take snaps and sweat out half my body weight. The one thing practice is good for is letting me clear my mind. But my dad made sure that wasn't possible today. Coach Loma is in his office with Jon Foster as I walk into the locker room. A few of the guys recognize him. He's wearing a subtle Tennessee polo shirt, and that name carries serious weight in this room.

"Dude, you see that?" Tory elbows me while he stands on the other side of the bench, bare-ass naked.

"I'd rather not," I joke.

"Ha! Funny," he deadpans.

He steps over the bench, pulling his practice gear out to get dressed. He doesn't press me again about the meeting happening a dozen feet away until Jon Foster leaves Coach's office.

"Are you seriously going to pretend you know nothing about that?" Tory's sitting now, straddling the bench and facing me while I suit up.

I drop my arms as soon as my pads are on and let my eyes stare at the back of my locker. I blink a few times and chew at the inside of my mouth.

"You know I wish I could be like you, right?" I say, turning to face my friend, whose face is screwed up and confused.

"You mean *so good looking?*"

I snort out a laugh. I needed that.

"No, man. I mean . . . I wish I wanted this. Like you with basketball. That's your passion." I glance toward Coach's office. He's on the phone with someone, but our eyes meet and he shoots me a crooked grin. I know he's excited about this visit.

"I knew what you meant. But seriously? You are like me, only in your way," Tory says, standing and slamming his locker door shut. He backs up a few steps, giving me room to lace my cleats.

"I am?" I'm not so sure about that. It would be so much easier to take what's being offered.

"Dude, you want to use your brain the way I want to break ankles on the hardwood and dunk on power forwards who are too slow. You have the same level of passion. You just happen to be good at two things. Guess I'm lucky I'm only good at one. Oh, I mean, I'm also an amazing lover, so there's that."

"*Pshhh*, fuck off!" I smack his chest as I stand.

Tory's words do their job somehow, and I jog out to the field with a clearer head. I guess it doesn't hurt to entertain these football scouts as a backup, in the event those forms I mailed today have nothing good to say about my character. If my dream comes in, though, I'm going to need another pep talk. I'll need to grow some balls for when Brainy Lucas lets down everyone rooting for Football Lucas.

NINE

If I didn't see her every morning in our shared class, I would start to wonder if June transferred out. Other than our forced contact, she's nonexistent in my world. It's exactly what I wanted—for her to leave me alone.

I hate it.

It's sick, but I think I miss the push and pull. I fought against myself all week to not do *something* in class. I flirted with the fantasy of attaching a paperclip to the end of her braid just so she'd get pissed at me. I also thought about showing off my test grade, since I aced it and saw over her shoulder that she got a B. And when I passed her in the office after school yesterday, I noticed that her shoe was untied. I was going to offer to tie it for her and then leave it in knots. Why I have to be such a childish bully in every scenario, I haven't a clue. But I know it has to do with missing that feeling I get when she and I are arguing, even if it's only giving each other a heated glare.

Everything about this week has me feeling off. My dad and Jon Foster, the mountain of offers I don't want, the pending deadline for hearing back on next steps for MIT. It's all too much, and I can tell it showed in the first half of tonight's game. We're up fourteen to seven at the half, but it should be double that. We're the better team.

"Coach is going to unload. Brace yourself," Tory jokes, spraying water from the sport bottle into his mouth as he sits next to me on the bench, the rest of the team filing into the locker room behind him.

"I'm playing like shit," I admit.

"*Pfff*, whatever. I'm the one who dropped your pass in the end zone."

"'Cause I threw it too high."

Tory's letting me off the hook, but I don't need him taking the fall for me. I'm letting our team down because my head is a mess. It's not fair. This game means something to a lot of the guys in this room. For them, their performance is the ticket to their dream. I can't half-ass things because I'm not feeling inspired or whatever. I'm letting the team down.

Coach storms through the door last, his assistants all lined up at the front of the room, their heads down as they wait for his volume. I tether my hands and press my thumbs together, ready to get reamed.

"D'Angelo!"

"Yes, Coach." Tory is the pillar of respect next to me.

"Check your hands, son. That was some sloppy-ass work out there. You need to wash the butter off?"

"No, sir." His response is quick, emotionless, exactly as it should be.

Coach grunts and turns his posture to face me directly. I look up to meet his hard stare.

"Fuller, nice work out there. Let's see if this O-line can get you more than a second to get a pass off next half."

And that's it. That's my ass-chewing. Tory got blamed for my shitty pass and he took it. The offensive line gets ripped apart for my lazy footwork. Meanwhile, I get an *atta boy*.

Coach spends five minutes yelling platitudes about how we "just don't seem to want it bad enough" and "we're the better team, and now's the time to prove it." It's all meaningless bullshit, but everyone around me seems oddly inspired. Coach leaves the locker room, and me and the rest of the seniors start to shout, hyping everyone to their feet as we stomp and clap and grunt until we're transformed into wild, rabid beasts. We fly out of the locker room and tear up the field with our aggression for another twenty-four minutes of play.

The third and fourth quarters pass like a dream, my body working on rote, my passes meeting hands in the right places while I somehow manage not to get flattened into the sod more than once. My head rings from the hit, but nothing I haven't handled before. That bullshit and hype session did its job on me too, even though the entire time, the voice in the back of my head is telling me I'm weak and not good enough.

The buzzer sounds, and it's maybe the best game of my life, but I feel like a total failure. It's because despite being great for my team, I'm letting myself down every day I don't tell my dad the truth about what I want. I'm a faker. A scared little boy.

"Yo, you may not like this game, but it fucking loves you, Fuller!" Tory leaps on my back and slaps my shoulder while I carry him across the field for our celebration. I clutch his knees and jog, trying to find my spirit. If I let myself, I'll break into tears right now. The feeling is that heavy, like a wet blanket over my shoulders and head. I can't give in to this sense of doom. I have to fight it until I can be brave enough to do what I want.

"Yeah!" I shout, forcing my body's chemistry to shift. My face contorts and I pound my chest as my friend slides from my back. I let myself go complete Neanderthal, my nostrils flaring as I pace the forty-yard line and bump chests with my teammates. The knot in my stomach eases, replaced by the familiar ease of competition and victory. I allow myself to eat up the compliments, to accept the "good games" and praise. I shake Jon Foster's hand as he steps to the sideline, and I smile when he tells me he'll "be in touch." I smile, though his offer is not the one I'm waiting for. I smile so my father sees it on my face, and I leave it there until I believe it to be true.

Families spill onto the field, dads high-fiving their sons, moms hugging them with pride. I blink around the scene and my focus goes to the one place I know I'll find my dad. Still standing, still analyzing, he's perched in the center of the stands, about a dozen rows up, his view unobstructed. The world around him is abuzz in celebration over this game that I play to make him happy, so he'll keep making Mom happy, and he's still disappointed. I see it on his face, in his mannerisms. His body is closed off, brow heavy and lost in thought. He's replaying that first half and wondering how he can rid me of bad performances like that in the future. He's rehearsing what he'll say about my game play to anyone who asks. He's making excuses that he will drill into my head until I believe them to be true. My mom is sitting, clutching her purse, ready to go home and pretend their marriage is good.

Rather than put myself through anything else tonight, I turn and throw an arm over Tory as we make our way to the locker room. They drove themselves here. They can drive home without talking to me first.

The buzz of pretending manages to last until almost everyone's cleared out, but by the time it's only Tory and me, my body can't fake it anymore. I drop my bag at my feet and fling my locker door shut so hard it bounces back open.

"Whoa, hostile much?" Tory chuckles as he reaches over and gently shuts the door. I flop down on the bench, elbows on my knees and head in my hands.

"I don't know, man. I'm sorry. I'm just so . . . so sick of it."

Tory props a foot on the bench next to me and places his hand on my back.

"I hear ya. This winning shit is so not my style." He doesn't laugh at his own joke, but I shake once under his touch to let him know I was amused. He didn't say it to be funny. He said it to point out how dramatic I'm being.

"Talk to your dad."

I shake with another laugh.

"I'm serious. Can I be real with you?"

I lift my eyes, not sure what expression I'll see on my friend's face. I'm not sure I'm relieved to see his mouth set in the hard line and his eyes serious, almost heavy. I breathe in through my nose and turn to face him as he straddles the bench about a foot away.

"You spend a lot of time making sure your parents are happy, and I know—" He holds up his hand before I can protest. He knows me so well he senses my knee-jerk need to defend my mom and keep her life intact. "I get it with your mom. I do, and I think you're a pretty awesome person for putting her first. But maybe, Lucas . . . she would love to see you put yourself first. Your dad might not get it right away, but your mom will. MIT? That shit's for *real!* Like, she would get to tell her friends her son's a rocket scientist and shit."

"I'd be on the engineering side, actually, focusing more on—"

He waves both hands in front of me, stopping me cold.

"I won't know half the shit you're about to say, and frankly, I don't care. You're smart. You'll do smart shit. Cool. I'm just saying your mom will be proud, and your dad will get over it. Think about it, at least. Because you cannot keep beating yourself up like this, and if you give in and do what your dad expects, you're going to resent the hell out of him—and maybe yourself a bit too."

I blink, stunned at the wisdom that just spilled from the mouth of this guy I've seen drink beer out of an actual bullet hole.

He leans forward and ruffles my hair like I'm a kid then stands and tugs his bag up his shoulder.

"And for fuck's sake, call June."

I grimace and he laughs, sticking out his tongue and pointing at me. He had to add that last little bit in there. We haven't talked about the whole drive-in debacle at Two-fers and the fact he drove her there just to goad me into feeling something.

"Party's on at our house, by the way. See you there?"

I nod, but I'm not sure I'm in the mood to party. I don't want to rush home either, so I end up gathering my things and climbing in my truck, listening to the low hum of the motor while I replay Tory's speech over and over in my head.

I'm putting off the inevitable. I'm going to get in to MIT. It's my destiny. I want it, too, so badly. Leaning forward, I turn on my stereo, tuning in the local pop station. It sounds like every high school dance I've been to, so I flip stations until I land on the local sports show. High school football is big out here, and in the case of Allensville and the dozen other county schools that make up our region, it's the second most popular talk sports topic, just behind Pacers basketball.

"Now, what did you think about the way Lucas Fuller lead his Fighting Eagles into that second half tonight?"

I lower the volume down before I can hear the response. My phone has already buzzed with a stream of messages from my dad. I haven't bothered to open them because the preview on my screen was enough to ward me off. It's his notes from the game. The radio guys are probably praising me while my dad's stream of text messages is ripping me apart. In reality, my performance was probably somewhere right in the middle of their assessments—perfectly average. I did the job.

I lean forward, feeling the weight cascade over my shoulders again, the claws of anxiety gripping my neck, squeezing. I draw in a breath just as my forehead hits the steering wheel. Right now, I would give anything to be able to talk to June. But she's leaving me alone, just as I asked her to.

TEN

I knew there was a chance June would be working. I told Tory I'd join him and the guys for bowling anyway, and so far, he has loved every minute of it.

"She's right there," he says, leaning into me while we lace up our shoes.

"Yep." I don't bother to look up. I won't give him the satisfaction of seeing me react. Besides, I spotted her as soon as she ducked into the back side of the lanes. She's probably back there hiding from me, and I'm fine with that.

"You really are something. Like a rock. Stoic." He chuckles as he slides his regular shoes under the seat and gets up to search for a ball.

Yeah, that's me. One big stoic rock.

I draw in a breath and let my hands fall to my knees before getting up and searching for a heavy ball. I don't bowl very well, so I like to sling the added weight in hopes the increased velocity helps the ball take out a few extra pins.

"You wanna go first?" Tory asks me as he drops his ball on the return and slides into one of the seats by the scoring computer. I nod *sure* and grab the only fourteen-pound ball I can find. I allow myself a quick glance toward the pins on my way to the return, and catch June's reflection in the ceiling mirror. She isn't working back there. She isn't doing *anything*, besides hiding.

"So are you depressed or just trying out the grunge look?" Tory pulls on one of the strings of my hoodie, cinching up the hole around my face.

"Ass hat," I say, stretching the hood back out. "I'm cold. And my hair's nuts this morning. I kind of rushed out of the house to avoid a session of football 101 with my dad."

Tory grimaces and drops his jokes about my lazy attire. I'm definitely not feeling myself lately. And maybe he's not wrong to mention depression. I wouldn't say I'm feeling low the way my mom does sometimes, but I'm definitely not feeling *up*. I'm sorting out a lot in my head lately, and my body is finally feeling the repercussions.

"Hey, Lucas. Great game last night. On the house." Morty, June's boss, slides a hot pizza on a nearby table, along with a stack of cups and a pitcher of beer.

"Thanks, Mort," I say, holding up a hand in appreciation.

"I sure do love how the people around here idolize you," Tory teases as he pats my shoulder and stands to pour himself a beer. I laugh along with him, but that adoration is part of the problem. If I don't go on and do something big in football, I won't only let my dad down, but I'll be disappointing people like Morty, too. That guilt doesn't stop me from snagging a slice of pizza, though.

Tory and I finish setting up the scoring system while Tory's twin, Hayden, and our friend Kade dig in and pour beers of their own. I opt for water.

"You think she knows we can all see her?"

Tory's asking about June. I shrug.

"I'm gonna tell her." He pulls out his phone and on instinct I reach out to stop him. The second my hand touches his wrist he freezes, and that know-it-all smirk rears its ugly head.

"Oh ho ho!" He leans back, pulling his phone close to his chest as if he needs to protect it from me. "Someone doesn't want me to get June Mabee's attention."

"That's not it at all, Tor. She's back there because she's trying to avoid us."

"You. She's trying to avoid *you*. June and *me?* We're tight. You're the one she has a problem with."

"*Pshh.*" I roll my eyes. "Whatever. Fine, tell her we can see her. Have at it."

"I will," he says, defiant, like he's ten and about to win a game of Sorry.

I do my best to ignore his back-and-forth texting, but when he howls in laughter I glare at him and he nods his head toward June, urging all of us to look. I stand when my friend does, and my eyes find June's panicked face on the other end of the lane. *Poor thing was just trying to get through her shift. Nice, Tory. Real nice.*

"I'm inviting her over. This is ridiculous," he says.

I wave a hand, knowing he's going to do whatever he wants anyhow, which he does.

I hover around the ball return, holding my open palm over the fan while Tory stands on one of the seats and cups his mouth, as if he needs any assistance in being loud.

"Maybe Mabee would like to come say hi to her friends?"

I cringe and glance with side eyes, almost certain I see June's shoulders scrunch up with embarrassment. My eyes fall back to the ball return, and I push my ball around a little to find the thumb hole.

"Oh, shit!" Tory's unnerved tone spikes my adrenaline, and I look up in time to see June's legs fly out from under her body, which cascades through the air, her head on a perfect path for impact with the corner of the gutter.

Fuck, she's hurt!

"June!" Her name flies from my lips out of habit and need. She hit her head—hard—and my heart thunders in response.

I sprint down the lane, my feet sliding along the slick floor the entire way until I'm at June's side. Her eyes are rolling, her pupils wide. This isn't good.

She's gasping for air. She probably got the wind knocked out of her on impact. I push her disheveled hair from her face and brace her head between my hands. She's squirming.

"June, careful. Don't move."

Her eyes search wildly and I hold her still, forcing her to focus on me. Her pupils have shrunk, which is a relief, but she's hell bent on moving. She starts to roll to her side and I decide I need to get her off this floor.

"You can't carry her on that. You'll slip, too!" Morty's worried about a lawsuit, so I shoot him a glare and do as I damn well please.

I scoop June into my arms, her body rolling into my chest as I lift her and fight to steady my feet. She wraps her arm around my shoulder, her fingers gripping my hoodie. I'm glad she has the strength and coordination to do that. It's a good sign. Her eyes flutter closed as she tucks her face against me, so I adjust my hold to grip her tighter against me. This floor is no joke. How I sprinted across it a second ago beats me.

"I can walk," she croaks.

"*Shhh*," I hush, laughing slightly. Still stubborn June, after all this time.

My right foot slides out about a foot so I bend my knees and stop. June clutches me.

"This shit is slippery," I say to my friends. They're about a dozen steps away, all standing with their legs spread, knees bent and arms out as if they are in any position to catch me or June if I tumble.

I cut my step length in half, sliding my feet as if I'm on ice. I've got this. I'm decent on a hockey rink.

"Almost there," I say, tucking my chin.

I take a gamble and lunge forward when I see unwaxed floor ahead. June flinches in my arms, and I check her face the second my legs are steady. Our eyes lock, and my insides rush with this overwhelming sense that I need to take care of this girl. My arms feel numb, and it's not because June is heavy. Hell, I lift things twice her size for a workout. No, this is more like a morphine drip. I'm a little sick from the feeling, but it lingers in my body, slapping me around on the insides.

"Tory, someone needs to drive her home, man. Get your car."

I kneel and set June on one of the nearby seats. I try to stand but June's hand grasps at my sweatshirt and her eyes flash wide. I'm not sure if she's feeling sick or uneasy or what, but I react with the same instincts I have for the last two minutes—as if she is mine, and I'm the only one in the world who can take care of her.

I crouch again and leave a hand on her shoulder, near the base of her neck. She clutches my arm as if she's holding on to find her center. She's definitely concussed.

"She's your neighbor, Lucas. Get over yourself and drive her home," Tory says.

I jerk my head in his direction and meet his stare. Driving June home is a bad idea. My mom should be home soon, and the odds of her seeing me with June in my truck are pretty high. The thought of putting her in a car with Tory, though, who has already finished his beer, or Hayden or Kade, who frankly aren't that far behind him on finishing theirs, feels daftly irresponsible.

My attention slips, as does my hold on June, and she drops to the floor, palms spread wide. She pukes a little on her shirt on her way down. Tory's right—I need to take her home. I toss Tory my keys and he takes off for the door to bring my truck around. Some dude who works with June, meanwhile, starts mopping up her mess right next to us. I grunt at him and he pauses while I scoop June up and hoist her against my chest. The smell of

Pine Sol is potent, and I'm half tempted to vomit from it. I can't imagine it's helping June in her state.

I push through the doors and Tory pulls my truck along the curb, shifting in park and racing around to the passenger side to help me load June inside. She grabs at the metal parts of the seat belt the moment I set her down, banging the pieces together as if they're magnets. I cover her hands with mine and her head pops up, eyes wide.

"You're not even close."

She lets go of the buckles and I finish the job, securing her in her seat. I shut the door and race to the driver's side.

"Text me and let me know how she is," Tory says as I pass him.

"Will do," I respond.

I pull away the moment my door is shut, buckling on our way out of the parking lot. June moans at my side, her body weight resting on the door and her head braced between the seat and the window. She's going to bump her head more if she stays like that. I keep one eye on her and one on the road, slowing when I notice potholes or dips. The railroad crossing is coming up, though, and there's not much I can do to avoid those.

"Hey, the tracks are coming up. I'll try to take them slow, but you might wanna pull your head from the window."

She straightens her body and I drop my speed to a crawl, doing my best to avoid any jerks or jolts. The rocking motion seems to make her sick again, though, because she moans and brings her forearm to her mouth as if that will hold everything in.

"I think we need to get you looked at."

I reach for her shoulder to help her sit upright as she falls toward the window again. Her head wobbles and rolls to the side and she blinks at me with sleepy eyes. I stop at the intersection closest to where we live and I meet her gaze. She looks high, and terrified. I can't leave her like this.

"You wait in the truck. I'll run in and get your mom," I say, slowly pulling through the intersection. Her hands peel away from her thighs and flatten against her forehead.

"She's not home," she says.

Fuck.

"Okay, well, I need your phone, then, so I can call her."

She reaches around her body, feeling for her phone. Her dexterity is a mess and she ends up flinging it to the floor.

"I'm so sorry," she croaks. Her voice teeters on a sob, and she leans forward to retrieve her phone. I touch her shoulder, stopping her as I pull to the side of the road. I scoot to the middle of the seat and bend down until I'm practically laying in her lap as I feel for the phone. Grasping it, I sit up and move back to my seat. I tap the screen to bring up her keypad and type in her birthday and her mom's—04080901. The device comes to life and I press her mom's contact info. June is staring at me with her mouth wide open and I realize that I basically just hacked her phone, like I'm a Jedi. Or a former best friend. *Her person.*

"Your birthday and your mom's birthday, same as the garage." I blink once as if it isn't a big deal that I remember any of that. She hangs on, though, her stare lingering, and eventually I drop my focus to my lap because the discomfort in my chest is becoming unbearable.

Her mom answers after three rings.

"Mrs. Mabee, it's Lucas. Fuller."

"Lucas . . . *Lucas!* Oh, my God, is everything okay? Is the house on fire?"

"It's all right, but June slipped at work. I was there with some of the guys, and I didn't want her driving." She gasps, and I sense it's part worry and a dash of relief.

"Thank you."

"Yeah, of course." I lean forward and sort through my thoughts, my head falling to my fist, which is wedged against my steering wheel. I know what I *should* do. I also know what I *want* to do, and that's help June. I want to be that guy who has character. I want to be her friend, and do the right thing. But my mom is going to make this into something it isn't, and then it's going to stir up old memories and rip open closed subjects.

"I can maybe get home in an hour. I'm pretty far, at the market on the north side, and I'm not sure how traffic is right now, but . . . would you mind waiting with her?"

June groans, and her head falls forward a little. She's nodding off.

"Sure, I can wait here. I kinda think she needs to go to the ER though?" *Shit, I'm really doing this.*

I roll my head to the side and eye June. I think she's trying to smile at me, but she also looks as if she's about to be sick.

"Did she vomit?"

"Yeah, she threw up once," I answer. I study her, looking for more signs of trauma. Her symptoms seem like a typical concussion, but I'm basing that off of shit I learned at football camp.

"Do you think you could take her? I can call in the insurance and maybe get there to relieve you if it takes too long?"

I blink a few times, anticipating that sinking feeling that's plagued my chest ever since June showed back up at our school. It doesn't come.

"I can do that. Yes."

"You're sure? It's not too much?" Her mom's voice is shaky, apologetic and vibrating with nerves.

"No, not a problem."

I shift the truck into drive and check the rearview mirror.

"Thank you, Lucas. We're both so grateful."

I swallow hard because her tone is earnest. She's not lying, and I wonder how someone could appreciate someone else on the other end of what our families have gone through.

"I will call you the second we're there," I say.

I end the call and slip June's phone into the nook near my stereo. I make a wide U-turn and check June as soon as I straighten the truck out.

"Your mom said she's at the market or something? Is she like a cashier?" I didn't realize she was working at a grocery store. I wonder if she has multiple jobs or maybe they're in debt.

"What? No, umm," June stammers. She brings a hand to her face, her fingertips on a hunt for an injury or swelling. The bruising is starting to make itself known. *I've been there, June.*

"She sells her photography. She's shooting on her own now, and it's a farmer's market up north. Good for business."

I nod, my gut tensing again with those pesky guilt pangs. Of course her mom is capable of running her own business. She's always been an incredible photographer. Before things turned sour between our families, she was going to take our family portrait when I turned sixteen, and I always kind of thought she'd do my senior photos.

"Am I going to die?"

June's question, uttered in the most pathetically frail voice, comes out of left field. I can't help the laugh that flies from my body. I flash my gaze to her, expecting to see her face break character. She has to be joking. I see quickly, thanks to the small worry line between her brows, that she is not.

"No, June," I assure her. I turn my attention back to the road, but give in to the need to care for her as I reach over and pat her knee.

Her phone rings and we both reach for it, our hands brushing. She slaps mine away.

"You're driving," she scolds.

I recoil and chuckle.

"Yeah, well, you thought you were dying so I thought I should maybe answer."

She grimaces at me, and normally she would follow that up with a playful punch in the arm. I don't get one, and I'm not sure whether it's because her head is jacked up or because I don't rate play-punch level anymore.

Her hands cradle her phone as she answers and puts her mom on speaker.

"Mom?"

"June? It's gonna be fine. We just want to make sure it's only a concussion, okay? Lucas? Are you there?"

I clear my throat and correct my posture, making sure my hands are at ten and two on the wheel, as if she can see me.

"Yes, ma'am."

"I called the advanced urgent care on Seventy-Fifth. She's on the waiting list so hopefully you can walk right in and get through. They have my card and insurance on file. If you don't mind taking her home after? I would never make it there in time."

Home. I mean, I figured I would need to bring us both home . . . together. My mom will be home by then. My chest tightens.

"Got it. I'll make sure I call you when we get out of the doc," I say, switching lanes to turn on Seventy-Fifth.

"Thanks," June's mom says.

I smile, something deep in my soul soothed by her gratitude. What a simple thing I'm doing. Anyone would do this. But *I'm* the one doing it, and it feels . . . nice.

"I'm a little freaked out," June says in a soft voice.

I start to answer, but when I glance her way I realize she's taken her mom off speaker and is talking to her one-on-one. Her eyes are drawn in, brows wrinkled, knee bobbing up and down. She shouldn't be fidgeting. Without pause, I reach toward her and take her hand in mine. I hold on tight.

The urgent care wait is, as predicted, a nightmare. Even with the call-ahead reservation, June and I are stuck in the waiting room for forty minutes. She's tired, and the last thing I can let her do is give in and doze off. That's dangerous for concussed people, masking signs of more serious injuries . . . like hemorrhaging.

I swallow and nudge June with my elbow, a move I've perfected over the last hour. She grumbles and tells me she's not sleeping, but she's tired. I don't mention the word *hemorrhage.* That will only freak her out more.

We finally get called back and I call her mom to keep her on the phone through the exam. It's a standard concussion, as expected, and I see the relief in June's relaxing muscles, her shoulders dropping from her ears, and her breathing slowing from the shallow, rapid pace she had going throughout the exam.

She lets me guide her back to the truck and I adjust the air vents to make sure she isn't getting blasted in the face. I'm keeping it cool to keep her awake. I get in and give her a reassuring smile, knowing deep down that in a few minutes I'm going to have to figure out a way to hide her from my mother. I know she's home. With a little luck, she's inside the house and maybe I can slip into the driveway without making a scene.

That hope is dashed when I turn down our road. I see my mom's SUV, the taillights glowing as she parks in the center of the driveway. She's wondering where I am, probably. Or she's wondering where my dad is, which . . . I have no idea. If I pull up with June right now, it is going to set off a domino effect of emotional baggage toppling around my life.

I stop my truck and kill the lights without thinking this through.

"Get out."

My mouth is so dry, and I feel like such an asshole, but the massive chaos in my chest is guiding me. I have to get out of this situation. I need to spare my mom the visual.

June jerks in her seat, clutching the fabric.

"Is something wrong?"

I start to shake my head, but my words contradict that.

"June, just fucking get out!"

Her hands fumble with the seat belt and then the door, and in seconds she's out of my truck, her medical papers clutched to her chest. The second her door shuts I turn around and speed away with my lights off until I reach the end of the road. I turn the corner and punch the steering wheel.

"Fuck!"

I punch it three more times after I pull to the side of the road. I push my hand through my hair, knocking the hoodie to the back of my neck. I'm hot, so I tug the sweatshirt from my body, getting tangled with the seat belt. The fiasco frustrates me and I growl until I'm basically left raging with a sweatshirt on the side of the road. I throw it at the passenger side once I'm free and stare at it while panting.

I just made June walk home after nearly knocking herself out and getting a concussion diagnosis. All because I'm scared.

My phone buzzes and I pull it from my back pocket, rubbing my palm over my face in an attempt to right my vision. It's my mom calling, and all I can manage to think is how June is probably a hundred feet from crossing her path. I feel sick, and I'm certain I'm an asshole. I'm only trying to be a good son, though, and somehow those two personas have become entwined.

I press ANSWER.

"Hey, Mom." I do my best to sound relaxed, to sound . . . far away.

"Hey, honey. Is everything all right? I just got home and the house looks empty. I was . . . worried."

I suck in my lips. She's lying. She's not worried, she's suspicious. As she should be. Because where is my dad?

"No, everything's fine. I had to run over to the field for something and got caught up talking to Coach. I'll head out soon."

My mom never speaks to my coach. And the odds of her and my father talking football without me being there is near zero.

"Oh, all right. Well, I picked up your favorite sub from the deli. I'll pop it in the fridge."

I smile at her thoughtfulness. I wish I were hungry.

"Thanks. Be home in a few," I say before ending the call. I toss my phone on top of my hoodie and stare at the seat June occupied only a few minutes ago. She probably passed behind my mom's vehicle while we were on the phone. My mom probably followed her movement in the mirror, waiting for her to enter her house. I wonder if June's mom is home by now.

To keep up with my lie, and maybe make myself feel a little less like a jerk, I shift into drive and navigate my way to the football field. Coach's car is in the lot, so I park next to it and head inside to sit with him while he combs through game film for our next opponent. It's not how I want to spend my Saturday, and I'm inundated with his thoughts about my performance—thoughts that are eerily reminiscent of my dad's notes—while I'm there.

I head home after about an hour, and June's house is quiet when I pull into my driveway. I force myself not to stare for long at their window, and I bury the urge to jog over there and check on her. Instead, I close the garage door, head inside, and eat my stale sandwich.

ELEVEN

Our kitchen usually smells of bacon and pancakes and fresh-brewed coffee on Mondays. It's part of the "routine" my mom is so hell-bent on keeping up. I can only think of two or three Mondays that have been bacon-less over the last two years. Which makes the lack of those things this morning a bit of a red flag.

I drop my backpack on the counter and glance around the house. It's quiet, and a quick peek in the garage lets me know my dad isn't home. My pulse ticks up as I piece together clues. *Did he come home last night?*

"I'm so sorry, Lucas. I have a meeting this morning and I got up late." My mom is fumbling with the coffee pot, her hands trembling at the sink. I step in and take the pot from her, filling it with water.

"It's fine. I'm not that hungry. I'll just grab a protein bar."

She nods and quickly turns her back while I take over coffee duty. My eyes narrow as I stare at her back. She's dressed for a meeting, and her hair is nice. It's a sad thing to admit to myself, but I need to get close to her to know for certain whether she spent the night drinking.

"I'll be home late tonight, but I left some cash by the fridge. You and Dad can order a pizza or something maybe?" She glances over her shoulder and I force a quick smile.

"Sure," I say, my hand still gripping the handle of the coffee pot as it begins to drip.

My mom busies herself sifting through a packet of papers before stuffing it in her satchel.

"You look nice, Mom," I say, noting how rattled she seems.

She flattens her hands on top of her bag and lets out a heavy breath before turning to face me and running her palms down the front of her blouse to smooth out any wrinkles. She smiles with closed lips. Her lipstick is subtle and applied perfectly. There aren't any signs of manic behavior or a night spent in tears.

"Thanks, Lucas. I have to talk in front of some really important people today. I'm a little—"

"You'll be amazing," I say, stepping close enough to kiss her cheek. I wish I could say it was to be a good son, but I breathe in deeply while I'm near as a test. The air is fresh and her body smells of her floral perfume and dry cleaning. No hint of alcohol.

I meet her eyes, and she widens them slightly, almost as if she's offering me a good look as proof. No redness. No puffiness or dark circles.

"Well, you'll knock them dead," I say.

"It's . . . it's a mortuary business presentation," she says, laughing lightly from one side of her mouth.

"Oh, wow. I did not see that coming," I say, rubbing my cheek and chuckling at my faux pas.

The coffee finishes its final drip and my mom steps around me to pour some in her thermos. She leans back and kisses my cheek this time and our eyes meet once more for a silent pact. *No, your father did not come home. And yes, I'm angry. But I am fine.*

"I'll see you later," she says, dragging her bag up her shoulder and jetting through the back door to the garage.

I pour myself the leftover coffee and grab a peanut-butter-flavored bar before grabbing my things and heading to the back yard. I left my cleats out there to air out, so I grab them and tuck them in my backpack before rounding the house and heading to the driveway. I rip open my energy bar and bite a third of it before I'm faced with June standing between our two driveways. I slow my chewing but the rest of me freezes in place. My eyes shift to the right, relieved the garage is shut and my mom is gone.

"I need a ride," June says.

I choke a little on my food.

"Why?" My chest hurts from the instant drum of panic. *Shit, shit, shit. What did I do? I got too close. I opened a dialogue. I . . . I fucking missed her.*

"My car is still at work and my mom had a job," she says. She gulps, and the movement in her throat is almost violent. She hates having to ask me for a favor and it makes me so goddamn sad.

I look toward my truck and then to the closed garage.

"Your mom just left," she says. She's reading my mind now. I wonder if she knows exactly how bad things are?

I chew at my lip while I think through my options. I could tell her it's not my problem, but that would be a dick thing to do. Besides, I don't want to. I *want* to help her. My mom is gone, and my dad is God knows where. The fact she's asking me for help after I kicked her to the curb and made her walk home with a concussion says a lot about her situation. She needs my help, emphasis *needs*.

"You fucking owe me," she pipes up.

I turn to face her as her finger jets out in an accusatory point. I swallow the last crumbs of my recent bite, my mouth suddenly going dry. *Wow! This is a ballsy side of June.* I tongue my cheek, a little impressed, and finally exhale as I look down at my feet and nod.

She tugs open the door the second I press my key fob to unlock my truck, and she is buckled and sitting in perfect posture by the time I open my door. I slip my bag behind my seat and pause in the open space between us. Less than twenty-four hours ago, I was holding her hand in this space. I lean in and yank down the folding console to build an armrest—*aka barrier*—between us.

Normally, I pull my letterman jacket off and leave it on the seat June is sitting in, but I'm not about to ask her to hold it. I'm already imagining the rumor mill that'll be kindled when we pull up together. I can't imagine what fuel her holding my letterman jacket would give to gossip. I hop into my side and jerk my door shut, but the second I do, June twists to the side and slams up the console, opening the space between us right-the-fuck back up.

I chuckle as my head falls to the side and my eyes take in the empty bench seat. *Unbelievable.*

I shake my head, laughing quietly, amused at how childish we've become. May as well get all the things off my chest if we're stuck together for two miles.

"You and Tory friends now?" I adjust the mirror while I ask, doing my best to look ambivalent. Inside, my chest is raging. Rather than look at her, I pull my phone out and slide through a few playlists, finding the most angry rap song I can dig up just to drown out her reply. I don't do it because I don't really care. I do it because I care *way too fucking much.*

She quakes with a small laugh of her own, and turns her attention out her window. I've turned the bass up as high as I can without blowing out my subs, and my truck vibrates with the beat. I zip us down the driveway, jerking the wheel and peeling out a little when I shift to drive. The quick move jars both of us, and I remember that June got knocked around pretty good yesterday. I glance to my right to check on her just as she lifts her chin to stare at me. She looks pissed, which means she feels fine. At least, that's what I tell myself.

Instead of giving in to the guilt and turning the music down and coddling her, I race through the few stop signs we hit on our way out of our neighborhood. I'm familiar enough with the cops to not get busted for a little rolling stop, though my last one was barely a tap of the brakes.

I'm literally counting down the seconds I have left in this situation when June hits me with more of her ballsy side. More like blindsides me.

"Why did you make me walk?"

My eyes widen. Maybe if I don't react, don't actually turn to face her, I can pretend I didn't hear. I maintain my focus on the road ahead, scanning for distractions. As we get closer to school and there are things like people crossing streets to snag my attention, I'm able to mask my reaction more easily. June, however, isn't letting this drop. I feel her stare. It's hot, and unwavering, and when we finally pull to a stop, I can't bear it any longer.

"June, just drop it," I say, turning toward her, my jaw tight and my eyes burning, hoping to startle her into submission.

She's breathing hard, and I glance down to see her hands balling into fists. She's not letting this go. Without warning, her hand flies to my stereo and she punches the power button off with her thumb. We're drenched in sudden silence with a mile or so left on our trip. I suck in my lips and reach to turn it back on as we roll forward, but June slaps my hand away, her fingernails grazing my wrist and leaving red marks in their wake.

What the—?

I bunch my face and twist to stare at her, wanting to call her ridiculous, despite how unfair that is since I'm just as bad. Before I say things I'll no doubt regret, a car makes a hard turn in front of us, nearly swiping the side of my truck. I swerve, and my arm flies against June's body, bracing her against the seat. She grabs on hard, her grip tight, as if I'm the only thing keeping her inside this truck. Every bit of the three or four seconds it actually takes stretches on for much longer. By the end of the slow-motion panic attack, June and I are left holding on to each other, and my eyes are strained with worry. I feel how tight my brow is, how drawn in my lids are. I will my face to relax before June draws any conclusions, and she unfurls her hands from my arm.

My heart is jacked up on adrenaline, and I'm nowhere near as careful as I should be as I zip us through the last intersection and pull into the school lot.

"You trying to get into another near accident?" June chides.

I hear her, but I don't let on.

Tory and Hayden are hanging by the front of their car, the spot always reserved for me there and waiting, right in front of everyone. June and I will be on display, ripe for speculation and assumptions. Whispers are probably already percolating on the lips of the few people who saw us pull in, though thankfully I don't see Ava lurking around. Or June's friend, Abby, who I'm sure wouldn't be shy about asking us questions and demanding *I* answer. Rather than make this morning worse, I pass by my usual spot and race toward the far corner, near the football field. *Way* out of sight.

We might end up a few minutes late to class, but I'll smooth that over. It's not as though either of us is a shitty student. We'll be excused.

June looks ready to leap from the truck before I shift to park, her bag clutched to her chest and her hand poised to open the door. It takes her maybe two seconds to exit by the time I fully stop, and she's practically sprinting ahead of me, although there's a nice limp to her gait thanks to her fall yesterday. I take my jacket off and toss it in my truck before grabbing my bag and heading after June. Not that I want to catch up to her; I don't want her to fall, but I can keep watch from back here.

I chuckle at how nuts all of this is, and maybe there's a bit of sadness in my amusement too. No matter how hard I try to lag behind June, my stride seems to double hers. Maybe it's because she's hurt, or maybe I'm unwittingly trying to catch her. Before I can dissect my feelings too much, June whips to her side.

"And yeah, Tory and I are friends now. *For now.* I mean, who knows." Her eyes flit to mine for a second then her gaze shifts back to the path ahead.

My blood is on instant boil. She cuts me off when we reach the doors to our building and again as she jerks open the one to our classroom. She slams her body into her seat, practically huffing, and I slip into mine, a little shell-shocked from the last ten seconds. I'm willing to let it go because she's justified in lashing out. I've been a total asshole. I shift in my seat, bracing my right foot against the leg of her chair because my body doesn't fit the space well. I guess my foot is the last straw for June. She pushes her chair back, clanking it against my desktop with the speed of a machete on track to decapitate someone. Our teacher is standing right in front of June's desk, the attendance sheet in her hand, her eyes screwed up as she probably wonders what the hell we're arguing about.

"Sorry, bag strap caught on something," June apologizes. She tugs on her bag at the side of her chair to embellish her fib, and the entire situation scratches at my immature soul. I shift my body and let my foot slam into the leg of her chair again, the force enough to make her hair sway and her body lurch.

Nice, Fuller. You're literally picking on a concussion patient.

My childish behavior doesn't spur another reaction from her, and when I try again a few minutes later, June seems to have completely moved on from our spat.

She's probably busy thinking about Tory, and how they're friends . . . *for now.*

Fuck.

TWELVE

"Yo, check it," Tory says, nudging my arm with his as he walks up next to me on our way to weights. He hands me his phone and I glance at some post on some app I never want to have.

"Yeah, what about it?"

"Nah, nah, nah . . ." He forces his phone back into my palm, realizing I didn't actually look at what he wanted. I stop walking and glare at him before looking down at his phone.

Some dude with the handle RedTedFred wrote "June and Tory totally dating." I grunt and hand the phone back to him, returning to my stride and pushing through the weight room doors.

"I thought it was funny is all," he says after a few seconds of me not reacting. He didn't think that. He wanted to make sure I saw it so he could use it as a tool to pry me open and make me admit to a whole bunch of feelings I'm not even sure I'm capable of anymore.

"I mean, I guess so. Except, aren't you into her best friend, Abby?" This is the one little fact I have held on to, something I've always had a feeling about. Tory has been pining after Abby Cortez for *way* too long. It's more than just the fact she rejects him. It's not "the hunt" when it comes to her. He likes her. Immensely.

"Nahhhh, not really," he says, turning his back to me as he flips open his locker to dress out. He stares at his phone for a few seconds, and I lift up on my toes to peek for confirmation. He's staring at that post, I assume not finding it quite as amusing.

Tory puts his phone away and locks up his things, turning and flattening his back on his closed locker door. He folds his arms over his chest.

"That rumor should be about you and June, you know. Don't think I didn't see you give her a ride."

"She's concussed," I respond. I was prepared for that question. I had a feeling Tory saw me pull in.

"Sure, but did *you* have to drive her?"

I sigh and flop down on the bench, lifting my right foot to re-tie my shoelace. I glance up at him while my hands work. "Actually, I did. I found her hovering around my truck this morning with nobody left to call."

I shrug and give my friend a crooked smile, feeling as though I won—for exactly three seconds.

"Okay, but I saw you with her when she was hurt. You can lie to yourself and everyone else in this damn place all you want. Hell, you can lie to June, even though deep down, I bet she knows the truth."

"And what's that?" I breathe out, not at all ready for his answer.

"You're in love with her, and you hate yourself."

He pats my shoulder with a heavy hand and shoots me the same smug smile I just gave him before heading out toward the free weights. I lag behind, caught off-guard by his blunt honesty. Tory didn't even wrap his advice in a joke like he usually does. Probably because he's being completely sincere.

I'm not in love with June. Have I *loved* her, in the sense of cared about her? Yes. Do I still? Honestly? Probably. Does the thought of him dating her make me a little mental?

Yes.

Do I hate myself?

Do I?

I slouch back against the wall and consider his dig. I have had that thought, sure, that I hate myself. I rarely like myself. I find fault in my choices, and I despise my weak will. I put my foot down over this June thing, yet I keep going along as if I'm fine playing college football and kissing a future high-tech career good-bye because it might ruffle my dad's feathers. If it were only feathers—

It will shatter him.

"You're a fucking loser, Lucas," I mutter to myself in the solace of the men's locker room.

I let my fist fall to my side and bang against the brick wall behind me.

I'm about to do it again, this time with more force so I can *feel* it, when our coach flings open the door and stops in his tracks.

"There you are. Office just called. You have a call from your mom. Run on up there and just drop in with your group when you're done." He squeezes my shoulder and continues on his way toward his office.

My heart jackhammers. In twelve years of public school, I don't think my mom has called the office once. At least, not to talk to me. I shake my head to wake myself from my pity session and head back outside. After a medium jog, I reach the office in less than a minute, and Maggie holds up a finger, waving me to round the front desk and stand by her.

"I've got your mom on hold. One sec," she says, punching a few buttons and handing me the receiver.

"Mom?" My body tingles with nerves. *Is she . . . sick? Did something happen to Dad?*

"Hey, Lucas. I got a really interesting call just now."

I lean against Maggie's desk, relieved and now unnerved for other reasons.

"Okay?"

"Did you apply to MIT?"

The phone slips from my hold and I catch it somewhere near my stomach, which is about where my heart is.

Shit!

"You all right?" Maggie asks.

I smile and nod and move to lean on the other end of her desk, as if that somehow is more private. I swallow hard and bring the receiver back to my face.

"I did." I roll my shoulders as I speak the words, owning them. It's the first time I'm admitting this to anyone other than Tory and the few people on campus I needed assistance from.

"Lucas!"

I scrunch my eyes closed.

"I know—"

"I'm so proud of you!" My mom's words lead me on a complete one-eighty. I was about to apologize.

"You are?"

"Yes! Honey, I think you got in!"

I stand, no longer needing to sit on the edge of the desk. My hand finds its way to my forehead and I breathe out a laugh that's part disbelief and maybe a little exhaustion. My eyes land on Maggie's and she holds up a thumb. She's one of the few people in on my plan, since she handles transcripts.

I shrug and mouth "Maybe."

"This woman, Candace, called and said she was in town. She wants to sit down with you for the MIT formal interview. I guess it's one of the boxes they need to check."

I start to pace the office.

"Yes, yes!" I'm blinking while I walk and think, my mind riffling through my day, searching out a window to make this possible—without alerting Coach or my dad.

"Okay, did she say when?"

I lick my instantly dry lips.

"I told her to be at the house at three. I know you have practice, but Lucas . . . it's MIT. We'll make it happen. Just blame me and say I need you for something, or tell Coach you left one of your cleats at home."

My mom never condones lying, especially not since my dad cheated on her. But the fact she's willing to indulge in a little fib for me, for this—my dream? It means everything to me.

"Got it, yeah. I can do that. And hey, Mom?"

"Yeah?" Her voice wavers with happiness. It's been a long time since I've heard her like this.

"Thank you," I say.

"Of course."

We hang up and I leave my hand on the receiver on Maggie's desk for a few extra seconds, simply taking it all in. I lift my head and meet Maggie's gaze, her hands cupping her mouth as she holds her breath.

"I have an interview. Today!" I whisper shout.

Maggie leaps from her desk and begins running in place, her hands in the air one second and reaching for me the next. She pulls me into a hug, and I'm not sure if she's possessed with super strength or something, but I swear she lifts me off the ground.

"Lucas! That's amazing!"

My heart is pounding so hard my ribs actually vibrate. I'm sweaty, and my body tingles with so much adrenaline I feel as though I need to sprint and climb buildings and sing from the rooftops.

"I've gotta get to class. I'll let you know tomorrow," I say, holding out a fist for her to bump. She does, tickled by the act as she giggles me out the door.

I'm practically skipping my way across campus, and there's no disguising the aching grin on my face when I meet back up with Tory. It's no use holding my news in, so I pull him to the side, and for the first time in a while, he looks at me as if he actually admires me.

I worm my way out of the start of practice using one of my mom's lies. I even went as far as hiding one of my cleats in my truck before practice so I could act with some authenticity. There's no way I can magically enter my house wearing a suit, but at least I'm not completely baked with sweat.

I tap nervously on my steering wheel as I drive, somehow hitting every stoplight on the way and getting stuck behind two or three cars at every stop sign. No rolling through anything today. I zip into the driveway and find the garage door open with a red car parked inside, my mom's SUV parked just outside. I cruise up slowly, pulling myself as close to both cars as I can, trying to not be seen, and I dash around to the back.

I can't imagine June's mom giving a shit about seeing me home during practice time, but I can't be too careful. I slip inside and catch voices in the other room.

"That you, Lucas?" my mom calls.

"Yeah, I'll be there in one second."

I don't have time for much, but at least I can wash my hands and maybe make the most of a gray practice shirt and football pants. I dip into the powder room and wash up, taking three deep breaths to settle my nerves, then head to the sitting room where I am instantly *way* underdressed. Focusing on my mom's proud smile instead of my unprofessional attire, I rid myself of any worries about the lack of shirt and tie and turn my attention to our guest.

"Lucas, nice to meet you. I'm Candace. Your mom explained how important your role is with your football team, so thank you for making this time work."

My eyes flutter a little as I take in the prep work my mom laid for me.

I take Candace's hand and give her a solid shake.

"Of course. My team understands. Besides, my absence gives someone else a chance to lead." *What a load of crap I just spilled.* Candace's eyes sparkle. She loved it.

"Great, well, this won't take too long. The university asks us to make formal visits when we're offering a student an opportunity to take part in one of our main trustee programs. I just have a few forms to give you—"

"Wait, I'm sorry. Are you saying—"

Candace leans back in her chair and clasps her hands in front of her body as she laughs. Her red dress vibrates as my eyes start to tunnel. I feel as though I might pass out, so I lean back in my own seat.

"Yes, Lucas. We'd like to welcome you to MIT."

I shift my gaze to my mom, who's covering what I assume is a massive smile.

"It's a full ride," Candace continues.

My heart stops. I don't need a heart anymore. I have a full ride.

"But you aren't formally enrolled until you complete all of this and pay a small deposit that unfortunately we can't gift to you. Something about accreditation or whatever." She waves her right hand while handing me a deep blue and maroon embossed folder with the other. I take it into my hands as if it's an ancient relic that could break at any moment.

"Understood," I say, flipping open the folder in my lap as my mom moves to stand behind me and read over my shoulder.

My mom pulls her glasses on and takes one of the forms in her hands. I'm grateful she's here because right at this moment I'm not sure I wouldn't be willing to sign my life away. I do my best to focus on Candace's mouth, holding on to key words as she explains everything I'm supposed to read and sign and return to the college. My mom's phone rings while I'm entranced in the way Candace's mouth says the word "Boston." It's not until she coughs to get my attention that I break from the trance and realize it's my dad on the phone.

"Oh, no, Todd. I'm not sure where he went." My mom holds up a hand to excuse herself so she can slip into the kitchen and tell her second lie. This one is going to hurt because she's lying to my father, the man she holds in contempt for lying to her. I can't let her live with that. I need to have this conversation with him on my own and let him know what I want out of my life.

"Well, I think that's about it," Candace says. I missed half of her words, but I got the important ones. My mom dashes back into the room to join us just as Candace stands, and we all shake hands.

My mom leads Candace back through the house to her car, and the second she pulls away, I reach for my mom's hand and bring it to my mouth to kiss the back of it. She cups my hand between both of hers and turns to face me with tears in her eyes.

"I'm sorry you had to lie."

Full ride. Full motherfucking ride.

"You're worth it," she says. bringing my hand to her mouth and kissing it. A single tear scales her cheek, it's fall slow then quick as it cascades over her skin. Her smile never wavers, and that tear was made of pride.

THIRTEEN

The first thing Coach says to me when my feet hit the field is "run." Twenty laps. That's five miles. I miss the rest of practice running, and Darren, my backup quarterback who throws like shit, has to take snaps all day. I couldn't care less.

The one thing that claws at me is the fact Coach is pissed I left something at home. He lectures me about being responsible and being a leader, though I have never, not once, been late or not showed.

No room for leniency when you're Todd Fuller's kid.

I'm sure this subject will come up when my dad meets with Coach. They talk way too often. And it's not as if I can even tell my dad he's making me look bad, because Coach Loma freaking loves hanging out with my father. They stroke each other's egos and relive their glory days through stories.

I push that stress to the side for the rest of the night. I drive home with my radio cranked and Kanye praising me. As confident as I was about getting in to MIT, never in a million years did I think the financial part would be worked out. There are still expenses, sure, but with tuition covered, I no longer need to depend on my dad's blessing.

I'm barely paying attention to the landscape as I pull into my driveway, and I don't notice Tory's car parked at the end of June's driveway until I shift my truck into park. My mind is catching up to him being bold enough to park there when I realize it's not only his car I'm staring at—it's him and June.

This is how rumors happen. I'm sure someone drove by and saw him sitting out here, at least *parked* here. If he doesn't care, though, why should I?

Because you don't want him to date June, you asshole.

I clear my throat—and my mind—and push open my door. Both feet are barely on the ground before my best friend harasses me.

"Hey, princess!" Tory calls.

I pause and focus on my reflection in my tinted windows. I give him way too much power over me. This doesn't bother me. I'll prove it.

The scent of pepperoni pizza hits my nose as I round the back of my truck, my arms weighed down with my gear and backpack. My stomach rumbles.

"You got your car back," I say, gesturing toward June's ride, which is serving as a lounge chair for her and Tory.

"I did," she says, patting her hand against the trunk. Her head rolls to the side but stops when our eyes meet. That post Tory showed me on social media flashes through my head, and for a millisecond, I think about mentioning it. The singular purpose would be to push her, though, in hopes that she would argue with me. We have to be done with that. *We are done with that, aren't we?*

"That's good." I can tell my answer surprises her. I shuffle forward a few more steps, stopping just short of the property line. Her eyes trail down my legs to my rolled down socks and slides.

"Your feet never grew after that big burst, huh?" She nods toward my feet and I glance down at them, lifting my toes.

I smirk.

"Yeah, well, it took me a few years to grow into my size thirteens," I say, a natural laugh flowing from my chest. It feels good to laugh. My body feels lighter somehow. It's been like this all day.

I'm tempted to step across the thin patch of grass that divides us and join them, but all of the easiness that was brewing in the dusk is erased by the sound of my father's truck pulling in behind me. My head falls on instinct, like a puppy about to be smacked in the nose with a newspaper. I roll my shoulders and tug my bags up higher. I shift my weight back and forth and give in to my fate, turning and heading toward my dad's truck as he stops short of the garage.

"Lucas?" His body is already out of the cab, the sound of the door slamming shut echoing in the garage.

"I was just talking with Tory," I start to explain, trying to erase June from this scene. There's no need to mention her to Mom.

"Mind telling me why Coach called me tonight?"

My mouth tightens. He doesn't care that June's here. I figured he'd at least wait until we were alone or inside.

"Well, I wasn't on that call, you were, so . . ." I'm flirting with danger using this tone, but I'm so fucking sick of my dad and the way he tries to manage my life.

"Tory, do you know why my son skipped out on an hour of practice today?" My dad leans to look at my friend beyond my shoulder. I step up in an attempt to block his view, which irritates the shit out of him.

"Thanks, Tor. You're a real fuckin' help," my dad barks, his stare sinking back to me. Of course my friend kept his mouth shut. What friend would answer that question? It's ridiculous.

"Let's go inside," I urge, my feet digging at the pavement with every step I take away from my father, from Tory—from June. It's as if I'm dragging a million invisible pounds, immoveable tonnage.

"This a joke to you, Luc?"

Something in my father's tone strikes through the center of my chest, halting my feet and suctioning me to the ground where I stand.

"Maybe Mrs. D'Angelo knows," June utters.

Suddenly, we're all looking at her. Only June is looking up at the stars. Tory snorts out a laugh, amused by her distraction. But there's something maybe only I notice about what she said, the *way* she said it. *Why would Tory's mom be relevant to this conversation?*

June inhales and slides from her perch on the back of her car. Her gaze falls back to the earth, to my father's face. He matches her bravado with his typical grit. He stretches out his arms to show how taut his suit is on his muscles, and his nostrils flare, an affectation he's perfected to put people on edge. The closer June comes, the more his grin stretches, pushing up into his eyes. She stops a few feet short of him and he waves a hand at her, puffing out a laugh as if she's some trivial teenager who's seeking attention.

She's not. She's never been the type.

"Get inside," my dad says, glaring at me as he passes by and climbs into his truck. The garage door opens as his tires begin their slow roll forward. Mom's home, and it strikes me as interesting that my dad wants to have this argument in front of her rather than out here in front of Tory and June.

"Call if you need me, Luc," Tory shouts. I glance over my shoulder and hold up a half-hearted peace sign. This isn't the first time Tory's been around to see my dad have a conniption over football. This is new to June, though.

I stand in my place, stuck between following my dad's orders and drifting to the other side of the driveway to take up Tory's place and lay back on June's car to look at the sky. As Tory's lights flash on and he backs out of the driveway, I let my focus linger until my eyes adjust to the brightness, and then my gaze lands on June.

Her arms are limp at her sides, and her eyes and mouth are pulled down toward her chin. I recognize the torture of guilt.

"I'm sorry," she says, her voice barely audible.

She means it.

I believe her.

"Don't be," I say, forcing a tight smile in place of the hurt and pain I know I'm wearing. I nod toward the pizza box still resting on her trunk. "Glad you got your car back."

I make my way into the garage, and before I can turn around one last time, my dad makes sure the door is already dropping.

My mom is working through some new recipe at the counter when the two of us lumber through the door. She pauses to wipe flour from her hands and leans in to kiss my dad's cheek. He grumbles in response, his affection practically robotic, and he jerks at his tie on his way to the stairs. I wait until he's entirely out of earshot before saying a word.

"I'm sorry. It's my fault he's like that," I admit. I dump my gear bag by the laundry room and swing my backpack up on the counter to pull out my lit assignment. I need to get some reading done tonight, but my eyes are begging for sleep.

"Lucas, your father is in charge of his own attitude. That has nothing to do with you." She flutters her eyes and shakes her head, giving both him and me a pass. I'm not sure he deserves one.

"He found out I wasn't at practice on time."

"Ohh." She takes a step back and covers her throat with one hand before glancing toward the stairs. "I see."

We knew this would be his reaction.

"He doesn't need to know you covered for me," I say, trying to ease her conscience. I've turned her into a hypocrite with one lie.

She waves a hand and turns her attention back to her recipe, the counter littered with rolled dumplings and slices of bacon. I wash my hands and dry them on the towel before stepping in next to her.

"Put me to work," I offer.

"Yeah?" Her grin lights me up.

I nod. She loves it when we do things like this together. I do, too. It takes me back to when I was a kid and our weekends were filled with Mom and Lucas activities. I never realized how absent my father was back then. My eyes are wide open now. He's never really been a fixture here. If it's not about football and his kid proving some legacy bullshit, he's not interested in this family.

"Take a strip of bacon . . ."

"Okay," I respond, copying her as she folds the bacon up in the thin layer of dough. She pinches the end and dips it into a bowl of oil and seasoning.

"Can we eat this now?" I joke.

She breathes out a slight laugh and moves toward the fridge, opening it with the only clean finger on her hand. Pulling out a plate of what I'm guessing was her first attempt at this recipe, she flashes me a quick grin and winks on her way to the microwave. She pops the plate in and punches two minutes on the timer. My mouth waters in anticipation.

"You rock."

"I know," she answers fast.

We work through a few more wraps and when the cooked ones are hot enough, she tells me to wash my hands and sit down and enjoy. The treats are as delicious as I imagined, and I have half the plate eaten in minutes. The room is quiet, save for the sound of my chewing her occasional rolling out of dough. She hums when she works sometimes, never a complete song. Only fragments.

"So tell me . . ." Her lips pucker as she works, her fingertips kneading the dough. If she weren't my mom, I would simply assume she was concentrating. But I know better. She has something on her mind, one of *those* topics. She always hems and haws her way into the hard things, like the time she brought up contraception when I turned fifteen.

"How has your senior year been? Besides all of that business with him upstairs, I mean." She wipes her hands then folds them and leans forward, giving me her full attention.

I pop a bacon wrap in my mouth and shrug.

"Fine, I guess."

She studies me, reading my face, waiting for me to break and admit that things aren't so great. I won't do that, though. Even if I am struggling with this whole MIT thing and June and . . . *June.* My mom doesn't need to know those details.

“I was worried when you told me she was in your class,” she says, working her way closer to the target subject.

June.

Whom I do not want to talk about.

“Yeah, but it’s been fine. We don’t interact much. And it’s mostly pleasantries.”

Her eyebrow quirks, and why wouldn’t it? What boy my age uses the word *pleasantries?*

“It’s fine,” I say, busying my stupid mouth with an entire wrap. Chewing is so much easier than talking.

My mom eventually stands tall and cools her stare. I finish my plate and help her clean the mess. She doesn’t bring June up again, and I don’t give her a window. I head upstairs as soon as we’re done and tiptoe my way by their bedroom door where my dad is watching *Sports Center*. I have a feeling he’s done talking tonight. And if for some reason he’s not and decides to wander toward my room to chat about me missing practice, maybe I’ll ask him what June meant when she brought up Mrs. D’Angelo. I have a feeling I know, but I don’t want to. Life is better in blissful ignorance. At least, it was last time.

FOURTEEN

Abby's in the driveway this morning. A part of me, a bigger part than I care to admit, was rooting for June to need another ride. I think I'm ready to talk to her. I want to explain why I've been distant. *Apologize for being so mean.* The more we interact, the less I believe she is truly aware of the forces against us. June would be sympathetic when it comes to my mom. That's just how her heart is. And maybe . . . maybe June doesn't know the details about her mom and my dad. I don't relish the role of being the one to tell her, but I would like to be the one who understands how she feels.

I wait for June to hop into the car with Abby, and when enough time has passed I grab my gear, lock up the house, and head to my truck. My parents left early this morning, my dad not interested in sharing more of his critique, I suppose. Or he didn't want me asking about June's D'Angelo comment in front of my mom. My mind keeps going back to that moment. There's something to it.

I ride to school in silence, something I do from time to time. Not every day feels like a song, and lately, my mornings have not required much of a soundtrack. Instead of pulling to the back and hiding like yesterday, I park next to the twins. It's clear Tory filled Hayden in on my dad's little show last night because they both stare at me with funeral expressions when I get out and join them.

"It's fine," I say, shaking the conversation off before it even gets started.

Hayden nods and pulls out his phone, busying himself and giving me the peace I want on the topic. Tory, however, keeps his gaze on me for a few extra seconds. Eventually, I cock my head to the side and sigh.

"I promise. I'm fine." I literally cross my heart with my finger to make it count.

"Okay." He shuts his mouth tight but keeps his eyes on me. I try to ignore them, pulling my phone out and scrolling through social media. He doesn't relent, though. No matter how hard I try to ignore his stare, it penetrates—like a laser cutting through my skull.

"What?" I huff, clicking my screen off and stuffing my phone back in my pocket. I sink my hands into my letterman jacket pockets, glad it's a little cool out today so I don't look like a douchebag for wearing it. I've been fucking self-conscious about it ever since June made that remark.

"You and June were civil last night. It was weird." He shrugs but I know that's not all he has to say.

"Yeah, well, we're both nearly adults. We can be grown-ups, I guess."

"Nah, you've made progress. Both of you. It was almost as if you enjoyed each other's company. I think that theory needs to be explored," he says, bringing his hand to his chin and scratching.

I give him side-eyes, and thankfully, the school bell saves me from delving into this theory he has. He chuckles and points a finger at me.

"You're lucky," he teases.

"Yeah. Real fuckin' lucky." I roll my eyes, thinking about my dad last night and the MIT offer burning a hole through my soul.

Tory walks with me until he peels away near the middle of campus. My eyes search through everyone ahead of me, looking for June. When I reach the building doors, I chance a look over my shoulder, kind of hoping she's behind me. I pause when I realize nobody is. I'm the last one through the door.

I must have missed her.

When I step into our classroom, the first thing that hits me is her empty seat. Puzzled, I scrunch my brow and dart my eyes around the rest of the room. It's possible she moved her seat, tired of our lame game of chair kicking and shoving. That doesn't seem to be the case, either.

My notion that she's just late for class is dashed by the time there are only fifteen minutes remaining. Worry sets in when the bell rings, because I know I saw her leave this morning. I saw Abby's car, and I know they made it here. The only thing I have yet to see on this campus, is June.

I pull my phone out and thumb through various posts and updates on my apps while I leave the science building and make my way toward the gym. Nobody is gossiping about anything out of the ordinary. Even Ava seems quiet for now. She's been distant ever since our dinner outing to Two-fers. I wasn't very responsive that night. Actually, I'm not sure if I spoke to her directly at all, except about what to order. Maybe she's moved on?

I'm nearly to the gym doors when I make one last pirouette to scan the center of campus. That's when I see June leave the independent study rooms near the office. Two weeks ago, I basically prayed for her to switch classes. And now, seeing it a reality sucks the air out of my chest.

She actually did it.

This is ironic in the Alanis Morissette sense of the word—I'm finally ready to be around June, and she's done being around me. I'm deep in thought over losing June in my first hour when I turn to head into the gym lobby and run into Ava. Or rather run *over* Ava. My size and swift turn add up to the best tackle of my life, the result me completely caging her to the ground with my arms and legs.

"What the fuck, Lucas!"

She pushes up at my chest and I lift myself enough to roll to the side and get off her. Her friends are gathered around giggling, and one of them says, "I bet he's like this in bed."

Ava smirks but I roll my eyes and get to my feet. I offer her a hand, and as she takes it I'm grounded by the thought that I don't think I would offer one to June. Or . . . I wouldn't have at the beginning of the school year.

"Why are you making that face?" Ava snarks.

I shake my head, realizing I was probably wearing my self-awareness shock.

"I . . . remembered something. That's all."

"*Mmm*," she responds. Her friends whisper and huddle behind her, like her coven, and she juts her hip, hooking a thumb in the band of her jeans.

"We need to talk." She lifts her chin, and I can tell she's practiced this confrontation in her mirror. I've seen her rehearse these types of things. Usually, she practices yelling at her mom.

"Sure. Fine. Whenever."

I don't have much to say to her. I probably owe her some sort of closure to whatever we were, but I don't want to drag us on anymore.

"Today. After school."

"I have practice," I respond. She knows this.

"Are you sure? Or are you going to ditch so you can sign your acceptance to"—she glances over her shoulder and leans forward to mouth the rest—"M-I-T?"

My eyes narrow and my brow lowers as the corner of her lip raises in a proud smirk. Sometimes, she's like a champion chess player. I'm not sure there's anyone better at blackmail in this county.

"How—"

I stop before I get into my question. She volunteers in the office. She sits with Maggie. She probably pulled my final transcripts. I exhale, knowing I have to jump through her hoops.

"Okay, but right after class. Walk with me to the locker room so I'm not late again." I cringe at myself having uttered that extra bit of information.

"You've been late?" Her mouth is practically watering. She wants to know the juicy gossip. Ava seems to secretly love when I get into it with my dad. I feel bad because her home life is total shit, and I think she mostly likes not feeling totally alone in her existence. She wants to commiserate. She also takes too much pleasure in my misery.

"Yeah, I had an appointment, and I don't like slacking on my obligations, so if you aren't in the quad a minute after the final bell, you're going to have to reschedule. I look to her friends, still gathered behind her back. "Have your people call mine."

I make the phone gesture and chuckle as I leave her in the lobby and head through the boys' locker room doors.

Tory is changing out by the time I get to my locker, and I can tell by his smug expression that he saw my little negotiation in the lobby.

"Thought you were done with that," he says.

I fling my door open.

"I *am* done with that."

"Well, that ain't done with you."

I look to my right and drop my chin, leveling him with a hard-lined mouth. After a few seconds, he breaks away and holds out his palms, whispering "Okay, fine."

I toss my backpack in and pull my shirt up over my head, and while my locker door blocks the view between us, I hit Tory with my burning question.

"You know why June switched her first hour?"

He's quiet, and after several long seconds pass, I realize he's not going to answer. I breathe out heavily and finish changing out before slamming my locker door shut and leaning against it to deal with his second smug look of the morning.

"Dude, I have no idea why Maybe Mabee"—this is what he has started calling her, and it's irritating—"dropped your ass. I mean class."

I purse my lips and hold up my middle finger. My friend holds his belly as he falls back with a booming laugh. I walk away, leaving him no choice but to catch up on our way to weights.

"Look, my guess is she's trying to do you a favor. She hasn't said anything to me about it, but I can ask in our last hour if you want. Or maybe, and here's a revelation, *you can ask her yourself.*" He covers his mouth and gasps as he walks backward then points at me.

I wait out his gloating session and decide not to bring the topic up with him again. Not because he's wrong, but because his advice is solid, and the last thing I have the guts to do.

FIFTEEN

I know what my dad is thinking. It's the reason he left after the third quarter.

You get the official offer from Tennessee and the next day, you put on this shit fest on the field?

It might not be his thoughts verbatim, but I guarantee it's in the ballpark.

My dad has left in the middle of three of my games, ever. Once was for an emergency appendectomy. The other time was to catch a plane for a meeting, something I now call into question. And tonight, about eighteen minutes ago. He wanted me to see it, too. It's why he stood and stared out on the field with his hands on his hips. He didn't even bother to glance down to signal anything to me on the sidelines. He was too embarrassed.

I was embarrassed for my mom. She had to weave through people she knew to keep up with him so the two of them could leave together in the middle of my game. The quarterback's parents . . . bailing.

I'm not getting in again. Our defense has been shit all night, almost as useless as my offensive line. I have a feeling that last sack cracked a rib. With two minutes left on the clock, Pinecrest would be dumb not to just run out the clock.

I'm not embarrassed by my game play. I did what I could with what I had. And I made Tory look good, and his dad is here. He doesn't get to make many games, so the fact the one he came to is one in which his son scored the only touchdown makes up for the three times my face was flattened into turf.

We let Pinecrest run the field, eating up downs, five yards at a time. At this point, I'll be happy if they don't score again and we can say we only lost by fourteen. My team gets excited when their quarterback throws a pass and our defense runs down the tight end, wrapping him up after seventeen yards. They scream and shout along the sideline, waving their arms in the air as they jump and turn to hype up what's left of the crowd. I let them go. I'm happier here on the other end, away from the action.

Helmet at my side, my eyes glaze over as I stare at the clock. I like that it counts the fractions of seconds. Feels like more is happening this way. It's like grains of sand spilling through the narrowing of an hourglass. When the buzzer sounds and fans rush the field, I force my legs to carry me toward the team. Instead of leading them, I opt to fall in step at the end of the line. Coach notices and I make up an excuse in my head for when he asks why I wasn't being a leader.

I wanted our hard-working defense to get the credit.

It'll be this private joke for me and me alone, and the best part is he'll wonder if I'm being sincere or mocking their shitty performance.

We shake hands with the other guys and I go through the motions, grabbing my sweat towel and following the dejected line of massive dudes all heading toward our bus. I glance to our stands as I cross the track, and though nearly everyone has cleared out—probably well before time was up—one person stayed.

June stayed.

I dart my eyes back to my path, holding steady on the Eagles jersey in front of me, the double zeros that our best receiver gets to wear. My helmet balanced on my head, I chew on my plastic mouth guard, anticipation building in my chest. I swear I can sense she's close as we get near the field exit, and I time it perfectly, glancing to my right as we pass through the few people who waited to see us off. Our eyes lock for a single beat, probably the first *real* heartbeat I've felt in months, maybe years.

She stayed. When everyone else left, she stayed.

I barely talk to a soul on our way back to the school, and Coach is too disgusted with us to talk when we get to our locker room. Instead of pausing by the white board as we all file in, he beelines straight to his office, slamming the door and dropping the blinds. His clipboard smashes into them a few seconds later, getting caught between a few of the slats and bending the thin metal. He leaves it there, a reminder and a warning to us to leave him the fuck alone or enter at our own risk.

"You up to party in the woods tonight?" Tory elbows me as we stop in front of our lockers. I pull my mouth in tight on one side and glance at him in my periphery before shaking my head.

"Yeah, I figured. For what it's worth, I think you played great tonight, and fuck Coach for thinking we're a better team than we really are." Tory holds out a fist and I drop mine on top. "I'll catch up with you tomorrow."

He takes off for the showers as I plop down on the bench to drag off my jersey and pads. I'm in no rush to be anywhere, and I'd rather let the hot water of the showers burn off my mood alone. I wait until almost everyone is done before heading in, and I think about Tory's words the entire time. He's right. I played well tonight. Yeah, maybe I could have had a little more fire in my throws, and definitely in my attitude. But none of that would have made a difference in the outcome. Our defense was no match for the Pinecrest offensive line. They must feed their boys beef and steroids for every meal. We kept up, and we should hold our heads up high for that.

My dad won't think so. He'll call my performance second rate. Then, he'll blame Coach and curse the program for not letting me shine. I'll have to listen to it all. Sit through every goddamn word and nod when expected. My mom will listen in from the kitchen, deep down wanting to tell my dad to lay off. She won't, though, because she saves her battles for her grudge, for snide remarks about infidelity and loyalty.

They're both letting me down.

I'm not sure when I decided I would look for June the second I got home. Maybe it was during that long shower, or perhaps during the quiet drive, void of music to disrupt my thoughts. I drove ten under the limit to get home, maybe knowing that the second I pulled into my driveway I would cross a line.

It feels foolish not to. All this time I've avoided June for two people who don't give a second thought to what I might need or want. My mom might support me going to MIT, but she sure doesn't seem concerned about me having to endure one more season of football lectures from Dad.

The brush back by the old Buick is thick and the weeds scratch my calves and snag my sweatpants while I cut through the tall grass on my way into the dark corner of June's back yard. I don't know how I knew she would be waiting for me. I didn't even hope for it. It was this understood safety net my gut told me would be here tonight. *June would be here.* And there she is.

I tug open the busted door and slip into the passenger seat. The lines in the dust from the last time I was in here are still there, only a faint sheen of new dirt filling in the lines. I leave the door open but bring my feet in, sitting back and exhaling. June rolls her window down, only a few inches but enough that the dank air clears out, making way for the evening breeze. For long minutes, it's nothing but me and June and the quiet.

It's a peaceful bliss, and exactly what I need. My mind feels calm, all of my stress at ease and the knot in my gut looser than it's been in weeks. Maybe all I need is this, a timeout in a familiar place with company who actually gives a shit, even though I don't deserve it.

My phone's ringtone plays Kanye and I yank it out, muting it the second I see it's Ava, probably wanting a lift to the party. She rings right back so I power my phone off and toss it onto the dusty dashboard before pressing my palms into my eyes. It feels as if I haven't slept in weeks. The bags under my eyes are like tiny pillows. I scratch at my head, feeling my wet hair run through my fingers. With another heavy exhale, I lean forward, resting my weight on my folded hands and the dash.

"I want to go to MIT." I nod at my faint reflection in the windshield, loving the way those words sound out loud. It's freeing to be able to admit what you want in front of someone.

"That's amazing," June answers almost immediately. I drop my head into my hands and roll it side to side while I toe at the rotting floor. I pull my mouth up into a crooked smile and look at her sideways.

"It is, isn't it?"

Her smile stretches wider, and I try to do the same with mine, but it only goes so far. I flatten my palms and lean forward, resting my head on the backs of my hands while I stare at her face, remembering all the things about it that fascinated me. I always loved the way her chin came to a soft point, and how her milky skin was the perfect canvas for her freckles, and the pink blush that took over her body at even the slightest embarrassment.

"I got an offer from Tennessee," I breathe out.

She nods, her expression steady, unchanged.

"That's awesome too," she says, and I shake with a quiet laugh.

"You're right. It is." I sit back and drop my hands into my lap. Leave it to June to boil things down to the truth: I have two great options in front of me.

"What do you want?" she asks.

My faint smile loses its hold and the heaviness creeps back into my chest.

"Does that matter?" I say with a quick shrug.

"It should."

I huff out a short laugh. Again, she's so right.

June fidgets with the marble ball on the Buick's shifter stick, twisting it until it comes off. She passes it between both hands a few times, tossing it, then holds it out toward me, as if presenting me with a ring. I take it, our hands brushing on the exchange. I'm left with the cool weight of the polished stone in my palm. I always loved this thing. When we were kids, I would pretend it was a jewel with magical powers or secretly worth millions. I even tossed it in the pool once to see if June could dive to the bottom to retrieve it.

"Thanks. I always wanted this thing."

"I know," she responds with a breathy laugh. "It's yours now."

My mouth tugs up for a short smile as I roll it around in my palm and stare at it.

"Or you could give it to Ava."

My mouth sours, but I do my best to appear unaffected by her words. I deserved that.

The silence bakes us for several long seconds. The breeze seems to have disappeared, and coupled with the passive-aggressive words June just uttered, my body feels a dozen degrees too warm.

"Why'd you leave physics?" I know why, and I'm sure that comment she just made has a little to do with it.

"Seemed it was for the best." I glance her way and catch an earnest shrug.

"Yeah," I sigh out.

I settle further into the seat, drawing one leg up while I toss the marble ball in my hand. I line it up with the shifter screw after a minute and twist it back into place. It doesn't feel as special as it used to. Or maybe I don't feel as worthy.

"I don't really want it," I say, flitting my eyes to her. "I just liked that it pissed your dad off."

We both spit out a short laugh.

"It did."

I'm suddenly caught looking at her. It's easier this time, so I indulge, not feeling guilty about it, and let my eyes hold hers through several full breaths. She seems to feel the same. The tension that's tethered our chests together, making it hard for me to breathe, has given us slack. Her gaze meanders around my features, and it tugs my lip up on one side. She's looking at the scar above my right eyebrow, the one from my monkey bar accident when we were kids. The faintest smile rests on her closed lips, and I swear I can hear the memories rushing through her mind, like the best story time ever.

"Ava's not my girlfriend, just so you know."

I'm not sure what possesses me to utter those words, but doing so immediately tightens the ropes around my chest. Breathing is no longer easy.

June doesn't blink, instead drawing in a long, steady breath through her nose.

"She seems like your girlfriend."

She probably does seem like it. She probably feels she is. I've led her on, used her to fill a void.

"She's not. She's just . . ."

What is she? She's a terrible person who bullies June. She was there when I was lonely. She put up with my moody bullshit so I stuck around.

"She's just this mistake I make sometimes."

That came out harsh.

June shakes her head.

"She's not a mistake," she corrects.

"Okay."

She's right. She was a choice I made, but now that I'm staring at the one person I always felt was home, every choice up until this point feels empty and gutless.

"I might not like her very much, but no girl deserves to be labeled a mistake. She's a lot of things, but mistake isn't one of them. Your moments with her had purpose, even if they were brief and not love. Your actions can be a mistake, but not the person."

She cries through the final few words. Other than me, Ava is the one person who has purposely hurt June over and over again, and here she is, defending her. More than that, she's putting me in my place. Most people would probably pile on and agree, and she'd have every right to argue I didn't go far enough. But that's not June. How she's managed to hold on to the high road while the rest of us have tunneled into the deep, I don't know. But she has.

"Okay," I say through faint laughter.

"Okay," she repeats. She wipes away another sniffle, and all I want to do is run my thumb across her cheek to dry her skin. It never moves beyond an urge thanks to the abrupt flash of lights from the back of my house. My dad slides open the back door to pace from one end of the patio to the other.

"He's probably looking for me," I say, squinting and glad I'm hidden in this car. He would never look for me here.

"Let him," June says. I glance to her and breathe out a laugh at the sight of her chest puffed up and her fist in her hand.

"I wish I could, but—"

"But he's the reason you can't go to MIT?" Her dose of honesty cuts like poison.

My eyes drop to her neck then flicker back up to meet her gaze, confirming her question.

"He went to Tennessee, and me and football—"

"You're living his dream," she says, her words overlapping with mine. She gets it. Of course she does.

"He'll come around."

My chest shakes with one silent laugh.

"Doubtful," I say, pushing open the door to head to my lecture. I spin and place my palms on the roof of the car, dipping my head into view to look at her one last time. My thoughts are disorganized and the words I'm searching for don't seem ready to come, leaving me with a mouth hung open and a chest squeezed so tight I feel as though I'm drowning.

"Thanks, June," I finally utter. At least those words are nice. Better than I've uttered over the last few weeks.

I rap on the top of the car and back up a step or two, tossing the door shut on my way. My dad's gone back inside and the lights are all off now. I pause at the edge of the deck, one foot perched on the first step. My house has a faint glow from the entry light and that's it, the kitchen void of life. My mom probably escaped to the bedroom, and maybe that's where my dad is for now. He'll wander back down the stairs to search for me after a few minutes, though; he's got too much to say. He's not going to feel settled until he has a chance to impart his wisdom on me.

Almost automatically, my head swivels to my left, toward the Mabee house. The lights there are all off. June probably headed inside. I was just with her but I want to be again. Not in the morning, or tomorrow, but now. *Right now.*

I back away from the deck and take quiet steps through the gravel into the grass, cutting across our yards until I'm staring up at her window, the blue glow of her lamp outlining the slats of her shutters. I glance around my feet for something to throw, gathering up five or six pebbles that won't cause permanent damage if I toss them. I shake them in my closed palm, like dice. I should probably blow on them for good luck, but I don't before launching them toward June's window. They scatter, pinging in all directions.

June opens the window a few seconds later, but her gaze is lost. She's not searching for what made the sound against her window; she's searching for me. Her focus is on my house—on the darkened back deck, my window.

Your actions can be a mistake, but not the person.

My eyes widen as I replay her words from a few minutes ago in my mind. June thinks she was a mistake—that *we* were a mistake. I drop my gaze and scan for more rocks, finding enough to make another attempt to get her attention, and I look up in time to see her pulling her shutters closed. I rear back and launch the stones at the side of her house, spraying the area around her window with the shrapnel. I immediately gather more rocks and bring my hand up to toss them and am unable to stop my motion when she opens the slats again. She flings both sides open and when the stones hit the surface and I realize that in seconds, I need to have the right words ready to say. I'm so terrible at this when it comes to her, and I can't mess this up.

"What are you doing? You can't run away to here. I mean, he'll find you," she says, making a joke about my dad.

"You were never a mistake." My heart is pounding so hard that I feel it in the tips of my fingers. I went with the most important words first, a reaction to my sudden worry that June thinks I classify her as anything other than important. It's my fault that she does, and only I can correct that.

My hands are balled into fists at my sides as I rock back and forth. June's mouth is open and she hasn't moved in five, six . . . now seven seconds.

"Okay," she finally says. Her mouth curves into a grin and she holds up two thumbs. She thinks I'm nuts.

"No, June." Shit, I can't do this from down here. There's too much distance; my words are going to get lost. I hold up a finger and rush toward her house with the same gusto I did when we were kids. The leap to the eave of the house is easier now, but my body is bigger and I sound like a gorilla climbing a playhouse. *God, I hope her mom is asleep.*

My hands find the familiar grip of her window ledge, a place they haven't been in years. I pull myself up as June takes a few steps back into her room. I'm not graceful, but manage to maneuver my body through her window one arm and leg at a time. I didn't think before doing. I simply acted. And now I'm here, in her room, my hands so fucking sweaty and my body pulsing with the rush of blood and beats of my heart. I bite the tip of my tongue and meet her gaze, breathing out a short laugh at my own expense. My God, what she must be thinking. I disappear for a couple of years then climb in through her window.

"When you said those things, about how no girl wants to be a mistake." I swallow hard and shake my head, my eyes never breaking from hers. "You meant you. You weren't talking about Ava."

I take a timid step forward and her hands ball at her sides. She's as nervous as I am, full of the same caution and fear. She looks to her side, to the mirror by her dresser. I follow her gaze and immediately see the pictures of us taped to the surface. My heart cracks wide open. She's never been far. She was here all along. I'm so stupid.

"I'm sorry, June."

Her eyes are still fixed on her mirror—on our memories—as I inch my way forward.

"You are not a mistake," I repeat. I'm close enough to feel the heat of her body.

"Got it. Thanks," she chokes out. She's putting up walls, waiting for me to sucker punch her with words. I've trained her to expect such. Shame on me.

I reach for her chin, squeezing the feeling back into my fist before opening my palm and brushing my fingertips along her chin. I lift her head with gentle pressure, tempting her gaze my way. When I'm able to hold her head between both palms, I tilt it enough to force our eyes to meet. My mouth goes dry, but even still, my words are there. Suddenly, I know what to say. I know everything.

"You are not a mistake," I repeat. No mistaking my message. I look deep into her green eyes, the glint of moonlight reflecting on their glassy surface. I don't mean to make her cry.

She nods her head, sucking in her lips once before uttering "Okay." One deep breath gathers her nerves, and the slight crooked smile fills me with so much happiness. I've missed her. I've missed *out* on her—on us. I'm so stupid.

I run my thumb under her eye, like I wanted to in the car, and stutter out a nervous laugh.

"Thanks," she says, eyes briefly flitting downward.

"Don't mention it," I say, doing the same to her other cheek.

The slight tremble in her lips catches my eye, and as they part, a tiny gasp escapes. I'm sunk.

My thumb roams from the curve of her cheek to the rise of her upper lip. I can feel her quiver under my touch and her eyes close when my thumb moves from her top lip to her bottom. I don't dare close mine—not yet. It feels as though minutes pass as my mouth inches closer to hers, and when our lips finally touch, my body is powered to life like a man about to die but saved by paddles to the chest.

This is what kissing a girl is supposed to feel like.

My nose grazes hers as I shift my position, tilting my head so I can kiss her deeper. I force myself to be gentle at first, starting with her upper lip and holding it between mine with a tender suckle. Her hands gather my shirt against my chest, bunching the cotton into her fists. The feel of her wanting me strips away my caution, and my eyes fall shut as my hands weave along her neck and into her hair, holding her mouth to mine. We suffocate in this kiss, and it's worth giving up air.

My tongue teases hers, my teeth caressing the softness of her lips. Hers hold on to mine, the threat of her bite rushing my bloodstream with her special brand of dopamine. I'm drunk on her, all at once. This kiss changes everything. It's the middle of the story—the one I told her I wish I could erase her from. I am a liar. I've never wanted June out of my story, out of my life. I've just been too afraid. She's worth the fight. I'm a better man with her. I'm stronger, kinder, smarter—braver.

Dizzy and maybe on the verge of passing out, I pull our mouths apart and rest my head on hers. We're both panting, and our mouths are raw and puffy from the force of our kiss. My hands cup her face, my fingers flexed and my muscles locked. I'm suddenly terrified this isn't real, or what we experienced was temporary—a dream, a blissfully indulgent dream. I rock us side to side in a silent dance.

"That was not a mistake," I whisper. My body shudders when her palms slide to my chest, her nails scratching at the cotton of my shirt, grabbing the fabric. Clinging.

"Okay," she whispers back. She rises up on her toes and presses her lips to mine, holding them still. Her kiss is unending, a steadiness to it she must sense I need. I know she feels my lips tremble. She must. Her teeth graze along my skin, dominant and sure. She doesn't slip away until I draw in a full breath, and when she does, she whispers "okay" again. She says it a few more times, each with a soft kiss somewhere on my chest or neck or shoulder. And somewhere along the way, maybe we both start to believe in this moment.

Naturally, I have to ruin it. I ruin everything. Like father, like son.

Our kiss breaks in slow motion as awareness crowds June's room, swirling around me and invading my head with panic. I do a poor job of masking it in my expression. I can tell because of the way June's brow draws in tight as I move toward the window I let myself in through.

"You don't have to go," she begs. I sense it, her desire. I have it, too, and it's the reason I need to go. I'm not quitting on us, but with the barriers in our way, I need to be smart, take it slow.

"My dad will be circling the property every hour on the hour."

We both let out a nervous laugh. I'm only half kidding.

I slide one leg out the window and hold my weight up on the ledge, careful to make eye contact one last time before I crawl my way back down her pitched eave.

"You can't tell anyone."

Her eyes dim, the green gone, nothing left but black. I asked her to be my secret, same as my dad did to her mom. Even sadder, I know she won't say a word.

SIXTEEN

I called Ava the second I got back to my house last night after being at June's. She'd left me a half dozen messages, each one progressively more belligerent, entitled and possessive. I was right that at first she wanted a ride to the party. Eventually, she wanted *me* at the party. Mostly, she didn't like not knowing where I was. When I called, she was her typical buzzed-at-a-party self. I told her I didn't want to do whatever she and I were doing anymore, and when she asked if I wanted more, I wasn't very nice.

I said, "Yes, but not with you."

She hung up.

I texted her an apology and told her she deserves better. She told me to *fuck off.*

When my phone buzzed at a decent hour this morning, I figured she was still hungover and angry-texting or wanting to complete our usual cycle of break-up then get back together. It wasn't Ava, though. It was Tory.

My friend must have taken it easy last night. Over the summer, I could basically set my alarm to noon the day after a party and still have hours on my own before Tory rolled out of bed hungover and hungry. This morning's message didn't even come equipped with a vomiting emoji, his signature post-party icon.

TORY: *Bowling?*

Dare I say, Tory is maturing.

I find myself ensnared in a strange set of obstacles now that my relationship with June has . . . *shifted.* I need to dissect basic questions and normal tasks, constantly asking myself whether June will be present and how I'd behave if I didn't know how her mouth tastes.

That's how I dealt with the *bowling* text. I didn't lie. I wrote back: *I hate bowling.*

I mostly do, though I'm decent at it. But I love pool. And I want to see June, desperately. I played to my strengths and somehow managed to not spark a million needling questions from my best friend on our way to Eight Lanes.

Abby's sitting at the counter when we walk in, and it helps keep my nerves in check seeing Tory get rattled. His crush on June's best friend has elevated. There's something different about the way he is with her and around her. And it's more than him liking the chase or hating her constant rejection. Maybe that's my ticket to getting him off my back about June. Every time he brings her up, I'll counter with a question about Abby.

"Maybe Mabee, what's up?"

June pops up from behind the counter, her eyes wide and darting to take in her new customers. I offer a one-sided smirk in apology for surprising her, but before she can speak, Tory's reaching over the counter and hugging her. My smile drops and I feel that tightness in my gut. It's fucking jealousy. Her eyes find mine over Tory's shoulder, and I swear she's telling me with her gaze to calm down.

"Nice game Friday, Luc," Abby says while she and June exchange glances. She winks at her friend. *Did June tell Abby about us?*

"Fuck off, Abby," I say, knowing she isn't really complimenting my game. We lost. And old Lucas, the one who doesn't kiss June, would call Abby out.

I slide onto the stool at the end of the counter, away from everyone else, mostly because I feel jittery. I'm overthinking things, but I can't help it. There's a newness to everything, despite the fact I've known June for years. I'm nervous and maybe embarrassed, in a good way.

"Can I get a water?" I nod toward the tap. I'm totally doing this to create physical separation between her and Tory. I hope I'm the only one aware of that.

She eyes me while sliding her feet toward the ice machine. She picks up the scoop and points it at me, her tongue pushed into her cheek.

"It's a buck for the cup."

Abby chuckles and when I look at her, she drops her eyes to the counter and takes a long drink through her straw, draining her cup until she's making the slurping sound.

"Ahh," she adds before sliding the cup forward and tapping it a few times on the counter. "Some of us get freebies."

June laughs at her friend's teasing. It's good. The normalcy. I just can't fuck it up.

I stare at Abby for a few hard seconds and chew at the inside of my mouth. She's a worthy opponent, twisting on her stool and crossing her legs as she stares back at me just as hard. I leave my eyes on her while I lean to the side, pull my wallet out and slip my debit card free. I toss it across the counter toward June, who slaps it down under her palm. She plays it up, waiting for me to turn to face her so she can study the front of my card, and then my face.

"Lucas *A.* Fuller." She over-pronounces my name, the way our principal did once in fourth grade when I dug a hole under the play yard fence during recess.

June flattens the card on the counter and flicks it toward me with her index finger. I manage to catch it in my lap before it falls to the floor.

"I'm afraid I can only take cash."

I laugh silently, enough that my shoulders shake. Chewing on my tongue so I don't break character. I peek at her from underneath the brim of my hat as she threatens to pour out the ice water she put in the cup, letting it go so far as to trickle into the sink. There's a part of her that truly enjoys this, and I'm not sure whether that's a good thing or bad thing. It's definitely a sexy thing. My thoughts keep going back to last night, to her mouth and the curves of her body that my hands traced. I close a fist under the counter to relieve the tension.

"Ah ah," I say, holding up my other palm.

I tuck my card back into my wallet while my eyes hold her hostage. It takes me a few tries to find the right card slot, but eventually the folded up dollar bill shows itself and drops on the counter. Of course, so does my fucking condom.

June's eyes zero in on it, and I'm only a millisecond behind her.

Fuck, fuck, fuck, fuck . . .

In a flash, June finishes filling my cup back up and refastens the lid.

"Here," she says, snapping it down on the counter. She tosses a wrapped straw next to it. My gaze moves from the straw to her face. All I want to do is explain, or apologize. I'm not even sure what to say. I mean, it's a responsible thing to have in one's wallet—*in my wallet.*

Shit.

June drags her palm over the counter before I can put my foot in my mouth and collects both the dollar and the condom. I swallow, and I don't even care that everyone saw it.

She drops the buck in the register drawer, then turns to face the twins and Abby while holding the condom packet between her thumb and index finger, as if it's a rare coin for people to *ooh* and *ahh* over. Tory and Hayden are stifling laughter, fists covering their mouths, and Abby just looks excited. She clearly can't wait to see what happens next.

They don't see the details like I do. I guess that's a good thing. It protects our secret. Only, now it breaks my heart a little too. June's hurt. Her cheeks are flushed, and not from being embarrassed, which is what everyone probably thinks. She's upset. Maybe jealous. I'm sure she's thinking about me and Ava.

I'm such a dick.

"Ribbed for her pleasure," she reads. She annunciates the same way she did my name and initial, ending with a click of her tongue. "Well."

She leans to her side, resting her elbow on the counter in front of me. Her eyelashes bat and her focus shifts from our friends to me. They got the performance. I am getting the truth. She pinches the edge of the packet and holds it out for me. I scratch at my neck and laugh nervously before grabbing the other side. June doesn't let go, and my eyes fly up to meet hers. I draw them in, begging her silently not to make this a big deal, or to make it something we talk about in front of everyone. *Please.*

Her lids weigh heavily and the corners of her mouth turn down. She lets go then backs away a step or two.

"I hope she enjoys it."

Our friends can no longer hold it in, and Tory spits out a laugh, reaching toward June to high five her for nailing me. He hates Ava, so of course he's all over this.

I stand, putting the condom back in my wallet then shoving it into my pocket. Abby is laughing pretty hard now too, and even Hayden—quiet, keep-the-peace Hayden—is repeating June's last line.

Lifting the water cup, I hold it out in a toast, and the laughter dies. They're all on the edges of their seats waiting to see what I'll say. I bite at the end of my straw.

"She better," I say, lips wrapping around the straw. I look to June as I suck, and a fire crackles between us. This push-pull isn't how our relationship should be. Maybe we're too far into our habits to break them. Or maybe it's my fault. I'm the one who set the rules, who asked her to keep us a secret.

"Gentlemen?" I tilt my head toward the pool table, and the twins follow me. Tory's eyes meet mine for a beat, and I see his disgust flash in the background. His expression is always easy to decipher, at least it is for me. Probably because I give him so much to judge.

"What do you say, boys? Five bucks a game?" I gather the balls on the table, racking them . . . *and avoiding Tory's glare.*

"I don't know, Luc. Pretty sure you just gave away your last dollar," Hayden says. He's teasing me, but I sense a little bite in his tone. *Ouch! And he's the timid one.*

"You'd have to beat me, and we both know that ain't happening." I flash a crooked grin at him and he flips me off.

"That was a little much, dude," Tory says as he basically body checks me with his bicep.

"She started it," I snap back. I can only look at him in short bursts. *This is normal Lucas behavior.* At least, that's what I keep telling myself.

"Come on. Five bucks a game. Who wants to go first?"

Tory grabs the stick from my hand and points it toward the counter where June is now alone and picking at a sandwich.

"It's me and Hayden this game. You get the winner. And we'll see if we let you place a wager." His mouth is a stern line, and his eyes move again from me to the girl beyond my shoulder. He's being serious, and deep down, I'm glad to see him respect June so much. I'm also fighting the urge to grab the collar of his T-shirt and tell him that taking care of June is my job.

"Fine. I'll go make nice. Maybe get a refill." I grab the cup from the edge of the pool table and let the burn of guilt torch my insides while I walk to the front counter. June is filling a cup with ice and water as I walk up.

"Employees don't have to follow that dollar rule, huh?" I joke. What I should have said was "I'm so sorry." Instead, I made a fucking joke.

Her gaze shifts to the twins then back to me, a smile the furthest thing from her face.

"You just missed it. I donated a condom to the register." Her monotone response is pretty clear. I should have gone with an apology.

She picks at her sandwich, her focus on nothing but the crust on her bread.

"June, don't be like that," I sigh out. That still was not an apology. Maybe I've played the asshole so long I don't know how to be the gentleman anymore.

June rips at her bread, pulling off the corner and popping it into her mouth before finally lifting her gaze to meet mine. Her jaw works slowly, her chew more of a distraction to her hurt and anger than anything. She forces a smirk onto her face while she leans into the counter.

"Be like what? Like your dirty little secret?" She takes a drink and tilts her head, one eye squinting as she hits me with an accusatory face. I deserve every bit of it.

I glance toward the game, which is still going, then run my palm over my face as I slide onto one of the stools.

"It's complicated."

She just keeps eating. The quiet between us is harder to take than the barbs and insults. I've spent enough time *not* talking to her. I don't want to go back to that.

"Excuse me," she says, wrapping up the rest of her sandwich and leaving it under the counter before tossing a towel on the counter and slipping away.

I spin in my seat, the twins' backs to me as they study a shot in their game of nine-ball. Taking my opportunity, I dash around the corner the way June headed, not finding her in the hallway. The only other option is the ladies' room, and this place is empty. I push open the door in time to catch her ducking into the last stall. I reach her before the latch drops, and push against the door. If I have to drop to the floor and crawl in there to get to her, I will. *Thank God, this isn't the men's room.*

"June, don't do this."

Why can't I just say I'm sorry? What is wrong with me?

June laughs at my attempt.

"You need to get out of here," she says in a raspy whisper. She pushes back hard, her feet sliding along the tile. I smile a little at her attempt to move me. I'm twice her size. Suddenly, though, my weight falls forward, through the door, as she gives up completely and steps back. *Well played, June.*

Fine. We'll do this in here. Where I can trap her.

I shut the door and latch it behind me, pretty confident I can defend her attempts to get past me. Not that I'll hold her in here if she asks to leave.

"What, because two pair of legs won't be a giveaway?" Her face contorts to match her snarky tone before she glances down at our feet.

I lean my head back with a heavy sigh and remind myself why this matters. June matters. Even if I think a condom is a trivial thing, to June, it isn't. And it shouldn't be. I hurt her.

For years.

My gaze drops to her and I lean forward, resting my palm against the wall on one side of her head. I'm blocking her from rushing out, and when her eyes dart to my arm, I drop it a little lower, afraid she's looking for a quick escape.

Great job, Lucas. You have to hold her hostage.

"Where should I begin?" I'm being serious, despite how vague my question sounds. I owe her so much. I want to tell her everything, to ask her what she knows. If I have to give her every detail of my mom's depression, of her addiction and nervous breakdown, here while surrounded by black and white tiles and the smell of industrial toilet cleaner, then that's what I'm going to do. I'm here for it. Let's do this.

"You said I'm not a mistake." Her voice breaks through that last word, and my bravado dissolves in an instant. She's trying so hard not to cry.

Without questioning it, I move my other hand to her face, stroking her cheek with my thumb and urging her to look me in the eyes.

"I did, and I meant it," I say when she finally does.

This is who I want to be. I need to remember what this man feels like. My mouth aches to kiss her, but it's not the right time. Words first. So many words are necessary.

"Out there," she says, dropping her eyes to the tight space between us. A single tear cuts down her cheek, pausing at the curl of her lip. I want to kiss it away. "I felt like a pretty big mistake out there. And every single second that passed just made me feel more and more like I . . . like me and you? We don't belong."

I can't look her in the eye. Her voice, so raw, cuts through me. I'm afraid when I lift my gaze from her chin I'll see more tears. I can't handle more tears. Not when I'm the reason they're there. Instead, I bring my head to rest against hers, pulling my hands in to cup her face so my thumbs can feel the streaks left behind on her cheeks. I won't erase them. I can't.

"June, nobody can know," I say, my mouth inches away from hers. If only I could kiss this all away.

"Is it Ava? So you can still sleep with her?"

My center of gravity sinks to the floor.

"No, June. Fuck Ava." My response is swift and my words come out harsh. I step back so she can see the proof in my expression, shaking my head and daring to meet her gaze. Her eyes are so fucking red, her cheeks puffy and tear-strewn. I did that.

"Exactly," she laughs out.

My instincts to shout and defend myself push against my insides. June isn't hearing me. Then again, why should she?

"I ended things with Ava. Completely." My teeth clench as my jaw tightens. So help me if Ava is telling people another story.

"*Mmm,*" June says, more tears spilling from her eyes. Her mouth is a hard line and her nostrils flair with fight. She's not going to make this easy. It shouldn't be. "That what you held on to the condom for?"

I exhale as my head falls to my shoulder. I'm a bit deflated. I want her to trust me. I guess I shouldn't expect to leap right to that kind of bond again.

"I didn't even know that was in there, June." I swallow down my frustration and glance to the side, letting my focus get lost on the bathroom graffiti. I don't know what else I can say to prove I'm a man of my word. All I want is for her to believe me, for her to know she matters—*to me.*

"Your dad is having an affair."

My gaze snaps to hers. Her hands cover her mouth and her eyes are glued to mine, unflinching. For a millisecond, I think I heard her wrong. In the next fraction of a breath, I mentally run through everything I know to be true. My dad had an affair. With her mom. He's been gone lately when he should be home. My family is teetering on a single card, and June just dropped an entire deck.

Now is not the time for this fight. This is not where she gets told everything I know. The women's bathroom of Eight Lanes is not where we swap and compare broken family tales.

I swallow hard, my mind replaying what June said, over and over. Her verbs were present tense. *Is having* is a lot different from *had.*

Before I make things worse, I spin on my heels and leave.

SEVENTEEN

I had to run home. My head was no clearer by the time I got there than when I left Eight Lanes, so I changed into more appropriate running wear and took off down our street, around the corner, and all the way to school.

I run when I'm stressed. I also run when I'm upset. This translates to an eleven-mile jog that lasts most of the afternoon. I take a break, climbing the bleachers to the top of the press box so I can stare at that goddamn football field for a while. All of those hits, hours of passing drills, my literal blood—all to make my old man happy. Turns out, he's big on getting greener grass in other places. Why do I even bother?

June wasn't lying. And she wasn't spreading a rumor or guessing at something she maybe suspected. I still know her well enough to sense when she's telling the truth. I pushed her to a point she wanted to hurt me, so she pulled out the sharpest tool she had. That one pierced me in the gut.

The sun is setting early, and there's a slight breeze in the air as I jog home then climb in the back of my truck. My sweat has mostly dried, leaving my skin cool. My mom's inside, and I can't face her. I don't want to be another man who lies in her house. My dad has that job all sewn up. Speaking of my dad, he isn't home.

Surprise.

The only person I can talk to right now is still at work. I have no idea when she gets off, and no clue if she'll even want to talk to me when she gets here. But when I crawled into the back of my truck and slid down to sit in the bed, I promised myself I'd wait.

Abby's headlights meet the glare of the setting sun at the end of my driveway. Our eyes meet, so I slump down lower, not really hiding but masking that I've been waiting for them to arrive. I hope she doesn't stay. I want June all to myself. She's the only one who can answer my questions and take away this awful feeling.

She swings the passenger door shut and drags her jacket along the ground as she takes micro steps in my direction. I breathe out a short, amused laugh, too quiet for her to hear. She looks like a kid about to get grounded for coloring on the walls. She's almost to me when Abby honks her horn, causing June to leap in the air and grab her chest.

"Shit!" she shouts.

My heart races, too, from being startled.

When she turns back to face me, a bashful smirk on her lips, I feel bad that I can't be light and happy with her. She got spooked by the car horn, and that should be funny, but nothing is funny right now. Nothing might ever be funny again.

"What's up, Maybe Mabee?" I sneer, glad it's dim enough to hide the details of my expression. That was my jealous side coming out. I hate that Tory calls her that.

June pauses at the end of my truck, her eyes dipping down, heavy with guilt. She didn't do anything wrong. She shouldn't feel this way. I guarantee my father isn't.

"I'm sorry," she utters, lifting her head to meet my gaze. She truly is sorry. I read it all over her face. She's not the one I need to hear it from.

I give her a nod, unsure what to say in response.

"Okay. Thanks." I shrug then twist the cap from the water bottle I've been nursing. I chug down the rest, put the lid back on, then toss the empty container to the middle of the driveway. June starts to move toward it.

"Let my dad pick it up. Maybe I'll throw the rest of his shit out here too." It's only partially a joke.

June pauses and looks back at me over her shoulder, her eyes studying my face. *Come on, Lucas. Smile. Show her you aren't completely broken.*

I must fail the test because she turns back to the bottle, picking it up and tossing it in her family's recycling bin. She drops her hands in her pockets when she turns to face me, her head tilted ever so slightly to the side. Her eyes are so soft, gentle and caring. Why can't I just scoop her up and hold her like I want to?

Because my mom is inside and might step near the window. She might see something that will break her. Me and the enemy's daughter. And then she will have to learn the hard truth. That my dad? He's screwing her over again.

"Can I climb in there with you?" June nods toward the space next to me. I stretch my hand out and flatten it on the metal bed, as if I'm taking that space up.

"Can't," I say. My face is numb, and I doubt I'm coming close to any form of an expression at all. I'm blank. Erased. Empty. "This—" I sweep my hand around, pointing to June then to me—"does not happen in front of people."

June blinks precisely once then steps forward, placing her palms on the tailgate, ready to hoist herself inside. My heart thumps erratically. I want her here. I want her here so goddamn badly. But it can't be *here.*

I rush to my feet and hold the side of my truck, swinging my legs over and onto the ground.

"Just get in," I grunt, gesturing to the passenger side.

She flips my tailgate up then slips into my cab, her eyes hovering on my every movement. She doesn't let up as I pull out of the driveway and race down our street. By the time we're a comfortable distance from my home, I pull to the side of the road and flip on my hazards. I can't drive any further with this feeling in my chest. It's an insatiable craving for more information. I need to know it all. *She* needs to know it all.

"Tell me how you know," I blurt out. I tighten my grip on the steering wheel, rolling my hands over the ridges. My hold is so tight I could cause a blister if I keep this up.

The only sound in the cab is June's deep breath. It's a thoughtful kind, the sort that comes with mapping out words and finding delicate ways to deliver bad news. She and I are both versed in this skill.

"I hate that I'm the one who knows this, Lucas." Her voice is soft, raspy even. She's struggling with this burden. I wonder how long she's carried it alone.

"I understand." I work to keep my voice calm. As raging as my heart is and as rabid as my temper has become since she first told me, none of this is June's fault. I have to remember that and not react *at* her.

She draws in another long breath and I hold mine.

"There are details that are hard—"

My eyes flutter closed and I hold out a palm.

"It's all hard. I know. Just . . . just tell me." I'm begging now.

"I was dropping something off at Tory's house while you all were at practice. I'd just put my car in park when I saw their garage open and a truck pull out."

No. This is not happening. No, no, no . . .

"Lots of people have trucks." My eyes flicker open but nothing seems in focus. I'm spinning, my thoughts bouncing from my best friend to our parents to my life two years ago to June.

No!

"They do," she says. I know more is coming. "Not ones with license plates framed in gold with *Tennessee Forever* etched on the top and bottom."

Everything in my body drops to my gut. My mouth is dry, and swallowing is impossible. My eyes are too dry to close. The taste on my tongue is sour, and my head thumps with the flood of adrenaline that courses through my body.

June twists in her seat, and I glance sideways, my weight held up on the steering wheel. Without it, I'd crumble to the floor.

"I saw them kiss, Lucas. Your dad and—"

"Don't." I stop her before I actually hear her speak it. I get the details. I've heard them before; I don't need them again. I glance up and hold my gaze on the roadway. It's mostly empty, minus the occasional car that passes. We're out of the glow of streetlights, and the sun has gone down completely. If I try hard enough, I wonder if I could make myself invisible.

"I don't want to know too much," she continues. "Details have a way of becoming nightmares and they poison everything."

I drop my gaze to my lap, letting my hands fall to the bottom curve of the wheel. I have to tell Tory. We'll both need to tell Hayden. This will wreck their senior year—and beyond. I would know.

"Just promise me that you are sure," I ask with a sideways glance. I can't gamble on this. It has to be certain.

"I wouldn't have ever said it if I wasn't one-hundred percent sure, Luc." She edges her palm closer to me, and I feel myself itch for the contact. I trace the form over her hand, the short nails on her fingertips, chewed off from stress biting I'm sure. She's had that habit since we were kids.

Leaning forward, I glare up through the windshield.

"There's supposed to be a meteor shower tonight. They said on the news that the best views are after midnight."

Stay with me, June. Spend the night with me right here and make everything all right. We'll look at the stars and ignore the trouble here on Earth.

"I don't have anywhere to be," she says. My mouth ticks up, a fraction of a smile. There was a tinge of joy in her voice.

"We need full dark." I lean back and roll my head to face her completely. Her lips curve into a faint grin as we hold our stare through the rush of several passing cars. It's the busiest this road has been in minutes. I think maybe the universe wanted to choose now to light up June's eyes.

"We should keep driving, then."

I hold her gaze for a few more seconds, blinking once, then turn my attention back to the road. I shift into drive and kill the hazards, careful to stay just under the limit along the way. The last thing I want to do tonight is get nailed for speeding.

We're off the beaten path. Old memories came to life, bright spots amid some awfully shitty news. June and I spent a summer treading this road and every tiny route around it on our bikes. I wonder when she's going to recognize where I'm taking us.

I veer onto a side road, and the thick trees give way to an open field. The abandoned drive-in theater comes into view, and I hear June exhale. She sees it. I'm sure she knows. I didn't plan this, but the opportunity to bring her here—to be *us* here—is too inviting. The pull of our past is strong. So many threads tether us together I could never cut them all.

June reaches forward and pushes the power button for my stereo, the Wilson Pickett song "Mustang Sally" spilling from my speakers. I need soothing music, and sometimes classic R&B is the only kind that works. I was listening to this during my run and cut it off right before the chorus, which June sings along with right now.

This was us, and here we are again—two kids singing classic tunes off-key while exploring the fringes.

"I heard this song last week with Tory," she says. Maybe it's childish of me, but her mention of him—of enjoying a song that's *ours* with my best friend—kills my desire to sing. June keeps right on going.

"Oh, yeah?" I'm not even hiding my jealousy now.

"He didn't know the words." She laughs. She's being nice. I can tell. I pucker my lips to hold in my embarrassed smile.

We're getting close to the drive-in spots, so I flip my high beams on so we can navigate the ghosts left behind. I hope they never completely tear this place down. If someone invested in it, I'd be willing to drive out here every Saturday night to see a movie. Probably not a solid business plan.

The old screen comes into view first, along with a few of the sound box posts. There's a rotted old couch in the middle of the lot, and the closer we get to it, the more certain I am it's riddled with bullet holes. Despite the spray-paint tags covering what's left of the old snack bar, this place is perfection in my eyes. June's, too.

"They're still here," she says, confirming why.

A lot of the speakers have broken away—or been stolen. But enough remain.

"Stop the car. Let's see if any work," she says, unbuckled and nearly out of the passenger seat before I stop the truck completely. We skid into a dirt patch and both leap onto the parking lot. The first several boxes I come to are busted, most of them missing cords. It takes at least two dozen failed attempts before June finally finds one that lights up when she flips it on.

"Oh, my God!" She celebrates by holding it out in front of her. The faint green glow that signals the speaker is working is the only thing I can clearly see. June's form is a scant outline lit by the moon.

I race toward her to test it out, reinvigorated to keep going when I see its connection is strong.

"Don't let go. I'll find one, too." I scurry in a new direction. I'm right up under the screen with only three or four left to try when my prayers are answered. The light flickers at first, but after a little push and pull on the wire, it lights up brightly. It seems like a trivial thing to pray for, but I need this escape tonight. I need June and our childhood and simple pleasures.

"Breaker niner-niner," I speak into the box. These things aren't supposed to work like this, but Tory showed me a special setting when we were kids. I dragged June out here to try it one night. It's like a rudimentary web of walkie talkies, or a group chat before that term existed. The power is some leftover line the town never dug up or turned off, and this town is too short-staffed to look for energy vampires.

"I cannot believe we found two that work!"

We laugh together, her voice coming through the small speaker embraced in my palms. It crackles and I hold incredibly still, not wanting to lose her.

"It's so dark, I can barely see you," she says.

I cup the speaker close to my mouth and let out my best evil laugh.

"Don't be a jerk. You know I don't like the dark." She doesn't, but she's always been better with it than me. She never made fun of me when we were kids, though she knew I didn't like the dark either.

"I wish someone would reopen this place," she says.

"Maybe I do that instead of go to MIT or Tennessee. Look, problem solved." I chuckle, but truthfully, the thought is appealing. Places like this are meant for worlds where profit doesn't matter.

"I think you really want to go to MIT," June says, yanking me back to reality.

"Yeah." I sigh after a long pause. She's right. I do. And anytime I think of giving in and going to Tennessee, I hate my dad a little bit more. As if my opinion of him could get any lower.

"Your dad has even less of a right dictating now," June says, practically reading my thoughts. I shift my weight and clear my throat, my head crowded with thoughts of my father, what June told me, and my obligation to do *something.*

"We can talk about other things," she says, and I'm relieved to have the life raft, but when it comes down to it, everything in our lives is knotted together. My dad. Her mom. My college options, her lack of them. The twins' parents.

The time June and I missed. Time that we could have spent out here, talking . . . like this.

"I'm sorry I was a jerk." This is the apology I should have given days ago. Weeks ago.

Months.

"I miss us, Lucas."

I hold the radio in my fist, resting it against my forehead, wishing it would magically become a time machine.

"What happened?" Her sniffles somehow come through crystal clear.

It's easy to say a lot happened. Even easier to blame everyone else. Life happened. Messy relationships got messier. Lies and betrayals interfered with innocence and coming-of-age. But what it all actually boils down to is June and me. We gave up on each other. Maybe *I* gave up first, but so did she. I didn't make it easy to hold on, and the more I pushed, the farther she went, until we were seas apart.

Strangers.

"Do you think you could help me with something?" I hold my breath, knowing what I'm about to ask her is big, the kind of thing I don't have a right to. It would be a gift if she grants it.

"One date," she says. It's not the response I was expecting, but the twist injects life back into my body. I'm smiling alone in the dark.

"With me, I mean," she continues. I love the way she rambles. "I want to go out on a real date, in front of people."

She wants to be seen. She *deserves* to. Why she would want to be with me leaves me clueless, especially after how awful I've been, but she's still here. She's asking. And how could my mom be more hurt by me going on a date with June than the repeat offenses of the man she took back after he cheated the first time. I wonder how many times he's been unfaithful.

"One date." I repeat the terms, and I can tell she's surprised I'm entertaining the idea by the way her breath puffs through the speaker.

"Yes. That's my offer. Take it or leave it."

I smirk at her confident voice. I bet she's forcing herself to stand up tall and rolling her shoulders.

"Deal. And June?"

The connection crackles, so I repeat my answer again.

"June? Can you hear me? I said yes. It's a deal. Did you get that?"

I hold my speaker to my ear, the fuzz growing more even, until soon it's just a soft hush of audio snow.

"Went dead!" she shouts across the lot.

I drop my box since it's useless now, and it bangs around the post where it hangs from the cord. I chuckle to myself and hang my head, scratching at the back of my neck, amused at the irony. June and I finally get our moment, and our chosen method of communication is some century-old hack in the middle of nowhere. Lifting my chin, I wait for my eyes to adjust on her figure. I wonder if she knows she's beautiful. I wonder if I have the guts to tell her.

I cup my mouth to make sure she hears me.

"I get to pick the place!" I shout.

My hands drop to my sides, a tingling sensation running from my neck all the way down to my fingertips.

"So you can pick somewhere nobody will see you with me?" June huffs out a laugh that's purposeful and jaded. She feels like a secret, and I get it.

We're too far apart for this, the details. It's time for real talk. The more we reconnect, the move obvious it becomes that neither of us has the full story. June obviously doesn't understand why I've been so cold and distant, which means she probably doesn't know about her mom's affair with my dad. If she did, her reaction when she discovered my dad's latest discretion would have been vastly different.

The hundred feet or so between us feels like forever under my feet. I'm not rushing, instead trying to gather the right words. She's sitting on a crate, her shoulders slumped and brow pinched.

"You ashamed of me, Lucas Fuller? Is that what all of this is about?"

What?

To hear her voice her broken feelings, to utter that word—*ashamed*—

spears my heart. She lifts her palms, showing an indifferent shrug, as if she's giving up, and everything in me solidifies.

No. We aren't quitting. Not this time. I'm going to have to tell her everything I know, and it's going to affect her the same way her news about my dad struck me. Probably worse. She'll push me away. But I won't go. I'll stay. Just like she did.

I tilt my head to the side.

"It's nothing like that, June." I shake my head.

"What's it like, then, Lucas? Because here's what it's like to me. We're best friends, then we're not. We live a hundred feet apart, and for two years, I see you only in passing, through open shutters and truck windows. I come back to school and we're enemies. I resent you, but only because you resent me, and I have no idea why—none of it. No clue. But then there are these few tiny moments when I see you. When I *really* see you. My Lucas shows up to take care of me, and he talks and he shares for one night. We kiss, then just . . . like . . . that."

She snaps her fingers and my eyes dart to the motion of her hand. I disappeared. Not like magic, though, because magic is wondrous and special. Nothing about the last two years deserves such an adjective.

"You can't tell anyone."

She throws my own words back at me, and I wince. I blink rapidly for a few seconds and draw in air through my nose. My gaze steady on hers, I try to see our world through her eyes. And then I try to predict how she's going to see things after I tell her the reasons behind it all.

"You're right," I say.

Her brow furrows as she blinks once. I don't think she's joking, either. I think she is actually surprised to hear me admit that to her.

She holds up her broken speaker and presses the button, which does nothing at all.

"I'm sorry, could you repeat that please?" she says into it. It makes me smile. June . . . she's funny. She's also honest and real. No pretense to what she wants or needs. What I see is what I get, and I feel lucky that I can have this amazing creature in my life. I'm in awe of her, actually. I find my head falling to the side again as I study her—the slope of her nose, pink lips, slender neck and tousled hair that falls over her shoulders in twisty waves, probably from braids she had in earlier. The girl I grew up with—the one who played in mud and rolled down the driveway, belly on a skateboard—she's still very much here. But so is this woman, a girl on the brink of eighteen.

Green eyes that I thought were cool because they were the color of a pond are now cool for entirely different reasons. They're wicked, and sexy, especially when her long lashes shade them, kissing her cheeks when she blinks. Once bony arms and legs are now lines that beg my eyes to trail up and down them, taking in the light dusting of freckles on her rounded shoulders—skin kissed by the sun. Her breasts would fit perfectly in each of my palms, and I drop my hands into my pockets at that thought, feeling both guilty for having it and hungry to test it.

"You . . . are right," I finally say, repeating the words she insists on hearing again.

She gives me a sideways look that makes me laugh.

"So, is that a yes? To the—"

"It's a yes to the date. And a yes that it won't be in a cave. I will take you somewhere that has actual living, breathing humans nearby. There might be food, and there will probably be a movie because this is Indiana and our options are slim."

Light and airy laughter falls from her lips.

"Come here," I say, extending my arm and calling her to me with a finger. I drop my hands back in my pockets to still my nerves when I realize my palms are sweating. June holds her stare on me, her mouth caught in a skeptical, open-mouthed smile that draws up one side of her lip.

"Please," I say.

She blinks. Lashes kiss cheeks. Fucking adorable.

She gets to her feet, brushing off the back of her jeans, then pushes her hands in her pockets too. I wonder if she's as nervous as I am. We've already kissed, but everything feels new. She twists her feet into the ground, swaying her hips side-to-side, playing coy. All I see are her curves, and the slight peek of skin where her jeans rest on her hips, her sweatshirt pulled up barely enough to give me this glimpse. I lick my bottom lip with the tip of my tongue, my mouth watering as the thought of running it along her taut stomach and navel flashes through my mind.

The second she's close enough, I close the remaining distance, grabbing her wrists and guiding her hands so they're flush against mine. Our fingers weave together, the feeling so natural. Our fit is perfect, palm-to-palm. I indulge in her beauty, my chest fluttering with the off-beat percussion of my heart. If she weren't holding on to my hands, I doubt I could feel them. I want this. And maybe that's what I was protecting myself from all along—from wanting something so fragile, so fraught with risk.

"I don't want—" I stop, closing my mouth and glancing down, my focus on her chin before I close my eyes. I have to get his right. "I don't want my family to fuck it up. I want to keep this ours for a little while."

I don't want to tell you the things I must. Details that will crush you. Don't make me yet. When I open my eyes, I try to simmer the burning resentments very much alive in my belly. I'm doing a poor job of hiding it when her eyes zero in on mine. It's not that she looks afraid, but that her expression is full of worry.

She steps into me so our elbows touch, and I practice measured patience. I'm sure she can feel my hands vibrating with urgency, fighting against their desire to rush around her waist and pull her into me. My heart is thumping against my breast plate with enough force to make it crack, and my lips tingle with expectation and hope.

June rises on her toes, her mouth so close to take, her gaze on mine.

Lashes dust skin. It's hypnotic.

"What's the favor?" I barely hear the words she speaks, drunk instead on the movements of her lips. The way they wrap around each word. The faint smile that follows. I flit my gaze up to her eyes, and I can only take in one at a time. We're so close. Inches. Breaths.

I need to kiss her.

"I'm going to interview for MIT. And Coach and my dad, they can't know." I glance down, to the tip of her nose. This is a difficult favor to ask, and honestly, it has nothing to do with taking her on a date. I needed to ask this of her regardless, and the option of saying no to taking her out disappeared the moment we kissed.

"They won't," she says. Her smirk settles my nerves. When I glance to her eyes, I see the pride she has in me. I can read her, the crinkled corners that are pushed up by her growing smile.

I let go of the breath I'm holding, and her hands squeeze against mine.

"I have a plan. You'll need to take my truck."

Her smile gets really big. I laugh and shake our joined hands.

"I'm gonna want it back in one piece."

She shakes her head.

"No promises."

I squint at her briefly, a crooked smile that teases on my mouth.

"Do you need help getting ready for the interview? Is it at school? Or do you go to an office?" Her questions spill out, almost as if she's been holding on to them, or has a list in her pocket that includes more.

I'm grinning like a fool when her eyes catch my face.

"What?" Her cheeks blush.

I need to kiss her.

Lifting our hands to my shoulders, I coax hers around my neck before drawing faint lines down her arms, tickling her skin enough to make her breathe out a hushed laugh. I rest my palms on her waist and she drops from her toes, standing flat, her height perfectly fitting under my chin. I close the remaining inches as she gazes up at me and runs her fingers through my hair.

"June?" Her eyes flit to mine briefly, mouth pulled into a tight, nervous smile that pierces the corners like arrows. Her gaze is gone as fast as it was on mine, her stare centered on my chest.

I lift my hand to her face, my thumb brushing over her bottom lip. So soft and supple, my mouth craves the feel of it. I want to suck her in, drink her, and devour her. I run the back of my hand along her jaw, then her cheek. I lift her chin so she has no choice but to look into my eyes unless she closes hers. I'm blessed either way—either the wild green or the feather of lashes.

I nod, a slight movement as my focus drops to her mouth for a fraction of a second. A tiny breath escapes and her bottom lip juts out. My muscles grow tense, the sensation of holding on tight as if I'm trying not to fall taking hold of my body. She's trembling. I feel her resistance out of nowhere, so I step back, giving us space. I hold her stare and search for clues, some warning of what's next. Some sign that it isn't what I fear it is.

"What happened?" Merely asking this question sends ripples through her body and she quivers where she stands.

No. Not now. Please not now.

I slowly shake my head.

"Why did you pull away? Lucas . . . I need to know."

My hands feel along her waist, the numbness returning. She's slipping away, and there is nothing I can do to hold on to her. I'm weak.

Useless.

"Please don't make me tell you. Don't make me say it."

I realize the moment the words leave my mouth that I have no choice. It has to be me, and I've now made sure that it happens tonight. I feel the moment slip away, like silk sheets sliding from a bed. My hands want to claw at them, clutch them and keep them here, but I have no power over my body anymore. I have no power over anything.

June looks sick. I shake my head harder, a fruitless effort that is met by her steeled expression. This is the point of no return. Dead man walking and all that.

"June," I plead, squeezing my eyes shut and hoping when I open them we'll be back in my truck, holding hands . . . *happy*.

My hands fall from her body and I'm not sure whether I did it willingly or simply lost the strength to hold on. I reach into my hair and grip it, tugging lightly, wanting the painful distraction and a reminder that I'm alive and need to get through this. I have to relive this for her.

Lifting my eyes to take in her face, I exhale the last of before and prepare for this painful now.

"This isn't my father's first affair."

She blinks. The connections are forming. I recognize the slight tug on her lips as they open. I'm torn between taking this slow and ripping off the Band-Aid. I honestly don't know which is the better choice, so I do what I would prefer. I will speak until she tells me to stop. Until she's had enough and can't take anymore.

"My dad was seeing your mom."

She blinks again.

"My mom caught them together."

Her eyes drop a tick to my chest.

"He begged my mom not to leave."

Her mouth closes, the places where our worlds intersect coming into view. This is why it had to be me to tell her. Nobody else would understand.

"My mom wanted him to make you and your mom move, but she settled for us never talking to you again."

I wanted to, June. I almost broke so many times. Somehow, it got easier, though. It got easier to avoid you, and I hate myself for that.

"She said she would tell everyone how your mom and my dad met."

I swallow hard. This is the detail I know she isn't expecting. It's the thing I regret most having shared with Ava. It's the biggest stain on my character, not hers.

"He hired her, June. She needed money to get away from your dad and still be able to afford . . . things. And my father paid. He paid over and over. And he said he wasn't the only one."

Her cheeks puff slightly. I think she might get sick.

"I didn't want you to know. I didn't want anyone to ever know. I didn't . . ."

Nothing else I say is going to fix things for her, and I doubt she can hear me now. I've been where she is, slipping away. She's scouring her mind for arguments against this, for other reasons and alternative timelines. This is the one we've lived, unfortunately. This is the path we are on. And I am the bearer of soul-crushing news.

EIGHTEEN

"We haven't seen the meteors yet."

June lies back on the roof of my truck. I should take her home. I've tried. She crawled up there an hour ago, and I don't get the sense she's coming down. Pushing her won't change the confusion swirling in her head.

She said she wanted to know everything, so I told her. Now, I fear I've filled her head too much. June and her mom are so close. They always have been, and from what I could tell from my self-imposed distance, they have only grown closer the last two years. Now, though, June has to be doubting everything.

I told her about the money exchange and the private investigator my mom hired when she suspected my dad was sleeping around. I showed her the screen shots of text messages I saved, proof to remind myself that my father is an utter disappointment. I needed something to shore up my will whenever I felt weak, to keep me from running next door and talking to June those first few months. I rarely look at them now, but I can't seem to delete them.

"The clouds are rolling in." I hook my thumbs in my pockets and glare up at the sky. This is my second attempt to make her concerned about the weather. I'm sure we won't get rain, I just want to snap June out of this state. It's like a switch flipped after I told her everything. She couldn't really run away, so she hopped on top of my truck.

"Sit with me?" She rolls her head lazily to the side, the smile that was flirting with her lips before we nearly kissed nowhere to be found. I'm not sure whether she's in denial or merely processing. I don't know how to navigate this without leading us back down the rocky road we were on before, as near enemies.

It's getting cold out, and June is probably freezing up there. I sigh and push my hands deep into the front pocket of my hoodie, the hood pulled tight around my face. I wish I had joggers on. These shorts were a good idea when I was sprinting around our neighborhood. That was two hours ago, though.

"You can grab my jacket from the floor of your truck. Use it to cover up?" She's being serious, and it's so fucking sweet. After the things I told her, she's still being sweet.

I smirk on one side of my mouth, breathing out a laugh.

"Okay, June." I open the passenger side and grab her jacket, flipping off the truck's headlights to save my battery and give us a better view. It doesn't take much to run my stereo, so I tune in some chill music then climb my way up top with June.

"Here," I say, handing her the jacket. I slide my legs next to hers and she glances from my knees back to my eyes.

"You're in shorts. I thought you could use it to cover up.

I shake my head and laugh. I'm fucking freezing, but what kind of gentleman would I be if I didn't take care of her first?

"I don't get cold." Those words carry double meaning.

"That's not true." So do June's. She winces, probably feeling bad, but she shouldn't.

"I didn't mean it like that," she adds. She's a terrible liar.

I let my head fall to the side but keep my gaze soft and on hers.

"Yes, you did." My voice is a whisper. Guilt has a way of muting me.

"I'm sorry."

Look how easy it is for her to apologize, you asshole.

"Don't be." I glance down her body to where her hands fist the bottom of her shirt. I unzip her jacket and spread it over her upper body like a blanket.

"Your mom is probably worried about you." She's not going to like that I brought her up. I had a hard time even *thinking* about my dad at first. I won't push too hard, but I won't let her fall into darkness.

I lean back on my palms and let my legs dangle down the windshield. I get dizzy if I crane my neck too long, but I give it a go and let my head fall back for a little while. I hope we see a shooting star. June deserves one. For a moment, I think I catch one out of the corner of my eye. I'm about to ask June if she saw it when her body shifts next to me and her head nestles onto my lap. Suddenly, I hope we don't see a meteor for hours. I don't look down, too afraid to jinx this.

"I'm probably not very soft," I joke.

"You're softer than you think," she teases back, her head squishing against my thigh. I think she's basically calling me a mushy pillow.

I can't help myself and look down, hoping to catch her smile. It's there, and it's breathtaking.

"Okay, then." I draw in a quick breath then let my head fall back again. The second my eyes settle on the black sky, a streak of stardust cuts through the center. Sometimes, it's hard not to believe in signs.

"Oh, my God!" June's voice is pure elation.

"Wow," I say, stretching the three letters out far longer than necessary. I'm reacting more to June's reaction than I am to the meteor, but she doesn't need to know that.

It's just June, me, the midnight sky, and the soft chirp of crickets. I don't even think I breathe for a whole minute. Not until her hand travels up my chest and the weight of her head lifts from my lap. I have no choice but to look down at her, and when her warm palm slides along my jawline and under the hood of my sweatshirt, my eyes threaten to close, soothed by her touch. I force them to remain open. June reaches into my hair, her fingers twisting around the strands. My lips part for their first breath in what feels like forever, and a heartbeat later, June's mouth is on mine.

My mouth first reacts in shock. I never pegged June as being bold. I worry she's trying to kiss away her fears, using intimacy to bury pain. That's what I did with Ava. I don't want that kind of relationship with June. Her kiss softens, and I wage a mental war with myself. I should pull away and make sure this is what she truly wants. Or maybe I should let her lead, simply follow. I know what half of my body wants me to do. Hell, ninety-eight percent of my body wants to let her do whatever she wants with and to me.

June's kisses rain along my jawline as her hands push my hood from my head. There's something intoxicating about the way her hands run through my hair, and I give in to the devil on my shoulder and guide her mouth back to mine so I can kiss her like I really want to. The moment our lips connect, I become ravenous. Every pass of my tongue against hers needs to be memorized. The way her teeth grab my bottom lip and tug drives me to do the same. It's as if we're in a silent competition over who needs this kiss more. Maybe we're both desperate for it. Like air.

We cradle each other's faces and June shifts so she's sitting on her knees. I lean back to give her room to straddle my lap and the second she sits on me, I lose myself completely. I'm so fucking hard. She's so soft and smooth and smells like honey and lemon. I'm sure she felt the groan that escaped my lips the second my cock came in contact with her body. All the sweatpants and jeans in the world couldn't deny the sensation I just experienced.

My weight back, I rest on my palms as June runs her fingers down the front of my hoodie. It's dark out, but the moon is bright enough to illuminate her eyes. They're hazed. Hungry. And I'm fighting my worst thoughts not to give in to my most base desires. Her lips are raw where I kissed them so hard a second ago, the bottom one pink and puffed out. Sexy and wanting. Her chin lifts a bit, revealing her slender neck, tempting me to run my mouth along it and taste, nibble. Her breasts sit up high, the tips poking through her cotton shirt. My mind conjures the sensation of flicking my tongue against that hard, pink tip.

June rocks her hips, and my eyes flutter closed briefly. "Fuuuuuuck," I groan, biting my bottom lip. If she does that too many times, I'm going to come in my shorts.

Her hands slip down to the bottom of my hoodie and I help her lift it over my head, tossing it behind me into the back of the truck. Her hands run along my sides, feeling the dips and curves of my muscles. If nothing else, my hard work in the gym has been for this. Her hands dip lower, toying with the hair below my belly button, teasing the band of my shorts. When her hand tugs the string holding them up, I come to long enough to cover her hand with mine and make sure this is something she means to do. I don't want to be her version of running.

To slow her down, I bring her hands to my mouth and kiss the insides of her wrists. Lifting her arms above her head, I let my fingers roam down the length of her arms, my eyes studying hers as my hands travel. When I reach her nipples, I let the pads of my thumbs run over the tips through her shirt, and she gasps. I continue my descent to the bottom of her work shirt, gathering it in my hands and dragging it up the length of her body. When I clear her head, she takes the garment from me and tosses it in the back of the truck with my hoodie.

She steadies herself, arms braced on my shoulders while her fingers play with my hair. I lock onto her gaze, searching for reservations, but all I see is the same hunger coursing through my body. My eyes close as my mouth falls to her neck, kissing along the curve to her shoulder while my hands slowly slide the straps of her bra down. I kiss each newly exposed bit of her, starting at her shoulder then moving to the center of her chest, each kiss lower until her bright pink nipples are right there for me to taste. I don't pause. I don't even think. I just lick, my tongue memorizing the soft tip it holds hostage. My mouth closes over the tip and I suck gently, blowing her cool as I back away.

June reacts, arching back. It takes seconds for me to peel her lacey white bra away completely, tossing it aside. My hand covers her right breast while my mouth finds home again on her left. I suck until a faint cry falls from her lips, and as they fall open, I clamp down on her nipple lightly with my teeth. Her body rolls with desire, and she rocks her hips against my erection.

Fucking hell, this is better than actual sex. And I *want* actual sex. With June. I want to erase everyone else and feel only her. I want to be inside her, to taste her and feel her breath pant heavily at my neck.

At some point tonight, she twisted her hair up into a knot at the back of her head. I want to see it flying wild. I want to wrap it around my hands and see the curls tickle against her breasts. I run my hand up her neck to the hair band and pull it free, tossing it God knows where. I let her mane fly in the breeze for a minute, then gather it into my palm so I can tug her head back enough to cause her to arch perfectly. Her neck is mine. Her breasts—*mine.* I saw my teeth against the hard peak, and she sinks her weight into me. I flick her nipple raw before giving in and biting it once.

Her hands slink around my neck, slipping to my shoulder blades as she pulls herself into me again. I feel my cock flex under her weight. I can't handle many more of those.

I sweep the stray hairs from her face when our eyes meet. Her lips fall open in a silent plea for me to quench their need to be kissed. I feel it, too. As long as I'm touching her, the world is right. Nothing makes sense except us.

This kiss is somehow hungrier than all the others. June literally dominates me, her need somehow outpacing mine, which seems damn near impossible; I feel as though I'm going to explode. Her hips rock and the hot center between her legs grinds against me. Needing to feel more of her, I drop my hands to her hips, guiding her back and forth over my hard-on. I can see her orgasm build in her face, her eyes rolling back and teeth gripping desperately at her lip, trying to hold on. I'm not sure if she knows she's humming, but the sound is fucking sexy as hell.

I'm intent on giving her what she wants, but before I grab her ass hard and pull her into me, she reaches between us and tugs at the string on my shorts. I'm too weak to stop her, and when her hand dips inside and finds the tip of my dick, the only word I can muster is her name.

She sits back enough to pull my pants lower on my hips, her head resting against mine. Our hot breath mingles with her words.

"I want to touch you," she says. I nod, shift so she can pull my cock free. The cold air shocks my system, but the sensation is instantly replaced with the warm touch of June's hand.

"Am I doing this right?" she asks, her fingers wrapped around me, squeezing with slight pressure and roaming up and down. My cock flexes at her touch and I nod.

"Yeah," I pant before grabbing the back of her head and bringing her mouth to mine. I kiss her hard while her hand flows up and down my shaft. She sits up tall on her knees, and the fact she wants to watch while she strokes me is so fucking hot. I slide my hand up the back of her thigh, and as she glides up my dick, my hand trails up her leg. I tease, flirting with her ass, and when I finally grab it her head falls back. She grips me harder, and I slide my hand in her back pocket. Her ass is perfect, round and firm. I sink my hand in as far as it will go so I can feel the place where it curves into her pussy.

June reaches for my other hand, and my breath stops in a panic. I lost myself in her touch, and I recoil my palm from her pocket, afraid I went too far. This is still June. There's an innocence to her that will always be there. It's part of what makes her so sexy. I hope I didn't ruin that.

Before I can even question things, though, she moves my hand to the front of her jeans, stopping at the button. I glance up to meet her hooded eyes. *Oh, fuck, yes.*

I tug the front of her jeans open, dropping her zipper with one hand while the other glides along the smooth skin of her lower back to her hip. My thumbs hook inside the band of her panties, and I yank both the cotton undies and jeans down her thighs. We shift so I can guide her to lie on her back, and she kicks her shoes from her feet and works her pants off completely, kicking them to the side.

I maneuver on my knees so I'm between her open legs, lifting my gaze to take in this beautiful creature lying before me, naked and writhing. This is June. *Fuck! June Mabee.* I've never seen a more sexual being. I can smell her desire and it sinks into my veins. My eyes trail from her navel to her breasts until our gazes lock. She nods and whimpers "Yes," and it's all I need for assurance.

I fumble for my wallet and pull out the condom, a new one. I hold it up to prove it to June, and she giggles, cupping her mouth. Her cheeks blush, such a pretty fucking sight on the roof of my truck under the moonlight.

She slides her hands under her hips while I slide the condom on, and I can tell she's both nervous and excited. Lowering myself so I'm on top of her, I leave enough room between us for her to arch and breathe. My weight on my forearms, I lean my head down to run my nose against hers then brush a soft kiss on her lips. I take my time, kissing her with teasing nibbles that I hope set her at ease. When our kiss deepens, I move to grab my cock and guide it inside of her. She sucks in a harsh breath when I push the tip in, so I pause.

"Okay?" My lips dance across hers with the question.

She nods, and utters, "Yes."

I take it slow, pushing into her until I feel her surround me completely. My mouth hangs open, my body rippling with tremors because she feels so fucking good. I let her get used to my size before pulling out and gliding in again. My movements are measured, steady and smooth. I don't want to hurt her, and it's almost painful taking it this slow. My mind is drunk on thoughts of me pounding into her, my dick slick with her wetness. The thought alone makes me flex and threaten to come.

I kiss along her neck to distract her as my rocking picks up speed. I suck a tiny hickey into the skin at the nape of her neck and blow on it when I'm done.

"I left a tiny bruise there so you'll see it in the morning and know this was real." I rock out of her and our eyes meet. The pain that was creasing them seems to have eased. She's approaching pleasure.

"Ready?" I ask. She nods again.

Lining my body up with hers, I push in deeper this time, my thumbs running along her cheeks to draw her eyes open. I lift my body enough to meet her eyes and share the smile she's etched on my face. I'm present for this, feeling every new moment right along with her. I may not be a virgin, but June is still my first in many ways. This isn't completely about sex. This night—our connection—is about love.

Love.

I draw back and rock into her again. She whimpers against my mouth, her teeth gripping my bottom lip. The sounds she makes drive me harder, and I sink into her completely. Groaning with every stretch of her body around mine, I slide in and out. We both get lost to the rhythm, and minutes pass of nothing but our moans and my body falling into hers. And then her legs wrap around my waist.

Oh, fuck.

I'm right on the edge. I'm going to come way too soon, and I don't want to ruin her first time, but I'm not sure I'm in control of anything anymore. I try to focus on nothing but her breathing, the light pant that leaves her mouth and hits my neck, the soft hum with every pump. When her teeth clamp down on my shoulder, I know I can give in to my own needs, and let myself feel it all—her pulsing around me, the sheen of sweat covering her skin, the embrace of her hands as she holds my hips tight, tugging them into her as she rolls with pleasure. One last whimper in my ear pushes me to climax, and my dick swells one last time, emptying inside of her.

We roll to the side and I pull off the condom, tying it up and tossing it into the dirt lot. If that was June's first time, I cannot wait to be her second, third . . . hundredth. She's insatiable, already tempting me to touch her again. I'm completely spent, but my cock is still rock hard, so she uses me and I let her.

I hold her hips while she climbs on top of me again, flattening my hard on against my body while she pleasures herself against it. This time, I get to see her body move, and if I were able to stop her and slip on another condom just so I could come inside her again, I would. But I'm out of condoms. And my muscles are still weak from seconds ago. But June—June is hot and young and ripe and breaking apart on top of me for my eyes alone, and she is fucking beautiful.

NINETEEN

The sun is up by the time I get June home. Her mom called and texted all night, but she kept sending her to voicemail. Eventually, she turned off her phone. I worried, but I was also, *well,* distracted. Now that we're in my driveway, and she's seen just how many times her mom messaged, and how many times her friend Abby did as well, I think we're both coming to our senses.

People were worried. I don't like that. Especially when I'm trying to earn trust again. No matter what June's mom was a part of, she's still June's parent. I want her to be all right with the two of us being together. It's going to be enough of a challenge to prepare my mom for this news.

"Tell me this will be okay," she says, sliding out of the passenger seat of my truck. I hold her hand in mine and kiss her wrist. I love this piece of her. It's both strong, full of life, yet delicate and fragile all at once.

"It will be, eventually. Don't be afraid of time."

I wish I could go back two years and tell myself this.

She steps up and crawls across the seat again, placing both palms on either side of my face, staring me in the eyes.

"And people say football players are idiots." I catch a glimpse of her smirk a millisecond before she leans in and kisses me.

"Who says that?" I play the part, laughing as she moves back to her seat.

She isn't ready to head inside. Not yet. I'll sit here as long as she needs, though I fear if we wait too long her mom may come yank me out of the truck and kick my teeth in. I've never doubted her loyalty and love for her daughter. It's her choice in men and marriage wrecking I take issue with.

We sit in silence for several minutes. I can tell by the way June's eyes flicker that she's trying to argue her way through the next several minutes, her lids twitching as her focus moves from one thing to another, never fully settling in. There isn't a plan for the conversations she's about to have. I suppose I could write one, but everyone's journey might be different.

"How come boys have it so easy? It's so hypocritical." She breathes out a smug but light-hearted laugh. "You're rolling in at the crack of dawn, too, but I don't see your mother out in the driveway waiting to rip your head off after she finishes hugging you."

She shifts her gaze to me, blinking over a wry smile, then turns her attention back to her house, the kitchen light glowing through the door's glass.

"I guess it's a matter of conditioning. My parents are kind of used to me not coming home on weekends," I say. I reach across the seat and roll my palm over for her to take again, an offer of strength. She's welcome to whatever she can drain from me. She moves her palm over mine and curls her fingers around my hand, squeezing tight.

"I don't want to do this," she says.

I can feel her pulse. Or maybe it's mine on her behalf.

"That's why I never said anything before." Guilt rushes up my esophagus, burning. I feel sick that I brought this to her forefront. It's my fault she has to deal with it now, in the pale light of morning.

The door to June's house opens while we're both staring at it, and her mom stops at the threshold, arms folded over her chest.

Shit.

I'm not sure whether June says it or I simply think it.

Her mom steps onto the driveway, marching toward us with angry steps, her arms still wrapped around her body. She stops abruptly about a dozen feet from June's side of the truck. The squiggled wrinkle in her forehead is more pronounced than when we were kids and in trouble. I don't think it's a matter of age this time, but rather severity of the crime.

"Wish me luck," June says. I give her one final kiss and watch as she heads into one of the hardest days of her life.

I'm content to sit here in my truck all day. I want to be here for her if things get sour, and I have a feeling they might. From experience.

My tiny bubble of peace and quiet bursts with a flicker of movement to my left, and even before I look to confirm it, I sense my mother's eyes on

June. I'm not sure how long she's been standing there staring, but I can tell by the soured expression on her face that she's seen more than enough.

I draw in a full breath and ready myself for the conversation to come. June is worth it, and my mom will understand. She loved June, and I know in her heart, she still does. She's simply blinded by the past, one painted by my father's broad, cruel brush strokes.

Rolling my eyes is probably not the best way to greet her as I climb out of my truck, but it's what happens to my face.

"Oh, am I inconveniencing you? I'm sorry, do you want to go back next door and spend time with the family you prefer? Maybe sign up to be a pimp?"

I pass by her and avoid making eye contact on my way. I hope June and her mom didn't hear any of that. I think they're far enough away by now, maybe even inside their house. I can't look to see because that would require turning around, and my mom is still hovering behind me. I pause at the door leading inside and look down at my feet, trying to catch enough in my periphery to know when my mom has cleared the garage door line. The second she's inside, I slap the button to lower the door and head into the house.

I've never been one to run from my mom when she's like this—manic and paranoid. I have massive empathy for her. I don't believe most of her behavior is entirely her fault. But I wish she would work on getting better. She stopped going to therapy on her own a year ago. I think maybe if she still went she'd have the courage to leave my dad. Maybe this time she will, when she finds out that he's having an affair again, with another parent of one of my friends. I should probably keep him away from Cannon, the new guy, and his family.

"Lucas, I'd like you to look at me." Her voice is stable, so I don't think she's going to ramble out more insults about June and her mom. I give in after pulling a Coke from the fridge, turning and opening it with my back resting on the counter.

"Look," she starts, pausing and pinching her brow while her eyes squeeze shut.

I wait patiently while she gathers her thoughts. This is where my parents differ. While my dad's style is more full steam ahead and scream, scream, scream, my mother is thoughtful and delicate. It doesn't mean she can't be a bit passive-aggressive, and I'm starting to realize she has a manipulative streak.

"I know you've been going through a lot," she says.

"*Mmm*, yeah. I have." My words come out snarky and her eyes snap to mine. I hold up a palm. "Sorry. Continue."

Now isn't the time to ask her where she was while dad was reaming me over football the other night. She probably doesn't even remember it. She avoids those conflicts. They aren't hers.

"Lucas, I get that you maybe miss June. You guys are seniors, and you're going to be heading in different directions soon. Who knows where she'll end up."

Junior college down the street. I don't say it out loud because I'm afraid it might make my mom happy to hear. She'll take pleasure in June's goals getting cut short, and that will make me mad. All of it will be built on my dad's bad deed, and *where is he?*

"She needed to talk, and I was literally the only person who could help." I'm not technically lying. If my mom doesn't dig for details, I won't have to either.

I take a sip of my drink and meet my mom's stare over the lip of the can. My belly is nervous, my stomach rolling with stress and nervous energy. I don't want to fuck this up. This is why I want to keep things secret. As soon as people find out about us, they'll find a way to ruin us.

"I'm glad you could listen. You were . . . late, is all." She's trying to be the bigger person. I can read behind her pursed lips and red-tinged eyes, though. She hates that she walked out and found me with June.

"I've been late before," I egg on. I don't know why I'm pushing. I shouldn't. The more I do, the likelier it is she'll break down, and that would be on me. It's only that I've placated everyone in this house for so long and frankly, I'm tired.

My mom shifts her weight, her arms folded much like June's mom's were.

"You have, yes. And maybe I'm being unfairly upset since it was June —" She stops abruptly, her mouth snapping shut but the words she almost said aren't far from the surface.

I suck in my lips to keep my words in, too. Knowing about my dad's new affair is this tempting card to play. I'm not that person, though—the kind who orchestrates chaos and sets others up. I won't let my mom live in the dark, but I also won't blurt the facts at her without some consideration first. Right now, it would be me lashing out. When I tell her about Dad, I need her ready to make a change. I need her strong enough to leave him, for good.

My mom's motivation has shriveled. I can tell she no longer wants to be angry with me. She's slipped more into the hurt category, but really, that's of her own making. She's the one who stayed after my father cheated. She didn't have to. I wish she hadn't. It's amazing what two years of maturing can do. The younger me was afraid of a world where his parents split up. I knew together they were a bad match. They have been for years. But divorce scared me. It came with unknowns, like who would I live with more often and when? Now that I consider it this way, my mom probably kept the peace and put up with the disrespect for my sake.

Looking at her through this new lens, I see how she struggles, even now. She's trying so hard to keep this elusive peace. She doesn't even realize that we're in the midst of war.

I set my soda down and move toward her. She flinches at first, which makes me sad and worried that my dad's bursts of anger make her that way.

"I want to dance," I offer, holding out a palm.

Her wide eyes jet to my hand then to my face, followed by a timid smile.

"Are you trying to make things better by bribing me? You know I love to dance with my son."

Her hand in mine, I spin her once and form the perfect frame for a little two-step.

"Mayyyybeeee," I tease. Her eyes are already clearer. I don't fool myself into believing she's not still thinking about where I was all night and who I was with, but the smile inching upward on her face is real.

I pause after a few steps and hold up a finger then reach into my pocket for my phone. I skim through a few songs on the latest playlist Tory put together for me, and I find the one song by Florida-Georgia Line that he forced me into halfway liking. I know it's the right choice when my mom's eyes light up.

"Oh, I love this one," she says.

"Of course you do." I chuckle. "Shall we?"

I hold my hand out again and my mom takes it, letting me spin her with a little more flourish this go round. I took a class with her a year ago because my dad never seemed to have the time, and we fall easily into our two-step pattern. For the next hour, we dance and laugh as if nothing in the world is wrong. That sense of impending doom remains in my gut, though. I think it's in hers too. Dancing can only cover up so much.

It's been years since I've messaged this number. I've wanted to for weeks. I'm pretty sure sleeping with someone is a major leap over the level of texting, so I push my anxiety to the side and pull up a new message for June.

I took a nap, and I'm sure she did, too. Her house has been still most of the day, or it was before I fell asleep. I want to make sure things with her mom went okay. I'm worried about her. And there's a slightly insecure part of me that hopes she doesn't think we made a mistake.

Of all the words in the English language to choose from, I decide to send her one of the shortest ones.

ME: *Hi.*

I pace my room, moving to my window to catch a glimpse of her inside her house. It's past four, and unless she plans on sleeping until tomorrow morning, she needs to wake up.

A minute, maybe two, passes with no response, and I start to wish there was a way to take back a text. When my phone buzzes, I freeze and clutch it in my palm.

JUNE: *Hi back.*

I haven't smiled this often in months, twenty-four of them, at least. I flop back on my bed, body still smelling of June. I haven't showered since we rolled in at the crack of dawn, and my hair is a crazy mess. When I woke, it formed a scarecrow-like shadow on my wall from the sun pouring through the window.

ME: *Don't suppose you can sneak over here to take a shower with me?*

Three dots show up, showing June is responding, then promptly disappear. I laugh out once and rub my tired eyes. Hard to think I can embarrass her now, after everything. I pull the neck of my sweatshirt up to my mouth so I can chew at it while I picture June in my shower, my hands on her soap-drenched body. I bet her hair feels like silk. I'd love to flow it over her tits and drink from them.

Fuck, I'm hard.

JUNE: *I'm not really in good standing at home right now. Rain check?*

ME: *Yes!*

I'm seriously going to *need* to shower after this. *Focus, Lucas. She's had a tough day.*

ME: *Was your mom upset?*

It takes her a few minutes to type, and I spend the time waiting by digging out our freshman yearbook from under my bed. I hang over the edge as I flip through the pages until I get to her picture. Her braids make me chuckle. She's matured a lot since she was fourteen and wearing braces. I flip a few pages back and study my own face, this time spitting out my laugh. Looking at our images through a totally unbiased lens I have to admit. June? She's way out of my league. There's a cuteness to her—both now and then—that I definitely lack. There's a gap in my teeth in my freshman picture, and the one I took before school this year is marred by a deep scowl. I haven't aged gracefully, but June aged into a goddess.

When my phone buzzes under my chest, I roll to my side to read.

JUNE: *We aren't exactly talking. I didn't know what to say and she was angry that I worried her. I feel bad because I don't like making her worry, but I'm also so mad that anything I say right now will be mean and nasty. I'm really sorry you had to go through this on your own. Maybe if I knew back then, we could have helped each other through it.*

I roll the phone in my palm and pull in my bottom lip. This is the dilemma I've had for the last two years—protect June and spare my mom's fragile emotions, or bring her into this web with me so we can suffocate together.

ME: *There have been many times when I almost called you. I thought you knew everything, though. And maybe I blamed you a little. I know. Not fair. And I'm ashamed and sorry.*

I let out a huge breath as I push send, and keep my gaze glued to the screen waiting for her return message. I've been wanting to say those words to her for a long time. Typing them was almost cathartic. Only now, I'm terrified to see her reaction. After five minutes of no response, I sit up on the end of my bed and shove my feet in my shoes. I'm torn between wanting to run to her house and pound on her door or run the other direction and punish myself for being so hateful to her for way too long. If she never writes me back again, I get what I deserve.

JUNE: *I understand . . .*

I fall back in my bed but leave my shoes on. She's still writing.

JUNE: *I'm sorry that took so long. I'm talking to Abby right now too. She requires a lot of attention LOL.*

My palm covers my face and my lips flap with a relieved exhale.

ME: *Tell Abby it's my turn.*

JUNE: *Have you met Abby?*

I laugh.

ME: *Good point.*

I hate that I can't see her right now. I'd propose a swap where Abby gets her on text and I get the phone or video call. I'm sure Abby would drive over here to interrupt, though, so I'm going to give myself the next best thing.

Kicking up to my feet, I head out of my room and creep downstairs, not wanting to get into any conversations with my parents. Although, my dad is gone—*shocker*—and my mom is sitting in her office with soft music playing. It's cover enough for me to slip out the back door and head to the Buick. Out of habit, I move to the passenger door, but I pause right before I answer her text. I'm *always* in that seat—even when we were kids. I round the back of the car through some incredibly sketchy weeds and take a seat behind the wheel. June can see my window from here, but I can also see hers. I sink down so I'm not totally obvious, just in case, and smile when I see her standing in front of a mirror on her wall.

ME: *You're beautiful.*

I can tell when she gets my message because she looks down at her hands, where I assume her phone is, and her body starts to twist side-to-side. I bet she's blushing. She glances back at her reflection, and I hope she sees what I do, all the things I've been blind to as well. That cute girl in braces is underneath it all but the exterior is an incredibly sexy woman.

JUNE: *Thank you. That . . . means a lot.*

ME: *It's the truth.*

Her body shakes and her shoulders lift to her ears. She's embarrassed, in a good way. It pleases me.

JUNE: *Will you do me a favor?*

ME: *I already said yes to the date.*

It's fun to watch her reactions. Her body shifts and I can almost hear the sigh she must let out. She pulls her palms up near her chest and types. She's so damn cute when she's frustrated.

JUNE: *This is different.*

ME: *I was kidding. Ask away. Anything.*

It strikes me while I wait for her to type and probably navigate talking to Abby at the same time that I meant that word—*anything.* It feels like a pretty fast leap to be willing to do anything for June. But also, this was such a long time coming. We've been waiting to get here for years. We detoured.

JUNE: *Will you help me practice talking to my mom? I don't know how to bring this up.*

My chest sinks into my body, my body heavy in the seat. I don't know that I ever had this conversation the right way with my parents. I feel unqualified to help her, but I also know I'm the only one who can.

ME: *I will try. I'm not very good at communication, I'm sure you know.*

JUNE: *You're better than you think.*

My mouth tugs up slightly.

ME: *So are you.*

My eyes widen when I read my own words.

ME: *I totally did not mean it like that.*

JUNE:

June's room is dim, the sun behind her house. Her lamp is on, and she must be sitting on her bed. I can see the curve of her shoulder where she's rolled up her sleeve. She's working a comb through her hair and braiding it. I want her to teach me how so I could do it for her. I never wanted to when we were kids. Well, I tried to weave Red Vines through her hair once but that doesn't count. I'm suddenly obsessed with the way her hair feels, and I want to touch it all the time.

ME: *Are you sure you want to get me started on the things I think you are REALLY good at? ;-)*

It takes about ten seconds for her to put Abby on hold to read my text. When her head falls forward into her palm, I let my laughter fill the Buick. I'm having so much fun out here spying on her.

JUNE: *Oh, my God, you are as bad as Abby. I'm not even going to tell you what she just asked me.*

I sit up, shifting my weight, my cock suddenly rock solid again. Damn, I'm in trouble.

ME: *I'm pretty sure you're going to tell me.*

My gaze moves to the window, to the tiny sliver of June's arm that I can see and the rope of braid that runs over her shoulder. She disappears in seconds, probably laying back, and even though my view is gone, I stay here, staring at that window. Maybe I'll climb up again.

She's talking to Abby about me, and that means our secret is not so secret anymore. It's weird, but I really don't care. There's a weight lifted from my shoulders, and I'm suddenly taking the deepest breaths I have in days . . . months. I want everyone to know she's mine. I don't even care that people will talk about us, warning her that I'm a player. Let them talk their shit. I have this strange faith in us. I mean, look what we came through already. Two years of hell and somehow we meet at the end? What are the odds?

JUNE: *She's asking about . . . uh . . . size.*

"Ha ha!" I laugh so loud that I immediately duck lower than the steering wheel. If anyone is outside, they surely heard me. I'm shocked June didn't hear me from inside.

ME: *And you said . . .*

I'm not sure whether she's dragging out her response this long on purpose to torture me, or she's simply mortified. I amuse myself by flipping through social media for a while, but eventually I'm left tapping my thumb nervously on the side of my phone, waiting for her to, *oh!*

JUNE: *Let's just say from what we have pieced together, you are way above average. OMG I can't believe I told you that.*

I lean on the old center console, resting my palm on the knob June tried to give me. I unscrew it to give my nervous hand something to do and type back: *Well, duh!*

She calls me *cocky* in response, which only solidifies my infatuation with my old best friend, all grown up. She's perfect. Funny, beautiful, smart —*mine.* That weight creeps back in, and this time it's not because of my fear of what my mom will think but rather a new fear, that this won't last.

That I'll lose her.

ME: *Hey*

Before I can send my message off, or even finish my pitiful insecurity memoir, my phone buzzes with a message from someone else. I don't recognize the number, and I'm relieved it isn't Ava. She's not going to be very nice about what's developed between June and me, but like the opinions of so many others, I don't give a shit.

I open the strange message.

PRIVATE LINE: *Hey asshole. It's Abby. I want you to know that if you fuck this up and break her heart, they won't find your body.*

I smirk but also hold my breath. She's joking, but she's also not. I actually like the threat, though. I appreciate it, that June has Abby in her life. I want her surrounded with people there to guard her heart and protect her from "assholes" like me.

ME: *Hi. You have my permission to leave zero evidence behind if I fuck this up. Abby, I'm serious about June. I'm realizing just how long I've felt this way.*

ABBY: *Ok. Good.*

ABBY: *You're still an asshole. Give it time ;-)*

I chuckle and switch screens back to June and our conversation. That *hey* I wrote is still there, a lonely word waiting for me to have the guts to say the rest. These words aren't meant for a text, though. I'll save them so I can speak them. She deserves to hear how special I think she is.

Instead of getting into my feelings, I decide to retrace our past—all of the good times. We spend the next four hours, until my battery is nearly drained, swapping stories about trouble we got in as kids, our favorite holidays, water fights and Halloween costumes. We debate favorite songs and she takes me down a tangent about the Buick I'm sitting in, how she wishes it ran so she could drive it. In the middle of it all, I send out a few feelers to friends who know things about cars, and I've already got plans in the works to restore this sucker. From what I can tell, it will take months.

Months.

I'm planning a life with June that exists in the months ahead. Dare I let myself think in years?

TWENTY

I'm nervous. I actually think my pits are sweating. *This is crazy!*

I woke up excited for my day, and I know it's because I want to see June. I probably could have waited around for her this morning, but I'm still navigating stuff with my mom and how to tell her, well, everything.

Tory keeps motioning for me to get out of my truck but I have no interest. If I go out there and stand with him and Hayden, the other guys are going to crowd around, and June might not be up for coming to see me. Besides, I need to get her my truck key. And I need to kiss her. I don't want Tory involved in that.

Abby pulls up with June in her passenger seat, and neither of them sees me at first. I slink down, resting on my console, cheek on my fist as I watch the two of them. Abby scares the shit out of me, but I like their friendship. She's good for June. I can't take credit for the strong girl she's become. June gets full credit, but Abby probably is due some influence points.

June flashes her eyes my direction and I lift my head from my hand long enough to hold out an open-palmed wave. Abby leans forward and glares at me, and I feel her threat. She made her point and I will abide by her rules. I can make that promise.

The two of them leave her car and stroll toward me, Abby peeling off when she reaches the twins. Tory leaps to his feet and brushes off the concrete bench he was just resting his feet on and Abby sticks up her nose. June gets in while I watch this strange scene unfold, and she's laughing.

"What's funny? I ask.

"Tory thinks being a gentleman is going to win Abby over," June says.

Win Abby over?

"Huh."

With my wrists balanced on the steering wheel, I lean back and observe my friend with this new layer of information. *He's finally actually going to admit to some feelings.*

"So, the key?" June brings my attention back to her and her open palm. She's awfully eager for this. *Hmm.*

"Oh, yeah. Here," I say, killing the engine and pulling the key free. She makes a grabby motion with her palm right before I drop the key in.

"I see that twinkle in your eyes. Don't get crazy." I cover her hand and wrap her palm around the key. She thinks I'm teasing her, but honestly? I'm a little nervous about giving her free rein to the only good thing to come out of my broken family situation. I fucking love this truck. June's more important, though. June and my future.

Does that mean I—

"Let me go over things one more time, just to make sure I have it down. At lunch, we both slip out the gate and you get in the car with MIT lady while I go to your truck and drive it to Two-fers."

All of this so I have an alibi. There are enough people to see my truck at Two-fers to explain why I'm not around for lunch or why I may be late getting back for class. Sadly, I won't be in trouble for being late; I'll be in trouble for skipping lunch to interview for MIT. Ridiculous.

I nod to June, but the second her mouth slips into a smile, my head rushes back to my last thought. *I'm fucking in love with June Mabee.*

"You'll do great," she says. I snap out of my daze and laugh. I'm unfazed by the pending interview. It's a formality. It's sweet that she is bolstering my confidence, though.

I turn my head to the side, rest it on my headrest and drink her in. I blink a few times, waiting for the moment to feel awkward or uncomfortable, but those feelings never come. All I feel is peace and comfort and fortune.

"I'm not really worried about the interview."

I'm worried about you changing your mind.

June twists in her seat to face me, tucking my keys in her bag before leaning forward and taking my hand in both of hers. She runs her delicate fingers over the rough edges of my skin—war wounds from the gridiron. My hands will never be the same. I turn my palm so our fingers weave together then run my thumb over the top of her hand. I smirk at it, but my head is lowered enough that she can't really see how happy this tiny touch makes me.

"Lucas, there is no way your dad can't be proud of his son getting into MIT," she says.

I nod and let out a breathy laugh. My dad will only see the betrayal. Pathetic. I've gotten to the point that I no longer remember a time when I idolized the man. I have doubts that I ever did. I know there were happy moments, like playing catch with him in the front yard, having him celebrate me by hoisting me on his shoulders and running in circles. Those memories are tainted now, my mind quick to rationalize his happiness as nothing more than opportunism. I've always been his second chance. He nudged me down his path, and because I was a boy, I followed, eating up the attention he showered me with when I was good at something he liked.

He never once pinned one of my report cards on the wall. My tests on the refrigerator were put there by Mom. And he called my near perfect SAT score "irrelevant." I'd love to tell him what's irrelevant to me.

The bell sounds, and June pulls her hands away after giving mine a gentle squeeze. We're on full display, and I'd told her—and myself—that we would ease our way into public. But now she's leaving, and I don't want to let her go without knowing how much I am in this with her.

She has her bag. Her hand is on the door handle. Move now, Lucas, or you get what you deserve.

Before she can crack the door more than an inch, I cross the center console and run my hand up her jaw, along her cheek and into her hair. Pulling her to me, our mouths collide as my eyes close so I can shut out the noise and enjoy *us.* I kiss her as if we're all alone, my tongue deep in her mouth, tasting her. My hand curls at her scalp, fingers tangled in her hair. I want more but this will have to do. June moans and it's enough to prod me to kiss her a few seconds longer. I'm sure we're putting on a show, but I couldn't care less.

I hold on to that thought as our lips part. The only thing that could burst this perfect bubble we've created is standing a dozen feet away from my truck. Ava's glare doesn't just penetrate, it cuts like a laser beam.

"Fuuuuuck," I groan, sinking my gaze to my lap. This is going to make today challenging. Ava will be spreading rumors the second her back is to us. She'll be dreaming of ways to attack June by the time her ass hits her chair in first hour. And she will be watching me like a hawk, which normally wouldn't bother me at all, but today . . . *today,* I don't want to be noticed. I have things to do. The last thing I need is Ava pointing out that

I'm heading off campus again, especially when she's pieced together why. *Thank you, shitty front desk privacy practices.*

"She'd find out eventually," June says. Her fingertips slide from my arm where she was still clinging to me. I glance her way, and one peek at her expression tells me she's scared. Ava is not going to be nice.

"Yeah," I sigh. I hold on to her gaze, more worried for her than my own selfish reasons.

"Does she know about MIT?"

My nostrils flare at her question. I don't want her to think I shared things with Ava. There's a difference between her nosy ass finding out shit and me confiding in her.

"She doesn't know shit!" My anger gets the best of me, and my response comes out more of a bark.

We both turn to check on Ava's progress. She's almost around the far corner to her first hour building. It's obvious by the way she's practically marching that she's full-on lit. I bet there are a dozen passive-aggressive social media posts aimed at me and June by now. It only takes her seconds to fire off those missiles.

June pushes her door open all the way and slides out, glancing to me over her shoulder.

"I'll see you at lunch," she says.

"I wish you were still in my first hour," I manage to squeak out before she closes the door behind her. Her eyes linger on mine as she walks backward a few steps, an impish smile playing at her lips. She lifts a shoulder, I guess shrugging to apologize that she's not there anymore. Or maybe she's telling me that it's too bad, I took too long.

I did. *Way* too long. I draw in a full breath and remind myself how much I have to lose. I'm thankful that the only casualty to my stubbornness is losing an hour with June every week day.

I thought I could wait out Tory, but I should know better. Dude would be fine getting detention for being late in order to box me in and force me to talk about June. He's standing at the front of my truck, nobody out in the parking lot but the two of us, so I give in and get out of the solace of my truck cab.

"I feel like I missed the middle of the movie. Bro, what am I missing? June hasn't said a word either."

I shrug him off but he punches my shoulder, kind of hard.

"Damn," I say, rubbing the spot he hit. "We've gotten past shit. That's all."

My friend laughs loud enough that the sound reverberates off of the corridor we walk through on our way into school.

"Lucas Fuller, finally coming to terms with the fact he's in love with June Mabee. What's it been, ten years?" I can feel his eyes boring into my cheek as we walk.

"*Pshh*, not that long. I didn't really know her that well until we were ten."

Tory stops in his tracks and I don't realize until I'm holding the door open for him. That's when my admission hits me, too. I turn to see his mouth agape, a tinge of a boastful grin touching the corners.

Shit.

I pinch the bridge of my nose and wince, looking down at my feet.

"Oh, no. You don't get to pass up on this. I heard you. Or rather . . . you heard me. And you were fine with those words. Lucas Fuller is in love with June Mabee." Tory doesn't have a quiet button. I'm not even sure my best friend knows how to whisper.

I bob my head up in time to catch Ava passing behind him on her way to the office and my stomach sinks.

"Could we take this outside?" I push the door open wider, and my friend finally moves his feet.

He pats my chest with a fat, open palm as he passes and utters a quick "Atta boy."

If I had more time to walk with him, I would turn the tables and question him about Abby. I'll have time for that later. For now, I'm glad he has to peel off to the left for class while I barrel straight ahead. Ava was heading to the office and it's filled my head with all sorts of mistrust. Somehow, she's going to make life miserable for June today. I feel it.

I pull my phone out while I walk, and hover over my text string with June. I want to warn her. I type out the whole scene for her, letting her know that Tory couldn't keep his volume down and Ava heard him say something, but then I stop and immediately delete. I can't tell her *what* Ava heard—that I love her. Or at least in Tory's mind I do.

No, I won't do that anymore. I'm not going to pretend I don't. That's the rule the old Lucas put in place. It's not only in Tory's mind. It's in my mind, too. In my heart. I love her. I love June. I don't want her spending her day worrying about Ava, which is all any warning text would do to her. And I sure as hell don't want to tell her I love her by text. I'm not sure I'm ready to let that thought move from inside my body to out of it. Of course, I blew that with Tory.

I'm the last one to slide into my seat in physics, right before the final bell sounds. We have a test today. I'm holding steady at a ninety-five in the class so blowing one test won't be the end of the world. I didn't study. I didn't even try. There was literally nothing in the world that was getting me to give up messaging June last night. I would have typed through a tornado.

My phone buzzes in my pocket so I give it a quick glance before tucking it away in my bag for the test. My heart hoped it was June, but I see Ava's name in the preview. Instead of letting *her* in my head, I drop my phone in my bag and decide to leave it there for the entire morning.

Getting dressed into interview clothes without having anyone notice proves a bit tricky. I didn't want to leave class early before lunch, so I packed the easiest pants and dress shirt I own. I'm pretty sure I wore these pants to my uncle's funeral over the summer. They're a little snug now. My quads have bulked up since I last pulled these suckers on.

I manage to slip out of my jeans and T-shirt and into the more formal wear in under a minute, rolling my regular clothes up and stuffing them in my backpack. The tie proves super problematic, however. I've never been good with them. My mom always has to redo them. I know I'm supposed to make it snug against my neck, but it makes me feel like I'm choking the whole time. After three attempts, I give up and leave the ends dangling at my chest as I jet toward the parking lot to meet June. I'm so relieved to see her at the front of the school, not because I'm nervous about the interview but because I need her help with this damn tie.

"*Psst*," I say, sneaking up behind her. She startles a little, which is cute.

She spots my tie situation right away, smirking and amused at how flummoxed I am by a strip of silk. I lift my chin as she grins.

"These things are tricky." She takes the mangled ends and gets to work fixing my neck situation.

"I fucking hate ties. They choke me." I swallow hard and tug at my collar.

"You're a big man," she responds, her words so matter-of-fact. Our eyes flit to one another and I catch the blush that creeps up her cheeks. My mouth edges up on one side with my devilish thoughts, and June slaps lightly at my chest.

"Shush, or I won't help you."

I lean back with a thick laugh that I do my best to apologize through. Clearing my throat, I stand up tall so she can finish making me look presentable. She tugs at the knotted tie a few times, either because she's making it straight or simply likes to jerk my body around. I think it might be a little of both.

My mom made sure my shirt was ready this morning. I haven't worn it in so long, the wrinkles looked impossible, but through whatever magic she has, she managed to have it looking crisp this morning. I rolled it for my backpack and somehow didn't ruin her work completely.

"There," June says, her hands loosely gripping my tie, almost as if she's afraid to let go. She glances up at me with a faint smile, and I'm hit with every ounce of feeling all at once. *I love this girl.*

"Wish me luck," I say, holding on to my view of her green eyes.

She shakes her head.

"You don't need it. Break a leg."

I laugh out once and roll my eyes before grabbing the gate just opened by one of the late-start seniors. June follows closely behind me and we pause just outside the gate so I can scan the lot.

"Ready?" I draw in a breath through my nose. I wish my heart would stop pounding. It's not the interview that has me wrecked by nerves, it's the fear that my dad or Coach will show up and catch me in the act. At least our principal is on my side for this. I emailed him about the interview late last night and he said he would make sure I was excused. He's not really a football fan.

June holds up my keys and jingles them.

"Let's do this," she says. We're practically jogging through parking lot. I spot the red car, Candace waiting inside, just like she was the first time I had to slip out for a meeting. June's already sprinted across the parking lot. She'll be pulling out soon, hopefully without anyone noticing it's her driving my truck and not me.

When I reach Candace's car, I give one final glance around the campus, and when I don't spot my coach or anyone who might mention they saw me doing this, I dip inside and finally exhale.

"Lucas, great to see you. I hope you like sushi." Candace gives me a nod and smile as I buckle up.

"I think I'm too nervous to taste. We could be going to a cardboard restaurant and I'd think it was five-star," I joke.

She laughs at my humility and tells me to relax, reminding me this is all a formality. I breathe out and flatten my palms on my thighs to play along.

"Right. Got it," I say, my insides still a twisted mess. Again, not nervous about the interview part.

We drive several blocks to the other side of town to a place called Tiny

Plates. I've never been here but I know my mom has. I wish I had time to text her and ask what I should order. She knows what I like.

"So tell me, Lucas . . . what drew you to MIT?"

She's making small talk but I know my answers still matter. I don't merely want to be their selection for this scholarship; I want to be the stand-out.

"I remember hearing one of my mom's old friends talk about the school when I was younger, and it stuck in my head. As I got older, I found out that me and math? We gel."

She laughs when I bring my hands together as if math and I are puzzle pieces.

"That's not something many people say," she muses.

"I guess not," I say, laughing lightly at myself. I regroup, though, and set my expression to a more serious one. "But the idea of doing something with this weird skill I have, maybe changing the world in some small way for the better? That's what I see at MIT. It enables so many good things."

Our gazes meet briefly, and she gives me a tight-lipped smile. That was a good answer, the kind the trustees will want to hear. I tuck it away and remember to repeat it in the next thirty minutes over my plate of raw fish rolls.

The restaurant is busy, but we find our party waiting at a table when we arrive. Candace introduces me to a tall man with an incredibly expensive-looking suit and an older woman with short-cropped hair dyed a purplish-gray. She's wearing a black suit with perfectly square frame glasses, and in any other situation I would probably observe how very *Men In Black* she appears. But my dad's old boss from the first law firm he worked for just sat down at a table on the other side of the room, and now the only thing running through my head is fear that he'll see me and feel the need to come say hi.

I twist in my chair, doing my best to shield myself from his view. I'm glad to see three other people join him, but it doesn't stop my imagination from conjuring what ifs.

Hey, Todd. Ran into Lucas at Tiny Plates while he was meeting with MIT. Wow! You must be so proud.

Of course, my dad wouldn't be. He'd be furious. And he'd come home ready to lay into me, which would probably be the final straw to get me to open my mouth about his current affair. It wouldn't be the way my mom should find out, and it would only make these final few months at home with my family worse—if I even had a family left.

"Lucas? You were mentioning in the car on the way here why you liked MIT?" Candace brings my thoughts back to the present, and I realize I spaced out a bit. I don't think for long, though, so I go to work covering my daydreaming.

"Yes, I was just thinking about our conversation, actually." Everyone at the table leans forward and I recite, nearly verbatim, what I told Candace in the car. For the next forty minutes, I switch off the part of my brain that seems to only be out to make my stomach sick, and I play the role of perfect MIT candidate. The two trustees insist on taking photos with me, and I don't worry about my reality again until Candace drops me off in front of school and asks if it's all right to post one of those photos on social media.

"Sure," I croak.

The odds of my dad knowing how to use social media are slim, so I rid myself of the extra worry and shake her hand before exiting the car.

"Oh, and hey, Lucas?" She's rolled the window down.

"Yes?"

I'm so close to getting inside. I'll make it to my next class and nobody will know anything. My truck is in its spot. June pulled it off. I can push off having it out with my dad and wrecking my mom for one more day.

"Welcome to MIT." A grin stretches the width of her face just before she drops her sunglasses down and drives away. I utter "Thanks" but I don't think she hears it.

It's official. A few signed documents is all that stands in my way. I laugh to myself, and as I make my way to class, passing through throngs of students, I catch a few of them looking at me oddly. It's probably because I'm still wearing dress clothes, but maybe it's also the enormous smile and skip in my step. I can't help it. I'm happy. There are things *I* want in my life. The school I dreamt of is within reach, a stepping stone to a life doing something I'm passionate about. The only thing left to do is kiss the girl I love to celebrate.

By the time the final bell rings, I've come around to embracing everything good, and not giving a second thought to the shit brewing beneath the surface. I practically skip toward the locker room, where June and I planned to do a quick key exchange. All of the warmth brewing in my chest grows cold, though, the second June turns her head and I spot her swollen black eye.

"What the fuck happened?" I kneel to inspect her skin. June tries to look away but I follow her face, moving to keep a good view. I also shoot a glare at Tory over her shoulder. He better not have been involved in this.

"I'm fine," June insists. She twists, but I reach up and gently coax her chin back in my direction.

"Your ex had a field day with her face," Tory says. I'm glad to hear he's pissed off, too, but his tone seems to indicate this is my fault. I stand and we have a mini stare-off. I glance down to the bag of ice in his hand, and because I'm an immature asshole, all I feel is jealous that *he* was here to get her ice and I wasn't. Which is not the point. And maybe he's right to take the tone he does with me.

"Gentlemen?"

We both shift our focus to Coach Loma as he walks up. My pulse races, excuses flying wildly around my head. He's going to want to know what happened here, and maybe he also knows I went rogue.

"I had an accident, Coach, and they happened to catch me before I fell all the way. I went end-over-end," June lies. I swallow down my guilt. I should cut her off and tell Coach what really happened. Ava deserves a world that knows what type of person she is.

June takes the ice and towel from Tory, pressing it to her eye.

"Lemme see what you've got going here," Coach says. He straight-arms me out of the way and bends to give June's face a closer look. Tory and I make eye contact above the two of them, and my friend's brow furrows. He doesn't understand why June would lie . . . or why I let her.

"You said you got this falling down the stairs?" Coach is asking June, but he glances to Tory and me with skepticism. His lips are pursed and his eyes squint a hint to show his suspicion.

June nods, lifting one shoulder in a shrug as if to say she's just a clumsy girl. *Fuck, I'm an asshole. Tell the truth, Lucas! Make Ava pay.*

"Mind if I get our trainer to come give you a look? Just a little concussion protocol, and since it happened on campus, we'll need to fill out an incident form." Coach takes things like this seriously. He's the father of four daughters.

"Okay," June says, her voice barely above a whisper.

We all stand, except for June, who flashes the inside of her palm to me to how me she has my key. She wants to give it to me now, but it can wait. It *should* wait. Clearly Coach Loma is ready for Tory and me to move along and get our asses to practice.

I meet June's gaze and lift my bag to bring it to my shoulder, but before I get it all the way up my arm, June yanks it back down to the ground. It's ridiculous, and I have to roll my eyes at her covert attempt.

"Oh, dang, sorry. I thought this was mine," she fibs. Her bag is pink. Mine is black. If anything, she just sold Coach on the idea that she's concussed. She manages to slip my key into the side pocket of my bag during the confusion, though.

"It's fine," I say, lifting my bag to my shoulder. I can't help the constant frown that's forced its way over the smile I was wearing most of the afternoon. Tory and I hover for a few more minutes, but Coach Loma conveniently steps into the space between us and June, essentially boxing us out.

"I guess . . . we're done here," Tory chuckles.

I can't laugh, though. I'm too angry. And guilty. And ashamed.

"She's okay. June's a tough one," Tory says, easing up on me as we head into the locker room. I drop my bag on the bench when we make it inside and it lands with a heavy *clunk*.

"What was that? She gave her a black eye, dude! Who does that?" I press my palms into my eyes and rehearse the conversation I need to have with Ava, one that makes it abundantly clear that she needs to back off when it comes to June.

"I mean, dudes in bars punch each other all the time. And I'm pretty sure I punched you in the face over pizza once." I drop my hands to meet Tory's gaze and he shrugs with a half-smile.

"We were ten," I clarify.

"Yeah, but I'd probably still fight you for pizza. I'm not very mature."

I breathe out a quick laugh, his joke releasing some of the tension. Tory swings open the door of his locker, dropping his backpack inside and pulling out his practice jersey and pads. I stare at his back for a few seconds, wishing there was an easy way for me to tell him about his mom and my dad. This whole thing gives me sickening flashbacks to when I struggled with this same question while looking at June.

"You checking out my ass?"

Tory caught me staring, and is now standing on his toes and glancing over his shoulder at his boxer briefs. I huff out a laugh, then rub my hand over my chin and give his rear a good look before shrugging.

"Eh. I've seen better."

Tory's face contorts. He's playing offended—or maybe he actually is—and does a few calf raises to flex his glutes.

"Nah, my ass is *fiiiine.*"

Damn, his confidence. I roll my eyes and we both dress out for practice.

For two hours, my mind shuts off. Coach never asks about my dad or mentions me leaving campus, and I almost forget that I did. It's only when I'm fishing the key out of my bag that my thoughts return to the fact I pulled off a pretty major secret meeting today. I check my phone, worried about June, but the only texts are from my mom, asking how the day went. I send her back a short reply, letting her know that it's official, and when she doesn't write back right away, I tuck my phone in my back pocket.

Zachery, one of the bigger guys on our defensive line, lingers on his way out of the locker room, stopping a few feet from my bench.

"Hey, Fuller? You hooking up with Mabee or what?"

I glance up and quirk a brow. It's none of his fucking business, but also . . . this is what June was talking about. She doesn't want to be kept a secret. She deserves better. And I'm proud she's willing to forgive me after the last two years of silence.

"She's my girlfriend."

The smirk on Zachery's face falls, and the joke he was probably waiting to make seems to be caught in his throat. I see him swallow it.

"Oh. Cool, man." He pulls his mouth into a tight smile and awkwardly exits the room.

"That was fuckin' weird," Tory says from behind me.

I nod. But now that Ava's involved, who knows what story she spun about me and June. And the fact I maybe told her things I shouldn't have about June's mom doesn't sit well in my gut. I'm an idiot when I'm drunk.

"Hey, you see anything on social?" I ask Tory as we gather our gear and head out to the parking lot. He flips through his phone while we walk, not really looking too deep into anything, which makes his lack of findings not very credible. I'd rather believe he's right, though, so I take his word for it and drive home under the pretense that Ava hasn't started the rumor mill yet.

That bubble bursts the second my headlights flash on the Mabee garage.

WHORE

The word is sprayed in red and it stretches from one end of June's garage to the other. I gnash my teeth and let a growl simmer in my chest, breathing out a "Fuck!" I kill the lights on my truck and let my temper heat to a boil. I'm tempted to peel out of here and race to Ava's house so I can drag her back and make her fix this. I probably would, too, except I know in my heart that June is inside suffering because of this. And taking care of her is priority number one.

My muscles are sore and tired, so my scale up the side of her house and eave isn't as smooth as last time. June's window is open when I get to the crest of the pitch, wrapping my hands around the sill of the window. I step through and find her sitting on the edge of her bed, her face void of emotion. *Drained.*

"June," I say, rushing across her room and dropping to my knees in front of her. I hold her face between my palms while her eyes hover on the cusp of forming tears.

"I'm so sorry," I say, running my thumb over her puffy skin. The bruising is worse now, the swelling down some.

"I'm so sorry," I say again. I repeat those words every time I take in a new piece of her. Her hair is damp, either from showering or crying. And her fingernails are stained pink on the tips, likely from scrubbing the garage door to no avail.

Fuck, Ava!

Her palms fall to my chest, gripping my shirt, and she falls into me, laying her unbruised cheek against my heart. Her body shakes and she finally lets out a sniffle. I slide one arm under her and lift her to me as I stand, cradling her trembling body while I shift to sit on her bed and hold her in my lap. My hand strokes her back, a smooth rhythm meant to bring her peace. Her face finds reprieve under my chin, and she shivers with another sob.

"I know, June. I'm so sorry. I'm so fucking sorry," I whisper at her ear. I rock her gently as tears well in my own eyes. Mine are a mixture of hurt and anger, like hers but different. I can't explain the vengeance swelling in my chest. I want Ava to pay for what she did. This is inexcusable. So was my act, though—sharing secrets that weren't meant for Ava's ears.

"She painted my house," June cries.

"I know," I say, my mouth against the side of her head.

She painted her house.

I squeeze my eyes shut and the moisture falls to my cheeks. June has been hurt so much in all of this. How could I not see what the last two years has done to her?

I hold her for nearly an hour, never once letting my biceps relax. I keep her nestled into me, my fingers drawing gentle lines up and down her bare arms until she seems to be feeling the call of sleep. Her tears have stopped.

"How was the interview?" Her voice is raspy, and it makes me laugh quietly that of everything she's been through, she's focused on me. I lean back, resting on her bed, but keep her tethered to me.

"There are more pressing things," I say, sweeping her hair into my palm. The waves fall through my fingers, but some of them stick, leaving me to gently smooth them out.

"Not really," June sighs. "I mean, if all this happened and you didn't get in, that would suck." I smirk and let out another tiny laugh. She's funny, even when she isn't feeling it.

She wriggles on top of me and holds herself up so our eyes meet. I dip my chin and she morphs her face into what I think is an attempt to wink. I shake my head slowly and laugh, running my thumb along the bruise. This eye is not meant to wink—or do much of anything—for a good two days.

"I'm in," I finally say, giving her something positive to celebrate. It feels selfish, but June doesn't see it that way, of course. She pushes down on my chest, giving my lungs a compression boost that clears them of oxygen, and sits up higher. I wrap my hands around her wrists.

"Shut up!" she whisper-shouts, but damn is it loud. I cover her mouth and suck in my own lips, trying not to laugh. *Wouldn't her mom love walking in on this?*

"*Shhh.* I can't go to MIT if your mom shoots me first," I tease. Sorta.

June and I both roll to our sides, her hands holding my cheeks.

"Lucas, I am so proud of you." Her eyes flash wide then blink as her focus moves around my face. She's waiting for me to be as elated as she is. I want to be. It's just—

"He'll come around," she finally says. She's trying so hard to be an optimist. I simply don't see it, though.

I shake my head and glance down to our legs, her knee between my thighs. I bet we've lain like this before, as kids. Maybe watching a movie, one of the scary ones we weren't supposed to see. I have vague recollections of my younger self wondering if I would ever be into girls and feel differently when lying with a girl like this.

That answer is a clear yes.

"I don't even care. I'm going, and my mom said with the scholarship money I'll get, they can pay the rest." *They, as if my dad will be involved with our family ever again.*

I twirl June's hair around my index finger, winding it then letting the twist fall loose. My chest is tight, and it's because of everything looming just outside this room—the garage, Ava, my parents, Tory's mom, *me and June.*

"My mom knows you helped," I admit. I decided to tell her, my way of inching into breaking the news to her that I'm not giving June up again. She was surprisingly receptive. I wouldn't say warm, but she wasn't angry.

June blinks at me a few times, her eyes darting from mine to my mouth and back. *I want to kiss you, too, June.*

"And she'll still let you go?" she finally says. She's joking, but I hear the tinge of hurt in her tone. She and my mom were close. I never thought about how much June must miss her.

"My mom doesn't hate you, June. She's just—"

"Hurt," she cuts in.

I stare into her pools of green, bathing in the emotion they hold. June's eyes are a witch's brew of poetry, mystery, pain, and joy. If it can be felt, it exists right there, in those eyes.

"Yeah, she's hurt. When she found out about the affair, she went through a pretty dark time." My throat gets dry and I try to swallow the scratchy feeling down. I don't talk about this time with my mom often. I don't have to. Tory *lived* through it with me, and he's honestly the only person I talk to about these things.

"You haven't told her about the new one, have you? The new affair?" June says.

I shake my head.

"I haven't told her."

I shift so our faces are close, nearly nose to nose. My eyes shut, the weight of what I've been carrying taking its toll. Maybe I'm finally in a place where I feel safe.

"Have you told Tory yet?" she asks.

I shake my head, my nose grazing hers.

"I'm sorry about . . . the word. On the garage." I hate that word, but more than that, I hate that it was Ava who wrote it. She did it with such malice, trying to cut deep. And I gave her the tools to be cruel.

"You told Ava about my mom and your dad," June whispers. It's not a question. She already knows.

All I can do is let out the breath I've been holding.

"I'm sorry. I don't even know why I did, but it slipped out once."

"*Shhh,*" June says, tenderly running her nose against mine. I think she is both trying to soothe me and prevent me from telling her more than she wants to hear.

"I'm sorry, June. I'm sorry, I'm sor—"

She stops my pleas for forgiveness with the gentle touch of her lips to mine. I open my mouth to let her own me, and she brushes another pass of her soft mouth against mine. We take our time, never pushing our kiss deeper. And at some point, her lips on mine still, I manage to find sleep.

TWENTY-ONE

My eyes pop open, my body rested and my mind at ease for the first time in months. June's room is partly illuminated by moonlight, part by the rising sun. It's a soft glow that shines on her skin, lighting up the tiny hairs on her arm. She looks like an angel this way.

It's early enough that I might be able to slip back inside my house without my mom realizing I was gone all night. She worries, and I think she'll probably continue to worry about me even when I'm all the way in Boston. Part of it probably stems from the times when my father doesn't come home. It's filled her with mistrust. Unlike her worries about him, though, for me she visualizes car wrecks or medical emergencies. Her mind runs wild. It's been conditioned to, I suppose.

June is deep asleep, and while I should take advantage of this early hour and get back to my house, I'm caught in the sight of her. Her breathing is a perfect beat, the small push of air that leaves her nose dusting the ends of her hair that have curled up on her pillow next to her face, moving them like a gentle breeze. Her lips pout when she sleeps, the top one curled up to reveal her top teeth. I stare at them for a full minute, considering blowing off my escape in exchange for a kiss. I don't want to break her peace, though. There's a hint of a smile on her lips that makes me believe she's having good dreams.

I slip my arm free from where it's buried under her neck and she stirs from the movement. Holding my breath, I wait until she nestles deeper into the covers and her pillow before I finally get up and make my way toward her window. We left it open all night, and it's made the room cool. She seems comfortable, though.

My body aches from sleeping in a bent position, but it's worth the massive kink in my neck. I held her through the night. I swear I was aware of every minute of it, too.

I make it to the roof mostly in near silence, but my decent from the eave into the driveway is a little clunky. I end up running through the middle rather than gracefully landing, which I suppose is better than falling. I check my truck on my way to my house, pulling my gear bag from the cab and tossing it in the back so it airs out before I have to get in and drive my ass to school. I still can't believe *that* is happening soon.

My mouth contorts into an uncontrollable yawn that strikes me because I *thought* the word sleep, I swear. It pauses me just long enough to catch sight of my letterman jacket. I smirk at the thought of giving it to June. She'll find the gesture both sweet and passive aggressive . . . in a playful way. She love-hates this thing.

I snag it before closing my door and trek back to the rooftop that just sent me dashing off balance down her driveway. I have to put the jacket on to have full use of my hands to climb back up and through her window, and she moves at the sound of my arms slipping free of the sleeves.

I drape the jacket on the back of her desk chair and twist it so the mascot on the back is the first thing she sees. I sneak out through her window, finding sure footing this time and making it down easily.

Proud of my stealthy moves, I take my time walking back to my house. A door slams shut behind me, though, and I jump and dash behind my truck. I doubt June woke and raced downstairs, so the only other option is that her mom came out the door. I duck low, doing my best to watch June's mom through the glass of my back and side windows. The sun is peeking out more, so I can see her profile fairly well. She doesn't look angry. In fact, she almost seems amused.

She pauses in front of her marred garage door for a few seconds, hands on her hips as she takes in the ugly landscape. Patting her hands together, she marches forward, punching in her garage code and heading into the cluttered space. I should help them clean that area out some day. I think there are a lot of things in there that belonged to June's dad, things I'm sure her mom is anxious to get rid of. Maybe a garage sale is in order.

She comes back out with a ladder and a bucket of paint, one of the large five-gallon types. She works at opening it for several minutes, and I struggle between getting caught lingering out here and rushing over to help.

I don't want questions, though, and I have the strange feeling that one look into my eyes would reveal that I spent the night with her daughter. I don't think I'm ready to rationalize that with her, given *everything else* we are all dealing with.

Thanks to a swift hammer swing into a screwdriver, she finally pops the lid loose and goes to work. I watch her brush and roll for twenty, maybe thirty minutes, feeling guilty the entire time because it's my fault in part that she has to cover such a word to begin with. Her paint job is patchy, probably a stopgap until she can get a professional to come out. But when she goes into her garage for another bucket of paint and drizzles what looks to be red around the garage, I'm baffled. I want to stick around long enough to see the end result. I'm so curious about what she's up to, but my mom will be up any minute.

Rather than make noise with my own garage, I crouch down and tiptoe to my back yard, slinking inside through the glass door. I make it up to my room without a sound, noting the sound of my dad snoring as I pass my parents' door. He's home this morning, and from the sounds of it, he was here all night. He doesn't snore unless he's had some serious sleep.

My brain suddenly wired, I ditch my clothes and pick out a fresh T-shirt. I'd shower, but me getting up early would set off all sorts of red flags in this house. Instead, I lay back on my bed and hold my phone to my chest, waiting for June to wake and comment on the gift I left behind.

I must have dozed off, because by the time my phone buzzes against my body, it's almost time to leave for school, and the message is from my mom, wanting to know why she saw June getting into her mom's van this morning in my letterman jacket. My thumbs hover to respond, but rather than over-think things, I decide to keep this bit of my life simple.

ME: *Because I gave it to her.*

I leave it at that and gather my wallet and keys so I can make a mad dash to school. I halt at the end of my driveway, noticing the finished work from what June's mom began in the wee hours. Bold, red and somehow perfectly centered, their family home now boasts a vivid middle finger, one that gives everyone a giant F-U as they pass by. I stop and stare for almost a full minute, fighting the urge to take a picture.

Not everything needs to be photographed. Some things are meant to only be remembered. This is one of those things.

I pull in to school after the bell rings and rush through the main office doors to catch up to everyone else. The last thing I need is someone noticing me rolling in late and mentioning it to Coach. Somehow, it would get around to me skipping out yesterday to meet with a college about something other than football.

When I push through the main office doors, I'm greeted by the familiar stare of a bright golden eagle, wings outstretched, claws ready to grip. Its view is quickly dashed by a curtain of dark brown hair, and my grin grows. June is wearing my jacket.

I jog forward in time to reach over top of her and push the second set of doors open wide. She slows her steps, stopping suddenly, causing me to crash into her. I wrap my arm around her midsection and carry her forward with me in the opposite direction of her independent study room. *Why did she have to switch classes?*

"Earl? Is that you?"

I spin her around, my hand caressing her check and sliding into her hair in one swift movement before my mouth covers her. I kiss her long and hard in front of the entire school population.

"This public enough for you?" I touch her lip with my thumb for good measure, and she smiles around it. Her eye looks better, but I can still see the aftermath of Ava's rage.

"It's getting there," she teases.

I keep her hand in mine as I walk backward, still coaxing her to follow me. I know she can't forever, but a few more steps at least.

"This jacket is really fucking hot," she says.

I burst out a heavy laugh.

"You love it," I tease.

"I love you," she says back. The words slip from her mouth with such ease, all in the same breath, and I feel instantly drunk.

June's eyes widen and I think she considers covering her mouth with her hand. No use doing that. There's no stuffing those words back inside. I don't want her to. I'm stunned to hear them, though. I hoped, and my gut tells me we're at the same place with how we feel about each other, but I truly didn't think we would be able to verbalize things for months. After you spend two years avoiding each other, the pendulum gets stuck rather than swings.

I practice the words in my head, wishing I could shed whatever guard June let down. The bell rings before I'm able, though, and I ready myself to watch her sprint away. I wouldn't blame her. Not at all. But I'm not going anywhere, not until I can find the courage to say those words back.

Students run into us, and despite what I expect, June doesn't leave. We're a slow-motion film caught in the middle of high-speed traffic. People whip around us, cutting between us in some cases, and our gazes never break. I will my smile to inch upward, to be more obvious so she knows her words had meaning, that they were received with equal love, that I needed to hear them. I have a feeling on the outside, it's a stupid—and likely crooked—grin on my face.

"I'm really tired," June begins. She's about to ramble. I can feel it. "I meant the jacket. I love your jacket. Oh, God. Um." She's fidgeting with her hands, and her smile is so wide it practically threatens her ears. She's panicking, and it's so damn cute. She squeezes her eyes shut and twists in place before finally shouting "Good-bye" and taking off toward her classroom.

"I love you, too" I whisper to nobody. It's even hard here, in the safe space of being alone. Maybe if I say it every hour on the hour, I'll be able to utter it loud and clear.

I practice three or four more times on my way to class, then tuck the words back inside my chest so I don't accidentally speak them to the wrong person. I doubt my physics teacher would be into it. She's married—to a woman. A female *rocket* scientist. Pretty sure high school jock head is not in her dream fantasy list.

I count down the hours until lunch, and when the bell rings after second hour, I'm ready to sprint toward the cafeteria like I did in first grade when being first in line felt like it meant something. Only this time? I'm running to kiss the girl I used to push on the swing set.

"Lucas. You're wanted at the office," one of the office aids says. The girl looks young, maybe a freshman, and she probably ran to get the notice here before the final bell. If it were Ava delivering it, I might blow it off, but this girl was sent for a genuine reason.

"Thanks," I say, taking the pass.

I scan the throngs of students filing into the cafeteria as I make my way toward the front office. I don't see June in the mix, and I pull my phone out to message her but am halted by the firm hand of my father on my shoulder.

"Luc, glad I caught you. It's a big day!"

I'm sure the shock on my face isn't pretty. My eyes are so wide they dry out.

"Big . . . day?" I haven't seen this man since he nearly disowned me for throwing what he deemed a shitty pass. And now it's a big day?

"Yeah, Tennessee. It's the admissions rep. It's a formality, really, but they like the pomp and circumstance."

I walk alongside him, my mouth still agape and my brow pinched. My dad punches my arm.

"Your acceptance, bozo. You got in. To Tennessee?" My dad seems puzzled that I have not been waiting with bated breath for this acceptance to happen. I have a four-point-seven GPA with honors. Of course I'm getting in. *I got into MIT.*

"Oh. *Oh!*" I force the biggest grin on my face, teeth showing and all. "Yeah. Of course. I guess it's the whole phone-call-during-school-formality-thing that's throwing me."

Why the fuck are we doing this?

It becomes clear as soon as we step inside the main office. It seems I'm not the only person who got into Tennessee. The D'Angelo twins did, too. They've been accepted into lots of schools with early decisions. They have decent grades and are basketball gods. I guess the excitement of three Allensville students getting into a major powerhouse like Tennessee is worthy of a PR photo for the district.

I'll play along. I know for a fact neither of the D'Angelo boys are going to end up in Tennessee. Hayden was only using the offer to play there as a bargaining chip to play somewhere on the West Coast, and Tory has no idea where he wants to go. He wants to be famous and that's about as far as he's gone in terms of hoops.

When the twins' mom walks in, my stomach rolls and my veins light on fire. This is why I'm here. Why my dad is here. *Why I'm not sitting next to June.*

"How long will this take?" I check my phone. Lunch is five minutes in already.

"Got a hot date or something?" my dad jokes. Tory snort-laughs and when my dad turns to face him, my friend waves his hand.

"Sorry, sir. Funny joke is all."

I meet Tory's gaze behind my dad's back, and he smirks because he thinks this is all about my secret relationship with June. I feel sick because for me, it's about the enormous secret my dad and his mom are keeping from the three of us.

Maggie waves us back to the principal's office, and we gather around his ornate desk that's littered with paper, crowding around his tiny phone to listen to this call on speaker. I tune nearly everything out and step to the back, hiding my phone in my palm so I can fire a text off to June and Abby that I got stuck in here. It's all too much to explain, so I leave it at that and continue with the formality of ridiculousness.

"Deeply honored, ma'am. Thank you," Tory says when he's told he's been accepted. He's good at bullshit. Me? Not so much. I feel my dad's stare before I turn and see it in person. It startles me, but I pull it together.

"Oh. Yes. Honor. Huge honor."

Tory snickers at my lackluster contribution and my dad sneers.

"So we'll be in touch with you as we get closer to official signing day. Excited to have you recognize the talent we have here at Allensville Public." Our principal's cheeks are cherries, his grin is so tight. He's loving the attention that comes with this. My dad is loving the mid-day excuse to see Tory and Hayden's mom. I love that whatever the fuck this was? It's done.

Unfortunately for me, my dad has taken the rest of the day off. It means that he doesn't only stick around for "lunch" with Mrs. D'Angelo, but he also whiles away the rest of the day in Coach Loma's office.

"Your dad sticking around for practice?" Tory leans into me as he asks.

"Guess so. I'm going to get my ass on the field because at least he can't talk to me out there." I rush dressing out, mad that I won't get to see June before she goes home. Sick that I have this festering secret burning a hole in my intestines. Tory deserves to know.

I sprint to the field and start warmups on my own, waving our trainer over to help me stretch when I see my dad pacing at the top of the hill. I close my eyes and will him to disappear, but when I reopen them, he's no longer alone. June is with him, and she's proudly wearing my jacket.

There was a day when this situation would have driven my anxiety up seventy notches. Now? I simply smirk and put one hand behind my head while I stretch so I can enjoy the show.

TWENTY-TWO

JUNE: *I told my mom. She's talking to your mom. She's going to bust your dad. Warning.*

I blink at the text, the one I've read a dozen times. The first pass freaked me out, but now an odd calmness has oozed its way into my body, like Pepto.

My dad is talking to Coach, his arm slung out of his truck window all casual-like. He's comfortable, living in his bubble where he thinks nobody can outsmart him. My eyes dim at the visual of him as he laughs. I think the reason I never gelled with Coach Loma is because he and my dad are too much alike. They laugh at the same bad jokes, and I don't think either of them truly listens. When one of them is talking, the other speaks right over them, like a layer cake of words that nobody ever hears.

It's maddening to be in the same room with them. They feed off each other, and I seem to be their favorite topic. More directly, *my future* is.

Coach Loma played college ball. They were both quarterbacks the same year. Unlike my dad, Coach played all four years. He went to a smaller division school, though, not the same cache, so to speak. While he never got hurt, I think he harbors a strange grudge about the whole thing. I wonder if he thinks my dad's opportunity was wasted on him, as though he would have been a better fit since he made it through four years injury-free.

My dad's engine fires up so I shift into drive and lead us home. The closer we get, the wilder my imagination runs. I have a vision of June's mom holding my mom down in an Olympic-style half nelson, or vice-versa. It makes my foot heavy on the gas because those are not the two people who should be tearing each other apart. The man deserving of their rage is shining his brights in my rearview mirror. It's rude, and he does it all the time because he's afraid he'll hit a deer. He's afraid a deer will dent his precious truck is more like it.

I pull into the driveway in time to see my mom and June's in a standoff in my garage. Suddenly, all that bravado I felt over getting this over and done with is out the window. I don't want to go through the next several minutes. I can't back away now, though. *Literally.* My dad has pulled in behind me.

I wait in the truck while he rushes out, his lights still on, illuminating the show. I kill mine and roll down my window so I can hear.

"Babe? What's going on here?" My dad is practically staring down June and her mom, almost as if he knows what they're up to. My hand subconsciously forms a fist. Did he threaten June today when I saw them talking? Something is behind that look he's giving her.

Dad turns to face Mom, his body marking the third point of the invisible triangle drawn between them all.

"Our neighbors were just leaving," my mom says.

My stomach tightens and I instantly grow defensive. I don't want my mom thinking any of this is on June.

I fly out of my truck and call her name, and when our eyes meet, I see the resolve in them. June isn't backing down. And neither is her mom.

"We weren't leaving, Todd. We were just getting to the bottom of this big fat fucking lie you've concocted. That's what we're doing." June's mom crosses her arms over her chest, and my body goes numb. She's intimidating, and I think I actually see my father shake in his boots.

"Kristen, you don't know what you're saying." This is my dad's favorite tactic, deflection. He rolls his eyes toward my mom as he talks to June's, as if to say this is just more of Kristen Mabee's usual drama. He'll follow this with some distraction, a little what-aboutism pointing to something my mom should be angry about instead. He'll fluster June's mom until her words come out jumbled and she's so frustrated with everything that she gives up and storms away. I've seen him do this in court.

Seems courtroom rules don't apply to suburban garages.

"Oh, I know what I'm doing. I'm ruining your day, that's what I'm doing," June's mom says, stepping a little closer to my dad, her arms still crossed in front of her. I think maybe . . . she's flexing her biceps.

My eyes rush to my mom, my concern that she won't be able to take everything she's about to learn. She's been broken so badly, and it took every bit of her strength to rebuild herself. I hate my dad for making her go through this again.

"You never helped me with my divorce out of the kindness of your heart. You were setting up an alibi," June's mom says. That was always the crux of my dad's web—that he was helping Mrs. Mabee with her divorce because she couldn't afford a lawyer up to par with her ex-husband's.

The closer June's mom steps, the more my father's feet itch to take a stride back. I can tell by the way he toes at the ground then puts pressure on the heel of his boot.

"Nicolas was going to leave you with pennies, Kristen. Of course I wanted to make sure your ex didn't absolutely ruin your life just because he had a lawyer and you didn't. I'm just sorry that you blurred the lines of my kindness. Babe—" My dad heads toward my mom now, a sense of desperation in his movements. His hands are out at his sides, making it seem as if there's nothing to see behind this curtain. But there's plenty to see. More than he's ready for.

"She's twisting reality. And I'm so sorry you have to hear it. What happened was a mistake, but I guess to her . . . it meant more."

I swallow hard. Of the millions of words and phrases my dad could decide upon, he goes with that one. I see June lurch forward, but before the words can leave her mouth it hits me—this is how I make amends for everything. It has to be me who undoes this.

"Is Mrs. D'Angelo a mistake too?" I step in between everyone. My hands ball at my sides as my eyes zero in on my father's. I stare so hard that his pupils shrink under my glare.

"The twins' mom?" My mom's voice breaks as she speaks. I look to her, expecting to see her crumble, but instead, she barrels toward my dad, shoving his shoulder with enough force that she may have dislocated it. I sure hope so.

"Who told you that? Did she?" My dad points at June as if she's some untrustworthy liar. I laugh at how sick that thought is. The only one fitting that description is wearing boots and a blazer.

"I did," June says proudly. She steps into the center with me, and for a moment, I feel the earth quake. It's in my imagination, clearly, but the effects of anger and panic rush my body to the point that I think a seismic event occurred.

"Baby, she's lying. I mean, come on!" Stripped down, without his lies to bolster him, my dad sounds pathetic. His lies are so blatant now. Looking at how fragile the entire story was, it's amazing it didn't collapse sooner.

"Tell me everything," my mom seethes. I move closer to her, ready to take her hand or hold her up if she needs it. She seems strong for now.

My dad is clearly not going to reveal the details, so instead, June's mom does the heavy lifting, with a little help from the rest of us filling in the gaps. My dad knew my mom was suspicious, so he used the Mabees' divorce as his distraction, volunteering to help June's mom so they would have to spend time together alone. He left clues behind, including some sketchy labels in his phone's contact list that made it seem he was texting June's mom instead of Hayden and Tory's.

Their affair has been going on for three years, starting from a class trip they both chaperoned. These new facts have ruined old memories.

There's a perfectly reasonable explanation for everything, like the money he was seen giving June's mom. It turns out that was her settlement, just enough to cover expenses. Some fucking lawyer he is.

My dad cooled things off for a while when my mom got sick. Her breakdown didn't scare him for the right reasons, though. Nobody says it, but I know in my gut he was afraid the twins' mom would feel guilty and confess. Or would refuse to keep the charade going. He didn't want to lose his cake and candy. Man's a pig.

"Get. Out!" My mom doesn't waste another second when she finishes taking in the missing details.

"Babe, you're not being rational." My dad is grasping at straws, and the fact he decided to attack my mom's mental state—her mental health that she has worked so hard to care for—is pathetic.

"So help me, God, Todd, if you do not run upstairs and grab a bag full of your shit and leave this house right now, I will throw your things out the window and advertise free yard sale goods." I smirk at my mom's words, biting my tongue and staving off the temptation to volunteer we make it a block sale and bring out June's dad's old shit too, along with the dregs of probably a dozen other deadbeat spouses from the block.

I'm so amused by this thought that I don't realize my best friend has joined us.

"Tory," June croaks. I turn slowly and meet his shattered expression.

Everyone was so revved up and ready to shout over one another a second ago, but now that Tory's here, there's a dull hum in the air. I can always tell when my friend is about ready to fight someone. He has a way of rocking back and forth on his feet while his nostrils flare. His jaw flexes, and his fingers twitch with nervous energy. Blood is pumping through him with too much force to form fists. It won't matter. He's so livid he could take a man down with his pinky and nothing more.

Tory lifts his chin enough that our eyes meet, and I try to impart everything I know without using words. His eyes flicker back to my dad as he steps toward me, his sights set on the weak man just beyond my shoulder. When he reaches me, he places his palm on my chest and pats it. My heart readjusts to the new rhythm he sets.

"I got this one," he says.

Tory continues to march up to my dad until they are standing toe-to-toe. My dad is a tall man, taller than the D'Angelos who are both well over six feet. At this moment, though, my father is tiny.

"Leave my family the fuck alone." There's an eerie calm to Tory's voice that seems to force my dad to listen. He nods. It's a slight movement, but I see it.

"Oh, and your son? He's going to MIT. You? You were a shitty football player." I barely have time to process those loaded words before my best friend punches my dad hard enough to spin his head around and break his jaw. My dad is left holding his mouth together while blood spews through his fingers.

Tory and I exchange glances as he passes by me on his way back to his car. I don't rush after him. He needs time alone—time to drive too fast and yell way too damn loud. He gets to be angry for as long as he'd like. He can even resent me. Whatever he needs to get through this. I'll be waiting for him on the other side.

TWENTY-THREE

Two years of my life ticked by. It feels as if my freshman year happened forever ago. But the last two weeks have passed in a rush. My dad was gone from the house that same night. And rather than a yard sale, my mom gathered most of my father's belongings and took them to Goodwill.

Seven trips and two hundred bucks in fees. She called it an extermination.

I'm not sure where things go from here. I have no desire to see my dad ever again, and since I'll be eighteen soon, I don't have to. June's mom hooked mine up with the guy who represented her dad in their divorce. Seems a little fucked up to me, but if it takes care of my mom's needs and June is all right with it, who am I to question it.

Maybe it's because I've been on this ride before, but I'm not as messed up as I was the first time my family went through this. Maybe it's because that time was a lie, and now it feels more like a dry run. I'm glad I'm holding it together, though, because it means I can be here for my friend.

I've been in June's bed every night for the last two weeks. I'd prefer to be there again tonight, but Tory asked for a favor. And since he is pretty much the king of the pity hill for the foreseeable future, I'm beholden to indulge him no matter what. I'm not in this alone, either.

"If I have to go stand on the shore of a freezing-cold lake, so do you," I say.

June is hovering at the edge of her window. I'm not sure why she doesn't just go through the front door. I think she's afraid her mom will see her leave and not let her come. Chicago is a far drive, and June wants to be there with me to support Tory.

"Take my hand. I'll show you where to step." I have been propped in this awkward stance on her rooftop for ten minutes. My calves are cramping. If she doesn't scale down with me soon, I'm going to seize up and tumble into her dead bushes.

"I'm really bad at this," she says between maniacal laughs.

"No shit, you are. It's been an hour," I tease.

She flashes her eyes to me and scowls.

"It's been like . . . five minutes."

"Ten," I correct. That doesn't win me many brownie points.

"Do you want me to carry you like a vampire boyfriend?" I tilt my head to the side and she nods. I laugh out and shake my hand again for her to take.

"Well, that's tough shit because I am not a vampire, nor do I possess vampire strength so I can skip up and down rooftops with you on my back. Now, take my damn hand."

Her lips pucker, and as infuriating as she is, she's also beautiful. After a few seconds, we both laugh. Our moment is broken, however, by a few sharp-edged pebbles.

"Hey!" I glance down and catch Abby loading up her hand for round two. She lets them fall and puts her hands on her hips.

"Get your asses in gear. I have a photoshoot in the morning so we have to make this crazy-ass trip before the sun comes up."

Abby must have some special gift that I lack, because she motivates June to scale down the roof without my help at all. I'm left shaking my head and chuckling as Abby pats her hands together and calls it a day's work.

It's a two-and-a-half-hour drive to Chicago from Allensville. I manage to get us there in two. Tory was virtually silent for the entire ride. Both of the twins are taking their parents' divorce hard. Even though their dad was on the road a lot, he was a big part of their lives. He was heartbroken by the news, though, and from what Hayden tells me, he's searching for an apartment near the city.

As angry as Tory and Hayden are with their mom, they also have this undeniable loyalty to her. It's hard for me to understand. Cutting my dad out of my life was a no-brainer. Maybe that's because he's a cruel-ass son-of-a-bitch. Tory and Hayden's mom has always been there for her boys.

There's an anger brewing in them, though, and for Tory, it's going to burst. He's always been this way, the kind of guy who holds it in rather than inconveniences others with his feelings. Now, *that* is something I can identify with.

It's freezing when we step out of the car. The beach by Lake Michigan is empty, minus a homeless man I'm pretty sure I just watched pee into a bottle then hoist it into the water like a keepsake.

Gross.

I follow Tory as he takes slow steps toward the edge of the pier. If he leaps in, I'm going to have to go in after him. I hate cold water. Plus, it's dark. I'll have to scream and make a scene, and the lighthouse will fire up like a Fourth-of-July spectacle.

"Dude, don't do anything stupid," I finally say. He glances at me over his shoulder, looking at me like I'm stupid.

"Just covering my bases. It's cold." I shrug and attempt to push my hands deeper into my jeans pockets. This hoodie is doing jack squat to hold back the wind. Why do people live in this town? Indiana's cold too, but this wind makes it feel like someone is throwing knives made of ice.

Tory stops a few steps shy of the edge, so I line up with him. He's still within arm's reach. Our friends' voices are a murmur behind us. They've opted to stay near the truck, a smart decision since the truck has a heater. June would have joined me, but I waved her off. Something inside told me this walk is for Tory and me alone.

"Why didn't you say anything?" he finally asks.

I've been waiting for this question, but I didn't want to offer up answers until he was ready. That's how Tory is—he stews and bottles emotions in. It's not healthy, but he wouldn't have heard me if I told him before he was ready to talk about this. He would have erased the conversation from existence. I lick my lips and hope my voice comes out audibly. I'm shivering, but I'm also afraid of this conversation. I've decided the only way through it all is to be honest.

"I'm a chicken shit."

I glance to my friend and he tilts his head back to stare at the stars. I blink, waiting for him to respond, but eventually decide that his silence is his acceptance of my answer.

"I'm so angry," he says, his voice clear and precise. How is he not freezing?

"I know. Me, too, but . . . different." I move my stare from his profile up to the sky. I get dizzy when I look up like this for too long, but I want to see what he sees. Right now, it's a swath of clouds covering the stars like gauze.

The moon is bright, along with a few of the stars. It's hard to see much this close to the city.

"I'm going to end up here. Just so you know." He blinks, not once pulling his gaze away from the stars. I've settled on watching his expression instead.

"Yeah? Next Chicago Bull?" I laugh lightly but shut my mouth when I note the serious set of his jaw.

"Who knows? But I'm going to come here for school. I just feel it. I don't know why." He levels his head again, his focus out on the black water that seems to disappear into nothingness along with the sky.

"I believe you. I think you can do anything, Tor. You're twice the athlete I am." I hold a fist out at my side, desperate for him to acknowledge it. Several seconds pass, and I notice that our friends are no longer talking behind us. They're watching the awkward show. I've come this far, so no sense in backing down. My arm burns with lactic acid while I hold my hand out, the knuckles turning blue and cracking from dry skin in the whipping cold wind. Finally, after a truly ridiculous number of minutes, Tory turns his head and dips his gaze to my hand. In a swift motion he drops his fist on top of mine and we both stuff our hands back into our pockets.

We remain side-by-side in silence for another full minute before Tory finally breaks and I get a glimpse of my friend again.

"I was going to see how long you could hold it out like that," he says.

"I know. Also, fuck off," I respond.

We don't make eye contact again, but we both laugh out once in unison. These little things, they are what make us uniquely tied to one another. It's not the tragedy of our parents' poor decisions that binds us, it's the fact there is no place I would rather be than right here, supporting him, in what I swear to God is the coldest place on Earth.

"Ready?" *Please, Tor, be ready. I want a heater so bad.*

"Just a few more minutes," he says.

I nod, my head bobbing continuously as I adjust my hands in my pockets and dip my chin into the neck of my sweatshirt.

"Okay, sure. Few minutes," I mutter.

"I'm fucking with you. We can go." He winks at me when our eyes meet, but he's quiet once again for the trip home.

The quiet is fine. I'll wait him out, because I know my friend is in there. He's hurting, but he isn't unsalvageable. And now he has June in his corner, too.

TWENTY-FOUR

In the course of a month, I somehow went from a guy afraid to hold June's hand in my driveway to one getting dressed up for a formal dance preceded by a photoshoot directed by both of our moms, recently-sworn-enemies-turned-besties. It's nuts, but more nuts? I still, for the life of me, cannot tie a fucking tie!

"Dude, you're pathetic," Tory says, swatting my hands from my neck so he can take over dressing me.

"I need to learn this."

"Why? So you can be the smarty-pants math nerd who wears ties? Nah. Be suave and sexy, and wear a shirt with the top two buttons open." Tory tugs on my tie and I'm shocked that in the matter of seconds he has it perfect.

"Was no tie seriously an option?" *Because I'll take this off right now.*

Tory drops his gaze to meet mine and the straight line his mouth forms answers my question.

June's mom is taking photos of us. It's a little overboard, but she's a photographer, so I suppose this is her way of showing her love for us all. We got ready in June's room so the girls could walk down my spiral stairs to meet us all at the bottom. June said something about the dreamy railings I have. If this makes everyone happy—*June happy*—then a foyer photoshoot it is.

Tory, Hayden, Cannon, and I give each other one final check then leave

June's house to head back to mine. I knock lightly at the front door and my mom lets us in.

"They're just about ready." My mom's smile is real, and it warms me to see it. These are the things she missed because of my father. Things *I* missed. Milestones that moms want to take photos of to keep in boxes in their closets. My mom deserves those photos. And I'm glad to be giving them to her now.

"What do you think?" June's mom asks, waving her hand around the scene she created in my house. I nod and purse my lips, honestly impressed. There are thousands of tiny lights strung through the iron railings of our staircase. It's very fairytale-like. Of course, as my eyes roam up the stairs, my thoughts turn to the deal June and I made before tonight—that she would be naked under her dress. I step forward and test the view, and my dick flexes in my pants.

"I think we're ready," June's mom says to mine.

"I'll get them." My mom is practically glowing as she rushes up the steps. I wonder if there's a part of her that wishes she had more kids—had a daughter. In many ways, June is like one to her. They used to be so close, and I see glimpses of getting that back. It will take time, which is fine by me because I'm invested in the long haul. I don't care if I have to find a way to fly home every other weekend to see her, June and I are making distance work.

Abby's the first to crack open the door upstairs, and in typical Abby fashion, she owns the runway. Every step is a pedestal for her to own. She's done so many commercials by now that this type of thing comes easily to her. What she doesn't see, however, is the pair of eyes next to me drinking her in.

"Just tell her," I whisper, cupping my mouth and leaning to the side to urge Tory to get off his ass and do something about the crush he has.

His eyes slide in my direction but quickly return to Abby.

"I'm good," he says. He's a liar. He's anything but.

Lola and Naomi, two of June and Abby's friends, make their way down the stairs next, opting for those girlfriend poses that are so popular on social media. I'm baffled by how many ways girls can form hearts with their arms and hands. Even more mystifying is how close the four of them are now, especially since Lola and Naomi were Team Ava at the beginning of the year.

I shift my feet the longer they drag their decent on, and when they reach the last step, I consider rushing upstairs to catch June alone before she steps out for everyone to see. I'm selfish, and I know she's going to blow me away. I want to keep her my secret, one more time, just for a moment.

That chance is lost when the door pops open and she steps out onto the landing. She's so goddamn beautiful that I forget altogether about being greedy. I want to show her off instead. She's a work of art meant to be shared. *Not touched!*

"You are beautiful," I mouth to her. Her cheeks blush and her long lashes flutter along with her stretching smile.

Unable to hold myself still, I move toward the stairs, and with every step she takes down, I take two up. The snapping and clicks of June's mother's camera is our soundtrack, the blast of bright light and flashes nearly blinding me before I reach her. I'd find her by memory if I had to. Somehow, my heart would simply know where to meet her.

June's gained six inches in heels, and it transforms her calf muscles in a way that makes them utterly bitable. I cannot wait to run my hand up that leg, all the way from her ankle to her—

"Look who's all grown up," I say once I reach her. June's eyes move over my body, taking in my clothes. I let her pick out everything, and she's stuffed me into this sweater vest and tie that make me feel like a boarding school bad boy. It seems to work for her, though, because her hands are quick to pull on the knot of my tie.

I hold her elbows in my palms and she rests her hands on my hips as we turn to give her mom the shot she wants. The camera whirs, and my eyes catch up to the lack of focus every time she washes the room in major wattage.

June's body is teeming with nerves. I feel her quiver in my palms so I snake my hand around her back and step in close, holding her to me as I lean her back and kiss her lipstick off her face. My fingertips flirt with the sway of fabric that drapes at the arch of her back, and when my hand slides underneath, I'm greeted with the curve of her ass.

"Fuuuuuck," I groan against her mouth, loud enough for only us to hear. I'm so hard right now, it's all I can do to shift my body away from the camera lens. I don't think *these* are the pictures June's mom has in mind.

When I tip her upright, our eyes meet, and every fear I've ever had washes away. Maybe I need June to remind me that love is possible. My examples in life were never stellar. And my choices up until June, less than.

There's a strength behind her eyes now that pulls me in. At night, she always begs me to stay until she falls asleep. She says it makes her feel safe. I stay for me as much as her, though. June . . . she's my home. I bend down to dust her shoulder in kisses, and am instantly overwhelmed.

"I love you, too," I utter against her skin, pressing a final kiss into the nape of her neck.

"I love you," she mouths back.

My mouth raises on the side only she can see.

The last picture her mom takes is of June tenderly wiping her lipstick from my mouth.

After what feels like a million retakes so June's mom can get "just the right light," Abby finally breaks us all free. Basically, she announces we're done, and nobody argues with her.

June clings to me as we enter the gym, the music blaring from inside. I think she's still half expecting a sucker punch from Ava. I don't think that's coming her way, though. Ava's been quiet, for the most part. I try my best to distract her from stressful thoughts with little compliments. It's also practically impossible to forget about what's under her dress, or rather . . . what isn't.

When "Midnight Hour" comes on, we both suspect the other one for having set it up. We both move to the center of the floor and dance like lost children of the sixties, which makes just about every other person in the room gag. One person is happy for us, though. And it solves the mystery when we catch Tory hovering near the speaker by the DJ, proud of his special request.

June and I sing off-key, and a few people try to join us but they can't keep up. Some private, inside jokes are meant to stay that way. Even Tory only gets it from the outside looking in.

The DJ lets the song roll on for longer than anyone other than June and I probably want it to, but when he breaks it off, it's for the one thing I have been truly dreading about tonight—*homecoming royalty.*

Our friend Cannon is the first to take the stage, set up by the twins. When he realizes he's standing up there alone while we all laugh at him, he throws up a middle finger that earns him a "Hey, buddy" over the microphone from our student council liaison, Mr. Simon.

The twins finally take the stage too, along with a few girls, including Ava. I can tell by the way June's body stiffens that Ava is the only thing she sees. Truth is, June's all that Ava is focusing on as well. It's obvious to anyone in this room that her stare is pointed at one person and one person only.

"She could not possibly hate me more," June says.

They begin to recite everyone's names so I clap while bending my head to hear June better.

"Ava?" As if there could be another person in this room who thinks poorly of June. She's the most adored person I know. It's impossible to hate her, unless, of course, your heart is made of ice.

"Yeah. She hasn't really bothered me since the whole spray paint and black eye incidents. What's weird, though, is I don't get why she hated me so much when you were dating her."

I hum out a half-laugh, half admission of guilt before turning my gaze to June.

"Oh, I know why," I say, smirking at the memory of Ava's party, when we were too young to understand what love really was. I swear I did, though. I know it now. I knew it then.

We both clap through the list of queen nominees, but June's eyes remain on my face, a quirk to her brow. She's not letting this go.

"Let's get out of here," I say, leaning into her to kiss the top of her head. Her hair smells so good, and the way it's pinned into these curls that fall down her neck and shoulders has me desperate to touch its softness. I want to run my fingers through it and leave it wild, spread around her body.

"But you're probably gonna win," June says, holding me in place.

I punch out a laugh.

"I don't really give a shit." With a half grin, I manage to persuade her after a brief pause, and soon, we're both on our way out of the gym. We're blessed with the announcement of Ava as queen just before the doors close completely. At least one thing went her way.

We make it all the way to my truck before June comes back to the question I *knew* she would not let go.

Twisting in her seat, her body primed and ready for me to taste from the arch of her foot all the way to the raw tips of her breasts that are so close to popping out of that dress, June manages to hold her desire in for a few more seconds. Long enough for her to repeat her question.

"Tell me, Lucas Fuller. Why does Ava Pryor hate me so much?"

I smirk. It's so simple, and I'm proud to say it.

"Because when she told me she was in love with me at her eighth grade birthday party, I told her I was in love with you. And deep down, she knows I never stopped."

And I haven't.

I've only gotten started.

EPILOGUE

This surprise is more intricate than the one I surprised June with at graduation.

Yeah, getting that Buick up and running, not to mentioned painted and restored to the level it is today, that was a feat. June's mom helped with the lie, pretending she sold it for scrap. I had a crash course in auto body and called in a ton of favors. But seeing June drive that car every day, the smile on her face when she holds her hand out the window, is worth the grease I may never fully get out of my fingernails.

This surprise, however, it requires a major leap of faith. On June's part . . . and her mom's.

June's last-minute acceptance into Boston College made this possible. I can't imagine a life in that city where she and I don't share the same bed at night. Honestly, the thought of sleeping with her without crawling through a window feels like a lottery win.

I have my laptop set up on my bed and I'm pacing when June finally shows up. She spent the day at her dad's house—a promise she made to herself to find room for him in her life. I think the fact my dad is such an asshole put hers in new light. He's *less* of an asshole. Not quite forgivable, but tolerable. Family.

Maybe one day I'll get there with my dad. I know he hopes for it. I just don't believe his motivations are pure. I've come to realize what a narcissist is, and Todd Fuller is the walking definition. If he wants to mend our relationship, it's because he wants to gain something from it. His efforts aren't driven by love.

My phone buzzes and I quickly read June's text, letting me know she's downstairs. I left the door unlocked when my mom left earlier. I pop my door open and shout "Come on up" before returning to pacing in circles. When she gets to the threshold of my door, I step in front of her and hold my hands to her shoulders, squaring her with me and meeting her eyes.

"Wow, serious gaze you got there, Fuller," she jokes. She lifts one hand to salute me and I shake it off.

"I need us to be serious for a minute."

June's eyes blink rapidly a few times and her smile falters. *Shit, I made her worry.*

"No, *good* serious. Not *bad* serious."

She nods, but she's still concerned. It's hard to be two damaged kids coming of age together and falling in love. Our baggage matches, too, so working through it sometimes feels more like driving in circles.

I exhale a laugh and shake out my arms and legs.

"Let's try this again. I have a surprise. But I'm afraid you won't like it."

June's mouth twists on one side.

"I'm not making this any better, am I?"

She shakes her head no.

I puff out air and look down at my feet. Tapping my toe a few times to gather my thoughts and refocus my approach to this, I decide things with us are always best if we start with a kiss. I lift my head and move my hands to her jaw, cradling her on either side, giving her a gentle tilt so I can kiss her deep. She walks back a step and I crash into her, sucking her top lip into my mouth and releasing it with a pop. Her lips are raw, and her eyes have trouble focusing. Mission accomplished.

"Right, so you were saying . . . surprise." She shakes off the daze, playing up how affected she is.

I step to the side, revealing my computer. Of course, in the time spent trying to get my opening lines just right, my screen has timed out, so instead June gets to see my fingerprints and the splatter from my iced coffee this morning.

I sigh in frustration and lean forward, running my finger over the track pad to bring the computer back to life. The screen is consumed by a photo of the coolest looking brick building and an apartment window on a neighborhood street in Boston.

"Ohhhh-kayyyy," June says, still not getting it.

"Click around. Tell me what you think," I say, motioning for her to sit. She does, pulling my laptop onto her thighs. I slide around her body, straddling her from behind so I can watch over her shoulder.

Her first click takes her inside the building. The next one shifts to images of the individual rooms. The space is bright and airy with ceilings that seem too tall to fit into that building when you see it from the outside. Exposed duct work and black iron steps set up a modern feel that is met with bright colors accenting the space and art on gallery-style walls.

"This is gorgeous," she says, falling in love a little more with every click.

"I thought so, too."

She gets to the room that I'm going to propose be ours, and stops. Her eyes roam the empty space, a large bed waiting for sheets and blankets, a desk made for this computer in her hands. June closes the laptop and slowly turns her head. I lean forward to save her the trip, kissing the side of her mouth right before our eyes meet.

"What do you say? Roommates?" I quirk a brow and hers slowly creeps up to match.

"I mean . . . yeah! But also, your mom—"

"Is fine with it," I finish.

"And mine—"

"Will be fine with it," I add.

She shakes with hesitant laughter at my second response.

"My mom said she would talk to her with us if we want. And if we room together, it cuts your room and board in half. And I'm not a bad cook, so I can make sure you eat actual food. Plus, you know I'm good at studying. You'll have a live-in tutor."

June shifts between my legs until she's on her knees and facing me. She pushes the center of my chest slightly with two fingers and I scoot back to make room for her but continue talking.

"Our utilities will be less. And the couple who owns the place, Dax and Conner, are super chill." I'm basically saying words right now. I'm not sure I'm even listening to myself. It's June's fault because she's moved her legs to the outside of mine, and she's lifting her T-shirt up and over her head. And my mom is gone for the rest of the day.

"And if we live together," she cuts in, reaching behind her back to unclasp her bra. The black lace falls down her arms and I help her toss it to the side.

"Exactly." I smirk before drawing her body onto mine, my mouth covering her bare tit to suck it raw and draw a whimper from her lips. She rolls her hips, and I can tell she wants me to do the same thing to her other breast. I hold back, though, just for a moment.

"Lucas, I'm dying," she whines.

"You aren't dying. You're distracting me. And it's working. Fuck, you're hot," I groan. She rocks her hips again, her center sinking onto my hard-on. I push up into her, needing the sensation to hold me over for a few more seconds.

"June," I say, bringing her focus to me. Her eyes flutter open but when we lock gazes, we're in sync. Her lips quiver, not from our touch but from fear. It's a big step asking your parent to bless your desire to try something incredibly adult. But June and I? We've been adulting emotionally for a really long time. What's the big deal about sharing an address?

"You really think she'll go for it?"

I nod. I happen to know she will. That's the surprise part. I already talked to her mom about everything. I made a fucking Power Point.

An impish grin sneaks onto June's mouth and I nod. After a breath she joins me, and soon, laughter spills out.

"Yes, Lucas. I will move in with you."

I hold out a fist and draw it into my body with a hushed "Yes." Then I promptly get to work pleasing her in every possible way. Just wait until I show her the ring I bought her with the money I got for my truck. That can wait a few years, though. Until she's ready.

Me? I'm not going anywhere.

THE END

ACKNOWLEDGMENTS

I swear the Varsity series was done. When I finished book 3, I clapped my hands together and sighed out one of those warm, gooey kind of sounds you make when you're pleased with the way your cake came out. I loved my cake. I baked a damn doozy.

Turns out, I loved Lucas Fuller more. Damn him!

Good thing he kept talking to me, I suppose. I worked on The Fuel Series, and he would pop up randomly in my thoughts: "Remember me? You didn't let me have much of a POV in Heartbreaker. I'm a bit ticked about that."

Truth be told, I go into every book with a gut feeling of how it needs to be told. And Heartbreaker *needed* to be told through June's eyes, her heart and with her words. But that didn't mean Captain wasn't waiting in the wings. I love the way these two books complement each other. They are peanut butter and jelly. So thank you, readers, for bringing Lucas up when given the chance and reminding me that he deserved his day in the sun. I hope you loved reading it.

This world—the Varsity world—has been a blast. High school, sports, young love, coming of age, self-discovery? This is what I live for. Thank you from the bottom of my heart for giving these books your time and holding my Varsity family in your hearts . . . or at least your Kindles and bookshelves.

I must thank my amazing family for their support in writing this book. I spent a lot of hours in various chairs and beds and couches and ballparks with my laptop while writing this book. Thank you, Tim and Carter, for letting my Mac accompany us on summer and college trips. Thank you, Autumn, for . . . *well* . . . basically everything LOL! Seriously, Lucas is here very much because of the support and love I get from you, professionally and otherwise. So grateful, my friend. Jen and Shelley, your time spent beta reading gives me strength. You always guide and champion me to the end. Mom, you *know* I can't do any of this without you. Frankly, the world gets these stories *because* of you. Any courage I have is from my mom. She is the maker of my backbone. And Brenda Letendre, you know I think you're a saint! I've sent you the reddest of hot manuscripts and you always put out the fires and manage to keep me breathing and at my best. Thank you!

Readers, I meant what I said at the beginning. This book is here because of you. I get to do this job . . . because of you. Us writers are mostly fragile little things, but you give us wings. At least, that's what you do for me. Thank you for always believing in my work, for wanting to go on these journeys with me, for trusting me with your time, and more often than not, your hearts. This is the part where I ask—*kinda beg*—for your review, if you feel so moved. But honestly, the fact that you're reading the acknowledgements and (hopefully) smiling is enough. (Though, I'm not going to turn down a review . . . ever.) Right now, cross both arms over your chest and squeeze. Feel it? That's me, giving you a hug. Feel free to use it when you need a good one. You've given me plenty.

VARSITY TIEBREAKER

VARSITY

Tiebreaker

Cover Design by Ginger Scott, Little Miss Write LLC

For Tory's biggest fans.
Y'all are gonna have to fight Ana for him.

ONE

TORY D'ANGELO

I've never really gotten the appeal of flowers. I mean, one, they're super fleeting. Every time my mom's gotten flowers, I swear they're dead within three days. Feels like a major waste of money. Of course, my mom's flowers probably came from the man she was having an affair with, so it's entirely possible my perspective is tainted. Even so, what do flowers say about a person's feelings for someone else?

I like you enough to pop into the grocery store and pick up this pre-arranged bundle of plant clippings wrapped in plastic.

I mean, yeah. Flowers are pretty and shit, but there are a lot of things that are pretty. Cakes are pretty, and you can eat those. A perfect three-pointer drained within seconds, nothing but net . . . that's a thing of beauty. Art, a really hot red dress, or hell, a puppy! All of that is as aesthetically pleasing as a bundle of flowers. Yet here I am, clipping the stems off some weedy-smelling plant shit over my kitchen trash while my best friend June tells me what a good idea this is.

"She's going to love them," June assures me while she reaches toward my bundle, tugging on the stem of something. She pulls it free and dumps it into the trash with the stems I chopped off at an angle because "angles take in the water better" or whatever.

"She won't love that one?" I cock a brow and laugh. I'm still not sold on any of this.

"That one's dead."

I form an O with my mouth and drop my chin to stare at the drooping flower where it lies in the trash.

"Huh." I nod.

June giggles then wraps her hands around the bouquet, holding it steady so I can slip the giant band around the stems again. I never thought my best friend would be a girl, let alone June Mabee. I've pretty much picked on her since she got boobs, probably before that if I'm being honest. I still call her Maybe Mabee. June and I collided in epic fashion a couple of months ago. We kicked off our senior year on a strange note, going through some really awful shit together. We're kinda honeymooning at the whole best friend thing, I guess, but she's not sick of me yet and turns out Maybe Mabee doles out some pretty solid advice. Though, I'm not totally sold on the whole flowers thing.

"You sure this isn't stupid? I feel really stupid." I'm sweating, and I've already showered from basketball practice, changed my shirt twice and put on a whole lot of deodorant. This is strange territory for me. To put it succinctly, I have a fucking crush. It's bizarre because hooking up with any girl at Public High—or in our whole town of Allensville, really—has never been an issue for me. June says it's because I'm used to being chased, and maybe that's true. But I also think it's because the girl I'm trying to impress has never, not once, shown an ounce of interest in my presence. In fact, if I had to make a guess, I would bet on her hating me.

"Abby is going to die . . . in a good way!" June's said that a lot, that little add-on of *in a good way.* Feels like a hedged bet to me.

Abby Cortez is June's *other* best friend.

Fine.

She's her *real* best friend, and I'm the new guy June hangs out with sometimes while she waits on her boyfriend, Lucas. *My* real best friend. Along with my twin brother, Hayden, we've become our own clique. Except for the little part about me being pretty sure Abby hates me. Oh, and me wanting to kiss her candy lips and wrap her legs around my waist just before I lay her back on the hood of my car.

This is complicated. But flowers is the key. June swears by it.

"You look amazing," June says, stepping into me and brushing something from the shoulder of my shirt. I went with a button down, mostly because this shirt is snug on my arms and chest, making me look a little bit beast-mode. I don't need June to tell me how much Abby likes man candy. She was digging on the new guy, Cannon, for a while, and she noted his arms and chest a few times. Apparently, though, he's moody as fuck. Thank God!

"Where's your brother?" June asks.

"Job interview," I answer, bending down to catch my reflection in the glass front of the oven. I actually have product in my hair. *Who am I?*

"Wow. D'Angelo boys are going to work?" June mocks.

I shrug as I stand and face her.

"It's hard to be around here, and Hayden's had a harder time than I have. I think he wants something to fill the free time." June's eyes soften, but she's careful not to let them dip into pity. We don't do that around here.

My dad moved out a month ago. It's still pretty fresh for all of us. My mom was having an affair with Lucas's dad, and when it all came out, it basically blew up both of our families.

"Have you guys talked to your dad lately?" June asks. Our pops said we could go to Indianapolis with him if we wanted to, but this is our senior year. We're primed to win state this basketball season, and we both decided we couldn't give up on that. Staying here means sticking out the next few months in a house with a parent we pretty much have lost all respect for.

"Our first family therapy session is next week, with *both* of them. It promises fireworks," I say. June grimaces in response.

"You sure it's not weird, me forcing some double-date with you and Luc?" I squint through my question, and a small part of me wants her to let me off the hook. I've never been afraid of rejection, but with Abby, I put it at a solid fifty-fifty that she kicks me in the nuts when I ask her out.

"Stop," June protests, laughing at my nervous behavior. "It's sweet. And it will make you both more comfortable. Plus, it's Eight Lanes. Bowling is the easiest first date ever."

"Says the Eight Lanes employee who bowls a two-hunny," I say, one brow arched.

June's laughter ticks up but stops when we're interrupted by the familiar rumble of Lucas's truck in the driveway. I start to jump in place because he is supposed to bring Abby to the house with him and suddenly I'm full of enough energy to power a lightning bolt.

"It's go time," I say under my breath. June squeezes my arm and offers me a reassuring smile.

Lucas busts through the door first, and I puff out my cheeks to indicate how stressed I am. But something about the look in his eyes freezes me to the floor. My jumping stops, and my heart does too.

"Abort. Mission," Lucas says, pointing at me then staring intently into his girlfriend's eyes.

"What the—" My protest is cut short when Abby follows Lucas through the door in a rush, her hand gripped firmly in my brother's. My eyes see nothing else. I'm blatantly staring at the place where my crush and my twin are fused together.

What the actual fuck?

"I got the job, yo!" my brother says. At least, it sounds like his voice. I couldn't testify he said the words because I'm not looking at his mouth. I'm looking at the way Abby is holding his elbow with her other hand, bouncing with excitement. That's two hands she has on him now. Two. Hands.

"Did you hear me, bro? I got the job!"

I shake my head—*literally* shake my head—and force my gaze to meet Hayden's. We are nearly physically identical, but our personalities are vastly different. Where I'm loud, he's quiet. My confidence is offset by his reservation. I believe I can make any girl fall in love with me. And Hayden . . . he's never had a girlfriend. Ever.

Until—

"You're looking at the new host at Two-fers," my brother says, holding up his new work shirt. It's bright red with two weenies embroidered on the pocket. It's ridiculous, and my natural instinct is to make fun of it, but I can't seem to find a single funny thing to say.

"Wow," I say, over-exaggerating this terribly small word.

"Right?" He pushes at my shoulder, pressing the shirt into me to take. I unfold it and stare at it while I fake laugh. I toss it on the counter and hold my hand up for him to slap, and we grip each other and pull in for a hug. My eyes catch June's over my brother's shoulder, and they are full of pity. *Motherfucking pity!*

"I hope it's cool that I invited Hayden to come with us?" Abby asks from somewhere behind me. I can't bear the thought of turning around and looking at her.

"Of course. Yeah, totally," I croak out. I cough to cover my weak-ass voice.

"I just gotta change, and we can go. What's with the flowers, dude?" my brother asks, pointing to my fisted palm that's nearly choking the bouquet to death with my grip.

"Oh," I say, lifting them and feeling suddenly numb. "I—"

"He lost a bet," June says, coming to my rescue.

Hayden nods, accepting her answer, then dashes up the stairs, leaving the rest of us here in this instantly shrinking space.

"That a new thing there?" June says to her friend in a half-whisper I wish I didn't hear.

"We've been talking a lot, with everything they're going through, and I don't know, it just sorta . . ." Abby's head waggles side-to-side, but it's the blush that colors her cheeks that has me defeated.

Just sorta.

The sudden need to rush from the room hits me, and I march across the kitchen toward June. "Here you go, a bet's a bet," I say, shoving the flowers I knew were a bad idea into her chest. She hugs them and lets out an "*oof.*"

I keep walking, making eyes at Lucas on my way out, knowing he'll follow me to his truck so I can scream obscenities and feel like a fool with only him as my witness.

"Wow, someone's a sore loser," Abby teases from over my shoulder.

I huff out a laugh, not even able to lob one of my normal comebacks because she's so dead-on. I *am* a sore loser. I'm also done catching feelings for some girl.

TWO

ABBY CORTEZ

It's not that June was quiet on the way to the bowling alley. It's that she's *still* quiet now that we're inside. Things between my best friend and Lucas mended quickly, and very dramatically. I mean, yeah, they've been meant for each other since grade school, but a whirlwind romance like they had, right on the tail of the unraveling of so many lies—I just hope their honeymoon period hasn't hit a brick wall so soon.

I've been searching for the right time to tell her my big news, but ever since we left the twins' house, June's been oddly busy. Quiet, yes, but also busy. Like now, for instance. While the rest of us are sitting on the table at lane eight waiting for June to bring us our bowling shoes, she's standing at the counter shining them. They're ugly bowling shoes! Why would we care if they glisten under the neon glow of this dump?

I'm dying to talk to my friend. I almost wish we hadn't planned this bowling thing. I'd *so* rather be curled up across from her on her bed, jammies and all, while I spill my guts of the things I'm anxious about. This is my moment. It's the one thing an actor hopes for, the big payoff after thousands of auditions. This deal means I might not be back for graduation, and prom is probably, definitely a no-go, but it's a *movie*. Totally worth it . . . *I think.*

It also probably means my dad's legal pursuits will get even nastier, if that's possible, but *damn it!* I've been wishing for this break since I was six years old and singing my ass off on the community center stage as Indiana's first Latina Annie. I got a perm for that shit, so if all this movie role requires is that I miss the last three months of my senior year, well, fuck it, man. Prom dresses are ugly anyway.

"Are we gonna bowl or open up a shoe store?" Tory shouts across the lanes toward June, who is still running a rag over the tops of the shoes on the counter. I knew I could count on Tory's impatience to break the ice. As sweet as his brother is, he's not a boat rocker. Tory D'Angelo, however, is the Ozzy Osborn of boats. He rocks things to the point of fire.

"I know how important your footwear is to you!" June shouts back to him. I laugh, but Tory only grumbles and sinks into the chair attached to the scoring computer.

"He's just mad because I'm a better bowler than he is," Hayden says, his voice crawling over my shoulder as he bends over the seat behind me. He lightly kisses my neck, then squeezes my shoulders. I exhale heavily, feeling my tension fall away with the pressure of his hands.

Never in a million years would I imagine a world where I am dating Hayden D'Angelo. The only thing less likely is a universe where me and Tory are a thing. But Hayden is just . . . so easy. He called me out of the blue weeks ago, and we've talked every night. He needs someone who understands what a messy divorce feels like; someone who isn't his brother, and isn't his friend who's going through the same thing with his own family. I'm that person. *Kid of a messy divorce* should be a bullet point on my resume. Nothing new to Hollywood, I suppose.

"Nines, right?" June holds a pair of shoes out for me, letting them dangle from the tethered laces hooked on her finger.

"Yep," I say, followed by a tight smile. She hits me with a matching expression. Something is definitely off. Besides, she knows I wear nines. She wears nines. I wear her shoes all the time!

Hayden's body falls into the seat attached to mine, his large frame making me instantly feel crowded. I slip my foot into my shoe and glance to the left at his, noting the size before he puts his foot inside.

Twelves.

I finish tying my laces, then slide my other shoes underneath my seat. Tory has typed in our names, and he put me at the end. I'm glad about that because me and sports of any kind are not on the same page. I'm not even sure how this ball comes off my fingers when the time is right. June has worked here for more than a year, and in that time, all I've ever done is drink sodas and roll pool balls back and forth in the bar area while waiting for her to get off.

Hayden leaves the space next to me and I glance up at him in time to catch his wink and smile. He's adorable, the way his hair squiggles down over his forehead and one eye is always squinting just a little more than the other. I've often heard that twins try to differentiate themselves from each other as they get older, sort of a way to stand out and break away from their carbon copy. I see the evidence of that when I stare at the D'Angelo boys. Hayden is a little sloppy sometimes, but in a cute way. He wears a lot of T-shirts, always half tucked under slightly wrinkled button downs, and his jeans are sometimes, maybe, just a little tiny bit too short. Again . . . in a cute way. He wears the beach boy look, if that's a thing in Indiana. As good as he is at basketball, I wouldn't flinch seeing him run by with a long board under his arm and board shorts slung low on his hips. I'm probably the only one who thinks that since basketball is religion in this state. The brothers share the same hazel eye color, the same light brown hair that's sometimes amber, sometimes gold, depending on the season, and the same body type that *oh-my-God!* The twins have always been hot. And they are identical. But through their own efforts, they're also very much not. Tory is polished. His hair is somehow always in the perfect place, even after a two-hour basketball practice or after pulling off a football helmet. His wardrobe looks like the ones I see on the commercial shoots I do. Things match, like the kind of match you see on department store mannequins or in catalogues. And he must time his shaving just right because where Hayden is always baby-face fresh, Tory is frat-boy stubble.

He's also frat-boy brash. In all the years we've known each other, Tory D'Angelo is the one person I can count on to always have something snarky to say, his own little flair for turning me off. Lately, though, he's been tempered. Not quiet, but just not . . . *Tory.* I've spent a lot of time talking with Hayden about his parents' fallout, and there's no way Tory isn't feeling it too. In his own way.

"Look at you, throwing an eleven-pounder, Mabee," Tory teases as June walks up with a bright green ball cupped in her hands. She curls one arm to form a bicep and Tory laughs.

"Can I use yours?" I ask her, standing and walking over to the ball return where she's just sat the green ball down. June twists her mouth up on one side and Tory snickers before turning his body away from me in his seat. I stare at the top of his head, doing my best to burn laser beam holes through his skull.

"What's so funny?" I object, shifting my stare from his head to June's face.

"It's just, eleven is kinda heavy," my friend says, tapping her finger on the 11 etched into the ball.

"It's fucking eleven pounds. That's like a cat!" I reach for the ball as she laughs at my comparison.

"You're not throwing a cat down the lane, Abby."

I glare at her while I poke my fingers awkwardly in the holes. They're enormous, and too far apart.

"I know I'm not throwing a fucking cat at pins, June. That would be cruel."

Her eyes widen as she glares at my hand along the smooth surface. Her mouth pops open, but before she can talk me out of it, I drop the ball on the return with a *clunk* and brush my hands off on one another, determined to throw the eleven-pounder.

"I'm using yours. Thanks," I say, taking the seat next to Tory. He gets up the second I sit.

"Are you seriously that appalled by my ball selection?" I shoot my question at him, but he keeps walking toward the balls to pick his own.

This vibe is strange, as if I've walked in mid-fight, or to an intervention that's not quite fully started. *What the f—?*

June slips into the seat Tory just vacated and types on the keyboard, changing Lucas's name to Princess. I smirk and puff out a laugh.

"Funny, right?" she says, pushing enter just before the boys come back with their balls.

Tory goes first, stepping up on the smooth wooden floor and positioning his feet with this super serious stance. He holds the ball in front of his body, lining it up, then takes three quick steps toward the pins, launching the ball down the lane dead center. Pins explode at the other end, leaving one standing on either side.

"Nice!" I say as he walks back toward us.

"It's a seven-ten split. Nothing nice about that," he huffs.

I shrug and glance to June, not knowing what the hell is so wrong with what I just said.

"It's really hard to knock both of those down now at once," June explains in a whisper.

I look back up to Tory as he stands with his hand hovering over the stream of air blowing from a vent on the ball return.

"Don't choke," I say just before his ball appears on the rack. He only offers me a sideways glance.

"I love when you two give each other shit," Hayden says, stepping up behind me and running his palms along my shoulders, then squeezing gently.

"Yeah, don't choke, bro!" Hayden tacks on. Tory's feet stop short of the arrows on the floor and his hand holding the ball lowers to his hip as he turns and looks at his brother, his head leaning to the side. Hayden bends down and rests his chin on my head, wrapping his arms around my neck and shoulders completely. Tory's body quakes with a short laugh.

"Fifty bucks says I nail it," Tory says. Even though he's talking to his brother, his eyes are on me, almost as if he wants me to take the bet. Hayden's arms relax and unwind from around me as he stands tall and pulls out his wallet.

"I've got twenty," he says to his brother.

Tory's mouth ticks up on one side. "So, you'll owe me thirty."

The pregnant pause as they dare each other is filled with the pumping beat of the pop music on the Eight Lanes' sound system.

"Deal," Hayden says.

Tory nods in agreement, and their little rivalry is sealed.

"He's going to blow it." Hayden's voice carries over my shoulder.

I lean in, resting my elbows and palms on the small counter in front of me, suddenly not sure whether I'm rooting for Tory to succeed or fail. He rolls his shoulders and positions the ball in front of him, just as he did before, only his body is lined up on the far right side of the lane. My gut knots as he begins his approach, and all I can envision is his ball roaring angrily down the right gutter.

I hold my breath with his release, a mixture of hexes and hopes coming from everyone else.

"Do it, Dude! Do it!" Lucas shouts as Tory's ball teeters along the very edge of the lane, practically skating without spin as it heads toward the single pin on the right.

"No way it kicks around. Not enough juice, bro. Not enough—" Hayden's curse is cut off by the flinging pin that strikes into and takes out its twin on the far side of the lane.

"Yes!" June and I both say together. I guess I was rooting for Tory to make it. I feel as though maybe he needs a win.

Tory saunters back to us and his brother steps out from behind me with his hand outstretched to congratulate his brother. After they shake, Tory comes in close and pats Hayden's chest with a heavy palm.

"Better hope you get tips at Two-fers," he says, his eyebrows lifting just before his gaze sinks down to where I'm sitting. "Unless you wanna make another deal? Double or nothing?"

The smile on my face flattens under the heat of his eyes. I don't get the sense he's bargaining with dollars anymore, and the insinuation pisses me off.

"I'm not on the table," I interject, turning to the side and crossing my legs. My bare knee pops through the ragged hole in my jeans and my green sweater falls down on one shoulder as I cross my arms over my chest.

A slow laugh brews in Tory's chest, soundless at first until it comes out loud as he holds his stomach.

"I don't know what your obsession is with me having you on a table, but that's not appropriate now, Cortez. You went and picked the wrong brother." It's a typical barb from him, the kind I'm used to mostly, but there's also an extra bite to it, and I can tell it's made everyone uncomfortable. Hayden shoves his brother, pushing into his shoulder and knocking Tory off balance.

"Not cool, Dude. Knock that shit off," he says, throwing the twenty dollars at his brother's chest. Tory catches it against his sweatshirt, crinkling it up in his palm. "I owe you thirty."

Hayden moves toward the balls to take his turn, brushing into his brother's shoulder, clearly on purpose. Tory's body twists from the force and his half smile lingers on his lips as he looks down at the money in his palm. His mouth finally shuts into a tepid straight line and he pushes the money into the back pocket of his jeans, the prize apparently no longer worth bragging about.

"Glad this isn't awkward or anything," Lucas says from behind me.

"He's just going through things," June adds, her eyes softening on mine. She's trying to communicate to me without words, using our *friend* code, hoping I understand. I do. Hayden is a talker, and he's opened up to me about how hard his parents' split and the ugly way it all came to a head has affected him. Tory locks it all inside. I identify with him more than he thinks.

Hayden takes his turn, only knocking down nine. When June vacates the seat next to me to get her ball, Hayden slides in, a tight look on his face from the reaction from his brother. I can tell by the way he avoids his brother completely that it bothers him, but I'm not sure I'm the person who should step in to ease the situation. I tend to inflame things with Tory.

"Of course she bowled a double," Hayden mutters as June spins on her heels and holds both hands up in the air to gloat.

"I mean, she does kinda work here," I say, leaning into him. He leans back, meshing our shoulders together.

"Gotta love it when your girl kicks your ass in a sport," Lucas grumbles teasingly, cradling his ball in both hands and bending forward to dust a kiss on June's lips.

"That was sexist, but the kiss was sweet, so I'll forgive you," my friend says. Hayden and I both laugh, but stop at the sound of Tory's feet slapping against the floor in his slick bowling shoes. I glance over my shoulder, expecting to see his goofy grin or his hand up to high-five June for putting Lucas in his place; but instead, my gaze locks with his and there isn't a smile to be found. His mouth is pure nothingness, a lifeless line. He's in a dark place.

I wait for him to wander down the row of balls and out of earshot before I mention my thoughts to Hayden while Lucas takes his turn.

"Do you think you should go talk to him?" I spare another glance as I lean in closer to Hayden. His hand flattens along my thigh, his fingers curling to scratch at the frayed threads of one of the holes in my jeans. It tickles, and I let out a little giggle that catches Tory's attention.

"Nah, he's just moody. Probably stressed about therapy next week." Hayden's words conflict with my gut and the look on Tory's face, but I don't need to poke my nose into more drama. I have enough of my own.

"You're up!" Hayden brings me back to the action on the lanes, and I stand, wiping my hands along my hips. I have no clue what I'm doing.

"Green ball, I'm gonna make you my bitch," I say, wrapping my hands around the ball June used. I bring it toward my stomach, masking the strain I feel because this shit is way heavier than I thought it was.

"Just remember, your goal is straight," June encourages, clasping her hands together like she's praying. She's probably hoping I don't launch this sucker at her feet.

"Need help?" Hayden gets up from his seat, and I can imagine how this whole scene plays out, with him standing behind me, holding my arms and helping me push the ball forward from between my knees like a child. It's a cliché romantic scenario but I'm having none of it. Hayden is sweet, and comforting. But we are not doing the romance thing. And I won't be handled like a baby.

"I got it!" The words come out forcefully, and his slight flinch tells me I might have offended him.

I work to soften it.

"If you help me, nobody is going to believe I got this strike all on my own."

Hayden's mouth curves on one side and he sits back down with a nod and a chuckle, knowing that I'm talking shit I can't back up. This is my way.

My focus returns to the line of pins sixty feet or so away from me. This ball in my hands feels twice as heavy as it did before, when I tested it. No matter. It's just a rock. And I just need to push this rock on the floor with enough umph to knock over one of those things at the end. Easy.

Doing my best to mimic the approach everyone made before me, I hold the ball in front of me and stretch my palm as wide as it will go, inserting my fingers in the damn holes that I can barely reach. After I line up my ball with what I estimate to be about the middle, I slide my slick bowling shoe-clad feet along the floor toward the line where the lane officially begins. My arm drops to my side, swinging as my hand clenches with every bit of strength I have not to drop this heavy fucker on my feet. The ball rocks back then swings forward across my hip and I let go when my body is lined up with the pins as good as it's going to.

"*Ohhh, shit!*"

Lucas's exclamation registers in my mind a fraction before I realize what I've done. My arm did not swing straight at all. Far from straight, actually. More of a veering extremely to the right. And the ball slipped out maybe a little later than I planned, causing it to fling rather than roll. Not that it matters, because it bounced two full lanes over, careening into the gutter of lane six, then swishing its way toward the dark pins still guarded by that thingamabob that lines them up.

I want to repeat what Lucas just shouted, but all I can seem to do is stare at my results with my mouth gaping open. The ball is slowing, and by the time the slow drawled "fuuuuck" leaves my lips, the green sphere that I was so sure I could handle is stalled in the middle of lane six's gutter.

"Here." Tory's tone isn't his usual tongue-in-cheek, and I'm sure my expression shows how surprised I am by it when I turn to face him. He's holding an orange ball, an eight stamped in its surface. His eyes dip and see what I'm noticing, so he shifts his hand and covers the number completely.

"It's just a ball. That one isn't made for you. This one is, though." He isn't laughing, and that's odd. No jokes about how I can't even handle throwing a ball straight. Tory D'Angelo must truly be broken because he's not even picking on the low hanging fruit to tease me. His low-key demeanor is unsettling.

"Ohhh-kayyyy." I cock my head slightly in trained suspicion. Tory breathes out a short laugh through is nose.

"Fingers go in the holes," he finally says through a crooked grin.

"Double entendre in that statement?" I plunge my fingers in and hook my thumb in the final hole, lifting the ball from Tory's palm in a brisk, confident movement. It's lighter, and the right fit.

"Just helping a girl out," he says, again avoiding the shot I teed up for him.

I turn my attention back to the still complete set of pins waiting for me, and shuffle my feet forward, pushing my shoes together and squinting as I align the ball with the center. Tory's still in my periphery, and I catch him walk away but do a full turn and come back, stopping a couple feet to my right.

"Can I?" he asks.

I turn my head to face him, finding his open palms waiting tentatively, slightly reaching toward me. I nod quickly.

"Go on," I say, twisting my lips.

"Oh, sure, you'll take his help," Hayden hollers. He's joking, but there's a hint of jealousy in the tone. *I think.*

"She wants help from winners," Tory says back, glancing to his brother briefly before meeting my gaze and winking at me. There's a sudden lightness to his face and his smile reaches his eyes.

Tory places one palm along my back and holds my shoulder with the other, pushing lightly as I scoot to my left with his guidance.

"You're lining your body up, but the ball is to your right, in your hand. You have to sort of correct for that. Make sense?"

It does. I nod.

He taps his foot into the side of my shoe a few times.

"Relax your legs, soldier. This isn't marching band."

A breathy laugh falls from my lips as I realize how tense I am. I do as he says, even adding a few inches of space between my feet, and bending my knees.

"Okay, so now . . . instead of the pins," he says, timidly moving closer to my shoulder until he's so near I can smell the spearmint of the gum he spit out in the parking lot on our way in. I don't flinch but I can't help but react to his closeness, turning my head to face him just as he does the same. When our eyes meet, he swallows hard. I can't help but see it. Hayden is watching, and I'm sure Tory doesn't want this to seem weird. It's not weird. Only, it *feels* weird.

"The arrows," he finally mutters, clearing his throat. His eyes shift out toward the lane, and I follow the direction of his gaze.

"What arrows?" I ask, scanning the pins. Tory leans in more and points toward the middle of the floor, where the small arrows are painted on the lane.

"Those aren't for decoration?" I ask.

His body shakes with a short laugh at my side. "No, Abby. Those aren't decoration."

I glance at him briefly, catching the smirk. I shrug in response, partly to signal that he should make some space. He seems to get my hint, and drops his hands down to the pockets of his jeans, shuffling backward.

"Well, go on, then," he says, nodding his head toward the pins.

Using Tory's technique, I take a deep breath and line my arm up with the center of the lane, using the arrows to guide me. With nothing to lose, I pace forward and let my arm swing the surprisingly light ball, letting it go in just the right spot. I leave my hand in the air and walk back as it rolls forward, aiming for dead center.

"Go, baby! Go, baby!" Hayden's voice echoes behind me, and soon his hands are on my hips. My ball makes contact and knocks over seven pins, and Hayden lifts me up, spinning me in his arms and swinging me around in a giant bear hug as if I just achieved world peace . . . at the Olympics.

I smile because I'm proud, even as Lucas reminds us all that it's only a seven.

I catch Tory's eyes over his brother's shoulder and he holds up his hands and gives me a golf clap with a nod.

"Thank you," I mouth.

My God, that is the first time I have ever said those words to this boy.

The strange undertone of competitiveness between the twins carries us through the next nine frames, but by the time we start the second one they seem to have settled whatever silent pissing match they had going on. June kicks all of our asses anyhow, breaking two-ten for the first time, which I guess is a really big deal in bowling.

When Tory gathers our shoes to return to the counter and Hayden and Lucas drift over to the pool tables, I pounce on the free moment with June so I can finally tell her my news. I sit in a seat opposite her and fold my legs under me.

"You know Jordan Shotcraft?" I know she does. She has seen every single one of his movies. He's *dad* hot, and married to one of our favorite singers, Lillian Ash.

"Oh, my God, did you get to meet him?" June is literally sitting on her hands and swinging her legs. She's gonna die when I tell her.

"Better," I say, letting my sly grin sit there to hold the moment. Her eyes widen slowly.

"No!" She grabs my arms and pulls them toward her, causing me to laugh and lose my balance. I unfurl my legs, but not in time to stop my fall. Before I hit the ground, though, Tory wraps his arm around my body from the empty seat next to me.

"I have that effect on women," he says, giving me his classic wink as he rights me in my seat. The mint scent from his gum is now replaced by the faint aroma of his cologne. It's different than Hayden's—maybe richer, woodsier, if that's a thing.

I'm trying to form a clever response when June kicks her feet forward and touches my knees with the toes of her shoes. I shift my focus to her and her eyes are still wide.

"Abby Cortez, you better tell me now. And if it's what I think it is, you better take me with you." Her head shakes on its own just to show me how firm she is about this.

"You're looking at Jordan Shotcraft's surprise teenaged daughter in his next rom com." June's screaming before I get the last word out, and within a blink, she's wrapped her arms around me, practically sitting in my lap.

My eyes tear with happiness. I squealed when I got the news, but seeing my friend's reaction just makes things so incredibly real.

June's reaction draws Lucas and Hayden back to our seats, so once everyone gathers around and June leaves my lap, I feed them the details.

"It was down to me and another unknown actress, and I guess they liked my attitude."

Tory snorts a laugh, so I shoot him a glare.

"You're hardly unknown," June says. "You're the face of Allensville Yogurt!"

"This stuff is *great!*" Lucas pipes in, pumping his arm just like I do in my biggest commercial deal to date. The yogurt company ad paid me the most of any job I've ever landed, even more than the modeling spreads that have been in major magazines. This movie deal, though . . . it's a game changer.

"Filming starts in early March," I say, leading to a noticeable hush from everyone.

"Wow," June says, shaking her head while keeping the smile plastered on her face. I knew this would be the hard part. We had plans, she and I.

"I know. Prom . . . and maybe graduation, but—"

My best friend grabs my hands and gives them a little shake.

"No buts. This is huge. *Massive!* We'll have our own celebrations, and you deserve this." Her boost to my doubts does the trick, and for the first time since I was offered the contract, I feel one-hundred percent ready to take this leap.

"I'm going to need to run a lot of lines over the next couple months," I say through nervous laughter.

"Okay." My friend nods, tears forming at the sides of her eyes from what I can tell is genuine pride. "No kissing scenes for me, though."

"Damn," Lucas adds, drawing a laugh from all of us.

"That's what Hayden's for," I say, turning my attention to the guy who probably deserved to get this news from me one-on-one. He doesn't seem upset, though. In fact, he stands and holds one hand to his chest, his other out in front of him.

"Romeo, Oh Romeo . . ." he starts, clearly showcasing his insincere acting skills.

I kick at him and he grabs my hand, pulling me to my feet and hugging me.

"I'm actually really bad at that stuff, but I'll do whatever I can," he assures.

"You sure you don't mind me taking over your weekends for a while?" I ask, already knowing my mom will be too busy working. When I feel the sway of his embrace pause, I peel back to look him in the eyes.

"Weekends, huh?" His mouth falls into a regretful grimace.

"Your new job," I respond, piecing it together. I guess I knew he'd have to work weekends a lot. Basketball practice and the season are pretty intense, so weekends are really his only chance to pick up hours.

"Hey, but Tory can fill in. Actually, of the two of us, he's the actor." Hayden moves to my side, his arm slung over my shoulder, and a sudden tightness grips my chest at his suggestion. Tory seems equally surprised by the suggestion, popping his head up fast and flitting his attention between me and his brother.

"Me?" He points to himself. "I mean, nah, I'm not the best to practice with."

"He's being modest. Yo, check it." Hayden drops his arm from around me and pulls his phone from his pocket, scrolling through his videos and pictures while I awkwardly smile at Tory and he awkwardly smiles back. "Yeah, here it is. Look."

Hayden holds his phone out for me to watch his screen, and a tall, skinny near-exact version of his younger self is standing at the center of a stage under a spotlight.

"If music be the food of love, play on." Tory is probably in seventh or eighth grade in this video, and the fact it's on his brother's phone still baffles me almost as much as that I'm watching him recite a monologue from Shakespeare's Twelfth Knight.

"Okay, okay, that's enough," Tory says, swiping the phone from his brother's hand and closing the video.

"Dude, you were good. He was good," Hayden says, glancing around at all of us. I wonder if the dent between my brows is as deep as the ones on Lucas and June's foreheads.

"You did theater?" I ask.

"Yeah, I mean nah. Not really." Tory leans against the bar top near our seating area and exhales heavily. "I auditioned for a bunch of things one summer. I thought maybe I'd try acting, but ya know . . ."

He holds out two open palms.

I tilt my head to the side.

"He always got in trouble for being a smart ass," Hayden blurts out, slapping his brother's chest. He takes his phone back and points at his brother. "Doesn't mean you weren't good, though."

Tory shrugs.

"So, will you?" I ask. I already regret it, but the panic of not being ready with my lines down by the time filming starts overrides the epic bad idea this is.

Tory's face wrinkles in hesitation as he takes a long breath.

"I don't know. I mean . . ." He glances to his brother first, then to June, almost as if he's taking a vote or eliciting permission. He doesn't bother to look to Lucas, making his own mind up instead.

"Fine, yeah. We can run lines. But don't make fun of me when I'm not that good." He stands straight and dives his hands into his pockets while he rigidly scrunches his shoulders.

"Don't worry. I'm sure there are plenty of other things I can make fun of you for," I say, falling into my more familiar role with this D'Angelo. A sharp laugh leaves his chest.

"No doubt," he says. He smiles at me with tightly closed lips, then pivots, pausing when June stands up in front of him. "No doubt," he repeats, for some reason speaking directly to her.

What a fucking weird day. I bowled a forty-one. I have a boyfriend. Tory D'Angelo has acting chops. And I just made plans to spend every free weekend in the books with him. Lord help me if I get a call to star in the reboot of the Twilight Zone.

THREE

TORY

It's amazing how many different ways June found to tell me that agreeing to read lines with Abby is a bad idea.

"It's sort of your fault I'm in this predicament, you know," I say, tossing her the ball at the end of my driveway. Hayden left to take Abby home and Lucas fell asleep on our couch while playing video games.

"How is this my fault?" She bounces the ball at her feet then lifts it overhead, jumping and pushing it toward the hoop on our garage. It falls several feet short, and I catch it, bouncing it to her to try again.

"You could have agreed to do the kissing scenes with her," I say, letting my imagination toy with the idea of those two making out in front of me. Can't lie; I've visualized it a few times since June made the joke.

She holds the ball against her hip and sneers at me.

"There probably aren't even any kissing scenes," she says, holding her glare on me for a beat before palming the ball with both hands and throwing it hard at the ground. It bounces toward me in a high arc, but I step back and catch it with one hand. I dribble out toward her, then spin and take a short jump shot, sinking it without touching the rim.

"I have to work a lot too. You know that. I'm saving for college, and as good as business is going for my mom, it's not booming so much that I can slack off."

June is trying to save enough that she's able to swing state school instead of junior college. With Lucas going to MIT after we graduate, I think she's a little worried about the long distance relationship thing. Even though she's focused on going somewhere affordable in Indiana, I wouldn't be surprised if she eventually ended up in Boston.

If I'm being honest with myself, I actually wanted to get trapped into helping Abby. I know it deep down. Even now, as I try to convince myself that it's not really about spending time with her. It is. It's *all* about spending time with her. I sure as hell won't say that out loud to anyone, though. Not even June.

"You know, you really don't have anything to worry about. I'm over it," I lie. I'm an excellent liar. I do it for my brother all the time, pretending I'm handling this divorce situation and public embarrassment over our mom's affair with my best friend's dad. It's easier for Hayden if I have my shit together. He's always been the worrier and the fixer, and he's got his head and hands full right now fixing our family. He doesn't need to add me to his list. As far as he knows, I'm handling it all just fine.

"Really?" June grabs the ball from my hands while I'm lost in thought.

"Really, what?" I take the ball back from her and toss it from one hand to the other. When she lunges for it again, I grip it hard and step back.

"You're over it," she says. She levels me with a stare that threatens to call me on my bullshit. I play it off with a cocky smile, dribbling the ball through my legs a few times before driving it toward our hoop, palming it with my right hand, and dunking it with enough force that the entire backboard rattles where it's bolted to the eave of our house.

"That's right," I say when my feet land on the ground. I brush my hands off and reach for June with an open palm to shake on it. She takes my hand in hers and squeezes tight. *Holy decent grip, Batman!*

"Bullshit," she says.

"*Pfft*, whatever. I shook on it," I say, letting go of her hand and turning around as I stretch my fingers wide. Yeah, it's bullshit, but what am I going to do? Tell Abby no? Tell her I'm not comfortable spending time with her because all I do is think about kissing her, which is super sketch since she's my brother's girl now? Yeah, I'm not saying all that. I'm tucking that shit deep into the pit of my soul and pretending it's all a dream.

June walks out to the street where the ball has rolled and stops it with her foot.

"Hayden's back!" she shouts, seconds before the Subaru I share with my brother roars into the driveway. June picks up the ball and bounces it near the sidewalk, clearly giving me and my brother space. She's anticipating Hayden to ask me questions about my behavior all day, but she doesn't know Hayden like I do. He's all about avoidance and pretending.

My brother pulls the car into our garage, into the gaping space left from the spot where our dad's SUV is usually parked.

"You wanna get in some one-on-one?" Hayden asks me, leaving the car door open so the stereo can blast Drake's latest drop into our garage. Mom hates it when we do this. Her bedroom is above the garage, and she's been sleeping a lot more than she's been working as a substitute at the nearby grade school. She doesn't dare yell at us about it, though. She kinda lost her authority, what with the daily hookups and all.

"Sure," I say, holding my hands open toward June, signaling for the ball. I glance at her in time to catch the warning look on her face. I roll my eyes and eventually she tosses me the ball.

"First to eleven cuz I'm hungry, yo," I say as I dribble out to the center of our vacant driveway.

June lingers inside our garage for a while, but she gives up after the first few possessions result in off-the-rim shots by both Hayden and myself. I think she was sticking around to make sure I didn't let my edge slip again. I got a little alpha in our bowling match.

"Dude, you talk to Coach yet about Thursday?" Hayden always talks through our games. It's fuckin' annoying.

"Yeah, I did Friday. He said to keep him posted when we have therapy. I mean, what's he gonna do, bench us?" I tip the ball out of Hayden's hands when he lets his guard down, and laugh.

"Damn it!" He's on me fast, trying to right his wrong. He's not nearly as aggressive as I am, but he's agile. Swift. He's always been faster, and his shots are prettier. Mine are a lot more effective, though.

"You figure out what you're gonna say?" he asks. His hands are stretched out and his footwork matches mine. I lower my shoulder and fake a drive, pulling back instead for a jump shot. Finally, one of us sinks something.

"One-oh, key it up," Hayden says.

I jog to the ball and bring it back to the top of our imaginary three-point line.

"I figure this lady, she'll ask us a bunch of questions. I'll just answer whatever I'm feeling at the time," I say.

I send a deep three up spontaneously since Hayden's distracted. It bangs off the rim. He hates that I don't have a plan. I'd bet he has a notebook full of bullet points he'll memorize before our session so he knows exactly what to say. I'm not sure that's the best way for therapy to go, though . . . planned out and shit.

"You think Dad really wants to go to these?" Hayden asks, dribbling out and faking a drive only to pull back and hit a fade-away shot. It's pretty, floating through the air without rotation and landing in the hoop with the grace of a butterfly.

Quiet. Agile. Pretty.

I lunge for the ball and push it into his chest, my competitive beast awakening.

"Simmer down, now," he teases, loving the fact that he knows how to push my buttons on the court.

"Shut up and set up," I grumble, only making him laugh harder.

We play the next few points without serious talk, climbing the score to five to six, his lead. Hayden can't stand leaving questions unanswered though, so when he calls for a water break and tosses the ball into the dry grass alongside our driveway, he brings up his question about our dad again. I chew on it while he heads toward the old fridge that keeps the water, beer and soda cold. He tosses me a water, but I waggle my finger to throw me a beer instead. He does, but takes a water for himself, making me look like the failing youth. Whatever. I want a beer.

"I think Dad's probably pretty hurt, so . . . no. I don't think he wants anything to do with Mom or therapy or talking about his feelings right now. Fuck, I don't want any of this. Do you?" I pop the cap off my beer and take a swig. The cool touch of the liquid on my tongue makes me go in for more. This is why people shouldn't drink beer when they're thirsty; half is gone before Hayden answers my question.

"I just want it all to go back to how it was. I wish we were all still oblivious, ya know?" He tips his water back and eyes me for my response. My face sours.

"Hayd . . . we ain't ever going back to what it was. Our old holiday card, picturesque fake-ass family? That was a lie. There's no putting the shit that came out back in the bottle, and I don't need a therapist to tell me I need to come to terms with that." My harsh words dent his fragile ego, and I feel a touch of guilt. I quickly drown that with more beer.

"Let's go," I say, setting my two-thirds empty bottle on a ledge in the garage before jogging out to the ball.

I turn back to the garage, expecting to see Hayden walking toward me, ready to ball, but he hasn't budged. He's caught in his feelings. I'm in insensitive dick mode. This isn't going to work. I sigh and prop the ball on my hip, no longer in the mood to play. I just want to drain our hot water in the shower and turn my skin lobster pink. I'm starting to feel the chill in the air.

"Look, man. This sucks for all of us. Probably sucks for Mom, too. And maybe things were broken that we didn't see. Either way, you and I are going to have to stick through this raw end of the deal. It's our senior year, Hayd. Senior fucking year. I'm not going to let them ruin that for me."

I move back into the garage and drop the ball at my feet, stopping its bounce with my foot and nudging it into the corner. I pick up my beer and hold it out to my brother on my way inside the house.

"You shouldn't let any of this ruin your happiness either, man." I take one more drink to toast my worthless wise words. Hayden's eyes stay on me the entire time, full of skepticism. I turn my back and head toward the garage door into our mudroom. When I pull the door wide, Hayden hits me with one more of the thoughts he just can't stop processing in his head. This one is super fucking unexpected.

"You're cool with me and Abby, right?"

I grip the door knob hard enough that my veins define in my forearm and grind my back teeth together.

"Yeah. I mean, if you're into her. Whatever, dude. Good for you, *pff*." I speak over my shoulder so I only have to pretend with half my face.

He doesn't respond, but I'm looking his way enough to catch the smile and nod. I leave it at that, letting the door fall shut behind me. I give June and Lucas a quick nod good-bye as they get ready to leave, and I keep my truth contained all the way upstairs, not letting it go until I step into the shower and practically drown myself in the spray of water falling from the nozzle. I let it fill my mouth over and over again, and I growl through it a few times while I know Hayden's still outside. Eventually, his music kicks on in his room on the other side of our shared bathroom, so I keep my show of frustration to the quiet kind, resting my palms flat on the wall and bending my head down low enough that the water cascades around my neck and face, blurring away any expression that remotely resembles jealousy. It takes me forty minutes to wash my feelings down the drain, about how long as it takes to run this house out of hot water.

FOUR

ABBY

There are a lot of reasons why December is my least favorite month.

One: It's my birthday month. The fifteenth. Right smack in the middle of the Christmas countdown, and usually in the middle of Hanukkah, which means I've never really had a birthday party with friends, and my presents from my relatives have become lump sums of cash that encompass both Christmas and birthday gifts in one.

Two: I hate being cold, and December in Indiana is gross. It's also often wet. My hair takes work to turn haphazard corkscrews into soft waves. December makes it all a moot point. December is for ponytails and buns.

Three: December is when my dad left. He left my mom with a mountain of debt. He left like a coward in the middle of the night. He left without warning, after a lot of years of ugly fighting. He took off before I got my first big commercial deal and modeling contract. When I did, two years after being off the radar, minus divorce papers and a virtual court appearance, he showed up with flowers and balloons for my birthday. More like he showed up with bribes, thinking he could win me over and become my manager. It's been one messy custody battle ever since. I've only had to visit him once in Miami, two years ago. In December.

Today marks the first day of the worst month on the calendar. December can suck a dick.

"Thanks for driving." June picked me up for school today in her mom's van. My car needs tires and my mom won't let me drive until I get new ones. Dad won't pay for them, which is part of their agreement, even though I have plenty of cash saved in my accounts.

"That's not the point," my mom keeps saying.

I don't know, though. Kinda feels like the point is I need tires and have found a way to be self-sustaining. I'm almost eighteen, and I plan on calling my own financial shots soon.

"It's nice getting to drive. I miss my car, though. The minivan doesn't really scream *cool*," June says as we pull into our usual spot at the front of the school.

"I don't know. I mean, you're cool enough to always get this prime real estate in the student lot without having to fight for it," I say, tipping the mirror to check the smoothness of today's twisty up-do. Strands are already falling away and framing my face like wispy baby doll hairs.

"I get this spot because it's right in front of the principal's office, and almost everyone else hides vape or pot in their car so nobody *wants* to park here." June kills the engine and gives me a sideways look.

"It's cool not to be the pot-smoking vaper," I say, folding my arms over my chest to hold my position. Laughter breaks free from June's lips almost immediately as she reaches over her seat to grab her backpack.

"Okay, Nancy Reagan." She gets out, thinking she proved a point.

I step out on my side and shut the door just as she locks it with the key fob.

"Joke's on you. I have no idea who Nancy Reagan is." I'm lying. I totally get her joke, but it's going to piss her off more that I don't, and then she'll forget all about not driving a cool car.

"Just say no?"

I glance up and purse my lips in feigned consideration, then shake my head when my gaze falls back to her.

"Ronald Reagan's wife? He was president in the eighties? And she was the First Lady? Just . . . say . . . no?" She's getting worked up. I live for this. My hand grips my phone in my pocket.

"No," I say, just as she requested.

She groans with frustration, and I pull my phone out to snap a photo of her at the perfect moment. My cherry on top.

"Damn it!" June chides.

I can't help but laugh hard.

"You were fucking with me, weren't you?" my friend demands. She'll get over it in seconds. She always does.

"Bitch, I totally know who Nancy Reagan is. Do you think I'm stupid?"

I snap one more photo, this time with her mouth open wide, ready to argue. She snaps it shut and grumbles, which only makes me laugh more.

"I'm making that one my lock-screen photo," I tease. She rolls her eyes, and I set the photo to save. I'll change it with a new one tomorrow, but today this photo gives me joy. More importantly, though, now June couldn't care less about driving a minivan and parking it front and center. That's old news.

On instinct, I duck and roll when an arm slinks over my shoulder. It takes me three full seconds to realize it's Hayden's arm doing the act. He's wearing his Allensville Public hoodie, number fourteen on the back. Tory's wearing his, too, only he's two. Must be a team thing.

"Sorry, didn't mean to scare you," Hayden says, cautiously opening his arm for me to tuck myself next to him on my own terms. I do, but the weight of his arm on my shoulders feels heavy—suffocating.

"What's with the twin matchy-matchy?" I ask, tugging on the cord from his hood. He shoves his free hand into the front pocket and puffs the sweatshirt out to look down at our school's logo. It's a cartoonish drawing of a massive eagle carrying away a bloody piece of prey. There's a constant debate among students whether it's a rabbit or another bird of some sort. Whatever it is, it's gross. There was a petition to change the mascot logo my freshman year, but apparently the guy who drew it is some famous local artist, so we're stuck with these gory sweatshirts and stuff.

"Did you forget? Game day!" Hayden steps to the side and pulls his arms free of his hoodie one at a time.

"Today is the first game?" I'm a bad girlfriend because saying I forgot wouldn't even be close to the truth. I never paid attention enough in the first place to even know it was game day.

"Yeah. You're coming, right?" He pulls the hoodie over his head, messing up his wavy hair. It's cute.

"Of course. June?" I turn to my friend who is already making out with Lucas against the back of his truck. They have a lot of time to make up for, but I swear they're always locked mouth-to-mouth.

I'm about to turn back to Hayden and tell him I'll be there, with or without June, when the tight fit of his dark gray hoodie swallows up my head and chokes at my neck.

"Uh, no. I don't . . ." I struggle to find air under the enormous fleece-lined sweater. My eyes finally find Hayden's smile, and I instantly feel guilty for wanting to rip this thing off of me. The messy bun that was already falling apart is also unraveling.

"I like seeing you in my number," Hayden says. I catch Tory's snicker just over his brother's shoulder, and when our eyes meet he covers his laugh with a fist to his mouth and a lame-ass cough.

"It's a little big on me," I say, following through and poking my arms into the sleeves after dropping my bag to my feet. Hayden reaches toward the top of my head and I strain to stare straight upward as he tugs free the band I was using to hold my hair in place.

"It's cute that it's big," he says, handing me my hair tie. I put it around my wrist, once I *find* my wrist.

"Okay, well, I'll get it back to you after first hour, I guess."

"Keep it. Wear it to the game," he interjects before I can conjure an excuse.

"Oh, uh, okay," I stammer.

June has snapped out of her love fest by Lucas's truck and steps up on the curb to stand behind me and comb out my wild hair with her fingers.

"Look who's got spirit," she says, sarcasm tainting every word. It was only a few months ago that I gave her shit for just sitting at the football games. I never forced a giant sweatshirt on her with a wild bloodbath pictorial painted on the chest, though.

"Haha, yeah, look at me. Woo!" I raise both of my hands and waggle them with pretend pompoms before bending down to pick up my bag and work the straps up over the massive thickness of the material I'm wearing. I can actually *feel* my hair growing out in all directions. I'm going to look like a palm tree by lunch hour.

"Okay, well, I'll see you at lunch, and after the game." Hayden flattens both of my cheeks with his palms, puckering my lips out as he bends down and kisses me. His kisses are sweet, and he sprinkles them often. Being with him feels a lot like dating a boy from the 1950's. He made a big deal about holding hands, and we've never really full-on made out. We kiss, but it's got this weird unwritten time limit on how long it goes on.

Hayden holds out a fist and pounds it against his brother's and Lucas's, and everyone heads their separate ways, leaving me and June alone to walk through the main hallway together. She's in independent study just down the hallway from my bio class. Lately, I feel as if this two-minute walk through throngs of students is the only time she and I have to catch up.

"So, are you going to tell me how all of this"—she pauses to tug at the sleeve of Hayden's hoodie—"happened?"

"He's nice," I say, which makes me immediately cringe because God, that sounds lame. Our story is a lot more complicated than *nice*, but I'm not totally sure I have a full handle on it so nice is the best I've got.

"Yeah, he always has been. Since when has that been your thing? I thought you were hooking up with that new—"

"Cannon?" I answer for her. "Cannon is hot. And I tried to get on his radar, but that boy has major shit going on, and he's so focused on baseball and the new coach at school. It was literally all he ever talked about."

"Yeah, okay, but then how did you get to Hayden?" June asks.

I sigh and roll up one of the sleeves at my wrist.

"We have a lot in common, and I'm sure you've had to help Lucas navigate a lot of this. Us fucked-up family kids have to guide each other, ya know?" I give her a sideways smile and she nods.

"Yeah, I get that. I've been sort of preoccupied with Lucas lately and we haven't talked much, but I thought surely Miss Love Sucks would have filled me in on settling down with a guy like Hayden D'Angelo," June says.

"That's my nickname? Miss Love Sucks?" I say it in a joking way, but there's a tender pang at my side. *Am I truly that jaded?*

"Well, it is now. I just made it up, but you know what I mean. You've never had a *boyfriend*, per se. You have had guys you're talking to, and then guys you are *seriously* talking to. You just jumped right into a label with this one." She laughs through her assessment of my love life, and I guess on most points, she's right.

"Huh," I respond, letting the hurt show a little.

"Hey, no, I didn't mean it like that," June says. We've reached the independent study room, but before she leaves me to step inside she softly touches my elbow and moves us to the other side of the walkway, away from the students rushing to beat the bell.

"I know, yeah. I guess I didn't realize all of that. I mean, Hayden and I *were* talking, and maybe that's what it was. We *talked*. We talked about the way my dad left, all of the shit I'm going through now, how he's filing all of this crap to get his name on my company even though I'm about to be eighteen."

I stop short of telling her the worst of it. I'm not ready to relive some things. Not until I absolutely have to.

"Abs, I'm so sorry. I didn't realize how bad things have gotten with your dad," June says, hugging me with one arm. I let her, because she's June and she is a kind soul, but I'd rather not be a thing people have to say *sorry* about.

"It is what it is," I say. That's such a dumb, meaningless phrase, yet it's the only thing that fits my situation. The only way my problems could go away would be with a time machine. I'd go back to being Annie and whisper in my ear: *"Don't dream big, little girl. That house of cards is mighty fragile."*

"It wasn't all about me, though," I continue, shaking away my own thoughts. "Hayden is having a hard time with his parents too. He feels angry, but he has no idea what to do with those feelings because he's not really the angry type."

I don't go into the guilt he feels because that's his dragon to battle. When he wants others to know everything, they will. And if he never wants that, then that's his choice. Our relationship is built on confiding in each other, creating a space to dump our baggage and move on. It's what gives us both peace—we are each what we need.

"No, he's not an angry kind of guy," June agrees. "I still remember in fourth grade when Hayden rescued the kittens underneath our grade school portable art room. His mom helped him nurse those things until they could get them adopted."

"I remember that! I totally wanted one, but my parents said our household wasn't the kind of place for kittens. No truer words than that!" I'm old enough now to realize a kitten would only have been one more thing for my parents to fight over.

"I'm glad you're happy," June slips in, bringing me back to the subject we're *actually* talking about—me and Hayden.

"Thanks," I say, the words basically an act of autopilot. I'm not sure I'm smiling right now, but the commotion of the last warning bell gets me off the hook. June rushes in, shouting something about missing lunch for an SAT meeting or something.

I ratchet up the sleeves of Hayden's sweatshirt and make my way to my classroom, squeezing in just before the teacher shuts the door, and like a heatwave, I'm pummeled with stares. Okay, maybe I'm not really pummeled, but there are a few people near the back of the class who are definitely eyeing me in this hoodie. There's going to be talk about it, like me dating someone is major TMZ news, but whatever.

I'm happy. *Right?*

FIVE

TORY

Hayden forgot about the SAT meeting. I remembered the moment he told Abby he'd meet her for lunch. I probably should have said something then, but I didn't. I didn't because I've got a super selfish streak, and I was planning on skipping the SAT meeting. I'm fine with the score I have. A solid nine-eighty works for the places I want to go. Besides, state schools are lenient on test scores when you drain threes like I do. I also knew Abby would skip it. She took her first test the same day I did, and she bragged about being two hundred points higher than me when our results came in. She also said she'd never take that test again.

I feel like a dick now that I'm in the moment, though. I'm clearly taking advantage of the fact my brother and all of our friends won't be here so I can have Abby all to myself. I didn't account for the fact Abby and I don't really hang on our own, though. It's always been in groups. When June and Lucas were going through their shit, Abby and I were the co-pilots, steering those two together. That's when my feelings got all fuckin' weird, too.

I pay the cart guy four bucks for the same chicken burrito, chips and drink I've been buying at this school for four years, then pull my phone from my pocket when it buzzes. I balance the cardboard food box in my other hand.

It's a text from Hayden.

Hey, totally forgot about this SAT thing. Tell Abby for me?

I was prepared for this. I type back my nonchalant response.

Got it.

Abby is sitting in her usual spot, the one in the far corner of the cafeteria where the windows meet and the sun peeks through the trees. She's pulled her knees up on the bench and keeps glancing over her shoulder, out the window, probably wondering where Hayden is. She's usually surrounded by people—Lola, Naomi, June, Lucas . . . me and my brother. She's become the top of the pyramid in our social structure, the one who isn't afraid to speak her mind and who would speak up for her friends in a heartbeat. I'm not sure where I fall in that hierarchy. I can't say she'd get in someone's face to defend me, but then again, I don't need her to. I'm pretty quick to handle my own defense.

"Seat taken?" It's not even clever, and she calls me on it with a look that says I'm a fucking dumbass. I straddle the bench on the other end from her, leaving a solid six feet of distance between us, and plop my wrapped burrito down between my knees.

"They're all in that SAT meeting," I say.

"Yeah, I know." She shrugs and pops one of the chips from her bag in her mouth.

I nod, suddenly kicked off the map of what I should say next.

"Cool." That's what comes out.

"You really sticking with that nine-eighty?"

I glance up at her with one raised brow and breathe out a laugh. I wonder how this became our way with each other—little digs, barbs and insults until enough of them add up to equal a conversation.

"Well, I mean, it's no eleven-eighty." I hold my palms up, arms out, beating her to her punchline.

"It sure the fuck isn't." Her eyes do that little righteous flutter with her words. I laugh it off and turn my focus to my burrito.

She continues to take nibbles at her chips, pushing the bread around from her sandwich. Meanwhile, I bear down and chomp about half of my burrito in three bites. A worry line seems to be permanently pressed into her forehead, and I stare at it for several seconds until she glances up and meets my glare.

"What's up with you?" I say through a full mouth.

She glowers.

"Nothing." Her short clipped answer is irritable, and it's also a lie.

"Come on. I'm good at listening," I say. I actually am. I rarely say shit that matters to people because sharing my thoughts and feelings is uncomfortable. It's turned me into a really good free therapist. Lucas unloads on me constantly.

Abby chews through a few more bites while she studies me with her bullshit meter running full blast. She finally gives in and disposes of her half-eaten meal in the crumpled-up paper it came in and slides a few feet closer to me on the bench. We're facing each other, her feet flat on the wood in front of me. I note the red heart doodled on the side of her right Van and the broken version drawn on the left. I feel like there's a story there.

"I turn eighteen in two weeks. I've had that date circled on my calendar for years because it's supposed to mean that the bullshit back-and-forth stuff between my parents, which has really only been about money, stops. It's supposed to mean *I* decide where I go, with whom, when and what my business amounts to. But—"

Abby's mouth pulls tight as she shrugs. My stomach sinks with sympathy.

"Eighteen means you're an adult though, right?" I shift in my seat, moving my foot up to the table so I can scoot a little closer. I'm not doing it for predatory reasons, which I think Abby might suspect given the way she just tucked her knees tighter into her chest. I'm doing it to make our bubble smaller, so she can talk and share without the nosy-ass ears floating around the lunchroom. There are a lot of those around this place, especially when it comes to Abby. She's considered "famous" around our parts.

"I'm more like a *half* adult," she says, laughing at her definition.

"How so?"

Her long lashes flit against her cheeks, golden brown like her hair, which she's tied into this messy knot at the base of her neck. She has the faintest dusting of freckles on her round cheeks, partly covered with makeup but never so thick that the real her doesn't shine through. She mashes her lips together, the satin red on her lips glimmering as she forms a wry smile.

"I guess my parents are considered *investors* in the start-up of my career. All the modeling classes, acting classes, photo sessions for headshots, clothes and makeup." She waggles her head side to side as she twirls her finger around her face with a giggle. It pulls a breathy smile from me in response.

"Okay, yeah. But that's also parenting, right? I mean, my mom and dad put Hayden and me in youth basketball for years, then club, and there were shoes—*oh how there have been shoes.*" I make the same head waggling motion and finger twirl she did, only this time at my feet, which are in loosely laced Jordan Ones that I literally shined up with a baby wipe this morning.

Abby is amused at my comparison, and she lets her legs fall loose from her hold, her feet landing on the ground as she straddles the bench in front of me, leaning forward and bracing her palms on the wood as if she's a gymnast about to lift herself into some sort of hand stand. She stares at the carved-out G+T for long seconds while her laughter fades.

"It wouldn't be a big deal if this was all just my mom. She's my manager, and I have never once felt like one of those abused child stars. I know what my savings account looks like, and I know she doesn't pull shady shit you see in the tabloids. It's always been me and her, and then the world. But the fact that my dad is like, I don't know, forcing his way on the team? It feels more like the custody hearings have turned into employment ones. I mean, the last time he actually came in with all these receipts from when I was six and seven."

I'm not sure she realizes she's trembling, but she is, so to stop her from digging any deeper in a place so public and so filled with the fumes of microwave pizza and Coke machines, I reach forward and rest my hand on top of hers. We both freeze, and I'm pretty sure my palm is already sweating. Her gaze lifts to meet mine, but I don't let go of her hand just yet. I don't make this touch a big deal, even though it sort of is. That's not why I did it, and I don't want to cheapen it. With our eyes locked on one another, I let the air fill with silence just long enough for a ragged, emotional breath to fall from her lips.

"You have every right to feel the way you do," I say.

"And how's that?" she fires back. Her hand shifts under mine, but she doesn't pull it away.

"You feel like your dad sees a business opportunity where he should see his daughter."

She swallows and keeps her gaze on mine for a beat before finally leaning back, pulling her hand away and glancing off to the side. With a snort sniffle, she runs the sleeve of my brother's hoodie across her eyes, erasing the tiny break that she let herself have.

I'm suddenly not hungry. I don't think I have ever *not* been hungry, but I couldn't eat the rest of my burrito if I were forced at gunpoint. It's not that I feel sick, but more that I feel . . . envious. I was fooling myself thinking that Abby was a passing crush I could easily dismiss. Two months of riding shotgun with her through all things June and Lucas was just long enough for me to get hooked on having her around. But while it's my advice she's listening to, it's my brother's fucking sweatshirt she's dabbing her tears with.

"So, see you at the game?" My move to leave is abrupt, especially after she just bared part of her soul. If I stay, though, I'm going to say things I don't mean out of sheer self-preservation. This is precisely why I don't do relationships. I do flirting and hookups. Feelings, well, they fucking feel.

"What, did you change your mind and suddenly decide that nine-eighty bare-minimum wasn't good enough?" Her nose wrinkles after her insult, but I think I get where it's coming from. She just hit me with a major share, and now I'm bailing. Better to lash out. Her and I aren't so different.

"Something like that," I say, holding up my lunch trash as a wave good-bye.

Abby's face shifts slightly, her wrinkled mouth and dimmed eyes morphing from the snarky expression that accompanies her tease to the look of a girl who just lost her brand new balloon to the sky.

"That hoodie"—I walk backward, pointing toward her chest—"looks good on you." I leave things there with a tight-lipped smile and a nod—a truce of sorts, not that Abby even knew we were in a battle. Hell, we weren't. I'm the only one in a conflict, and it's with my own damn self.

I manage to turn my back to her and toss my trash out without pausing to get one more jab in to fully take things back to our version of normal. For now, I'd like to leave things nice. I wasn't counting on her wanting to leave things that way, too.

"I'll be sure to cheer for you, even if I'm wearing Hayden's number," she shouts.

I spin on my heel and give her a thumbs up, but keep moving away from her because if I turn around, I'll keep trying to win her over. And she's not mine to be won.

SIX

ABBY

I haven't been to a basketball game since freshman year. Football is easier for me to follow. I guess it's easier to go along with the crowd at those games, too. Our basketball team has always been better than our football team, and it's packed inside. I wasn't about to cram in here alone, and June had to work, so I dragged Naomi and Lola with me. I talked Lola into coming because I knew Cannon would be here, and now that I'm not trying to get with him, she is. *Good luck!* That boy is like a miserable, grumpy ice sculpture focused on only one thing—getting drafted by a major league team right out of high school.

Lola peels away from Naomi and me the minute Cannon walks in with his cousin Zack, and she manages to get him to laugh at something she says when they sit down a few rows away from us. I must admit I'm a little dumbstruck—I didn't make him laugh once in all of the beer-keg party meetups we had. And I'm fucking funny, dammit!

"He's mesmerized by her tits," Naomi says in a hushed voice at my side. I laugh softly and tap her leg with the back of my palm. She's only trying to make me feel better about not being able to get Cannon to drop his scowl despite weeks of effort.

"Lola's charming. Give her credit," I say.

Naomi wobbles her head but gives in with a sing-songy "Oh-kay."

"But yes, her tits are mesmerizing," I add, both to give props to what nature gave that girl and to let Naomi off the hook after calling her out for shaming our friend.

"Sigh, she does have great tits," Naomi adds in a hum. We both rest our chins on our fists, elbows propped on our knees while we stare at Lola's bright red sweater with envy. After a few seconds, we give in and laugh.

"You have *nothing* to be envious of in that department," Naomi says, elbowing the side of my boob. I wince because *fucking ow!*

"Thanks," I say, adjusting my bra under this giant sweatshirt I'm still swimming in. The plus of wearing Hayden's hoodie is that it's long enough to cover my ass, which means leggings are a go. I can almost endure the carnage drawing on my chest for this level of comfort, plus my fuzzy boots look super cute. My arms are still carrying folds of material, though, and with the heat on in the gym, I'm starting to get kinda hot.

"There's your boy!" Naomi teases, leaning into my side as our team comes rushing onto the floor. They jog two laps around the perimeter of the gym, and Hayden looks up and winks at me as he passes the second time. I hold up my hand and scrunch out a wave with the few fingers I manage to get loose from the cuff of the sweatshirt.

"He's pretty into you, huh?" Naomi's voice is dreamy. All I can do is laugh.

"I don't know about that. Hayden and I just sort of happened. Like it was easy, you know? It's nice to have someone to talk to about all of life's shit." My gaze slides over to the other D'Angelo while I say that, and I note the far more serious face Tory wears compared to his brother.

"Yeah, okay, but . . . tell me about his body, girl. Give me the details! Those boys are so freaking hot, and getting to kiss one is like winning the lottery." Naomi is practically licking her lips, which . . . gross.

I shake my head with a soft laugh and glance from her back out to the floor where the guys are all stretching.

"It's not like that with us." My smile slips a little as that realization sinks in. Hayden's attention slides to me a few more times and I make sure to prop my smile up every time, but eventually I can't hold it anymore.

"Oh, yeah, I'm sure all you do is hold hands," Naomi teases.

"No," I retort, scrunching my face. "We kiss. We kiss a lot. All the time."

We kiss some.

"You're telling me you haven't gotten all up on that boy?"

I turn to face my friend, her eyes wide and chin dipped low as she waits for my answer. All I can do is shrug, which I know is not the kind of story she wants. I'm far from a prude, and I'm not uncomfortable talking about being with guys. I've slept with two boys, almost three. The third and near sex partner was my co-star in the yogurt commercial, and I had the sense to realize that every time I saw that commercial I would be reminded of him. We had zero in common other than being pretty on camera. His name was Jake. There was no future for Jake and Abby. Not that I have a future with anyone. Serious is not really my thing, and forever love is a myth. I have yet to get close to a family that is still whole. Marriages just don't last forever. There's an expiration date, and it always comes due at the shittiest time.

"Wow, Abby Cortez is taking it slow," Naomi says, leaning back on her self-righteous elbows.

I furrow my brow because that's not the case at all. At least, it certainly isn't intentional. I just don't really . . . *want* to move things fast.

"I'm just busy," I respond, turning my head briefly to the side. I let my focus stray back to the gym floor, pausing on Hayden's back, his perfectly toned arms, broad shoulders, long legs. The boy is built for hands to roam around his skin. His hair flops around as he jogs, and I know there are a dozen freshmen girls in this gym just staring at it. I should want to run my fingers through it and grab hold tight. Yet somehow, I just don't. I think it's because Hayden and I know each other so well. At least, we've known each other for so long, and that's almost the same. I see the seventh grader underneath who got gum stuck in his braces and who spilled chocolate milk on my favorite backpack. That history, it's part of the reason I like him so much. Hayden is a comfortable home in the turmoil of my life, and I might just be his safe place, too.

Lola comes back up to join us by the time the game starts, and I can tell by the way her mouth is set tight that she didn't get much more than the one laugh out of tight-ass Cannon. I hold my hand out as she moves to sit on my other side and we squeeze each other.

"Don't take it personally. I seriously think that boy might be broken. You are beautiful," I say.

Her eyes soften and her bottom lip plumps with a pouty expression.

"Thanks, friend," she says, hugging my arm as she slides into the space next to me.

A roaring thunder brings all of us to our feet, and soon we're stomping on the bleachers to join the sound of our boys' squad circled on the floor, all taking one knee and bending forward as they slam their palms against the hardwood and shout out the letters P-R-I-D-E. When they all jump up at once, the crowd hoots with them. I'll get that part down for the next game, but I dig the spirit. It's fun.

Mr. Newsome's brother does the announcing for our school. He's retired military, and has one of those voices that booms. I've only ever heard him do the football games, so I'm not prepared for the fanfare he gives the basketball team. It's clear where his loyalties lie.

"Ladies and gentlemen, welcome to the Madhouse on Main, home of your District Seven defending champs, The Allensville Public Eagles!"

I'm surprised by the volume of my own screamed response. My hands cup my mouth to boost the volume as Coach Newsome announces the players on the other team. We're playing some Catholic school from the city, which means they're either going to suck or kick our asses. There's no in between when it comes to private school athletic talent.

So far, it looks like they have us on height. But every single player just sorta looks lanky and easy to push over. Maybe I'm projecting my bias.

By the time he gets to announcing our team, I'm on my feet again and stomping along with the girls. Hayden and Tory get saved for the very end, which I'm guessing is a testament to how good they are. The same team chant follows each player's name, but when Tory's name and number gets said, there's a new chant that takes over, a long, deep-voiced *boo?*

"Why are they booing him?" Naomi asks.

I shake my head, having no idea. Everyone is cupping their mouths and making the same awful sound, but they seem so happy about it. Even his team is bellowing, and Tory seems to feed off it, skipping his way down the line of players and pounding fists with every one until he gets to his brother, where he stops so they both can jump high and bump chests.

Tory takes his spot at the end of the line, cracking his neck in both directions while someone plays Jay-Z on in the backdrop of the announcement of the rules and good sportsmanship. He's antsy, like a bull being held behind bars with a steak waving in front of him. His eyes are fixated on the nothingness at the center of the court, almost as though he's playing out the entire game in his mind. Where Hayden smiles, Tory growls. Everything about him is harder, meaner—cut with a sharp edge to keep people from getting too close.

Keep people from getting burned.

I will myself to look away, but before his form leaves my periphery entirely, his movement draws me back in. He reaches over his back and tugs at the collar of his warmup shirt, pulling it up and over his head in one smooth movement, his jersey underneath rising up enough to expose his entire abs and chest, and I feel flushed.

I'm sure the other girls noticed, too, but a quick glance to both sides doesn't reveal either of them to have a noticeable reaction. I laugh silently to myself—*at myself.* It's not as though I haven't admired both D'Angelo brothers before. Hell, half the town has. The reason our football car washes do so well isn't the cheer squad that lines up on the street corners holding signs, it's the two Italian-American boys with *oh-my-God* bods who wash anything that rolls in with their shirts off and their shorts slung low. I'm guilty for dropping several twenties at those car wash fundraisers.

I lean forward, crossing my arms over my knees while I bite on my thumb and bring my flared-up cheeks under control. Before I get comfortable, though, the crowd stands for the national anthem, so I'm stuck with the guilty color on my cheeks. I dart my glance in all directions but Tory's, like a petty thief covering my tracks, but I doubt anyone realizes it but me.

The student running the sound set up at the front table slips a few times while moving his phone close to the mic. It's such an embarrassing rigged-up system, no doubt dwarfed by the tech over at the private school we're playing against. But that's what Allensville is—a place where you take what you have and find a way to make it work.

I settle my gaze back on the line of boys as the music finally crackles out of our decade-old speakers. The hot red blood that was pushed to the very top of my cheeks is almost back where it should be when Tory comes into view, sucking the calm from my chest with one glance and replacing it with searing hot sin. I'm overcome with guilt because one body width to his right stands the boy I'm dating, his brother. But my eyes are locked here, and I'm sure Hayden can tell. Tory doesn't blink, not once through the nearly two minutes it takes for the Star Spangled Banner to play. His body vibrates with his home-brewed energy and his chin tips more than once in what I imagine is a silent acknowledgement that he sees me staring at him and intends to remember that I did. I wonder whether it's evidence to hold against me down the road or for his own personal ego gain. None of the nonsense in my head can force me to turn away, though.

Tory's lips part just as the song winds down and a slight curve forms in his mouth, dimpling his cheeks. Rather than run scared, I make the same face at him, because really . . . he's looking at me, too. This forbidden flirting game is a two-way street that we are both driving on dangerously.

I could almost convince myself that I'm imagining this were it not for the slight titter as he clearly nods at me before turning his back and huddling with his team. Once cut loose from his stare, I'm suddenly aware that Lola and Naomi probably noticed my little game of chicken. I have milliseconds to clean it up before it becomes a big deal.

"He is such a punk," I say with a shake of my head, confident my girls will instantly agree.

"He has always wanted to get with you. He's probably just jealous." Lola spills first, standing to adjust her jeans along her hips. She steps down one row to turn and face me and Naomi, her hands on her hips.

"He just likes the game. It's so annoying. Hayden is nothing like him," I add, meaning every word. Tory has always loved the game. I don't think I've been to a single party over four years of high school madness where he hasn't tried to get me to make out with him. A person doesn't keep coming back for the rejection if they don't like to play. And his lame pick-up attempts over the years have been so annoying. Hayden was so adult about it all—so easy. We were hanging out on the bleachers at school having one of our long talks when he reached out and took my hand in his, looked me in the eyes and said, "I really like you." How simple is that? I said it back, we kissed, and when he called me his girlfriend to the lady at the diner the next day, all of the noise in my heart and head just stopped. One two-minute stare down with Tory, though, and a hive of bees are swarming in my chest.

This guy named Danny, who has always been the tallest kid in school, matches up against the big guy for Vanguard (that's the name of the private school, I guess. Or it's their mascot. I can't tell for sure, but it's the only thing people from their school are yelling.) Danny wins the tip-off easily, pushing the ball in the air straight into Tory's hands. This is where everything aggressive in his fabric takes over and drives. Watching him work with his brother out there on the court is like watching a pair of ice dancers. They have this unspoken choreography that plays out on the floor, from one quick pass to another until Tory launches the ball in the air for Hayden to grab and hammer home. People are on their feet as the twins manage to score six straight points in less than a minute, and I find myself shouting Tory's name as he makes a steal and races down the court. Everyone expects an encore of the last shot, where he fed his brother under the hoop and Hayden laid it in with a gentle finger roll, but that's just what Tory wants. Everyone barrels down the court, but he stops short, giving him just the edge he needs to set up and catapult the ball in the air with the smoothest body movement I've ever seen. I'm not sure whether everyone has gone silent or I've temporarily lost the ability to hear, but the only sound that accompanies my view of Tory's ball soaring in a perfect arc is my hitched breath, which I hold midway for good luck. The net swishes with his three-point shot, and the players on the bench go absolutely nuts.

Tory's signature smirk crawls up into his cheek as he turns, and for a brief moment our eyes meet and I get an overwhelming sense that he's showing off . . . *for me.*

The complete dominance doesn't last forever, and by the time the first quarter ends, we're only up by six. With my focus back where it should be, I stand and take advantage of the short break between quarters, tagging along with Lola to search for something sweet at the snack bar. I give her money while she stands in line and then rush to the dimly lit restroom, happy to find it completely empty.

It's here, in the last stall of the gym lobby women's restroom, that the first hint of something ominous finds my ears. I only recognize it because of the nightmares I've had most of my life. The deep moan that the wind makes—as though it's alive, when a thunderstorm like this one crawls along the Indiana landscape—is undeniable. The forecast said rain, and it's December, so this sound is unexpected—*unwelcome.* The last tornado to touch down remotely near Allensville in December happened eleven years ago.

It sounded just like this.

I finish my business quickly, rushing my hands under the sink water, and kicking open the door with a flourish that cracks the handle against the wall outside. My pulse is thumping throughout my entire body, but the beat is loudest in my head. It's annoying because right now, more than any time ever in my life, I need to hear. My ears are the one sense I can count on against the dark sky outside.

I pop open the side door and breathe in the moisture, the air thick with dirt and destruction. A rumble echoes along the ground, different from thunder. This sound can be felt; the earth is being moved by nature, and the beast is coming for us.

"Tornado!" I scream over my shoulder, disobeying all the rules of calm civility I've been taught through every storm drill we've practiced at this school. That shit is out the window, because that wind is picking up, and the whistle is getting steadier—louder.

Lola is the first to react, dropping the pretzel and cheese she just spent a few bucks on before rushing over to see what I'm seeing.

"She's right! Shelter!" Her voice crackles with panic. My voice disappears.

The next few seconds happen in blinks. I'm rushing toward the middle of the gym. Players are pushing, and whistles are blowing.

"Hey!" One of the referees grabs my arm, but his grip loosens the second more shouts echo my initial warning. His admonition quickly turns into crisis management as he motions me toward the double doors on the other end of the gym. His whistles morph into the kind that guide people where to go, and order in this chaos still feels achievable.

And then the lights flicker.

That's when the screaming begins, somewhere along my route to the school's storm shelter, a large, concrete corridor with zero windows and emergency lights buried in the walls. A blur of purple jerseys, the ones worn by the Vanguard team, surrounds me as their team runs past to safety, and a stray elbow cracks my nose with enough force that I'm instantly dizzy and on my ass.

The hit was hard enough that I might have passed out if it weren't for the straight-up terror coursing through my veins. I manage to stumble to my knees when I'm instantly swept up in someone's arms.

"I'm bleeding," I mutter, my hand awkwardly assessing my nose. I expect a gush, but miraculously it's only a few spots on my palm.

"You're okay," the familiar voice says.

My hand flattens against the chest of my rescuer, over the emblazoned number 2, damp with sweat with a wildly kicking heart underneath. I look up enough to see Tory's worried eyes scanning for a way in. Too many people cram into one opening, and the lights have completely gone out. The backups will kick on, but not right away.

Tory bypasses the crowd still pushing to enter the tight hallway, running with me against his chest toward the men's locker room. He pushes it open with his foot and weaves around rows of lockers and tiled walls until we're in the center of the cluster of showers. He sets me down in front of a main pipe, and I wrap my hands and legs around it on instinct. He crouches down with me, his body cocooning mine while he reaches around my body and grabs the same pipe with both hands. The heavy weight of his head leans into the back of mine, and for the first time ever, I hear fear in his ragged breathing.

"It'll pass soon," I say, somehow able to get words to leave my quaking lips.

He doesn't give me a verbal response, but I feel him pull in tighter around me. I do the same, and within seconds we're practically one with the metal pipe that runs deep into the ground. The vibration against the palm of my hands is making me numb, but worse—I can no longer hear the screams from other students in the gym or nearby hallway. The storm, it's too loud.

A large branch, or perhaps a piece of a nearby building, crashes against the heavy metal door that leads outside, and I flinch. Tory's hands slide from above and below where mine are gripping to cover mine. His hands are nearly double the size of mine, his fingers filling in the gaps where I wrap around the pole, locking me against the metal. His head shifts just enough to bring his chin over my shoulder, and strangely, he begins to hum. I focus on the sound, learning the tune as he gives it to me in faltering bits and pieces. It's vaguely familiar, and I've found my breathing has started to follow along.

"So, hoist up the John B's sail," he sings in a soft murmur. If I didn't know how scared he was, I'd assume he's nervous. He shouldn't be; his singing voice, even this soft, is really nice.

"See how the main sail sets," he continues, this time the faintest touch of his lip brushing against my ear. It isn't on purpose, but every single nerve in my body tunes in as my skin reacts with a rush of pebbles that trail down my arms and legs.

The wind is crying outside our walls, and panic takes hold of my emotions. I shudder out cries as more debris smacks against the walls outside, but Tory continues to hum his sweet song against my ear. His voice shakes every so often, but nothing deters him from keeping up the rhythm and pace.

And then it happens.

There's a difference in the way his mouth touches my exposed neck. It's purposeful, even if feather light. There's a taste taken with his lips, and he lingers for longer than a second, long enough for him to consider what his lips should do next. I'm frozen, less scared of the storm for this brief moment and more afraid of what's happening and the question beating down my conscience. *Do I want it to continue?*

As if he can read my thoughts, Tory's head tilts just enough to remove his mouth from my skin, the cool spot left from his lips drawing all my focus. The wind seems to be at its peak, a relentless hiss beating its way inside. Fear crawls back inside my chest, and Tory's body rocks me side to side in slow movements, as if we're lost at sea.

"Call for the captain ashore, let me go home . . ." His voice is a little stronger with this part and I blurt out a short laugh mixed with tears at the sentiment in his words.

"I want to go home!" I shout as the building quakes around us and we both start laughing hysterically, a mania taking hold in the moment.

"You know this song?" His voice is loud at my ear.

He seems so happy that I recognize whatever this is that I shout back, "Sure!"

The heavy patter of rain fills in the gaps left behind as the wind shifts direction, the destruction headed somewhere else. As the pounding subsides, Tory shifts enough to check my face, but his arms are still locking me down, his muscles still flexed as if ready to hold us both to the earth.

"You're such a bullshitter," he says, his voice raspy and mixed with laughter that's probably leftover from the massive dose of adrenaline.

"Thanks, and I'm glad you survived, too!" I bite back.

"No, the song. You have no idea what that is," he explains, finally easing his grip and scooting back enough for me to unglue myself from the pipe.

I stand, ass damp from the shower-wet floor, which I guess is a small price to pay for not losing the roof over our heads. I glance down and meet his sideways look and crooked smile as he stills with legs outstretched and palms flat behind him.

"You seemed so excited that I knew it, so I went along."

I smile and extend a hand to help him to his feet, and he studies my palm for a few seconds with an amused look on his face. I'm about to rescind the offer for help when his eyes flit to mine and he grasps my hand, barely using it to get to his feet. His hold is firm, and he doesn't let go right away, the pressure of his thumb against my knuckle bringing the raised bumps back to life along my neck and spine.

"Are you okay?" Tory steps close enough to have to look down at me from his height. My stomach tightens and I'm not sure whether it's because he's got me feeling strangely nervous or because of the question he just asked. I haven't heard those three words in a very long time, from anyone, about anything.

"I will be," I say, which isn't the answer I meant to utter at all, but it's the one that's honest.

His slight smile remains, even as his lips close tight and his eyes wrinkle at the sides with thought. The bustling of students and parents and players filing out of the hallway adjacent to us draws his attention behind me briefly, and I take that opportunity to glance at our still connected hands. I shouldn't be holding his hand like this. The acceptable time has passed. I'm not fighting to get free, though.

"I liked it, the song," I say, bringing his attention back to me. He shakes his head with confusion and our hands naturally part. Perhaps both of us realize that things were venturing into awkward territory.

"Come on, people will be worried if they don't see us," he says, his hand pressing softly against the center of my back, directly over his brother's number.

"Sloop John B, by the way. That song I was singing? Beach Boys version, not the really old folk version." There's a giddiness in his tone when he talks about the song as we find our way back to the door leading into the gym. I had no idea about this side of him.

"You have a great voice," I say, squeezing out one more compliment before we go back to trading snarky insults in public.

His feet stop briefly and I jump, nervously afraid he's seen something bad. When I catch the expression on his face, though, I realize I'm the one who surprised him.

"Thanks. My dad played that on the guitar when we were kids. It's the one song he taught me that I really mastered." A proud grin pushes into his cheeks, but it's fleeting as he's still racked with nervous energy.

"Maybe you'll play it for me sometime."

Those are the last words I get out before we open the locker room door and step into the panic and mess. The gym is intact, mostly, though a large section of the metal roof is either missing or bent. It's hard to tell with the harsh glow of the emergency lights. The floor is soaking wet, and people are shouting random names in search of each other. It's chaos, and I find myself drifting silently through the midst of it with Tory at my side.

I don't hear my name being called, but I recognize the way it's formed on Hayden's lips as he rotates slowly, scanning the crowd with his hands cupping his mouth. His face is pale, and his eyes are deep, dark circles. He's like a ghost of himself, a shadow left in the wake of a rare December tornado. When he spots me, he rushes in my direction and instantly folds me in his arms. I can't understand the words he's muttering into the top of my head, and I don't feel settled at all. If anything, I somehow feel more scattered than when the wind was threatening to tear down the walls. I also feel guilty, because the only thing playing through my mind is the slow hum of that sweet song and my inappropriate hope that Tory might sing it to me again.

SEVEN

TORY

Hayden and I spend most of the morning clearing the debris from Mom's front yard. Somehow, the damage from last night's surprise twister is minimal. The gym roof is the worst of it, along with flooding in some classrooms, and the shingles on the nearby Coffee Shack. It's enough to cancel school for the day, until they figure out where to put the displaced teachers.

The rest of the damage was sustained by the old maple trees that line the entire main drag through town—fifty or sixty years' worth of growth wiped out in five minutes. When I drove in to meet up with June and Lucas for lunch, I counted maybe six still standing out of the more than twenty that should be. Most of the businesses look fine; the streets are messy as hell.

I'm a few minutes late, and it looks as though my friends have already ordered and gotten their food, which is fine because really, I just came to talk.

I slide into the booth to join them and dive right into the meat of my problems.

"I fucked up."

June and Lucas don't even flinch.

"Did you guys hear me?"

Both of them are staring down at their bowls of pasta. I've been eating at this joint my entire life and I know the pasta here is shit. They're teaming up on me, which is seriously irritating.

"Hey!" I smack my palm on the table between their two drinks. June flinches and drops her fork, quickly running a napkin over her mouth to clean the splatter of sauce left behind. Lucas merely glances up, still masticating the world's worst penne.

"We're listening." June clears her throat and sets her napkin to the side, folding her hands on the table in front of her. After a few seconds she elbows Lucas, and he huffs, but sets down his fork and pushes his bowl away.

"Yeah, what she said. We're listening," he says with a preteen-girlish roll of his eyes.

"Wow. I didn't realize I was such a burden. I mean, it's not like I didn't spend the last three months listening to both of your bullshit." I move to slide from the booth, but Lucas juts out his leg and leans forward with a stiff arm, staring me down.

"Relax, dude."

I glare at him for a hard second, still considering barreling through his barrier and jetting out of here, but then who'd I have to talk to about this? I breathe out long and hard but slide my way back into the booth, centering myself across from them.

"We didn't mean it," June starts, but before her apology gets wings, Lucas makes sure it crashes and burns.

"Speak for yourself," he cuts in. "I meant it. Tor, you've been telling us the same thing for the last five days. It's this endless circle of 'I wasn't really that into her' followed by 'I really blew my chance.' Just . . . pick one."

By the time Lucas is done, June's glare at him does the job so I don't have to. When he slowly turns to meet her gaze he flinches a little in his seat.

"What? You know I'm right."

June just shakes her head then turns her attention back to me.

"Anyway, please, Tory. You can talk to us, or *me* at least," June says. Lucas snorts out a laugh and shakes his head, pulling out his phone to scroll through social media.

June waves her hand to bring my attention solely to her. I take another deep breath and shift in my seat, leaning forward on my elbows and resting my forehead into my hands so I can knead away at my temples.

"I'm guessing you haven't talked to Abby." I stop rubbing my head long enough to raise my brow and glance up at June.

She tilts her head sideways and squints her eyes.

"I have not." Her voice sounds suspicious.

"Okay, maybe I'm not fucked, then," I say, leaning back into the soft, squishy padded back and let my shoulders sag. Damn, they were up to my ears tense.

"You're going to have to give me details if you want my advice, Tory." June's method has always been no-nonsense. I think it's kinda why we clicked all of a sudden. She's helped me get my shit together more than she realizes. We both assist Coach Newsome's class for our last hour, which means we basically sit in the back and do whatever. I don't think June would let me out of that room, though, without checking to make sure I actually did my homework or studied for whatever test is coming up. This might just be the first semester I pull off a 4.0.

"Things got pretty chaotic at the game last night, with the tornado and shit. Everyone was running toward the back hallway, through those main doors—you know the ones?"

June nods, and Lucas puts his phone down—I guess he's over his pouty fit and ready to listen.

"Abby was there watching the game, and in the rush, she took an elbow to the nose. She was a little stunned and getting pushed around so I picked her up and took her with me." I sound like a fucking hero if I stop the story here, and given the way June's looking at me, I'm half tempted.

"Seems like the human thing to do, man," Lucas says.

"And then I took her into the locker room. Alone." I'm unable to finish before Lucas pipes in again.

"Aww, shit!" He laughs, holding a fist to his mouth as if that somehow mutes it.

"Not like that, dude. Just, fucking listen, all right?" I scold him.

"Sure, yeah." He snickers. June gives him another elbow.

"Thank you," I say to her, recalibrating myself to finish the story and get to the hard part. I crack my neck to the side and bring both of my hands together and rest them on the table. "There were so many people cramming through that space, I was afraid we weren't going to get inside in time. It was the first thing I could think of, because of the pipes."

"Okay, might be a bit of a stretch, since those pipes only go down a foot or so, but whatever." Lucas adds his color commentary. I shoot him a look and keep going.

"We were both holding on and she was so freaked out, and maybe I was too, so I started . . . like . . . humming this song that calms me down and shit."

The snort that leaves Lucas's nose is epic, only outdone by the cackling laugh that actually forces him to hold his hand over his chest. June pushes him toward the window, to the other end of their seat, but he laughs right through her efforts. She eventually gives up and leaves her boyfriend's side of the booth and takes my hand, dragging me to a table and chairs on the other end of the diner.

"Oh, come on!" Lucas shouts. June holds up a flat palm.

"I'll deal with him later," she says, her eyes square on mine. There isn't an ounce of judgement in her expression.

I swallow.

"I'm not gonna lie, I was scared, too. The walls were buzzing, and the emergency lights were a joke. All I could feel was her body shaking, and I just sorta . . . started . . . singing."

"You sing?" June whisper shouts.

I level her with narrowed eyes and tight lips.

"Right, sorry," she says, clearing her throat. "Continue."

I squirm a little in my seat because this next part, this is the part that's bad. June is like my church, though, the place I can come to repent and ask forgiveness, so I hit her with the truth.

"I was holding her against my chest, kinda from behind, and her hair smelled like apricots or fruit or something, and her neck was wide open, and it just felt like I should rest my chin on her shoulder."

Her eyes sag and her bottom lip protrudes, her face turning into that one girls make when they have to leave a puppy.

"The first time was totally an accident," I say, skipping ahead.

She shakes her head quickly and twirls her finger, signaling for me to rewind. I sit back in my chair and slink down, stretching my legs out and leaning to one side with my arm slung over the back.

"I was keeping my mouth so close to her ear because I wanted her to hear me. I thought maybe it would calm her or whatever. It was like a graze, I guess."

"A graze," June repeats, her mouth all twisted in disappointment. I may as well spill it now.

"Yeah, that one was a graze. Then I fucking kissed her neck." I shrug under the heat of her blistering glare. "I told you. I fucked up."

"Oh, Tory." Her voice is low, but not angry. It's the goddamned pity again.

"I know." I huff, standing and rounding the chair. I'm about to push it in when a waitress walks up with a glass of water and a straw for me.

"Oh, you're not staying?" The girl looks familiar, sophomore class maybe. I don't want to look like a jerk, so I grab the back of the seat I just left and look down to regroup. I manage to shift my frustrated scowl into something more pleasant, lifting my chin and flashing her the biggest smile I can muster.

"Just heading to the restroom. Give me a burger, cheddar, and skip the side." I keep my mouth locked in the tight-lipped smile while she sets down my water and scribbles my pretty basic order on her pad. I think maybe she's new here; I should tip her good. I blink a few times, silently counting the seconds, until she looks back up at me and tells me my food will "be right up."

There's a happy sway to her hips that bobs her ponytail from side-to-side as she walks away and I laugh lightly before returning my gaze to June. "Why couldn't I get stuck on a girl like that?"

"Because she just got her driver's license and you're narrowing down your college choice," June replies.

I point at her and nod in agreement, then excuse myself to the restroom to follow through with my charade. My hair is a mess, having rushed from yard work to the diner without a break in between. I spend a few minutes at the sink, soaking my hands and running my fingers through my hair, wishing like hell I had a hat. I'd dry my hands on the front of my shirt, but now that I glance down at it, there's dirt all over the front. I grab a towel from the dispenser and pat my hands dry before taking the towel to my shirt to clear some of the dirt off and, *what the—?* My pants are worse. Who am I? I bend at my waist and brush along the seams of my joggers, actual leaves and twigs getting knocked to the floor.

"Ha." I laugh out loud at myself.

I give up when major chunks of nature are no longer stuck to me, and wad the towel into a ball and toss it across the room into the trash bin. Guilty or not, I do feel lighter now that I've bared my soul to June. I'll just go back and take her lecture or her advice on how to get over crushes—*like she ever did*—and then I'll go home and crash face down in my sheets to make up for the zero sleep I got last night. I tossed and turned with stress for seven hours, and I was pretty close to barging into Hayden's room and begging him either for forgiveness or his girlfriend. The end goal changed every ten minutes.

The bathroom door opens with surprising ease and I almost crack heads with the person coming in while I'm exiting.

"Oh, shoot!"

There's a strange element to being a twin that people don't talk about.

Even when you're used to it, it's still surprising to look right back at yourself. I had a slight warning, though, because *shoot* is a total Hayden word.

His palm grasps my shoulder hard, and at first I prepare myself for a fist in the jaw, but he shakes me instead.

"Damn, you scared me," he says, gripping his hand to his chest. He's all cleaned up, a nice white T-shirt and jeans. It's kinda like we traded places during the tornado, like one of those movies, only I'm still stuck wanting his girl and he's still got her. All I got was his frumpy-ass look while he got my style.

"Sorry. Hey, I didn't know you were coming." I scratch at my head as I swap places with him, stepping out while he steps in.

"Yeah, so much for a day off, I guess," he says.

"We've got practice?" My face screws up with surprise because Coach texted us all this morning, telling us to work out and do sprints for the next two days and be ready to hit the gym at the junior high on Thursday. Ours is basically a shipwreck.

"Nah, I picked up a shift, and Mom gave me her car," he says. It's then that I notice the infamous red weenie shirt clutched in his fist. "First official day on the job!"

"Nice. I'll let you change," I say with a quick smile to excuse myself.

My back barely turned, Hayden catches the door.

"Oh, and Abby came with. We were going to hang but then, duty calls! She thought maybe you'd be up for running lines? If not, it's cool. I can take her home."

I don't want to turn around. If I do, I'm either going to tell him that the phrase *duty calls* means he has to take a shit, or I'm going to massively fail at bluffing as I stammer my way through an excuse to avoid being alone with Abby.

"Sure," I say, because of the third option—the one where I *want* to spend time with her and I can play loyal as long as my back is turned.

"Cool. I'll be home around nine, I guess."

I hold up a thumb and walk away, mentally doing the math on the number of hours left before nine. It's barely twelve-thirty.

I get back to the booth where things started, my burger probably still several minutes away from being ready. Abby is twisting where she stands, eyes on the spot where her gym shoe digs at the floor. She's dressed for the gym in tight black leggings and a black workout tee, a white long-sleeved shirt tied around her waist. Unlike me, she's got her hair tucked neatly under a hat, and I can't help but wonder if that's so she can hide underneath the brim.

"I guess I'm driving you back to our place?" My words come out convincingly nonchalant, but June reads below the surface. My friend shakes her head at me slowly, a warning I ignore as I fish out my wallet and toss a twenty on the table. "Just take my burger home. I'm not hungry anyway."

"I'll eat it," Lucas says, winking at me. Clearly, June filled him in on the details he missed. "I'll probably be over in an hour too. I don't mind doing my own thing while you guys study or whatever it is."

"Run lines," Abby corrects. She tips her head up sharply and her eyes shift from Lucas to me, but they're impossible to read. Maybe I'm overreacting, because I could swear she's her usual self, short-tempered and pretentious, and appalled that Lucas wouldn't understand her world.

"Right, study," Lucas says, just to be a dick. I chuckle, mostly to fit in but also because that was funny.

"Ready?" Abby's entire body has turned to face me, and she's completely void of tension, at least it seems so on her end. I, however, am an impossible knot.

"Sure, yeah," I say, picking up my water cup and gulping down half of it. I set it back on the table and clutch my keys in my pocket, nodding toward the door. Abby walks away first, not bothering to wait for me, and I breathe out a laugh as I follow, a little thankful for the normalcy.

"So, see you at one?" Lucas calls after us.

That's hardly an hour. It's less than thirty minutes from now. But I know he should show up. If he's there, everything will stay above board, maybe even my imagination. If he doesn't show, I might get all sappy and shit and pull out my guitar.

"Sounds good, bruh." I hold up my hand as I push through the door, the tiny bell ringing at the top as I leave. I'm pretty sure that means June gets her wings.

EIGHT

ABBY

Stick to the plan, Abby.

I woke up with a renewed sense of business as usual when it comes to Tory D'Angelo and me. If only he'd participate in said plan. This works much better when he acts like a dog, tossing out misogynistic jokes while acting like every girl wants him.

Every girl does want him.

I sense he's trying, though. His cocky swagger is only at mid-strength. He called the guy with the double-sized spoiler and whirring muffler who tried to race us a douche, then laughed when the guy had to stop short because a minivan pulled out in front of him. Other than that, he's acting as if I'm not sitting here, a foot away from him in his bucket seat.

I kiss his brother sitting in this seat. What am I thinking? What am I doing? Why am I even dating someone? I'm not emotionally equipped for this stuff.

We get to the main drag of town and traffic halts, a line of twenty or more cars in front of us. Tory rolls down his window and climbs halfway out from his seat, sitting on the ledge. I lean toward the middle of our seats as if somehow, I can see better from here.

"They're removing some of the downed trees. Looks like they're almost done," he says, slipping back inside before I have a chance to move away. His brows draw in a little and his mouth sits on the cusp of laughter as our eyes meet.

"You wanna have a look?" He points over his shoulder and out his window.

"*Pfft.*" I huff, glowering before blinking my gaze back to the windshield and situating myself away from him again. This little tiff almost feels normal. If only I didn't know that his stare was loitering on the side of my face. Every breath I take has thought behind it, knowing he's watching. I work to hold my mouth in check, my face expressionless, despite the burning sensation of his eyes staring at my lips. My pulse is racing, and I'm getting hot even though it's forty degrees outside and the heater in this car is shit. A perfect storm of my mood triggers clashes in my chest, and finally, I just snap.

"Can't you just go around?" I jerk my head to face him, catching the twitch in his eyes. I think he's both nervous I caught him staring and jumpy at my tone. I sounded mean just now. I'm fucking hot, and . . . confused. And I want out of this car.

My hand moves toward the door handle with my panicked thoughts, and on impulse I push my door open a few inches.

"What, are you gonna go help them hurry things along, lumberjack Abby?" Tory adds in a wry smile and I tug my door closed again, crossing my arms in a humph as I fall back into the seat. His laughter grows, but he glances up at the rearview mirror and then over his shoulder, flipping on his turn signal.

"Hang on. I know a way around." He hangs a quick U-turn, then speeds back past the diner, where June and Lucas are just getting in Lucas's truck. The minivan is gone, so Hayden must have already rushed off to work. He was pretty excited about his first day, and even more excited about a paycheck in a few weeks.

"How come you don't have a job?" I ask.

Tory doesn't answer right away, and at first, I think maybe he didn't hear me, but as he checks the mirror again, I note his grimace and pinched brow. My question came out kinda judgmental, I guess. It's not like I have a real job, either. I have gigs, and all of this sort of fell in my lap. My dad signed me up for a summer acting class when I was six, mostly to get me out of the house, but I got hooked. That little class registration, of course, is the cornerstone of his legal argument for deserving a portion of my company. I think the summer fee might have been thirty-five bucks.

Tory makes a sharp turn into an older neighborhood where most of the homes have front porches and cute yards with huge trees now barren for winter. Flower beds are all emptied for the freeze, but you can see the outlines where they probably bloom bright reds and yellows in the spring. Winding pathways lead to swings and sitting areas where kids no doubt run through sprinklers while parents drink lemonade. I've always wanted to live in a house like one of these. I crave that Hallmark lifestyle. Maybe I just crave a normal family.

"I should be spending my free time on basketball," Tory finally says, drawing my attention back to the driver's seat. His eyes are hazed as he stares at the road ahead, and while my first reaction is to be defensive under the assumption that he's talking about me taking up his free time, I realize he's alluding to something deeper.

"You guys are going to get back in the gym, right?"

There's a long pause before his answer, and I wonder if he's thinking about last night, too. Less about the disaster and more about . . . us.

Tory leans his weight to the side and rests one hand on the steering wheel, wincing.

"We'll be in the junior high gym until the new year, which is lame as hell. You know I dunked there in eighth grade?" He flashes a child-like smile at me, and I get that while he's being funny, he's also sorta bragging about it.

"Wow. Big time," I tease.

Maybe I don't have to be *quite* so cold with him. It feels as if we're in a new place, friendship-wise. It happened with June, so perhaps we're all coming around to each other and maturing.

"It's been hard to focus, with all of the drama. I'm sure you get an earful from Hayden, and I'm fine, so let's talk about you." He glances my way with a tight-lipped grin that tells me his last little bit was complete bullshit. He's not fine at all.

"You know, it's not like I have a set number of hours to hear about people's struggles. If you need to talk, I can listen to you, too," I say.

"Nah, it'd be like reading the same book twice, back-to-back. Who does that?" he says with a snort laugh.

I stare at him and blink slowly, my mind picturing the book on my nightstand that I'm reading right now—the second time through. He does a quick double take when he realizes I'm staring at him, and by his third glance, he gets it.

"Oh, shit. You do that? I'm sorry. I mean . . . that's cool. What do I know? I read *Sports Illustrated*." He shrugs and looks back to the road.

"You look at the swim suit issue," I crack.

His body shakes with quiet laughter and he eventually nods.

"Yeah, I do."

I muse at his humility. It's rather charming, which is the opposite of the objective I set. I'm not supposed to find Tory likeable. The plan is to aim for tolerable. But likeable goes with friendship, so maybe I can shift my end goal.

"Hey, if you want, we can trade. You can run lines with me, and I'll play you some one-on-one." I throw this out there not to flirt, because Tory knows damn well that I am not athletic in the least.

He blurts out a quick laugh.

"Yeah, okay, Abby."

His eyes soften when he says my name, and I feel it in the dead center of my chest. Time to move that goal line back where it was.

With only a mile or two left until we reach his house, we spend the last few minutes letting the radio fill in the dead air in the car. It's nothing but commercials for pot roast sales at the grocery store, snow tires at DJ's Pit Crew, and a laundry list of side effects for some drug that helps you keep your hair. I'm thankful when we pull in the driveway and see Lucas's truck.

He's already pulled a ball out of Tory's garage and is shooting hoops in his driveway as we pull in. A pile of branches and debris forms a mountain near the street, and I survey the new bare spots in the D'Angelo front yard before Tory shuts off his car. His house seems intact from here. We lost a patio cover, but it was basically only a board held up by two crooked posts, so I'm shocked it didn't fly away sooner.

We both get out and Tory jogs over to his friend, stealing the ball from him and palming it in one hand to dunk it easily. He's graceful in the air.

"Dude, how'd you get here so fast?" Tory asks. He punts the ball and catches it off the bounce, then passes it back to Lucas. I lean on the back of Tory's car, dropping my purse between my feet, to watch boys be boys.

"They got Main all cleared right after you took the detour," Lucas says. "We saw you guys drive by. Dropped June off on the way, and maybe, just maybe, I sped a little to beat you here."

"Just a little, huh?" Tory slaps the ball from Lucas's hands again and jogs to the end of his driveway, putting up a shot that bangs off of the rim.

"Oh, so close," Lucas teases.

Tory flips him off, then moves my direction.

"Come on, let's go see what this movie you're in is all about," he says.

I grab my purse, noting how Lucas isn't far behind as we march into the garage and enter through the back kitchen door. I sense that Lucas is trying to protect Tory from me. Or maybe to watch Hayden's back, like I'm some super predator out to double-cross twin hotties.

Shit. Am I?

Tory stops at the fridge, bending over and reaching in deep for a bottle of water. He offers one to me, which I take, then holds up another for Lucas.

"I'm good. Mind if I hit up your PlayStation?" He's already flopped on the couch and turned on the TV.

Tory's glare shifts from Lucas to me and he shakes his head slightly.

"I don't even need to answer that, I guess," he says.

A laugh puffs out as I take my first drink from the water bottle. Tory nods to my purse, where I've stashed the script I have to memorize. I've actually got a lot of the early part down. I read it over and over every night, picturing the scenes in my head. My mind works like a movie in many ways, where I can visualize something as if I've already seen it. It's like memorizing your favorite parts of movies, only this one hasn't been made yet.

I pull the script out and plop it on the counter. Tory spins it around and reads through the direction. He flips through the first few pages, eventually setting his water down and taking the script in both hands as he leans back against the opposite counter. I slide into an open stool and sit on my hands, which are suddenly super clammy.

"So, your character—" he questions.

"Roni," I fill in. "Veronica, but Roni for short."

"Got it." He nods.

I wait while he reads on, getting a good ten pages in before flipping back to the opening scene. I'm the first thing people see in this film, assuming this part doesn't get left on the editing room floor. It's a tough scene, where Roni is smoking crack with two guys from her high school, her inner dialogue about how she's tired of her mom's boyfriend abusing her.

"This is some fucked up shit," he says, pinching the bridge of his nose and squeezing his eyes shut. "I thought you said this was a romantic comedy?"

"It gets funny near the end," I deadpan.

Tory's eyes pop open and he stares at me for a solid second before laughing.

"Jordan Shotcraft, huh? Yeah, I guess I can see it. His stuff is always this mix of serious and light." He drops his chin and his eyes scan the first page again in silence. Eventually, he looks back up at me, a crooked smile playing at his mouth.

"You know you're going to be stupid famous after this, right?" He rubs the back of his neck as he glares at me with one squinted eye. I'm oddly not very good at dreaming big. I take big breaks one at a time, never expecting them. It keeps me sheltered from disappointment. Landing this role was a big deal, but in my gut, I still expect something to go wrong—movie shelved, me replaced mid-shoot, Jordan getting struck with some huge scandal that renders our movie a flop and sends me into obscurity.

I lift one shoulder, signaling a *whatever,* then deliver my first line.

"The drift to sleep comes on sweet and slow, like drinking molasses. I do this so the high erases all of the fucked up things in my life, like tar oozing over gravel."

My gaze drifts off to another place entirely. I'm not secure enough in my lines yet to be able to look at Tory's face, and I kind of want to take on that feeling of being adrift mentally. After a few seconds pass without him reading anything, though, I'm forced to look at him.

"Oh!" He startles. "Sorry, I . . . just . . . damn!"

"Stop. I don't even know what I'm doing." My chest, though, flutters with butterflies at the compliment. I like that he thinks I'm a little bit good at this.

Tory's gaze sticks on my face for one beat too long, and I get up from my seat to pace, partly to run away from it. I take a few steps around the kitchen island and back while he reads more stage direction. It's an odd juxtaposition with the cacophony of gunfire barreling through the television a dozen or so feet away.

"Hey, Lucas? You mind maybe . . ." Tory cups his ears with both hands. Lucas gives him a blank stare, then jars himself when it dawns on him.

"Oh! My bad," he says, leaning over the arm of the couch and opening a drawer to pull out headphones. It takes him a minute or two to get them synced, and Tory whispers an apology to me while we wait, watching him wrangle with the Bluetooth settings. He gives us a thumbs up and we shoot the same gesture back.

"Jesus, he's a child," I mutter.

Tory laughs quietly.

"Don't tell June that," he says.

"I'm sure she knows. Anyhow, let's start from the cop's first line, yeah?" I pace again, feeling more in character this way, even though on screen I'll be nearly passed out on an abandoned couch in the middle of a fake desert for this scene.

"Hey . . . hey!" Tory gets into character for me, reaching out and shaking an imaginary shoulder.

"Go away, Paul! My mom doesn't want you touching me anymore!" I let loose now that Lucas isn't listening. Strangely, I have no problem watching my own work on-screen later, but having someone hear me deliver lines live and in person makes me sweat like a pig.

"Miss, I don't know who Paul is, but you're under arrest." Tory stands and makes his way closer to me. I freeze at the end of the island and turn my back to him slightly, putting both my hands behind my back, ready for his fake cuffing.

"Fuck you, Officer Friendly!" I slur my words and anticipate a timid touch to my wrists, but Tory grabs them firmly, wrapping one of his hands entirely around both my arms and tugging.

I shirk, both as part of my character and as a natural reaction to his aggressive touch. His hold on me loosens, but I push my arms harder into his palm, encouraging him to keep playing along. Now fully in character, I turn fast and force my face inches from his, my nose close enough to scrape along his cheek. The black in his eyes bleeds into the hazel of his irises, and his nostrils flare with a sharp breath.

"I said I'm done with strange men thinking they can touch me." I speak in a low growl, gritting my teeth and preparing myself to actually bite into Tory's shoulder. Before things get that far, though, his grip falls away from my wrists and he takes a step back, blowing out and running his palm through his hair.

"Damn, sorry. You . . . that was intense," he says, flexing his hand—the one that held me forcefully—a few times at his waist.

Realizing how into it I was, I blush and retreat back to my stool.

"I'm sorry, I was just feeling it. I guess I know this part really well. We can probably skip ahead—"

"No, no. I just need to get some balls I guess and step up to your level." He shakes with a short laugh and rubs at his forehead while reading through the next few lines in the scene.

"I'm not so sure I want you to bite me, if that's cool?" His brow wrinkles while he reads ahead and gives me his request.

"Fair enough." I laugh out. "How about I stick to my seat and you stay on the other side of this thing?" I tap my long, freshly manicured nails on his counter, and he smirks with a nod.

"Deal," he agrees, jumping right back into the text.

We manage to get through my first six scenes in a little over two hours, and we're so absorbed with the story that we don't realize Lucas has pulled the headphones from his head and put his feet up on the couch to nap. Neither of us is sure whether he listened in for any of the performance, and the only reason we discovered Sleeping Beauty is because he snores like a donkey.

"Oh, my God! June is a saint," I say, slipping from my seat and moving closer to Lucas. His lips are actually vibrating with his breath.

"That's nothing. Back in junior high, he sleepwalked. Fucker showed up at our front door at two a.m. in nothing but these cartoon character briefs."

I cover my mouth to mute the laugh his story evokes.

"You're shitting me," I whisper.

Tory shakes his head.

"My dad took a picture, then drove him home. I still have it somewhere. I save that sucker for a rainy day, when I need to call in a *huge* favor."

"Well, then, you should probably find it," I say, suddenly desperate to see it for myself.

I make my way back into the kitchen, twisting the cap off of the new water bottle Tory gave me a few minutes ago. My throat is dry, and my brain is a little fried. Turns out rehearsing lines *is* a lot like studying.

"Hey," I blurt out, remembering a question I had for Tory but forgot to ask. "Why did you think I knew that song you were singing?"

I promised myself I wouldn't bring up our moment in the locker room, but I'm really curious. Maybe it's how good Tory was with his lines that made me think about him singing. He's amazingly natural at performing.

He smiles with his cheeks full of the water he just drank and holds up a finger while he pauses to swallow.

"You actually said the next line in the song. When you yelled, 'I want to go home'? That's the next line." That same music-nerd smile is back. I like this secret side to him.

"Shut up!" I look at him sideways.

He crosses his heart, but I keep my stare steady and my eyes slitted.

"Sing it again," I say, falling into another trap I promised myself I wouldn't. I shouldn't hear him sing again. Hearing it the first time is what stirred up all the weirdness in my head. Yet, I really hope he does.

"You know what? Come here." He motions his head toward the stairs and jogs up them, stopping midway to see if I'm following. I hesitate for a beat, but the temptation and the possibility that his guitar is upstairs are too strong.

We round the short wall that divides the stairs from a small loft space with floor-to-ceiling bookshelves, and Tory runs his thumb along a row of tightly packed albums. I take this opportunity to nose around his upstairs, a place I've never been, not even for one of their infamous parties. It's a strikingly modest home inside despite the grandeur of the outside façade. I guess it's the large open space in the living room where the fireplace towers up twenty feet, a monument of ivory rock with a massive rustic beam sliced through the middle for the world's most ostentatious mantle. The obligatory family portrait sits atop it, the twins maybe seven or eight in the photograph-turned-painting. I was a little surprised to still see it there when we walked in.

Up here, things are tighter, the space more intimate. This loft area has a built-in desk with a computer I assume Tory and Hayden have to share. Their school bags are both tossed in the corner, and phone cords poke out from a charging station on the wall. To the right is a set of double doors—I'm guessing the master bedroom—and behind me, on the opposite end of the house, above the garage, are two doors divided by a bathroom. I already know what Hayden's looks like. He took me on a video chat tour when we first started talking. His room is spotless, like a military man. Something tells me Tory's is probably on the other end of the spectrum.

"Found it!" His exclamation draws me back in. I step closer as he pulls a record from a sleeve. There are probably a hundred or more albums organized on these shelves.

"Wow, this is some collection," I say as he tips the lid up on a sleek black turntable. Tory leans to his side and brings his eyes level with the record as he gently sets it down on the player. A small speaker tucked between a row of books crackles when he turns the device on, and he quickly turns the dial to keep the volume low.

"*Shhh*," he says, holding a finger to his lips, then pointing toward the stairs where Lucas is still sawing dreamy logs.

"I don't think he could hear it at full volume over that racket he's making," I say.

Tory's smile is sweet, and he holds his soft gaze on me for a single blink of his eyes before returning his attention to the record, which is now spinning. He picks up the arm and rests it gently on his thumb, finally engaging it somewhere in the middle of the album. I recognize the melody almost instantly, not that I've heard this song more than once.

"Beach Boys, *Pet Sounds*. Maybe one of the greatest albums of all time." He grins after that statement, maybe expecting me to challenge him. I couldn't. My knowledge of music is limited. I could, however, debate him until Sunday on classic film.

"I think my dad likes this stuff," I say, falling for the sway of the melody.

It sounds just as it did when Tory sang it, minus the threat of a tornado and plus the digital mastering of a music studio.

Tory clicks his tongue against his teeth and shuffles his feet closer to me, holding out a palm. I stare at it for a good, long, awkward while, but finally place my hand in his. He threads our fingers together and pulls me in, his other hand gingerly resting at my waist like a gentleman.

"Time for a music lesson," he says, careful to look anywhere but directly into my eyes. I'm thankful. This, so far, feels safe.

"School me, Salvatore," I say, sparking a short laugh from him.

"Your dad likes this stuff because this stuff is good. Music made in the sixties has backbone. Words mattered, and sound was a constant experiment. Most real music fans would list a dozen albums from this era on a best-of list before even touching something contemporary."

While he's looking away from me, I'm drawn to stare at his eyes. I have no idea who this is that I'm dancing with, but this is not the guy who hands me red cups at parties and asks me when we're gonna bang. This guy is . . . strange. He's interesting, and he has passions. Secret passions that beg the question—

"Why are you not doing something in music?" I ask. We rock slowly in an extremely chaste slow dance, and Tory merely flits his gaze to me, long enough to acknowledge my question.

He shrugs the shoulder that's under my hand as he looks away again.

"I like basketball more," he says.

I blink a few times, staring at the lashes of his too-near-to-me eyes while I wait for him to explain further. I realize soon, though, that it's that simple. He has a passion for his game and keeps music as a love.

"Huh," I say.

His eyes move to mine again, then leave immediately.

"*Huh,* what?"

"Huh, that you have, like, hobbies, I guess." I laugh through my nose. A slight shift in my body and a tiny step from him as we both laugh brings us closer, and suddenly my chin is resting on top of my own hand, which is now comfortable on his shoulder.

We turn together, our laughter silences. The song soothes, and if I could manage to hold myself up, I could fall asleep right here. This is not appropriate.

"Show me some of the others," I say, slipping out of his arms and moving my attention to the rows of albums on the shelves. He lets me go easily, probably glad I broke things up. I think maybe music can be a drug. I think maybe surviving a tornado with someone is a bit of a drug, too. That's it.

"What kind of music do you like?" he asks, pulling a few albums out sideways to peer at the covers, standing at the other end of the long row.

"Everything, I guess. I mean . . . I don't know. I guess I listen to what's popular." I kinda feel schooled standing in front of a collection like this.

"Well, when you were little, was there a song, maybe a hit, that you just *had* to *have* so you could play it over and over again?" His finger is teasing the corner of a silver album cover.

I suck in my lip and think back to junior high, and then the years before. I don't think my life really has a soundtrack, and that's maybe a little sad. Before I realize it, my forehead is creased from the weight of my frown.

"You know what, let me try this," Tory says, letting me off the hook. I step closer to peek at what he's pulling out, but he holds up his hand and shoos me away.

"Okay, fine," I relent, sitting down on the thick carpet in the center of the wooden floor. I let my fingertips pet the strands while Tory does his thing, carefully putting the first album away and blowing dust from the new one. He hovers over the player as he lowers the needle, and a familiar beat flows through the speakers. I nod with the rhythm as Tory kneels down and eventually sits facing me. He leans back, digging his hands into the plush cream rug and pulls his knees up, swaying them with the beat. As I stare at the dead leaf stuck on the knee of his pants, I smile; recognition is settling in.

"This . . . yes! My mom used to play this all the time on our way to auditions. She said it was her 'power jam!'" I exclaim. I sing along with a few of the words until I get to the title of the song in the chorus and Tory sings along with me.

"'Rhythm Nation'!"

He exhales a celebratory type of laugh, his head falling back as if he's proud to have unearthed another thing I like. Perhaps I have a soundtrack after all.

"My dad was *in love* with Janet Jackson. She came to the state fair when Hayd and I were like six or something, and he dragged us along. Hayden fell asleep but I stood on my chair and just watched my dad sing every word and stare at her like she was some goddess." His gaze drifts off, caught in his memory, and the longer he's gone away, the more I realize what these albums—what us playing them right now—is all about. He misses his dad, misses being a family.

"It will get easier," I say.

"Huh?" He stirs, shaking away the dust of wherever he'd been as he looks at me. "Oh, yeah, I know."

"I won't say it gets better; it doesn't. It just gets easier." I hold his stare and feel a little sorry that I maybe dashed a flicker of hope. "It's an amazing collection." I change the subject and look toward the bookcase again. Tory follows suit. A heavy breath lifts and collapses his chest.

"All of these are my dad's. If he leaves permanently, they'll go with him. But I won't be here anymore, I guess, so it's whatever." His gaze shifts to me for a beat, then to the floor. He sits forward and brings his hands to his lap as his legs fold together. Right now, we're two kids playing records, but the longer we sit in silence, Janet marching along in the backdrop, simple leaves the situation and complicated seeps in.

"My brother treating you right?" His head cocks his head to the side and his eyes level me with a look that feels like it's hiding more.

"Yeah," I say. Nervous energy jolts at my insides, so I shift my position and tuck my legs under my body, leaning to one side. I'm careful to keep my focus on the floor, on the albums, on my own fingers and knuckles and skin. The song fades out, a new one begins, and I rush around mentally in search of something new to say while also silently begging Tory to ask me easier questions than the ones I fear are dancing around his head.

"He's a good guy," he continues.

"Uh huh." I nod.

My pulse is drowning in my ears, the beat heavy, leaving me dizzy. I spare a quick glance up to meet Tory's gaze, hoping maybe he's looking elsewhere. Or maybe simply smiling, happy to see his brother happy. Me happy. But that's not what I get at all. My chest squeezes when our eyes lock, his mouth a soft smile that hints at regret. My lips part and I draw in a quick breath, thinking for a moment that I'll say something—*anything*—that acknowledges there is something unspoken and heavy in the room.

"Hey, I heard the music."

Lucas's welcome presence breaks the tension, and I take the out, climbing to my feet and putting more distance between Tory and me. Tory stretches out his legs and crosses them at the ankles, tipping his chin to grin at his friend.

"Just dusting off some of my dad's gems," he says.

He and Lucas seem to speak without words, staring at each other with knowing smiles that verge on the cusp of words, as if they're about to trade insults with each other or something.

"Right, well . . . I'm going to take off and thought since I'm leaving, maybe Abby needs a ride home?" Lucas turns his attention to me, his eyes wide in a way that signals I'm to leave now. It feels oddly parental, but also . . . he's right.

"Sounds good, yeah. We got through a lot. Just let me get my stuff in the kitchen," I say, moving toward the stairs. I get a few steps down before pausing and making eye contact with Tory again, his expression erased from any of the strangeness from before. "Hey, thank you, by the way. I feel really solid on this now."

"Don't mention it," Tory says, moving his focus back to Lucas so they can continue whatever weird-ass staring match they have going on. "We can pick it up again Saturday."

My mouth pops open, ready to turn down the offer, but before I'm able to push out the words, something inside me makes me stop. I say nothing and instead descend the rest of the way into the kitchen, shoveling the script into my purse and hooking it over my shoulder in a smooth, brisk move through the rest of the house. I'm sitting in Lucas's truck before I take another breath. Lucas, however, doesn't come down for another fifteen minutes.

NINE

TORY

I didn't need a lecture. I knew exactly what I was doing, where the line was, and how I was walking all over it.

Lucas gave me one anyway. I guess that's his job, though. I'm used to getting different kinds of lectures from my best friend. Usually, he tells me not to eat something that says *fire hot* or drink one shot too many before jumping from the roof into the pool. Dumb shit.

Abby's a different story. I know what I'm doing, and I know it's wrong. My feelings are wrong, the goddamn dreams I'm having are wrong, and this animosity I'm developing against my brother is wrong. It's not his fault that he figured out how to talk to Abby like a human before I did. Hell, he had no clue I had a *real* thing for her. I flirt with everyone. Abby's just the only one to ever shoot me down, over and over. Me hitting on her and her telling me to eff off became our routine, a one-act show that we perform at every party and in every class we have together.

And then, I don't know . . .

I even liked the rejection. It was attention, a push-pull that was a challenge, yeah, but also, she has this edge that feels, I don't know . . . a lot like me?

I have to stop this cycle, though, otherwise I'm going to spin out. I slept through Wednesday, and I've been about as social as a toad all day at school, but I can't completely turn away from the outside world just because I have a crush that hurts to deal with. It's time to find my groove again, especially since Hayden and I are heading right from practice to our first family therapy session. If I bring this mood in there, nobody is going to make progress, which is what my mom keeps preaching this is all about. *Making progress.* Some fucking family goal.

The junior high moved their players outside for practice, which has all of these twelve- and thirteen-year-olds pissed as hell at us. One kid calls me a douchebag on my way into the locker room I long ago outgrew.

"Yeah, you too, kid," I say back, getting a rise out of Hayden and a few of the other guys nearby.

I dump my gym bag on the bench and change out of my jeans and sweatshirt into shorts and a T-shirt, then take a seat to wipe down the bottoms of my basketball shoes. Hayden drops his stuff next to me and I catch the photo on his phone screen of him with his arms wrapped around Abby. The angle is weird because it's a selfie. Couple shit.

Deep breath, Tory. Deep breath.

"Hey, nice job landing Cortez, man. You tap that yet?" Chaz, whose real name is Chad but insists on forcing everyone to use the stupid z, tabs his shoes against my brother's back as he walks by and takes a seat on the next bench over.

"Oh, ha, yeah. Thanks, man. And I don't-I don't talk about that stuff." Hayden's respectful, but his grin is super evasive and full of innuendo. I drop my shoes to the floor and let them land with a heavy smack against the concrete. Chaz and Hayden both look my direction.

"Sorry." I shrug.

Not sorry.

"That's gotta really piss you off, right?" Chaz's question lingers unanswered. I don't bother to look up because I assume he's just goading my brother about not getting laid or some shit. Frankly, I'm glad Hayden isn't talking about it. If he's gotten to that level with Abby, I'm going to have a really hard time ejecting that visual from my head.

"Ah, I see. Silent treatment, huh?" Chaz keeps going, and I finally look up to catch him leaning forward, arms resting on his knees so he can stare at me like a major asshole.

My brow wrinkles.

"What the fuck?" I glare at him for a full second, then lean forward and slip my feet into my shoes, lacing them tight around my ankles.

"Ha! Baby Hayden sweeping in and taking what big brother thought was his. Yo, your brother hates you right now," Chaz taunts, thinking he's super clever playing around with the meaningless fact that I slid out of my mom's vagina a full minute before Hayden did. What an ass!

I stand without reacting, finding inner strength I didn't know I had, and stop with my stance square with Chaz. I palm the side of his face a few times with a playful force.

"Why don't you just run along now and get the water for us starters, yeah?" I wink and flash a tight smile before turning and heading into the gym, catching the deep *oooooh* that sounds behind me from my teammates. Hayden's voice better be in that mix.

After jogging a few laps around the gym that once seemed so big when I was little, we all circle up at center court and begin our stretches. The tension left from my little moment with Chaz is still very much present, and there's hardly a sound other than the occasional snicker from someone trying damn hard to keep their mouth shut. Coach Newsome is a nice guy, but he doesn't do drama during practice. He calls stuff like this "playtime" and I've seen him kick guys out of the gym—and once, off the team—for letting girl trouble interfere with the business on the court.

I turn to face Hayden and nod for him to go first for our hamstring stretches. He lies in front of me and lifts his right leg, holding it straight for me to push toward his body. I try not to look down because I know he's staring right at me.

"Hey, thanks for running lines with Abby the other day. She said you were actually pretty good at it," Hayden says.

I blink slowly, tempted to leave my eyes shut. *He's talking. Why is he talking?*

I glance down and nod my chin.

"Yeah, no prob." His focus hangs on to my eyes, a hint of suspicion in the way they dim. I raise my brows and shake my head a little in question, calling him on his silent question. I know he's got one.

"You do hate it, don't you?"

Fuck.

I sigh and roll my neck and lean forward, stretching him a little more, probably to punish him. He takes it.

"Hayden, I don't *anything.* I'm just trying to get through practice then to this therapy shit that's not going to work so I can go home and go to sleep. That's literally all I have going on in my head right now." I let go of his leg and purse my lips when our eyes meet. His head tilts just a hair, trying to read me better. I snap my fingers, calling for his other leg.

I assume he's letting things go when he gives me his left leg and I look away, repeating the stretch in blessed silence. Once he's done, I squat to lay as he stands to work on me. I give him my leg while my head rests on my threaded fingers and I look off to the side. But before he pushes my leg forward, he grasps my foot in both hands, his fingers squeezing into the top of my foot hard enough that I feel it through my thick-ass shoe.

"Hey," I protest, jerking my foot but unable to break free.

Hayden's jaw is set and his eyes are searing into me, and I wonder if he has a hidden camera near dad's albums.

"You need to take it easy on Mom." This is so out of left field that the only reaction I can possibly have is laughter.

"You're fucking kidding me, right?" I shake my head, amused. Hayden clearly isn't joking, though. I'm so struck by it because no matter how many ways I bend the truth, I'm still on Dad's side.

"You don't hear her cry at night? Your cold shoulder is killing her," my brother says, finally pushing my leg forward to stretch.

I stare at him with my mouth agape.

"*I'm* killing her." I repeat this as if it might suddenly make sense. It doesn't.

I switch legs.

"Just . . ." My brother pauses, grimacing as he pushes forward on my leg. Hayden doesn't like conflict. He never has. And he's partly right—*though, no fucking way I'll admit that.* My parents have never been picture perfect, and they fought all the time. They also made up a lot, too. Dad went out of his way to make sure my mom had whatever she wanted. She just didn't want him.

"I won't pick sides in therapy. Is that what you're asking?" I chew at the inside of my mouth and wait for him to admit it. He finally agrees, nodding once and letting go of my leg. I hold my hand up, partly for a lift but also for a gentleman's agreement of sorts. I pat my brother's back a few times with a heavy hand and Chaz can't help the commentary.

"Aww, you guys work it out?" he says.

"Yeah, we took care of things while you were over there on the bench," I reply, not bothering to look his direction. My brother snorts out a laugh.

We muddle through practice, as good as practice can be in a gym that feels too small for our bodies and with rims that can be lowered to my height. We work on plays mostly, which is boring for the guys like Chaz who barely have a role, so at least I get to watch him stand around and whine with the irked look on his face.

I was hoping for more of an outlet though, because even after we leave the gym there's a clenched fist in my chest, like I want to scream or hit something. It's the anxiety from this impending doom that Hayden and I are driving toward. He's driving, actually. I'm riding shotgun, preparing mental lists of all the passive aggressive things I'll want to say but won't because I promised.

"You don't have to speed there," I say the closer we get.

"We're late, so . . . kinda do."

Hayden's back teeth are gnashed. I recognize it because I do the same damn thing when I'm stressed. I'm doing it now. We have different reasons, though. Hayden hates being late. I hate having to do shit I don't believe in.

We pull in, parking between the minivan and my dad's truck. How incredibly prophetic. Hayden rushes out of the car, but I take a moment to myself to let what's happening really sink in. I can't remember the last time I truly idolized both of my parents. I still do my dad, I guess. I just don't see him now, haven't really in a while. Even when he was at home, he was never *home*. He travels a lot for work at a job that bought the house we live in free and clear and has kept both of my parents in new cars for my entire life. Hayden and I share because my brother is practical and insists on it. Dad told me on the side that he'd get me my own ride, but it never felt that important. Wish I'd taken him up on it now, though. If I had, I'd still be on my way to this session while Hayden was here right on time, waiting for my ass to show up.

My brother raps his knuckles on my window. I don't bother to look, breathing out hard enough to flap my lips as I push the door open and join him out of the car.

"I was enjoying the last bit of quiet I'll have for a while," I say.

"Like you have ever wanted things quiet," my brother scoffs.

Touché.

Our parents are in the waiting room for the family therapist, Dr. Majestic. I thought my dad was shitting me when he texted me the info for Hayden and me to come, but no, that's really this doctor's name. It's going to take superhero powers to fix the broken things in this household. Dr. Majestic sounds a lot more like a villain.

"Son," my dad says, reaching toward me first to shake my hand. We make the same uncomfortable, fake smiles at each other because neither of us wants to be here. We're a lot alike, stubborn with a veil of easygoing.

"Hey, Dad," Hayden says after a few seconds, nodding to our pops.

"Hey, kiddo."

"*Psh*," our mom sounds.

"What, I can't call him kiddo? I suppose that's babying him?" My dad is on edge, which is not promising for the next fifty minutes. I looked up the fees and at four hundred an hour, I hope my parents spend less time on childish sounds and button-pushing when we get in the room.

None of us are sitting, which is typical. We're the family that, when we go out to eat, hovers impatiently around the hostess stand even if the wait is an hour. We have this unspoken strategy that standing makes other people uncomfortable so they seat us faster. It works.

"Gio? Natalia?" My parents turn in sync.

"*Hmm*?" they both say.

My eyes fall to the floor and I lead the way toward the incredibly tall woman standing with her door held wide open, welcoming—like the gates to hell. I glance up when I pass her and give her a crooked smile. She probably thinks it's my way of greeting her and expressing how upset I am over all of this, but really, I just think it's cool she's my height.

The rest of the family files in after me, the four of us cramming onto a sofa made for three. The black leather is stiff and it squeaks with our weight, a sound that repeats each time any of us moves. This won't be distracting at all.

"I have other chairs," Dr. Majestic says, indicating a high-back recliner pushed against the wall.

"I'm on it," I say, happily volunteering. I grab the chair by the arms and slide it a few feet forward so it's now part of the circle of death. I get in and immediately pull the handle, kicking my feet up and crossing my ankles.

"Salvatore." My mom's voice has that scold-tinge to it, like when I was a kid and made a farty noise in the back seat of the car during a long drive somewhere. I give her a sideways look and consider putting up a challenge. Hayden clears his throat and I give in.

"Fine," I say, lowering the foot rest and sitting up enough to rest my elbows on the arms and fold my hands together on my lap. I'm ready for testimony.

"All right, first . . . I'd like to congratulate you all on this very important first step. I want you to take a minute and congratulate yourselves, quietly or silently. Thank yourselves for this. I know coming here isn't easy, and the fact you rose to the challenge means you all have something invested in this family unity."

My dad breaks first, puffing out a short laugh that he quickly covers with a cough. My mom gives him a stern look, which he pretends not to see. I enjoy the show while my brother shrinks, his head falling into his shoulders as he sits on the rubbery sofa between them. I can't believe I'm here.

Congratulations, Tory. You did it.

Yeah, this Dr. Majestic is full of it.

"I'm familiar with your file and I understand the circumstances, but I've found that the things we report on paper are often not the *real* story. Why don't we start at the root, being open and honest. Shall we?" Dr. Majestic scans the room, getting nonverbal commitments from each of us. I shrug, just like my dad, while Hayden and my mom nod.

"Good. Tory, let's start with you."

Aww, fuck.

"How has your parents' split made you feel?"

The heat from four pairs of eyes is instantly on me.

"Ha!" I laugh out, mostly from the audacity of the question. My mouth hangs open, and I look first to my dad, who is of absolutely no help, his eyes clearly saying he doesn't want to be here. I move to Hayden next, who has a poker face that would save any gambler, and then there's Mom—oh-so hopeful, expectant Mom. She wants me to be her good little boy.

My head swings back to the front and I deadpan to our doctor with dim eyes and a sour mouth. "Fine. I guess."

"Tory," my mom cuts in.

"No," the doctor says, halting her. "Let him talk."

I raise a brow and turn my head a hint to the side while staring at her.

"I did talk. That's all I've got." So far, my plan on how to handle this is falling to shit, but I have yet to break my promise to Hayden, so, hey—win!

"Why do you think you answered that way?" She's not going to make this easy. She's needling, chewing on the tip of her pen and leaning in as if I'm about to get raw.

"There are a lot of germs on your pen," I say, pointing to the spot where her teeth have locked onto the clicking part. She lets go, smirking slightly as she leans back in her chair, which matches mine. I wonder if she ever gets to put her feet up.

"I bet you're known as the funny one."

Wow, she's a genius.

"Among other things," I say, winking.

"Tory." This time, the stern warning comes from my father. I shift and release my hold on my hands, exhaling on his command.

I rub my face, digging into my eyes that feel puffy from too much sleep. Resting my face on my palm, leaning on the arm of the chair, I stare in thought at the strands of the very expensive-looking rug that's centered in this room. It doesn't fill it completely, just enough to stretch under the sofa, the doctor's desk and these two chairs. My chair is an intruder.

"I don't know, maybe I'm disappointed." I grimace and glance up to meet the doctor's approving eyes.

"Go on," she says.

I draw a long breath through my nose and shake my head, letting my stare wander off again into the swirling pattern on the carpet.

"He's not the favorite anymore; that's how he feels," Hayden says, his unexpected contribution widening my eyes so much they actually burn.

"Hayden," my mom says, a totally different tone than the one she used with my name. This one is nurturing, and perhaps a bit pathetic.

"That's how I feel, anyway. I feel like my brother was always the king, and now that life at home isn't picture-perfect, he's less . . . shiny." My brother's eyes flit to mine a few times, but he doesn't stick around long. Probably because I'm full-on gawking.

"I was a king?" I laugh at the statement, thrusting down on the chair handle and kicking my feet up again because *fuck this!* "Go on. Please."

My dad's brow is pulled in tight, maybe as surprised by this outburst as I am. I'm starting to think, though, that maybe this is calculated. My brother doesn't back down, holding my stare as long as I hold his. The longer I look into eyes just like mine, the more animosity stews in my belly. Hayden's eyes, however, haze with a sinister fog. That bit in the gym, the stretching of my legs and asking me to be on my best behavior here, it was never about Mom or this session. It was about Abby, and those things Chaz put in his head.

My lips curl of their own accord, my chest gradually bubbling with laughter until it finally erupts and I'm practically cackling, minutes into our family therapy session. Look who's the crazy man in here!

I smile with a wide open mouth and look off to the side, trying to form words.

"Unbelievable." That's the only thing I can say.

"Why do you think your brother was our favorite?" our mom asks, twisting to the side to face my brother.

"Because I am?" I even surprise myself with the words. I don't mean it, but now I'm just pissed.

"Tory," my dad says, only the second time he's spoken since we got in here, and both times it was my name.

I push my feet down again and look my father in the eyes. He doesn't want to make any of this work. He's going through the motions. There's no way he is forgiving my mom for what she did. And there's probably no way I'll ever be able to either. This is where the ride ends. My dad isn't coming to any more of our games, driving in from the city when he's not traveling. He's taking his albums, too. And maybe I'll see him a weekend here and there.

All of those frames in my mind are just bullshit. Me hoisting up my first MVP trophy and him holding me on his shoulder, him placing my hand on the right strings to make a G chord on the guitar, him telling me to be careful who I love because if I pick wrong, she's going to chew my heart up and spit it out. He wasn't talking about me on that last one; he was sharing experience.

"You know what?" I stand, knowing my pocket is light of keys and that my shit is still in the car. I've taken busses before, and it's not that cold out tonight. I could use a walk. "I'm done. You guys figure out whatever you need to in here. I'm going to take care of things my way."

I get to the door before my dad stands to utter my name a third time. I stop him before he does.

"Don't act like you want to be here," I say. His confession is all over his face, his eyes relenting first, followed by the tight line of his lips and the sag in his shoulders. He used to seem like this strong, amazing man. Now he's just a shell.

I push open the door and meet the gaze of the front secretary. She doesn't speak, and she doesn't even look surprised to see someone making a run for it. I bet this happens all the time. I hold up a hand and tell her to have a good evening, then step out onto the cold sidewalk in my practice jersey and shorts, still cold from old sweat. I tug on the car handle, glad my brother forgot to lock our car again, and pull out my sweatshirt, throwing it over my head and slamming the door behind me. I stand at the edge of the parking lot for a minute, looking up and down the street for signs of a bus line. Traffic is steady but light. I look over my shoulder one last time, giving my brother a last shot at redemption, but he isn't coming after me.

I want to choke him, but I also understand this is all coming from somewhere else. Hayden isn't good with change, and this has been a major adjustment. He's lashing out, and I'm the one who can take it. But I won't pretend there wasn't a trace of something else in that long gape he steamrolled me with.

Just start walking.

My legs travel north at first, but unsure how to get around the highway, I end up doubling back a few roads over. I finally find a creek bed that runs underneath most of the big streets between where I am and our neighborhood. I amuse myself for a while with my breath, puffing out thick, icy smoke then slicing it in half with my hand. That works for about half a mile and then I get anxious at my own lack of direction. I start to run, thankful for my lung capacity, and after about three miles, find myself in the last place I ever thought I would be at a time like this—at the end of Abby Cortez's driveway.

TEN

ABBY

We look like hoarders. Between legal contracts for some of my residuals, contracts from the production company for the film, travel plans, waivers, and the files upon files from my parents' custody battle, I'm just glad nobody in this house smokes. There is so much paper for kindling, we would go up in flames.

"Abby, babe, I swear there's a knock on our door. Can you . . ?" My mom's glasses are perched at the end of her nose, her fingers dug deep into her temple, and the light above her like a heavy spot on whatever it is she's reading. It's something from my dad, but she doesn't talk about it with me if she can avoid it.

"You need to eat, and then you need to go to bed, Ma," I say, hopscotching my way through the living room over papers and a few scattered pieces of laundry.

"I will. I just have to finish this last—"

"Yeah, yeah. You always say that. Just one more page," I tease. My mom looks up at me and smiles with her eyes, her mouth too tired to make the trip.

"Soon. I promise," she says. I wonder if she remembers the pencil she shoved in her hair to hold it up out of her eyes.

"Okay," I holler, turning around while opening the front door.

Tory D'Angelo looks back at me, and he looks like he's been in a fight. Only he hasn't been hit, he's only been emotionally tortured.

"Mom, I'll be right in," I say, stepping out to our front porch to talk with him. My mom hasn't seen either of the twins in years. She doesn't even know I'm dating one of them. All we talk about lately are travel plans and court dates. Seems like a confusing way to bring my love life up to her, what with an evening visit from the brother I'm *not* dating.

"Hey, something wrong?" I lead Tory down to the first step, motioning for him to sit next to me.

"I think I need to stand. I'm too amped up," he says, his feet in constant movement between the two stairs of our porch. He's a constant whirl of up and down, and he looks like he's just finished a marathon.

"You, uh, out for a run?" His hair is slick with sweat. He glances up, straining his eyes, and runs his hand through his hair a few times to push it from his forehead. A crooked smile plays at his lips for a flash of a second.

"This is kinda weird, I know." His eyes flutter closed and he tangles his hands behind his neck for a stretch, exhaling while bouncing on his toes a few times. When his eyes open on mine again, he seems more settled, less like a stray dog who just dodged a shit ton of traffic.

"Let's just say therapy did not go well." A sarcastic smile plays at his lips, tightly closed and pulled up in the corners.

"It never does," I say, making him laugh lightly.

My plan to keep our talk outside falls apart as my mom opens the door and leans against the door frame, holding her own tired body up.

"It's freezing out. Come inside. I'll make some cocoa." She dips her chin so she can peer at me over her glasses, brows raised as she shifts her eyes to my male visitor a couple times, hinting for an explanation.

"Mom, you remember Tory D'Angelo, right? He threw up at June's fourth grade birthday party."

"Come on," Tory whispers in exasperation.

I glance at him and shrug. It's the one thing I know will stick in my mom's memory.

"Oh, yes, the green cake. Glad to see you're feeling better," my mom jokes.

Her reaction manages to pull a laugh from Tory and he drags his tired legs up the step and across my porch, reaching out his hand.

"Much better. You sure about that cocoa, though?" He cocks a brow, somehow able to charm a real hard-ass like my mom with his personality. Her lips pucker with the smile of a blushing school girl, but he doesn't have her completely fooled.

Patting her hand on his cheek a few times, she says, "I'll get you a bib."

My mom leads us inside and Tory glances at me with a wry smile.

"I see where you get it," he says.

As my mom is riffling through our cabinets looking for stray packets of hot chocolate, Tory takes a meandering tour of the state of my home. Our house isn't as big as his, and it isn't fancy by any means, but it is historic.

"It was my grandparents' house on Mom's side. My grandfather built it," I say, feeling the need to narrate his experience. He runs a hand along a wooden sill under a stained glass window that overlooks our dining table.

"It must be a pretty cool feeling to stand back when you hammer in that last nail and see a house you put together." He continues to touch the little details, like the corner nook bookcase that holds my grandmother's dishes, and the chair railing that lines almost every wall, from the front door on to the back of the house.

Eventually, he turns his attention to the table, littered with documents and my mom's two spare pair of reading glasses haphazardly tossed in the mix. It's strange having him here, especially when Hayden usually stops at the door. It's as if I've unintentionally built two worlds, one where the boy I'm dating kisses me in his car and takes me out for burgers, and this one, where shit feels hard. Tory, he can walk in between.

"This is the best I could do," my mom says, walking over with two mugs in her hand, the strings from what look like tea bags dangling from the side. She carefully sets them on the edge of the table before clearing a little space by stacking folder on top of folder.

"You like tea?" I quirk a brow at Tory.

"Love it," he answers, for my mom's benefit, while shaking his head no to me. I pucker a smile.

We pull out chairs and sit, the rounded corner of the table barely dividing us, and I lift my mug to dunk the bag up and down. I wiggle my brows to Tory to hint that he can do the same until my mom leaves. He does.

"Tory, it was very nice to meet the older version of you. Please, if you're going to throw up, the powder room is . . ." My mom points to the door under the stairwell.

"Thank you, Ms. Cortez," Tory plays along.

"Call me Denise," she insists. She turns her focus to me.

"Baby, I'm done. I'll see you in the morning." My mom moves to stand behind me so she can kiss the top of my head. As she does, I reach an arm up and hug her from behind.

"Don't forget the pencil," I say as she shuffles away. A glance over my shoulder catches her pulling it out and tossing it on the small table where we drop our keys. She heads up the stairs with heavy thumps, and when she's out of sight, Tory puts his mug down and pulls off his sweatshirt.

"We like the heat in the winter." I grimace.

"It's fine," he says, his head finally free from the fabric. He runs his hand through his hair a few times to straighten it, then rolls the sweatshirt up and sets it on the table. He's still wearing his practice jersey and shorts.

"Long day?" I look him up and down.

He blows out a long stream of air and stares at me, the amped part of him finally seeming calm.

"Longest ever," he says.

He twists in his chair so he faces the table and pulls my script toward him, the pages now curling from me reading and carrying it around.

"You up for a little reading?" he asks.

I shake my head.

"I don't think you have it in you," I respond.

His lips pout for a second but eventually he nods and pushes the paper away, clearly exhausted.

"You're probably right."

I study him while he scans the contents of my table, all the ugly and exciting things about my life on display. It's like the ingredients for Abby soup, a little sweet and a little sour.

"Want to talk about therapy?" He's staring at the latest argument my father submitted, but I'd rather talk about him than me.

"I'm not sure," he says, distracted and distant.

"Okay, so . . ." I let my voice trail off.

We sit in silence, Tory glancing over the highlights of my parents' divorce while my stomach knots in this shameful squeeze, knowing how much worse I've made it all. I've never quite gotten over the sense that some of their relationship's demise was my fault. The frenzied legal state it's at now is most *definitely* my fault. It's because I'm selfish, and that might be what ruins me—my mom for sure. I have a feeling Tory's in that place now, the very beginning of it. I wish he knew his brother was right there with him. They could help each other. I had to swim through the swamp on my own.

"I should put that on my resume," I say, needing to break the quiet.

"Huh?" He pushes away the page he was reading with a flick of his finger and turns his attention back to me, his hands resting in his lap.

"Bargaining chip. That's what I am in this whole thing. I'm a bargaining chip for my parents. I don't really blame my mom, because she's the one who has also been a parent along with being a manager, but it still feels kinda like—" I cut my words short when Tory interrupts.

"Like every other kid we know gets to grow up normal and we got ripped off?"

"Exactly," I say. My forehead pinches as I consider that for a moment. "Though, pretty much all of our friends are from fractured families, so we really aren't missing out."

"We're missing out," he says swiftly. "They're just missing out, too."

He stands and wanders around my kitchen, moving on to the hallway plastered in framed photos of me through the years. Most of them are headshots, but some are pictures from performances. My favorite is the one of me in tap shoes with a giant heart covered in sequins around my head.

"You were always a diva, weren't you?" he teases, tapping his finger on the glass of the frame. I move in closer to cut the glare and take in my ear-to-ear, full-teeth-showing smile.

"I'm certainly *always on,*" I joke.

"Not always," he replies. I look to my right and meet his waiting stare. It isn't that he suddenly sees me, but rather that he maybe always has and finally understands my fabric.

"Therapy . . ." I work to bring things back to him and his needs, but he's having none of it.

"Show me more," he says, moving down the wall and pivoting at the stairs. "Your room up here?"

He points.

"Yeah," I croak out.

He takes the steps slowly, probably not wanting to ruin his good graces with my mom. I follow, noting how he takes time to look at every photo on the way up. The ones here are more personal, family portraits that include people who are no longer alive. My favorite is the last one near the top of the steps, which attracts Tory's attention. He pauses there, waiting for me to catch up to him as I climb the last three or four stairs.

"You in a wedding or something?" he asks.

"No, it was my fifteenth. We went down to Miami for my *quinceañera*. Most of my family is down there, which is why my mom prefers to be up here because my aunts and cousins are nosy, and bossy. But that's also where my *abuela* lived." I run my finger along her form in the photo. I felt so grown up on that day, so celebrated and loved. My father even showed up, and for a full weekend, he and my mom didn't argue once.

"You said *lived,*" Tory notes.

I nod softly and turn to meet his gaze.

"She died last year. She was in a nursing home down in Florida, and Mom and I hadn't been to see her in almost a year." I feel the burn of tears threaten to expose themselves, so I clear my throat and move past Tory to lead him toward my room.

Hayden hasn't been up here. My mom is never home when he picks me up. I never invite him inside, and he never asks, yet more than anything I want to show Tory this personal window into my world.

We're both hushed as we move in the opposite direction from my mother's door. The spare room between is overrun with paperwork and costumes. It was supposed to be our business office, but it's become more of a dumping ground for things that don't require our immediate attention or that don't fit me anymore.

I push down on the door handle to make the click as quiet as possible, then slip inside, Tory knowing he should hurry. I close the door behind him and flip on the small purple lamp next to my bed. It paints my room in color. I don't bother to kick away the clothes I left on the floor or hide the makeup scattered around my vanity, and Tory doesn't even seem to notice any of it's there. He continues his trip through my life in pictures, now standing in front of the corkboard next to my closet door. It's filled with pictures, most of them things I've printed out from my phone.

"Why is June always so grumpy?" He points to the one I took the night of his party a few months back, when June got locked in the garage with Lucas. I laugh and pull my phone from my pocket to sort through and find more images of my friend.

"It's sort of this thing I do with her. I take random pictures of her expressions. I won't lie, I love to catch her when she's pissed off. It pushes her buttons, and maybe I like the negative reinforcement." I laugh, handing him my phone.

He takes it, sliding through a few of them and wincing at the ones that are truly bad.

"I know," I say, covering my face in fake shame. "But it's not like I print all of them."

"June knows you do this?" He turns the phone to show me the one in which her cheeks are puffed out and her face is red. She was about to punch me in the shoulder for that one.

I smile and nod.

"She does. I give her the right to rip them off the board if she hates them. She knows they make me happy, though."

Tory's face scrunches and his brows lift as he shakes his head, not totally understanding my most important female relationship. He doesn't have to. I'm sure he has weird traditions with Lucas or his brother, and I *so* don't want to know about them.

He hands me back my phone, but on the exchange, my hand covers his, and we both jerk back, like we touched a hot skillet mid-air. My phone tumbles to the floor, and I giggle with embarrassment while he apologizes profusely and we both bend down to retrieve it. We stop when our heads are an inch from banging into one another and I brace myself, grabbing his shoulders and falling forward to my knees.

"Whoa," he hums, steadying me with his hands on my hips.

My adrenaline-fueled smile mixes with a breathy laugh until I look up and we come face-to-face. Every molecule between us is palpable; the air has a taste to it, somewhere between sweetness and intoxicating liquor. My lips part with a breath and his eyes flit to my open mouth. We're slow dancing without moving, facing each other on our knees, alone in my room, which I purposely cloaked in mood lighting. I can't lie to myself any more. I'm painfully attracted to Tory D'Angelo. I'm also regrettably committed to his brother.

We're young, and relationships at our age are so fluid, and if it were anyone else, this would just be a life lesson, a moment of growth or an innocent mistake fanned by teenage hormones. But it's Tory, and then Hayden.

I swallow hard. His gaze falls to my throat and back to my eyes.

"What happened at therapy?"

In his world, it's the worst possible time for this question, but it's also probably the best. Things are going on between us that need time to sort themselves out, just as I'm sure there are things happening in his head that need attention. I'm not sure if he realizes it or not, but Tory needs someone to listen.

"No judgement," I continue.

We're inches apart, a breath away from making dangerous decisions.

"Why are you with my brother?" His stare is unrelenting. My stomach is sick but at the same time, my heart is pounding. I am the center of a tug-of-war, the part of the rope that is fraying. I don't know how to keep it from splitting, but I do know that his question cuts to the very core of it all. He reaches forward and tucks a strand of hair behind my ear, and his hand never leaves, his thumb tracing the small inch of space along my temple, then making a slow pass along the cut of my jaw toward my lips. I turn into it and let my eyes close, waiting for the alarm to sound in my head that makes me stop.

"Don't," I say, getting to my feet and shaking my head. "You're just avoiding the question, and I know you're struggling, too. We can be friends, Tory. Just like June and you are friends."

He falls back on his calves and positions himself like a catcher, arms resting on his knees, head cocked to one side and a faint yet intensely confident smile playing at his lips.

"Abby . . . you and I can't be friends like that, and you know it." He blinks once, slowly, and I'm tempted to push him off balance and watch him land on his ass.

"I told Hayden I'd call him. You should go," I say.

A quick inhale flares his nostrils and his body shakes once with a short laugh. He gets to his feet, his eyes making a slow drag around my room as if he's memorizing it to infiltrate the space at some later date. He nods eventually and moves toward my door, stopping to look at my board of photos one more time. He tugs one loose and pinches it, holding it close to his face for a long second before tossing it on the floor between us.

"You tell me we look like friends in that photo," he says, leaving me with a short, challenging glare. He pats his hand on the edge of my doorframe as he leaves my room and peers over his shoulder.

"I'll show myself out."

I remain frozen until I hear the click of the door downstairs. My space still smells like him, my skin still vibrates from the place his hand touched my skin, my heart still pounds so hard I feel it in my throat.

My phone vibrates in my pocket and I pull it out, knowing I'll see the image of Hayden's smile to show that he's calling. I glance at the screen just long enough to swipe to answer, then fix my eyes on the Polaroid of me and Tory at last month's school carnival. I paid ten dollars to smash a plate of whipped cream into his face to raise money for the basketball team, and I got to keep this photo as a memento. Have I never really looked at it before? Or was I just ignoring it all along.

"Hey, Abs. Sorry it's so late. Our session was . . ." He pauses to let out an exasperated breath. "It was kinda brutal."

"I heard," I say, the words coming out on autopilot, the logical answer rather than the smart one. My attention is on the photo Tory tossed to the ground. I kneel and pick it up, turning it right-side up so I can absorb the way we're looking at one another. His face is covered in cream—minus the two holes I wiped for his eyes because I felt bad—and the enormous smile formed by his laugh. I'm laughing hard, too, truly happy with red cheeks and a dot of cream on my nose. The evidence is in the nuances; not only our display of happiness, but the way our hands happened to be wrestling with one another, threaded together so comfortably in a perfect fit. His eyes are soft and affectionate, looking at me not like the girl he makes sure to hit on at a party, but like the girl he stares at in class.

"Abby? You there?"

I stand with the photo and move back to my board, startled into movement by Hayden's voice. I push the sticky side back against the board, putting it back in its place.

"Yeah, sorry, I was balancing my phone while doing something else," I say. I'm vague.

"Oh, I asked how you heard?" There's a bite to his question and I wince, realizing what I said.

"June and I were texting. Tory stopped by her house."

I just lied. I lied and I feel like shit for it, and at the same time I am terrified that Tory won't back up my lie and I don't even have his phone number to call him and tell him to. I don't fix it, though. I leave that lie where it is and let it buy me time.

"Oh," he answers, the quiet after his short response telling me he doesn't fully buy it.

"You wanna talk about it?" I kick off the fuzzy shoes I wear around the house and slip my feet into my unlaced tennies in anticipation.

"If you're not too tired." I'm sure he's already driving toward my house.

"Of course not," I say, flipping off my light and quietly closing my door.

"You want to start telling me about it now, or wait until you get here?" I ask, anticipating his response.

"I'm almost there," he says.

Hayden opens up better in person. He also only really opens up to me. That happens when someone finds you on the wrong side of a bridge railing with an incredibly steep drop over some very jagged rocks, drunk from too many shots at a party you didn't want to go to in the first place.

Not Hayden.

Me.

"I'm at the end of the block," he says.

"Okay," I say, making my slow descent down the stairs.

I'd gotten the call for the audition, and I went to the party in the woods to celebrate. Sean McCaffey's parties are legendary. He's rich, and he owns the land he throws his parties on—massive bonfires and expensive-ass booze. I went alone because June swore she'd met her party quota for life, and she's turned Lucas into a homebody. Naomi and Lola weren't around to play my wing woman, so I went expecting to know a few people there and with the understanding I would only stay an hour.

The guy I met that night was cute, and two hours passed with many drinks and a lot of talk. I was feeling a good buzz, and we hooked up. I didn't go all the way, and I was fully aware of my choices and consent. What I wasn't aware of was his motives.

He left that party with three photos of me—three *compromising* photos. On his phone. It only took thirty minutes for the bribe to hit my phone. What's crazy is I knew I was too drunk to drive; that's why I was walking home in the first place. The idea to climb out over the bridge railing was an impulsive one. A destructive choice would have kept my keys in my hand and my ass behind the wheel. All I could think about, though, for those four miles I wandered in darkness, throwing up twice, was that my dad was going to use this against my mom.

Hayden found me before reason left my head and I jumped. He brought me home, and when I woke up in his car sitting in my driveway, I spilled my guts. He spilled his. We cried, and not a single night has passed that we haven't talked on the phone just to give each other an out, an excuse to mess up and hate ourselves for a little while.

"I'm out front," he says, my hand cupping the phone to my ear.

"Be right there," I say, ending our call and grabbing the sweater hanging on the finial at the bottom of the staircase. I slip my arms inside to stay warm and rush to the dining table to pick up my keys. I stop dead in my tracks, though, because sitting right next to them is a black sweatshirt that someone left behind, and I can't help but sense that he did that on purpose.

ELEVEN

TORY

"Did you sleep out here all night?" Lucas flips up the tailgate on his truck with a thrust in case I didn't hear him blare out his question.

I pull my feet up and lift my knees, rubbing my eyes from the bright-ass sun. My hat must have fallen off because my hair feels ratty like I was raised in a cave. Goddamn, I feel like shit.

"Only half the night," I say, rocking myself into a sitting position. Lucas tosses his backpack into the back of his truck and rests his arms against the frame, looking at me like I'm a toddler in a baby pool.

"Oh, well, that makes sense, then," he cuts, his mouth a tight light.

I rub my face to help focus my eyes, then crank my neck right and left, trying to work out the kinks before flattening my wild hair under my black hat.

"Therapy didn't go well. Kinda hate Hayden right now. I maybe went to Abby's last night and made things all fuckin' weird, and I hate that I have to live with my mom. That a good enough reason to sleep in your truck for six hours?" I lift one brow and hit him with a sleepy stare.

He holds my gaze for a second then nods.

"Yeah, that seems right. Come on, get in." He smacks the side of his truck to rile me more.

I stand and kick my legs over the edge of the bed to jump to the ground, then slide into the much more ergonomic passenger seat and recline back as far as it will go.

"Are you going to sleep on the way to school?" Lucas asks, cranking his engine to a roar.

"No, I'm going to sleep on our way to the gas station where I plan on getting a forty-four ounce Dew." I look at him, one eye shut.

"We're gonna be late," Lucas argues.

I shrug and silently dare him to come up with a better excuse. He can't, so I tip the brim of my hat lower to shadow my eyes while he drives the four miles to the gas station near our school. We both run in and grab donuts, and I fulfill my Dew destiny, chugging a quarter of it from the exit to the passenger door.

"Better," I breathe out.

Lucas chuckles and backs us out of the lot, taking us the rest of the way to school.

As much as I need the caffeine jolt, I have an ulterior motive for being late to school this morning—I want to avoid running into Hayden. I've gotten tired of conflict. Lately, it feels that's all my life is, a connect-the-dot puzzle from fight to skirmish.

Seems Hayden has his own reasons to walk into class late, though. He knows I won't skip completely; I take my sports eligibility seriously during basketball season. Lucas backs his truck in so my side is butted up next to my brother in the driver's seat of our car. Abby is sitting next to him, and she's doing that thing where she only looks my direction but not actually *at* me.

This day is going to be epically bad.

"You want me to just lock you in? You can sleep on the jump seats in the back," Lucas kids.

While he thinks he's being funny, I take a second to actually consider the idea, looking over my shoulder and assessing the room. It's a tight fit, but as tired as I am, I'm pretty sure I wouldn't even notice. I glance back to my friend, who's looking at me sideways.

"That was a joke," he explains.

I know.

I grimace and pop the lock on my seat belt, leaning forward and resting my arms and head on his dash to stretch out my lower back. I managed to slip into our house to get a shower and a change of clothes, but sleeping in a truck bed didn't do much for my wardrobe. My long-sleeved shirt is wrinkled, and there's a line of dirt on the side of my jeans from the back of Lucas's truck.

"Go on in. I'm gonna get this over with," I say, wiping my palm down the side of my face and over my mouth. I open my door and make a slow trip toward the passenger side of the car, opening the door for Abby.

"Can you give us a minute," I say, pinching the bridge of my nose and doing my best to not crowd her.

"Sure," she says in a whisper.

I look her direction just enough to catch her give Hayden a look and ask if he'll be okay. What does she think? That I'm a monster? I wonder what version of events he told her.

She turns her body to the side and her bare legs cut in front of mine. She's wearing a long, tight skirt and a blazer, as if she's ready for a job interview. I open the door wider to give her space and she stands, straightening her skirt and jacket. Her hair is pinned up in loose curls, and she smells like candy. I saw her car, so I know she drove herself here. She's just been waiting for me with Hayden, keeping him company, making sure he gets all the attention he can because, apparently, I'm some attention whore who has ruined his life.

I'm determined to pay no attention to Abby but she makes it impossible when she clears her throat and shuffles in her heels to face me, adjusting the collar of the shirt she's wearing. She stares into my eyes with a terrified gaze and swallows.

"How do I look?"

My cold stare breaks down and my eyes narrow with inexplicable guilt. She looks beautiful. Her permanently golden brown skin is flawless, her lips pout and glow, her eyes are dewy but still the most stunning mix of brown and gold. She looks scared, yet also strong.

"Court today?" I assume, my eyes sloping with empathy.

She nods.

"How do I look?" she asks again. I scan down the lapel of her jacket to the spot where her hand is needling at a button near the bottom. She drops it as soon as she sees I've noticed. I move my focus back up to her face.

"You look ready," I say. My response draws a hesitant smile from her and she gives me a tiny nod.

"Be nice," she whispers, careful to keep her words between us.

I agree with a slow blink and wait as she grabs her bag from the floor of the car and pulls it up on her shoulder. I don't allow myself the pleasure of watching her hips sway as her heels click down the walkway into the front office, but I imagine it. I get into the car as soon as she disappears into the building and close the door behind me, knowing Hayden and I will probably sit here for a while.

Neither of us is ready to talk. Hayden has yet to kill the engine, so the car hums enough to keep the heater on and the speakers at a low buzz. I lean forward and turn up the volume to see what he's playing, expecting his usual barrage of R&B. It's the one place where my dad, brother and I differ in our tastes. I don't mind it, but I never got into that part of my dad's music obsession the way Hayden did. I think my brother spent an entire summer memorizing every lyric to, like, fifty songs.

I'm a little surprised to hear the song I sang for Abby spill through the speakers, and I narrow my eyes as I look at his phone screen.

"Branching out?" I ask.

My brother shrugs.

"Abby wanted to hear the Beach Boys this morning," he says. My stomach tightens, a little bit hopeful and a little bit sick. Hayden's hands fall from the steering wheel to his thighs and his head rolls against his head rest, his eyes making the slow, suspicious trip to mine. "She said you showed her Dad's record collection."

"Huh, yeah. Didn't think she cared that much," I say, trying to pass off what was a memorable thing as a meaningless one. I sense by the long, silent breaths Hayden takes while staring at me that he isn't buying it.

Whatever. I'm not the one who threw his sibling under the bus at therapy. I think maybe it's my turn to talk, and give him a long look.

"Oh, and hey . . . what the fuck was that shit you pulled yesterday?" My temper isn't even a little bit controlled. I've gone and blended my love of sarcasm with my own boiling rage at how unfair life is being. My brother's reaction is completely unsatisfying.

"You know how I get with conflict. I wanted to say something to end the bickering—"

"That's bullshit," I cut in.

His mouth shuts into a hard, straight line and all of the pretend sincerity he was trying out fades away. He shifts his head, his eyes moving to the stereo controls. After a few long seconds, he finally lifts his hand and pushes in the power button, shutting off our distraction.

"You know what's bullshit?" he says. "What's bullshit is that you and I are basically the same person physically, but for whatever reason, Dad has always preferred your version of us to mine."

Wow.

"Dude, you're way off base," I reply. Hayden quickly laughs me off.

"I'm right on base, Tor, and deep down"—his gaze shifts back to mine and he bites the tip of his tongue, actual hate simmering in his smile—"you know I am."

My brow drawn in, I shake my head and laugh quietly, mentally shuffling through so many times in our lives when Dad was equal with us to a fault. I'm a better player than Hayden. It isn't even a question, and if I asked him right now, he wouldn't be able to lie and argue with me about it. When it comes to the court, I am dominant. He is decent. But my entire life has been held back to his level because Dad didn't want the "dynamic duo" to be split up. He didn't want Hayden left behind. I know in my heart that my dad just wanted Hayden to feel equal, but I always felt I had to carry him, which slowed me down.

"You do know that you and I are two different people, right? I mean, we look alike, but that's it. I am me, and you are you." It's a harsh response but I'm growing tired of working so hard to make sure Hayden is happy. I love my brother, but damn, sometimes my parents were too obsessed with the idea of coddling his sensitive ego.

"Oh, I'm well aware." He shifts in the driver's seat, turning to the side and folding his arms over his chest. "Think about Dad's bookcase. There's a row of albums, and then the top shelves are all of your special moments—your first place triathlon plaque from junior high, your invitation to Duke's high school basketball showcase, the photo of you, Dad, and Phil Jackson. And where are my things? They're on the bottom, Tor. They're on the goddamn floor."

I picture the space in my mind, conjuring some detail that will prove my brother wrong, but there isn't one. He's right. I can't believe any of it was intentional, but at the same time, the split is so obvious that how could it not be on purpose?

It seems insignificant to apologize. It also doesn't seem the right fit for the situation; it's not my apology to make. I've been holding my dad on this pedestal because of my mom's affair, but really, they both are flawed people. We're all flawed.

"You want some room on my shelf, maybe?" I squint, looking into the morning sun, and Hayden laughs.

"Sure, I'll take some shelf space."

We look at each other briefly, the new awkward truth sitting thick and heavy between us. He's still mad, and I'm still pissed off about therapy, but I also feel really shitty about the stuff he just said. I can also tell that he feels bad about the way it came out.

"I should have saved that for another time. Maybe I need some one-on-one sessions with Dr. Majestic," he says.

"Can we talk about that name for a minute? Really? Our family therapist is named Dr. Majestic?" This is my way of accepting his olive branch. Avoidance and humor—this is something we both definitely got from Dad.

"Right?" Hayden finally turns our car off, and I take the signal as it's finally safe to get out and go beg for late slips instead of detentions from the front office. He gets out of the driver's side, and with our bags slung over our shoulders, we walk in tandem, mirror images in many ways, opposites in others.

"Not gonna lie, I was picturing, like, major octopus tentacles to pop out of her shoulder blades or something," Hayden continues.

"Why does it always have to be octopus tentacles? Every bad guy—full-on tentacles."

"Why does it have to be a bad *guy*? Why not a bad *woman?*" he argues.

"Touché, brother. Touché."

We slip in the office door and put on our most charming smiles, bashfully wincing when Maggie, the best front office manager a high school senior could ask for, spots us. She was the queen of orange slices when Hayd and I were kids. I don't think we played a single game without her showing up with bags full. Her son, Nicolas, is in our grade, and he played most things with us when it was all about participation and less about athleticism. He's horribly uncoordinated, but dude is going to graduate high school with something like forty-eight college credits out of the way, so who cares if he can't throw a ball. Pretty sure he's going to build rocket ships.

Maggie spots us while she's on the phone and leans her head to one side, eyes hazed enough to admonish us. She writes out our slips while talking to the person on the phone, then puts them on hold when she brings them to us.

"If I ever find out you two are late for doing something stupid like smoking pot or robbing a liquor store, I'm going to whoop your tooshies, you got it?" She points at me instead of Hayden when she says that, which makes my brother laugh.

"Yes, ma'am," he says, taking his slip.

My brow knit tight, I bunch up my face and pinch the edge of my late slip between my fingers. Maggie doesn't let go right away, keeping her other hand pointing at me as she tugs the slip to bring me in closer.

"That's right, Tory, I'm talking to you. Of you two, I know you're the one I've got to keep my eye on." Her smirk breaks through just in time because I was about to get irrationally butthurt over her opinion. She finally lets go of my slip and pats my cheek in her overly coddling Midwestern mom way. "Oh, I'm teasing you."

"Thanks, Maggie," I say, my pulse beating fast from my emotional roller coaster.

"But I'm serious about the pot. No pot, you two!" She lectures over her shoulder on her way back to the phone. Hayden salutes her and pushes through the door into campus with his back. I follow along and wait until we get outside before I react out loud.

"I mean, it's kinda late about the pot. Been there, done that, over it," I say.

"Over it, huh?" Hayden says, slapping my back.

I'm pretty sure he and I both lit up a month ago out at one of McCaffey's parties. I guess that's recent to some people, but for me, shit I did a month ago is in an entirely different lifetime.

"Yeah," I sigh. "I'm over it."

He gives me a sideways look, daring me to prove him wrong. I lift a brow and reach out my hand to shake on it and he takes it.

"All right then. I'm gonna hold you to it," he says.

I shrug it off as if it's no big deal, but in reality, I just haven't been to a party in weeks. I'm the king of both enforcing and caving to peer pressure in those situations. Hayden has the resolve of stone, so for him this really is no problem. I might have to become a permanent introvert.

"Oh, hey." He stops me just before we split up and head toward different buildings. "Abby's birthday is in a few days. I want to do something special, but I'm stuck. This place is kinda void of special things. Got any ideas?"

Instantly, all of that good will we just forged collapses in my chest. I manage to keep that feeling from exposing itself on my face, though, and bundle it all up into a thoughtful expression. What kind of man am I? This is one of those forks in life's road. I decide to take the path I know will make Abby happiest.

"You know what? You said she really liked that one song you were playing. Maybe you should learn it on the guitar, play it for her," I suggest, the petty child that lives in my gut kicking me.

"Oh, I don't know, man. You're a way better player than I am. I could never really get it down," he says, overwhelmed at the idea. Thing is, that song is really easy to play. And Hayden and I sing about the same. He's just a lot shyer about stuff like that.

"Nah, I'll teach you. It'll take an hour, two tops." I cross my fingers over my chest and feel the scorch of my decision.

"Seriously?" There's a flavor to Hayden's surprise that reeks of suspicion. My brother isn't stupid, and while our little talk this morning focused on his envy over my relationship with our dad and my ignorance to it all, I can't forget that his first words to me were about how I spent time with his girlfriend and made an impression.

"Sure," I say. "What the hell else do I have to do? Go to McCaffey's and smoke pot?"

His lips purse into a tight smile and one brow ticks up.

"I swear, it will be easy. She'll love it, and you can talk about how many hours you put in to learn it just for her and blah, blah, blah." I want to throw up just thinking about her reaction. She'll think it's sweet and thoughtful, and she'll instantly realize how my brother picked up on her clues of liking the song but I didn't. He'll come away as the good guy and I'll be the chump. As it should be.

TWELVE

ABBY

Anymore, I don't really know how to judge whether or not things go well with the lawyers. It might be my new hardened belief that court mediators and custody lawyers are greedy bastards. It's probably not fair to lump them all together like that, but my experiences have been so tainted that it's hard not to.

Sitting in that room while my mom and our lawyer hashed out what seemed like a fair deal for my father's investment—*in me, the daughter he left*—was demoralizing. Add in his claims that he spent nearly a hundred thousand dollars making some sordid photos of me disappear, and today was basically an out-of-body experience.

I wasn't the girl in those blurred-out photos that my dad's lawyer kept referencing in his argument. I was dressed for business, a professional with a huge future only a few weeks away from beginning. That man made me sound like a wild party girl who shows up in tabloids, even hinting that there's no guarantee there aren't *more* photos of me like this flying around. "Or worse, video," he said.

I've told my mother everything. I promised her it was just this one time, which it was—I've never been so stupid as to flash my flesh for the camera. But I was drunk and feeling invincible because I just landed the part of my dreams. I was feeling carefree and romantic with a mysterious guy who was paying so much attention to me, and it felt good. I hate that I keep blaming myself for this mess. My mom keeps nearly convincing me that I'm not the one to blame, that the guy who took advantage of me is. Yet all it took was that one seed of doubt planted by my dad's calculated lawyer to fuck up everything.

Or worse, video.

That one tiny phrase is on repeat in my head, as is the sick expression that weighed on my mother's face, sagging her eyes, souring her mouth and tightening her body where it sat. She shifted her feet when he said those words, her heeled shoes scraping along on the floor beneath her chair like chalk on a board as her ankles uncrossed and crossed again.

Our car ride home was quiet. That's usually a sign things didn't go well. When my mom leaves one of those meetings feeling confident, we stop for smoothies. Today, we drove straight home and she took a bath—for an hour.

She's back at it now, hunched over at the table, emailing statements back and forth with our attorney until she gets the wording just right.

"I'm sorry," I say, paused at the coffee maker, the bag of grounds in my hands.

She blinks up at me, one pair of glasses on the tip of her nose, another pair tucked in her hair. I point at it and she looks straight up at her brow, feeling around the top of her head until she uncovers them.

"Oh." She laughs, pulling them from her twisted-up hair and tossing them on the table. "I spent an hour looking for those."

"Found 'em," I say.

She gives me a very tired, slightly crooked smile. Both of our bodies are numb from the emotional beating we took today. It kills my mom to have to talk about me like I'm a commodity, especially when I'm in the room. Even worse, it's probably hard to have her parenting judged on my mistakes, especially when the other parent couldn't even bother to fly in for this meeting.

"Stop saying you're sorry," she says, finally, resting her chin on her fist.

I shrug.

"But I am."

My mom slowly shakes her head.

"Well, forgive yourself, then, because I have no reason to. My daughter is perfect. Mistakes are part of growing. As parents, we are here to guide you and support you through your highs and lows, even if there's a financial responsibility tied to it. Your dad . . ." She straightens her spine and draws in a deep breath.

That's another thing my mom is good about. She limits the bad things she says to me about my father. I did not inherit her ability to take the high road. I like to battle in the trenches and go low. Mostly, though, I do it to stand up for my friends who are like my mom and won't get ugly.

That's how fights are done—ugly.

"Okay, well, how about this? I'm sorry I didn't make him pay for the privilege of taking my photo in the first place." It's actually a thought I've had a lot, about how this guy didn't even earn what I gave him. I'm starting to think the only reason I made out with him was because his name was Jake and he reminded me of my yogurt commercial crush with the same name.

"If that makes you feel better." My mom chuckles.

She pushes her glasses back up her nose and continues with her work while I begin a pot of coffee. A light rap at the door catches my attention and I look over my shoulder to see if my mom heard it too. She's so deep in her work, though, that I dump the water in the coffee maker and wipe my hands on my way to the door.

Hayden is standing close enough that his nose looks way too big for his head through the fisheye lens on the peep hole. It makes me laugh, and I continue being amused while I open the door.

"Were you trying to look through it the wrong way?" I ask, playfully pushing at his chest. He's dressed for practice, and I'm not sure why he isn't there now.

"I was, but it doesn't work that way." He tips forward on his toes and kisses my forehead. He hands me a single rose from behind his back and my face heats from the sweet gesture, knowing that my mom will make a big deal about it. I may as well bring her into the loop on my dating life.

"What's this for?" I ask, pushing the door open wider to invite him in.

"Early birthday gift. I have something better planned, but I wanted to stop by and give you this on my way to practice," he says, clearing up my question on where he's headed.

"Still at the junior high?" I assume.

"Yeah." He sighs as he steps into the house, and my reactions are too slow to undo the trouble I see coming.

"Back so soon? You must really like tea," my mom says, slinging one arm over her chair.

A squiggle forms on Hayden's forehead.

"This is Hayden, Mom." I make eyes at her, silently signaling all of the complicated shit I have to say about him, his brother, and that she got to see one of them all grown up before the other, when it probably should have been the other way around.

And . . . shit. This is bad.

My mom's brow lowers and her mouth bunches as she pulls her glasses from her face.

"Ah, yes. Reading glasses made you all blurry but I can see the difference now." She's joking, but Hayden isn't in on it. It takes a while to get a grasp on my mom's humor.

"Very funny, Mom. Yes, they're still twins," I say, placing my palm on Hayden's chest as if he's an exhibit. I glance to him and whisper, "I'll explain this later."

He laughs out "okay" and continues toward my mom with his hand outstretched.

"It's nice to see you, Ms. Cortez. It's been a few," he says.

My mom's head tilts to the side as they shake, her mouth hung open with questions just waiting to spill out. She looks from him to me, to the rose in my hand, then back to him again, and her mouth curves up in an amused smile.

"Nice to see you again, too," she says, that smile growing into a full grin. "So grown up."

I turn my back on the situation because she's about to get nosy and pushy, and embarrassing. I find a tall glass in the cabinet and fill it with water for my rose.

"So, tell me, Hayden. How long have you two been sneaking around behind my back?" Again, my mom is kidding. This is her way of both making Hayden shit himself and getting dirt on the stuff I haven't told her. I exhale and turn to face them with my back against the sink.

Hayden falls right into her plan, stuttering his way through some semblance of an answer. "Oh . . . I didn't mean to disrespect . . . Not that I'm disrespecting your daughter, but I meant your house . . . or rules. Yes, rules!"

My mom finally gets up and places her palm on what I am certain is Hayden's wildly beating chest.

"Relax, child. I'm messing with you. I figured you'd tell me more about my daughter's life than she does," she says, shooting me a glare that only I can see. She's joking in front of Hayden, but deep down she's upset that she had no idea that a *we* existed between us.

I haven't had a real boyfriend, well, maybe ever. It's a topic my mom and I talk about when we watch romantic comedies or teen movies where all girls seem to want are boyfriends.

"Where is your boyfriend?" she always asks.

My consistent response: "I don't have one."

She pushes me about it because deep down she's afraid that her and my dad's ugly relationship is ruining my perspective on love and matters of the heart. And honestly? It is. When I think about love, I can't help but associate it with animosity, jealousy, regret, hatred, destruction. My list is endless and so very negative. But I can't tell her that. Besides, I'm not so sure it's a bad thing that I got to see love for what it is—a dangerous gamble, high on distraction and low on reward.

There's no risk in dating Hayden. He's kind and I know I can confide in him, and I like that he needs to lean on me right now. But I know I don't love him. I don't think I could. I'm not sure I'm capable of it . . . at all. I like him a whole lot, and he likes me. But love? No. The only danger I've found in being with Hayden is one that I've only recently realized. And I don't understand why it's happening.

"Tory." My mom says his name and it shakes me from my thoughts, bringing me back to the conversation unfolding between Hayden and my mom.

"Right, that's your brother's name," my mom says, snapping her fingers as if Hayden just filled in a gap in her memory. My mom is playing along now for my benefit, which means she picked up my silent plea. She doesn't forget anything. It's half the reason we've been able to fight my dad's legal team so well. My mom has a photographic memory, and she's a touch of a hoarder, saving every remotely important piece of paper on the planet to back up those memories. There's no way Tory's name slipped her mind.

"You know, it's amazing how damned near identical you and your brother are," my mom says. I kind of wish she would drop the comparison conversation because lately it feels as if Tory and Hayden are doing plenty of it on their own. And I'd rather quit thinking about one of them.

"The only difference is I'm a little better looking," Hayden responds, his joke getting a short chuckle from my mom.

The slightest hint of a smile remains on her lips long after Hayden turns his attention back to me. I find myself caught in the look on her face, trying to decipher it while Hayden is talking.

"Earth to Abby," he says, waving a hand in front of me and cupping my shoulder. I jerk and reengage with the world.

"Sorry, you were saying something about Saturday night."

He laughs at my pathetic summary.

"Umm, yeah. That's your birthday. I was talking about taking you out. To celebrate?"

My mom has suddenly given us space, disappearing into the mudroom in the back of the house, folding things I'm sure are already folded and staying just close enough to the door that she can hear every word we say.

"I'm simple. We can just go to dinner or something." Truthfully, after the day I've had, my birthday feels completely insignificant. I looked forward to the independence of being eighteen, but it's looking more and more as though my dad will be an unwelcome business partner until I'm successful enough to pay for lawyers who can fire him.

"Okay, well, it might be a little better than simple, but I promise you'll enjoy it," he says, pulling me into arms that have been nothing but safe and a home for my restless mind. This time, though, his embrace does nothing to stop my racing thoughts.

"Hey, is that Tory's?"

My stomach drops at his question, my mouth watering in reaction to the dose of adrenaline injected into my veins. That fucking sweatshirt! He left it here like a Trojan horse and it will put me right smack in the center of whatever bullshit pissing contest is happening between him and his brother.

"Oh, yeah. I'm not sure why I have it, but—"

"I'll take it to him," Hayden says, grabbing it forcefully before I can come up with a lie as to why it's here.

"Great."

I'm too weak to elaborate. Too scared to invite more conflict. Too afraid to lose this other version of myself that I get to be with Hayden. And that's what this is all about. It sinks in suddenly. With Hayden, I'm the girl who can have a steady relationship and a person to call, and I'm the person who solves someone else's problems. My problems are in the background, easier to ignore tucked neatly in the shadow of something normal—like just being a high school senior planning to celebrate her birthday with her boyfriend.

Hayden leaves for practice with the token left behind by his brother in hand, such a trivial piece of clothing to spawn such an intense shift in my world. One more hug from arms that feel a little colder than before and leave me feeling nothing, and Hayden is gone.

THIRTEEN

TORY

I've texted my brother six times with no answer. I hung out with June and Lucas after school so I had them drop me off and told Hayden I didn't need a ride. I didn't hear back then, and the five texts after have all gone unread. Normally, I'd lie for him about being late to practice, but I think I've made enough concessions in the last twelve hours to hold me over on favors for a little while. He can come up with his own excuse for this one. Besides, it's not like he or I would ever get benched. Coach sits us and he might as well spot the other team twenty points.

I toss my phone into my temporary locker and fling the door shut, jogging out the door to begin warm-ups with the team. Our shoes squeak a little more than normal on the junior high floors, and we set a playful rhythm as we jog our laps around the gym. I'm comfortable in the pattern, laughing with Chaz, who actually isn't being a dick for once, when something quickly throws our rubber sole musical off beat.

"Hey!" My brother's fast pace is accompanied by screeching steps that spin me around as I run. I take a few steps backward before my own sweatshirt is thrown at my face, followed by my brother's fist.

"You left something at Abby's house, you fucking snake!"

I'm still a bit wobbly from the first punch, struggling to get my feet under my weight as they scurry. Hayden seizes the moment, shoving me backward completely, and I fall on my ass. Hard!

"What the fuck, Hayden!" I run the back of my hand across my nose, getting a streak of blood on my skin. The bright red fuels my own rage. So much for high roads and forgiveness.

I scramble to my feet as my brother charges me with his shoulders lowered, like a bull seeing red. I brace myself for impact, catching him around his midsection and lifting him in the air before throwing him to the ground. Our bodies tangle, a fury of awkward punches and flails. He smacks my ribs and sides so hard I get the wind knocked out of me, but I'm undeterred. I'm finally able to get my knees on his arms, pinning him to the floor as I straddle his body. I'll only be able to hold him like this for a second, three tops.

"Hayden, what is going on?" I hold his wrists to the ground and lean all of my weight on him as I look into his raging eyes.

"You tell me, brother. You tell me!" He thrusts me off and grabs the sweatshirt from the floor, once again throwing it at my face.

I know what it is. I know why he's pissed, but this reaction—in front of everyone—feels a bit excessive. It's not like anything happened. *Not that I didn't try.*

Maybe his reaction is more on target than I give him credit for.

"Abby get cold or something and you just need to warm her up? Or you leave that over there when you were sneaking around behind my back?"

Chaz snickers in a low breath, loving this drama between me and my brother. We should both forget about our issues and take out Chaz right now.

"Hayden, I'm not sneaking anything. And if you don't know your girlfriend well enough that you have these kinds of trust issues, then maybe you need to step off and deal with that." I toss my sweatshirt into a corner then tug down my jersey before testing the blood on my nose again. My cheek is puffy, and I'm sure there's a bruise forming under my eye.

"We about done here?" Coach Newsome steps into the space between Hayden and me. My brother and I are maybe eight inches taller than the man, and we each outweigh him by forty pounds. His physical authority isn't intimidating, but he has this disappointing tinge to his expression that tends to dominate whenever he needs to use it. He's using it now, his mouth a flat line and his eyes drooping with disgust. He tucks his clipboard under his arm to clap. I've seen this move before too. He does this to referees when they blow calls. Hell, he's gotten thrown out of games for mocking them like this. Pretty sure Hayden and I don't have the authority to throw him out of anything.

"Sorry, Coach," Hayden says, getting to his feet.

"Yeah, sorry," I reiterate.

His clapping continues, long enough for us to feel truly uncomfortable.

"You two figure this shit out. You're done here today. We're going to work on some defense, and since you're both shitty at defense, you'll just be in my way anyway. So, go on. Get out of here. Maybe Monday will be a different story. Last game before the holiday break, then our invitational tournament. Try not to ruin Christmas, yeah?"

He glares at both of us over the top of his black-rimmed glasses. His brows are thick caterpillars that meet in the middle when his eyes narrow like this, and it makes him look meaner. His method works because I feel like an asshole, and I can tell Hayden does, too. His shoulders sag, and his body drags as he walks over to the place where I threw my sweatshirt. He picks it up and shakes off the dust from the floor, then holds it out for me without making eye contact.

"Thanks," I mutter.

We both head into the locker room like puppies caught chewing the new couch, tails tucked between our legs and chins buried into the nooks of our neck.

Neither of us says a word as we switch out our shoes and stuff our belongings into our matching gym bags. Dad bought these for us for the start of the season last year. I'm not sure why they feel so symbolic now, but the fact they're exactly the same seems important. Inside, they are so incredibly different.

I sit down on the bench with a heavy exhale and stare at the empty locker in front of me for a few seconds while my brother zips up his bag. Eventually, I get the courage to swivel my head in his direction. His jaw is tight and his movements are rigid. He's still mad, and now that the heat of the moment has passed, I realize he probably should be.

"Dude, I'm sorry," I say in a low voice.

"It's fine," he says, tugging the strap of his bag up his arm and popping his gaze to mine just long enough to show me that he's no longer in the mood to talk about this.

I breathe out and get to my feet, stepping in front of him before he's able to just walk out the door. I hold the side of my fist against his chest and he looks down at it with narrowed eyes.

"Don't do that. I mean it. Abby and I are . . . friends. That's it. And I'm sorry if it seemed disrespectful." The words feel like acid on my tongue.

Hayden covers my fist with his hand, wrapping his fingers around it then tossing it from his body. His eyes shift to meet mine and we stare hard at one another, each of us knowing there is a layer of bullshit coating the things we're saying to each other.

"Like I said. It's fine," he grits out.

He makes his way to the door and I wait for it to slam closed behind him before I scream out "*fuuuuuck!*" so loudly that the word bounces off the walls around me. I follow his footsteps through the door, expecting our car to be long gone, but it's not. Hayden is idling near the curb by the exit.

I get in and Hayden begins driving before I buckle up. We ride the few miles in silence, and he pulls into the driveway at an uncomfortable speed, taking the bump in the curb hard enough to scrape the chassis of the car. I shoot him a glare because we share this thing, but he doesn't seem to notice.

"Get out," he finally utters.

I don't immediately, instead subjecting myself to the hot fumes of his temper and letting them reignite my own. But for once in my goddamn life, I manage to not engage.

"Whatever," I say, kicking open the door and dragging my bag out from the floor. I slam the door closed behind me and Hayden speeds backward a beat later, tires squealing when he shifts back into drive and peels down our street. I stare at the space he vacated for a few seconds and replay the last thirty minutes in my head.

My mom is home. She almost always is. She's had the same part-part-time job at Craft Mart for years. She works, and when they get in new displays, her job is to build them then do the sample craft for people to see on the tables by the entrance. Her degree is in elementary education, but I think her emphasis was on crafts. Hayden and I always turned in the best projects in grade school. Mom did every single one of them.

In a fantasy family, I would be able to walk in, call her name out then go tell her about my problems. She'd be able to help me work out a solution. Instead, she's part of my mess. Hayden talks to her a lot more than I do. Now that I think about it, I don't think my mom and I have spoken for maybe a full week—perhaps even two—not counting therapy, of course.

I glance through the van windows on my way into the house. There's a pack of cigarettes in the center cupholder, the top ripped open and the end of one poking through the hole. She's smoking again. She's tried to quit about a dozen times. My dad hates it, so she keeps it to the van. I can't help but think she's stress smoking in the van out of respect for him, and her delusion that he's coming back.

He's not. I knew the minute he moved out. I guess even I clung to a thread of hope, though.

The kitchen is messy, bread left out from toast my mom must have made, so I dump my bag in the laundry room and spend a few minutes cleaning the house. This is another one of those things my father took care of, despite the fact my mom hardly works and has always had time to keep up with the house. He's fastidious; Hayden got this trait. I'm normally more like my mom when it comes to neatness. I'm trying to shed any quality we share, so might as well start with tidying up.

The more I dust and straighten, the more caught up I get in making this place look as if Dad were still living here. I tuck the cord behind the coffee maker the way he would. The mugs in the cabinet all get turned with their handles facing the same way, and the random bags from shopping that my mom has just thrown into a drawer get neatly rolled into balls to save space.

I continue making little changes around the living room, dragging the dust cloth up the stair railing after I finish with the tables and shelves downstairs. My dad would use this wood shine stuff in a spray bottle when he did this. I couldn't find any downstairs, but the rag smelled like it so it will have to do. I cleanse our space in the scent of something familiar, clearing away the layer of dust that's formed on the record player top and along the spines of Dad's albums. I pick up one of my trophies from the end of the book case and run the rag around the dusty base, pausing to read the inscription.

MOST VALUABLE PLAYER

I set the rag down and kneel, looking for the matching statuette on the bottom shelf, finding it quickly and holding them both in my palms side by side.

LEADERSHIP AWARD

Those are the words on Hayden's statue. It's not even a real thing that teams give out. It's a made-up recognition to make sure our family wasn't sent home with one trophy in a house with two boys.

Fuck, he's right.

I pull out more of his things, reading the engravings and certificates more closely than I ever have before. Every single piece of hardware out on display is the equivalent of second place, a make-up award. When we were little, it probably didn't register with him, *but come on!* There's no way that by the time he was eleven or twelve he didn't see the difference in our accolades. I can't believe it's taken him this long to act out on it.

My eyes glaze over, staring at the neatly lined up set of awards with my name on them. My mom's TV hums in the background, the noise muffled through her closed doors. She's probably taking a nap.

I pull trophies and frames down from the top shelf—*my* shelf. I'm gentle at first, but the farther down the row I get, the less I care about these gold-painted plastic pieces of junk. By the time I get to the middle section, I'm done with it all, and I run my forearm along the rest of the space, sweeping everything to the floor in a clattering mess.

The space now cleared, I refill it with Hayden's things. My movements grow more and more manic until I'm basically throwing his things up on the shelf while my eyes burn with a cocktail of anger and guilt. The top shelf becomes crowded with these trinkets that helped form the animosity my brother now exhibits against me.

Even his photos were kept down here. I lift up the one from our freshman year, his skinny arms barely filling out the varsity jersey, and as I hold it up to study, a folded piece of paper slides out from the back of the frame.

Setting the photo in the very center of the bookcase, I straighten out the paper, instantly recognizing the logo on the letterhead. I applied for Olsen Training Academy in eighth grade. It's a boarding school in Texas where sports are treated with the same weight as math and science. It's a factory for elite athletes, and more than half of the athletes that go through the program end up playing in the pros for whatever sport they specialize in. Almost all of them play in college. Dad helped me apply, and I bugged my parents every day for three months asking if they'd gotten a call, an email . . . *a letter.*

I fall to my ass and sit, holding the letter in both hands as I imagine this life I could have had, my *almost* life.

Provisional acceptance.

I was one visit to the campus away. An interview that I no doubt would have aced. There's no way my dad knew about this, because he was the one who encouraged me. He was ready to travel with me, to buy a second home or a condo near the campus so my family could visit. It was my mother-fucking dream!

There's no way to fashion a second-place trophy for this. If I went to Olsen, I went alone. Hayden stayed behind. I went top shelf and he went bottom.

Without pause, I take my phone from my back pocket and glance to the still-closed doors behind me, my mind vacillating between who to blame—Hayden or my mom—while I listen to the rings sound. My dad answers by the fourth ring.

"Tory, hey. Something wrong? Aren't you in practice?" He knows I should be.

"Dad, I think maybe I need to come stay with you. For a little while at least. I just . . ." I break down, swallowing hard and feeling my lungs tighten as the air leaves them and my body grows numb. This is what betrayal feels like to the utmost degree. This is how he felt when he found out about Mom's affair.

"You're going to have to drive back for school on your own," he says, giving me the only roadblock to the plan. I have a thousand dollars saved from various birthday and holiday gifts and shitty summer job I took at the local pool.

"Okay," I agree, getting to my feet and moving to my room to pack my things. "Can you pick me up soon? Like . . . now? I'll buy a piece of shit car."

"On my way," he says.

I end the call, not sure whether my dad likes the win that comes with me choosing address sides or he senses the urgency in my voice. Maybe it's the aftermath of our pitiful therapy session. Whatever the motivation, I'm glad he's coming. And I'm glad I'm getting out of this place. It's suffocating me.

FOURTEEN

ABBY

It's been a while since I've felt like myself. I told June all I really wanted for my birthday weekend—because yes, I get an entire weekend, and yes, Friday nights are weekend-eligible—was to do something that felt like the old me.

"Anything you want," she said.

She regretted it the moment the last word left her lips. She could read *party* all over my face. I don't care what she says, though. Deep down, June needs tonight, too. She misses us.

"Are you sure you don't mind driving?" She doesn't, but it makes me feel polite to ask. I like getting ready at June's house. There aren't papers all over her table, and her mom is in a pretty good place. Mine is buried in the fight to give me a life without my father's greed picking away at it. Tonight, I want to forget that version of myself.

"I'm not going to drink, and the van has plenty of room," she says while running a brush through her hair. I smile because she's repeating my talking points.

"Exactly," I say, leaning close to the small mirror on the back of her door so I can perfect the shade under my eyes.

It feels nice to dress up like this. I've been a lot of versions of myself lately—the girl who wears her boyfriend's oversized sweatshirt, the business woman who gets accused of having a sex tape, the actress who doesn't know what her character is supposed to look like. It's nice for once to just be me. My makeup, my skinny jeans and cut-off sweatshirt—my body, my rules. I can feel my confidence coming back already. It's amazing how much your own unique look can make you feel at home in your skin. My look isn't everyone's, but it's mine.

June's mom holds the door open for us as we leave, hanging out the door as if we're still the same little girls she sent off to walk to school by themselves for the very first time in second grade. I'm tempted to hold June's hand in solidarity.

"Don't do stupid things!" Mrs. Mabee shouts. She says that to me a lot.

"Nothing you wouldn't do," I shout back before getting into the passenger side. She shakes her head at my usual response.

Again—normal.

We head to Naomi's to pick her up, then stop at Lola's work as she finishes her shift. She's a server at the Pancake House, this truck stop joint open twenty-four hours a day, which means she has unlimited access to bacon. I don't care who a person is, if they say they don't like bacon I immediately throw them in the *sketch* category. Because of birthday weekend, Lola swiped me an entire to-go box full. I'm already five pieces in.

"Abby, if you don't slow down you're going to be vomiting before you even get close to a shot of tequila," June says, turning right on the old dirt road a few miles out of town.

"Well, guess what? I'm drinking beer tonight," I say, winking as I take a bite of my sixth piece. June takes it out of my hand and finishes it for me, part for my own good and part because, well, it's bacon.

It's barely ten at night and the party is already crowded enough that we can hear it with June's windows down. I crack my window and breathe in the scent of burning wood. There's a huge clearing on McCaffey's property and he always has these huge bonfires. It's an amazing sight to break through the trees and see the bright orange flames off in the distance. June spots Lucas's truck quickly, so she pulls the van up next to him and we all get out.

"Happy birthday, Abs," Lucas says, pulling me in for a side hug and handing me a cup full of beer.

"Just what I always wanted. Thanks," I say, taking my first gulp and feeling the tension in my neck and shoulders ease.

Tonight, there is no lawsuit. I'm on the brink of stardom. And there is nothing in my life to bring me down. I almost believe these words when a lifted red truck pulls up across the clearing, the chrome bumper catching the flicker of the flames as Tory hops out of the driver's side and Cannon and a few other guys climb out of the back carrying a keg.

Tory stops and leans against the front of the truck, one knee bent as his foot rests on the bumper, his hands sunk in the pockets of his jeans. He's wearing a red and black flannel over a black shirt, and his normally perfectly sculpted hair is windblown and messy. I recognize his dad's truck, which makes me wonder why he's driving it.

I bring my cup of beer to my lips and taste it with my tongue, tipping it back slowly while staring at Tory over the rim. He's not even pretending not to look at me. It's like a dare, to see if I can handle the attention. Well, I can. And he can keep on looking from over there. Hayden works tonight, which means I am one-hundred percent about my girlfriends. I plan on spending the night gossiping mercilessly, dancing to music under the stars, and telling dumb stories without endings that make me and my friends exhaust ourselves with buzzed laughter.

"You heard he moved out, right?" June says, bumping into my side.

"Huh?" I pull my cup away and shift my gaze to her.

I'm already breaking my rules. I'm not supposed to care. But Tory moved out and Hayden hasn't said anything. Seems kinda weird.

"Oh." She winces. Her mouth gets tight and she forces that pretend smile on her lips, trying to convince me that it's not a big deal.

I lightly punch her arm.

"Don't do that. Spill it," I say.

She wiggles her head side-to-side and shrugs at me.

"Hey, I'm gonna go talk to Tor for a bit. I'll be right back," Lucas says, kissing her softly and glancing at me mid-kiss. I can tell by the awkward bend in his brow that there's more to this story than just Tory moving out. I let him get several steps away before I grill my friend.

"What's going on?" I ask.

June's mouth twists up.

"June," I beg.

"I guess there was a sweatshirt or something?" She shrinks into her shoulders as she talks, and I immediately roll my eyes.

"Oh, my God," I say, waving my hand in the air in a big circle. It lands at the bridge of my nose and I pinch.

"Tory came by once for a visit, just to talk, while he was out for a run a few days ago. He took his sweatshirt off and forgot it. Hayden saw it today and said he was going to give it back to him. I had a feeling he was getting the wrong idea."

"Abby, he sucker punched him in the middle of practice," June says.

My head pops up and my mouth hangs open.

"For real?" I challenge, hoping she's exaggerating.

She nods toward Tory across the field.

"Go check out his eye. It's purple."

I look back toward him, squinting to see if I can make anything out from the light of the flames. It's too dark to see for sure. I knew something like this would happen. I had the worst feeling when Hayden left, and he's been off today. We've barely talked, other than him telling me he had to work tonight. I just figured he was stuck in his feelings, and I didn't want to push.

That's become the problem. He's always in his feelings or my life is chaotic, so instead of having the tough talk about what we're even doing together, I just kick the can down the road for the next day, and then the next.

"So, he moved out because they got in a fight . . . over me?" I look back to June and her expression isn't definitive, one eye scrunched and her mouth twisted up along with it.

"Sorta?" She says it like a question. "I don't think it's a permanent thing. He told Lucas he was driving here from his dad's tonight. I think he's just staying there until things get sorted out, or until graduation, or—"

"Until graduation?" I blurt out.

I hand June my beer and roll down the sleeves of my sweatshirt to cover my chilled knuckles. I hug myself to keep the midriff of my shirt from blowing up in the cross breeze as I cut in front of the fire. The warmth feels good, and moves into my cheeks, injecting more of that confidence I've been missing in my spine. I catch Tory mid-conversation with Lucas and Cannon, and something about the way I march up must signal to the other guys that they should leave. They split without me even having to ask.

"You wanna tell me why you're living with your dad?" I cross my arms over my chest and stare at his smirk. Shit, his eye is pretty fucked up. The bruise is worse on his cheek. He can tell I'm staring at it, so he reaches up and touches it lightly with the tips of his fingers.

"It doesn't hurt anymore. Sometimes, I almost forget it's there." His hands drop to his pockets and he lowers his gaze to the ground, glancing back up at me with his eyes more than his face. "Hayden didn't like that you had my sweatshirt. That's basically all there is to that story."

His gaze lingers as he chews at the tip of his tongue, his lips curved with a hint of a drunken smile.

"You drive after a few?" I jut my hip out and stare at him with judgement.

"Just one beer. I'm fine," he says.

My eyes haze and I hold them on him until he has to look away.

"What? Fine, okay, maybe two. And I just rolled up to McCaffey's house to haul down the keg. No main roads. And I'm sleeping here, so just . . . don't worry about me, birthday girl." He leans forward and touches the tip of his finger to my nose, then walks away.

I'm left there all alone, wondering how I got here, to a place where I'm both livid that he belittled me and care that he's upset with me. This is Tory D'Angelo. I walk away from *him,* not the other way around.

Determined and pissed, I follow in his path and slide up next to him at the keg, waiting while he fills a cup. I partly expect him to give me the one he's working on, but he doesn't. Instead, he turns to make space and holds his hand out to signal it's my turn as he takes a long gulp. Seems the old Abby *and* the old Tory are both making appearances tonight.

"Where's your boyfriend?"

He says it with such animus, I wonder if he found out Hayden knew about his mother's affair when it first started. This rivalry brewing between them has to be about more than just me. Hayden has been struggling with major guilt over hiding his mom's secret for so long. Nobody knows he knew. He saw them together at football camp their freshman year, and a few unexplainable lunch-time visits when he ran into Lucas's dad at his house fanned his hunch that the fling was not a one-time occurrence. Since his parents' relationship blew up, Hayden feels his lack of action made everything worse. I've tried to tell him it didn't, it only postponed the inevitable.

I finish filling my cup and take a few steps back, opening space between us so people can get through.

"Hayden's at work. He know you packed up and moved out?" I take a slow sip, smiling with my lips against the cup.

We stare at one another while two freshmen come up and fill their cups between us. It's amusing to watch them blush and act out for Tory's benefit. So hungry for attention.

"Ladies," he says, throwing them a bone.

"H-Hi," one of them says while the other giggles. They're barely fifteen. No way they're finishing a whole beer. I wonder if the daycare camp bus dropped them off here by mistake.

"Careful, ladies. He's all talk," I say, shrugging with one shoulder as I cash in my win.

The girls rush away, whispering to one another. Tory and I just gave them a story to tell for the rest of the year. He's the hot guy and I'm the bitch.

"All talk, huh?" He tips the rest of his beer back, chugging it in one smooth movement then tossing his cup to the ground. I hold my ground even though he's getting closer, even though people are watching us, even though I shouldn't. I'm daring him right back, and a little part of me wants to. It's the beer thinking.

Tory runs his finger up my cheek then tucks my hair behind my ear. He leans in and dips down, pausing at my ear as if he's about to share a dirty secret. My body tenses, and shivers run up and down my skin. I straighten my posture and shift my feet slightly, hoping he doesn't notice the nervous movements. With his lips close enough to my skin that he could taste me if he wants to, I listen to only his breath. It's warm.

"You look absolutely beautiful."

His mouth hovers there, dangerously close for a full second that feels like several more. He backs away, letting his eyes seer into mine as he straightens tall and walks backward, leaving me where I stand—frozen and oddly heartbroken.

I have zero comebacks. Worse, I can't rectify how badly it turns out I wanted—no, *needed*—to hear it. Mr. All Talk just said the perfect words, and a tear forms in the corner of my eye. I hate crying, but I've suddenly realized how absolutely miserable I have become. My life is a mess, and I'm trying to make it better by being some guy's girlfriend because as messy as I am, he's worse. This is co-dependency at its absolute worst.

"You all right?" June slides her arm through mine and I swipe the back of my hand over my eyes and nose.

"Yeah," I say, smiling at her—performing. "Just cold. Let's get some of that fire, yeah?"

She grins, then escorts me to a flat log parked near the open pit, a perfect spot for me to curl up my legs and think. So far, this isn't the girls' night I pictured, but maybe it's the girls' night I need.

FIFTEEN

TORY

Two things happen when you have about an hour to buy a used car. One, you don't really pick based on the right set of criteria. You scan the lot by price point and then narrow things down based on mileage and the little car know-how you possess to get a sense of what might break and what you can fix. And then two, you get mercilessly screwed by the dealer.

I had a thousand bucks of my own, two with the grand my dad pitched in. Shocker—this piece of crap old cop car rang up just under the cap. I have just enough left to fill the tank. I promised my dad I'd get a job as soon as the season's done so I can take on the insurance. Hayden pays a portion of the Subaru's, and I can't let him better me.

The strange look I get from my mom as I pull into our driveway tells me the body of this car is as bad as I thought. You can almost read the word POLICE on the side; the buffing job and primer cover-up was an afterthought. The one thing this car has going for it, though, is the engine. I'll be able to leave this place fast when I need to.

I came back because my dad said it was a good idea. Our family has a lot of drama happening, and a split like this—two against two—sets up a real roadblock for any hope of peace in the future. I didn't tell him about the letter I found Thursday afternoon. I'm still processing it in my own head, and like he said, I'm not sure if adding more fuel to our dumpster fire of a family is best right now.

I'm not here for all selfless reasons, though. I also came back because Abby's birthday is today, and June is throwing a party for her tomorrow. I want to be there for it, even if my brother spends the time secretly plotting to push me out a window. I'll go back to Dad's next weekend. Space is necessary for me and Hayden. I don't want to hate him, and right now . . . I do.

"Wow, that's . . . some ride," my mom says as I step out of the car. The heavy door squeals as I shut it.

"It gets the job done," I say, stopping when my feet are squared with hers. We face off for a few seconds, my arm weighed down with my bag of clothes that I intend to shuffle back and forth. I see how unsure she is of what to do in her eyes. They keep scanning me, making sure nothing's broken and that I'm as she remembered. Thing is, though . . . I'm not. I've changed in the last two months. And the old me will never fully come back.

"You have laundry?" Her voice is hopeful.

"I was gone for a day, Mom."

"Oh, right," she nods. She steps forward and squeezes my biceps, her attempt at some sort of affection. She hugs Hayden all the time.

"Are you hungry?" She lets her hands drop from my arms and heads in through the garage. I follow behind her.

"No. I ate at Dad's."

"Oh," she says. I can hear the disappointment in her tone.

"He had muffins, so I grabbed one," I say. That's a lie. Dad made me bacon and eggs, but for whatever reason, it seems that would be showing off.

"Well, I can make some sandwiches for lunch, or maybe we can go out?" She turns to face me, hope widening her eyes. I don't think I have ever gone to lunch with just my mom. She's trying so hard, though.

"Maybe. I'll see if I'm hungry," I say, popping her hope balloon with a pin. It's already noon, and I'm not planning on leaving my room.

"Hayden should be home by three." She must know something about our fight. She hasn't mentioned the purple line under my eye, and she has to suspect something made me rush out of this house and head to Indy.

I only nod at her information, and after a long, painfully quiet stare, she moves on, apparently deciding to drop it.

"Well, I'll be down here, going through some old things in the garage. If you decide you want that lunch . . ."

I've already begun my trip up the stairs.

"I'll let you know," I say.

I'm being cold. I'm also being civil. I can't be both warm and polite right now. The two qualities are mutually exclusive.

My bedroom looks like I left for college. My mom must have come in and cleaned up. The only reason she knows I left for my dad's is because he told her. If he hadn't, I sorta wonder if she would have noticed.

I toss my bag to the floor and faceplant into my comforter, pulling my pillow down to bury my head. My dad's rental isn't set up for guests yet. He wasn't planning on Hayden or me coming, so when I got there, my only bed option was the crappy couch that came with the place. Staging furniture is a lot like hotel lobby furniture. Stiff as fuck.

I didn't wake up hungover, which is a refreshing change after a McCaffey party. I didn't get back from the woods until two in the morning. I quit drinking after my short talk with Abby. Instead, I sat in my dad's truck for four hours and watched her have a good time with her friends. She laughed, and I haven't seen her do that in a long while.

She isn't who she's supposed to be when she's with my brother. And yeah, that thought is steeped in jealousy on the surface, but what makes it honest is I don't think she would be who she's supposed to be with me, either. While we're all growing up, Abby's already there. She has her life mapped out and is full of ambition and drive. I'm broke because I blew my birthday money on an old squad car.

Before the urge leaves my mind, I pull my phone from my back pocket and prop myself up on my elbows over my pillow, scrolling through my contacts until I land on June's info. I'm not sure whether she'll think this is a good idea or a bad one, but she must know that things in my life are chaotic at best. I haven't filled her or Lucas in on the latest revelations. I need to process them on my own first.

ME: *Hey.*

I let that message sit there for a while like a test to see if she's even around. I know she's normally at the bowling alley at this time on a Saturday, but since it's Abby's birthday weekend, maybe she took the day off. She writes back after a full minute.

JUNE: *Well hi, stranger. You in Indy?*

I rub my eyes, still puffy from the long night and face still sore from my brother's punch.

ME: *Long story, but no. Trying to keep some peace.*

I pause while she types, but before she can send her reply, I get my real motive out of the way.

ME: *I need to call Abby. Number?*

All signs that June is responding stop, so I drop my chin to my pillow and stare at the message screen with the weight of rocks in my stomach. It finally rings and I cringe. I'm so much better typing than I am talking. At least it's June.

"Look, I just want to apologize to her." I don't bother with hellos because I know June doesn't plan to, either. She'll dive right into how I told her I would be okay and that I was over it and how I'm clearly not. I keep telling her she needs to consider psychology in college. It's not that she's good as much as she loves to dig her hands into other people's heads and find out their business.

"I wasn't going to say anything," she says, a playful lilt to her voice. She's such a bad liar.

"Yeah, right." I laugh.

"Fine. I just don't want to see you get hurt."

"Well, too late," I respond, rolling to my back and pressing my fist against my head.

The line is silent for a few long seconds, and finally I hear her breathe out a mixture of concession and pity—there it is again, goddamn pity.

"Just try not to make things worse for yourself, okay?" She's serious about her position, and all I can do is laugh because of course I'm going to make things worse. I'm going to torture myself endlessly until I get over whatever this infatuation is that has its hooks so deep in my skin that it actually burns.

"Fine, got it. No making things worse." My response is snarky, and I can tell June is not amused.

"*Hmmm,*" she hums into the line.

"All right," she finally gives in. "I'll text you her contact. But only because I admire you not dropping into her DMs like some creeper. Oh, and hey, you know we're having her birthday dinner here tomorrow, right? You *are* coming to that, aren't you?"

"I guess that depends on how this phone call goes."

"Tory! You can't not come. It will be weirder if you're not here. And my mom made cake, and she has these games planned, and it only works if we have enough people show up—"

"I'll be there." I say it just to shut her up. She's spiraling and Lucas is way more equipped to deal with that than I am. "I promise. I'll be there."

I promised. *Shit.*

"Okay, well . . . good luck."

"Thanks," I say.

We end our call and a few seconds later, Abby's contact info shows up on my phone. I let my finger hover over the call icon for several minutes, running through all the reasons I could use as an excuse for calling. I told June I want to apologize, but that's a lie. I just want to hear Abby's voice, and maybe talk for a while without all of the noise that comes between us. I want to hear about her court case, and about her in general. I want to do nothing but listen.

With my eyes closed, I let my finger fall to the phone, and then hold my breath as it rings. I move to my side so I can rest on the phone and keep it close. I'm about to give up when she finally answers.

"This is Abby Cortez."

Instantly, my lips twitch with a sharp smile. She's so professional. Much better than my "Yo, what up" greeting.

"Hello, Miss Cortez. This is Salvatore D'Angelo. I was calling with some important information." I put on a deeper voice, expecting it to make her laugh, but there isn't a response for several seconds. Finally, she sighs.

"What do you want, Tory?"

Ouch. She doesn't want to know all the things I want. They aren't mine to have. And while I thought, for a while there, that maybe there was some reciprocation in her feelings, I'm pretty sure it was all on my side.

"Sorry," I say, going with my lie to June. Seems I do need to apologize to her after all. "I just . . . I wanted to call and apologize. I made you uncomfortable, maybe more than once, and I'm just . . . I'm sorry."

"How's your eye?" She doesn't miss a beat in responding.

I breathe out a laugh and roll to my back again, touching the tender skin with my free hand.

"Hurts like a motherfucker." I laugh out.

Quiet takes over again, and my smile falls back to the flat line that's taking up permanent residence on my face.

"I told Hayden it was just an innocent thing. I don't think it had anything to do with you; I think he's just having a hard time lately." She's giving my brother an excuse. One, my sweatshirt being at her house was not innocent. I was a breath away from kissing her that day. And two, she's wrong about Hayden. His issues with me are deeply personal.

"Right," I say, letting it rest there. She doesn't need my baggage. And when it comes to my brother, I'm going to be the bigger man for as long as I can. My anger will come out when it's good and ready.

"He's taking me out tonight," she says. My stomach rolls with a sick envy. I forgot that I told him to play her that song. I never got around to teaching him how.

"Oh, that's right. Happy birthday." I feel like an asshole.

"You told me last night," she says right back.

I did. I also told her she's beautiful. No matter what she is to me, or to my brother, I don't take that bit back. She deserved to hear it, and I had a right to tell her. Admiration is not a breach of loyalty. It is, however, a poisoned knife that cuts deep into my chest. It hurts to admire her so much.

"So, hey, how's the script coming?" I put on my best light and happy voice.

"It's . . . coming," she says, hesitantly. I was supposed to practice with her a lot more than I have. It's my fault we haven't.

"I bet it's better than you think. Why don't you give me some lines," I say.

"What, like . . . now?" Her tone is so offended it makes me laugh.

"No, like maybe later, after you film. Like an encore," I joke.

"Ha ha, Tory D'Angelo."

I catch myself grinning, a happiness taking over my body that I haven't felt in eons. I like the way she says my name. She's always done that when we spar. I think it's her way of showing she's my superior, yelling at me like a parent or teacher would.

"How about we read a little now," I suggest.

"What, on the phone?"

I pause with my mouth open, about to make another smart-ass remark, but I pivot.

"Yeah, why not. Maybe shoot me a few pics of the scene and I'll put you on speaker and we can read. I'll even lock the door so nobody will hear how awful I am and how great you are." I sit up, hopeful she's game.

"I don't think I'm allowed to send pictures of it," she hedges.

"I'll delete them as soon as we're done. Cross my heart." I wait while she mulls it over, and I can tell she wants to.

"You trust me?" I add.

Her pause is brief.

"Yes," she whispers.

I feel that one small word in my chest, and I'm grinning. There's something special about her trusting me, even about something like this. June was right to warn me—this is gonna hurt.

"Okay, send it my way. I'm locking the door now." I don't pretend but actually do it, mostly because I don't want my mom coming in unexpectedly just because she's nosy.

My phone dings with her delivery and I put her on speaker so I can open my images and expand enough to read.

"Got it," I say. "So, you want me to be Jordan Shotcraft?"

"Tory . . . nobody can be Jordan Shotcraft except Jordan Shotcraft." She has a point.

"Okay, smartass. I mean, isn't that his character, this Max guy?" I thumb through a few of the lines, getting the sense that most of the work will be on her. This should be easy.

"Yeah, this is the one section I'm struggling with." She sounds stressed. I'm glad she's letting me help.

"Okay, then. Let's go. Ready?" I have the first line, but I don't want to start reading until she's ready for it.

She draws in a sharp breath before whimpering a tentative, "Yes."

I sit on my bed with the phone cradled in my lap, my legs folded and my hands suddenly sweaty. I can't imagine doing this in front of an audience. No wonder my acting career peaked with junior high and community theater.

"Look . . . kid . . ." The script says pause for dramatic effect, so I am . . . I think. "I'm not really good at this father thing. I think you'd agree, so how about this. Give me a number."

"A number." Abby bites out the line, a near growl to her words.

"Yeah, you know . . . an amount. I'll set you up with whatever you think you need. I can give you money. You'll be good. You don't need me—"

"Money!" Her anger is thicker this time. "Ha! Yeah, sure, fine. Go ahead and cut me a check. Cut me out of your life. That's how things work for Max Stewart. Buy your way out of responsibility."

"Christine, you know this is for the best." I feel like such an amateur reading with her. I'm barely finished with a line when she begins hers. The conversation feels so real, so raw. It also feels vaguely personal.

"Yeah."

There's a long pause, and I wait through it. It's meant to be there, but the longer it drags on, the more on edge I get. Something's off.

"Maybe it is. For the best, I mean," she croaks. It's not quite the line as written, but it's close enough.

"It is," I hum.

"And maybe, maybe you'll regret it one day. Maybe I'll be so famous that you'll wish you took the job of dad when it was yours to have. But it won't be there anymore. That job is closed, no more applications being accepted. Eliminated."

She's definitely veering now.

"Abby, do you want—"

"And then you can swoop in and play hero just so you can get your foot in the door, earn off of your investment. Those are your words, not mine! Your fucking investment. That's all I am to you!"

I can hear the tears through her words, and I get why this section has been so hard for her to get through. I've read ahead, and while it's nothing like the words she just spilled out from her soul, it does ring very familiar. This story has a happy ending, though. I know it does because I looked ahead when we read the first time. Abby's relationship with her father, however, is just one big loop.

"I'm on my way," I say, not giving her a chance to tell me no.

I grab my keys and wallet, and stuff my phone in my back pocket, jetting down the stairs, out the door and by my mom without a word. I fire up my shitty squad car and test out the engine, getting to Abby's house in less than three minutes by blowing one stop sign and rolling through three others.

At her curb, I slam the car in park and dash through the lawn and up her steps, pounding my fist on her front door. She opens it after only seconds, and I step inside and take her into my arms, and let her cry big, fat, ugly tears into my chest.

"I know," I say, running my hand over her head and through her hair, rocking her softly while we embrace in the doorway.

"I can't do this," she fights. I assume she means the movie, and that's just crazy talk. She's too good to let this emotional hump stop her.

"Yes, you can. Don't give him that much power over you. Your choices, your decisions," I say.

She goes quiet, breathing hard, her mouth open on my cotton shirt. She's making a wet circle in the middle of my chest with her spit and tears. In all my years of knowing Abby Cortez, I don't think I've ever seen her truly cry.

"Someone took nude pictures of me, and he paid them off. I owe him," she says, her voice raw and embarrassed. She hides her face against me, turning inward even more. I'm glad because I'm sure the expression on my face is violent and frightening. I feel hot, and it's a struggle for me to keep my touch so gentle while my muscles are flexing, ready to rip someone's head off.

"You don't owe him jack shit, Abby. Taking care of you is his job." I'm probably a little more forceful than she needs to hear in her fragile state of mind.

"He's moving here. To fucking Allensville. He's moving his whole

Miami life, his whole Miami girlfriend, to the town he called a shithole and pledged to never step foot in again." She pushes off from my chest just enough so she can form fists with her hands and level them against my chest. I can take it. I hold her elbows while she beats against me, letting out her rage. "He's coming here so he can get a better handle on my business. He thinks my mom doesn't do enough. I should be earning more! He's coming to milk me dry, not to be a dad!"

I bend down enough to look her square in the eyes, my palms cradling her face. I swipe away the tears collecting on her cheeks and wait for her breathing to slow while she sniffles and focuses through her blurred vision. She nervously steps side-to-side in my hold.

"Abby, listen to me. You . . . deserve better. You hear me?"

She shakes her head. It's going to take more to make her get it. I tighten my lips and shake my own head.

"No, you need to listen, to hear! You are worth a thousand suns. Your dad screwed up, and not like a business man, but like a human. He screwed up the day he wrote you and your mom off, and he doesn't get a second shot at that. He's not the man for the job. Hell, you and your mom—you don't *need* a man. Look at what you two strong women have done! You . . . you're going to be in a fucking Jordan Shotcraft film! Like, in theaters, where I'll have to buy some twenty-dollar ticket or some shit."

She laughs through lighter tears and sniffles.

"That's right. Smile, Abby Cortez. Let him try to steal your spotlight, take dollars out of your pocket. He's just using you to fill his empty void. And he did it to himself. He gave up the chance to have a real heart, a real life, the day he took off for Miami. He can move here and fight you in court so he can get paid and it will never be enough because he won't have you. Not having you . . . it is fucking torture, Abby Cortez."

Her eyes blink away tears and open on mine, and I swallow hard. That last part, that's about me. There's no way she doesn't know it. She has to know.

"Abby . . ."

My attempt to get back on track is cut short when she steps up on her toes, clutching my now damp shirt in her hands, and presses her lips to mine. I'm frozen from the touch, my hands falling away from her face but never going far, hovering in shock somewhere around her shoulders until I regain control over them. I move them to her neck, burying them in her hair, my fingers curling at the sensation of her silky hair between them. I've dreamt this exact feeling.

Her mouth is salty from tears and her lips are soft and quivering, but they don't back down. I coax her head to the side to deepen our kiss, and our tongues connect when she opens to me. A sweet hum escapes her throat, and it makes my lungs crash in disbelief that this is happening. Her hands have moved up my body to my neck, gripping at my shoulders to lift herself higher, to bring us closer, and then without warning, she falls several steps away and covers her mouth with the back of her hand.

Her chest is heaving with labored breaths. Mine is too. That kiss, it was forbidden. We crossed the line that took us from good people to the selfish kind. She was weak, and I took advantage. I should have told her no; I should have stopped her. But I wanted it, too. I wanted to kiss her even if that kiss was only about making her feel better right then, for a moment. I wanted to be her medicine, to be the thing that made her smile and made her believe she really is all of those things I said she was.

She is. But now, she's not going to believe it. One kiss took it all away. She'll think I said it solely for the outcome, which, while I'd kiss her back time and time again, my intent was only to give her back her fire.

"I'm sorry. Abby . . . I'm . . ." I hold out my open palm, the sting of my bruised eye burning more than before. Her lips are puffy and smeared with the same pink that's probably on mine. I run my wrist across my mouth to erase it, so she doesn't have to see what we've done. Still, she turns away.

"I'll let you go. I hope you have a happy birthday." My gravelly voice betrays me, and there's no way to hide the hurt.

June was right, and I get my phone out to call her on my way back to my car. I can't do it, though, and while I drive away, I toss my phone into the passenger seat and stew in my own shame. I'm no better than Hayden. He took something from me, and I just took something from him.

SIXTEEN

ABBY

I'm such a fake.

Hayden is standing in my doorway, dressed so nice—*in a suit!* He told me to wear something fancy, so I put on my last awards show dress. It's black and plain, and feels kind of simple now that I see him downstairs, clutching the rest of the roses meant for my birthday.

I kissed his brother.

I suck in my bottom lip at the memory; the tingle hasn't left for hours. It was wrong to kiss him like that. Things were so raw and he was saying all those words that just made me *feel.*

I'm going to break his brother's heart.

I can't hide up here all night, and maybe I'll go downstairs and feel differently. Maybe my heart will swell, Hayden's kiss suddenly feeling different—feeling like Tory's.

Nothing has ever felt like Tory's kiss.

My mom left Hayden in the doorway while she got back to her work, and he's fidgeting. My dad's news about moving back to Allensville really threw things into a frenzy for her. It's easier to have hope when the problem is several hundred miles south of you.

My father will hate it here. He'll leave, eventually. This is the best plan I have come up with so far—wait him out. Some plan.

Unable to avoid my fate much longer, I make my way down the stairs, catching Hayden's gaze about halfway down. He looks at me like I'm something special. Why can't it light me up inside?

"Wow," he mouths. I tighten my smile.

"You sure this is okay? You're in a suit, and this thing was on double clearance at Boutique Bin," I say, fanning out the skirt to one side.

"You could make a paper bag look good," he teases, tipping my chin up with light pressure from his thumb. His lips hover over mine for a beat, and he smiles just before kissing me. It's sweet. It isn't Tory's kiss. I need to stop comparing.

I need to stop *thinking*.

"Everything all right here?" He motions toward my mom after handing me my flowers. I hug them close to smell them and glance over to my mom, who is making piles out of the piles.

"My dad's moving here," I say with a shrug. It's an inevitable obstacle that I'm going to have to accept.

"Your mom is letting him in?"

I scrunch my brow and flash my gaze back to him, taking a second to realize he's confused.

"Oh, no," I laugh out. "Not for a million bucks. No. Besides, his girlfriend is coming too. It's part of his plan to be 'more involved.'"

"I'd let him have the floor for a million dollars," my mom hollers from a room away.

My lips bunch in skepticism and I shake my head silently at Hayden, because as tempting as money might be, my mom knows the trade-off would be letting the devil inside. You don't invite them in. You wear garlic and shit.

"Let me put these in water," I say, handing him the small purse I packed for the night with my phone, wallet, and keys.

I slip past my mom and move toward the cabinet to find a vase. I flip through a few, the noise annoying her, and she finally joins me, digging one out from beneath the sink. It's a tall, slender, blue glass cylinder, a gift that came with flowers from June a couple of years ago when my mom got home from the hospital after a car crash resulted in a broken wrist. She's basically ambidextrous now because she refused to stop working. She booked me two national ad campaigns in that cast.

When the vase is full of water, I dump in the flowers and move it to the center of our dining table. My mom quirks a brow at my choice of placement.

"Just trying to liven up all of this," I say, waving my hand around the mess.

"Ah, yes . . . it's much lovelier now. Thank you," she jokes. "Now, go on. Go enjoy your birthday."

"Birthday weekend," I correct as she moves around the table and places her palms on my cheeks. She squeezes them enough to force my lips to pout and she plants a big mother-has-the-right-to kiss on my lips.

"Weekend. Correct," she says, giving Hayden a sideways look to make sure he's on board.

She moves her gaze back to me, and before she lets her hands fall away from my face, she stares at my eyes with a questioning look, her eyes pulling in to the center and her lips pinched, on the verge of speaking.

"What?" I ask.

Her eyes flit to Hayden and back to me quickly, a silent clue that hits my stomach hard. I'm not sure what she's insinuating, but my mom and I are very close. There's every possibility that she can read my thoughts. At the very least, she can tell that my body language with the twin I am dating is very different from the one I'm not.

"Be good to yourself, baby girl. Be selfish." She pats my cheek lightly.

My gut rolls with the weight of guilt because I *was* selfish. Very selfish.

"Can I take your jacket?" I quickly switch the topic, never reacting to her advice, but she can tell I heard it, knows it sunk in. She's always been able to read me like that.

"Sure," she says, backing away and moving toward the mudroom where she keeps most of her winter things.

She comes out with her black wool pea coat, which is probably the nicest thing she owns. Her letting me wear it is a sign of trust. She let me borrow it once before, to a party, where I stupidly left it hanging on a hook in a house full of pot smoke and underage drinking. I went to retrieve it the next day, thankful it wasn't covered in spilled drinks or worse, but the moment I got it into my car I knew it would never pass her inspection. It reeked. I took a hotdog ad for Twofers just to pay for the dry cleaning.

I slip my arms inside as she holds it open for me and pull the belt around my waist, knotting it in the front. There's a small chance of snow tonight. If it happens, I don't want the little black dress to be all I've got.

"You ready? Reservations are at seven," Hayden says, holding out his arm like a gentleman.

I glance to my mom one more time, and she continues with the same begging look she had when she told me to be selfish. I ignore it and wish her a good night as I let Hayden walk me out to his car.

"This one's all mine now," he says.

I already know. I saw Tory's junker earlier. Hayden doesn't need to know any of that, though.

"Oh, yeah? No more sign-up sheet for who gets to take the car?" I joke as he opens the passenger door for me and I slip inside. He smiles at my joke, but that's about as big of a laugh as it gets.

I figure we're going somewhere nice for dinner, but I don't expect the rooftop grill on the way to Indy. Hayden keeps me guessing for most of the trip, but I figure it out when the only other option is driving completely into the city. He pulls into the lot, tucking his car neatly between an Escalade and a Porsche. He can't afford this.

"Hayden, this is very sweet, but we don't have to go here," I say.

"I know we don't *have* to, but I want to give you a special night." He leans toward me and runs his thumb along my cheek. All I can think is how I wish it were Tory, and how I'm basically using him for a nice dinner because I'm too big of a chicken shit to end this.

"Thank you," I croak out.

He gets out and rounds the car to open my door for me, taking my hand and leading me inside. A glass elevator takes us up to the roof where he's reserved a table in the corner that overlooks the downtown lights. I don't know what he had to do to nab this seat, but I feel as though I'm becoming a way overpriced date. This is too much.

"Madam," he says, putting on a silly voice as he pulls out my chair. Before I sit, a hostess steps in and takes my jacket for me, draping it over an open seat nearby. Heaters hang over our heads from cords strung across the patio amidst the zigzagging lights. It's warm, but maybe I'm warmer because of how uncomfortable I am with this entire situation. My eyes dart around in a paranoid fashion, and I don't even hear when the waiter steps up to take our drink orders. Hayden must have answered something for me.

"You're in shock?" He reaches forward and holds out an open palm, a crooked smile showing his teeth.

I put my hand in his and hope to feel *something.* He closes his fingers around my hand, and it's as if I'm dead. My heart is pounding but only due to this sensation of feeling trapped.

"So, confession time," he begins.

"Huh?" I shoot my gaze to his, my eyes wider than a cat caught in a hound dog's path.

He chuckles and squeezes my hand a little, shaking it against the table softly to work out my nerves. I'm sure he thinks I'm just caught off guard by the fancy restaurant, but that's not it. I've been to dozens of restaurants like this, meeting with casting directors and agents. As stressful as those dinners may have been, they were nothing compared to this one.

"So, my confession," he starts again, and I'm so terrified that he is going to blurt out the L word that I interject with a confession of my own.

"I don't think I can do this anymore." My mouth goes dry, my voice cracking on the last word.

"You . . . can't do *this?*" His touch on my hand has relaxed, his fingers unfurling and letting go. I squeeze back because I care about him.

"Hayden, I'm not . . . I don't want . . ." My jumbled words are not enough. I am no good without a plan, and this is about as spontaneous as I've ever been. I don't know what to say to make things clear, but I do know it's killing me to see the cracks forming in his happiness. His smile has disintegrated, and the dimple in his cheek has become a deep divot between his brows.

"I'm so sorry," I say, tears pooling in my eyes. I shake my head and kneed at his hands, trying to bring life back into them. They've gone cold.

His focus is off, as if he's looking through me more than at me. He leans back in his seat, finally pulling his hands away completely.

"Tell me, is it *him?*"

My insides twist and burst with pain. I don't know how to answer this because the right answer is both yes and no.

I shake my head lightly, my bottom lip trembling.

"I don't know." I won't lie to him. I've lied enough already.

He slumps even more and looks off to the side with a sharp laugh. Our waiter walks up with a tray, holding two sparkling drinks, and Hayden holds up a hand.

"I'm so sorry, but something's come up," he says to the man.

Hayden stands and paces around his chair, catching the attention of others sitting nearby. He pauses behind his seat and grips the back with both hands as he bends his head down with a derisive chuckle.

"We can go," I say, jetting to my feet and grabbing my jacket.

"Yeah. Sure," he says, his focus still on the floor.

I'm too warm to wear my mom's coat. My skin is on fire, so I layer the jacket over my arm and stand perfectly still, my hands gripping tightly at one another underneath the wool while I stare at Hayden, waiting for him to make his next move. He laughs again, a light, ominous sound tainted with the bad blood between him and Tory.

"I brought my dad's old guitar, the one he left behind. It's in the trunk, and after dinner . . . I was going to play that song for you, the one you had me play in the car." His head pops up and his eyes meet mine. There's no hiding the red sting and glossiness taking them over. "It was Tory's idea."

I gurgle out a small cry, biting hard on my lip to stop it from progressing.

Hayden nods, puzzle pieces coming together. I am a terrible person.

"Come on, let's get you home, birthday girl," he says, and even though his voice is still sweet, there's a note that rests below his tone that carries a brewing mixture of hurt and anger. He's been dealing with it for some time, but I may have just added the final ingredient. Call me the master chef of broken hearts.

Hayden ushers me out ahead of him, and we are both deathly silent for the elevator ride down. It takes several minutes for the valet to retrieve his car, and I note every five-and ten-dollar bill he's doled out since we arrived. His eyes remain straight ahead on the road and mine on the blur of life that passes by out my passenger window. The radio is set on some news channel, the volume low so the only sound to pass the time is a mumbling noise that's broken up by the occasional commercial.

He speeds a little to cut the time, obviously as anxious to leave me as I am him. If I stay in this car with him any longer, I will fold and profess that I was wrong, that I need him and want to be with him, and the only reason would be because I don't want to see him suffer. But that is not heeding my mom's advice.

Be selfish.

My mom was never selfish. She stayed with a man who cheated on her numerous times, and made sure he came home to a perfect house, with clean laundry, a hot dinner, and all of the bills paid. My mom was the first to go to college in our family, and her business degree was squandered as a housewife. Most of my dad's investments turned into money pits. He mortgaged our house—the one my *abuelo* built—to pay off his own debts, so my mom took on an accounting job to pay it off. It's in only her name now, but what was once hers free and clear still has more than a hundred thousand owed. All this, yet my dad is the one who feels he's not getting his due.

My mother was selfless to a fault. She was naïve, and she was a doormat. I don't think she's ever really known love. But I—I might.

Hayden pulls into my driveway but stops short. He's already in far enough. I understand.

"Hey," he says, stopping me before I get out. I pause with one leg out of the car, my purse and my mother's coat clutched in my lap. "He's going to break you, just so you know. My brother?" He shakes his head, his mouth a tight line. "He doesn't know any other way," he says. "Happy birthday, Abby."

I smile and nod, not able to find words to reply to everything he just said. My chest aches and my lungs hunger for me to scream, but I'm too weak. I shut the car door behind myself and wait at the end of my driveway as Hayden pulls out. He doesn't speed away, and he even signals at the end of the street. He's heading toward his home, and I can't stop the barrage of thoughts rushing through my head of what he's going to do when he gets there. I don't know whether Tory's home or not, but it's only a matter of time before the two of them collide again. This time, it's all my fault.

SEVENTEEN

TORY

I haven't shot pool with Lucas in ages. It's what I needed tonight. He knew it.

We got to Eight Lanes when June's shift began, and we've racked up maybe forty games of nine-ball in three hours. Because June's here, we're not taking advantage of our usual *look-the-other-way* pitchers of beer. I have to respect the way Lucas respects June. She doesn't like him breaking rules at her place of employment, so he waits until she's not around. I mean, a free pitcher is a tough thing to give up entirely.

I won the last round, so I offer to buy Lucas a slice and refill our Dr. Pepper at the counter while he racks up to break the next game, but June's off work soon. I'm officially third-wheeling. I've done it enough that my Spidey senses alert me. He's waffling in his response because the good friend in him wants to say yes, but he's got a girl to spend time with. They've missed out on enough time as it is.

"Actually," I say before he has to find an excuse. "I'm pretty tired."

It's eight-thirty. He knows this is bullshit.

"A'ight man, you sure?" He's grateful I gave him an out.

I fake a yawn and pick up the empty soda pitcher.

"Yeah, I might head back to my dad's. He wants me to stay here and keep the peace, but I'm not doing a very good job of it." I walk backward a few steps, grimacing. Lucas knows things with me and Hayden are bad. I told him about the camp letter I found, and he was as shocked as I was. He remembers how excited I was when my parents let me apply. It cost three hunny just for the shot. I did not, however, alert Lucas to the details from earlier—the kiss. I'm not in the mood to be judged tonight. He won't mean to do it, but he will. The dude's poker face is shit.

"You gonna come back for the party tomorrow, then?" he asks.

I wince with a tight smile and waggle my head side-to-side before setting the pitcher down at the register near June.

"Tory!" June grunts from behind me. She leans over the counter and pulls on my shirt, tugging me back with a short choke. Her mom's put a lot of work into the party, and yeah, yeah . . . games. But the thought of being in a circle that tight with her and my brother just burns my throat. I don't think I can do it. Call me a pussy, but I just . . . can't.

"You know I wanna be there," I say, which is a very non-answer answer. I grab my collar and tug my shirt out of her hand and straighten it on my body as I turn to face her. I love this shirt, it's all black and says the word DOMINATE in the center in dark gray. Now it's all kinked.

"Tory," she repeats my name, this time a little more forgiving.

I take a deep breath. It's hard to say no to June. She has this way of making people do things they don't really want to do, like buy flowers for a girl who will never be theirs.

"I'll try," I say. I'll probably cave and show up briefly just to make June happy. I really don't want to, though.

"Okay," she says, leaning over the counter and throwing her arms around my neck. As I lean in, she kisses the top of my head.

"That was all her, dude. You saw it," I say to Lucas, holding my hands up innocently. He laughs because he thinks I'm joking, but lately I've been hit enough over women that I'm not taking any chances.

"I'll see you guys," I say, grabbing my beanie from the counter and stuffing it on my head. It's crisp outside, the sky clear and full of stars. It's a no-moon night, so the glitter in the sky shows off a little more than normal. It also makes the drive home pitch black.

I go slow, taking a route that passes Abby's house because I'm a sucker and the torture reminds me that a part of her wanted me, too. Her car is gone, which maybe means her mom finally caved and took it in for new tires. Things for her are about to get really hard, and as messy as my parents' relationship is, the one between her mom and dad has years of complications woven into it. She's only shared the tip of the iceberg with me.

I stayed locked in my room until Hayden left, but I saw him haul out my dad's guitar, so he's at least going to try. Even his poor skills on the thing are going to make her swoon. I get in our driveway, parked in the place where our—I mean *his*—car normally rests, and sit there for a few minutes with my engine off.

Maybe this is all I need to get myself to grow up. I need to take ball more seriously, and I have to send some emails to coaches on my own. My dad was doing the work for us, but it's probably not on his mind right now. I want to get out of this place, go somewhere warm maybe. Basketball in California sounds nicer and nicer.

I leave my car, renewed about my direction. I'm so wide awake and sober on a Saturday night that I might get started making my plans tonight. I practically skip through the garage, my mom's van unmoved for the entire day. I find her already asleep upstairs, her TV on low and a box of things she brought up from the garage on the bed in front of her. I recognize my Little League jersey right away, and pull it loose from the pile. Hayden's is snagged on it, so I bring them both in my hands, noting how they're both Youth mediums. He's number one and I was number two, which makes me smile and laugh to myself. I bet he loved being number one just this once. I remember how excited he was when dad threw the jersey at him. I'd asked to be number two, but not to be nice. I wanted to be Derek Jeter.

My mom lets out a light snore, so I set the shirts on the bed and pull her blanket over her arms. She's still wearing the same clothes she had on earlier. She's probably been cleaning all day, or reliving better times by going through boxes like this one. The sight makes me both happy and deeply sad.

I back out of her room and pull her door closed, not wanting to disturb her. Hayden's door is wide open, and I think about closing his door too, but instead pause at the entrance and look at all of the things inside to remind me who he really is. His closet door is open, exposing his perfectly hung shirts and pants. Who hangs their joggers? Hayden does. The space smells clean, like lemon, and not because mom whisked through with her laundry basket, grumbling while she picked up socks and boxers, but because Hayden actually cleans things. We have matching quilts; they're made of old jerseys that we wore throughout the years. His is tucked in and even, ready for military inspection. Mine has a peanut butter stain on it from a protein bar I ate two weeks ago, and I don't think I've ever folded a thing in my life.

I'm smiling as I back out of his room, somehow a bit of the hostility I've been clinging to easing. But the carefree moment is quickly replaced with the tight squeeze of suspicion when I step into my room and find

Dad's old guitar resting on my bed. My light smile drops, the corners of my mouth like arrows pointing to my feet. I stand over the instrument and run my finger along the D-string, making it vibrate with an eerie buzz. I know Hayden took this with him. At some point, though, he brought it back. He left it here for me to find.

Glancing back over my shoulder, I half expect to find him standing in my doorway, waiting to punch my other eye out. The hallway is dark and silent, though. A quick check on social media brings Hayden up blank. He's turned his location settings off, which usually means he's out at McCaffey's place. Nobody shares their location out there, mostly so the people who aren't invited don't know their way in. Hayden is probably drinking, or maybe taking advantage of McCaffey's side business—the cat sells the best weed in the county. I shouldn't care what Hayden does, *but damn it, I do*. The guy can hold his beer but that's about it. I fish around in my bag for my keys and toss my beanie on my desk, hurrying down the stairs and through the garage toward my junker so I can just get eyes on him. I'm nearly halfway across the driveway when Abby's headlights flash off and on and catch my attention.

Shading my eyes, I take cautious steps down my driveway as she kicks open her door and throws it closed behind her. She's parked across the street in an open alley space like some undercover cop on surveillance. She's wearing a black dress that swings around her knees, her feet stuffed in bright white tennis shoes, and her arms covered in some obnoxious pink sweatshirt that she's only pulled over her arms, the front left bunched across her chest.

"This is your fault," she says, her voice raw as if she's been crying.

I figured tonight did not go as planned when I saw the guitar on my bed. I can understand why Hayden would be marching toward me with a hot fist and fire in his eyes, but Abby? She kissed me. Yeah, I kissed back, but this, for once . . . this isn't my fault.

"Abby, I know you're upset, but now is really not the time."

I don't get a chance to say more before she levels me with both hands in the dead center of my chest. She pushes me so hard that I fall back a few steps and she legit ricochets.

"I broke up with him. Are you happy? I'm a terrible person and I just ripped your brother's heart in half and threw away so much trust. You satisfied?" She comes at me again, this time grunting on impact. I don't budge, but only because I see her coming and brace myself.

"Abby, you aren't a horrible person. I think Hayden's at McCaffey's. I'm just gonna make sure he's—"

Another shove knocks the wind out of me.

"Goddamnit!" I grab her wrists as she lunges at me again.

She literally growls and tugs down hard, my grip quickly releasing as she rips away from me. She takes off one of her shoes and throws it at my head and I swat it away, but not in time to block the second one. It hits me square in my still-black eye.

"Abby . . . stop!" I whisper-shout.

She's swaying forward and back, her arms dangling in front of her, the sweatshirt bunched around her wrists. She has to be freezing with her bare shoulders and bare feet. I can see her breath, it tangles with mine in the air as we both pant.

"Just stop." I hold my hands out flat, like I'm ordering an audience to be seated.

She blows at the stray hairs that have fallen in her face. Sniffling, she runs her sleeve along her nose, yanking the sweatshirt up her skin only for it to slide down to her wrists again as she stands there a total mess, body rocking with this unleashed rage that I think is meant for me. Her head shakes and she points at me, only lifting her arm halfway.

"God damn you, Tory D'Angelo." Her words quiver, either from the cold or from the fumes of emotion left in her tank.

My hands are balled into fists, and I'm incredibly uneasy. My world tilts more by the second just from staring into Abby's eyes. It's so dark that it's impossible to see the golden hue, but I spot the red in the whites. Her features are heavy, a pairing of exhaustion and fear that I only recognize because maybe I feel it, too.

"Why did you break up, Abby?"

I touch the inside of my wrist to my lip that feels fat from where her shoe hit me. She blinks at my question.

"You know why," she says, her voice low and discreet. If none of the neighbors have come out to see what's happening after the shoe bit, they aren't coming out now. I think my mom might have indulged in a little wine during her walk through memory lane, so we'd have to practically be murdering each other with screams for her to come look.

"No, I don't. I have learned that I don't know shit, Abby. I can't afford to pretend or assume. I need you to tell me." My hands flex from outstretched to fists and back again. My legs tingle, either ready to collapse or to carry me on a marathon. And still, Abby stands out of arm's reach and rocks, and stares, and lets that one tear run down her cheek and fall into the small divot on her neck above her collar bone. It's lit by the stars, like a diamond gliding along her smooth skin.

"Why did you break up with Hayden, Abby?" My mouth quivers in anticipation, and the longer she stands facing me, her mouth unable to say the words, the more I want to reach inside her and pull them out.

She finally shakes her head.

"You know why," she repeats.

I shake my head, prepared to say *I don't*, but words fail me as she takes one step, followed by another, until she's nearly standing with her feet on top of mine.

Her tiny frame fits under my chin, and as I glare down at her she raises her face to the sky, her hair sliding out of her face like ribbons, her bare shoulders covered in bumps from the cold air. Clouds are beginning to move in, killing the only light we have, but before the stars are completely gone, I run the back of my fingers along the side of her bare neck, over her shoulder and down her arm. I lift her hand in mine, doing the same with the other as I duck low enough to tuck my head underneath the sweatshirt that tethers her arms together in the sleeves. Her hands rest on my shoulders and she steps up on my feet, her lips soft and fragile, timid and scared. Open. Ready.

My head falls to rest on hers just as she lifts her chin, and our lips touch just barely. Electric. It's as if I've been stung.

"Why did you break up with Hayden?" I repeat again, this time only a whisper, my lips brushing against hers as I speak.

Her head tilts an inch or two to the right.

"You know why," she breathes, and that's enough. Because I do.

Our lips connect as if they're starving for the life only we can give to each other. I lift her up and she wraps her legs around me while I walk us both back into the garage, our mouths never once breaking their hold. This is how I've wanted to kiss her since the first time she shot me down. I've dreamt of this kiss during our late-night talks with June and Lucas. I stared at these perfect lips and imagined what they taste like.

Honey and peaches.

Her skin is cold, so I smack my palm against the garage door control, closing it behind us. I set her down on the hood of my mom's van long enough for her to toss her sweatshirt from her arms and for me to run my hands up her jaw and into her hair.

We pause to breathe, teeth clinging to each other's lips as we peel apart, chests heaving and fingers clawing into our clothing. Abby lifts her chin, her eyes flitting upward to meet mine under the haze of her long, thick lashes. She's classic pin-up, even dressed down. The girl was born to be a star, and it makes me so angry that her father is trying to chip away at her brightness.

She studies me with a serious face, lips parted enough to take needed breaths, her breasts lifting with each intake of air. I glance down at them just enough, the allure impossible to ignore. Abby reacts by lifting her chest higher and sliding closer to me, her knees parting until I stand between them.

Her nervous lips grow more confident, sneering at me as she lifts her chin enough to give me her neck. Like a hungry vampire, I take the bait, pulling her body against me, opening her legs wide, and running my hand down the length of her hair until I've found enough to grip and pull her head back with a gentle tug. She whimpers when I do, her hands grabbing the loops on my jeans and pulling me close to feel how hard I am for her. I grunt at the sensation and the idea of being so ready against her softest parts.

I dust kisses along her jaw and neck, and she arches as I move lower, her breasts pushing up toward me, begging me to taste them. My tongue traces along the fabric of her dress, across the curve of her tits, my teeth grabbing at whatever cloth I can, wanting to tear away her dress. I settle for placing kisses over her clothes, nipping the curves until my lips find the hard peak underneath. I bite through the material, and her shoulder blades lift from the cold metal of the car.

Unable to do everything I want here in the garage, I pull her into me, my cock straining under my jeans, wanting to bust out and plunge deep into her like the barbaric asshole I am. My hands grab under her thighs and lift her up, swinging her around toward the mudroom door. The house is dark, so I'm careful not to move too fast or run us into anything that might wake my buzzed and sleeping mom. I'm not about to let her go, though. I've kissed this girl before and when she pushed away, it nearly broke me.

"Do you want to see my room?" I ask against her mouth in a whisper. She nods and licks my lips, taking the top one between her teeth and clamping down with seductive pressure. I hope I can carry us up the stairs without passing out from the things she is doing to me.

We both hold our breath at the upstairs landing, passing by the albums and empty shelves where my trophies used to sit. I threw them out, though I saw that my mom saved the bag from the trash and left it in the garage.

I'm quiet with my door, letting it click slowly and twisting the lock behind her back as I hold her up against it.

Her legs relax their grip around my waist and she slides from my body, down the door, and for a beat, I'm afraid she's about to tell me this is all a big mistake. Not that it isn't. It's a clusterfuck on the scale of mistakes, but I'm already in it. I was in it the moment June talked me into buying flowers and Abby showed up with my brother.

Hayden would probably say I've been handed everything in my life, but that's a lie. I've worked my ass off for every honor I earned, fought my way through expectations and my own failures to show I have grit. Abby was never mine to easily have. I don't deserve her. But damn, do I plan to fight for her, to fight to keep her, and prove to her there's something worth being with inside of me.

With lust-heavy eyes holding me hostage, Abby brings her hands up her body, crossing her arms over her chest, and walking her fingers up to the thin straps of her sleeves. She slides them each over her shoulders at the same time, her dress slipping down her body until she catches it just over her breasts. A coy smile paints her lips, the bottom one caught in her teeth.

Fuck me.

I cover her hands with mine, coaxing her hands to let go of the fabric. The silky material slips from her fingers slowly, revealing a new inch of her skin a second at a time until it slips down to her hips all at once. It's not the kind of dress you wear a bra with, and I knew that when my mouth ran along the smooth material, but it's still a control-altering sight to see Abby like this.

Vulnerable.

Never—not once—is that a word I would associate with her. But she is right now. She is for me, baring her skin and extending her trust.

Taking her hands one at a time, I lift them above her head, pressing the back of her wrists flat against the door as I step in close, my chest pressing against hers. She leaves them above her head, letting me trace slow lines down the tender skin inside her arms, over the nape of her neck and down her breasts until my thumbs find the aching peaks of her nipples. I gently stroke them in circles, and she reacts by scratching at my skin. I pause long enough to tug my shirt up and over my head and toss it to the floor, and my touch returns to her pink tips within seconds.

I gently roll the budding nipples between my thumbs and fingers to start, adding pressure as her body reacts. God, I bet she's wet as fuck.

Stepping up on her toes, she nips at my chin, and I drop my head enough to take her mouth with mine, my hands working her breasts while she runs her palms along my sides and to my back, finally reaching inside the back of my jeans and tracing from the curve of my ass and hips to the front. Her fingertips graze along the tip of my dick and it flexes from the slight touch, causing me to growl against her mouth. Her lips smile against mine. She's proud of her control. So much for vulnerable.

She easily unsnaps my jeans, pulling on the open waistband to bring my zipper down fast. When her hand reaches in and wraps around my width, I shiver in response, my cock flexing again. Lowering myself in front of her, I kiss my way down her neck and the center of her chest until my mouth finds the perfect hard tip of her breast. I clutch it with my teeth, rougher than I probably should, but she seems to like it. My tongue flicks against it a few times before my hands snake around her legs and lift her ass so I can spin her and carry her to my bed.

With one hand, I reach to toss away my total bachelor-style blanket before setting her down atop my deep blue sheets. Her body is like snow against the deep color, like the stars that were just moments ago bright in the navy sky. I allow myself a pause to look down at her, one knee on the bed between her legs, her arms bunching up the pillow above her head while a wanting smile turns up the corners of her mouth.

She hums.

I obey.

I've never had a girl in my room. I've *had* girls, but never in a way that was so slow and perfect and matching every fantasy I've had. I want to take my time, but every nerve in my body wants to rush. And then she groans and rocks her hips, still cloaked under the rest of her dress.

Not wanting to ruin her trust, I step to the table next to my bed and take out a condom. I hold it up, meeting her gaze with a question. She reaches out to take the foil packet from me, tears it open and hands it back.

I'm genuinely nervous. Every ounce of bravado that has ever come before is gone; the only thing left is a nervous young man standing before the most beautiful girl in the world, desperate to be hers completely on her birthday.

Moving back to the end of the bed, I hold the open packet in my teeth while I push down my jeans and boxers, stepping out of them before pulling out the condom and rolling it on. My heated gaze begins at her breasts and trails down to the space between her knees, which open when I look at them. I lower myself to my knees and run my palms up her bare thighs, collecting the fabric of her dress along the way. Once I reach the top along her waist, I curl my fingers and drag the black cloth down the length of her, her curves like the soothing waves of a crystal ocean, kissed by the sun. Her black lace panties barely hide a thing, her skin smooth and shaven, a small gold stud fitted in the skin below her belly button.

I touch the stud with my finger, then travel lower until my hand runs along the edge of the lace, dipping lower along the soaking wet cotton strip between her legs. I push it to the side and dip my finger inside her, reveling in the way her body curls from my touch. I push into her again, causing her to moan and her hips to rock.

Unable to stand not being inside her any longer, I slide both hands to her hips and curl my fingers into the lacy straps along her hips, rolling her panties down her hips and legs until she's able to kick them away. Her pink skin is swollen, dusted with a small strip of hair that begs to be kissed. I bend down, holding myself above her hips, just so I can press a kiss against her soft center, dragging my tongue along her swollen pussy just once before pulling her legs down the length of the bed so she's poised and ready for me to enter.

"Tell me you want this," I say, needing to hear it for my own ego.

"I want *you,*" she moans, and that's all it takes for me to push forward and drive through the center of her.

"Ahh," she cries out, grabbing the pillow above her head and covering her face to muffle her cries from pleasure.

I slide out of her completely, wanting to feel the same sensation again, and her reaction is the same, a muffled cry as her body pushes against me, urging me deeper. I do it again, and again, until I'm no longer able to leave the warmth of her pussy, the sweet tightness and the way it hugs my cock. My hands grip at her legs, pulling her into me with every thrust and eventually, she pushes her own body up, sitting on the end of the bed while I push my dick in and out so hard that I'm afraid I won't last more than a few seconds.

That, however, is not Abby's plan. Now sitting before me, she pushes me back until I'm on the floor and she crawls on top of me, lowering herself on my throbbing cock and riding me cautiously, her hands pressed against my chest to pin me down while she controls every single sensation I'm allowed to feel.

My hands reach up to touch her, but she stops them as her hips rock, pinning them to my sides as she leans over me and rolls her hips in the most intoxicating motion, her body sliding down mine and taking all of me before almost letting me leave her completely.

Her hair has fallen all around us, hiding us from the outside world while our bodies take what they want from each other. My hands beg to touch her, and I fight against her willingly until she relents and lets me run my palms along her breasts and back, cupping her ass and pushing her into me hard until she pulses and squeezes around me.

I push myself up with one hand so we're both sitting while she rocks her hips against me and I penetrate her again and again, filling her completely, until she leans back and bites her knuckles in a breathy cry of pleasure. I pull her body into me, close enough to bite at her neck and quiet my own sounds as I come hard, throbbing with every wave of pleasure.

She falls against my chest, her hair damp with sweat, my body beading with moisture, every bit of me sticking to every part of her, and she stays just like this, with me inside, for long minutes until soft laughter brings her eyes to mine.

"I cannot believe I finally let Tory D'Angelo have me," she jokes, referring to every single time I've hit on her without expectation that this—that *us*—could ever be real.

"You've always had me. Only seems fair," I say, my response not as funny as she expects.

Her amused smile shifts to something else entirely. I don't think she was expecting such honesty from me, or such adoration, and frankly, I'm a little surprised to have said it. But it's true. Every word of it. Also, there is no way I'm giving her up to spare my brother's feelings. He can have the fucking basketball academy. I want the queen.

EIGHTEEN

ABBY

I knew what I was doing when I left my house and drove to the D'Angelo's after Hayden dropped me off. I knew he wouldn't be home. How could he go home? Too great a chance that Tory would be there.

And Tory would be there, eventually.

I sat in my car and vacillated between wanting to scream and tell him to leave me alone forever and wanting to wrap my everything around his heart and smother it until it was mine. I seem to have leaned into the latter.

I didn't want to leave. He didn't want me to go. Everything about the way he touched me was so different from any touch I had before—*from Hayden's*. My heart was different. What we committed was a sin—an indulgence—but it was also what both of our hearts wanted.

It was selfish.

I left in the early morning hours, one final kiss from him as I wrapped myself in one of his T-shirts and an old pair of sweats, and with the shoes I threw at him during my tirade. Even now, as I lay wide awake after only a few hours of sleep, I feel him everywhere—*still.*

It's my party at June's today. I can smell the menudo on the stove downstairs. My grandma always made it for the holidays, so it's become one of my birthday favorites. It's really the only thing my mom mastered from my grandmother's kitchen. Warm soup is one of the very few good things about December. I guess now I have two good things.

My neck is covered in love bites left behind from Tory. I noticed them when I got home, so I laid my turtleneck dress out for the day, knowing I'd need something that isn't suspiciously modest. It's a sixties style, a dark orange short swing dress that I pair with knee-high brown leather boots. I might have worn it even if I didn't have guilty marks to hide all over my skin.

After a quick shower, I lock myself in my room to dry my hair paper straight and put mascara on my lashes to distract from the major sleepy puffs I sport on my face.

I make my way downstairs with a watering mouth, anxious to take a taste from the pot I know must be near ready. I'm stalled at the bottom of the steps, though, when I see my father's back as he stirs over the stove.

"Get away from my soup," I bite out.

In the courtroom, I'm a quiet girl. In person, though—I'm me. There's no judge here to keep tally on the way I disrespect my father. He's disrespected me my entire life by basically cutting himself out of everything that doesn't make a profit.

I flash my gaze to my mom who stands behind the table, thankfully cleared of all of her homework to fight the man in our house. She's dressed and ready to go to June's house, which means he is an unexpected guest.

My father turns to face me, holding a fat spoon in front of his lips, blowing across the steam. I hate the way his lips pucker. I hope mine look nothing like his. He opens wide and floats the spoon over his tongue, his mouth closing over it like a child waiting for the airplane full of oatmeal.

"*Mmm*, Denise. This is just like your mother's." It's disgraceful to hear him talk about my grandmother, knowing how he could have helped her or checked in on her in Florida but refused since she was no longer his family.

"Thanks. We have to leave, so—" My mom swings her open palm toward to door, ushering my father out.

He drops the spoon in the sink and runs his sleeve over his lips before reaching into his coat pocket to pull out a thick envelope. Neither of us are naïve enough to believe there's money inside.

"I just wanted to drop by to give you this," he says, tossing the envelope on the table. "You can read it if you want, but basically, I own fifty percent." He winks at me, as if I'm supposed to be pleased that he owns half of my soul.

My mom rips the envelope open and unfurls the papers, scanning quickly as my father heads for the door.

"Judge said it was the easiest ruling he's ever made," he says.

My mom collapses into the nearby chair, not even bothering to respond to his smug remarks as he leaves.

"Is he right? Is that . . . *it?*" I ask.

She brushes her hand in my direction to hush me, her eyes pinched with worry as she reads. She flips through the papers at a maddening pace, then finally gives up, tossing them into the center of the table.

"I give up," she says, shrugging. Her eyes lazily focus on the pages. I move close enough to read some of the language, but it's so *lawyer-ized* that I can't get through the first paragraph without getting lost.

The soup rolls to a boil, so I rush to the stove and turn it off, stirring to keep the rich ingredients from burning. It'll be too hot to put in the car for a few minutes, so I move it to one of the empty burners and leave it there to cool while I return to my mom, stepping in behind her to squeeze the tension from her shoulders.

"Baby girl, no. It's your birthday. I'm fine," she says, patting my hands. I don't budge, and eventually she lets me continue massaging.

"Your muscles say you aren't fine," I say.

She shakes with a quick laugh.

Normally, something like having my dad show up and drop a bomb like this would ruin my day—definitely my birthday weekend. But I'm different today. Optimistic, and maybe a bit . . . bold.

Selfish.

"You know what?" I stop rubbing her shoulders and gather up the papers, twisting them into a kindling stick that I march over to the stove. I turn the burner back on high and hold the paper against the coils until the end catches fire. My mom leaps from her chair and rushes to me, but I hold the papers up high, keeping her at bay long enough for the flame to take hold and eat away half of whatever the fuck this shit stack is that my dad left. I drop the smoking pages into the sink and run the water over what's left, scooping the soupy mess out and tossing it in the trash like a rodent I just killed.

I wash my hands and glance over my shoulder, meeting my mom's wide eyes.

"Oh, like he doesn't have a million copies. And like his lawyer didn't send one to ours. That . . . that felt good." I shut the faucet off and dry my hands on a towel, tossing it to the counter with a bit of zest when I'm done.

The shocked awe on my mother's face shifts into pride after a few breaths, a curve taking to her lips.

"You told me to be selfish," I say, knowing she'll appreciate the credit. Though she doesn't realize just how greedy I've been.

June's house is already full by the time we pull up. I park us in the street and my mom hefts the pot from the back seat of my car. She gets halfway up the driveway before Tory runs out and takes it from her. Our gazes meet for one intimate glance.

"Thank you, babe. Not too much cake for you today, okay?" she teases him, knowing which of the two she's dealing with this time. My mom doesn't miss clues, which means she'll probably sense that something is up when Hayden shows up, if he even does. If he doesn't, well, everyone is going to wonder what's going on.

His car is the only vehicle missing. Lola and Naomi both parked in the garage. They spent the night with June baking and preparing for my day. I was supposed to stop in to help after my date, but well . . .

"There's my girl!" June's mom, Kristen, rushes over to me, her hands shielded by oven mitts. She gives me a half hug, not wanting to get flour and frosting on my sweater dress. Her arms are covered in ingredients.

"You look adorable," she says, looking me up and down. I sashay in acknowledgement just as Tory comes back into my space. Our eyes meet again, and I catch the knowing grin on his lips. He's very aware of the reason I'm wearing this dress.

I follow everyone through the kitchen into the main room that the Mabees have set up to be wide open for whatever silly games June has planned. There's a long table pushed all the way against the wall opposite of the fireplace, and it is filled with every type of frosted cookie and cake I can imagine.

"The maple cupcakes are surprisingly good. The oatmeal cookies . . . eh." June wiggles her palm in the air.

"Noted," I say, moving right in for one of the cupcakes. I reach for the perfect-looking desert on one of the tiered plates, another hand reaching for it a blink afterward, resulting in a near tug-of-war.

"What, you think because it's your birthday you can come in here and swoop the best cupcake?" Tory's finger grazes mine where we touch, a hidden token to let me know he's thinking of me—of last night.

Neither of us gives in right away, precariously holding the cake hostage over the Mabees' wooden floor.

"I tell you what, I'll split it with you," he offers.

I shake my head and smirk.

"Uh uh."

He puckers his lips into a tight smile, enjoying our playful spar. This is always where we were at our best—sharp tongues, poised for flirting.

"You want it all, huh?" His finger strokes along mine again.

"Always," I reply. His eyes dare me for a few seconds until others arrive to scour the table for treats near us. He lets go one finger at a time, and I casually bring the treat to my lips, unwrapping the paper from the bottom before I take a bite.

"Worth it?" he asks, one brow raised.

"Totally," I say, licking my lips.

Rather than look frustrated, he chuckles, hesitantly reaching an outstretched finger toward my face. I follow the tip of his finger, crossing my eyes as it lands on my nose and he wipes off a small dollop of frosting I left behind. He sucks the frosting from his finger, leaving it between his lips then showing me his teeth.

It's hot. And I no longer want to be at this party, but instead in his messy-ass bed with his body against mine. Naked. So very fucking naked.

My mom and June's have taken over running the kitchen, lining up sandwiches and my menudo, and with everyone else distracted, I take advantage of the perfect moment to slip away and pray Tory follows.

Tearing my cupcake in half, I hold out a bite as an offering for him. When he leans forward to take it in his mouth, I pull it back and pop it in mine, a suggestive smile on my closed lips as I chew. I wiggle the remaining piece in front of me, then draw him close with a finger as I walk backward to the small hallway that leads to the powder room. I lead him all the way inside, and he shuts the door behind him, locking it.

"You want my cupcake, Tory D'Angelo?" I hold it out for him, and he lets out a breathy growl as he rushes into me, taking my arms and pinning them out against the wall, the cupcake falling somewhere on the floor. His mouth covers mine possessively, his tongue tasting me, our teeth scraping against each other's hungry lips. He runs his hands along my arms and down my waist, bending down so he can continue the trip to the back of my thighs, lifting up my skirt enough to cup my ass.

"You are so much fun to touch," he whispers against my ear, biting the lobe and sucking it hard.

His hands are digging into my ass, palms to skin, and I want nothing more than to unzip him here and now and have him push me against the wall. That's not going to happen, though. I might be a terrible, selfish heartbreaker, but I'm not about to defile my best friend's powder room.

Ten bucks says she'd do it to mine in a heartbeat.

"I like this dress," he says, licking up the side of my neck and then covering my mouth with his for one last raw and needy kiss. I push him away, needing air, and we pant while dirty thoughts run rampant through both our minds.

"I had to wear this dress," I say, pushing the light switch down before we open the door. "You left your mark all over my body."

He bites near my ear as he wraps both arms around my stomach, holding me to him from behind. I can feel what our kissing has done to him, and it makes it difficult to leave this tiny, dark room.

I crack the door, though, knowing I have to be present for my own party, and when I'm sure the coast is clear, I slip out, spinning and meeting his confused eyes.

"You leave in about five minutes. Deal?"

He blinks a few times, then nods, shutting the door while I straighten my dress and the panties he basically hijacked up my ass.

We didn't talk about it, but I assume we're both on board with keeping this thing between us private . . . for now. I don't think Tory's family could handle a girl coming between him and his brother, though I did, and I am. With my dad finally in town, I'm not prepared to handle the backlash from our friends, either. No matter how you position *us*, we're the bad guys.

I'm funneling through the various scenarios, mentally making plans for how and when Tory and I *will* come out when the reason why we shouldn't stares me right in the face.

"Happy birthday weekend, Abs," Hayden says.

My eyes jet about the room as I'm hit with the sensation that I'm riding the Tilt-a-Whirl and I'm not buckled in. Hayden's palm finds my elbow, steadying me as he leans in and kisses my cheek.

"I'm not going to make you uncomfortable," he whispers. "I didn't want you to have to explain."

I straighten my spine and mentally flog myself for being the asshole that I am. I can't believe he's doing this to make sure *I'm* not the one who has to explain things and save face.

"Hey, June? It sounds like maybe there's a leak in—" Tory stops after taking only two steps into the room. All eyes zoom to him, Hayden's carrying the most intent.

"Hey, bro," he says. The hostility in his tone is apparent, but it's to be expected. Their recent struggles to get along aren't secret. *I'm* the secret part, on so many levels.

"You came," Tory says, a tight grin stitched on his lips. He nods and avoids looking me in the eyes. Hayden's hands are on my shoulders, and though he said he came here as a kind gesture to me, his friendly touch isn't meant to be kind at all.

"Of course. Can't miss my girl's party," Hayden says.

I catch the crinkle on Tory's brow as he turns to take a few more samples from the desert table.

"Cool. Well, I'll be in the kitchen, helping the moms." He pops a candied pecan in his mouth from the few gathered in his palm and glares at his brother, saving a small bit of that look for me as he passes.

Shit, shit, shit, shit.

I can't even talk to June about this right now. I haven't caught her up, and I'm not sure I even want to. I'm not proud of how I handled all this, but the thought that Tory thinks Hayden is here under any pretense other than to just show up and play the part is ripping at my guts. He's assuming that we aren't really broken up, or that somehow Hayden was mistaken. I look like a massive player just toying with two brothers, which, ugh, maybe I am.

"Hayden, good to see you," my mom says, walking by with a platter of sandwiches in one hand, tugging on Hayden's sleeve sweetly with the other.

This is awful. I want to crawl into a hole, any hole. I'll take a keyhole, smoosh myself inside and just live in a fucking doorknob.

June starts clapping—it's her annoying method of getting attention—and we all turn to face her.

"Thank you, guys, for coming together today to celebrate our favorite diva . . ." She fans a hand out toward me. *I guess I'm the diva?* "Abby, you're a woman now."

"She's been a woman for a while," Lucas says under his breath. June swings an arm at his chest and he spills a bit of punch on his shirt. *Good.*

"Now, we said no presents because let's face it, Abby's got enough shit," June jokes. She's right, my closet is packed and I don't really do trinkets and things. Mostly, though, I don't like the awkward attention that comes along with getting a gift. The giver watches you open it, holding their breath and waiting for this perfect reaction. I don't think I could ever give someone the absolute perfect reaction and the pressure of it stresses me out. Even on Christmas, I ask for cash. Cash is easy to react to. *"Hey, thanks for the cash!"*

"But I did a little thing," June continues.

Shit. A gift.

"It's nothing extraordinary, Abs, so don't expect much. But I may have gotten a little help from your mom to borrow a few things from your room for this occasion." June walks over a large manila envelope, holding it in her flat palms as if she is presenting me with the crown. I quirk my lip up in a half-hearted smile.

"Should I be nervous?" I am nervous. She took shit from my room!

"I don't think so," she answers. Yeah, that's a vague answer.

With a deep breath, I take the envelope in my hands, straightening the clasp to pull the flap free. I reach in and feel the coils of a spiral notebook, and for a brief moment, my heart stops at the thought that she's somehow dug up my fourth grade diary.

My center of gravity shifts a little with the dose of panic, but things right themselves when I slide the booklet from the envelope and see exactly what my friend has done. It's a calendar—of June's various pissed off faces.

Damn it. I love it.

My mouth hangs open in search of the right reaction, but June fills in the words for me.

"Right? It's your most favorite thing, isn't it?" She flips the cover open for me and points to January. It's a photo of her chewing, her eyes all screwed up and angry that I'm taking her pic. There's a dab of pizza sauce on her chin."

"Aww, the memories," I say teasingly, covering my heart and looking my best friend in the eyes.

"It's literally the one thing I knew you needed in your life—a humiliating collection, sorted by month, of pictures of me." She's wearing a wry smile, and without pause, I reach for my phone from my back pocket and snap what is probably a blurry shot of her face.

"Already starting on the next calendar, I see," June says in a flat tone.

"I think we could sell these," I say, flipping through the rest of the months while my birthday guests crowd around. *Most* of my guests, at least.

Tory's taken a seat on the sofa on the other side of the room, a clear invisible wall between him and his brother—between him and *me* and his brother. It feels thick and ruled by silence. I lift my eyes to his, finding him waiting, staring. I try to form a smile, but it's faint and sad. It matches the one he gives back to me.

June claps again and as she wrangles everyone's attention, I walk my new favorite calendar ever over to Tory, handing it to him and being careful to keep a friend-type of distance between us even though every cell in my body is battling to make contact with him.

"Did you know about this?" I ask, remembering how he looked around my room at my photos of June, and the one of him and me.

"Nope. She did this all on her own," he says, looking up with a half-smile. We stay locked in a stare for a full breath, both looking away when the noise of the room makes us realize we aren't alone.

"Tory, I need you to be a part of this," June hollers.

"She's like a teacher," he says, twisting up his lips and pulling in his brow.

"That's what I've always said!" I step back to make room for him as he leaves the sofa and rounds the small coffee table. I'm careful to keep extra distance between us, walking slower than him, and curving to the other side of the room. I feel confident that I have everyone fooled—everyone but Hayden, whose glare at his brother is marked by a notable heavy brow and dimmed eyes that look like a predator ready to strike.

"So, before we eat," June says, these first few words receiving a collective groan from a room full of hungry bellies. "I know, it smells good. It's almost ready! Just waiting on the wings."

June went all out, making all my favorites. Other than the soup my mom made, everything else in this spread falls in one of two categories—bakery item or bar food.

"Everyone take a paper. Mom is passing them out."

My chest constricts because games are not really my thing, but June seemed excited so I told her it was fine as long as it's not something hard or a pain in the ass to organize. When I take the paper from her mom and read through the first few questions, I wish I let her set up kickball instead.

"Now, no cheating. We have a timer, so you cannot start writing until I say *go.*" June's directions are background noise while I scan the list of personal questions about me. My birthday, which everyone should get right. My favorite thing at Holiday Theme Park—*easily the glitter cotton candy.* My favorite color, favorite time of the day, favorite thing to wear, first crush . . .

I swallow and fold my own paper, moving over to the dessert spread to pick at a few more treats while I wait for June to finish this game. I'll be shocked if anyone gets more than two. I'm not sure even June knows all the answers. My mom doesn't, and that thought makes me sad. Over the last few years, we've been so consumed with my career and fighting for our independence from my dad that the personal things have sort of fallen to the side.

"And . . . go!"

Instant silence follows June's directions, and I turn while I nibble on a chocolate pretzel to see everyone feverishly writing answers. June has her paper flattened against a wall so she can write quickly, which . . . *why didn't she just cheat and do it beforehand? She picked the damn questions.*

Hayden and Lucas seem to be teaming up, making each other laugh over their answers. Lola and Naomi seem to be working really hard, and my mom and June's mom are concentrating and giving thought to each answer. Even if they get them wrong, I bet there will be some element of rightness. Tory is hovering in the back of the crowd, his paper folded in his hand. He slips it under some mail in the nook space by the refrigerator where the Mabees keep their keys and phone chargers, then opens the fridge to pull a cold water bottle out from the bottom drawer. He glances my way as he turns, but his attention doesn't stick. He's either good at pretending or detaching himself on purpose, trying not to get hurt.

What June said would be three minutes of time feels as if it stretches on for ten, but finally, she tells everyone to put their pencils down and she collects the papers. She begins reading the responses, and a lot of them are funny. This part of the game . . . it's okay.

"Abby's favorite time of day is any time that Abby is right," June reads.

"That's kind of true. Give that a half point," I say.

"Score," Lucas shouts, pulling in a fist pump.

My mom ends up getting the most right, even more than my best friend, which soothes me some, but I'm curious about the one paper that wasn't turned in. I wonder if he tried at all.

"Okay, food is finally ready," June's mother announces.

Everyone files toward the table to collect plates and bowls so they can filter down the line and stuff themselves in my honor. Tory is near the front of the line, and I smile to myself at the sight of him filling a large bowl of menudo. He'll love it. It's impossible not to. Waiting my turn, I back up a few steps into the kitchen while nobody notices and walk my fingers over to the paper Tory tried to dismiss.

I pull it into my hand and open the fridge, bending down to act as if I'm getting a drink or searching for something down low. It's silly that I feel like I have to hide just to read his answers, but I do. And as I read on, I'm even more certain.

He's gotten every answer right. My favorite color is pink, but not just pink—pale pink. My favorite glitter cotton candy is jotted down. Sunsets are my favorite time of day, and my first crush was Peter Pan. I liked the idea of someone sweeping me away for an adventure. Hearing my name mentioned, I quickly fold the paper up small enough to tuck it in my hand

and pull a water bottle out for myself, shutting the fridge and moving back into the room full of people.

"Do you want to tell everyone the right answers?" June asks. I discreetly stuff Tory's paper into my purse and set my water down on the floor by the chair I've chosen to be my throne for the day.

"No, I think I like the mystery. Besides, maybe some of you have answers I like better." My response gets a laugh, and Lucas pipes in to take credit for changing my mind on some things.

I fill my bowl with my mother's soup, knowing this is probably the only other thing I will eat today and I will eat servings until it is gone. I take my seat again and nudge my purse under my chair with my foot, glancing up to see Tory staring at it. His eyes flit to mine and we lock gazes for a quiet moment when everyone else is too busy to notice.

"Thank you," I mouth.

His lips curve up slightly at the corners and he blinks slowly with a careful nod. I don't know how he knows me so well, but perhaps he's been paying attention. I'm starting to wish I had been all along.

NINETEEN

TORY

This is hard. Loving a girl is hard. I'm in love with a girl, with Abby Cortez.

And it is fucking hard.

My brother and I drove in separate cars this morning. We left the house a minute apart, to give each other space. It's all starting to feel so trivial. And wasteful. Gas is expensive.

Something has to get figured out between me and Hayden before our game tonight. I've never actually seen Coach this upset at us. At other guys? Sure. But Hayd and I are exceptions. I guess getting away with four years of shit is finally catching up to us. Either that, or maybe this time our problems are too much for a team to take.

We play St. Agnes today. It's a big game, the first in our division. If we can run up the score against them, we have a good chance of taking the holiday tournament and maybe coming out the top seed in our division for state. We won't beat St. Agnes if Hayden and I aren't in sync, and it's less about the team and more about how much it's affecting me emotionally. I hate hating my brother. I can't do it anymore.

Part of making amends is going to mean letting go of Abby. I just don't see a way that she and I can be something without it ruining everything else. I promised myself I would fight to keep her, but maybe the honorable thing and the best way to love her is to let her go. Maybe in another life . . . another time and place. This round, we are just off. The world isn't ready for us.

It's hard to commit to being honorable when I read her texts, though. She wants to know how I knew everything about her on that birthday list, and I have to shake my head because I don't really have an answer. I just do. I know so much about her, more than I realized. All from watching her, from paying attention to her little details, the things that make her tick. She wears more pale pink than any other color, and when she wears it on her lips, her smile is always brighter and her laugh a little more real. I knew the Peter Pan thing because she mentioned it once in fifth grade, that she thought Peter Pan was cute. Some of the boys in our class laughed at her; she punched one of them. She got sick eating the damn glitter cotton candy during our eighth grade trip to Holiday Park, but she said it was worth it when she threw up. I've been watching Abby Cortez for years; I just didn't realize that the lens I was looking through was one of love.

I leave my last hour early. I told June to tell Coach I am going to get things right with Hayden. She was glad to hear me say it, and since we're both his assistants for last hour, she said she'd handle it.

Hayden has study hall this period, and unfortunately the teacher in there is a former drill sergeant. I don't say that to make commentary on the woman's demeanor, I'm being real—she was in the Army for fifteen years. How our school was lucky enough to land her, I'll never know. I had study hall last year, and she and I . . . let's just say we don't gel.

I see my brother's backpack dangling from the back of a chair, so I know he's within earshot if I can manage to get his attention through the small crack in the door. She'll be closing it soon.

"Hayden," I whisper, giving my voice enough volume to carry but not gain unwanted attention. It does zero good.

I look both ways and move in closer, smooshing my face through the door to whisper it again.

"Psst, Hayden!" I move away fast and flatten my back to the wall. My heart is thumping. I swear, this woman terrifies me.

I crane my neck to peek through the open part and catch my brother's eyes as he leans back. He grimaces and waves his hand, shooing me away.

Goddamnit.

"Come here," I whisper a little louder, again darting away. I think that's all I've got in me. If I try one more time, she'll grab my tongue mid-speech and lord knows what that woman will do to it. Probably nothing, but something about her glare instills that kind of fear in me.

I wait with my back against the wall for almost a full minute, and I'm about to give up when the door opens and my brother steps out. He walks past me, toward the restrooms.

"Come on," he says over his shoulder.

I follow. We get inside and move to the window along the back wall where people put out their cigarette butts and snuff out the ends of their blunts.

"What's up? Something wrong at home? You need money? What?" He can barely make eye contact with me while he talks, and he keeps pacing, clearly not wanting to be here.

"This is gonna take a lot longer than a bathroom break. I hope you know that," I say. He huffs and moves to the sink, running his hands through the water, then through his hair.

"Better not. Hurry up," he grumbles.

The urge to rush him and tackle his ass against the wall and sink and nasty floor is definitely simmering in my legs. It wouldn't take much.

Drawing in a calming breath through my nose, I say the only thing I believe will work, that will get him to actually stop and listen.

"I love you."

He shakes his head like a cartoon mouse getting smacked with a broom. His mouth hangs open, unprepared to deliver a reaction. Those are not the words he was expecting, and that's why they needed to be said.

"Thanks, I guess," he finally says, stretching his lips out over his teeth and awkwardly mashing them together. He's uncomfortable, which is weird because we're brothers—it shouldn't be hard to say those words to each other. But after Abby's party I struggled to remember the last time he and I had. I couldn't think of it, which means it's been too long.

I step into him, and he flinches a little when I raise my hands. Placing my palms on either shoulder, I look him in the eyes and let the uncomfortable quiet strangle us as we're forced to look at ourselves, at our own faces on someone else. It takes several seconds for him to return to character, for a softness to shine through this hardened armor on his face, but it happens. Slowly, it happens.

"I love you," I repeat.

He swallows at hearing it the second time. His eyes shift to the side then back to me.

"I love you too, man."

We both breathe out hard, our chests in sync with every in and out movement our lungs make. Once I think he's ready for more, I tell him the part that's even harder for me to say.

"I'm sorry." My mouth waters delivering the words because while I truly am for many things, I'm not sorry one bit for others. That doesn't matter, though. I realized last night that forgiveness doesn't get put on a scale.

It's going to take my brother some time to work through hearing these words, and I don't expect to hear them back, though it sure would be nice. He folds his arms over his chest, closing himself off as he steps back until he can lean against the wall.

I maintain eye contact with him the entire time, even when he can't hold it on his end, looking down often and rubbing his finger in the corner of his eye. Ready, he finally snaps his gaze up to mine and tilts his head to one side.

"Abby?" I hate that he starts here. It's not the place to begin.

With tight lips, I shake my head and look down.

"It's nothing," I lie. I don't swallow the painful rock lodged in my throat for fear he'll see it. It's my one big tell. I lift my chin and lean my head to the side to match his.

He smirks and puffs out a short laugh, moving his hands to his pockets and relaxing a little more.

"Guess she ruined both of us, huh?"

I shrug in response.

"Something like that," I say.

He studies me, looking for the cracks in my answer, the way to really get to the core. I'm not yet ready for core sharing when it comes to her. I'm giving her up for him, and it's going to take me a long time to not be truly bitter about it.

"I have to ask you something, and . . . it's . . . " I pause, rubbing my hand over my mouth while I fight through the wave of anger that still courses through my body over the things I've discovered in the last few days. "This is hard for me to talk about. Hard to wrap my mind around, but Hayden . . . I found the Olsen Academy letter, man."

His eyes widen fast. His mouth remains a straight line, though. He's been practicing for this moment, probably for years. Still, the unexpected timing was too much to prepare for now that I confront him about it in our gross-ass high school bathroom.

"Don't give me the story. I want the truth. I can take the truth, okay? It's this awful resentment we've both fostered that I can't handle. Tell me. Tell it to me straight." I brace myself for his response, which takes him several seconds to form.

"It was a really shitty thing to do, Tor. I'm sorry," he says. I wasn't expecting him to start so humble. It makes it easier to hear, somehow. His ability to admit that he did take something precious from me somehow makes the wound sting less. It stings all the same.

I nod and slowly spin where I stand, rocking on my feet. My head falls back and I look up at the ceiling tiles, marred with dangling pencils and gum.

"It was in fact a pretty shitty thing to do, Hayd. I'll give you that. You nailed the description spot on." I suck in my lips hard, making a near impenetrable straight line that holds in the other things I'm tempted to say.

Hayden groans, lowering his chin to his chest and letting his head fall into his open hands. His fingers scratch at his scalp, and it takes me a few seconds to realize that he's . . . he's crying. When he raises his head, I'm met with red eyes and a sour face.

"Tory, I messed up. I messed up, and it messed up everything, and I don't know how to make it right." His confession churns my stomach.

"Messed up how?" I question.

Another deep breath for both of us. Hayden brings his fist to his mouth, holding it to his bottom lip while he blinks at me, trying to get the words out. My fingers itch to grab his wrist and yank his fist away, but he needs it right now. He needs to hide a little, as silly as that seems.

"I saw mom and Mr. Fuller," he admits.

My brow pulls in so tight I can feel the fold above the bridge of my nose.

"Like, at our house?" I question.

"Freshman year, at football camp. When they first—" He can't finish that statement and nobody wants him to. It's an awful image.

"Hayd." I shift to lean against the sink. I press my palms into my eyes, dizzy from this information. I pull one hand away and lift a brow as I look at my brother. "You knew? You knew all this time?"

He shakes his head.

"I wasn't sure. I thought it was only that first time and maybe that was it, but then this summer—"

"Oh, my God, summer. They kept it going over summer," I groan. I flip around and grip the sink, taking in my own sick expression in the scratched-up mirror.

"When your letter came, I thought if you and Dad left, I'd be there alone with Mom, and then . . . " His shoulders rise up to his ears as he shakes his head. "I deleted the email, but then the letter came and I wanted to throw it away, but also, I knew it was important to you. I've thought about throwing that thing away every day for nearly four years."

"Why didn't you?" I mumble, once again dropping my chin to my chest as I lean over the sink. "God, Hayd. I wish I'd never known. It would have been better than this."

I can't help but play through the what ifs of my life, a thing I have been doing constantly since I found out Hayden sabotaged my shot. Yeah, Mom and Dad probably would have split up a long time ago, and Hayden and I probably would have lived apart, but I'd be at Olsen and on my way to D1 somewhere big, maybe more. But I wouldn't have had Abby. Probably not ever.

My hands grip the porcelain and I shake it a few times, knowing if I want I could probably rip the sink from the wall. I stand straight and let my hands fall to my sides while I just breathe.

"It all got away from me, and then it seemed for so long like things were just . . . fine." Everything about the look in his eyes is the opposite of fine. My brother made some selfish, stupid choices, but they've taken a toll on him. This is why he's struggling so much. While I can get mad and let anger rule me for a little while, he's still trying to tuck everything that's wrong into this little box to keep it safe, keep our family whole.

"I love you." I say it with my gaze toward the floor. The same words I started this with, and maybe I'm saying them because I need to remind myself a bit, too.

"I swear to God, brother, if you're about to hug me," he says, trying out my brand of humor, a default mode I prefer over emotional moments. I laugh at the attempt. *Not bad.*

"I'm gonna hug you," I say, moving in closer. He recoils, but only for show.

"It's coming, big man. Might as well let it happen. Feel the love," I ramble on, getting close enough that we can touch.

We stare at one another with limp bodies and tired hearts, for once truly the same in almost every single way. We embrace mutually, and I hug him with as much force as he hugs me. My hand grips his shirt over his shoulder, and we rock a little because that keeps us from crying. After simultaneously slapping each other's back, the secret bro way of signaling it's time to stop hugging, we pull apart and back away from one another.

"You should probably get back to study hall. She'll red card you for the game because she's mean like that," I say to him.

He nods with a short sniff, toughening up his posture to enter the same way he left.

"No more shit on the court, okay?" I hold out my hand for him to take, and he does so without hesitation.

"Nothing but the good kind of trouble." He shoots me a brief crooked smile. That's what Coach refers to us as when we're on the court together. We're trouble for the other team. Too much to guard, too fast to catch.

I wait for Hayden to leave first, sticking around in the bathroom until the period ends and I can head to the gym and dress out for the game. I'm going to have to talk to Abby first, if I can get her alone. I have to make her world right while also making things right with Hayden, but I'm not sure I'm strong enough to do what needs to be done. She makes me forget the line.

TWENTY

ABBY

I'm leaving.

Wednesday.

The moment school breaks for the long holiday, my mom and I are locking up the house and driving up to Toronto for what will be months. I'm leaving, just when things are happening. Just when things feel right.

I'm leaving.

I got the call this morning, and there's not a way to say no when producers who took a chance on you for their big budget movie say they need you a month earlier than expected. Leaving will give us space from my dad, too. He's renting a house about four miles away and about four times the size of ours. He's doing it to show off, and it's gross. It's also an irresponsible thing to do with his money, which does not bode well for him being involved in my finances at all.

Now that I'm eighteen, I'm allowed to file suits of my own, and I intend to break my company into pieces and give him the worthless part while forming a new one with only my mom and me. He doesn't know it's coming, and he'll be really ugly about it, but I'll be in Toronto, with my mom. And he doesn't have a passport.

This all leads back to this moment. The one I'm about to have.

I'm leaving, and I have to tell Tory.

He texted me to wait outside the locker room at four. It's about five minutes past and I feel a bit foolish, and a bit like a predator who hangs around boys locker rooms to catch peeks of their asses. I've seen two so far, and I will never be able to erase those visual assaults from my eyes.

I'm about to text him to catch me later, a little thankful that maybe I can put this talk off a little longer, when the door pops open again. I look up briefly, trying to avoid seeing something I don't want to see, but it's Tory jogging up the steps and out to me.

He scans the area around us before bending forward, leaning his palms on the concrete bench I'm sitting on, and holding my lips with a soft kiss. I tilt up as he hovers above me for a few seconds, his mouth lingering, sucking in my top lip just a little then letting go. He leans back to sit next to me, kicking one leg over the bench to straddle it while I sit in front of him.

"You sticking around for our game?" His eyes crinkle, a hopeful expression.

"Wouldn't miss it," I say.

"Good, good." He nods, his tight-lipped grin pushing into his cheeks.

I'm leaving. I am leaving.

He looks down at the concrete between us, tapping his fingertips manically while he chews at the inside of his cheek.

"What's going on?" I reach up and touch his cheek, and he lifts his eyes, giving me a half smile that doesn't stick around long. He keeps his gaze on me, though, all kinds of worries and thoughts rushing behind it.

Tory reaches up and cups my face, pulling me in for another kiss, once again chaste, the same fated feelings attached. His hands fall back to the bench, gripping the sides as he sits up tall and holds on as if he has to hold himself to this spot on the earth.

"It's Hayden," he says.

My heart rushes with so many chemically induced and heart-wrenching emotions that for a moment I think I might overdose on feelings.

"Did he find out about . . . us?" I keep playing our night together over and over in my head, thinking about how close Hayden's room was to us, how he could have come home at any moment, how guilty my face must have seemed when he came to my party. He's sharper and more intuitive than we give him credit for.

"No, at least, I don't think so. He knows how I feel, but I know how he feels so I guess it's a wash." He shrugs, despondent and lifeless. He squints from the sun as he brings his gaze back to me, his words suddenly stalled. I have the power to save him from having to say any more.

"So . . . I'm leaving Wednesday."

His brows lift and his breath halts for a beat.

"Yeah, I know," I say, looking down to where his hand is still curved around the edge of the concrete. I place mine on top of it, threading my fingers with his until his grip loosens and he rolls his palm over to completely give me his hand. I play with his fingers, wishing I had the time to really study them, to learn how they look with mine, how they look on me, around my waist and near me while I sleep.

"I got the call last night. Something about budget, and getting my shots early before Jordan has to film something else. The good news is it means I'll be back for prom and graduation." I dip my head to catch his eyes again and grin at the word *prom.* It doesn't seem to do much for him, though.

"So you're leaving, for like . . . a while." He draws in a deep breath and leans back.

"Probably four months. I'll have a tutor."

I should be excited about this, but I dread every moment. My big break feels like a crash and burn, and it's making me rethink my dreams and goals. I'm giving up one of the most important times in my life. I'm giving up this feeling—*love.* I'm falling in love with Tory, and walking away before it has a chance to take hold.

"Maybe it's for the best . . . with Hayden and all," he says, his eyes meeting mine in fits. They're glassy, but he masks it, coughing and hazing them as he purposely looks back toward the sun.

"Maybe," I choke out.

"Another time, maybe. Or life. Or maybe our future selves. I don't know," he rambles, squeezing the bridge of his nose and holding his breath. He averts his eyes as he stands, and I stand with him, feeling the need to wrap him in my arms and hold him here, to me.

"We're in warm-ups, and I just slipped out. But you'll be at the game, right? You'll stay?" His arm swings out and his fingers latch on to mine, like fragile hooks holding together too much weight.

"I'll stay," I promise. I will, and it will hurt. Because I am leaving.

Tory leans in and presses his lips to my cheek this time, pausing there long enough to graze his nose along my jaw and plant one more kiss on the bare skin peeking out from the large neck of my sweatshirt.

"See you after, then."

Our fingers slip apart and he walks away backward for the first several steps. He turns around to jog, disappearing down the steps to the locker room door, slipping inside and never once looking back.

I talked June into coming to the game. She was the second person I told that I was leaving early, so she hardly even grumbles about having to sit on these bleachers with me. Of all the things I'm going to miss out on for months, time with her ranks as one of the highest.

"One thing I do like about basketball over football is it's inside, even if it's crowded," she says.

"It's because our basketball team is a million times better than football," I gloat.

"You're biased," she retorts.

We take our seats at center court but in the very top of the bleachers. I learned last time that it's nice to have a wall to rest your back against. Plus, I kinda like keeping everyone else in my line of sight. You never know where the haters are gonna come from.

I haven't filled June in on Hayden yet. That's the other reason I want her and I to have this time together.

"I'm more impartial than biased now, by the way," I say, leaning into her. She pulls her water bottle from her mouth and it makes a pop. Her mouth hangs on to the O shape.

"You broke up?" I can't tell if she's really shocked or just playing the part.

"Come on, you know you were shocked to see us together in the first place. And yeah, it just wasn't right, and with me leaving and all . . . " *And with me being in love with his brother*. That part stays in my head.

"Yeah, I guess I can see that. Are things good between you, though? I mean, when did this happen? At your party?" She studies me for a second, reading the truth in my wincing face.

"Oh, shit. Before?"

I nod and sigh.

"Oh, that must have been hard or weird or . . . hard *and* weird?" She turns her attention back to the court where both teams are lining up for the tip-off.

"Hard and weird pretty much sums it up." I chuckle. The whistle blows and Tory sails over the St. Agnes player, pushing the ball through the air to his brother who rushes it down the court for a fast two points. June and I both stand and shout.

"Okay, I can get into this basketball game thing," she says. Tory steals the ball the moment she finishes her statement, this time taking it all the way himself but stopping at the three-point line and putting up a shot that floats through the air in perfect silence. When he sinks it, we stand again, a roar erupting.

"Yes! Go Tory! Go Hayden! Go Eagles!" June is red-faced, screaming, and I tug her arm to drag her back down to sit with me.

"Slow down there, mama Eagle," I tease.

"It's just . . . this is so exciting. Things happen so fast, and there's not all these timeouts and measurements and—"

We stand again for another steal, this one by someone other than one of the twins. Another layup, and our team is up seven to zero with less than a minute burned.

We're giggling from the excitement, and it injects much needed joy into my body. For a little while, I'm able to forget that I'm leaving something new and special, and that I hurt someone kind and soft, and that I'm going to miss my best friend. For the next hour, I simply exist in this bubble, in a world where the boy I love and the boy I admire absolutely put on a show together on the court, and I'm lucky enough to watch it unfold. Hayden and Tory bond before my eyes. They celebrate each other, and they work as this singular unit that positively cannot function without the other half.

And then it hits me. Maybe they can't.

"In another life," I mutter, not realizing my thoughts spill out loud.

"Hmm?" June leans in.

I shake her off, claiming to be talking about the other team, but the way she continues to look at the side of my face makes me believe she knows better. She also knows not to push.

The game ends with us on top by twenty-seven points. It was basically a blow-out, led by the D'Angelo boys. A reporter from the local paper asks them to stick around for a short interview and a picture, so June and I move down to the bottom row to listen in. The questions are pretty typical, but the D'Angelo answers are not. They goof with each other, poking fun in a way that also praises, and whenever the reporter tries to bring the spotlight to Tory, he instantly shifts it, giving credit to Hayden. Before they get up, one of their teammates rushes by with a cup of ice water and splashes it across the backs of their necks, and they take off after him into the locker room.

"I guess we can just hang around outside," June says.

I follow her out the doors and glance to my car. I can't wait around and see them both. Whatever balance they have happening between them, it's necessary. It's how they'll get through the next few weeks and months. It's how they're going to navigate their lives. They don't need me to stick around to tell them both nice game.

"Actually," I begin. June's head falls to the side, a frown tackling her lips. "I know, I know, it's just that I have so much to do. I have to pack!"

"You haven't packed?" She's shocked. I actually have, but there are still a few things I could work on before leaving. I won't be at school tomorrow or Wednesday either, so in many ways, this really is good-bye.

"I know, and you know how I am with shoes," I joke, reaching around her shoulders to hug her tight. She squeezes me.

"They have a weight limit for the plane, you know."

"Good thing we're driving."

"Ha, well . . . tires can only hold so much, too."

My lips pucker a smile that turns into laughter, the kind that settles between two friends who would rather part like this than through tears.

I back away, wanting to run before the boys come out.

"I'll call you before we go. We'll talk. And we'll talk every day, okay?" She's the one promise I know I can keep. I need her too much.

"You better. And I want coordinated video chats that just happen to have Jordan in the background," she says.

I pull my phone from my pocket to wave it, catching her in one last photo before I go.

"Unbelievable," she retorts.

I grin, turning to walk the rest of the way to my car, and I cradle the phone in my lap once inside and look at the cross-eyed, open-mouthed face my friend is making. I save this one as my backdrop, and pledge to let it help me get through four months apart.

As I pull out, the team files out through the locker room doors, a certain two walking out last. I pause at the parking lot exit, my blinker on, ready to turn. It would be so easy to turn around, and I almost do.

But I don't.

TWENTY-ONE

TORY

I should have gone to say good-bye. Hayden did. He even bought Abby a gift—a keychain with one of those little director's clapper boards on the end. He wrote her name on it. It was thoughtful. I'm not very good at thoughtful right now. I'm nice and settled in on pathetic.

It just seemed better to let things end where we left them. Nothing definitive, just an air of possibility. No painful tears. No explanations to Hayden or our friends—*ourselves.*

She hit the road yesterday. Hayden called out of school to see her off. I went to class, and not because I love being one of the handful who shows up on half days before holiday break to watch various versions of *The Grinch*, but because school was a damn good place to hide for the day.

There's no hiding from Thursdays, though. It seems a month since I stormed out of Dr. Majestic's office. In one week, I've managed to unearth four years of secrets my brother has been keeping, bought a car, moved some of my shit to my dad's place, and fallen in love. Oh, and I hit rock bottom in terms of ever wanting to fall in love again.

All in all, a pretty well-rounded week leading up to therapy.

In a show of faith, or maybe in an act of naiveté, I drove Hayden to therapy tonight. He wanted to have the full cop experience. I think he was a little disappointed when I didn't actually have a siren and the flashy lights. They rip that shit out before auction. I do have a spotlight, though. That'll come in handy the next time I take this thing off-road out on McCaffey's land.

The drive in was good. I only hope we survive the drive home, because the longer the four of us sit in this waiting room just . . . *waiting*, the more palpable the tension becomes. Right now, it's thick enough to melt the paint off the walls.

"D'Angelos. Welcome," Dr. Majestic says.

"Wouldn't it be great if she wore a wizard hat for one of these?" Hayden whispers behind my back. Dad and I both snicker.

"Tory!" My mom hushes me with her finger to her lips, and in a sign of normality, my father and brother straighten their posture and pretend they don't know me.

"Unbelievable," I mumble, elbowing my brother in the ribs. He grunts but laughs through it, proud he can still say things and blame them on me. This has been happening since we learned to talk.

We take the same seats as last time, only the doctor planned ahead and pre-moved the recliner for me. I give her a nod and flop into my seat, toying with the handle on the side to kick my feet up. My brother and dad chuckle but I stop when my mom gives me side eyes.

"Fine," I grumble. I'm trying to keep it light on purpose—because I still don't want to be here. Maybe I can will this time to fly by and be painless.

"Let's pick up where we left off," Dr. Majestic begins, and there goes any hope that this will go easy.

"Tory, we didn't get to work through some of your speed bumps before you left."

"Speed bumps?" I question.

"She calls our conflicts speed bumps. She says it makes them easier to acknowledge," Hayden says, one brow raised.

I lock eyes with him.

"Ah. Speed bumps. Okay, well, no speed bumps for me. Smooth sailing, or driving rather. I'm a racetrack." I show my hands and lift my shoulders, playing the part of an easy-going man, though I really have no idea what one of those looks like.

"I see," she says, crossing her legs, clicking her pen open, and leaning forward, wrists crossed atop her knees. She has this way of drawing her breath in through her nose that makes her mouth look like it's about to unleash a barrage of new questions. But all that happens is more silence, and more studying of my silence.

"Yep," I finally say.

She nods, but still no words.

My head swivels to face my brother, who simply blinks back at me. *No help at all.* My dad is growing uncomfortable watching me under scrutiny and shifts his posture on his end of the couch.

"Honey, it's fine. This is a safe space." My mom finally gives.

The match to my lighter fluid.

"Safe space?" My voice is loud. I have no in-between.

"Yes, you are safe to be honest here," she says, which sets off a fit of laughter in my brother's belly. It brews slowly. Coming out through his tight lips, it spits until he finally has to cough it out.

"Are you all right?" My mom turns to him, coddling like she normally does, only this time my brother shirks off her attention.

"Oh, I'm totally fine. Race car ready just like Tory," he says, and I smirk at his quick response and comradery.

"Me, too. More of a pace car, but smooth ride," my dad adds in.

Unable to handle being ganged up on, my mom throws up her hands and covers her face. It's a move we've seen her do often, crumbling in the face of confrontation to get everyone to stop. Thing is, that visual got my brother to tuck away the things he saw and knew. It forced him to be afraid of setting off a massive landslide of dominoes. And that . . . *that* is one hell of a speed bump.

"Natalia, do you want to share how this is making you feel?"

My mom milks the moment, her breath quivering with overdone emotion, until she waits too long and my brother takes over for her.

"It makes her nervous because she can't control any of it. She can't mess up and just make things go away," he says.

"That's not it at all, Hayden."

"Oh, it is. And it's more than that," my brother unleashes. "Mom, I knew. I saw you and Mr. Fuller. I saw you at camp, and I saw the signs that it was still happening when we got home, and I saw the signs again months ago when I figured *surely, they've ended things by now.* But no, you just kept living double lives, throwing everything we are in the garbage because it wasn't enough, and I spent four years pretending it was normal because I didn't want our little bubble to burst."

"Unbelievable," my dad says under his breath, closing himself off more. He's flawed too, just differently.

"Are you saying you didn't know?" My brother lashes into him now, and while my instinct is to defend my dad, I think maybe that is *my* flaw. I pick sides without hearing the full story.

"Yes, Hayden. I just wrote it all off, figured she could go have her fun and I'd do all the work." My dad waves his hand dismissively. He's making a bad joke of all of this, out of us in a way, and his words only make my brother grow bolder.

"First of all, you're lying. She didn't hide it well, and there's no way you weren't suspicious. Hell, Dad, I had a girlfriend for like, six weeks, and I knew Tory was with her behind my back."

My mouth widens and my lungs deflate with the sucker punch. It's fair, but it's also not the topic. And it's over with Abby, because I chose Hayden.

"Tory," my mom comes to life again in time to scold me.

I stand up and cup my ears as I glare at her.

"Oh, no. You do not get to judge me," I say, only to have Hayden take over my point.

"Handle your own problems, Mom. Handle this—*us*! This is your mess. You and Dad, you're in a marriage. Tory and I are fucking eighteen and dating and figuring out who we are. You should have gotten all of your mistakes out of your system by now."

"Yeah," I agree, pausing at the word *mistake*. I lower myself to my seat and fade into the background, letting the chaos move forward without me. I glance over to the doctor while my family's shouting silences in my own head. She's listening, but she isn't writing down a damn word. It's the expression buried underneath the professional façade that really piques my interest. She's getting us to do just what she wants, what we *need* to do more of. She's getting us to talk. To listen.

For an hour, we yell over one another, Hayden doing most of the talking to the point that his voice is ragged by the time our session is done. My parents leave in their separate cars, my dad driving back to the city and my mom to our home. I still feel confident my dad's albums will leave the house soon. I'm pretty sure there isn't a resolution to their marriage in any of this, but maybe there's one for us as a family. Maybe there will be a way for things to be civil, and for Hayden and I to quit carrying the weight.

Hayden and I leave the office after my parents are gone, walking quietly to my car. I turn it on and maneuver the aux cord while my brother buckles up so I can shuffle to his personal playlist for the ride back. One of his favorite Motown songs comes on and he turns to face me with a suspicious line on his mouth.

"You pick this on purpose?" he asks.

I hold up my phone and show him the playlist labeled HAYDEN'S SHIT. He laughs, taking my phone and scrolling through the songs.

"You're missing some good ones," he says.

I grab my phone back and smirk.

"I've got like fifty. Let me learn to like all of these first and then we'll talk about you adding some."

I shift into reverse and check my mirrors.

"Maybe you make me a playlist of your shit," he says.

"Can do, only my stuff isn't shit. Just your stuff," I tease.

"Ahhh, you like my shit and you know it. I've seen you singing Wilson Pickett." He crosses his arms, confident that he's right.

"*June* likes Wilson Pickett, and she made me listen to it," I reply.

I pull us out onto the main road and we get a mile or so down the road before I finally throw him a bone.

"All right, fine. The Wilson Pickett stuff is pretty good."

"See? I knew it!" He rocks in his seat, mouthing the words to whatever song this is now. Something about loving somebody's baby. I'm sure after a month of driving back and forth from Dad's with this playlist, I'll know the words, too.

"You know, Dad's cool with you coming out, too. We could go the same weekend sometimes, or . . . separate. If you want some one-on-one time, I get it." I glance at him while I drive, gauging his reaction. The best I can gather is that it's thoughtful, his tight lips not frowning but not quite smiling, either.

"Maybe," he finally answers.

"I hope so," I say, and I mean it.

We make it the rest of the way with nothing but HAYDEN'S SHIT serenading us, and the more songs that play, the more I soften to his favorite sounds. We pull in the driveway and sit with my car running just so the current song can finish out. I kill the engine just as it ends, and we let the mood we've built embrace us for a little while longer.

"Why her?" I finally ask. I think that's my speed bump. It's definitely the question I've been asking myself when I can't sleep at night, when I shower, when I drive, when I should be learning in class. I think, given Dr. Majestic's definition, that equates to an emotional speed bump. It's too high for me to get over on my own.

Hayden's silence makes my chest tighten.

"She just . . . *listened*," he finally says.

My eyes drop, along with my heart. I can't fault him for falling for her for that. Abby does listen. It might be what forced me to finally see her through different eyes. Through *possible* eyes. While Hayden was opening up to her about the things happening in our family, I was shutting down, but it doesn't mean I wasn't talking to her. I talked, just in my own way. While we bonded over Lucas and June, I made snide jokes about love being a farce and she made them right along with me. But she was always sure to leave me with a glimmer of hope before we parted. Like when Lucas and June finally got together and she leaned into me and said, "See, some people get their happy endings." She's not as cynical as she pretends.

"Did you love her, at least?" I wasn't sure about asking this question tonight. It feels like an overreach, a step maybe neither of us is ready for. But now that I'm in the moment, my belly hungry to be settled, my heart anxious to be soothed, I have to ask.

"I thought I did," Hayden admits, sinking down in his seat and leaning his head against the window to look up at the stars. I do the same. The sky's lit up again, like it was the night Abby came over.

"You still think so?" I ask.

"Nah," he responds quickly. I'm a little surprised to hear his answer, and I roll my head against the glass to look at him through the corner of my eyes.

"No?" I echo.

He shakes his head.

"I think I needed her, and that's not quite the same," he says, rolling his head to look at me.

"How about you?" I figured this question would come. I've been ready to answer it for a while.

"Yeah. I did. I do." I shift to look at him more head on. I can tell my admission catches him off guard as he sits up and pulls in his brow.

"You love her?" He makes it sound so impossible.

"I love her. I was about to ask her out the day you showed up holding hands," I confess.

"Fuuu—" His mouth hangs open as it hits him. "The flowers."

"The flowers." I nod. "The motherfucking flowers."

We both lean back into our windows and stare up at the stars. My window is fogged from my breath, so I pull my sleeve down over my wrist and rub it clear.

"I'm really sorry, Tor. If I had known—"

"It's all right. I never said," I cut in. I hold my fist out in the space between us without looking to him, and he reaches over to pound mine just by feel. We're back in step. I don't know how long we were out of it, but in a strange way, it was Abby who put us back together.

TWENTY-TWO

ABBY

Christmas in Toronto is unreal. I've seen snow lots but never like this. It's more like someone came through at night and replaced everything in the city with frozen blocks of ice. It's beautiful, but it's painful.

I've slipped twice so far. Not bad falls, but enough to leave a bruise on my hip. Mom wasn't so lucky. She fell and cracked her wrist on a curb. I guess if you're going to be stuck in a cast for four to six weeks, it might as well be in the cold.

Mom and I promised each other no holiday gifts, but I did get her this pack of cast wraps so she could bling out her plaster arm. She seems to have taken to the rainbow peace symbols for her first week of wear.

She broke the rules and got me a gift, too. Hers was a package too, but a major step above some pack of fun acrylic sticker. She gave me a settlement package. In my favor. She'd hired a private investigator the moment I confessed about the nude photo bribe. It took the guy a while to earn his fee, but he finally came through in spades. Seems Jake from the party got a payday a week or two before he met me—a wired deposit from my dad. The chips fall into place easily when you're willing to really look at them, but even as my mom was telling me, I didn't want to see things clearly. It was too ugly. Regardless, it was true.

My dad paid Jake to dupe me into those pics—to the tune of twenty grand. The hundred grand never went anywhere; it was all for show. Oh, and since I was seventeen at the time, and Jake was nineteen? Well, leverage. Zero prison time traded for never, ever seeing us again. It's going to take me a while to be able to open up about all of the betrayal. I've been able to tell June, but even with her, I can't get through the details without shutting down.

On a positive note, though, my company is now mine, and mine alone. My mom is setting up the structure, but she insists on being listed as an employee. She keeps saying being fireable is the one thing that ensures good parents don't go bad, but I'm pretty sure that's more of a soul-and-ethics sorta thing. If I ever make it truly big, the first thing I'm going to do is pay off the debt on her house. She'll sleep easy knowing that the walls my abuelo put up are hers forever. I want to secure that legacy for her.

With the break in shoots, Mom and I decide to make a short trip home for New Year's. June's mom is throwing a party, and apparently June went and invited a lot of people. I'm gone a week and a half and my friend becomes a party animal. Hayden says it's because she liked throwing my birthday party so much. She and her mom are good at catering and planning and decorating and, well, all of the things I'm *not* good at.

My mom's been sleeping so little that she finally conks out on the couch. I don't dare move her. She's getting too skinny, a thought that makes me sound like my abuela in my head. I drag the comforter from her bed over her and hit the mute button on the TV. The light will comfort her if she wakes in a strange location. With my phone, wallet, and key from the nearby table, I tiptoe out of the apartment. The busy sidewalk is freshly covered with a sparkling dusting of snow. It's nice to see before the morning traffic makes things so dirty.

It may be freezing here, but one thing my mom and I are suckers for is ice cream. We found this unique little place called Sweet Jesus on our first day in town. It's housed in an old church, and the ice cream is the best calorie gain I've ever experienced. Our goal is to have one of everything on the menu before we quit filming in March, but at this rate, I'll be through the list by the middle of January. I can always double up, I suppose.

The sidewalks are busy and the city is bright with holiday lights. The line for ice cream, even in the snow, is out the door. I take my spot and huddle against the building to stay warm in my fuzzy coat.

I palm my phone, hiding my face deep in the fur of my hood and scroll through pictures on my friends' feeds. It's hard to find photos of Tory, but it doesn't stop me from constantly searching. He usually fights it like he is in this one I stopped on. It's a selfie Hayden took, and Tory is hiding most of his face with his palm, his tongue sticking out far enough to touch his chin. It's enough to see his lips.

Excited to share my news about coming home, I flip to my contacts and stop on Hayden's name. We didn't talk for a few days after I left, but he texted out of the blue one night saying he needed someone to listen. It made me smile, and it's made me less lonely to have him only a text away. He gives me little updates about his brother, but I don't ask about him much. It seems they're in a good place, and I don't want to stir up anything that's better left put to rest. My feelings and hurt and scars over Tory aren't for Hayden to hear. Besides, I like just listening.

I press the call button by his name and bring the phone to my ear. I hate when people walk around on video chat, talking to one another in crowds for everyone to hear. I refuse to be that, even though *everyone* I work with—including Jordan Shotwell—is one of those people. I caught my mom doing it the other day and duly chastised her.

After four rings, I'm close to giving up, but Hayden picks up, sounding winded.

"Hey! One sec," he says, the phone muffling with his movement.

"Hey, I'll be right back!" he shouts to someone there with him.

I hear a door shut and the background noise disappears.

"Sorry, we were ballin'. I needed a break. Good timing!" He's panting a little, and I hear his water bottle filling up in the distance. I picture their fridge, the kitchen counter I sat at with Tory when I first practiced the part I'm playing now. I'm glad he rehearsed with me. If I hadn't started early I never would have been prepared for the schedule change.

"Just you and Tory?" I ask, wondering if his brother came inside, too.

"Us, and"—he stops while he takes a drink—"Cannon, his cousin Zack, and Chaz."

"I thought you hated Chaz?" I protest.

"I thought you hated Cannon," he fires back.

"I do!" I realize I'm being loud so I duck my head back between my shoulders and pull the zipper up on my coat, holding my phone inside the insulated cubby I've made for one.

Hayden laughs and says something about needing a fourth or whatever. Their tournament is next week. It starts the day I leave, so I won't be able to catch any games, which bums me out.

"How's Mr. Shotwell?" He asks this every time. My friends are more star-struck than I am, but maybe that's because I have to maintain a level of cool. I wouldn't be able to produce tears in front of the man if I stopped to realize how mega-huge his fame really was.

"I didn't get to see him when we wrapped. I think he's back in New Zealand until we start back up again in two weeks."

"Wow, New Zealand. He invite you to his posh palace to yacht and dine and all that stuff?" Hayden teases.

"Yes, we're besties." I roll my eyes.

"Two weeks off, huh? What are you going to do?"

"Well . . ." I lead. "Guess who gets on a plane tomorrow?"

"Jordan Shotwell," he answers, purposely being wrong.

"You're an ass," I throw back at him.

"I'm kidding. You. You're getting on a plane. When do you get in?"

"Not until like four. And we have to do some legal things before the weekend, but I hope maybe I'll get to see you guys by Saturday?" I say *we* in a generic sense, but I'm pretty sure Hayden gets the implication.

"That can probably be arranged. You know June has a shift, but she gets off at two. Maybe . . . we bowl?" He throws that idea out there because after my first showing, I swore to him I was retiring, knowing I would never best my big honkin' forty-one.

"I don't know. I'm officially on the Champion's Tour, and my sponsors don't like me falling back to amateur status."

"You know the Champion's Tour is for seniors, right? Like fifty-five-plus?"

"You're kidding!" I protest.

I've moved through the door of the parlor, so I tuck myself into a corner to finish our conversation before it's my turn to order the Unicorn Dust Sundae, my flavor choice of the day.

"All right, bowling it is," I relent, actually a little excited about my sophomore attempt at the game.

"It's on. I better get back before they try and take on Cannon without me. Dude's six-foot-three and absolute trash at basketball," Hayden says.

"Okay. Tell everyone I say hi."

He ends the call with a quick, "I will," and I wonder if he means it.

I get to Eight Lanes early. I texted Hayden after our call a few days ago and told him to keep my arrival a surprise for everyone else. To make it work, I have to slip in while June's on break. It's been easy to hide from her in lane one because every other lane is full of league bowlers. I've spent the last thirty minutes watching them from afar to pick up tips.

The secret is in the swag. I need one of those wrist-guard thingies, and this lotion that goes on your thumb. And some of them have balls that actually glow. I want a ball that glows.

I'm mesmerized by a man next to me. Bud Fox. I know that because it says so on his ball. And on the front pocket of his bowling shirt. And on his ball bag. I bet his name is tattooed on his wife. I'd say she could do better but really, in terms of bowlers, I don't think she can. Bud Fox is epic. I wonder if he's on the tour.

"Hey, sorry I'm late," Hayden says, slipping into the seat next to me. I startle, then shift instantly into a breathy squeal. It's good to see him.

I wrap my arms around his midsection and hug him tight, my head falling against his chest. Nothing about our embrace is weird, and I don't give it a second thought until minutes later when I realize it happened and we both acted natural.

"Okay, so June will probably wander over first. I don't know how you want to play this, but if you'd like to surprise them all at once, you can always hide behind the ball rack, I guess?" He points over his shoulder to the curved wall filled with colored spheres.

"Yeah, that works," I say, getting to my feet and stretching. I feel as though I've been on the go since I first left home. Two weeks of flights and filming and freezing temps has left me a little achy. I might be ready for that Champion's Tour after all.

"She's coming," Hayden whispers.

I crouch down and waddle my way behind the rack, sitting on my knees when I'm well out of sight. I hear June's voice a few seconds later and my legs twitch with the desire to spring up and see my friend. I hold tight instead and listen.

"Lucas is almost here. He said Tory was dragging ass. I think the whole driving back and forth thing is getting to him," she says.

I lower my head. He's still keeping up with the splitting time thing between his parents. Hayden hasn't mentioned it. He decided to stay at his mom's; I don't know why I figured Tory did, too.

"I know. I think he's just trying to make sure my dad isn't alone. He's got a few work trips coming up in January, so Tory should be home for a solid block then."

"You want me to get the names up?" June asks.

"I got it. Let me know when you see the guys," Hayden says. I lean forward to catch his eyes and he's doing the same from his seat. When we connect he gives me a thumbs up. I can't believe I'm really going to pull this off. I can't believe I'm going to see Tory. I haven't seen him since he sat with me on that concrete bench and told me he couldn't hurt his brother.

"I see them," June says. My pulse explodes into a splatter of beats. My mouth waters as if I'm about to be sick, and I feel faint. I'm not sure I can really see this through. I move from my knees to my ass so I can bend my head down and breathe. I completely fill my lungs once . . . twice . . . and the ringing in my ears stops.

"Hey, man. How was the drive?" I recognize Hayden, so I hold my breath, waiting for the voice I've been craving.

"Brutal. I think it's the soundtrack," Tory says. I smile automatically. It's good to hear him and his brother joke. It's good to hear *him.*

"You're just being stubborn," Hayden says.

There's a bit of chatter while everyone shuttles around getting balls and swapping out shoes. I can't quite tell if it's a good time to just pop out, so I lean forward again, hoping to catch Hayden in his seat. I lurch out from around the corner just as Tory leans down to pick out his ball, and our eyes stall on one another for almost a full second before I scream and fall back.

With my hand over my thundering chest, I blow up at my hair, looking at the only great kiss I've ever had. The dent on his forehead tells me he's not quite sure what to make of this situation, but the longer it's there, the more I realize he isn't happy to see me. I don't think he's sad.

I don't think he's anything.

"Abby?" June leans over the wall, her hair flopping down in braids on either side of her face.

"Surprise!" I whimper, waving my hands in the air.

Tory puts his ball down and steps toward me, reaching out a hand. I stare at his palm for a beat before taking it. The moment we touch will be a sign of where things stand. His hand completely wraps around mine as he yanks me to my feet. He steadies me with his other hand, resting it on my shoulder, but while that hand drifts away once I'm upright, the one pressed against my palm still holds on tight. His eyes haven't left mine, either.

"I'm home . . . Yay!" I celebrate in a quiet, playful voice, my cheeks burning from all the attention I've gotten myself. I really blundered this.

"Abby!" June rushes me, ripping my hand from Tory's so she can somehow lift me and twirl me around. I've got twenty pounds on her, so I'm not sure where her strength comes from, but it's nice to feel so loved.

"Hey, Cortez," Lucas says, waiting his turn. June holds my hand while I hug Lucas, and she keeps a hold on me while Hayden adds my name to the scoring screen.

"You knew about this?" Tory asks his brother.

A wave of nausea knocks me into a seat. June comes with me, glancing at me with concern. I play it off by kicking off my shoes and swapping them out for bowling ones.

"Yeah, she wanted to surprise you guys," Hayden answers, not even looking at his brother as he readies the screen.

I look up as Tory's eyes shift to me, and the hurt in them is undeniable.

"You talk a lot?" He's asking me, but Hayden doesn't realize this. He answers without giving it much thought.

"Sometimes. Just when we have time. Hey, you're up first." He shifts in his seat so his legs are out to the side and nods to his brother.

Tory walks back to the rack where he left the ball after I ruined my surprise entrance. He picks it up as though it's made of Styrofoam, then takes long strides toward our lane. Without taking aim, he hoists the ball at the pins but sends it flying through the air a good ten feet before it thumps down on the alley.

"Ooops," he says, laughing in that menacing style of his, the one he uses when he means to push buttons. He claps his hands together, like a gymnast dusting off chalk, and then pivots when he's under the screen to look up at his score. The ball took out one pin, so he plays this up just to be an ass.

"This was a bad idea," I mutter. June is the only one close enough to hear, but she doesn't react other than sliding her foot over to rest against mine.

Tory finishes his turn and moves to the stools behind our seating area, propping himself on his elbows. I stare at him until it's my turn, willing him to look back at me, but he doesn't. Not once.

I manage to knock six pins down my first time, and seven my second. Lucas turns into my biggest champion, rooting for me like an obnoxious wrestling fan every time I take the ball in hand. When the game is halfway through, Tory finally leaves the shelter he's hiding in and joins the rest of us.

Things finally find a natural ease, and I'm sure to everyone else, everything feels normal. But if any of them stopped to pay attention, they'd realize that amid our banter and celebration, Tory and I haven't exchanged a glance, a word, or a touch, not once since the game began.

It's my final turn of the first game, and after a series of single pin frames, I'm four pins away from beating my whopping forty-one record. I take a deep breath, the rumbling echo of Lucas pounding the floor like football fans do on the bleachers as my backdrop. My pal Bud Fox hushes him more than once, but Lucas doesn't listen, continuing his homemade thunder.

I glance over my shoulder on a whim, just to see if Tory is watching, but he's looking down at his phone. Dejected, I line up the ball, using his advice and aligning myself with the middle arrows. I shuffle forward and release, my thumb getting stuck and sending the ball in a sidespin down the right side of the lane.

"Come on, baby. Come on, baby," Lucas hums behind me. I think he's genuinely invested in my outcome. I'm only sad that Tory isn't watching.

I take slow steps backward, stopping right in front of Lucas, who is down on one knee as if he somehow has the power to steer my ball down the lane in spite of my poor toss. My ball hits two pins in the front, and a third behind them, but not with enough force to fully knock it down. My hips roll along with the movement as the pin rolls on its base, finally falling to the side at the perfect angle and taking its neighbor down with it.

"Yeah!" Lucas rushes up behind me and lifts me from under my arms. My feet kick wildly as I laugh.

"I have never seen anyone so excited over a forty-two," June jokes, waiting to high five me the minute Lucas puts me down.

I get another high five from Hayden, and I move to the back seats where Tory is sitting, hoping he'll have some sort of reaction. He's on his phone, the device pressed to his ear. His eyes flit up, never fully meeting mine, and he holds up a finger as he stands and walks around the counter to the stools he was hiding on for half the game.

"You guys wanna go again?" Hayden stands with one knee on the seat at the computer. I glance to June who nods.

"I'm in," Lucas says.

We all turn our focus to Tory, waiting while he finishes his call. He holds his phone in his palm for a second, staring at the blank screen before acknowledging us.

"Hey, sorry guys. I'm out. Cannon is coming by to get me, but we'll catch up more. Yeah?" His gaze swings to me, his eyes finally reaching mine.

"Sure," I rasp.

A polite smile barely makes a dent in his face and he holds up a hand, moving on to our other friends, who all seem as dismissed and offended as I am.

Tory swaps out his footwear and carries the bowling shoes to the counter before heading out the exit. My friends hold their tongues until he leaves, doling out theories over why he might be upset as soon as he's gone.

None of them are right, and I know they're not, but I listen with feigned concern and continue to indulge their theories throughout our next game. Lucas and June leave after we enjoy a round of wings, on the house because Morty, the alley's manager, says I'm the biggest star to ever come out of Allensville. Not quite ready to go home, I wander over to the pool tables and lift a cue in challenge to Hayden. Truth be told, for once I might need *him* to listen.

"I'm pretty bad at pool," he says, taking the stick and helping me rack the balls.

"I'm not that great, either. It should be a real duel," I say.

He simpers at me and takes the cue ball in his palm, setting it on the felt and offering for me to break. I bend, looking the part, and run the stick through my fingers like a violinist uses a bow. My results aren't nearly as impressive as I don't hit the ball squarely, sending it immediately off to the side and into a corner pocket.

"Mulligan?" I arch a brow.

Hayden laughs, pulling the ball out and rolling it to me.

"Sure."

My second attempt is a little better, scattering the balls around the table but not sinking a single one. Hayden walks around, eyeing different angles, but before he lines up what I think is his best shot, he stands up tall and sets his stick down flat, his palms on the table's edge.

"Tory's in love with you."

I blink, frozen by his words. I'm not even sure I heard them right. And I can't tell by his expression whether he's guessing or saying something backed by fact.

"I'm sorry, what?" I shake my head and squint my eyes.

"He told me. Right after you left, after the awesome therapy session I told you about that first time we talked when you were in Toronto."

"Tory . . . said he's in love with me." I repeat the words, still not believing them. Not that I think it's impossible, I just know what Tory said before I left. How deeply he cares about his relationship with Hayden. And also, how little credit he gives the idea of love. About as much as I do.

Hayden takes one of the balls in his hand and rolls it against the felt, ricocheting it off the bumper and back into his hand. Our game is done. That's fine; it was only an excuse anyhow.

"Look, Abby . . ." He rolls the ball again, but I cut it off before it makes it to his hand this time, catching it in my own. His gaze lifts to meet mine and he exhales. "Tory is in love with you. He told me, and I know he's not going to do anything about it. I can't let that happen. Me and him . . . we're in a good place."

I blink away the threat of tears.

"Why doesn't he tell me?" I ask.

Hayden levels me with a sideways look, his mouth a flat line. He doesn't have to say the words. Tory won't hurt Hayden.

"What do I do with this? What . . ." My words run out.

Hayden leaves his cue and rounds the table, stepping directly in front of me and lifting my chin so he can look in my eyes.

"You tell him you love him, too."

A sloppy laugh falls from my lips, part nerves and part sob. I nod to him and he pulls me into a hug. Hayden and I were always better friends. Tory was right the first time he said it—he and I, we would always be more.

TWENTY-THREE

TORY

My dad left yesterday for a business trip to Canada. Playing bachelor was fun for exactly twelve hours. I drank one of his beers but the novelty wore off before I went in for another. I walked around in my boxers for a while, but ultimately, I just ended up cleaning the apartment. Being alone is turning me into Hayden.

A buzz from my phone wakes me from a near nap, my third of the day, so I tap the screen awake to read the text.

HAYDEN: *June says if you don't come to her New Year's party she is never talking to you again.*

I blink twice at the message and decide to call his bluff.

ME: *That's a lie. She'd never cut me out.*

When it takes him a few minutes to respond, I sit up. I don't really believe she would, but I don't like the idea of disappointing her. I'm sure she understands that I don't want to see Abby. I know Hayden must. Why does it feel like he's pushing so hard?

My phone buzzes with a photo attachment from him, and I open it to see a picture of June flipping me off. I shake with a short laugh.

ME: *Fine. I'm coming.*

I toss my phone into the center of the bed and pace the empty guest room. Hayden has been here once, and only to see it. It's not very homey, but that's not really in my dad's skill set. It seems a waste for him to buy us a bunch of shit here anyhow, since who knows where we'll be next fall. I should find out about my offers soon. Hayden's picking between Colorado and Nevada. I could go with him. Both coaches expressed interest in me, too, but I think it might be good to have our own college experiences. I'm more interested in staying in the Midwest. Who knows, maybe we'll play each other in the Big Dance.

It's after ten, so I better hit the road before drunks start to spill out onto the backroads I take on my way into Allensville. Tossing a few staples into my duffle, I rush through a shower and land on my gray sweater that buttons at the neck and a pair of dark blue jeans. I look dressed up enough to pass for New Year's formal, I think. Besides, I know there's no way June will get Lucas in anything fancier than this.

It takes me more than an hour to get into town, the highway dotted with patrol cars waiting to pull people over. I keep to the speed limit exactly. When I turn onto June's street, almost every space along the road is blocked. I cruise by her and Lucas's driveways, and they're full of cars as well.

"Damn, this is a real party," I say to myself.

It takes me two passes to find an open space that I can wedge my car into. It's not the best parking job, but it will do. I plan on leaving early anyhow. I just need to make my friends happy and show some face time. I reach into my bag and grab my cologne, giving my neck a quick spray before getting out of the car. I like to let the scent linger in there; it masks whatever that strange smell is that's been there since I bought the thing.

The music is thumping loud enough to be heard four houses down. I hope the Mabees invited all the neighbors, otherwise they're going to get a noise complaint. People can be real assholes about partying on New Year's. I mean, the entire premise of the holiday is to stay up until midnight.

I'm halfway up the driveway when my palms start to sweat. I know what it is: it's seeing Abby's car. I've been avoiding her. She messaged me twice after bowling and I put her off, making excuses. It's the reason I ran to Indy to stay at my Dad's. Seeing her—and knowing she's stayed in touch with Hayden—cut something open inside of me—fresh wounds over old ones. My jealousy reared its head, and I don't like the monster that emotion turned me into.

I'm nearly to the door when someone tugs on my arm and pulls me into the hedges that line June's house. My fists clench, ready to fend off some drunk asshole, but before I take a swing I realize it's my brother.

"Dude, it's wet over here. What the hell?" I brush droplets from my pants and sleeves, then lift my foot to check my shoes for mud.

"I told Abby," he says. I look up at him and wonder if that's supposed to make sense.

"That it's wet out here and she shouldn't romp around in the bushes? Yeah, man. Good call. You really saved her." I look back down to the clump of mud on my Nikes. These things were pristine.

"Jackass. I told her you love her," he says. My eyes shoot up again, and my fists reform.

"What the fuck, dude?" My body is overrun with the falling sensation, the same one I got in that creepy elevator ride at the amusement park that drops you several stories at a time over and over just for fun. I don't like the ride, and I don't like this feeling now.

Hayden grabs my shoulders and his fingers dig in enough that I'm forced to give him my attention. I'm also a breath away from starting a lawn brawl with him.

"She loves you, too. You know she does. Hell, I know she does. And I'm truly, one-hundred percent happy about that."

I stare at him, at a loss for words. The elevator in my gut pauses for a moment while I register everything, but it yo-yos again when my mind processes what comes next in the chain of events.

"No, I went down that road, and it was . . ."

"It wasn't the right time," he fills in.

It's not what I was going to say, but his point is more valid. Chasing Abby Cortez was a rush. Tasting her was a dream, and loving her was an epiphany. The only thing that made it not possible was the damage it created between me and the man squeezing my arms out of their sockets.

"You would be okay with this?" I turn my head in skepticism.

"Tor, you have June. And you know what? *I* have Abby." I happen to glance over his shoulder through the window as he says those words, spying inside just as June rushes through the main room with a stack of plates in her hand, playing hostess.

"She has to regret the idea of throwing this party," I say, changing the subject.

Hayden turns to see what I'm seeing, then laughs.

"She does, especially since her mom is totally lit. The adults are all drinking and the rule was that the seniors should stick to soda," he says.

"That didn't happen," I predict. He shakes his head in response as we take in the scene inside.

I could find more ways to stall, and I think my brother would let me because he knows how very little I enjoy being vulnerable. But Abby cuts across the room we're studying, dressed in a dark gray sweater almost exactly like mine and leggings that hug her curves. The sight of her makes my fingers flex, imagining the path they could take from her knee up to her breasts. Her hair is down in waves, and her lips sport her favorite shade of pink. She flips her hair over one shoulder with a laugh, and for a moment my breath stops, her eyes looking right at me.

"It's too bright in there. She can't see out," Hayden assures me.

My shoulders relax, but my muscles tense again almost immediately because I know I'm about to do something about what my brother said.

"You're sure?" I ask again, needing the extra push.

"Tory . . . go," he says in a low voice, pushing me forward.

I leave the brush and stomp the mud from my shoes, waiting while my brother does the same. Taking away my choice, he opens the door, pushing it wide enough that people see me trailing behind him. If I turned and ran now, Abby would hear about it. She'd look for me, wondering where I went.

I follow Hayden inside and close the door behind me, surveying the room for familiar faces. June spots me first, rushing up to me in her frenzied state. I'm a little proud when I smell a hint of beer on her breath. She's always been such a straight-laced partier.

"Lucas is out back. There's a fire pit. But it's almost midnight so he better get his ass inside," she says, her mouth near my ear so I can hear over the pounding club-style music. It's an assault on the ears.

"She's upstairs," Hayden says, glancing up and encouraging me to follow his eyes. I look in that direction and see Abby leaning her back against the railing. She's surrounded by people, probably waiting in line to go to the bathroom or something. I'm not sure I should be so public about this just yet.

"Two minutes," my brother says, cupping his mouth so I can hear him. I scan the room for a clock and verify the time. It's actually only around a minute now.

The music dies, and someone switches on a television, the volume cranked to announce the countdown for everyone in the house. My gaze again moves up the stairs in search of Abby, and this time, she's looking down at the people gathered around me. I will her to find me, and she almost does a few times, but her gaze never completely settles on mine.

Without time to spare, I push through the crowd gathered in the living room to see the big screen mounted on June's wall. The count is at twenty by the time I get to the steps, and I slice through people on my way up, evading a few shoves along the way.

The count hits fifteen when I'm about four steps below Abby, fourteen when she finally turns and sees me. Twelve when she weaves through the crowd, heading deeper into the dark hallway toward June's room. It's seven by the time I catch her, and five when my hand finds her slender wrist. By three, we've stumbled into June's room, her door closed by two.

One.

"I love you," I say, not waiting a second longer to get the words out of my heart and into her ears. It's midnight on New Year's Eve and I should pull her into me and kiss her senseless. But saying those words was far more important.

Her arms remain stiff at her sides, her brow pinched, and her lips quivering—trembling the way they did the first time I felt them against mine.

"It's okay if you don't feel the same. It's okay if you want me to leave. I will. I'll leave right now, and I'll be fine with that because I got to tell you I love you. But if there's a chance you feel the same way, if there's the remotest chance that your heart kicks a little when you see me, that your breath maybe dropped when I said those words, then I swear to God, Abby Cortez, you better kiss me in this new year. If I love you and you love me, I want to start this right."

Her eyes dip to my chest, then flicker back up to my face. She's nervous, and I'm not sure whether she's weighing her options or looking for an easy way out. "Auld Lang Syne" blares from downstairs, and most of the party is either kissing or shouting *Happy New Year* while repeatedly blowing those dumb paper horns. My confidence wavers with every second that passes, though I couldn't possibly give her a better speech than the one I somehow just delivered. My gaze dips down to the floor and I move to step to the side so she can leave.

"I love you, too," she utters, her voice meek and shaky.

I raise my chin.

"I love you," she says again, this time the wavering gone.

"I love you," I say to her again, enjoying this volley of words. I take a step toward her and she does the same.

"I love you."

"I love you."

We repeat in rapid succession as we erase the distance between us until she leaps into my arms and I catch her as her legs wrap around my waist, our mouths finding their homes against one another's. We are a perfect fit. Our kiss is natural and explosive. Every time is like this, a rush and a comfort, a death and a birth.

"I love you," I utter against her, my mouth suddenly unable to stop speaking these three small words. The way her mouth feels when it smiles against me is as potent as her kiss.

She kisses along my jaw as I hold her against my body and walk us toward June's bed. Her mouth finds my ear and her arms encase my head as she mouths those three words to me again. She straddles my lap as I sit us down, and my hands glide up her sweater, pulling it off in one swift move. She pulls mine off next, and her bra is not far behind.

"June is going to kill you," I say, chuckling against her mouth as she tugs on the button of my jeans.

My thumbs are already hooked in the waist of her leggings, lowering them over her hips and over her ass as she pushes me down to lay flat on my back. She flips her hair up and her hungry eyes meet mine.

"Let her try," she hums, a devilish curve accented in her favorite color. Dropping her lips to my chest, she kisses her way down my stomach until she reaches my open pants. My eyes roll back at the sensation of her hand on my hard cock, and when her tongue runs along the tip I nearly pass out.

"What do you want, Tory D'Angelo?" She's a vixen, her mouth poised over me, tempting me with my own biggest weakness—every man's thinnest defense.

Knowing the only thing that will truly satisfy me is satisfying her, I sit up and trail my hands to her ass, grabbing the bare skin with a firm grip that makes her gasp.

"I want to be inside you." I lift her and trade positions, her back now on the bed and her body under my control. She wriggles out of her leggings and panties while I kick off my jeans and search for my wallet to pull out a condom. I tear it open and work it down my length while her knees part, and her trust makes me pause and gaze at her naked flesh. I love how absolutely bold she is with her body. There is no shame in anything she does with me, nor should there be.

She brings her finger to her mouth, biting on it in such an unbelievably seductive way, and I accept the invitation. Lowering myself until our bodies align, I hold my weight up on my elbows so my hands are free to draw gentle lines along her face.

"Goddamn, are you beautiful," I say, drawing another pale pink smile from her lips. I bite the plump bottom of her mouth teasingly, holding it hostage in my teeth until my own smile makes me lose my grip.

"You're covered in my lipstick." She giggles, drawing lines of her own along my shoulders and neck until her palms stop at my jaw.

"Then I'm wearing your favorite color," I say. Her eyes blink to mine and she stares into them, wordless for several seconds.

"You see me," she says.

"I do," I agree, my hands gathering up the soft waves of her hair at the side of her face. I lower my head until it rests on hers, and her eyes close as she hums.

"I love you, Tory D'Angelo." Her next sound is a sigh of pleasure as I push into her with a slow, deep stroke.

The minutes tick by, and we let them, milking every moment for what it offers. I taste each whimper she makes, kissing her lips raw and tangling her hair in knots around my hands. The party rages on below, the thumping music picking up again to carry on until someone down the road complains. Here, in my best friend's room, I fall in love for a second time with the same girl I did the first. I fall in love with every touch, with every word, and with each gasp for air we share until our bodies are limp and wrung of energy.

By two in the morning, Abby is fast asleep against my chest, our naked bodies fused together from hunger and passion played out for hours. By three I fall asleep and dream about her. And by four, she's waking me up to do it all again.

EPILOGUE

ABBY

Keeping us a secret wasn't easy. I didn't want to lose a minute of time with Tory before I had to board the plane again, but I also didn't want to ruin something so fragile and new by throwing it under the microscope of our group of friends. Hayden is the only one who knew, and he promised to keep our relationship to himself until we were ready to welcome more opinions. He believed in us, and that was enough.

We decided prom would be our big coming out. Only now that I'm standing on the top step of Lucas's winding staircase, June's mom's studio lights casting me in a glow powerful enough to spawn angels, announcing that I've been in a loving relationship with Tory, Hayden's brother, for more than three months, seems terrifying.

"Why is your mom so obsessed with taking photos of us walking down stairs in high heels?" I ask my friend. She laughs from just over my shoulder.

"Just a little longer," she promises. She said that thirty minutes ago.

We've been lined up in this same position for about twenty minutes, taking turns standing in different spots. When we started, the guys were all paired with us, and Tory kept pinching my ass. He's making me regret picking the short black dress. I know I look good in it, though. It works with my curves, and I tested to make sure it wouldn't ride up while I danced. I intend to put these shoes and this dress to work. Tory has promised me he'll salsa. We'll see how long before he bows out.

"Okay, now just one more for each couple," June's mom begs. Collectively we groan, but none of us really mind making Kristen Mabee happy. June and Lucas go first, so I take a break from smiling and duck into Lucas's room.

Most of our parents are here in the house, and June's mom has been patient letting my mom art direct some of my shots. It's a habit for her, having been on set with me for so many test shots.

The D'Angelos both came, and Natalia even helped me with my dress. Their divorce is almost final, but oddly their relationship has never been better. Tory said his dad comes to the house every Sunday for dinner, and they usually end up sitting around the table as a family for two hours just talking after the food is gone. Some people are just meant to be friends.

My dad moved back to Miami, and I filed a restraining order and an injunction, extra protection on top of what he pledged in our settlement. With some luck and a lot of legal maneuvers, he should never bother me or my mom again. I had to do something for peace of mind while I was away at college. I don't worry about my dad hurting her, but I do worry about the harassment. I think his DNA is just woven to make him cruel.

"We're up," Tory says with a soft knock on the door.

I suck in one last, deep breath and work the nervous energy out through my fingertips.

"Show time?" I say to him.

"Now or never," he responds. We pause at the door, and when our eyes meet, we laugh. The idea of never coming clean about us has crossed both of our minds. Keeping secrets is hard, especially one like this that deserves so much public display of affection.

"Ready," he declares, running his hand down my arm, his fingers finding mine and weaving through all the empty spaces. I turn into him and straighten his tie, flitting my gaze up to find him smirking.

"Now we're ready," I say. We squeeze each other's palms and step through the door, making our way to the landing, then down a few steps.

"Great. Okay . . . Tory?" June's mom immediately begins directing.

"Yeah?" my boyfriend responds.

"Maybe come down a step so you're lower; it will balance out your height," she explains.

"Oh, yeah, sure," he says, taking a step and turning to face me with a wiggle of his brow.

"Oh, but first? I want to tell you all one thing."

All eyes jet to us, including those couples I don't know well. Our group has blossomed while I've been gone. Life has rolled on. Hayden is dating

Lola. Naomi met a girl. Cannon apparently has a soul and possibly decent taste in women. And Tory—he's still head over heels in love with me. And he's about to show the world.

In one smooth movement, Tory tugs me into his arms and leans me back into a daring dip, the fingers of one hand splayed on my bare back, the other griping my thigh. He holds my leg up against him and kisses me in front of every person we care about in Allensville, Indiana.

"Holy fucking shit!" Lucas's words are the first to ring in my ears, and I laugh against Tory's lips.

"Wooooo!" June shouts. Her mom whistles with her fingers.

There's actual applause, which seems like overkill, but the adulations only make me want to kiss him more.

I'm dizzy by the time he tips me upright, and he holds my body close to his while the stars circle my head. We spend the next several minutes basically being interviewed by our friends, and there are actual *awes* when Tory gives Hayden full credit for us ever happening. It's credit due, though, because without his gentle pushes, I'm not sure either of us would have ever given in.

The party bus finally honks outside, saving us from more prying questions, like the one I fear June is about to ask. She put two and two together, and I'm judging by the distance her brow travels up her forehead, she realizes that Tory and I totally had sex on her bed.

The D'Angelos paid for the enormous Hummer to drive us all to the prom. Even though the distance to the ballroom is short, we still manage to test out every gadget and feature. By the time we roll up to the dance, we have the disco ball spinning and the neon lights changing colors. I think the guys would be happy with their dates for hours in this small, intimate space, but I for one have plans to dance until my feet cave in.

Answering my prayers, Jennifer Lopez's "Let's Get Loud" is kicking as we make our way in, and before Tory can plant his ass in a chair, I wrap his tie around my hand and lead him out onto the dance floor.

"Not gonna lie. You intimidate me a little, Cortez," he says, tugging his tie loose when I let go. He unbuttons the top button of his dress shirt and stretches his arms like he's getting ready to compete in a triathlon.

"Your arms aren't as important as your hips," I say, shouting over the music. His eyes slant, playfully frightened. "Here."

I put my hands on his hips and stand about a foot away so he can follow my movement. It's basically a figure eight, only it isn't just two dimensional, it's three. When I roll my hips, Tory's head falls back in a fit of laughter.

"What?" I ask.

He points to my body, drawing his finger up and down.

"There is no way I can do that," he says.

I look at him sideways, knowing he can. He just needs the right encouragement.

Taking his hands in mine, I place them on my hips and look him in the eyes as I proceed to move again. After a few beats, his feet are moving with mine, and by the time the song is really in its groove, he's gotten it down, at least enough to hold me close and let our bodies grind. I knew he would like this. I can teach him the fancier stuff later.

The DJ carries right into another salsa song, so we stay on the dance floor, our bodies damp from both the exertion and the sexiness that comes with being this close to one another and moving like this while clothed. I catch June attempting to follow my steps while dancing with Lucas, so I pause with Tory and give an impromptu lesson. By the third song, I've managed to teach four couples to do a basic step, and the vibe is singing to my heart as we all sway to the rhythm.

The tempo finally slows, and I'm grateful to have a moment to hold Tory to me and barely move. It also gives me time to prepare for the second big reveal Tory and I planned for tonight—this one for each other.

"Do you want to do it now?" I ask, knowing he'll get what I mean.

"Hmmm, I'm not sure. What if—"

"We're different?" I finish for him.

He peels back enough to look me in the eyes, his mouth set with worry.

After we'd been dating for two months, the college talk started to take on realistic consequences. With our past, and with the mistakes we've seen our parents make, we didn't want to fall into the trap of having one of us give up a dream to follow the other person to theirs. We came to the decision that we would narrow down our schools and share our decisions with one another at the same time—tonight.

"There is no wrong decision. And I will love you no matter what coast you're on," I say, moving into him and pressing a soft kiss to his lips.

He hugs me tightly against his chest and spins us around.

"I don't know . . . ugh," he grumbles playfully. I can tell there are sincere nerves under the surface of his jokes.

To assuage them, I cup his cheek and stand on the tips of my toes, touching his nose to mine.

"I love you, no matter what." I repeat the core of our pledge. I'm not sure when we started saying it to each other, but it's become habit. It's become a promise. It's our future.

No matter what.

"Okay, on the count of three," he says, his chest rising with a deep breath. I follow suit and fill my own lungs.

"One," I say.

"Two," he follows.

We pause; there's no turning back. A promise to each other means no cheating. We said we would share at the same time, and if we make it to three, we must. We don't hang each other out to dry.

Our eyes lock, and I wait until certainty passes through the hazel oceans of his irises. His mouth turns up, and his cheeks lift. He's ready.

"Three," I say, immediately followed by the word, "Chicago."

"Northwestern."

Our nerves have vanished.

Two schools, twenty miles apart. A train ride.

There were endless combinations that could have been. He didn't know my final five, and I didn't know his. Maybe fate whispered to us in our dreams. Or maybe sometimes, friends are also meant to be in love forever.

THE END

ACKNOWLEDGMENTS

I fell in love with Tory D'Angelo somewhere around the first 30 pages of Varsity Heartbreaker. To keep this smart-ass boy at bay while I finished writing his best friend's story (well, *both* best friends, since June is also his best friend) was no easy task. He was persuasive and insistent in my head, talking to me when I was trying to sleep at night with his cute little "oh, and I'm gonna be funny, right? And unpredictably thoughtful? And you'll write me hot, right? Like, abs and all that shit but also perfect hair, and…I like nice clothes. Give me good style."

Tory got his way. And I hope you guys did too. I hope you enjoyed his angsty ride through his senior year, his ups and downs, and the way love and life played out. I was just the chick at the keyboard for this one. That story is all him. And of course, Cannon is already talking.

As always, full credit goes to my team that holds me up. This starts with my rock, my sweet Autumn. Bless you for having the same F'd up sleeping schedule I do, my friend. And thank you for every single thing you do for me. It's far beyond the PA and publicist job title. It's really more of a confidence whisperer/life coach/guide. My betas, Jen, Shelley, TeriLyn—I love you and am so glad you tolerate the pieced-together way I send you things. One day you'll get the whole thing at once (probably not, but it felt good to put that in writing). Brenda Letendre and Tina Scott, your edits help me find my best foot and put it forward. Lost without you.

If you enjoyed this book, I would be SO VERY GRATEFUL if you could leave a review. The book market is a lot like swimming through mud sometimes, and getting the word out in this increasingly noisy world is becoming so hard. I am incredibly thankful to my readers and supporters for every boost they give. It's those viral shares, the recommendations to friends, that help get my stories seen, and I don't for one minute take any of that for granted. I get to do this because you give me your time and your passion—you tell others to give my books a try. My stories are for you and you alone. Well, maybe a little for me, too, but without you all, there's really no heart. You are the heart—my heart. Thank you for letting it beat so wildly!

VARSITY RULEBREAKER

VARSITY

Rulebreaker

Cover Design by Ginger Scott, Little Miss Write LLC

Cover photo by Michelle Lancaster

Cover model Andy Murray

For Ruthie.
I could not have done this without you.

ONE

CANNON JENNINGS

I'm perfectly content ringing in the new year with a sparkler and leftover pizza. Unfortunately, my cousin Zack is an extrovert. He *needs* to feed off the energy of others. I prefer to eliminate distractions.

"It's one party, Can. You need to pull the stick out of your ass and enjoy one night. One party will not derail your future."

Zack has been on me about loosening up for weeks. Deep down, he's probably right . . . to an extent. If I keep grinding like this through my entire senior year, I'll burn out before I even land at summer camp wherever I get signed. But when you've dreamed of pitching for Vandy since you were six years old and it's legit within your reach, it's hard to let up off the gas, even just a little.

"Come on, man. It's New Year's Eve." Zack's head falls to one side and his lip juts out.

"Are you gonna fuckin' cry?" I toss my glove to the corner of the sofa and get to my feet. Zack rubs his hands together while shuffling his feet in this weird-ass jig.

"I'm not going if you're going to do that," I say, pointing at his lower half. He freezes and instantly stands tall, rolling his shoulders and clearing his throat.

"Sorry. Must have been overcome with shock that Cannon Jennings is actually going to do something social," he says.

"*Pffi*," I huff at him. I grab my keys and my lucky hat and we both head out to my car.

Zack is overexaggerating. I've been social. I went to a party a week ago, and I've made some decent friends. I've done pretty well for being the new guy at school. I moved in with my cousin over the summer as part of the grand plan my dad and my uncle, Zack's dad, devised to maximize the attention we both could get for offers to play college ball. Zack has caught for as long as I have pitched, and we used to play together when we were younger. But Zack's family moved to Indiana for work right after junior high, and it broke up our dream duo. We've both done all right without the other, but we've got one more year to really show our stuff, and Allensville Public High just hired a new coach—with Division One coaching experience. It means I'm sleeping on the futon in the spare room at Zack's while my parents sell our place in New Mexico. Once they do, we'll move into a rental together—and I'll have a bed that doesn't fold up during the day.

"I don't know June very well," I mention as we pull up to the Mabee house. We only live two blocks from them, so the drive was easy.

"Yeah, but you know Lucas, so it's all good," Zack reassures me.

He gets out of the car with an actual skip in his step, still cradling the six-pack of micro brew he snuck from his dad.

I let myself enjoy the quiet of the car for one more breath. He's right. I've gotten to know Lucas pretty well, and the D'Angelo twins. They're all pretty decent athletes, and it's nice to mess around and do things with a group of guys who aren't all about baseball. I gel with Tory D'Angelo the most. He's got plans to play basketball in college, so he gets my constant focus. I swear, as much as my cousin Zack *says* he wants to play college ball, he doesn't seem to have the obsessive passion that I think it takes.

My cousin raps on the window, tired of waiting on me, so I get out and put on my best *happy-to-be-here* face.

It's a strange collection of people inside. Someone who clearly is someone's father opens the door for us, and he eyes the beer in Zack's hand as we enter.

"Maybe we shouldn't have brought beer," I whisper to my cousin, but he ignores me, weaving through the house and into the garage, where an extra refrigerator is stuffed with drinks. He pulls a beer out and hands it to me, taking one for himself, too. I arch a brow, not sure this is allowed.

"It's fine. June said as long as we don't make it obvious around the adults, we're good to go." Zack pops the cap off and takes a swig, gesturing for me to do the same. I do, but only because drinking half this beer might settle the knots in my chest. I'm not so great at social things.

We weave through the house to the back yard where I recognize more faces. My shoulders relax when I spot Lucas sitting near the fire pit with space next to him. I nod in his direction, letting Zack know where he can find me, and head toward the flames. Lucas's girlfriend, June, beats me to the open seat by two seconds, and I'm about to bail when an absolute goddess steps in behind them.

I don't know a lot of people in town or at school, but how I've missed this face, I have no idea. She's tall, maybe only an inch or two shorter than my six-foot-three, and her long blonde hair looks like molten gold as she stands near the fire. I can't tell if her eyes are gray or blue, but I need to get closer to settle the debate in my head. She's supermodel hot, but playing it down in a pair of baggy jeans and an old baseball jersey worn over a hoodie to keep her warm. I bet her dressed-down look keeps her under the radar. Most of the fucking douchebags at this school only want to keep score and see who can date the hot girl first. Lucky for me, she showed up tonight dressed for the part of *exactly my type.*

"Jeter fan, huh?" I say, stepping up next to her and tugging on her jersey sleeve.

A short laugh puffs from her naturally pink lips while she takes a small sip from her cup. I suspect she's actually drinking soda, so I casually set my beer on a small patio table behind me.

"Yankee fan. Jeter's all right," she says, a wry smile on her mouth. I hold her stare for a full breath, partly to challenge her and also to get a good handle on the color of her eyes. Blue, and maybe a little green too.

I match her smirk with one of my own, letting it crawl up into my cheeks before glancing down at the small patch emblazoned on the right sleeve of the jersey. This thing came from a game.

"Bullshit," I say, nodding toward it.

She twists her head to the side and tucks her chin, noting the authentication patch with a slight breath and a smile.

"You got me," she says, her eyes flitting up to mine. I again hold them for a long second, this time because I like the way it feels when I challenge her to return my stare. She's a worthy opponent, and I'm the first to break.

"You a fan?" she asks.

"Of the Yankees? Fuck no. But Jeter's special; he's like a level above the Yankees. He's folklore," I say.

Our baseball banter must annoy Lucas and June because they make a lame excuse to leave us alone. We take over their seats, propping our feet on the lip of the firepit and settling in so we can glance at one another.

"I have another one of these . . . signed," she says, pulling down the front of the jersey to even out the Yankees logo.

I lift my brows, impressed. Also, I catch a hint of her accent, which I'm pretty sure is from the heart of New York, possibly one of the boroughs.

"Super fan, I take it?"

She wobbles her head side to side, playfully, and her eyes dance with this proud kind of joy you only get when you have a childhood full of memories at the ballpark. I know because I've got them, too. Between spring nights at New Mexico State and spring breaks spent in Arizona hunting autographs from my favorite MLB stars at training camps, I've got a pretty full childhood of baseball fairy tales of my own. I can't wait to write my name into those stories.

"I'm Cannon. I'm new here," I say, holding out my hand.

She blinks at it, her lips parted for a few seconds before speaking. She finally takes my palm in hers, her grip impressive.

"I'm Hollis, and I'm new here too."

Definitely from New York.

"Long Island?" I question.

She quirks a brow and blows out from her lips.

"Heck no. Staten Island, baby." She's teasing me, and it's cute as hell. I should have known; Long Islanders are Mets fans.

"Ah, right. Well, nice to meet you, Hollis. I'm from New Mexico. Not nearly as exciting as your big city," I say with a shrug.

"I don't know," she says, leaning her head back and looking up at the sky. I follow her gaze to the stars and the embers popping in the air above us. "You probably have some pretty epic views where you're from."

She's right. We do. Or, at least, we did. I guess these are my views now. Lots of . . . trees.

"We're both from Allensville now, don't you think?" I put that idea out there while we stare up at the black sky, speckled with salt diamonds and masked by smoke.

She sighs.

"Yeah, I guess we are." She drops her chin to her chest and I do the same. "We came from both ends and met in the middle."

She has a way of letting this faint smile linger on her lips after she finishes talking, and I'm having a hard time looking away. Normally, I'd be embarrassed by my overt infatuation with a girl. I'm shitty at flirting. But Hollis, she makes this pretty easy.

"So, what brought you here? To the middle?" I ask.

Her brow pulls in with thought, but that faint smile is still there. She's calculating something. Maybe it's how much to tell a guy she just met.

"Family . . . er, work. My dad moved here for work." I sense that she's conflicted by something, so I don't pry. She probably misses a lot of things from home. I get that. I miss my parents, but at least they'll be here eventually. Can't really move New York to the middle of Indiana.

"We moved here for family too, sorta. I came to play ball with my cousin. He's here, somewhere." I glance over my shoulder, only to find that everyone in the back yard has disappeared. We're completely alone out here.

"I'd introduce you, but . . ." I hold out open palms when I look back to her, and she giggles. The sound she makes pushes my half smile up high into my cheeks, and I quickly realize I'm grinning like a fool. I don't stop, though. I let the ache remain on my foolish face because maybe I've just met my soulmate in pinstripes.

"We must have missed the memo," she says, looking beyond me and into the house.

It was after eleven when Zack and I left the house, so the countdown is probably on for the new year.

"You wanna go in?" I ask her, moving my gaze back to her eyes. This time, she dares me, studying my face intently as if waiting to call my bluff. I don't have one. I'll literally go wherever she tells me to. I'm hoping—

"I don't like crowds. You cool ringing in the new year out here with some girl from Staten Island?"

Foolish grin makes its second appearance on my face, so I lick my lips to tame it just a little.

"For sure," I say, leaning forward with my feet on the ground and elbows on my knees. "Though, you're an Allensville girl now, aren't you?"

She breathes out a laugh and stands, stretching her arms to the sky. It lifts her jersey and sweatshirt just enough that I get a glimpse of her cream-colored skin and the silver stud in her belly button. I never thought that would be my thing, but it's totally my thing. Maybe it's only my thing on beautiful blondes from Staten Island.

"Let me get used to being an Indiana girl for a while, then we can move on to the local titles, yeah?" She sounds so tough when she talks, and the contrast with her angelic face would be almost comical if it weren't so goddamn mesmerizing.

I stand so I can match her height, and maybe get a better read on whether it's okay to kiss a girl I just met at a party I didn't want to go to. I kinda think maybe it is, but only because she didn't want to be here either. And because she's wearing a Jeter jersey. And because I'm pretty sure her eyes have put a spell on me.

With a foot of space between us, I measure how close we come in height while she glances around me to the house filled with people who have started counting down from ten. I was right to guess we're only two or three inches apart. She licks the corner of her lips and smiles, her cheeks suddenly red, and not from the heat of the fire.

"Happy New Year, Hollis from Indiana," I say, my lips in a closed-lip smile to stem off the hungry vibrations urging my body to lunge at her and taste her tongue.

"Happy New Year, Cannon from Indiana," she returns, biting her lower lip but only briefly. She's trying to keep up the act that she's tougher than I am. Maybe she is.

I step toward her, my movement slow and cautious while I read her body language. She doesn't move away, and her hands don't nervously fidget at her sides. They're tucked in the pocket of her hoodie, the front of the jersey lifted so she can slip them inside the warmth underneath. She's so calm I'd almost think she's sleeping with her eyes open, but I know she's not. She's staring at me with a dare—a welcoming dare.

I take another small step, lifting my hand to her chin and touching the pad of my thumb to the soft skin just below her pouting lip. I brush away her hair and bring my other hand up to cup her face.

"Happy New Year," I whisper one last time, mostly to test the waters and see if she flinches. She merely breathes the words back and closes the remaining inches between our mouths until we're locked in an electrifying kiss that feels like fucking home. I lift her chin, coaxing her mouth open just enough for me to slip my tongue inside to taste her sweet mouth. Her lips move with me, and her hands come up to grab at the front of my own hoodie, tugging on the strings as she slips away slowly with a giggle.

My face is numb in the wake of our kiss. It was ten seconds of my life, but quickly rockets up on my top-five moments list.

"Thanks for the New Year's kiss, Cannon. I have to get home, but . . . maybe we can hang out sometime?" She lets go of the strings, her finger drawing a line down the center of my chest as she backs away.

"Most definitely," I say, a bit stupefied that I've been so quickly whipped by a girl I barely know. Maybe it's the haze of New Year's Eve, or maybe I really have been overworking myself and I'm exhausted. Whatever it is, I'm grinning like an idiot again and it doesn't go away for the rest of the night.

I've never had a coach want to hold a meeting with his potential players on January second, but that's what makes coming here an even better decision. Coach Taylor has a reputation for being stern. His last job was at some private school in New York, and they took state twice, back-to-back. He sent us all texts on New Year's Day telling us he wanted to get started with workouts before tryouts come up. There was a subtle overtone that the serious players would be here, so Zack and I arrived before anyone else just to prove we're a cut above dedicated.

It's cold as hell outside, so Coach invited us all to the small clubhouse behind the dugout. This might be a great program I'm walking into, but the facility is shit. Back home, we had brand new everything. My school was barely eight years old, which in terms of a high school lifespan is infant-like. This place was built in fifty-seven. The clubhouse has a plate on the door that says DEDICATED IN 1965. I'm not sure we aren't breathing in lead and asbestos.

"Gentlemen," Coach says, clearing his throat and getting our attention. There's another cough from the back, but I can't quite see who it's from. From the way it sounded, it came off a little bit snarky, like someone making fun of the new coach's style. Coach seems to have picked up on the same nuance because he's staring back there with a scowl on his face.

Bad idea, dude, whoever you are.

"First, thank you all for coming in today. The bad news is this isn't just a meeting. We'll be running two miles too. I'd like to see you all come in under ten minutes by the time season starts."

The collective groan is comical. Me and Zack, though, we keep our mouths shut. Some of the guys showed up in slip-ons, and I have a sneaking suspicion Coach is not going to care. They'll be running either in those or barefoot. Zack and I always dress. In fact, we have our gear and cleats in the car just in case.

Coach spends the next few minutes going over basics, like I had to do at my old school. I've already taken care of the things on the list like my physical and the waiver forms. I zone out through most of his talk, but perk up when he mentions competing for roster spots. Zack doesn't flinch, probably because he's been the starting catcher since freshman year. He's solid. I am too. Hell, from what Zack told me, I will probably be the ace this year; but still, it's never good to assume. There's always someone busting their ass out there. I have to work harder.

"I'll be pairing you guys for head-to-heads and training. Competition fosters greatness, and I don't believe positions are guaranteed; they are earned. You understand me?"

"Yes, sir," we all say. Funny how we know we're supposed to.

"Okay, so listen for your names to be called. This will be your group until we move into official tryouts next month and I have our final roster. I'm keeping fifteen, and other than pitchers, some of you might not get to play. If you're okay with that, stick around. If not, well, thanks for coming in today."

Nobody leaves, but I can tell a few of the guys sitting in front of Zack and me want to. I glance sideways at Zack and he lifts his brows.

"This guy isn't fucking around," he says.

I breathe out a laugh and shake my head.

"Jennings," Coach says.

Zack and I both answer.

"Oh, right. I meant Cannon first. Pitcher only, right?" Coach peers at me, his finger pushing up the brim of his hat just enough to bring his eyes out of the shadow. They're crystal blue and a bit like lasers, wrinkled at the corners from squinting in the sun for years, I imagine.

"Yes, sir," I respond.

He nods and makes a note on his clipboard.

"Jennings, Zack," he says, reading my cousin's name as it's probably written. "You'll be working with Hollis."

Hollis? I casually glance around the room, not seeing the girl of my dreams. Maybe I didn't hear it right.

The first thing I notice on Zack is the way his forehead creases, a dent between his brows. His mouth is parked in an O shape, so I slide my right foot into his to jostle him from this sudden trance.

"Hollis, uhm, okay. Sure." He heard the same name I did. He also did not say *yes, sir,* and given the way Coach narrowed his eyes on him, it was not the right move.

Coach holds his clipboard against his chest, folding his arms over it and leaning his head to the side. I think if he could give Zack a detention for that answer, he would.

"Is there a problem with that?" Coach's brows are lifted in expectation. I tap my foot against Zack again, willing him to respond.

"No, sir. No," he sputters out.

"Good," Coach says. "You might learn a thing or two from her."

From her. Oh . . . fuck.

"You mind working out with a girl, Jennings?" Her voice is as rich with her Staten Island roots as it was when I kissed her two nights ago. Puzzle pieces fly together: her accent, Coach's accent. His eyes, her eyes. New to town, her dad moved for work.

I turn just enough to catch her pulling her catcher's helmet and mask from her head, her blonde hair tied up in a knot at the base of her neck.

"Gear's a little tight, but it should do," she says, handing it to her dad.

Fuck me, that's her dad.

"Thanks for taking it for a ride," he says, nodding to his daughter.

Fuck me, that's his daughter.

"Sure, but next time remember . . . it's *ladies* and gentlemen when you're talking to us, 'kay?" she says, reaching forward and playfully punching his arm. Guess I know where the laugh came from when he started his speech. Pretty sure he's not going to punish her for it, either, on account of her being right and all. Oh, and being his freaking spawn.

"Hey, Cannon from Indiana," she says, the same mischievous bend to her lips that made me feel absolutely drunk on her mouth forty-eight hours ago.

I don't dare respond with the same flirtatious tone I used last time, instead opting to nod as she backs away with a wink. I think I just got played.

"Your partner is leaving without you, son," Coach says to Zack. My cousin is still a bit stiff from the shock of having to fight for his position against his new coach's daughter. Talk about delicate.

"Oh, yeah. Thank you. I'll catch up," Zack says, his words all jumbled and hesitant. His confidence literally just crawled away and sank through the cracks of the clubhouse's concrete floor.

Not wanting the same fate, I grab my bag from under the bench so I can escape without taking more blows to my ego. I'm nearly out, too, when Coach stops me by hollering my name. I turn with my back flat on the door, my mouth suddenly dry with the mystery of the unknown.

"I see you know my daughter."

There's a pregnant pause that's thick enough to choke our football team's offensive line. I keep expecting him to say more, to ask a question or shoot me some warning to stay away from her, which of course I will absolutely obey. He doesn't. Just that one statement, along with his laser stare from his weathered death eyes.

"A little. We just met," I say, finally, my delayed response clearly exposing my nerves.

"Hmm," he says with a nod.

I pull my lips in tight, mostly to keep from saying anything else.

"Go on," he says, after another painful pause.

Yes, sir. I only think it this time.

I round the clubhouse and look out on the track, where Hollis is about to lap someone. Zack hasn't even finished tying his laces. My cousin is in trouble, but not as much as I am. If I want to make it to Vanderbilt, or anywhere *like* Vandy, I need to be at the top of my game. One midnight kiss, though, and my season is cursed. So help me if that vixen ends up calling my pitches.

TWO

HOLLIS TAYLOR

For a bedroom filled with so much crap, it's weird how I can't seem to find anything. We've been moved in for a month. That's thirty days I've had to dump my clothes out of trash bags and put them into actual drawers. I miss my gym, though, and I found a place to lift and work out that I want to try. The only thing stopping me is locating my Nikes. I'm probably compounding things by the piles I'm making in the center of my floor while I search.

"Mom!" She's going to rip me a new one the second she walks in, but her lecture is worth the use of her location superpowers. My mom can find anything. My dad reported a credit card missing last Christmas, before consulting her. The moment she found out he lost it, she walked straight out of the house and to the driveway where she began surveying the bushes. She plucked it from some branches in seconds and held it up proudly. He'd been holding it in his teeth while wheeling in the trash receptacles the night before and must have spit it out and forgot. She remembered; she *always* remembers.

"Jesus H. Ch—"

"I know. I'm working on it," I lie, cutting off my mom's assessment of my room mid-blaspheme.

She digs her fingertips into her forehead with both hands as she steps over the pile in the entryway and into the center of my room. Chin down and jaw tight, she holds back all the little comments I know she'd like to make about *how could she have raised such a slob*.

"Nikes," I say. It's best to give her a task.

She breathes out through her nose loud enough that I fully understand how irritated she is. She makes a slow quarter-turn while she scans the perimeter of my room and stops abruptly, letting out another huff that indicates I would have seen them myself if I only got my shit together.

"They are on your PlayStation, for whatever reason," she says through a grimace.

"That's right!" I leap over the new pile I made and grab my shoes before leaping toward my mom and kissing her on the cheek. "You're the best."

"*Mmm hmm*," she hums.

"Keys?" I know, it's a big ask considering the state of my room. My parents are suckers, though. With her tongue over her front teeth, she sucks in and reluctantly hands me the keys to the van.

"Tonight, this gets taken care of, okay?" She doesn't bother to look me in the eyes, and it's probably because she knows I'll fail at her ultimatum. I'll try to unpack, though. I truly will.

"Deal," I say, catching the short laugh that leaves her chest, showing her doubt.

I dart from my room, shoes in one hand and keys in the other while my mom lingers in my room and opens my drawers. I bet most of my things are put away by the time I get back.

"Off to try that workout place. I'll let you know," I shout at my dad as I hit the driveway. He gives me a quick wave while playing street hockey with my little brother, Ben. He's taking shots at my brother with whiffle balls. Ben is eight, and he wants to be a goalie. My dad tried to talk him into catching instead, but Ben is obsessed with the ice. He's going to outgrow my dad's hockey-coaching skills soon, but until then, Coach Travis Taylor will be splitting time between the ice and the grass.

I slip my feet into my untied shoes before backing the van out, my dad moving my brother's goal out of the way while I pull into the road. It's going to take me a while to line up the view I'm used to seeing with the one I will for the rest of my senior year. Both my old street and this one are tree-lined, and both houses have a certain nineteen-seventies charm about them with banged up vinyl siding and pretend shutters glued on either side of the windows. But where a two-minute jaunt down a Staten Island road took me to Sal's Meats and Cheese, Al's Liquors, Rose's Deli, and Rick Manning's Boxing Elite—the gym I grew up on—the only thing two minutes down this street is more trees. They're nothing but winter sticks now, but I bet when spring rolls around, it's pretty.

Having a real yard is nice too. And Dad promised Mom a pool in the ground. The above-grounder we had back home—our *old* home—leaked twice a season. Even when I take off for college, my family will stay put. That's what this deal is about, finding a good place to settle in and raise Ben. While I loved being so close to the city, it made my parents nervous. They said Ben isn't tough like I am, which I guess I can kinda see. He doesn't get bullied or nothin', but he's quiet. Whatever their logic is or was, it ended up with us living here.

At least I get to be part of a better team during my senior year. Xavier Prep back home was competitive, but only against other small schools. We won state in a tiny division that means nothing to colleges because our school was more about academics. We didn't exactly have the largest pool of ball players to choose from, either. And the parents on the board were not keen on the idea of me playing on a team with boys. It didn't seem to bother them enough to fund a softball team—not that I wanted to switch sports—but the topic sure dominated the conversation at parent meetings.

"What's she gonna do, play football next?"

"I suppose Coach Grady will bring his daughter in to QB?"

"She's going to get hurt."

My dad and I heard that last argument time and time again, and it irks me the most. Nobody knows how much I can endure, not even my father. Some trials in life are survived and meant to be kept close to the chest, used to build armor and grow strength. I'm strong on my own, but the battles I've come through on my journey to do something I love have definitely shaped my fortitude. They're my stories to either tell or keep tucked inside, and I see no reason to share them with anyone.

After ten minutes of weaving through streets and stop-sign intersections, I spot A&P Fitness. It's promising, especially because the building doesn't look like some slick treadmill factory. Rick's was a boxing gym, so I'm used to working with free weights and jump ropes. The occasional speed bag is fun too. I pull into a spot near the door, between two sedans. I should probably back out and move somewhere else; the fit is tight. But before I shift into reverse, a jacked-up pickup slides into the spot behind me. I won't be here long; this is only an exploratory visit.

I grab my dad's ear pods from the center console and head inside. I'm greeted by a heavy boom that echoes around the brick walls, and I flinch a little.

"It's just the tire," says an older man from behind a desk. I'd guess he's in his late sixties, but maybe he's just a smoker. His skin is pretty tan and wrinkled. Straw-like blond hair pokes through the sides and back of his trucker cap, and his arms fill the sleeves of his Notre Dame T-shirt. He's fit for a senior. I have a good idea this place belongs to him.

"Ah," I say, glancing around the gym again until I find a familiar body squatting to lift the side of a monster tire. His body was the first thing I noticed about Cannon at the New Year's party. Tacky and predictable, maybe, but he's not built like the guys back home. He's taller. And pretty stacked for a pitcher. I see why now that I watch him pushing up what must weigh 400 pounds with ease. His gaze hits mine briefly across the tire's tread.

"Hi," I mouth, holding up a hand. His cheeks sink in, his jaw clenching as he grunts and hoists the tire over again. The boom doesn't startle me this time. Cannon looks away, tearing tape from his hands with his teeth.

"You know the Jennings boys?"

"Huh?" I jerk back to the muscle-man behind the counter. "Oh. A little. I'm new here, like Cannon. From Indiana."

I giggle lightly to myself, but he just looks at me like I'm nuts.

"You're from Indiana?" The man quirks a brow, and I realize how stupid that sounded.

"No, it's just a nickname. Sorry, inside joke," I mumble.

"Ah," he grunts. He centers himself at his register and I spot the half-empty pack of cigarettes left on the chair he was sitting in. My assessment is spot on so far.

"You wanna a day pass, sugar?"

I roll my shoulders from habit. Some men have always talked to women that way, but it still makes me want to vomit and punch them when they do it to me. That's what you get when your mom teaches women's studies for an online university. I hear the same lessons every semester, and the one about the cycle of labeling hits home.

"Sure, pumpkin," I shoot back. His eyes dart up, away from his register drawer, probably not sure he heard me right. I wink to let him know he did, and he laughs through one side of his mouth—the one with a well-chewed toothpick hanging out.

"Alright, then," he says. I hand over my card and he rings me up for a five-dollar pass while I scan the board behind him for the monthly rates. There's an old black-and-white photo tacked on a corkboard, and even though I don't quite see the similarities, I take a gamble.

"That you?" I motion to it.

He glances behind him and pulls the pin from the board, bringing the photo closer.

"In my prime," he says, fond memories tugging up the corners of his mouth, toothpick and all. He leans forward on both elbows, studying the photo closely.

"You know, I could have put those Jennings punks in their place back in my day. Joker flips that tire like he's something, but I'd like to see him move the whole goddamn tractor!" His joke echoes loud enough that Cannon turns his head and grimaces. I can tell this banter must be normal between them.

"Well, I'll try and put him in his place for ya. What do you say?" I expect more of a laugh than I get, but there's a slight smirk and hint of a nod. He's daring me to try, or at least, I decide that's what that gesture means.

I move over to the area near Cannon, dropping my things on the metal chair in the corner and pulling one of the jump ropes from a hook on the concrete wall. He paces around the tire with his hands threaded behind his neck, a good deal of sweat discoloring his gray T-shirt, his hair slick and floppy and super sexy. His hands fall to the bottom of his shirt as he turns to face me, and he lifts the front to wipe the moisture from his face, giving me a good view of his perfectly sculpted abs and widening chest. He's disciplined, and that is sexier than the damp waves of hair falling into his eyes, but just barely.

"This is a cool place," I say, swinging the rope out to untangle it as I hold on to either end.

"I guess," Cannon laughs out, a bit abruptly for someone whose tongue was in my mouth a couple of days ago. My gaze ices over as he turns away.

"Oh, I get it," I say, lining the rope up with the front of my feet. I glance up to briefly catch his eyes on mine.

"What?" he grunts, grabbing a water bottle from the floor near my things. He twists the top and guzzles down every last drop.

"Nothing. Just that you're one of those," I say with a shrug. Swinging the rope out, I wait for it to come back at my feet and I jump, a methodical double bounce to my feet as I whirl the heavy rubber rope in circles around my body to get my heart rate up.

"One of what?" He doesn't make the *pfft* sound after his words, but it's implied in the sour look he wears. Standing, he grabs a rope and moves about ten feet away, turning to face me as he jumps rope a little faster than me.

I wobble my head side-to-side and glance up, catching sight of the loose blonde hairs that have crept out from my head band and hair tie. I blow at them, maintaining my jumping speed. I'm not winded in the least. Back home, we lived on a hill. Dad made me sprint up it ten times in a row before I was allowed to sit at the dinner table. This rope, it's nothing.

"One of those guys who kisses girls for fun, then acts like a total prick the next time he sees them." The *thwap* of my rope against the concrete floor picks up its pace as I take away the double bounce and jump fast enough to hear the wind caused by my rope whirling through the air.

Cannon's rope stops completely.

"Okay, now, hey," he says, a defensive shake to his head. "That's not fair."

He runs the side of his fist over his brow to blot away sweat, his rope clutched against his hip in his other hand.

"Okay, how?" I continue to swing and jump, my heart rate picking up. Like hell am I gonna let my breathing pattern reflect that, though. I'll pass out first.

"How? *Pfft*!" Aannd there it is. His forehead dents and he puffs out a heavy laugh. I can't wait for the excuse he's trying to form. I see his brain working in overdrive behind his scrunched-up eyes. He's still pretty, just a little less so because I don't like boys who act like assholes to make themselves feel cool or whatever.

"You didn't tell me you were Coach's daughter!" He points at me with the same hand that holds the rope, and it swings harshly as he gesticulates. I can't help but laugh, which only pushes more of his buttons. Irritated, he grabs my rope mid-air and tangles it around his palm, ripping the ends from my grasp.

"I'm sorry, was I supposed to offer up my resume?" I giggle at the thought and imagine that scenario playing out.

Hi, I'm Hollis Taylor. I'm almost eighteen, and my favorite foods are fried zucchini and every kind of cheese. My parents are Dina and Travis Taylor, and they're forty-two and forty-three, respectively. Oh, and my father, he's a coach. Oh, you play baseball? Me, too! No, not for fun. Like you! No, I don't think I should play softball. Why? Because I like baseball. Oh, but it's for boys? Huh, I didn't know that. Is there a sign somewhere that says NO GIRLS ALLOWED?

"You don't understand," he grunts out, interrupting the argument going down in my head. Cannon continues to pace with both of our ropes tangled in one hand.

"Spot me?" I say, moving on to the squat rack. I shuffle the plates around, pulling out the forty-fives while he fusses with the mess he made with the ropes.

I've got my bar ready to lift by the time he's done, but he stops about ten feet short of the rack, his hands on his hips, shirt soaked with sweat and his black joggers pushed up on his calves in that super cute way.

"No, I'm not going to spot you. I can't . . . I mean, you're—"

"Coach's daughter," I say with a roll of the eyes. I step under the bar and find the right fit along my shoulders. I wait a beat to see if he gives in, and when he doesn't budge I step forward with the bar balanced along my back and shoulders and steady my feet. I get through two whole squats before he mutters, *"Fuck"* to himself and steps in to assist me.

We don't talk through my first set, and he shakes his head when I offer to trade off and on with him. I tend to step side to side when my muscles recover, keeping the burn at bay and making the most of the tingles as blood rushes to the skin. I catch Cannon's eyes on my feet, though, so I abruptly stop to get his attention. I tap a toe until he looks me in the eyes. God, his face is beautiful. His eyes are this deep ocean blue, and his hair is the kind that I'm sure looks good right out of bed. I smile at him with tight lips, silently urging him to spill it, whatever his unexplainable issue seems to be. His expression tightens, his eyes pinch, and his gaze dips to my neck for a full breath.

"My cousin Zack, he's our catcher. Our *starting* catcher."

"Well, I mean, that's not really decided yet, so . . ." I know where this is going. I'm used to it. It's partly the reason we're *in* Indiana.

"No, you don't get it. Zack and me, we're family, and we've had this plan for years, to do this together. Our dads have had this plan. Zack, he gets the best out of me. Throwing to him is basically the entire reason I'm out here. And, I mean, just because your dad is the coach . . ." His eyes droop with this desperate plea for me to bend to his will, without forcing him to finish that sentence—*that incredibly offensive, full-of-false-assumptions sentence.* If I were another guy, he wouldn't say these things. He'd tell Zack to suck it up and compete. Double standards are so obvious to the one getting stung by them; meanwhile, the perpetrators are ignorant to their own biases.

I guess I'm glad I got the sweet kiss before this conversation. It was a nice kiss, and I choose to keep it separate from this display before me.

Maybe I'll pretend they are two completely different people—the New Year's Cannon and this sexist one who doesn't want a girl in his boys' club. Nodding silently to myself, I glance to the floor as I close the distance between us until I'm close enough to flatten my palm on the cold wet cotton clinging to his chest. He's rock hard beneath my touch. Damn if both Cannons aren't built to perfection.

With hooded eyes, I lift my chin just as he tucks his, the feel of his heartbeat strong underneath my hand. I tap out its rhythm a few times and his gaze flits briefly to my fingertips, then back to my eyes. The slight tick up on the right side of his lips probably means he thinks things are going his way. They're not. Not even close.

"Cannon Jennings from Indiana by way of New Mexico, you have no idea what I'm capable of, so I wouldn't rush to judge. Maybe I'm the catcher who makes you great. Or maybe I make someone else great, and you, you ride pine a lot more than you're prepared to."

My lips close with the satisfied curve that comes along with saying the perfect thing at the perfect time in the perfect way. I let the smile linger as I back away until my shoulders run into the cool metal of the bar and I situate myself, ready for a second set. I lift an eyebrow. In the face of my challenge to pick a side, he does, leaning forward to spit on the concrete, just beyond his shoes.

"This is bullshit," he says, shaking his head as if I've actually broken some sort of law by being good at a game. He tosses his empty water bottle in a nearby recycle bin with a flick and picks up his keys and a towel from the wall on the other side of the gym. He holds up a hand to wave at the old man behind the counter; he grunts in return. Bright light spills into the gym as Cannon pushes through the heavy metal door without bothering to give me a final glance. It slams closed behind him, and I move with the weight on my shoulders to begin my second set alone.

It's the same every time. Every team. And I'll prove him, Zack, the whole fucking roster, wrong, the way I always do. It's a shame I had to kiss him first. And that he had to be so damn good at it.

THREE

CANNON

I didn't tell Zack about my little run-in with Hollis. Pete doesn't exactly make newcomers feel welcome at the gym, so I'm thinking she won't be back anyway. Hell, the only reason Pete can stand me is that Zack's been coming here for three years.

I noticed he charged Hollis for a day pass. I've never seen him do that once. *Ha!* He certainly never charged me before my parents were able to get automatic payments set up for him. That's probably half the reason he likes me, honestly. My mom works in programming and she built him a website. Until last month, Pete just collected cash and stuffed it into a zipper bag to take to the bank every Friday.

Practice and workouts start for real today. Not that the impromptu January second practice wasn't real. Two miles is a lot longer than I thought it was; I was pretty gassed and still several seconds over. It's going to take some work to pull off two miles in under ten minutes, but not nearly as much work as it'll take Zack.

Where my body is long, he's squatty. His legs are built for catching, power pedestals digging into the ground, ready to stop everything and pounce for a throw to second—not necessarily the kind of legs that hustle around bases. He's always been a great hitter, though, so his lack of speed shouldn't hold him back. The whole situation is stressing him the fuck out, though. He hasn't stopped badgering me with questions I don't have the answers to since the team meeting and running drill three days ago.

"You don't think she's actually on the team, do you?"

"Isn't there some sort of rule against this?"

"What happens if she gets hit with a bat?"

"Can she really handle your slider? I mean, come on."

I feel another question coming on, perched on the tip of his tongue, waiting to plunge out of his mouth while we sit here in the school parking lot. It's our first day back after winter break, too early for him to start in on this shit. I have a statistics class I need to get my head ready for; I can't be all jacked up with my cousin's anxiety.

"You think she was the starter at her old school?" He's asked me this one already, twice. He already confirmed Hollis didn't play softball at her last school by scouring her social media, going back years. It's always been baseball for her. She's always been special it seems, racing through the doors that "daddy ball" opened for her—all-star teams, batting cleanup, MVP. It's bullshit is what it is, and I get why Zack's pissed. But I wish he'd start doing something about it rather than just *talking*—er, *whining*.

"Who?" I answer my cousin finally, mostly to be a dick.

He punches my arm with the side of his fist.

"Come on, man."

I scowl at the throb left in the wake of his hit.

"Piss off. You're lucky I'm left-handed." I rub the spot and breathe out, overexaggerating the exhale so maybe Zack will finally get it. I don't have the answers to his questions, and I have my own questions.

"I don't know. Why don't you look up their season," I suggest.

"Smart, yeah." He's already got his phone in his palm, his thumbs typing in the search bar.

Eventually, I step out of the car and toss the keys to my cousin at the curb. Zack's not great at getting up early, so he eats breakfast during our car rides to school. I don't like how other people drive, and prefer being behind the wheel anyhow.

I miss my truck. Dad's driving it out here in two or three weeks with a bunch of our stuff, so I'll have my own wheels soon enough. How we're all going to fit in Uncle Joel and Aunt Meg's house until our rental is ready, I have no clue. It'll be a chaotic two months, and these few weeks before tryouts are going to be painful.

"Can, hey, look at this," Zack says, slapping at my arm and shoving his phone in my face. He can't seem to quit swatting me.

I shirk away from him but take his phone and speed read the story he pulled up from some news site.

XAVIER PREP BOARD OF DIRECTORS VOTES 7-1 TO ACCEPT

RESIGNATION FROM COACH CREDITED WITH TURNING SCHOOL'S BASEBALL PROGRAM AROUND

I skim through the first few paragraphs, losing interest as it goes into detail about private-school politics and unhappy parents. I wouldn't call this *breaking news.* I scroll down to the end to see the comments, noting maybe a dozen, mostly from players' parents praising the board for making the decision.

"So, he's a winning coach who doesn't do politics. He resigned and they told him not to let the door hit him on the way out. Not sure what you want me to take away from this," I say, handing the phone back to my cousin. I don't want to entertain his trip down this rabbit hole, but I admit to myself that it is a little odd that a school would be so okay losing a coach like him, especially one with college experience.

It doesn't matter whether I indulge or not; Zack is going to kick this can around with or without me.

"It means something's up with him, that's what it means. Think about it —a coach goes, what, thirty-six and four, two state titles, and he gets shit-canned? Nah, bruh. Something's off with that, and I bet it has to do with daddy's little girl."

Our friends Hayden, Tory and Lucas are sitting on the brick wall by the front office, so I kick my leg over to sit on the end and turn my back to my conspiracy-theory-spinning cousin.

"Who's daddy's girl?" Tory nods, lifting a curious brow. He's taking this in a *whole different* direction.

"You talkin' about Abby?" Lucas sticks his tongue out and nudges Tory, who only slaps his friend's arm away. It gets uncomfortably quiet after Lucas's ill-timed joke. I haven't been hanging out with these guys for long, but from the bits I've seen the last few weeks, I'm pretty sure Abby moved on to the D'Angelo twins after she and I tried hooking up.

Let's just say Abby Cortez and I were a bit like oil and water. From what I heard, it was basically one huge love triangle bomb with the twins, too. That girl is all drama. She took off for some acting gig, and all I know is nobody talks about her dating either of them. I have a feeling Tory isn't telling the whole story, though. He was pretty into her, but his brother is *here,* and Abby is long gone. Brotherly loyalty and shit, I guess.

I'm glad the bell rings before Zack can bring the conversation back to Hollis. As far as I know, nobody's aware of the New Year's kiss. I'm not up on bragging, and now that Hollis is the enemy, I'd prefer not to throw a meaningless kiss into the mix, especially if I'm supposed to throw ninety-mile-per-hour fastballs at her face.

I hold out a fist and pound my knuckles against Zack's then the other guys' before heading to the far west end of campus. It took me a while to learn my way around this place. My old school was all inside, three stories with glass windows and stairwells, super modern and spotless. Allensville Public is laid out like a prison, complete with graffiti. The windows don't even open anymore thanks to years of paint layers. And the brick buildings are scattered so far apart it's impossible to get to class on time when you have to motor from one end to the other. I quit trying last semester, and other than a few scowls from a very picky biology teacher, nobody cares if you wander in during attendance.

I slip into statistics as the door closes. Nobody notices. The teacher doesn't even look up. His glasses are pulled down on the tip of his nose and he's scratching at the back of his neck while struggling to read his tablet.

"Sherman *Poo . . . scooter?*" There are snickers at his attempt because even though most of us in here are seniors, we also possess third-grade senses of humor. Dude said poo. It's funny.

"Uh, it's Sharmaine? And my last name is Poscotier—*puh-sca-tee-ay.*" The voice comes from a girl in the front row. From the back, all I can see is the irritated head waggle that shakes her long, blonde ponytail. Her tone is enough to inspire me to take a seat in the very back, though. No way I want to be paired with that—*ever.* Pooscooter.

"Right." The teacher nods. There's a smirk peeking out from his overgrown beard and mustache that makes me wonder if he's making a mental note to mess her name up for the rest of the year. If he does, he will win the spot of favorite teacher ever on my list.

"Alright, and Jennings? Did Jennings finally make it?"

I must have missed his first trip through the roster.

"Present," I say, lifting my palm slightly from the desktop. The girl in front of me tucks her head into her shoulder while she twirls a lock of her red hair around a pen. I lean forward enough to catch her eyes and make her blush at getting caught peeking.

"Hi," I whisper. She whispers *Hi* back and hunches down in her chair. She shouldn't be embarrassed. It's cute when girls check me out; the ultimate compliment, really. I could spend a few more seconds silently flirting with her, but that plan is cut short the moment the teacher attempts another name.

"And Taylor. Or is it Hollis?"

A whirlwind hits me, both mentally and physically, as Hollis flings open the closed door behind me, announcing her arrival in a hurried, disheveled, and chaotic scene. You'd think a hurricane was brewing on the other side of the door, her hair wild and her plaid flannel shirt falling off one arm almost completely.

"Hollis, yeah. That's me. I'm . . . Hollis." She's panting, and her eyes land on the open seat next to me. A look of relief colors her face and she takes it, dropping her heavy backpack at her feet and immediately twisting her hair up in a bun on top of her head. She pokes a pencil in to hold it in place.

"Phew, that was rough. How's it goin'?" She blows up at the loose hairs on her forehead, her cheeks red.

I lean forward and grip the front of my desk, keeping my eyes on the wood grain and my periphery as closed off from her as I can. It takes her about three seconds to tap my shoulder with the eraser end of her pencil.

"Hey!" she whisper shouts.

I sigh heavily and slowly turn my head to the right, forcing a smile and quick nod to respond. She leans to her side to cut the distance between us.

"What'd I miss?" She's already got a notebook out, her hands opening the cover while she stares at me.

"We took a quiz," I joke, shrugging. For a flash, she believes me. I can see it in the way her eyebrows lift and her pupils bleed into the blue of her eyes.

"Ass," she bites back after a few seconds, moving back into her own space and writing the date at the top of her paper. She must be a good student. That's a *very good student* kinda move.

There are seven open seats in this class. An entire row on the far right. Of all the seats, she took this one, but it doesn't mean I have to stay here. While our teacher flips on a digital screen at the front of the room, I grab the strap on my backpack and twist to the side, ready to make my break for the farthest desk from Pooscooter and Hollis. Before I can make my escape, though, the teacher flashes a layout on the screen that already has us labeled in our seats.

"Welcome to statistics, brought to you by the Allensville School District's latest technology grant. I'm Dr. Vanetta, but you can call me Dr. V for short. If you could all be cool and do me the solid of staying in your seats, I won't have to butcher your names ever again, *unless I want to.*"

Most of the class chuckles at his introduction, and maybe later, when I'm not pissed off at getting stuck next to *daddy's girl,* I'll laugh about it, too.

Right now, I'm focused on making myself as closed off as possible, to the point that the guy to my left is sliding his seat from me inches at a time as I encroach on his space.

"This is my first year here, and last semester was my first as a high school teacher. I'm used to college kids, so my expectations are kinda high. Prepare yourselves to work," he says, switching the screen over to the syllabus. I note the label at the top—PAGE 1 of 12. *Jeeeezusss!*

I take my phone out and click to the class listing on my school app, pulling up the documents Dr. V is flying through on the screen. The guy is pretty funny, but he wasn't kidding about expectations. He's quickly losing his bid to become my favorite teacher. To my right, Hollis is feverishly scribbling, and I could probably clue her in on how to use the app, but she said it herself—I'm an ass.

It takes almost the entire class period for Dr. V to get through his expectations for this semester. I decided somewhere around the fourth assignment that I would be fine taking a C in this class. It won't affect where I go; I'll be signed long before that final grade locks in.

While Hollis squeezes her hand and flexes her fingers from writing cramps, I lean back and zone out, mentally preparing for the next month of conditioning before tryouts. It's almost impossible to ignore my biggest hurdle, though, especially since she's constantly moving right next to me. I don't know whether she's jacked up on caffeine or ADHD or nervous or *WTF!* Her knee has not stopped bopping since she started taking notes, almost as if her hand's in a race with her leg to burn calories. If this is what she's like on the field, I'm screwed. I'm used to a focused catcher. At my old school, I threw to a guy who was almost three hundred pounds. He wasn't great at running down balls but he somehow blocked everything, and he could lock me in when I was getting wild. Zack's got that gift, with the scrappiness to make fucking amazing plays behind the plate. I don't know why he's so freaked out about losing the starting position to Hollis. He's made the all-region team the last two years and he's proven himself. He'll do it again.

"Pshh." My scoff slips out as I laugh silently to myself and lean forward on my elbows. Hollis's knee stops gyrating, so I quirk a brow and give her a glance.

"What's funny?" she whispers.

My mouth begins its slow curve because suddenly, so many things amuse me. My tongue pokes out over my bottom lip and I lock it down with my teeth, nodding.

"Just ready for today." My grin is lopsided and arrogant, and Hollis's brow dips as she studies me, as if looking for the loophole.

"Better be," she says, her knee returning to its constant tapping out of Morse code.

We must have made enough noise to catch Dr. V's attention because he abruptly stops talking. His posture is pretty ready for conflict with his hands clasped in front of his body and his shoulders rolled back, chest puffed and chin high. He's looking at us through his lenses now—they've moved from the tip of his nose to the bridge.

"Mister . . ." He muses for a moment, leaning to the right to check my name on the tablet that shows the seating chart. "Jennings. Right. I made a note by your name. Athlete, I see. You'll be needing to stay eligible for the season. Let me guess, do you two play doubles tennis?"

He waggles his finger between Hollis and me. I shift in my desk, feeling the rush of blood travel down my neck and spine. I don't like being made an example of, and Mr. V is officially out of the running for favorite teacher.

"We play baseball, sir." Hollis speaks up. I wince because of the way she says it, so sure of herself. Her knee has stopped moving again, and her hands are clasped on top of her notebook, mimicking Mr. V's in a way. A confident smile plays at her lips, and while she seems to grow taller in her seat, I find I'm shrinking in mine.

"Oh, that's . . . progressive. I didn't know we had a girl on the team," he says, engaging and leaning one elbow on his podium.

"We don't, yet," I blurt out. It's my temper—a knee-jerk reaction when I'm embarrassed.

"We will," Hollis pipes in, turning to face me with the smug mask tightly pressed to her face. She blinks slowly and I shift again in my seat as I make eye contact with her. I hate that I don't fit in these things, my legs too long to completely bend my knees under the tabletop, and my body too tall to rest my arms comfortably on the desk. I look like a monster breaking out of a cage. I'm not sure how Hollis fits so easily. Girls are just flexible I guess.

"Interesting," Mr. V says, actually running his palm over his beard while evil ideas appear to swirl in his head. "You two are perfect for my first statistics question. Let's give it a try, shall we?"

His question lingers in our silent classroom while nobody steps in. I finally shake my head and say, "Sure."

"Great. Here's the data set."

He quickly pushes the screen to the side, exposing a whiteboard underneath. He takes a red marker to the board to write with the same fervor Hollis just did, explaining the details as he writes. Hollis doesn't seem to be taking notes, and I wonder if the attention is chipping away at her brave face.

"First, we have you, Mr. Jennings," he says, drawing the male symbol on the board. "And over here, we have Miss—"

"Just call me Hollis," she interjects.

Her boldness earns a smile that barely breaks through the beard.

"Hollis it is," he says, drawing the female symbol on the other side. He next writes the number fifty on the board between our names, tapping his marker against the number a few times to punctuate it before turning to face us.

"There is one spot open on the baseball team, and both Hollis and Mr. Jennings are trying to take it."

He takes out a coin.

"Let's assign heads to you Hollis, and Mr. Jennings, you're tails." He dips his head, peering over his glasses, waiting for us to agree. We both nod. I have no idea where this is going.

Flipping the coin in the air, he waits with an open mouth, eyes eager to see how it lands in his hand before flipping it against his forearm.

"One of you will make the team, and one of you will not. Based on this coin, would you say there is a fifty-percent chance it will be you?"

I shrug and nod as Hollis does the same. Mr. V peels back his fingers to expose the coin, walking through the desks to stand between us so we can verify the coin. It's tails. I smile as if I actually did something to earn the win.

"Congratulations, you've made the team. Hollis, I am sorry," he says, leaning to her side. Taking this entire scene in stride, Hollis snaps her fingers in front of her, a gesture that says, "Darn." One side of his mouth lifts with his short laugh.

"Ah, but wait. You know what? Let's do this again. And for fun, let's put some theory behind it. What are the chances I will land on tails again?" Pinching the coin between his thumb and finger, he twists it around in front of us so we can see both sides. "Mr. Jennings, what are your chances now? Can I land this on tails again?"

I stare in thought at the coin, not sure how to wrap my mind around his question. "Maybe," I eventually say.

"But what are the chances? More? Less?"

His eyes bore into me waiting for my answer. I let my mouth hang open, mentally playing out the game and testing the odds in my own mind.

"Fifty percent. It's exactly the same," Hollis answers.

Mr. V's smile gets bigger this time as he strolls backward, flipping the coin in the air again and catching it, finishing with a swift slap against his arm. He cups it in place, waiting until he returns to the front of the class, and before looking, grills me one more time.

"Is it the same? Or is it harder for you because now you're trying to win a second time?"

I swallow, but his question makes sense, and that's what I was thinking.

"Yeah, it is. I've already done it once, so the odds of doing it again, twice in a row, are smaller," I say.

His smile lingers, but becomes stale. I sense that I'm not right.

Bringing his arm up in front of his eyes, he slowly un-cups the coin and shifts his focus to the emblem that landed on top.

"Tails again," he says, smirking.

I breathe out and relax in my seat, suddenly aware of how tense my muscles were in anticipation.

"Looks like you were lucky," he says, and I chuckle in agreement, completely hooked into his trap. "Or was it luck? I wonder."

He tosses the coin in the air and it lands in his palm once again. He holds it out in his fist, staring at me.

"What are the odds?" His face is devoid of emotion, zero expectation. He looks at me as if he doesn't know the exact answer. I take a guess, doing my own form of math by taking the three tosses and dividing them into thirds.

"Thirty-three percent," I throw out with a shrug.

"You don't seem certain." His mouth is a flat line, and he maintains eye contact with me as he flops the coin on his arm once again. His gaze shifts to Hollis.

"It's the same as the first time. It's always the same. Every time you toss it there is a fifty-fifty shot that it will land on heads," she says.

I sit forward wearing a grin that stretches into my cheeks because I think she's wrong. But with the coin still covered under his palm, Dr. V stretches out a finger to point at her and winks.

"Exactly," he says, uncovering the coin. Once again, it's tails.

"Seems this experiment proves my point." I fold my arms over my chest and lean back, one foot braced on the chair leg in front of me. Dr. V dips his chin and pulls in his brow.

"The sample size is too small," Hollis says, again calling his attention to her.

"I could do this a thousand times. Every time, there is a fifty-fifty chance that the coin will land in Mr. Jennings's favor. And to spare you all the pain of watching me do this nine hundred and ninety-seven more times . . ." He slides the digital screen back, switching to a slide that details some famous coin-flipping experiment. The chart shows dozens of trials with samples of thousands. The red color bars are nearly dead even with all of the blue ones. Fifty-fifty, I'm guessing.

"Okay, but baseball isn't like that," I argue. I can feel Hollis's eyes on me to my right, but I ignore them, pushing ahead to dispute this experiment.

"How so?" Dr. V questions.

"Well, we aren't coins. I'm not going out there and flipping to see which end I land on. I'm going out there to work," I explain.

"Hollis? Do you go out there to work?" he queries her. I get the point he's trying to make, but still, he has to see mine.

"Of course. Some might say I go out there and work harder." Her snide tone draws my glare, and when our eyes meet she sneers at me, her feminist claws ready to take out my eyeballs.

I sigh.

"That's not what I'm saying. I'm saying there are variables that don't work with the fifty-fifty method. You have my speed versus her speed. You have my weight and height, and then the natural differences between male and female athletes. I'm going to be stronger. It's a fact."

Anticipating Dr. V's counterpoint, I hold up my palm.

"And yes, not all male athletes are going to be stronger than all female athletes, or faster or whatever. But on the average, those are the facts." I finish my point with a slight head shake, my chest pounding with adrenaline. I've gotten worked up over statistics, and I have to give it to the guy—he made this interesting. Maybe he's not my *least* favorite teacher.

The bell rings, but nobody leaves their seats. All eyes are on me and Hollis, waiting for more arguing, more coin flips, more . . . something. I swing my backpack around from between my knees and stand, initiating everyone else, but before the clamor becomes too distracting, Dr. V throws out one more morsel for me to chew on.

"Mr. Jennings, given everything you just learned, and your points in response, care to give me your best guess on the odds that you will have a female on the Allensville Public baseball team this season?"

He's baiting me, not even looking at me after his question, instead turning his focus on erasing the whiteboard and prepping the room for his next class. There are variables I haven't mentioned, namely that Hollis's dad is the coach, which sort of takes odds right off the table. I'm pretty sure that argument won't be popular with him, though, and I know how Hollis will feel about it. I'm pretty sure she regrets kissing me as much as I regret kissing her.

"It's not fifty-fifty," I say, tugging my bag up my shoulder.

"You sure about that?" he asks, glancing at me over his shoulder.

My eyes meet Hollis's waiting gaze as I turn to my right, a steady tremor of anger brewing behind her sky-blue eyes. Her mouth is a tight line. She pulls the pencil from her hair, letting the twisted blonde waves fall around her face. Her nostrils flare.

Daddy's girl.

"Yeah, pretty sure."

Hollis's eyes haze as her lips curve ever so slightly to meet my challenge. I'm sure to Dr. V my answer sounds like another cocky chauvinist pig out to tell girls what they can't do. But the faint smile Hollis flashes me just before her eyes blink rapidly in disgust says she gets my real point, that this whole thing is rigged, and she's a guarantee, no matter what the other variables are.

I'm going to have to get Zack in shape enough to force a fifty-fifty toss-up for playing time.

FOUR

HOLLIS

I knew today would be hard. I didn't think it'd actually suck. Cannon Jennings is an asshole. I'm sick and tired of assholes. We left a bunch behind in New York, and I hoped we wouldn't get a new crop here. Worse yet, Cannon isn't even a local. He's an outsider too, he just doesn't have tits. Such hypocrisy.

I'm used to being independent. Growing up in New York does that to a girl. You learn to ride trains young. Biking around city blocks to meet up with friends when you're nine or ten is a basic rite of passage. And hanging out in front of the 7-11 until three in the morning with a bunch of teenagers is totally normal. Walking into a middle-America high school cafeteria without knowing a soul, though? Nothing normal about this.

I managed to kill seven minutes standing on line for a slice of pizza and an apple juice. I'm half-tempted to find a corner to lean against and eat on the run. The only person in this entire room I sorta know is June, and that's only because my mom reached out to the school's parent group to find me friends before we moved. June emailed me a few times before I got here, and insisted I show up for her New Year's party.

The New Year's party, scene of my first mistake with Cannon Jennings. He dropped a clue when we first met, told me he moved out here to play ball with his cousin. I was so charmed by his unbelievably handsome face that I didn't put the facts together that playing ball was what I was here for, too. That we'd be playing ball together. *Teammates.*

I'm about to go for the wall-leaning option when my gaze lands on a waving hand. June's smile is like a lighthouse in a really foggy sea. I don't know why I feel so intimidated by the students here. I think it's because the culture is so different. Back home, my friends were loud. And new people were rare. We all grew up together, and everybody knew everybody else. The only time things got sticky was when I started high school at Xavier. There was a sense of privilege there, a thread of extremely conservative traditions—that's not how the Taylor household runs. We're not hippies, but we're definitely progressive. Hell, my dad sees no reason I can't play D1 baseball. I know the realities, though, so I'm aiming for a two-year school, to keep baseball in my heart a little longer. If I have to give in and switch to softball for a full ride somewhere, then so be it.

June kicks a chair out to make room for me when I get close to her table. She's chewing a bite from her sandwich, so she cups her mouth to talk.

"This is Lola." She points above the head of a really pretty blonde girl with magazine-style beach waves.

"Hi," she squeaks before puckering her lips around the straw of her soda. She smiles around it. She seems sweet.

"Hi, I'm Hollis. I like your hair," I say, pointing at it.

"Oh, thanks," she says with a giggle, pulling a few of the strands out to the side and glancing at her periphery. Her eyes are more white than blue at this point. She's funny. "I have one of those curling irons that basically does all the work for you. I just hold my hand in the air while I eat breakfast, and voila!"

"Cool," I say, unscrewing the cap from my juice. I turn it over to read the words on the inside, a weird habit I've been doing ever since I had my first Snapple. I like it when companies leave you with little positive messages. There's nothing on this cap but an inspection number, though. Guess I'm glad it was inspected.

"I can do your hair sometime, if you want," Lola says, bringing my attention back to her. I laugh out some of my juice and catch the dribble at my chin with my long sleeve.

"Sorry," I say, coughing out the last of the choke. "I'm just, well, I'm a lot of work."

I pull my hair down from the makeshift bun I made while waiting on the pizza line. Jagged curls flop in various directions, and several strands jut straight out from my shoulder. Lola reaches toward me with a fork and combs out the wildest pieces. I'm left stunned, eyes wide and brows high.

"Nah, my magic curling iron can do anything. We'll try it sometime."

She tosses the fork-turned-comb onto June's tray and sits back in her chair, seeming satisfied, and once again wraps her lips around her straw, drawing in a long sip.

"Okay," I relent, running my fingers through my hair a few more times to get the wild strays away from my face.

"So, how's your first day?" June asks. Once again I laugh, this time mid-bite. I cover my mouth with a napkin and finish chewing.

"Oh, it's been epic," I say, sparking their intrigue. Both lean in, eyebrows drown into Vs.

"Well, let's see. I'm taking an English class that is the exact same curriculum I *just* finished in New York, and because of my late transfer, the only credited elective I could get into was culinary. I hate cooking, and I hate cleaning dirty dishes more."

They both scrunch their faces to echo my disappointment.

"Sorry. That sucks," June empathizes. They both lean back, I think a little disappointed in my definition of epic, but I draw them back in with my last bullet point.

"Oh! And do you guys know Cannon Jennings?"

The flat-lined mouths and blinking eyes staring back at me tell me they do, and that their impression matches mine.

"Right, well, so . . . he's an ass." I sum him up neatly, not going into all the details. I don't need to bore my new friends—my *only* friends—with baseball politics and details of a sexist sports culture. My assertion seems to be on point, because within a blink they're sharing their experiences with him.

"He literally patted me on the head once when I was sitting next to him at a basketball game. I was trying to get to know him and asked a question about the game. He turned to me with an open palm and patted me like a puppy." Lola's innocent features are suddenly fierce, a bit of a snarl to her lips; I like her even more.

"He led my friend Abby on for weeks, but then she got tired of his games," June says. "It all worked out because now she's filming a movie in Toronto, and thinks she's totally meant to be with someone else."

"You said games," I echo, picking up on that word especially. "What do you mean, games?"

June shrugs and takes a bite of her sandwich, glancing up in search of an example.

"Okay, so like, when he's at a party or hanging out with the guys, he acts one way, but then when you get him on his own, he's totally a different person. He held my friend's hand and cuddled up to her at parties then ignored her existence the next day. Abby says he's moody, and I think that's the best description. Maybe he's only chill when he's buzzed at a kegger. I don't know."

Her examples fit the mold I've made for Cannon in my head. Our kiss was a caught-in-the-moment thing, but still, the switch he flipped between attitudes is unreal. Maybe his behavior isn't all driven by the fact I'm encroaching on his turf. Maybe he's just a douchebag.

By the time our lunch hour ends, I feel relaxed and a little more accepted. When I look around at the other girls, I still feel as though I stick out in this place, but that's not going to change. I like high-top shoes without laces and baggy sweatpants, and shirts stolen from my dad's college collection. I don't wear bras, unless they are sports bras, opting for camisoles or nothing at all. I want to feel I can breathe under my clothes, and I don't want to wake up early just to change the girl I am. The only rule I might break is letting Lola curl my hair, and mostly on a dare because I don't think it can be done. Plus, her hair is pretty freakin' bomb.

The end of my day is pretty easy. I opted for study hall instead of taking an early release. I did it to be able to take weight training at the end of the day. It was the only way I could avoid spending two full hours hanging out in my dad's office. It's bad enough being his daughter, I didn't need to add to the optics by being glued to his side. I'm riding the high of decent lunch company and the comfort of knowing that tomorrow I will have a place to sit, when the warm fuzzies turn into blistering acid. Cannon is sitting in the back of the study hall room, hat brim tipped down over his forehead to shade his eyes, probably so he can sleep. I recognize a guy from the New Year's party sitting next to him, one of the twins I've heard about. I'm about to slip by unnoticed when the guy's eyes land on mine, causing him to sit up straight and slap Cannon's hat from his head.

"Dude!" The few people already here turn to look as Cannon chastises him, and I take advantage of his attention on his friend, darting to the other side of the room and making my way up front. I slip into a desk, pulling out my phone to double check my schedule that I have the right room. My hope is dashed quickly, though it was a longshot that there were two study hall locations at the same time. Tucking my chin into my shoulder, I peer behind me to see if Cannon has gone back to hibernating. His eyes are glued to mine the moment I glance in his direction. His mouth a hard line, and he gives a slow shake of his head as if he's disappointed in me.

It's the other way around, buddy.

Not wanting to let him in my head, or give him the satisfaction of feeling he matters, I shrug and shift my gaze to his friend. I nod a silent hello that makes his friend chuckle and nod back. I'm pretty sure he's gotten the full story from Cannon, only neither of them have seen me play. Today is important, and I knew it would be. I've been in this position before, the one who has to prove herself to an overly skeptical crowd. The hardest part is that no matter how hard I work and how good I am, there are some who will still wear their blinders and refuse to acknowledge they maybe had me pegged all wrong.

Renewed, and amped with the familiar sense of drive, I turn back into my seat and pull my notebook from my bag, flipping to the middle to write my goals for the next five days. I got this habit from my dad. He's always done it in his scorebooks and on lineup sheets. He doesn't write down criticisms for his players, but instead takes the things he thinks they're failing at and makes notes for himself, for the work *he* needs to do to make them better. It's one of the things that makes him great at his job, and that's not simply my opinion as his daughter. He won a few awards from the university he coached at for his player-driven dedication. It's his approach, always looking for the things he can do rather than blaming someone else for failing on their end. It doesn't mean he doesn't expect his players to pull their weight. In fact, most of his players end up making their own notes, taking ownership of their weaknesses and goals. It's a proven method that has made his winning record one of the best in East Coast baseball. It'll work here, if the people in this program embrace it. The guy napping under his hat about twenty feet behind me gives me doubts.

The teacher for our study hall kicks out the door stop to shut the door before he beelines to the desk at the front of the room, laptop in hand. After a quick run through roll call, he ignores us completely, immersed in whatever he's working on. If he weren't typing constantly, I'd think the guy was watching porn. His eyebrows keep flickering in reaction to whatever he's reading, and I'm distracted by it for longer than I'd ever admit. I find my focus again before the hour is done, sketching out five goals for today's workouts. The physical stuff I'll knock out without a problem, but that last item—*make Cannon see me as his equal*—will be ongoing, I fear.

I wouldn't care so much if it weren't for the fact Cannon is our ace. I haven't even seen him throw in person yet, just the videos my dad watched from the scouting sites. I know his numbers and what he throws; I memorized all that before we got here so I'd be ready to catch him. I would never admit this to my dad, but I'm a little worried about Zack. The pitcher-catcher relationship is special, and they've had a childhood of playing catch to gel. They have blood ties. The only thing I have going for me is my hunch that I might be able to amp up Cannon's adrenaline, pissing him off enough to gain a mile or two per hour on his fastball. I note that in the margin before the class ends, packing up and breaking between Cannon and his friend before they reach the door. My shoulders brush their arms as I pass, something I make sure of and do not acknowledge. I grin over it, childish as the move was, and I maintain the high all the way to the girls' locker room.

It would be easy to dump my things in my dad's office, but again, I need that separation. It has to be noticeable for this to work. It's one of the things I learned from Xavier; one of the things we did wrong, though I don't know if that would have mattered. There was hostility brewing there for some people that ran deeper than the appearance of nepotism. I'm encouraged to see three other girls dress out with me. I'd braced myself to be the only girl in the weight room. It's nice to have sisters. I don't know them yet, so I rush to catch up to the last one in the locker room after I finish getting dressed. I reach her just as she hits the door with her palm.

"Hey, wait up!" I yell.

She pauses at the door, spinning to show me a bright smile that makes me feel as though she needs a friend in this class, too.

"Hey! Oh, my God, I'm so glad I'm not the only girl." She holds the door open wide and I slip by her, noting her slender arms and legs as I pass. I don't think she's done this sort of thing before, but I don't know that for certain, and I would be a hypocrite if I assumed.

"I feel that. I'm Hollis." I hold out my hand as I walk backward along the short sidewalk between the locker rooms and weight room. She's amused by my formality, another habit I got from my dad, I guess, but she takes my hand and gives me a fish-like shake. I bury the creeped-out expression I want to make and commit myself to taking this girl under my wing in here. Goal one, learn how to shake with authority.

"I'm Maddy. And I have *no idea* what I'm doing." She laughs through her words.

"Okay." I nod, still walking backward.

I sense the building is getting close, so I shift to turn and my chin slams into a thick bicep. An arm curls around me from the other side, catching me mid-collision. The smell is familiar, and it takes the same amount of time for me to place it as it does for him to speak.

"You gotta be fucking kidding me." Cannon's hand instantly lets go of my midriff, as if repulsed at the realization that I'm the body he caught. I jump back, equally repulsed to be caught by him, and angry with my hormones for fluttering at his touch.

"I don't have to do anything to you," I respond. Checkmate for having the right comeback, but boo for making my goal even harder to achieve.

The three of us stand in an awkward triangle, Maddy caught in the middle of Cannon and my silent showdown. She's tugging nervously at the bottom of her T-shirt. I see the movement in my periphery because I refuse to fully look away from Cannon.

"Hi—ey," Maddy interjects, thrusting her palm between the two of us. *Oh, God . . . she's going to shake his hand.*

Cannon's gaze drops to the pale, spindly fingers quivering in front of him, and I flash my attention to my new friend, warning her to retreat with a buzzing shake of my head. She must be young. I think she's a freshman. I never should have put the handshake idea in her head.

"Hi," Cannon says, his head cocked and eyes now on Maddy. I can't tell whether he thinks this is a joke or not, but he tentatively takes her hand, his eyes flinching when he experiences the same thing I did.

Oh, man. I squeeze my eyes shut and pinch the bridge of my nose.

"I'm Maddy," I hear her say.

"Cannon," he responds. I open my eyes in time to see their hands fall away, and I'm not sure who I'm more glad for that it's over.

"You should get better friends, Maddy," he adds, before flinging open the weight room door and letting it slam in my face.

Maddy. I'm more glad for Maddy.

"He is beautiful," she hums, her eyes entranced in the space he left behind.

"He's a pig," I say without pause. I hold the door open for my infatuated friend, and as she passes me, a flash of jealousy hits my gut. I want to ignore it, but I've got a lifetime of experience acknowledging my feelings, and there's no mistaking that's what I felt. It was brief, and it was irrational. But it was there. And it's because even as awful as Cannon is behaving, Maddy is right. He is beautiful.

On the outside.

FIVE

CANNON

What are the odds that Hollis Taylor is in fifty percent of my classes? Scratch that; I'm tired of dwelling on odds of fifty percent. From now on, I avoid fifty-fifty like the plague! But seriously, do I have to start *and* end my day with her?

Hollis is basically a hot but disheveled mess. By the time we had weight lifting together, she'd essentially tied her hair up in an actual knot. I'm pretty sure I saw a binder clip holding that shit up. And yeah, I was staring when she turned her back. That's the problem with the *hot* mess part. She was wearing black leggings and a gray T-shirt that was about two sizes too big, and it shouldn't have been sexy, but on her it just . . . was. There was something about the way she rolled the sleeves up tight over her toned shoulders that I couldn't ignore. She's tan, which is a rarity for this town, especially in the winter. Back home in New Mexico, everyone is always outside. Sun-kissed skin is a year-round feature. Everyone here looks pale. Hollis defies the gray, though, which means she must thrive outside. I guess New York tempers you for freezing cold weather.

It's blustery today, maybe forty-five degrees out. My arm hurts just thinking about throwing a bullpen, but Zack and my uncle keep telling me I'll get used to it. I guess if I could get acclimated to regularly playing in ninety-degrees back home, then forty shouldn't be a problem. By late April when playoffs hit, it should be about perfect. I just need to stay healthy.

Zack's waiting for me outside the clubhouse, already dressed out and ready for workouts. I nod and grin, holding up my fist to pound as I pass.

"First one dressed and ready, nice job," I say before spotting Hollis already hitting the track beyond his shoulder.

"Second," he says with an eyeroll. Everything about him is closed off, already defeated.

"Hey, you're the starting catcher. Go show him why," I encourage. My cousin fakes a smile that lasts for a fraction, then hoists his gear bag over his shoulder and trails backward toward the track.

"Your stuff's in the corner," he says. His last class is near the front of the building, and he did me a major solid by hauling my things across campus.

"See you out there," I say.

He merely nods and takes off in a rhythmic jog, the weight of his catching equipment smacking against his side with every step.

There are only a handful of guys in the clubhouse when I enter, so my cousin is still a shining example of being on time by being early. Hollis and I came from the same spot on campus, so I'm not sure how she beat me here.

For the most part, I know most of the guys doing the workouts. It's the same team as last year, minus one senior who wasn't very good. We should be tight this year, contenders, as long as we put the right people on the field. I can't imagine Coach Taylor going the *everyone gets to play* route just so his daughter gets a turn, but my cousin's worry is messing with my head. Today should put a lot of that to bed, though. We're gonna be on the field, and I'm throwing to both of them. Weaknesses will show themselves.

I pull on my compression pants and shirt and slip my shorts on over the top. Then I grab my cleats and push my feet into my turf shoes for the time being. There are only two other guys who are just pitchers like me. The rest of the rotation is made up of position players who throw decently. I like having a small squad to work with. It means I get more attention from our pitching coach, more work in, and better looks from the schools I'm targeting.

I wait by the door for Jay and Roland, the other two in my group. When they grab their gloves and jog my way, I push through the door, the bright sun making me squint, and the steady wind drying out what's exposed of my eyes. *Goddamn, I miss the Southwest.*

We jog in sync down to the track and dump our gloves and cleats in a pile before starting our first lap. Our pace is steady but slow. By the time we round the curve, Hollis and my cousin are at the field, throwing.

Atta boy.

My gaze once again drawn forward, my eyes land smack on Coach's. Arms crossed over his chest, he squints against the sun, his face hard. I'd say expressionless if it weren't for the obvious ire slightly pulling down the corners of his mouth. I'm not sure what makes me speak up. Maybe I still feel the curse of my day and schedule, or maybe Zack is in my head. I stretch my hands out at my sides, palms up, and my lips move with the word just as my brain shoots a warning to my vocal chords. *Noooo! Don't . . . do . . . it!*

"What?" The simple question spills from my mouth, loud enough that it's distinguishable, undeniable that it came from me, hostile and oppositional—all qualities that get you cut before you even make it to tryouts if you don't throw like I do.

My feet keep going, though my partners pick up the pace, distancing themselves from me. I don't blame them. I manage to pull my stare from Coach as I round the corner and kick it in a little faster through the straightaway. When I pass Jay and Roland, they up their pace to match me, and by the time we round the next curve and hit the final straightaway, we're near a sprint, a shotgun race to see who crosses the finish line first. Roland edges me out by a foot, and I beat Jay by a full two strides.

Chests pounding, the three of us rest our folded hands over our heads, slowing from a jog to a walk as we make our way back to our pile of gloves and shoes, cheeks red and mouths panting.

"Jennings!"

The guys don't even spare me a glance. It was a long shot that he'd let this pass. Things always seem to start off this way with me. By the end of the season, I'm coach's favorite, but for whatever reason, I always go into relationships adversarial. It's a flaw. I'm aware. I hate it. Still, *every fucking time!*

This one, it's on Zack. And Hollis. I wish none of it concerned me, only Zack is the entire reason I'm here. Me and Zack, that's how it was always meant to go down. Our fathers have this shared dream, and yeah, maybe there is some vicarious living happening, but regardless, it's had years of hope invested in it. That's too much importance to be ruined by some chick out to prove a point, and her pissed-off, protective father.

"I'll see you guys in the bullpen." I nod. Jay lifts his hand up, but neither of them glances over their shoulders. They're safe. My fuck up, my punishment.

"Coach?" I say as I jog to where he stands at the edge of the track. Assistant Coach Dixon gives me a short nod, a hint of a smirk buried under his mustache. At least he's amused by my hot head. I won't have to do the make-up work with him.

"Ten percent of the population is left-handed. You know that?" Coach Taylor's jaw rolls as he chews at a piece of gum. His eyes are trained on the track, his focus on the clump of fielders making their way around it at different paces.

"Something like that, yeah. I read that somewhere maybe," I answer, even though I haven't. It's just a fact that seems about right.

"I bet you think that makes you special," he spits out, and my mouth pops open in awe. I close it quickly, disciplined enough to know that anything I say next will surely be incriminating. He snaps his gum once as his head swivels my direction, his eyes full of years of experience dealing with players like me.

"No, sir," I decide on. It's the right response, and I can tell by the way he draws his mouth into a tight, satisfied smile. Despite this little spat, I know that I am, in fact, special. I know that throwing the way I do is rare, and I know he is aware of how rare it is. I know in my gut that this is simply him showboating to get the upper hand. But he's tugging this little thread that leaves me unsure whether he means what he says. I get the insinuation—he's not afraid to cut me. Right now, I'm not sure he is.

"Run it again."

I blink, still out of breath from my two-hundred meter sprint. He pops his gum and gnashes his back teeth, flashing his canines.

"Now?"

Damn it, Cannon. Of course, now.

Coach shifts his stance, his shoulders squaring up with me, his arms still crossed over the taught coaching shirt stretched over his chest. He's in shape, not a has-been.

"Right, now. Okay." I exhale, letting my lips flap with the air. I'm probably going to throw up, but I get the sense he would be impressed by that.

Dropping my things at his feet, I jog over to the curve where I started last time. Just before I kick into a run, Coach calls out, "Two and a half minutes will put you on pace!"

I crane my neck back and stumble a little. That's what a ten-minute-two-miler breaks down to over two laps. I planned to work up to that, maybe by next week. Mouth agape, I manage to stop myself from questioning this time, nod, and hope he's too far away to see the *WTF* written all over my face.

"I'll tell you when," he says, lifting his arm and tapping on his digital watch. He's actually going to time this.

I nod and kick out my legs, already tightening from cooling down. I get the idea that this—sprints—running in general—gets the blood moving, makes stretching more effective, and preps the heart rate. What I'm doing right now, though, is purely to satisfy his ego. It's bullshit, but I'm gonna do it anyway.

He shouts *Go* as the largest group of fielders passes me for their second lap. I use their pace to kick me into overdrive, burning past them until I leave them well behind by mid-straightaway. My cheeks puffing in and out on a steady count, I mentally coach myself into the first turn, feeling the burn threaten my chest and numbness tickle my calves and thighs.

"A quarter through. Do this. A quarter through," I grunt out, nobody around to hear me.

Beads of sweat slide down my forehead as Coach comes into view at the end of the track. He holds up his arm when I hit the curve again, tapping on his watch.

"Two seconds slow," he shouts.

Fuck me all to hell.

My brain tells my legs to move faster, but I don't know if they are. I pump my elbows back, hoping for slingshot, and lengthen my stride, thankful for my long legs. If I had to do this with more steps, I think I'd die.

I'm completely gassed by the time I get to the next curve, and now I'm basically falling my way through the rest of the run. I lean my weight forward, using it, grasping at every advantage, my breath coming out in heavy grunts and pants. I sound like a woman birthing a forty-pound baby. My arms begin to flail at fifty meters, my balance threatening at thirty, but I hold on through the finish line, giving in to gravity and tucking my shoulders as I fall into an awkward double summersault that gashes up my knee and leaves my forearm with one hell of a raspberry.

Finally stopped, I let my arms flop to my sides, my legs out like a scarecrow, my chest rising and falling like a giant, blood-filled heart. That's what I am right now, and I'm not sure whether I'm going to pass out, vomit, or burst open.

Coach's shadow shades my eyes, and I run my forearm over my matted, sweaty hair and forehead as he drops my ball cap on my chest. I clutch it, too tired to put it on my head, too exhausted to sit up. I shield my eyes from the sun with a chopped hand at my brow, my eyes wanting to close, my body begging me to sleep, right here, just for a minute or two.

"Eight-fifty-eight," he says, followed by a snap of his gum. He gives it another chew and spits it out into the dead grass near the long jump pit.

"What?" I breathe out, not sure what he means. Afraid he'll mistake my question for more attitude, I force myself to sit up, palms flat behind me, legs lifeless and stretched out before me. I shake my head and widen my eyes.

"Sorry. I mean, I don't understand."

He's smirking. *Smug prick.*

"You ran an eight-fifty-eight two-mile pace. I lied about your first lap."

He reaches down to help me to my feet. I puff out a sharp laugh, my chest giving out a breath it's been working hard to find. I stare at his outstretched palm for a few seconds, working my way up to a full sit, my elbows propped on my knees. A drop of sweat falls from my brow into my eye, and I squint before taking the bottom of my soaking T-shirt to my face. Then I grip his hand and haul myself to my feet.

I slide my hat over my damp hair, tucking the sides in as we slowly cross the space between the track and the ball fields.

"You sure it was eight-fifty-eight?" I quirk a brow as I look at him sideways.

He lifts his watch to show me the time.

I have to stop walking to get a good look at it, and after a full two seconds of staring, I laugh out loud enough that the guys stop throwing and look at me.

"Hot damn! Woo!"

"Personal best, I'm guessing?" Coach questions.

I continue to laugh silently, a little in disbelief, and I nod.

"Uh, yeah. You might say that. My dad is going to think it's an honest to God miracle," I confess. My response pulls a laugh from him, a genuine one that's raspy and accompanied by a smile that reaches his eyes.

I bend down and grab my glove and cleats, my body suddenly full of a zest, as though I could do that again if I really had to. I'm not going to offer, but I do feel that little additive pride gives my steps, and I'm not completely empty.

"Cannon," he says as we near the bullpens. It's the first time he's said my first name, and the significance is not lost on me.

I nod and straighten my hat, pulling down on the sides to offer more shade and curve to the brim.

"Tomorrow when you come out here to run, know what you're capable of, and don't sell yourself short. Every workout and drill and warmup and stretch is an opportunity to be better. Don't waste your own time on mediocre."

I let my eyes meet his directly, feeling the burn of the uncomfortable stare, letting him look behind mine to see that I hear him, that I'm sorry, and that I'm about to prove to him that I am indeed special.

"Yes, sir," I say, a little stunned at how damn good this guy is. It took two and a half minutes for me to buy in completely. And I'm in—one-hundred percent—when it comes to this team and this coach. What I'm *not* in for just yet is the catcher waiting in the bullpen with her helmet and mask balanced on her head, her hip jutted out, shin guards covering her legs, and chest protector layered over her Yankees practice shirt.

Coach lingers behind me, waiting to see what I do. My cousin is already catching Jay, and I know that's on purpose. I can tell he's pissed, based on the extra zip he gives to every ball he throws.

"You about ready, champ?" Hollis shouts. It's both infuriating and sexy, and my brain is doped up on serotonin from just pulling off a miracle.

"Lemme get on my cleats," I shout back, a neutral response that doesn't raise Coach's eyebrow or tick off Zack.

It's going to be weird throwing to someone else right next to him. I'm already mentally preparing myself to pretend he isn't there, that this is just some camp or a different team entirely. It's a game of catch, with a girl who swears she can handle my heat. If I can run two laps like my life depended on it—and I think maybe it did, just a little—then I can do this.

She jerks her mask down and crouches behind the plate while I slip out of one set of shoes and into my cleats. Pounding her glove a few times, she stretches her legs out to the side one at a time, clearly showing off how flexible she is. I catch Zack trying to do the same, and it's not smooth. He stops trying after losing his balance on his left.

Relax, buddy. You don't have to do everything she does. You're good at doing it your way.

Dropping my turf shoes on the bench, I step up on the bullpen mound and dig in at the rubber. Grass overgrows much of it. This field needs some love. I roll my shoulders and hold the ball up for Hollis to see, making sure she's ready for a warm-up toss. I throw it at half speed, not surprised when it pops in her glove above her head. She stands and rolls the ball in her hand a few times, and I hold my glove out for her to toss it back. We're going to be here all day at this rate.

I knew she could play. I didn't expect her to come out here and be weak or not at least hang. I expected Zack to blow her away, but I figured she would be able to handle a little bit of catch. This game is nothing like softball. It's fragile and dangerous, and tiny mistakes in calculation result in disasters, in a blink. What I expected from Hollis was a gamble, a risky move for the sake of proving a point. My assumptions topple the second she sends the ball right back to my glove, hitting me square in the chest, the pop on my end as loud as it was on hers.

The sound is resounding enough that Zack stops mid-throw, distracted by the game of catch happening next to him. He eventually tosses the ball back to Jay, but I can tell he isn't invested. I also see right through his lame attempt at tightening his mask so he can watch Hollis and me throw for a full minute. He's crouched, fumbling with his gear, eyes lasered on the ball zinging between Hollis and me with increasing speed. Either seeing enough or realizing how obvious he is, he puts his helmet back on and drops to his squat, returning to Jay who was as lost in Hollis as the rest of us.

"Damn, girl," he says. A second later my cousin pounds his mitt, forcing his partner's attention back to him. Hollis just keeps doing her job, pretending not to notice any of it. She has to, though. Her mask hides most of her features, so underneath there must live a bit of arrogance. Not that it isn't warranted. *Damn.*

I shake out my arm after our last toss and situate myself on the mound, ready to really throw, motioning that I'm starting with a four-seam. She lowers and pats her glove, flashing it open and closed where she wants it. She seems ready. Every little nuance is as it should be. This is the true test, and I'm glad Zack isn't watching. No matter what happens, I'll have to make him believe he has nothing to worry about, that she can't handle this. To be honest, I'm not sure what I'm hoping for right now. If she can't handle it, she's going to get hurt.

I raise my leg and draw my hands in to my chest, then extend my arms with my stride as I push off and let it fly. It's an inside pitch for a lefty, and meets her target right at the corner of the plate. A strike if they don't swing, a probable double if they do. It's exactly what she called for, exactly where she wanted it. And she handled it like it was nothing.

These odds are not fifty-fifty.

SIX

HOLLIS

It's not like my dad to take Fridays off from workouts. He believes in using every inch given, and there are no rules against holding "optional" workouts seven days a week. Of course, everyone knows the unwritten rule of workout attendance—it's *silently* mandatory. Not today. Today, my dad sent out a text blast around lunch hour letting everyone know they were on their own.

Apparently, for most of the team, this means bypassing the field completely after the last bell of the day and heading home, or to this hill everyone keeps talking about. I thought for a while I would be the only person to show up, but about five minutes into my run, Cannon arrives. I went a full mile today, to make sure I could still do it, and I'm about to hit my final stretch, my legs pleading with me to give them the rest I've been promising them for the last seven-eighths of a mile.

I slow to a steady jog and eventually a fast walk, my hands folded atop my head to give my lungs a good stretch. The sky is blanketed with a deep gray, the clouds thick and threatening to dump rain or snow, or a little of both. You can really see the weather out here. Back home, it was more of a surprise. The news told you the storm was coming, but the height of the borough's buildings made it easier to ignore the oncoming threat. More times than I can count, I got caught blocks away with nothing but my bike to get me home. Something tells me rain and snowfall are a little different out here.

Cannon nods to acknowledge me. It's . . . strange. We spent the week barely exchanging words. We talk more to one another in statistics than on the field, but that's basically a proximity thing. I did the mental measurements and we're less than two feet apart in stats. Out here, it's sixty feet, six inches.

"Those clouds gonna do anything?" I force the question out because I want this to be pleasant. I don't want him to finish his run and just go home. I'd actually like to practice, and that's damn near impossible on my own. Not that I haven't done it.

Finishing the laces on his shoes, Cannon rolls his compression pants into his socks and tugs down the pant legs of the joggers he's wearing on top. He glances up as he stands, squinting from the reflection thrown off the clouds.

"Fifty-fifty," he says.

His gaze is on me for a solid five seconds before I get his joke.

"Oh," I breathe out with a laugh. "Right."

He grants me a short laugh of his own, accompanied by the slightest tick up on one side of his mouth. It pushes a dimple into his cheek and for a flash, I get a glimpse of the boy I kissed to ring in this year. It's gone before he turns toward the straightaway of the track for his run.

I let him get about fifty meters into it before my legs relent and let me take on another two laps. I've already cooled down, so the tightness in my hips keeps me from sprinting to catch up for the first half-lap, but I'm loose by the time I hit the curve and we round it together, crossing in front of the home stands with our strides in sync.

We both glance to our sides, making eye contact for a stride or two.

"You already ran," he pants out. He's breathing harder than I am. I gloat internally.

"Didn't want you to run alone. It's good to have someone push you." My pulse is picking up again, partly from the cardio, but mostly from this awkward conversation. I decide to let the rest of this run finish in silence, and Cannon seems all right with that, picking up his pace for the second lap. I have to double my steps to keep up. He's only an inch or two taller, but it feels as though his stride is twice the length of mine now that we're really running.

We cross the finish line and I'm a solid ten meters behind. I expect to see him turn and gloat, but instead, he lifts his arms up to match mine and utters "Good run" through pants.

I nod. It was.

We walk in large circles until our heart rates find their way back to normal, and pick up our gear. I didn't come out here expecting a bullpen, and he's probably on his day off from throwing, but I'm both tense and pleased that he makes his way into the dugout with me.

"Think you can manage to throw strikes?" He jerks his head toward the batting cages as he drops his bag on the bench.

I set my gear on the opposite end and unzip the pouch with my batting gloves inside, pulling them on while I study the nearby netting. I twist my mouth as if I'm really giving his question thought.

"Guess I can throw 'bout as accurate as you can," I respond, looking back at him with a shrug. He laughs, a genuine one, but it's short. Like a punch.

He follows me into the cages and I move a tee into position. He lets out an exasperated sigh.

"What?" I glance up, tugging the tee's neck to the right height. "Hate tee work?"

"It's torture," he says with flat eyes.

"Then you're not doing it right."

The laugh that crackles from his body is less genuine this time. I drag a bucket of balls to my side and balance a ball on the tee, gesturing with an open palm to let him go first.

"Nope." He moves back to the corner where he can lean his weight against one of the poles, crossing his feet and pulling out his phone, probably skimming through social media.

"You wanna go second?" I ask.

"I don't wanna go at all. I'll wait for you to throw," he responds without looking.

I shake my head as my gaze moves away from him. He's gonna be in a world of hurt next week when my dad moves on to hitting drills. He doesn't believe in skipping steps, even if your only job is pitching.

The best pitchers are the best they can be at everything else.

He put that mantra out there often at my last school. For the most part, the players bought into it all. My ex, Jordan, bought into it hardcore, which is probably the only reason my dad was all right with us dating. He was mediocre as pitchers go, but he was always at his best. Drive counts for a lot more than talent in my dad's eyes. Too bad that sentiment wasn't shared by Jordan's father.

I push that thought out of my head and instead focus on my target, digging my feet in at a comfortable distance and taking a few slow-motion practice swings without my bat. I glance at Cannon as I reach down for my bat, but his attention is still on his screen, probably flipping through pictures of our classmates doing stupid shit and documenting it all for public consumption. I hate social media. It's the downfall of my generation.

Eyes back on the ball in front of me, I rotate my hips and bring my bat back, twisting with a hard swing, leaving my feet in place. Cannon must have stopped his social binge long enough to catch me because he repeats the same simmering chuckle he gave before.

"That's your batting stance?" He cocks a brow.

I open my mouth to explain how tee drills work, but then decide it doesn't matter. I close it into a straight, unaffected line while meeting his stare with a harder one. The familiar competitive growl in my belly mixes with the constant need to prove myself as I place another ball on the tee and repeat the same drill. This time, Cannon snorts a laugh through his nostrils, and by the time I glance up, he's back to his mindless phone skimming.

It shouldn't surprise me, and I guess really, it doesn't. It disappoints me, though, and that takes me off-guard. I expected more from him, and I'm not sure why. Maybe it's because he was so receptive on the track, or because up until this point, other than a really good kiss, Cannon Jennings has been nothing but an arrogant prick.

I power through about twenty more swings, noting the half-empty bucket. I could move on to regular swings, but because I'm stubborn—or because I can't help but engage with this guy—I try one more time to show him the way.

"You sure you don't want a turn?"

I study him until he finally blinks up from the screen. Our eyes would look so good together, I think. If only his didn't make me absolutely mental.

With a slight eyeroll, he bends and tucks his phone under his mitt to protect it and lines up to swing left-handed. I smirk because it always looks weird to me. Honestly, I'd give anything to be able to do it. I look like a fool when I do anything left-handed.

"Don't move your feet," I say, pausing with the ball in my palm, an inch or so away.

He grimaces because he thinks my method is stupid, but he'll understand next week when my dad makes him do this about a hundred times.

I place the ball and adjust the height of the tee up just a tick for his height. He lines his bat up with a few slow swings, stopping right before impact, then clears his throat as he wriggles his heels into the turf and loads for his first swing. Topping the ball with his bat, it dribbles from the tee and travels about six feet to the center of the cage. It takes every ounce of self-control for me not to revel. Holding in the laugh proves impossible.

"Fuck off," he retorts, not bothering to wait for me to load the next ball and instead doing it himself. He repeats everything as before, and the result is the same, including my reaction.

"This is stupid," he says, tossing his bat to the side and undoing a Velcro strap on his batting glove. I reach forward and grab his wrist, my need to coach stronger than my instincts for what is probably a bad idea. His arm petrifies under my touch, forearm flexed with threat. I unwind my fingers one at a time while my eyes are fixed on where they just were. Blood rushes back in to fill the pale spots left behind from my hard grip.

"Sorry. I meant you shouldn't quit after two tries. It's a drill, and you've never—"

"I know how batting practice works, coach. Thank you, but I'm good." He offers a salute along with his sharp tongue and bends down, pulling his batting gloves completely off his hands. He picks up his mitt and cradles it under his arm, holding it like a kid holds a teddy bear but with a tinge of aggression. Phone in hand again, he resumes his position against the pole, leaning impatiently, put out that he has to wait for me to finish my drills before we can get on to doing something he likes. Something he's good at.

Stunned at how quickly he can turn into a child, it takes me a few seconds to regain the ability to move.

"Have you always been this sensitive? Or is that a new thing?" I bend down to get a ball in my hand so my eyes aren't insulted by his sour puss expression, but it's still there when I look up. Rather than back down, I glare right back at him, placing the ball on the tee before taking deliberate steps back. Holding my palms out, I offer him a chance to prove me wrong.

He laughs through his nose and looks to the side, squinting as he stares off into the distance where the mound—his comfort zone—sits empty, dirt swirling in the air around it as the wind kicks up. Cocking his head to the side, he levels me with one more hard gaze before giving in, his gritted teeth and flexed jaw evidence of how much he doesn't want to fall into my trap.

After picking up his bat, he sidles up to the tee, lining up his feet in a position I know in my gut is too far back. I clear my throat rather than say something immediately, which comes off totally passive aggressive. He pushes my buttons and brings out the fighter in me. It's maddening.

"What?" His shoulders sag, the bat resting heavily on the left one as his hands loosen their grip.

I run my hand over my mouth and chin, giving myself a few seconds to plot the perfect words before they leave my lips.

"So, the point of this drill is torque and bat speed. And the reason you're not making the right contact is because . . ." I pause and hold my open hands out while my eyes widen to stop him from thinking I'm being insulting. "I know you know how to make good contact. I know you can hit. I'm only trying to correct this one little thing, that's all."

He gives me a slight nod, tiny enough that if I blinked I would have missed it.

I step up next to him and nudge his front foot with my toe, guiding him forward a few inches. Pacing around his body, I grab the barrel of his bat and pull it around as I walk the trajectory it would take for a normal swing. He lets me guide his hands while his eyes narrow and follow my movement with suspicion. His forearms flex as they rotate and though I don't want to, I swallow at the sight; I know he sees me do it.

"You want to make contact . . . right . . . here." I stop the bat just as it meets the ball, holding it firm and glancing up to make sure he's looking. His focus isn't on the mechanics I'm demonstrating at all. It's on me. More specifically, he's zeroed in on my eyes. He was just waiting for me to finish my silly little show, until I looked up to find his jaded, pursed lips and completely intolerant expression.

"You think this is stupid. I got it," I say, letting go of the bat and backing away. I'm so damn mad at myself for trying. I don't know why I don't give up when I'm faced with these situations. I'm forever that girl who thinks she can change people's minds.

I'm about to give him his out, tell him we can do it his way, go straight to hitting from live pitches, when he rears back and rotates his hips, bat following and making hard contact as it drives the ball like a bullet into the metal posts at the other end.

We both stare at the point of impact for a few seconds, and I breathe out a little laugh to accompany my half smile. I'm not sure whether I'm more surprised by the result or his effort. Rather than attempt more conversation, I decide to simply feed him another ball, silently placing it on the tee and stepping back as he moves his feet into position—the *right* position.

Another swing. More great contact.

I nod, whispering a "Yes" under my breath. He's still brooding, and any celebration on my part is going to come off as gloating. Not that it isn't warranted, because I *was* right, but making a big deal out of that won't make things better. It'll only drive the wedge back in that uncomfortable place between us.

We continue on with this pattern, wordlessly working out and going through my usual round of drills. Cannon lets me set the pace and go first so he can copy everything I do. He doesn't resist when I nudge his feet, but I never once breathe a word aloud. It's odd, but it's working, so I don't fight it.

After the fifth time of picking up all the balls, Cannon kicks the remaining few into the far corner and takes the bucket in his hand, carrying it to the screen at the end so he can throw to me.

"You ready?" His voice startles me because we've been carrying on in silence for so long.

"Yeah," I respond, settling into my comfortable hitting position and nodding for him to begin.

I have noticed a lot of things about Cannon that I will never tell him. It's enough that he's already had his lips on mine, but beyond being the best kiss I've ever had, he also has the kind of voice you wish could wake you up in the morning and put you to bed at night. It affects me more when he says very few words.

Like now, when he said, "You ready?" It came out in this deep timbre that just hung in the air, the sound of the *y* at the end lingering a little longer than it would from any other mouth. And then there's his movement. He pitches as if he's putting on a contemporary ballet, every tick of his muscles purposeful, each pause met with a fluid extension of his arms and legs. The way he draws his leg up and separates his arms before exploding with a slingshot of power that sends the ball exactly where it's meant to go—exactly where I asked for it—is pure perfection.

His talent is undeniable, but there's an undertone of truly primal appeal that I have been fighting every single time we throw together. I find myself growing jealous of the times he works out with his cousin, and not because I think Zack is a threat to my playing time. I'm envious that he gets to watch Cannon work.

Those movements are now on display, and for his first three or four pitches, I'm thrown off *my* game. A smug satisfaction tugs his lip up on one side, and it's enough to shake me out of my awe. I send his next pitch barreling back at him, my ball striking the metal of the L-screen shielding him. He flinches and I shoot him a smirk of my own, flipping the bat in my hand for show. He shakes his head, and looks down at his feet with a quiet laugh that I instantly add to my short list of traits I admire about him.

Lips puckered, he flexes and digs in to throw me another pitch, contributing to this game of batting-practice chess that our competitive sides decided to play. I swing way too early, fooled by the slowed-down ball that seems to float by long after my bat slices through the zone.

"Whoa!" I grin at the path the ball took over the plate, impressed with a pitch my dad should know he can throw.

"You like that?" He tips his chin up, the shadow of his hat leaving his eyes for just a moment.

"That wasn't bad," I say, not wanting to inflate his ego too much.

"Not bad." He chuckles. "Not bad, she says," he continues on, a teasing spirit to his tone. It is hard not to find *this* Cannon Jennings utterly charming.

Swinging his arms around at his sides, he puts on a serious face, leaning forward as if getting a sign from his catcher. I play along and drop my bat to the side, crouching down and giving him the sign for slider, which is what I *think* that was. One of his eyes closes more than the other and his lip ticks up. I heed the warning and shoot to my feet, grabbing my bat and readying myself for the pitch. This one sails through even slower, somehow fooling me so badly that I swing hard enough to tie up my legs and trip myself. It's mortifying, and to add insult to injury, Cannon laughs like a madman at the other end of the cage, rearing his head back and holding his glove against his gut.

"Glad you're amused," I grumble, brushing my palms along the fresh raspberries scraped into my kneecaps, noting the new hole in my favorite pair of joggers.

By the time I'm upright and on my feet, Cannon has made his way to my side. I jerk, surprised by his instant—*and very close*—presence. He tilts his head, maybe curious at my reaction, then lifts his hand, a ball balanced at the tips of his fingers.

"That pitch," he begins, blinking his focus to the ball. Mine follows as he slowly rotates the ball in the air between us, the seams moving at an angle away from me. "It's not quite a full curve. I throw it more like a slider, so the ball tends to . . . go . . . like . . . this." He bends as he gives his description, walking the ball through the air and over the plate along the same trail it took the two times he threw it.

"You make that up?" I ask. He's crouched down, his quad muscles completely filling out his joggers, thighs tight and thick like a man. I swallow at the sight of them. He must notice because he rises, clearing his throat. I've just objectified him. I scrunch my face, embarrassed, while he's not looking.

"My dad used to throw it when he was in college. He showed me how when I was in Little League." He tips his head up and hits me with dazzling eyes that are warmed by this fond memory. It's sweet, and genuine. His mouth quirks up, dimpling his cheek. "I threw that sucker all the way to the championship one year."

He laughs once, eyes narrowing over his growing smile as he looks back to the ball in his hand. He rolls it in his fingers.

"You win?" I ask.

He glances up through dark lashes. My list of things I like about him is ever-growing, though admittedly superficial. His chest quakes with one more short laugh before he shakes his head, tossing the ball in his hand and gripping it with a firm palm, fingers spread along the seams just where they're meant to go.

"Nah. We ended up facing this team from Albuquerque full of massive seventh-graders with no fear. They knocked that pitch over the fence seven times."

I wait a breath before giving in to the laugh his story pulls from me.

"Ouch," I say, tapping my bat on the plate a few times, signaling I'm ready to try and send one over the fence too.

"Yeah, but I've gotten a lot better at it since then," he teases.

"We'll see," I fire back.

We're bonding, and it's nice. I like Cannon, beyond the obvious attraction, which really is a bad idea on all levels. We could be friends, and I meant what I said in our statistics class that first day—I might be able to help him. As much as his dad taught him about the game, mine's taught me a lot, too. About how to make good pitchers *better*.

"Give me what you've got, Smalls," I shout, a little *Sandlot* throw-back that makes him chuckle.

Muscles primed, I shift my weight, ready to hit that strange curveball of his, but instead of getting ready to throw it, Cannon drops the ball into the bucket at his side, his gaze off to the side.

"This your idea of only being an hour?"

I didn't see Zack walk up, and my stomach sours with the instant intensity brought to the air with his company. Everything about Cannon's posture changes with his cousin's presence, and that friendly banter between us grinds to a halt.

"Just taking some swings," Cannon says, acting as if he's packing up and getting ready to go.

"We just started, actually," I interject. Cannon doesn't look at me, instead continuing to kick balls toward the bucket to put them away. Neither of them responds to me, which only makes the beast grow in my belly, the one that tells me to scream and call 'em as I see 'em.

"Cannon." I assert his name, like a teacher would. *Like my dad would.* He spares me a sharp glare over his shoulder. "Aren't you gonna take a turn?"

"Bahahaha!" His cousin accentuates his over-the-top cackle by grabbing his stomach and arching back. I assume he's making a joke at Cannon's expense, because he's a pitcher and pitchers rarely hit. But that's not the case at all.

"What, are you gonna throw to him?" His eyes are squinty, his lips pulled in so tight that there are deep divots where they pucker on either side. It's a truly ugly face.

I open my mouth, the beast ready to engage, then snap it shut, not giving in to the urge. I shift my gaze to Cannon and lift my brow as he hoists the bucket of balls and sets it on a metal chair that looks as though it's been beaten by more than a fair share of line drives and bats.

"I'm done here." His answer is definitive, short and clipped, the kind of response a trainer gives a dog.

A punchy laugh escapes my chest. I'm dumbfounded, and within thirty seconds, I'm also alone. The Jennings boys cross the field without a single glance or goodbye, and I hate that I'm hurt by it. This is always what I expect, yet somehow never fully see coming. I should probably let it go, see them on the field again Monday with renewed armor around my *feelings.*

But that's never quite been me either. I'm always up for a fight, a trait both of my parents have sewn into my fabric. Before they make it to their car, I hustle and pack up my own gear, double-timing it to my mom's van that my dad left behind for me to get home.

I'm pretty sure Zack and Cannon don't notice me in their rearview as they speed out of the lot, fishtailing through the dirt shoulder. Masked by the cloud of dust left in their wake, I feel around the underside of the van's bumper until I find the lockbox where my dad stuck the key. I drop my gear in the back and jump behind the wheel, zipping out of the lot while the trail of dust still lingers in the air, showing me the way. Tail lights in view, I slow enough to not be obvious and follow them. We stop at a house nestled in the woods, the driveway filled with shirtless guys playing basketball and surrounded by the kind of girls who only want to hang out and watch them.

Any other girl would either slink low in the driver's seat and pass on by or park and find a friend to ogle with. Maybe that's because they don't have a basketball rolling around their back seat like I do.

The thundering in my chest slows when I recognize Lucas, and I find my footing as I slip one foot out of the driver's side and spot June sitting with a group of girls on Lucas's open tailgate. It would be so simple to hop in the back with her, the ease of it so inviting that my fingers twitch at the feel of the ball. I'm tempted to play this a different way. Be a different kind of girl. Take the easy route.

Don't ever betray the person you are.

My dad's words echo around my head amid my mental battle. He gave up a lot so I never have to diminish who I am. And I'm not the girl who sits on the sidelines. I'm the girl who puts herself in the game, who changes the rules.

I hop out of the van and open the back door. Ball in hand, I slam the sliding door shut and jog across the street, dribbling along the way. It's been awhile, but every step I take bolsters my confidence and comfort with the ball. June's head pops up when she sees me. Waving her hand, she announces my arrival, inviting me to join her, *over where the girls are.* I smile back and stay the course.

Zack and Cannon were only a few paces ahead of me, and I jog three steps to close the gap, tapping my apparent nemesis on the shoulder until his toes square with mine after he turns. Zack doesn't even flinch in surprise, as if he expected me; his smirk dares to suggest he may have even lured me.

"I've got next game," I announce, fully taking the bait if that's the case. I've learned not to ask permission. They never grant you access if you're timid. That's not how you change minds and break into their exclusive clubs.

Of course, I'm not here on principal. I'm here because my feelings were hurt. Stupid feelings for a stupid boy with stupid, stupid features that I've been thinking about way too often. And while it's his cousin I'm in a standoff with, it's Cannon I want to convince. I'm just not sure of what.

SEVEN

CANNON

Hollis Taylor might be more like my cousin than I thought. This is a total Zack move, following people who pissed him off so they have to deal with looking him in the eyes.

I have to look *her* in the eyes, and I don't really want to. Before my cousin showed up, we were . . . I'm not sure what we were, but we weren't holding this invisible grudge that's there now. I have to stop making this my problem, but it's hard when my uncle and Zack will not stop talking about what a huge problem this is, and not only for them.

"Your senior year is going to be overshadowed by some novelty publicity stunt."

That's their talking point. They want to rile me up to make sure I'm invested in their battle, but really, there is some truth to it. Allensville Public is not a small school. It's not one of the mega schools that gets TV coverage, but it's a decent size in a town caught between factories to the south and the big city to the west. A girl behind the plate is the kind of human interest story the media eats up, which makes it hard to shine when you're the one on the mound.

All of that shit shouldn't matter. Deep down, I know it doesn't. Coaches at D-ones aren't looking at news stories, they're looking at numbers. And I've got the stats.

"Alright, how 'bout this—you can have Tory but I get Hayden. I'll take Cannon and you get Lucas." I give my cousin side-eyes because I do not want to be a part of this showdown. Too late, though. He just shoved the ball into my chest.

Hollis tosses her ball to the side, and one of Lucas's friends nudges it into the dead grass with his foot. Friday afternoon basketball at Hayden and Tory's has become a habit for Zack and me. I usually look forward to it, mostly because the twins end up putting on a show and it comes down to the rest of us getting out of the way and passing them the ball to do epic shit. I have a feeling that's not how this game is going to go.

"You know what? I'll be nice. You take it up top first." My cousin jerks the ball from my hands and bounces it to Hollis who accepts it with a firm slap of her palms. She's locked in on this as much as Zack is.

My cousin points to me then Lucas, coaching me on whom to guard. It's a little irritating but he's so far gone in his head, I agree. Hayden and Tory eye each other, and when I get close enough to Lucas to strong-arm him while Hollis dribbles around the perimeter of the three-point line, he mutters, "What the fuck?"

I shake my head.

"My cousin is threatened by a girl. Coach Taylor's her dad, and she catches, and it's a whole shit show." I glance up in frustration while Lucas snorts out a laugh.

"Right, well . . . this should be good," Lucas responds.

We both shuffle our feet, me guarding him while he jukes for an open position on the makeshift court in the D'Angelo driveway. Hollis dribbles back, crossing the ball behind her body a few times, then once through her legs.

"Oh, look at you. Fancy," my cousin teases, swiping at the ball and easily knocking it away. He coughs out a boastful laugh while she rushes to regain control. She manages, but it's clear by the way the whites of her eyes turn redder that Zack is getting under her skin.

Lucas rushes to the other side of the court, clapping his hands then opening his palms for a pass while Hollis works to shirk off my cousin's handsy defense. She sends a hard chest pass in Lucas's direction, but I've already read the play and intercept it, dribbling up top and passing the ball off to Zack to set up.

"Atta boy, Can. *Yup yup!*" My cousin is obnoxious in his celebration. I've joined these guys for dozens of Friday afternoon games, and while Zack is usually the loudest guy out here, he's trash talking with a little extra venom today. It's obvious, and also embarrassing for him.

Hollis hasn't said a word, but I can tell she's reaching a boiling point by the way she holds her lips closed tight, almost puckering as she zeroes in on nothing but the ball. She's stuck to my cousin like glue, reaching in when he drives to the right. He toys with her for way longer than necessary, then spins, dashing around her on the left and driving the ball to the hoop for a layup. He holds out a fist for me to pound as he jogs by while Tory inbounds the ball back to Hollis.

The ball back in play, Tory gives me a quick glance, a silent commentary on Zack's showboating, and I can tell he wants to put my cousin in his place. I'm not sure he realizes this game has nothing to do with the rest of us.

Sensing that Tory's ready, Hollis passes the ball back to him in a rush, and we all step back as he puts up an instant three-pointer that sinks through the hoop without a sound.

"Oh, damn!" Tory boasts, moving in on Zack with his chest puffed out. My cousin laughs him off and pats his chest with his flat palm. Tory's gone stoic, no longer playing a game for fun. I'm not sure this is the result my cousin wanted. Regardless, it's the one he's getting.

For a few minutes, the game shifts into its normal pattern—the Hayden and Tory show. Zack passes the ball to Hayden, and the faceoff ensues. Each of them drives in against one another in a boisterous round of one-on-one, forgetting that the rest of us are on the court. It's then that I catch the smile on Hollis's face. She came here to prove a point, but now, she's just having fun. *I'm* having fun. Every time I manage to get a pass, I flip it over to Hayden and watch him do his thing. Hollis does the same with Tory, even picking up his signal to set him up for a dunk. The two of them slap hands after he finally lets go of the rim, and the tightness eases in my chest.

This game is back to being what it should be, a way to blow off steam and just *be*. A place away from baseball, away from my goals, away from plans and parents. Right here, for this little slice of afternoon, we get to be a bunch of punk-ass teenagers. The rules are unwritten, but they are always followed.

Until now.

I didn't realize how long it had been since the ball met Zack's hands, but the moment it finally does, the tone of everything changes. Hollis isn't set on her feet yet. She's still hailing Tory's last shot, laughing with her new friends, not even looking as my cousin lowers his shoulder and drills right through her.

I hear the moment the breath leaves her chest, an audible *pop* from inside her ribs, her mouth an instant O shape, her cheeks pale and eyes frightened while a muffled moan crawls up her throat and out her mouth. She falls to her elbows, a good chunk of skin peeling away from the right one. She's too busy gripping her chest and trying to refill her lungs to notice the blood trailing down her arm and dripping onto the D'Angelo driveway.

"What the fuck is your deal, Jennings?"

Tory pushes my cousin back a few steps with a hard shove, and Zack's nostrils flare in response. Stepping into Tory's personal space, my cousin moves close enough for their chests to nearly touch.

"Part of the game, isn't it? I mean, we don't change the rules because—"

"Because I'm a girl?" Hollis interjects, suddenly on her feet and urging Tory to back out of a fight meant for her. She joins the standoff and Tory gives her space, but only a little, his pulse amped up enough to make his jaw twitch.

"You're the one who wanted to play." Zack holds the ball against his hip as they stare each other down, both panting from a mix of anger and racing heart rates. The blood on Hollis's arm is drying, but the thick beading left behind is a pretty good indication of the cut at the heart of the trail.

"Just learning your rules, Zack."

I don't know if my cousin expects her to cry or what, but she's clearly not intimidated by a little pushing and shoving. Hell, I've bruised her up with enough wild pitches over the last week that I could have told him she had thick skin, both literally *and* figuratively. Zack rolls the ball back and forth between his hands, eyes searing into Hollis, tongue held between his teeth, smile faint and ominous.

"Dude, just stop this," I mutter at his side. He doesn't bother to look at me, dismissing me with a flick of his hand.

"What? Hollis is good with it. Aren't you? We don't have a problem here." He nods at her, prompting her to fold or call his bluff. Only, he isn't bluffing. I've seen Zack get like this before. When we were little and playing against club kids from the rich teams, he stood his ground over fights he clearly picked. It always felt as if we were on the righteous side back then, but now he comes off like a dick.

"Yeah. We're good," Hollis says, nodding slowly. Her eyes lazily sweep from Zack to Tory, then to me. She's summing up everyone present, and I'm not sure what label she's assigning me.

"We'll call that a foul, then. Your ball," Zack says, letting it fall from his fingers into a lazy bounce in her direction.

"How very *honest* of you," Hollis bites back.

She doesn't pause for long, catching us all off guard by faking a shot then driving in around Zack for a left-handed layup. Her move draws praise, some of the guys waiting for the next game whistle, and both D'Angelo brothers bump fists with her. It was impressive, and it was actions instead of words. I expect it to only light more gas in Zack's belly, but he seems equally impressed, nodding with big movements as he says, "Okay, I see you."

For the next ten minutes of play, everything and everyone seems to find a rhythm. Zack holds a stiff forearm against Hollis while he dribbles in, but he never crosses the line into flagrant fouling. It's a contact sport, and it stays contact—hands smacking against arms when shots are fired, inadvertent scratches, tripped-up feet, trash talking spilling equally from all our mouths. I block one of Hollis's shots on a double-team and she nails me right back, punching the ball between my legs and right into Tory's hands. We've battled so hard, nobody's noticed the dark clouds creeping in and the sudden drop in temperature. The only thing that could shake our moods would be the clouds opening up and dumping icy rain on our game—or what my cousin does . . . right . . . now.

Hollis has the ball, working it around the imaginary three-point line, Zack stuck to her like second skin, hands reaching in but never quite fast enough to throw her off or find the steal. Our shoes are loud against the pavement, screeching when we stop hard, and sliding against loose gravel. Tory is nearly impossible to guard, but I'm doing my best, always somehow in contact with his body, be it an elbow matching the one he's got in my ribs or our legs fighting for position. The game's tied, and maybe that's what pushes Zack over the edge. Maybe he was waiting for his moment.

Or maybe . . . maybe he's desperate and angrier and more insecure than I realized.

After long seconds of faking grabs at the ball and getting nowhere, Zack swings his hand around Hollis's side, his hand slapping against her ass with enough force that the sound of skin-on-skin bites through the heavy wind despite the padding of her joggers. He yaps in laughter, practically beating his chest when the ball juts out from the top of her foot, her world visibly thrown.

My arms suddenly go slack, no longer struggling to hold on for defense. Tory's do the same, no longer itching for the ball. Only the people in our game actually see it—*feel* it—but the awfulness of it all actually chokes me.

The ball now in his possession, my cousin rushes the lane, no one engaged enough to stop him, and dunks the ball with enough force that the rim vibrates along with the slow rumble coming from the clouds above.

"I gotta get home. I think it's going to rain," Hollis says, her gaze at no one in particular and her announcement cursory, an excuse to let us all leave and pretend everything is normal. Maybe it is. Maybe that was something playful, like the way Tory slaps Hayden's ass when he does a good job. Maybe I didn't see what I think I saw, or feel what I should have.

The fact Hollis is already in her van and swinging around for a U-turn tells me my instincts are sickly attuned.

I glance to the right, everyone suddenly broken up, gone in different directions—away from my cousin who is still shooting and smiling, proud of his big win. Hollis's ball still sits in the grass. I walk over and kick it up into my hands, rotating it until I see her name carved into the side in thick black pen marks. I trace it with my thumb, a sourness coating my stomach that I immediately try to convince myself is only in my head. I glance out to the road in time to make eye contact with Hollis as she drives by, and I know better.

This problem between her and my cousin? It's only going to get worse. And I'm in the very middle.

EIGHT

HOLLIS

I've gotten better at pretending for my parents. For a while, I still had a lot of tells. They could sense that something was under my skin because of the way I picked at my dinner plate or only gave short answers. I've found that sticking with my natural knack of being a smart-ass can carry me through any interaction without questions.

I came home from basketball Friday and pulled into the driveway seconds before my father did. Mask in place, I rushed from the car and ran toward him, greeting him as he stepped out of his truck, and leaping at him like one of those flying monkeys at the Bronx zoo. He had exactly two seconds to prepare for my weight, but he still caught me effortlessly, despite how awkward it looks when we do this now.

I get my height from him, so when I was a kid, I outgrew my mom carrying me pretty quickly. Since my dad's limbs are proportional with mine, he could always manage. Whenever I fell asleep downstairs or was sick or twisted an ankle, Dad was charged with hauling me around. We started doing this again last year when my mom bet he couldn't lift me anymore. Now it's our thing.

Sometimes, I need to be daddy's girl. Other times, I think he needs me to be. Friday night, maybe we both needed it a little.

With most of the weekend over, I've been able to put what happened with Zack into the appropriate mental box, locking it up and tucking it in that part of my brain I don't deal with until I want to. *Until I have to.*

We're not a very formal family. No big Sunday dinners when we all sit around the table and share. Usually, Dad grabs a pizza and we all take slices as we come and go. Sometimes, there's a game on in the living room, and we end up piled on the couch.

This is one of those Sundays when my mom is grading and my dad is nodding off on the couch, having drunk one too many beers while tinkering in the garage. My brother still goes to bed early, so I'm on my own. Having bargained that filling a dresser with clothes, one step closer to fully unpacking, was worth another week of van privileges, I have wheels at my disposal. The problem is I have no idea where to go.

After a good fifteen minutes of roaming aimlessly around neighborhoods, looking at leftover Christmas lights that are yet to be taken down, I pop out from a side street, suddenly on the main drag through town. The glowing orange A&P sign flickers in the mist lingering after the long weekend rains. The roads are slick with frozen mud. So far, winter storms here aren't the picturesque kind. I wait for the few cars to pass before crawling the van out onto the road. I'm used to driving in New York weather, but I've been told over and over again by my dad that the roads and weather here mix differently.

I immediately recognize the lone car parked in front of the gym, and despite the uncertainty of which Jennings drove it here, I pull in and park right next to it. I'm not dressed for a workout, my dad's old college sweatpants rolled up at my waist and my shirt the black Billie Eilish long-sleeved tee I got for my birthday at a concert last year. With one deep breath, I resolve to keep what happened Friday tucked away in my mental box, no matter who is inside, and push open the door, glad I at least have socks on with my bright pink knitted boots.

A bell jingles when I walk in, and the old man I met the first time I came here cranes his neck, peeling his eyes away from the Packers playoff game on the small TV mounted in the corner.

"Aw, hell. You again?" he grumbles. I *think* he's teasing.

I nod toward the TV as he pulls himself up from the chair he was planted in and makes his way to the register.

"What's the score?"

"Packers are up by a touchdown," he says, his groggy words wrapping around the well-chewed toothpick dangling from his bottom lip. The clank of metal plates knocking together hits the nerve at the back of my neck but I manage the strength not to turn and look in the direction of the noise. I don't want to know just yet who is to my left.

"Good." I nod.

He squints in apparent skepticism, a hint of a smile creeping into his dry, cracked lips, evidence from his lunch or dinner caught in his overgrown mustache. A deep cough crackles in his chest twice as he tucks his chin. He coughs with the lungs of a lifelong smoker. I recognize the same distinct sound that came from my grandfather's chest. Leaning on his elbow, he slouches at the counter and observes me with one eye, the other squinted shut.

"You a Packer fan?"

Oh, the temptation to lie, but I just can't.

"Oh, no way. Giants all the way! I'd just rather we play you next week than the Seahawks." I blink at him as he stares at me for a few seconds in dead silence, then huffs out a laugh, standing upright and slapping his palm on the countertop.

"Well, hot damn. I like you, sweetheart. I hate your Giants, but I do believe I like you." He pops open his register and hands me a five-dollar bill, and I look at it strangely, take it tentatively.

"I'm . . . flattered?" I'm really just confused, and maybe a little offended.

I cock my head, missing the opportunity to correct him on the *sweetheart* bit because I'm so thrown by what came after. And then I hear the voice of the Jennings I hoped drove that car here tonight.

"He's giving you a refund because he shouldn't have charged you in the first place. Aren't you, Pete?" Cannon is close by. I feel the heat radiating from his body from his workout, and a certain amount of oxygen leaves the space he enters.

I hold the fiver up between Pete and me and glance from Lincoln to the old man. I flatten it on the counter and slide it his way. "Take it off my tab. I'd like to get a monthly membership."

He gives me a sideways grin and slides the money toward him with a single finger.

"I'll bring the other forty-five when I come next time," I say.

He nods, pulling a clipboard up from behind the counter and tossing it down in front of me. A crumpled paper stuck to the top reads: ENROLLMENT FORM. He taps it with his finger, and I note the small tattoo above his knuckle, two small letters—G and F—faded in green.

"Put your info on here. I've got a fancy program that bills you so I don't have to handle cash. Something about taxes or some shit." He laughs, a little sinister, as if he's maybe gotten away with skipping taxes a few times in the past.

"Sure," I say, glancing up at him while pulling the paperwork and pen close to my body. I fill in my name and tap it with the ball point of the pen until he looks at it.

"Something wrong?" he asks.

"No, just want to make sure you take a good look at my name so you can commit it to memory and quit calling me *sweetheart.*" I raise a brow and leave my mouth flat and serious. A short laugh punches out of his chest, but he nods.

"I'll do my best," he says, eyeing the six-foot-plus guy standing next to me whom I have yet to completely acknowledge. I have mixed feelings after Friday. Cannon left our hitting session because Zack told him to, his mood suddenly changing to fit his cousin's stereotypical grudge. Then, when Zack turned our basketball game into a blatant and very public example of sexual harassment, Cannon just stood there. I don't expect knights on white horses; I'm not naïve. I do expect guys of my generation to be a little more enlightened. I remind myself, though, that Cannon hasn't walked in my shoes.

I fill the paper out and spin the clipboard around for Pete to take, but before he carries it off to head back to his chair—and the Packers—I stop him.

"Who's GF?" I gesture the pen I'm still holding toward his right hand. He turns his palm over and looks at his finger, his eyes getting lost for a breath before a tepid smile sinks into his mouth, rounding his cheeks.

"Gini Forenzi. Best damn cook this side of the Mississippi." He leaves his gaze on the fading initials then curls his hand into a fist, almost as if to hold on to them and keep them around a little longer. He knocks on the countertop with the same hand, and I can tell that's the end of that conversation.

My hope that Cannon has moved back to the weights is extinguished the moment I turn around. Hands in the pockets of his black shorts, his white T-shirt soaked with sweat, he jerks his head to the side to flip his curling hair from his eyes.

"Aren't you freezing in here?" It's the only question I feel like asking.

"Give it an hour, you'll be peeling layers off too." His voice carries over the volume on the TV and he looks toward the back of Pete's head. The old man promptly grips a remote and raises the sound a few more notches.

"My place, my thermostat. You don't like it, get your own gym," he grumbles.

My eyes widen and I can't help but laugh as I look back to Cannon. He shrugs at the response.

"Pete lives upstairs, and he keeps things . . . *warm.*"

Warm. Yes, that's the word for what I'm feeling right now. It has nothing to do with Pete and his thermostat, though. My stomach feels the same way it does when I take sips of my father's whiskey on holidays. I'm on shaky ground, and I'm not sure why. I think it's because I want to let Cannon off the hook, but after spending the last forty-eight hours renewing my bad impression of him, it's hard to flip back again.

"You wanna spot me?" He backs away toward the bench he has set up, and at a quick assessment, it looks as though he's lifting about two-twenty-five.

"Sure." I shrug, that line I drew over the weekend blurring with my first step toward him.

He straddles the bench, pulling up the legs of his shorts as he sits, and it's impossible not to gawk at his thick, defined quads. He might be right about the heat in here. I already regret the long-sleeved tee. I push the sleeves up and move into position at the bar while he leans back, resting his head in front of my knees. His hair flops back and if I were in shorts, it would tickle me.

I left without a hair band, so I stuff my hair into the neck of my shirt to keep it out of my face. When I look down and meet Cannon's waiting gaze, I notice the amusement threatening to break his lips into a chuckle.

"What?" My New York accent is thick tonight.

"You are always tying your hair in literal knots. Why do you even have it long?"

I blow at a stray lock that's already fallen over my face, and it's enough to pull out the laugh he's been holding on to.

"You make a good point, Jennings," I say, pushing the rogue hairs back into my collar, then tugging the neck of my shirt forward to keep them locked behind me for a few extra seconds. I hope.

I wrap my hands around the center of the bar while he places his on the outsides, making eye contact with me when he's comfortable. He nods and blows out, and suddenly I notice his lips. Full, a maroon red brought out by the blend of the cold air outside and the oven Pete's made inside. His cheeks are rosy, and there's a faint trace of stubble along his jawline. I don't think he could quite grow a beard, but for some reason, I imagine a version of him ten years from now that has one.

With a hard upward thrust, Cannon brings me back to the present, pushing the bar from his chest with a grunt. My fingers remain loose but poised, ready to help. Nobody at Xavier ever lifted this much weight. My dad lifts this much. *Sometimes.*

His pace is unflinching, the bar lowering with ease, rising with an equal push every time. He doesn't struggle until the end of his fifth rep, and even then, he only needs a little verbal encouragement from me.

"You got this. This is nothing for you, come on!" I boost. His eyes flit to mine while he holds his breath, his pupils a deep black from the effort, the ring of blue around them practically glowing, as if he's more machine than man. Perhaps he is, because when he reaches the top, he leaves his eyes on mine as he grunts out, "Again!"

I hold his intense stare, gauging his command, rooting out whether he's simply showing off for me or working to improve . . . *for him.*

I nod when I realize he's going to do this no matter what my response is, and I tighten my hold on the bar, not wanting him to injure himself on my watch. The bar falls more easily this time, his resistance weakened, and as it bounces off his chest, his drained power becomes evident.

"Come on!" he shouts at himself. I help with the lift just enough to give him an edge, his left arm stronger than his right; most of my work is to keep the bar level.

"Almost there," I say, even though he's only a quarter in to the return.

"Come on, push!" His eyes lock on mine again with my shout, and the doubt clears away behind them. He growls as his grip tightens, my hands sliding toward his, holding his fingers in place, not so much lifting as guiding him up. The muscles and tendons on his forearms and biceps roll in waves, working in unison to pass this hurdle. The moment the bar rolls back onto the rack, a hard breath rushes from his mouth, puffing his cheeks before his arms fall limp at his sides.

The smile that stretches his maroon lips is instant, and so very wide. Dimples mark both cheeks and the rush of blood comes back into his face as laughter billows in his throat and through his mouth in apparent relief.

"God*damn*, that was hard," he admits.

My hands are still on the bar as I stare down at him, my hair no longer obeying where I put it, instead sticking to my neck and face. I barely did any work and I'm sweating. Cannon was right, but it's the feel of his hands underneath mine, trusting mine, working *with* mine, that makes me rush with heat.

I suddenly need distance between us. I fall back a few steps to another bench, sitting down to pull my long-sleeved shirt over my head, and wiping away the sweat from my neck and forehead. I'm in my sports bra, which is never weird for me, and usually isn't a big deal for other guys in gyms. But my bare arms and midriff are Cannon's primary focus as he stares at me upside down, his head tilted up and his hair falling from the end of the bench while he stares at me from his lying position.

Leaning back, I place my palms on the bench behind me and stretch a little, fully aware of what this position does to my breasts and stomach. I'm basically a peacock right now, tits for feathers. I'm not a Victoria Secret model, my size modest, but B-cups pronounced from my muscle can draw attention. I've never really wanted someone to look. It's antithetical to what I preach. Fuck hypocrisy, though, because this is the first time since our kiss that Cannon Jennings has looked at me and licked his lips.

"You wanna go next?" He asks the question while still meeting my gaze from upside down. It's somehow easier to look him in the eyes this way.

I nod and get up just as he does. We cross paths, our arms brushing as we pass and he moves to stand at the bar while I position myself on my back, feet flat on the ground and my eyes fighting not to look past the bar and into his. I focus on my hands while shifting my butt on the bench until my lower back finds comfort. I test my grip while Cannon removes most of the weight. He's about to take another twenty-five plate off when I stop him.

"I can do that," I say. It's my max. It took me all summer to get up to one-twenty-five, and I was stubborn about it. I can tell Cannon has reservations by the way his gaze sticks to mine, his head slightly angled. His doubt fuels me.

"I said I can do that, so let's go, pitcher boy." He flinches at my tease but shakes his head while smiling.

"Pretty sure in the short time I've known you I've learned when I can and can't tell you to do things," he mutters.

"And that would be never. You can never tell me what to do," I respond, my mouth a tight, serious line for exactly two seconds before I let my laugh break through.

"I'm pretty sure you're not joking about that." He winces in one eye and smiles crooked. I nod toward the bar and try my damnedest to focus on this heavy-ass weight I'm about to lift up from my chest.

"Alright, Staten Island girl, show me what you got!" His encouragement is genuine, and it's enough to get me through the first thrust, lifting the bar off the rack and into position above my chest. Now comes the hard part.

I flit my gaze to his in a brief panic, and his grip tightens on the bar as he senses I need more help than I let on. He doesn't bail me out, though, which I appreciate. He's going to make me follow through with this.

"Come on. First one; we can get to three," he says, his voice low as he bends forward and speaks at me.

"Four," I grunt back. I can feel his assistance, his hold taking enough of the weight off for me not to crush my ribs, and as I let the bar hit my chest, I'm able to rebound it back up. I grit my teeth and tense my jaw so much that I feel the strain in the sides of my neck as my hands wobble their way back toward him, my elbows locking at the top.

"Okay, that was one. Let's get to three and then we can negotiate that fourth one, deal?" He lifts one eyebrow and I try to laugh. My exertion only allows me a quick nod, though.

"Fine," I bark out.

He chuckles and shakes his head, guiding my hands back down as I work on the second rep. Determined not to get weaker, I groan loudly, the same way my dad does when he maxes out, and the air in my lungs buoys me enough to finish the second rep with a little more energy. Not wanting to lose it, I nod at him to go right into the third. My muscles burn, and sweat glistens on my arms. It's the middle of winter in Indiana but I am burning up.

"You got this," Cannon chants.

His voice invades my head and I take my eyes away from my hands for just a blip. His eyes are focused on my hands, on the bar that is too heavy for me at this point but that he believes I can move. He nods, but our gazes don't quite meet. I'm glad because if they did, I might drop everything.

Lost in his blues, I blow out hard as the weight lands against my breasts. This exercise is so much harder for women. I can't imagine men lifting weights precariously over their balls. It wouldn't happen. I push and grind and my elbows are tingling by the time I straighten them again, arms locked and spent. I don't let go of my grip, though. I don't let the flex slip away either, because now is the time to negotiate. A small part of me wants Cannon to insist and give me permission to not walk the walk I so carelessly talked. But that is not his style. Yet one more thing for the list.

"You ready for this fourth one?" His eyes shift just enough to meet mine, and I can read the challenge in them. It's different than the taunting way his cousin stares at me, or the way parents at Xavier looked on when I took the field. Cannon is looking at me as though he legitimately believes I can do this.

I nod again and pant out a "Yes" as together we bring the bar back down to my body. Cannon helps way more this time, taking a good twenty-percent of the weight for me by the time I reach my chest. The way up is a different story.

"Time to battle," he coaches, easing up so I feel the struggle.

His assistance isn't gone, but he isn't helping me at the same level he did the first three reps. This time, my arms have little to give, so I dig in with my feet and crush the arch of my back against the bench for every extra little ounce of leverage I can get. I start to cry out as the bar falls to one side then the other. Each time, Cannon gives me a nudge back to balanced, continually uttering encouragement.

"You're so close. It's almost there. One more . . . just one more push." He takes over when I'm about an inch from getting the bar back on the rack, and the moment my arms are free, I let them dangle to my sides as relief and pride flush my body.

Cannon claps a single clap and brings his closed palms up to his lips, hiding his grin.

"I can do that," I say, echoing my proclamation from minutes before. My lips a lazy, open-mouthed smile, I say it again, my eyes meeting Cannon's as he backs away a few steps. "I can do that."

"You just *did* that," he corrects.

His cheeks dimple with his closed-mouth smile, and I cash that expression in as mine—I earned those dimples. Still a little breathless, and hot as hell, I maintain our stare until it becomes uncomfortable. Cannon is the first to look away, glancing down at his feet as he shuffles back until his shoulders touch the wall.

I swivel my legs around the bench as I sit up, straddling it and facing the other direction so we're now looking at one another. His stoic armor slips as his focus moves from my face to my neck, then to my bare midriff. When he looks me in the eyes again, he sees he's caught and rubs his palm over his chin as he lets out a bashful laugh.

"I like the belly button ring," he says, gesturing lazily at my stomach. I tuck my chin to my chest and stretch my skin.

"Oh, yeah. I forget I have it sometimes." I shrug when I look back up at him and he gives a slight shake to his head, breathing out across his faint smile.

"What?" I press.

His eyes dip to my stomach again and his lips part, his expression a little more predatory, definitely interested. I allow myself a glance toward his stomach, and then lower. Training shorts don't mask much, and Cannon is definitely into belly button rings.

I flick my finger against the metal to get his attention, but he doesn't waver, his gaze still on my bare skin, soaking me in like a boy told not to eat desert before dinner.

"I didn't plan on working out." I tap the bottom of my pink boots against the concrete floor a few times, drawing Cannon's stare there instead. He tilts his head back with a short laugh.

"That's a first. Pretty sure Pete's never had anyone lifting in princess gear before!" He lets his hands fall into his pockets as he shifts his weight against the wall, crossing his feet at the ankles.

I lift my toes to gaze at the glitter accents on the knitting, and smirk.

"My little brother bought these for me as a joke because me and pink aren't really a thing. Turns out though . . ." I draw my legs up and fold them on the bench, sitting so my hands can hold on to the tops of my feet. "I really love these things."

I gaze up at Cannon with a cheesy grin and he pushes away from the wall, nodding at my shoes. "They're pretty dope."

I wait for him to pass, irrationally pleased that he approves of my girly footwear. He's taking down the weights from my bar, so I stand and help him. We work wordlessly for a few minutes, leaving things nice by the rack before moving on to free weights. I kick the tire I saw him flipping when I first visited the gym.

"I'd like to try this sometime," I say.

He finds a good spot to stand for his bicep curls then glances from the tire to me and back again. "Shouldn't be a problem for you," he says, sizing me up like an equal. As he begins lifting, I stand by and watch for a few minutes, letting myself live this moment. I'm always either the cool teammate or the girl some boy who has no interest in team sports is into. Other than Jordan, guys in my game don't want to cross boundaries, and my relationship with my ex was living proof of what a disaster it is to blur the lines. But maybe . . . maybe I can be both the kinda girl you kiss at a party *and* the kind you throw with on the diamond.

Lost in this blissful fantasy, I set my feet up a few feet from Cannon, facing the wall-length mirrors as I begin my reps. My weights are about half the size of his, and my biceps are definitely not in the same league, but I keep pace, doing the same number of reps and resting in sync with him. We're about to begin our third sets when his eyes finally find mine in our reflection. He studies me while his arms begin their work.

"Hey, about Friday." He starts a conversation, maybe hoping I'll take it over and navigate the rough waters. What he doesn't get, though, is that this is a conversation I don't want to have. He's in the boat alone.

"Don't." My response is swift and clipped, forming instant ice. "It . . . It's fine." *Not fine.*

The awkward silence seeps back in, and my motivation to lift weights—to even be here—wanes. Butterflies are gone, replaced by lead and rocks that sit heavy in my gut.

"It's just that Zack . . ."

I let my arms fall, heavy with the weights, and look up at Pete's cobweb-covered ceiling tiles.

"Please, just don't," I grumble.

I roll my head to the side, eyes meeting his. He's grimacing as if embarrassed of his cousin, but Zack isn't his job. Cannon is responsible for Cannon.

"It's usually a boys' club out there . . ." He trails off, because there's no great way to finish that statement.

"Except for the girls who sit around and stare at you guys with awe like you're gods. Bare-chested gods." That was smug. My chest is getting tight. This happens when I get frustrated and conflicted. I'm not a very pretty angry person.

"Come on, that's not fair. So what that some of the girls like to hang out and watch us? So what if our shirts are off? And so what if, you know what? Some of us like the attention, and some of them like to give it to us. Fuck, Hollis. You need to seriously loosen up. Not everything is a protest for women's equality. And you can take your shirt off too, ya know. No rules against that out there." He rolls his eyes, a sneer to his lips as he turns away. He's proud of himself, and that tightness in my chest is close to suffocating. The only relief will be letting it burst.

Cannon dumps his weights on the rack and I follow a step behind, dumping mine right next to his. He huffs and moves them to the right place, which is actually a nice thing to do but the way he does it ticks me off, so I groan, balling my fists at my sides.

"Why did you have to ruin this?" I lament.

"Ruin what, Hollis? I was just trying to talk to you, about Zack and what he did—"

"You were making an excuse for him," I cut in, leveling him with the truth.

His mouth opens but promptly shuts. His eyes shift their focus from my right one to my left, his mind working behind them. I pat my closed fist against my hip, antsy and unsure whether I should wait for him to speak or get this weight off my chest.

"I swear, Hollis, I'm not making excuses for him. He was . . . not cool. Friday was not cool," he says, and I instantly regret letting him go first.

I laugh out and look up again, my jaw slack and my spirit dashed. How can I be so attracted to a guy who I also want throttle until he understands what it's like to be a girl in this world?

My head falls forward and I nod, a pathetic laugh drifting through my parted lips, the faint smile I'm wearing only there to mask that I'm nowhere near happy or really amused.

"You're right, Cannon. Way to sum that all up. Zack was not cool. And perhaps *Friday* was not cool either. That's what happened. Not cool," I rattle off, laughing a little more with every word I breathe because this is so ridiculous. I should have stayed home and tried to paint my dad's nails while he slept or put popcorn in his nostrils.

"You don't make this easy," he finally breaks in. His words stop me cold, my mouth closing while I stare, unblinking, at the space to the right of him, unable to bring my eyes to him fully.

"*I* don't make this easy," I rephrase. I just want him to hear it, in my tongue.

Crossing my line of sight with a heavy sigh, he grabs what must be his towel from a weight rack and slaps it against the metal with one hand. I'm no longer warm in this room. My bones are cold, my skin covered in bumps. Things got cold in here real fast.

"You just stood there, Cannon. Seems you decided to take it easy. I don't make it anything," I say.

He rolls his neck before balling the towel up and throwing it on top of his gym bag in the corner. I recognize his stuff from last time, bag unzipped with his clothes and phone inside. My eyes dart to the place where the towel now rests on top of his slides and sweat pants.

"Your cousin doesn't like me, because . . ." I shrug, not having to say it; we both know. I'm a threat. Short and sweet, very simple. "And he chose to deal with his dislike by demeaning me in front of others, by sexualizing me to point out that I am different from the rest of you. That he has a power I could never have, and that makes me weak and him strong."

"Hollis." The way he says my name and lets his head tilt makes my stomach churn, and not because of the belittling tone underneath, but because for a little while there, I had fantasies of him tilting his head and saying my name for wholly different reasons.

My eyes flutter closed as he speaks the rest, the words I saw coming.

"You're overreacting. It was hardly a statement. He just slapped your . . ."

The fact he can't finish tells me he knows he's wrong, that his line is bullshit. I open my eyes and point at him, wishing I could handle getting close enough to push into the center of his chest. My legs are lead, though. Most of me doesn't want to be near him.

"And you stood there and let him get away with it." I hold his gaze for several long, uncomfortable seconds, long enough for my legs to regain their feeling. I stay locked on his face while I move back toward the benches, to my abandoned long-sleeved tee that I want to crawl inside of and disappear into. Too mad to stick around to put it back on, I instead grab it, glaring at Cannon until I have to crane my neck to do so. I let my anger spill out onto Pete as I pass, knocking on his counter while I walk by and check the score as I utter, "Suck it, Green Bay." That wasn't fair, but I don't like being prodded into uncomfortable conversations. I knew I wasn't ready to talk about Friday, and especially not with Cannon.

His cousin may have felt threatened before, but he has no idea what's gunning for him now. I'm not going to make this look close anymore, and I won't offer advice. I'm going to humiliate him out there at workouts, and when tryouts come in two weeks, I'll make it hard for my dad to justify keeping him on the roster at all. And if Cannon can't throw what I need him to, then he's next. It won't be me calling in a favor from Daddy, either. It will be me showing everyone the difference between serious talent and a bunch of boys playing a game.

NINE

CANNON

She was right, righter than she even realizes.

It's Monday morning and I have yet to call my cousin out on acting like a douchebag. Not only did I stand there and watch him belittle her, but I'm still standing by and doing nothing. I thought about it all night, and it's still heavy on my mind now that I'm sitting across the table from him, watching him slurp up oatmeal like a kid still learning how to use utensils.

"Tryouts in two weeks. Who's ready?" Uncle Joel lands his heavy palms on Zack's shoulders and my cousin abruptly drops his spoon. The weight is both literal and psychological.

"We should have a pretty good team," I say, not wanting to give away too many details. I'm not sure what Uncle Joel knows beyond Coach Taylor has a daughter playing. My uncle joined the board recently, probably to have leverage. I don't think my cousin has been totally forthcoming about his insecurities, though, and I sure as shit ain't going to expose them over breakfast.

"They got you throwing to Zack?" He squeezes my cousin's shoulders when he asks that question, and his eyes grill mine from across the table.

"Got me throwing to everybody," I say. It's not a lie, and it's enough to pull a chuckle from my uncle's mouth while I leave the table with my bowl and empty glass to find solace at the sink with my back turned to them.

"Rumor is coach's daughter isn't awful. How 'bout that?" He's baiting Zack. I can tell. He knows more than he's admitting.

"She's all right," my cousin says. His chair screeches along the floor behind me, so I move out of his way at the sink, anticipating him. Our eyes meet briefly at the dishwasher, and a silent agreement passes between us.

Mouths. Shut.

"You throw to her at all yet, Cannon?" Now he's baiting me. I don't like it. This isn't how things work between my dad and me. We say what we mean and don't equivocate. It's a blunt and honest relationship that has never led to fights or distrust, and I'm sad that my cousin doesn't get to have the same thing.

"Eh, a little," I say with a shrug. I don't make eye contact with him on purpose, and his enduring silence gives me the sense that he knows why I'm not looking at him.

My backpack is near the stairs, so I move over to it and unzip and rezip the top for no reason other than to bide time while Zack catches up to me.

"Well, maybe I'll stop in and check out the lay of the land today. I've got a free afternoon," my uncle says.

My cousin's eyes close as he exhales next to me.

"Sounds good. We gotta go," Zack responds, keeping the keys in his palm this time and jetting right toward the front door. I lag behind, and my pulse actually races with fear that my uncle will try to pull one more piece of intel out of me before I can get away. I breathe out in relief at the sound of the door falling closed behind me.

"Take it you wanna drive this morning?" I meet his eyes over the roof of the car.

He nods, getting in without pause and firing up the engine before I have a chance to shut my door. We don't talk most of the way to school, but I can tell he's stewing.

"I think I'm throwing to you today," I finally speak.

"Uh huh." Zack's response is clipped.

It's bullshit, and we both know it. I have no idea who I'm throwing to. I only know that I threw with Hollis on Thursday and Coach likes to rotate us.

"Workouts are pretty regimented anyhow. There's not a lot to see, so your dad will probably get bored and leave in the first ten minutes." I don't know why I'm hell-bent on easing his anxiety, especially since I'm embarrassed for him after Friday's basketball incident. And he clearly isn't interested in anything I have to say this morning.

The car hits the dip into the school lot forcefully and I have to palm the dash to steady myself. Zack's driving like an ass.

"Fuck, dude. Easy," I finally grit out.

"*Pfft*," he breathes.

I sink into my seat and focus out my window on anything that isn't my cousin. When I see Hollis and her dad pull around to the back of the school in their van, I make a silent wish that Zack missed it. I'm not ready for him to launch into some snide remark about how nice it must be to live with Coach and get rides to school with him. I won't be able to indulge his grudge if he tests me right now.

Luckily, he's not in the mood to talk. We pull into our spot and he leaves the car before I unbuckle. I laugh quietly to myself as he stomps through the main doors and disappears, probably getting to class earlier than he ever has in his entire life. Turning my attention to the front, my gaze meets Tory's and he nods, leaving our group of friends and walking toward my side of the car. I kick open the door just as he steps up.

"Hey, man. I see Zack is still on his one-man douchebag mission," Tory says, pulling a short laugh from me as we slap hands. I shift in the seat while he folds his arms over the window frame on the door and glances around the lot.

"That was pretty fucked up, yo," Tory says, and I know he's talking about Friday.

"Yeah." I sigh. I don't have much to add because his synopsis captured Friday to a tee. *Fucked. Up.*

"This is about him, just so you know," Tory says, and I turn to look him in the eyes. "Don't get caught up in it and think you have to do whatever he does or defend him. I've learned a lot of things this last year, and key is knowing how to take care of your own shit. Don't get yourself neck deep in his to the point you drown in your own."

"Colorful," I say, chuckling.

"Yeah, well." He shrugs, opening my door fully while I grab my bag from the floor and step out of the car.

We hang close, Tory probably sensing that I'm not ready to talk about Zack's shit with a full group. It would be impossible for people not to bring it up. I'm surprised his ass slap isn't trending on social media. For Hollis's sake, I'm glad it's not.

Hollis.

I've been so caught up in my morning that for a brief bit I forgot I have to sit three feet from her in about ten minutes. I spent most of the night tossing and turning, playing out how this morning would go. I tried out jokes and flat-out apologies. Every scenario I imagined ended in her telling me to fuck off. Maybe I should just get that over with and say it before she has a chance to.

"See? That's how it starts," Tory says, pulling me out of my head.

"What?" I ask.

"You, taking on your cousin's shit. You're trying to work it out. I can read it all over your face."

"*Pshh*, nah. That's not it." I push away from our car and wander closer to the main doors. Tory tags along, waving off his brother who's hanging out with the girls.

"Spill," Tory says when we're far enough away from everyone for there to be no ears around to hear.

I wrinkle my face, a little in self-disgust but mostly because talking about things in my head with anyone but my dad isn't something I do. And even with my dad, it's mostly school, college, or baseball talk.

"My first hour is with Hollis. Think you can pretend to be my uncle and call me in sick?" I lift a brow at him, half serious about my request.

Tory's shoulders lift with his laugh.

"That's what happens when you kiss a total stranger. Things get messy." He pulls the tab on his energy drink and sucks down half of it, peering at me over the can.

My eyes narrow.

"How'd you know about that?" I query.

He pulls the can away and belches while shrugging.

"Saw you through the window." He holds his can out for me, and I take a shot of caffeine. I'm going to need a jolt of something to get through this.

"Yeah, well, that's only half the reason this is all so complicated. I'm not sure I can avoid drowning in Zack's shit because we have the same mess. Our issues bleed together, and then our dads are involved, and his is on the board for the booster club, and then . . ."

"I'm gonna stop you here," Tory says, hand on my shoulder with a heavy pat. "All that you just said?" He circles his finger in the air between us. "None of that means anything to me, or makes sense. But I can almost guarantee that you and Zack are not in the same shoes. You're making his problems yours, and that is only going to fuck with your head, my friend."

He flicks my forehead with a snap, and it hurts.

"Ow! Dick," I say, swiping at his hand but missing it. He laughs, then finishes the rest of his drink, tossing the can in the recycle bin by the office.

Our friends catch up to us, and June makes her way next to me. The bell is seconds from rescuing me, but it's as if she has it under her control and won't let it ring until she invades my head and space.

"How are you?" I'm immediately thrown by her sincere question and my brow puzzles. I was prepared for a lecture, part two of the things Hollis said to me at the gym last night.

"I'm . . . fine," I say, turning my head further and looking at her sideways. She doesn't budge, her eyes slanting more, and her stare unforgiving. She's a high school senior with mom powers; I swear she's looking right through me.

"I don't know," I finally give.

June loops her arm through mine and squeezes my bicep. She and I aren't close, not really, but she's always struck me as soft and kind. I can see why Lucas loves her. She's . . . *intuitive.*

"Nobody blames you," she finally says, the bell sounding behind her words.

My forehead dents as we move through the corridor, but not because I don't understand what she means. I understand perfectly. What hits me is the way she cut right to the heart of my stress. They don't blame me, but there is one person who does. And she's already sitting in her seat by the time I make it to my classroom door.

I'm a little shell shocked by the time I land in my seat, and I dump my bag by my feet and let my forehead fall into my palms. Rubbing my eyes, I ready myself for the hard part—*the hardest, really.*

My hair curly from my morning shower, I roll my head to the side in my hands and wait, staring on while Hollis busies herself with dozens of little tasks that I recognize as diversions, ways to keep herself from looking at me. Finally, the heat of my attention too much perhaps, she flattens her pen against her notebook and presses her palms on her desk, splaying her fingers out while she draws in a deep breath.

Her head turns and our eyes meet. Mine were waiting. Before she can open her mouth to keep this grudge going, I end it.

"I'm sorry."

Her lips are parted, the path her words were on suddenly diverted with something so simple. An apology. One she deserves from more than only me for sure, but one I owe her. And the only one I have the power to give.

My lips tighten in a subtle smile as I lock in anything else that might slip out on accident. There aren't any *buts* that need to be added. No excuses to make for people who aren't me. As Tory said, I'm taking care of my own shit.

She blinks a few times, hesitantly staring back.

"That's it. No excuses. I'm sorry, and you are right," I expand. The class quiets around us, and Mr. V dims the lights, flicking on the screen up front. He's giving instructions but I'm not listening. I'm determined not to look away from her until she gives me permission, even if it isn't full absolution.

Hollis clears her throat as she shifts in her seat, bringing her hands together on top of her notebook and moving her gaze to her own hands. She taps her thumbs together a few times and flits her gaze to me a few times, as if coming to a decision. I feel a bit as if I'm on trial with a super biased jury.

Leaning to her right, she glances first up to the monitor and our teacher, then to the floor, where her backpack rests beside her leg. Tugging on the top zipper, she reaches in, feeling around for something, her eyes remaining up front—always the perfect student. The scene makes me smile, even if I feel a bit shunned. She straightens again, a pack of gum cupped in her palm. She works it open in her lap and pulls out a stick, unwrapping it without looking and popping it in her mouth. She turns to me mid-chew, one eyebrow raised and holds the pack out for me.

"Gum?" she asks.

I breathe out a quiet laugh and shift my focus from the pack back to her, studying her eyes and her features for a second or two.

"Sure," I respond, reaching over and pulling out the piece on top. Her gaze sticks to mine through it all, as I unwrap the stick while staring back at her, and even while I pop it in my mouth and begin to chew. I smile with closed lips when the gum goes soft, and she does the same, our jaws in sync as they work slowly.

"Thanks," I whisper.

She responds with a slow blink, her lashes dusting the tops of her cheeks while her mouth curves up into them.

That's all it took. My chest is open, and I can breathe. Hollis is as comfortable with saying I'm forgiven as I was apologizing, and a stick of gum is her olive branch. Now, if only this feeling can stick all the way through practice. Somehow, I'm doubtful.

My relief is short-lived. By the time Zack and I make it to the track to get our laps in, Uncle Joel already stands in the middle of the field next to

Coach. I'm not sure which I want more—super powers that let me listen in from a distance, or to never know what they're saying. Zack probably feels the same.

We hit the track at the same time, and even though I finish before him, he's not far behind. I turn to congratulate him with a raised hand as we walk back to our gear, but his eyes are fixed on his father so I let it fall to my side.

Zack slings his heavy catchers' bag over his shoulder, not bothering to roll it. I'm not sure whether it's an act of showing off how strong he is, even after a run, or if he's so angry about his dad showing up that his veins are pumping super-human blood.

"Hey, it's gonna be fine," I say at his back. He's not waiting for me, but I get it.

He turns his head to the side, his eyes not fully reaching me as he nods. I slow my steps and let him gain some distance, maybe subconsciously wanting him to seem more dedicated than me, like he has hustle. By the time I reach the dugout, he's already fastened on his leg guards and is jogging out on the field to stretch with Hollis and the other catchers. I let my gaze wander toward Uncle Joel while I switch out my shoes, glancing up and peeking from under the brim of my hat. He's intently watching his son, arms crossed, while he remains stoic at Coach Taylor's side.

Nothing about this is good for anyone. Coaches aren't interested in parental opinions, but because Joel is who he is, and because he has a say in hiring and firing and funding this program, Hollis's dad entertains the conversation. His sunglasses shield his eyes, but I can read enough into the hard line of his mouth to know he hates every minute of this forced conversation.

No longer able to stall, I grab my glove and kick my gear bag into the corner before jogging out to stretch with the other pitchers. I catch the end of Joel and Coach's talk as I run by.

"Lots of talent, like you said, Coach," Joel says just before putting a hand on Coach's shoulder, somewhere between a friendly pat on the back and an intimidating intrusion of his personal space. "But hey, I know you'll make the right choice."

"The *best* choice," Hollis's dad adds as he draws his lips in for a tight smile. There's an *F-U* behind those lips, and Joel knows it. I glance away before I'm caught staring, but listen to the end.

"Of course. But we all know who the best is," Joel closes with, walking backward in my periphery. I shut my eyes, wincing through my last few steps until I join the rest of my teammates.

That weight I cleared out with Hollis this morning has been replaced by something heavier that takes up every inch of space inside. I feel as though my arms can't move independent of my gut, my pulse controls the pace of my legs, and my head is going to either deflate or pop without warning.

Somehow, I get through my stretches without bending over to vomit, and I remind myself to breathe, hearing Tory and June's advice in my head. I'm in charge of me, and Zack's shit is his. Only, I'm living with all of this, and his dad and my dad, and Zack—*family*—is the whole reason I'm here in the first place. Lines are hard to draw, and while I get what Tory meant, I don't think he understands how tangled everything is when it comes to this season—this team. Maybe I did get Hollis's forgiveness today, but if I can't walk this line just right, I'll end up betraying my family, and that apology will require a lot more than a pact made over some Doublemint.

"Jennings!"

I turn to answer the same time Zack does, both of us responding with, "Yes, Coach" from either end of the field. Coach Taylor lifts his hand and pinches the bridge of his nose just under his glasses.

"Sorry, I keep forgetting. Cannon," he says, gesturing for me to rush over.

I pick up my glove and do as asked, noting that my cousin watches my every move while finishing his stretches.

"I'm gonna have you throw to Hollis today," he says the moment I step up to him.

My mouth goes dry. My uncle is pacing around the dugout just beyond his shoulder.

I squint from the sun as I look at him. It's bright as fuck out today, the sky filled with puffy white clouds. I never wear glasses, though. I don't like the feeling of anything on me when I'm throwing. Extra swag is always a distraction. If I could get away with ditching the cap, I would.

"You sure about that, Coach?" I question. I know immediately that he's sure, and that I should shut my damn mouth, but that sick feeling taking over my insides made me ask.

He doesn't respond with words, only a look, one I have to read through the sheen of his Oakleys.

"Right, okay." I nod and head toward the bullpen. I get about ten steps into my jog when Coach stops me.

"We're on the mound today."

I pause mid-step and spin on my right foot, coming back toward him. He's making a point, and I'm part of the performance. There are seven of us out here who can throw, and at least three who are going somewhere after this year. He could have led with any duo, but he chose me and Hollis on purpose. I'm the best, but Roland or Jay would have been great choices for this exhibition. *Jay has a better curveball!*

My inner-dialogue continues on a constant stream while Coach calls Hollis out and points to the plate. She rushes into the dugout to grab her mask and chest protector while I kick at the rubber and push the dirt exactly the way I like it. She has no idea that Zack's dad is the weird guy wearing the crisp white dress shirt and deep blue tie hovering around the bench while she gets dressed. She doesn't even glance his direction despite the fact he is practically memorizing everything about her with that judgmental stare.

It's then that I realize exactly why Uncle Joel is out here. *Someone said something.*

I know it wasn't Zack. He was hoping to just win the starting job and have this never be an issue. Too late for that, though. It's the only issue in Joel's sights. My uncle rubs his chin, looking on while Hollis rushes into place, shaking dirt from her mask before pulling it over her head and face. She pats her glove a few times to tell me she's ready, and I circle the mound, stepping up a few feet behind the rubber to do some warm-up tosses while she stands.

I shoot a glance at my uncle before throwing. His arms are crossed firmly over his chest and he's chewing at the inside of his mouth. It's an old habit from his playing days when a wad of tobacco was always tucked inside his lip.

There's no way out other than marching off this field in protest or quitting to go play tennis, a sport I absolutely suck at, so I shuffle step toward Hollis and throw the ball. It hits her glove and creates a poof of dust before she pulls it free and sends it back to me on a zipline. I sneak another look in my uncle's direction while I set my feet again and note how sunk in his cheek is. He's chewing on it harder. He was hoping the rumors weren't true, but it's hard not to see that Hollis is the real deal.

She's not only good, she's *better.*

She and I continue our warmups until the rest of the team moves into the dugout, displacing Uncle Joel. He moves behind the backstop, just over Hollis's right shoulder, and takes a seat in the bleachers, his tie blowing across his body with the breeze. He has to be cold. Even with the sun and clouds reflecting the heat, it's maybe fifty out here. I'm wearing thermal compression pants and a long sleeves, and I feel the slight wind cut through the threads.

"Jennings," Coach shouts. This time I'm the only one who answers, Zack sitting on the bench with his water jug balanced on his knee. My cousin's eyes reach mine when I respond to our coach and the look of betrayal absolutely slays me.

"Yes?" I swallow, thankful I'm out here on the mound alone so no one can read the subtleties in my expression.

"Think you can handle three live batters? I'm looking to give you all three apiece today." He glances to his right where Jay and Roland stand waiting to go next.

I nod, choking down the bile.

"Sure," I say, dipping my chin and kicking the dirt out a little more to find my perfect fit.

I signal to Hollis that I'm ready to throw a few warm-up pitches for real, and she crouches down, ready to take them. We start with a few straight fastballs, and I easily hit her location. I shut out the sounds of players taking position behind me, ignoring my infielders throwing the ball a few feet away. I throw a change up and a curve next, one a little off target, forcing Hollis to drop to a knee to block it. The ball kicks away from her when she does, and she stands, jogging over to get it. I catch the pleased smirk on my uncle's face behind her, his shoulders shaking with laughter at the "silly girl trying to play a man's game."

Suddenly, I'm at another crossroads, not sure whether I want Hollis to shine or fail miserably. Maybe she'll be mediocre, and Zack will be a little *less* mediocre. There's no win in this situation.

"Johnson," Coach calls out. One of the guys I don't know well grabs a helmet and rushes out to the batter's box, the first unlucky supporting cast member in this play called *Get This Nosey-Ass Board Member Parent Off My Field.*

My guess is Johnson is a freshman, maybe a sophomore. His knees are quaking, and it's not only his pants blowing in the wind. Those suckers are skin tight. Hollis glances up at him then back to me, pounding her mitt before reaching down and giving me the sign for a two-seam right down the center.

I nod before winding up and rocketing the ball to her without as much as a blink from Johnson in the box. Hollis throws the ball right back to me while Johnson steps out and adjusts the Velcro on his gloves, as if that's what made him freeze and forget to swing.

I let myself be amused for a moment, also glad that this first batter is nothing special. Hollis handling my straight fastballs is meaningless. Hell, I could affix a glove to a folding chair for this, no catcher necessary. Nothing about this impresses my uncle, which means so far, my cousin is off the hook for having to prove anything in front of his dad.

It takes three pitches to strike Johnson out, and Coach forces the poor guy to stay up there and try to bunt for three more throws. He can't get a single one fair, though, so before my pitch count gets needlessly high, Coach lets him off the hook.

"Madden, you're up," he shouts, patting Johnson on the back as he runs by. If anyone is quitting to join the tennis team today, it might be him. Dude looks shell shocked.

Marcus Madden is another story. I know it, and so does Hollis. Marcus and I played fall ball out here together, along with Zack, which means Uncle Joel knows a thing or two about Marcus's swing. There are two guys who can put the ball over the fence if you're not careful, and Marcus is one of them.

As Marcus takes a few practice swings, my uncle sits up tall, rolling his shoulders and clasping his hands in front of him, elbows on his knees. He rubs his palms together greedily, and I can't help but imagine he's making a wish for one of those dingers right now. Either that or a harsh foul ball right into Hollis's head.

I grumble to myself, my voice a hum only I can hear, then step up on the rubber with my glove shadowing my chin while I look in for Hollis's signs. She asks for another straight fast ball, and I shake her off on instinct because I know better. Maybe I should let it go and get this over with, let Marcus round the bases and gloat. Hollis gives me the sign again and I suck in a hard breath, this time giving in.

"Fine," I mutter.

She moves her glove a few inches inside, crowding Marcus, which is smart, but maybe not pushing him tight enough. I wind up and let loose, both hoping it's enough and *just* enough at the same time. His swing is awkward, and the ball clips off the bat near his hands.

Coach whistles at me, and I turn as he tosses me a new ball. Hollis stands and kicks the other ball behind her before getting set for me to throw again. Her sign is exactly the same, and she sets up in the same spot. I'm tempted to shake her off, but after staring at her for a solid five seconds I decide, "What the hell."

I wind up again and throw the exact same pitch, getting the exact same result. This time Hollis scoops the foul tip and tosses the ball back to me in one smooth move. If this were a real game, I'd be gloating right about now. Ahead in the count, the clutch hitter one strike away. But it's not a game, and my uncle is now standing. So is my cousin.

My eyes shift to Coach but he keeps his gaze firmly affixed to the clipboard he's balancing on the dugout fence. This is his daughter's call, and he trusts her to make the right one.

"Give him hell, Madden," my uncle taunts from behind the plate. A few of the guys in the dugout lean forward to see who the obnoxious parent is. Coach glares in Joel's direction, the sun glinting off of his sunglasses as the tendons in his neck flex. I'd laugh my uncle off if he were actually doing this in jest, but he's not. The same ugly side his son has when he's challenged is coming out right now.

Hollis flashes me the sign for my slider while everyone else is occupied with Zack's dad. It's a smart call, and if I were on my own, it's what I'd want to throw. Marcus digs in with his palm out to me to give him time. While he's a good hitter, his ego is a bit much. During games, he can drag his at bat out with annoying rituals and time-outs. He's been warned by umps for being excessive, but knows there's nothing anyone can do about it. You hit the ball like he does, you can call time-out to paint your nails with glitter if you want and coaches won't care.

Once he's ready, I waste a few extra seconds staring from behind my glove just to eat at his nerves. He's lined up as if he's anticipating me going back inside. It's a gamble, but one he had to take. If I do, he'll be ready to punish me for it. But I'm not. My only task now will be not to miss.

I wind up and throw, my world switching into slow motion as my back leg swings around with my follow-through, my eyes up while my hand cuts through the air and skims along my shin. I get my glove up and ready, because I know better than to stand there defenseless. But there's no need; the ball cuts exactly where I want it to go, trailing away from Marcus as he swings through hard enough to lose his balance and land on one knee.

Hollis stands and pushes the mask up on her head, flashing me a proud grin that I can't help but mimic. My uncle catches it, too, so I let it drop as soon as she throws me the ball and shouts toward the dugout.

"Next!"

She stands there with her gloved hand on her hip, mask pulled up while wild strands of hair blow in the strengthening wind. They've come loose from what is probably an actual knot she tied with her hair under her helmet. Dirt lines her cheeks, darkened by sweat. And through it all, her blue eyes glitter like sapphires, the one beautiful thing she cannot cover up and hide no matter how hard she tries.

There's something exceptional about her, and I admit that to myself right now. She's not just beautiful, though goddamn is she. It's something more than that—this vibe she has that seems so invincible. While Marcus wears his confidence like an arrogant bastard, Hollis wears it like a queen, every jewel in her crown owned. All of the compliments in the world would be meaningless to her, though. All she cares about is her own expectations for herself. I wonder if she ever falls short like I do.

"Jennings."

The sound of my name shakes me from my trance and I shout, "Huh?" to my coach, only to realize that for once he means the other Jennings.

"Grab a helmet," Coach orders.

Zack stands dumbfounded for a beat, his body rigid like a deer's at the sound of a predator.

I blink.

"Well, go on," Coach barks, his East Coast accent suddenly thick over so few words.

I gulp as Zack rushes to grab his helmet, stuffing it on his head and slipping his bat from his bag. He rushes out toward the plate, forgetting that he still wears his leg guards, and Coach has to remind him by clearing his throat, then pointing at them.

"Oh, for Christ's sake," my uncle mutters, his volume loud enough that I hear him easily. I'm sure most of us did. I recognize the way Zack's jaw tightens and his lips come together in a tight seal. Uncle Joel was merciless when Zack struck out growing up, and as we get older, my cousin bottles his anger in and buries it under that same expression.

I feel trapped, so many outcomes possible in the next few minutes. Nobody knows what I can throw better than the guy at the plate. Zack and I have been apart for two years, but when we came back together, it was seamless. That is, until Hollis ripped things open. I stare into her eyes sixty feet away. She's squinting with thought, probably working out how we navigate this situation her dad purposefully put us in. She bangs her glove against her hip a few times to clear the dirt away then squats, glaring up at my cousin as he takes a few warm-up swings.

Zack is a solid hitter. If I throw anything near the plate without something wicked on it, he'll get a piece of it. And maybe that's what should happen. Maybe I throw for a duel, several pitches wasted, so no matter who comes out of this as the winner, really, we both do. But something tells me Coach Taylor has a nose for bullshit play. He'll see right through it, and do I really want to be *soft?* This is too important for me, but if I humiliate Zack, his world will be crushed, and I can't live with that either.

He creeps into the batter's box, digging his heavy feet into the loose dirt and twisting on his toes. This guy has had the same swing for years, and it's dramatic and filled with all the little mannerisms he's grown up watching the pros do on TV. Uncle Joel eats it up.

"Come on, son!" My uncle claps three times before hooking his fingers into the backstop. He won't be sitting down.

Hollis signals for a fast ball, then sets up low and outside. She's right. My cousin has trouble hitting the outside pitches because of his wannabe-pro-style swing. He's too far from the plate, which makes him vulnerable. I nod, knowing it's the right thing to do for me, but it's going to make Zack look foolish.

I wind up and send the ball flying at Hollis with my usual amount of pepper, but I miss her spot, giving Zack just enough to foul off and please his dad.

"Atta boy. Come on, show him what you've been working on for two years!" My uncle cups his hands to clap this time, amplifying the slapping sound. It's his way of boasting.

Hollis stands and tosses the ball back to me after sliding her mask up on her head. She holds a palm out along with her open mitt. There's a stink on her face, a sourness that has her lips sneering while her nose scrunches up. We've thrown enough together for her to know when I miss my spot on purpose. Damn her father for putting me in this situation. I know he's trying to prove a point to my uncle, but I'm the one feeling the stress.

I turn and kick at the rubber to ignore her stare, though I swear I feel the heat of it in my back. The smart move is to throw my slider, because that pitch starts out looking like the perfect strike then veers right into my cousin's dead zone. Hollis must be in my head because that's exactly what she calls. I breathe in through my nose and pause for a few seconds before shaking her off. Instead of calling a different pitch, though, she gives me the sign again. I shake my head one more time. Any pitch but this one. It will make Zack look stupid. I've gotten so much better at it over the last two years, and he hasn't seen it enough to know it's coming.

Hollis drops her chin, eyes on the plate and her glove hanging limp on her hand. She snaps her head up again to meet my stare while I remain hidden behind my glove. I wish it were bigger, big enough to hide my entire body. I've muted my uncle's clapping, but every now and then it breaks through. I wonder if Zack's immune to it by now. He doesn't seem to be fazed, digging his feet into the dirt while he anticipates my next pitch. He's like a bull waiting to be let loose in the ring.

Hollis gives me the same sign one more time, and when I shake her off yet again, she pulls her mask off and rushes toward me. I can see her gritting teeth by the time she's halfway to me.

"What the fuck are you doing, Jennings?"

Wow, no mincing words.

"I'm not feeling that pitch," I lie.

"Bullshit. You're being a chicken. It's the right pitch to throw. If this were a game, you'd throw it," she seethes.

She pulls her mask down over her face and runs back to the plate, crouching down and giving me the same sign as the last four, insistent and not waiting for me to nod in agreement. She sets up and snaps her glove for the ball a few times, no longer giving me the luxury of throwing anything but what she wants. If I don't throw this, it's going to look like a huge miss on my part. Stuck, I pivot and lift my knee, giving her the perfect slider that leaves my cousin whiffing the bat through the strike zone, not even close.

"Oh, come on! Dude, you hit that! You know how to hit that, don't you?" My uncle comes off like a drunk Little League dad, and if he were any other parent, Coach Taylor would toss him off the field. But my uncle approves his paycheck. Enough *nay* votes at the board meeting would make the principal nervous, and nervous principals fire people to make problems go away. Coach Taylor is stuck, just as I am. The only way he can make his point is by setting Zack up to fail. But I don't want to be the one who stabs my cousin in the back. I don't think I can live with that.

Hollis throws the ball back and gives me a quick sign for the same pitch, again. It's the right call, *again.* I nod, letting her know she's right, but there's no way in hell I'm throwing that pitch. My cousin needs this win a lot more than the rest of us. He's the one who has to sit at the dinner table with my uncle tonight. Uncle Joel will brag when my dad calls tomorrow too, probably embellishing the tale of his son's at bat against me, but I'll text my dad to let him know I missed on purpose. My dad will get it. He knows how his brother is; Uncle Joel is . . . *intense.* Besides, family comes first.

Right now, winding up and bringing my arms in then separating them with my stride, family comes first. The claps echo in some faraway place, the sound growing faster as the ball exits my nimble fingers. The threads spin line over line. It's an easy-to-spot four-seam fastball that my cousin can't miss. Hollis is already shifting her knees to adjust, her glove moving back to the center of the plate in a prayer that Zack swings through and misses.

He won't, though.

He doesn't.

My cousin tosses his bat over his shoulder with his typical ego-driven flair as he holds up a fist and begins his slow trot around the bases. I maybe shouldn't have made it quite so easy. The ball barely cleared the fence, but barely is always enough when it comes to home runs. My muffled ears clear and my Uncle's whistles break through the barrier first.

I feign disappointment, pulling my hat down on my face for a moment during his victory lap. I smile behind it, just for a second, and that's how I know I made the right choice. By the time I slide it back in place, Hollis has walked off the field and into the dugout, throwing her glove with enough juice to take out five or six bats balanced against the fence.

"Hey!" her dad shouts, snapping his fingers twice. She jerks her head toward him, her face stained with dirt, her eyes slits that glow with her anger. After a short standoff with her dad, her shoulders slump, and eventually, she looks down, pulling her mask and helmet off completely and undoing the knot in her hair. She stares at the water-stained concrete of the dugout for the next several minutes, and I'm glad, because the minute she looks at me, I'm going to quit thinking I made the right choice with that pitch.

TEN

HOLLIS

I've never understood why people pace. What does walking back and forth in patterns do to solve problems? Nothing, that's what. It does absolutely nothing. Yet here I am, not even sure who I'm the most angry with, and I am pacing.

I bet my dad is in his room doing the same exact thing, maybe even having the same exact silent conversation with himself. This is all so pointless.

Cannon doesn't trust me. That's the one thing I keep coming back to. If I'm ever going to catch for him in a game, when it truly matters, he needs to trust me. That's not the pitch I told him to throw today, yet he threw it anyway. My conclusions are either a lack of trust or he knew Zack would hit it. He did his cousin a favor, and maybe—*maybe*—I should understand the family bond thing better. But wouldn't it mean more if Zack actually earned it?

There aren't enough miles to be walked in this house to get my brain to stop. I need a better distraction, and homework is not going to cut it. I'll be lucky to slow my mind enough by midnight to finish writing the lit paper that's due in fourteen hours.

"Gah!" I grunt out, throwing my copy of *Macbeth* on the center of my bed. I stare at the cover and laugh maniacally, though quietly. How appropriate that I'm reading a story about the struggle for political power and how it tears people up from the inside out. *Scotland's got nothin' on the politics of high school baseball.*

Restless, I ditch the quiet solitude of my room, closing my door behind me so my mom doesn't mention the boxes still to be unpacked. My dad has finally parked himself on the couch, his feet up on the coffee table and some microbrew bottle in his hand. My mom's sitting at the kitchen table with the reflection of her laptop glowing in her reading glasses. I grab the van keys from the counter and try to be smooth, soundless, but they jingle just enough to turn my parents' heads my way.

My mom pulls her glasses down to the tip of her nose and raises a brow.

"Stir crazy," I answer her questioning look. "I won't be out late, and I will drive carefully, and yes, I am working on finishing my room."

That last bit's a lie.

She grimaces and says "Uh huh, sure."

"Thanks," I say through an exaggerated smile, palming the keys and heading on my way.

"If you see Jennings, let him know I wanna talk to him before workouts tomorrow," my dad says as I leave. I glance at him, but he's already turned his attention back to the television.

"Which one?" I ask.

"Either," he says before taking a long sip of his beer.

His ominous threat gives me a little boost as I leave the house. It's tacky to be happy about other people getting in trouble, but I'm all right with being a little tacky right now. It's better than some of the things I've wished on Zack and Cannon over the last hour. Nothing *too* bad—jock itch or premature baldness. Or getting cut from the team. I know that last wish won't come true. They're too good, and my dad would get called out for retribution. Zack's dad would make sure of it. I've had enough of other player parents getting involved to suit me for a lifetime.

I've yet to check out the bowling alley that June works at. She's been encouraging me to come visit during her work hours for the last week, and now seems like the perfect time. I could use another female to vent to. I shoot her a text to make sure she's there then head toward the main part of town. The lot is pretty full when I pull in. Cheesy eighties music blares through the doors every time someone comes or goes. It reminds me of a joint back home where I used to get slices of pizza with my dad after games.

I check my phone before going in to see if June responded, but nothing yet. She's probably busy. Buzzed on the nostalgia of hearing Madonna's "Like a Virgin," which my dad always points out was my mom's favorite song growing up, I'm smiling by the time I push open the door. The overhead lights are dimmed, and neon-colored lights line the lanes and walls of this place. It's a bit of a dump, but in that perfect kind of way. The carpet is obnoxious swirls of color, some of them glowing more than others from the black light shining along the main walkways. My white socks and shoes are vivid, as is the NYU emblem on my sweatshirt.

I make my way to the counter where a few people are in line for shoes, and I'm relieved when I see June rushing around to check people in. Stepping to the side, I lean against the counter and wait for her to have a free moment to talk. She catches sight of me on one of her trips to grab shoes and a smile lights up her face. Mine does the same, proof that I really needed this—*a person.*

"Hey! Look who finally showed up!" June holds up a finger and rushes back to her register to cash someone out. She clears the line in about two minutes and comes back to me with two large cups filled with Coke.

"Perk of knowing the junior assistant manager." She smirks. I take the straw and pull the wrapper off, blowing the bit left on the end up in the air for her to catch.

"Fancy," I say, sucking in a big drink.

"Mondays are league nights, so it gets pretty busy. You have to come back on a Sunday morning. We can literally bowl while I'm on the clock if you want," she offers.

"Oh, tempting. I'll have to take you up on that. You know, I was Staten Island sixth grade champ with a pretty wicked one-forty-one," I brag. I haven't bowled since junior high, so I'm pretty sure I'd have to work to match that score again.

"Well, I'd only take you by a hundred or so," June teases. I laugh out hard but stop when I realize she's not kidding.

"Another perk of the job, I guess, huh?" I say.

She cracks her knuckles dramatically to show off, then winks.

"Hey, I'll set you up with pool if you wanna stick around and hang out when I'm done here. We can grab a late dinner." She pulls a box of pool balls out from under the counter as more people walk up to her register. I ate dinner already, but I could really use the girl time, so I nod and smile, taking the balls and my drink into the pool hall area, away from most of the crowds.

The neon lights don't glow in here. It's peacefully dim, the room just dark enough to conceal Cannon until I've unboxed the balls at the pool table that's apparently directly behind him. He jumps at the sound, and his movement makes me yelp and grab my chest.

"Oh, shit!" I say through a nervous laugh. My heart is pounding at a marathon runner's pace. "I didn't see you."

He was wearing his hoodie up over his hair but he pulled it back when I startled him. My gut says he's here hiding. For about four seconds, I'm distracted by the adorable way his hair flops around, before I remember that I want to punch him.

"My dad wants you to see him before practice," I say without transition. Cannon's eyes scrunch up. "Just, he said if I saw you before tomorrow's practice. I didn't think I would this soon, and ya know . . . I don't want to forget."

"Uh huh," he deadpans with a slow roll of his eyes. He turns his attention back to the other table, rolling one of the balls across the table and back again.

"Don't throw shade at me just because my dad isn't happy with you. I have nothing to do with his coaching decisions." I mumble the words, irritated at the obvious insinuation Cannon makes. Most people—*all people*—assume that I'm basically my dad's assistant. I must get favors. He must be willing to punish people just for me, right? I mean, I couldn't possibly earn things on my own, and no way does my dad has ethical standards.

"*Pshh*, whatever," I mutter at my own thoughts.

"You just don't get it," Cannon says, suddenly facing me, tossing the cue ball in his palm.

I abandon the balls on my table and lean into the side with my arms crossed.

"Don't get what? That you don't trust me to call your pitches or that you would rather make your cousin look good than let him earn it on his own?" I can tell I've hit a nerve by the way his eyes flinch. He doesn't back away, though, abandoning his ball to the other table and stepping into my personal space until he's close enough for me to smell the mint on his breath.

"Did you take a minute to consider what the rest of the night would have been like for Zack if I struck him out? You saw my uncle out there. Imagine that at home, where there is no place to run off to." His eyes pierce mine, a penetrating stare that challenges me, and my stomach churns at his point.

"That why you're here? Hiding from your uncle?" I change the subject and shove a cue at his chest.

"Something like that," he says, his voice low, words trailing off as if he just realized we're close enough to share each other's breaths. He wraps his hand around the stick I gave him and his eyes flit to my mouth then back up to my gaze.

"You any good?" His head tilts with his question, but I think maybe he's challenging me as an excuse to put distance between us. The break is welcome. When he's close, I don't think clearly.

"I'm all right." I shrug and face the table to properly rack the balls. I'm being coy. My family has a pool table. Or rather, we did. When I was old enough to hold the stick right, my dad put me up on a bar stool and let me play. I'm not a shark or anything, but I know my way around a game of nine-ball.

Cannon meanders to the opposite end of the table, working the chalk cube at the end of his stick.

"What's the wager?" he says, glancing up at me before tossing the chalk in my direction. I catch it in my palm and squeeze it tight while I hold his stare for a beat. I could play this two ways. It could be a game, for fun, for something silly or maybe even slightly flirtatious. Lord knows there's a thousand butterflies beating in my chest rooting for me to take that route. But the tiger in my soul is even more demanding and pushes me to make a point while I still can.

My tongue gently tastes my upper lip before I suck in and grab hold of it with my teeth, locking in the nervous laugh that's dying to escape my throat. I'm going to make a business deal. The most gorgeous guy I've ever met is daring me to change the course of our relationship over a game of pool I have a really good chance at winning, and I'm going to instead opt to teach him a lesson.

My God, what is wrong with me?

He's literally my kryptonite right now, black long-sleeved shirt with three open buttons at the top, dark fitted jeans that rest low on his hips and show off that tempting bit of skin just above the band of his boxer briefs. His feet are stuffed into unlaced white Vans, and damn it all to hell, even his ankles are cute. Unlike me, he's taken a shower since that shit-show of a practice. His hair is damp, curling into loose waves that he keeps brushing away from his eyes. All of that is enough to make me get all stupid with my choices, but it's whatever that smell is that accompanies him most of the time that's thick and fresh and alluring as fuck right now.

Good thing I'm as close to repulsive looking right now as I can get. I'm still wearing dad's sweatpants rolled down to fit my waist and my Yankees

World Series sweatshirt. That knot that Cannon likes to affectionately tease me about is a doozy right now, to the point it's going to take a bottle of conditioner to work it out. I did wash my face, though, so there's that.

Tongue in my cheek, a little amused by my own gall, I let a short, airy laugh slip through my nostrils and dig in.

"What do *you* want if you win?" I need him invested for this to work. He props his stick up against the side of the table, folding his arm and leaning into the edge right next to his cue.

"*Hmm*, I mean . . . there are so many options." His voice is definitely indicative of a guy taking the bait, despite my super grungy look.

I'm really about to ruin this. Damn me and my morals.

"What if . . ." I let my words linger in the air and haze my eyes just enough to tempt him, draw him in. When his lip ticks up, I go for the kill.

"If you can beat me, I'll let you name your terms at any time you wish." It dawns on me as I say this to him that I must feel a decent level of trust when it comes to Cannon Jennings. An open-ended bet like this, especially given my past, is normally way outside my comfort zone. Yet, there's a little fire in my belly at the thought of losing and Cannon coming to collect. And the way he's looking at me, chewing at the inside of his cheek while he considers my offer, that fire is getting . . . hotter.

"Any terms," he reiterates.

I nod but hold up a palm in pause, hedging my offer just a little.

"Within reason," I add, one eyebrow raised.

Cannon's chest lifts with an amused laugh. I lock in on his blue eyes and will myself not to blink, even while he does, once . . . *twice*. His lashes are so long for a guy, like tools used to put whomever is looking at them under a spell. It's close to working on me. I'm a little jealous because mine are so blonde that sometimes they're hard to see except in the sun. Not his—his are *all* I see right now.

"I accept," he says, stepping back and spinning his cue over his wrist a few times.

I point my finger in a circle to mock his circus trick.

"I'm a little worried if that's how you think this game is done," I say.

He shoots me a tight-lipped glare before dropping the base of his stick to the floor with a heavy *thunk*.

"And what is your ask?" He leans over the table and swivels his stick into position, gliding it across his knuckles. I'll admit, he looks comfortable at the head of the table. This might not go the way I want. It's that emphasis on *might,* though, that prompts me to speak up.

"If I win, you have to let Zack know you went easy on him."

And there it is. I did it; said it. Put the challenge on the table. I thought I'd feel better about backing him into this corner, but now that I see the blood leave his cheeks and the corners of his mouth turn down as he slowly stands upright, this doesn't feel like *winning* at all.

I manage to hold my position despite his look of betrayal. What do I owe his cousin? Nothing! That fucker disparaged me in front of my peers. No, he sexually harassed me. He crossed a line, physically, to purposely demean me because he felt small. I owe Zack absolutely nothing, and he deserves to know that his big achievement at practice today wasn't very big at all. All it was is one big, fat gift he doesn't deserve.

My mouth curves the opposite way, a forced smirk inching up into my cheeks and working against the sourness I'm feeling from my neck down to the bottom of my guts. Crossing my arms over my chest, I hug my stick and jut one hip out in a challenge.

"Well?" I lift a brow.

His stare is decisive. No more blinking lashes to lull me into submission. I'm being dissected solely by the dominant glow of his swimming-pool blue eyes. His nose is pink from being out in today's sun and reflective clouds. His wet hair is drying right before my eyes into touchable waves that I imagine in my fingers. I'm thankful my arms are crossed to hide them because I can feel them twitch.

"Fine."

I flinch at his sudden acquiescence, most of me prepared for him to bail on this little wager. By the way he rounds the table and motions for me to step back, I tremble at the knees. Cue ball palmed in his left hand, stick grasped in his right, he steps into the space between me and the table and comes close enough that I can feel the warmth of the breath he exhales from his nose.

"Pardon," he says, and I step back several feet to lean against a pub table.

Cannon positions the ball a little off-center then dabs one more dusting of chalk on the end of his cue, blowing the excess away while he looks at me, his eyes focused away from the tip of the stick and onto my gaze. His mouth quirks on one side, and it's in that small look that I know I'm done. I'm so fucking screwed.

He leans over the table in a smooth pivot, drawing the stick back and getting the feel of the slide before letting it rip, knocking the balls in all directions and immediately sinking one of each—a solid and a stripe. His eyes centered on the table, he rounds it, his tongue sticking out the way Michael Jordan's always did when he was deciding whether to put the game away with a dunk or a little fadeaway from the top of the key.

"You got a preference?" he asks.

"I . . . well . . ." I stumble on my words, his sudden confidence nailing me to the floor.

He chuckles then bends down, lining up a shot at a solid.

"It's all right," he says, leaning his head to one side to glance up at me and wink. "It won't matter."

And it doesn't. He proceeds to sink his initial target, and then every other solid ball on the table, sometimes two at a time. I half expect him to drain the eight-ball without even looking. He has to work at it a little, though, what with so many of my balls still on the table and in his way. He calls the side pocket and when the ball falls in easily, I breathe out heavily enough to flap my lips, then I drop my stick.

"Two out of three?" I scrunch my lips up with my pathetic attempt to regain my edge.

"You think it will matter?" He lays his stick on the table and saunters toward me.

My nervous knee twitches, and I find myself rocking where I stand to keep my legs busy and my blood flowing. Cannon stops about a foot away from me, and looks down at the floor as he slips his hands into the pockets of his jeans. I draw in his scent, letting it numb my nerves like the venom of a scorpion. I got sloppy, arrogant even. And that trust I felt so sure of wanes a little now that he's calling in his bet. I gave him a free pass to surprise me, to ask something of me or dare me or— That's the thing. It's the unknown; I did that. *I did that!*

My hands balled into fists at my sides, I roll my shoulders back and lift my chin, determined not to let my worry shine through.

"Bet's a bet," I say, shaking my head with tight lips. I had no idea I was going up against a pool shark.

"That it is," he says, glancing up while keeping his head low. The way he peers at me through the strands of his hair that now shadow his eyes is both ominous and so freaking enticing.

"Five a.m., Saint Peter's Gulch. Tomorrow." He leans in and for a moment I think he's going to kiss me, but instead he pauses while forward on his toes. "I'll let you know what you owe there and then."

I swallow and he sees it, his eyes darting to that place on my throat that betrays my bravado.

"Fine," I gurgle out.

He laughs lightly and falls back to give me space.

"Relax, Hollis. I'm sure you'll be able to handle it." With one last wink, he brings his hands from his pockets and claps them a few times to remove any leftover chalk. I force myself not to look over my shoulder as he leaves, and I keep that promise to myself, spending the next twenty minutes playing out the rest of the balls on our table and realizing I never had a chance.

ELEVEN

CANNON

I used to have a huge grudge against my parents for forcing me to spend my summer days at the elementary school's recreation program. There were exactly three things I enjoyed about those summers up until seventh grade—all-you-can-drink chocolate milk from the cafeteria lady, time with Sydney Chistensen in the "kissing tunnel" where we kissed like sock puppets, and the pool table.

To say I got good at playing pool is an understatement. I won goddamn ribbons for it. For Christmas one year, I asked Santa for a Predator pool cue instead of the latest Louisville model. My dad was stunned, but good ole Santa came through. I still have that thing, gold case and all, assuming it survives the move here in the storage pod.

Uncle Joel said my dad will be able to head here a couple of days earlier than planned, possibly by Friday. The minute my dad gets here and we unload my truck, I take him to the airport so he can head back to New Mexico and make that drive all over again with my mom and more of our stuff. I'm so close to having a little bit of normal around me. Granted, we'll have to cram our "normal" into a shared set of bedrooms adjoined by a bathroom, but I'll be able to survive my living quarters if it means I have my own truck again. Sharing Zack's very unsexy sedan is seriously grating on my nerves. I'm used to being able to get in and just drive for however long or far I want, but with Zack, I have to constantly worry about how much gas is left in the tank, or if he needs to get somewhere or wants to be with me. *I'm never alone!*

I don't want him knowing about my morning plans, especially since I still can't believe I made them. I've spent the last five minutes silently working the car keys out of the pocket of his jeans that are on the floor. First, I had to find the right pair of jeans. I should have planned ahead last night, but Zack and I didn't hang. I got a lift to Eight Lanes from Tory and after my pool game against Hollis and my dramatic exit, I couldn't have her find me waiting around out front for someone to come back and pick me up, so I walked home. Three miles is a lot farther than you think when it's thirty-one degrees outside.

Of course, I walked in and Zack asked where the heck I'd been. I just held up my cell phone and told him I was talking to my dad. Thank God for video games because he half-heard me and nodded before going right back to shooting some alien thing.

Finally, with the keys loose and clutched in my palm, I creep out my cousin's door, thankful he's still snoring. I'll be bunking with him when my parents get here, and it's going to suck boatloads. I'm a light sleeper, and Zack basically holds a party in his nose every night.

I manage to slip out the front door without making a single sound and roll Zack's car back in neutral with the lights off so I don't disturb anyone. I told Hollis I'd be there at five, and it's a thirty-minute drive. I'm not sure she knows where she's going or what this place is, but if she shows up it means she really wants to be there. I don't know why that matters to me but it does. It's the entire reason I put this out there.

After a quick stop at the service station to drop the last twenty bucks from my dad's deposit into the tank, I race down the highway to make up time, almost missing the turnoff. The sign for the gulch state park is broken in half. When Zack dragged me up here for sledding before Christmas, he mentioned they don't fund this place anymore. I'm tempted to park under the sign and look out for Hollis to make sure she doesn't miss it, but I'm also worried she found her way and is already there, waiting for me.

Zack's car doesn't take the side road as well as my truck will, so I'm slow along the winding road that weaves through the stick-like trees, old snow frozen into solid ice blocks on the ground. It's still pretty out here, the frozen water like jewels that shine under the full moon along the landscape. Everything in town and on the highway has turned to icy mud. The sun won't be up for two hours, but we had to make this trip early to get home before school. *Before Zack knows I'm gone.*

The moon is bright enough to light my way and I travel mostly by memory, though I pull over a few times to check my location on my phone to make sure I haven't gone too far. The piled-rock walls come into view after about ten minutes of driving through the thickest section of trees. Steam puffs out from the exhaust of a familiar minivan parked close to the small ramada.

She came.

I pull into the graveled spot next to her, suddenly feeling my nerves. I blow out one hard breath and kill my engine, stepping out at the same time she does. We meet at the back of my car, our air mixing in a swirl of steam. She's shoved her gloved hands under her arms, and her body is wrapped in this obnoxiously yellow puffy coat. No knot in the hair this morning; instead, she wears a black sock hat pulled down just above her brow and over her ears, the length of her hair wrapped around her neck like a warmer.

"You know it's not snowing, right?" I tease her, but really, she's adorable like this, bouncing on her toes for warmth, tight jeans down her legs, feet stuffed in rubber-toed boots. She looks like winter—my kind of winter.

"It's somehow colder out here, ya know? Like, I mean, I've been cold in the city, and wind off the Atlantic is *ooof!*" She widens her eyes in expression. "But whatever this Midwestern stuff is, it's a whole different kinda cold. My breath is a solid. Skipped right over the gaseous state."

She puckers her lips and puffs out a few times, a tiny train engine coughing out steam. I see the fog clearly, but mostly I'm looking at her lips.

"I see you're tougher than I am?" She pulls one gloved hand loose from under her arm and gestures at my body, not quite as fully wrapped as hers.

I could play it tough, but that's not what this morning is supposed to be about at all. Unzipping my jacket, I twist the front inside-out and step closer for her to feel inside. She looks at me like I'm a total creep, which, considering how Zack has been toward her, I get.

"Feel my shoulder. I promise, just trust me," I say.

With twisted lips, she studies me for a beat, and her hesitant expression makes my chest ache just a little. I don't want to be the kind of guy that *anyone* makes that kind of face at, especially not her.

After a heavy sigh, she narrows her eyes and tightens her lips, still not sure whether she can trust me. If we can't get past this test, we're in trouble for the rest of the morning. She pulls her hand free from the glove then slips it under my jacket, nervous fingers tracing up over my shoulder as I cautiously fold the jacket back over her hand and my chest.

"It's made for snowboarders. Lots of warmth without the bulk. I think it's the same material they make bullet proof vests out of," I say.

Her lip ticks up and her eyes blink a few times before her gaze hits mine.

"Does that mean I can shoot you?"

"Ha!" I punch out a laugh, but the silence that follows during our brief stare leaves me a little unsteady. She's kidding, but there's maybe a one percent slice of honesty in that barb.

An entirely new feeling takes over when she pulls her hand away. Her movement is slower, and I feel the tiny vibration in her thumb along my chest. She's nervous, too, and not because she thinks I'm going to shoot her.

"We should get to it. I don't want to make you late," I say, nodding toward the head of the trail.

"You mean you don't want Zack to know you're gone," she corrects. She's intuitive—*and right.*

"That too," I admit, glancing over my shoulder, my mouth a straight line to mark my guilt. I slow my steps to look at her a little longer and feel the burn left behind from her calling me on my bullshit. Maybe I crave the punishment to absolve me of my sins when it comes to her.

Eyes forward again, I pull a small flashlight from my pocket and click it on, lighting the way to the edge of the canyon. The walk isn't long, but it feels like a mile with the silence that swallows us. The only noises are the crunch under our feet and the occasional snap of branches.

The makeshift ladder seems scarier now in the faint light of the moon, the pole slick with the deep frost that comes before dawn. I grip the metal pegs that jut out from the pole in my bare hands, the cold stinging my skin. I let go for a minute and rub my hands together, as if that'll help.

"Wait a minute. *We're climbing up that?*" Hollis points up.

"It's worth it," I say, starting my climb without giving in to the cautionary tale beating in my chest. The metal stings and I'm glad Hollis has gloves because at least she'll be able to tolerate the cold. The height thing, however, might be a different story.

She beings to climb behind me when I'm a full body-length ahead, and we both keep a steady pace. The wind is colder the higher we go, and by the time I reach the wooden platform at the top, it's chilling. Maybe this was a bad idea.

"I hope you know my dad will kill both of us if either of us gets hurt," she says, hoisting herself up to join me in the small standing-room space.

"Good thing we'll go down together, then—literally," I respond, tugging at the sturdy straps dangling loose around the tall pole at the edge of the platform. I keep my gaze on Hollis while I untangle the contraption, and it's hard not to laugh when her eyes widen so big that I see mostly the whites.

"Oh, hell no," she says through nervous laughter, shaking her head.

I tug on the zipline harness built for two with all my weight to prove that this thing is sturdy. I made Zack prove it to me. And if this can hold both of us, I'm pretty sure Hollis and I will be fine.

"I did this last month with Zack. It's a serious thrill, and besides"—I stretch the straps out and step through one section before holding out the remaining two loops for her—"A bet's a bet."

I hit her with a daring grin. The wind is strong enough that it whips the hair sticking out of my knit hat. Hollis's hair twists like tentacles, blonde ribbons curving around her neck then stretching out into the air like fingers. Her nose is pink and her cheeks are red. Her eyes, however, are not quite as wide as before. With a slight tilt of her head, she studies me for a moment more, then places her palms on my shoulders for balance, stepping through the straps.

The second she enters my space, my chemistry changes, and I think maybe hers does, too. There's nowhere for either of us to go, our bodies quite literally tied together on a perch about a hundred feet in the air. Her mouth rests at the base of my neck, and the tiny gasp she lets out tickles against my skin. It's the one part of me that's not sheltered from the cold, and she's managed to scorch it with one breath.

"Hold on," I say, my mouth suddenly dry. I tug the straps around her back and they cinch together with mine.

I peel back my upper body enough to look her in the eyes.

"May I?" I glance down to the space between us, where the last buckles are loose and need to be fastened.

She blinks nervously, but I can tell she isn't scared. She's something else, and I hope maybe what she feels is the same kind of reaction I'm having inside my chest.

"Make it tight," she laughs out.

I breathe out through my nose and smile before looking down between us. Her hands grip my shoulders tightly and she rests her forehead against mine so she can watch as I lock us in together. When I'm done, I freeze in place for a moment, not ready to look up and meet her stare again. She's close, and we're touching, and I've felt her nose brush against mine twice since we've positioned ourselves like this.

Three times.

Four.

Her lips part with another breath, fear exhaled and a leap of faith drawn in.

"Ready?" I ask, still not moving my head away from hers. She nods against me.

My hands tentatively move to her waist, never moving from the invisible guideline drawn by the top of her jeans. She leans into me and circles her arms around my body, and when the weight of her chin rests on my shoulder, I let my muscles relax and flatten my palms on her back.

This is different than kissing as strangers. This is a literal leap, a sign of trust that goes way beyond. When I made this trip with Zack it was more about the thrill and being boys together who like to do daring, dumb shit. I may not have admitted it fully to myself until right now, but I dared Hollis to come out here because I want her to trust me.

"I've got you," I promise just as I push us off from the ledge. Her fingers dig into me at first, but after a few seconds of gliding across the frozen stream below, she relaxes. And then the joyous laughter begins.

"Oh, my God!" she cries out, her head swiveling from where it rests on my shoulder. We're halfway across the line, moving at a good speed, when she drops her hands down to my chest and leans back enough to see everything.

"This is amazing!" Her smile is all teeth and glee, like a kid seeing a true winter wonderland.

I had fun here with Zack, but this trip with Hollis is special. I haven't looked at the scenery once; the only thing my eyes want to watch is her. We rotate as we travel, and her eyes blink from the wind and cold, but the dimples pushed up into her cheeks only grow deeper. The moonlight traces her lashes, lighting them up like flecks of gold. Her eyes glimmer like diamonds, her lips like candy, I lock in on them for a little too long, and she catches me. When her tongue passes over her bottom lip, I give in and meet her waiting stare. Damn that this zipline isn't longer.

"Brace yourself," I warn, glancing up in time to catch the safety rope as we glide over the second pedestal.

I wrap the rope around my forearm with one hand, and stop us as gracefully as I can. Hollis lets out a small grunt then breaks into laughter, her arms limp at her sides.

"Worth it?" I ask.

Her smile hasn't dipped once, and she adds in an emphatic "Yes" with a nod before tilting her head to the sky, ready to climb to the next platform and make our trip back.

My chest is enlarged with pride, but other parts of me are swollen from something else, and unfastening our straps while trying to hide my painful erection is borderline comical. Thankfully, Hollis steps out quickly when I loosen the belt to create slack.

She's already at the top of the next platform by the time I free myself, and the solo trip up the peg ladder gives me a chance to calm down and let the cold air work its magic before I gladly torture myself again.

This time Hollis helps, more familiar with the process and less afraid of what comes next. I expect her to hold on to me less so she can enjoy the ride and take in more of the skyline, a soft glow of the sun hinting at its impending rise. It's like a line of glowing bright blue ink tracing along the slight hills. Rather than looking around completely, though, she holds on exactly as before. Her hands rest more comfortable around my neck this time, and as we slip away from the solid wood base and into the air, her fingers twist some of my hair. Everything I thought I had in check explodes, including my self-discipline.

Slipping back enough to force her eyes to meet mine, I do my best to read what they say. She doesn't blink, her focus moving from my left eye to my right, as mine do hers. Her fingers curl my hair again, letting the short pieces slip through her knuckles while her nails scratch at the base of my neck. My palms at her waist, I give myself permission to stroke along her sides with my thumbs as we glide across the landscape at twenty-something miles per hour.

I sense the end of the ride coming, and reach out instinctively to slow our stop. I catch her against my body when my feet find solid ground, then let the safety rope go, remaining steady where I am for fear she'll let go completely. Our feet tangle on the wooden planks, hers tucked inside my wide base. Either my eyes have adjusted or the sky is getting brighter because I can see every freckle that dots her cheeks and nose. I'm mesmerized by them, but equally as rapt that she seems as taken with mine.

I had no idea how much I actually won in our silly pool game. I don't think I knew how much I *wanted* until this very moment. As her lips part, her tongue dashing out bravely into the cold to taste her skin, I'm overwhelmed with desire to take everything I can. I won't break this trust, though. Of everything that this morning brings, her letting me help her fly is the most important.

Her fingers curl into fists at the back of my neck, and I'm so damn afraid she'll let go and tear us apart. She doesn't, though. Before I make a move to unfasten our straps, she lifts up on her toes ever so slightly, just enough to bring our heights in line. Her eyes skim down fleetingly to my mouth as she closes the distance between us, and her gaze hits mine again just as her soft lids flutter to close. She leans in, the ultimate of trust, and presses her mouth to mine in a chaste, soft kiss that I let her control completely. My only moment of greed is a soft suck of her plump bottom lip, and it's pure torture forcing myself to let go, but I do.

Our lips part but her forehead remains on mine. I unbuckle our straps and eventually, the harness falls to our feet. Before Hollis steps back, she kisses me one more time, this one on my cheek.

"Thank you, Cannon," she whispers.

"You're welcome," I reply, knowing our words should be reversed.

Despite spending the last hour in the freezing cold, I keep the shower temperature tepid while I erase the feel of her lips on mine and the visual of her body from my mind. It's a good thing we drove back separately, because I don't think my body could handle these thoughts with Hollis just a foot away from me in the warm car. My imagination is bad enough. The minute I pictured laying her down in the back seat, the ride home got really uncomfortable—*and fast.*

Finally somewhat coherent and no longer hard for a girl I'm keeping at arm's length, I kill the shower and wrap a towel around my waist. When I come face-to-face with Zack's sinister smile on the other side of the door, I expect him to make some joke about me draining the hot water or spending so much time alone in the bathroom. But that's not what's on his mind at all.

"The board is meeting about Coach Taylor." He grins, arrogant pride seeping from the pores of his skin.

"Why?" I ask, when really my inner-voice is saying, *What did you do?*

"There are some questions about his techniques, and maybe how he makes his rosters." My cousin passes me in the doorway and we trade sides as I step into the hall.

"But he hasn't made any rosters yet," I explain, my mouth watering with sickness.

Zack's smile grows more ominous just before he winks.

"Exactly," he says, closing the door on this conversation, *and my face.*

I spent the morning trying to earn Hollis's trust and prove my integrity, and with one conversation with his father behind my back, Zack is threatening to burn that trust to the ground. All because a girl might be better at something than he is.

No *might*. She *is* better. And I need to start standing up for her, despite my family.

TWELVE

HOLLIS

I wasn't sure my body would warm up after I climbed that pole this morning, but somehow, now I can't seem to cool it down. I've been simmering from the inside out ever since I left the gulch this morning, and sitting next to Cannon in class earlier today rekindled everything.

Things have been pleasantly awkward since. I quite like pleasantly awkward. This time, the aftermath of our kiss is more promising. We went into that with eyes wide open. The only thing that can ruin this euphoria is currently finishing up his second lap, alongside Cannon.

"Looks like I beat you out here today, Double-D," Zack says as he slows to a walk, pacing around me in wide circles while I stretch before my run. I glower up at him from my squatting stretch, waiting for him to finish his lame bra-size joke.

"Oh, no. Not like that. Double-D—Daddy's Daughter." He laughs at his lame joke and I dim my eyes. I mean, that's basically a statement of fact. Most humans are their father's child, biologically at least. I get what he's insinuating, though. Nothing new. Before I can defend myself, Cannon walks up behind him and knocks his hat from his head.

"Don't be a dick."

I look down at my toes to hide my smile. I don't need anyone fighting my battles, but after my morning, it's reassuring to see Cannon do it.

Zack picks his hat up from the track and puts it on backward, which is one of my father's pet peeves. I could warn him, but he deserves what he gets. He shoots me a sour look before he leaves the track and makes his way to the field. Cannon sticks around, but I sense his uneasiness in the way he keeps checking to see if his cousin is watching us.

"You don't have to wait for me," I say, my stomach twisting with gooey butterfly feelings and insecurities galore. *Of course he isn't waiting for me.*

"Hey, I just . . ." He swings his arm into mine as I stand and our fingers catch briefly.

Lightning bolts.

A breathy laugh slips out from his guilty smile. It's sweet, as is the way he's stammering and having trouble looking me in the eyes. Perhaps we got a redo on our first kiss. This one is going much better.

"I want to apologize for him, my cousin?" He points over his shoulder with his thumb. He glances behind him but I reassure him before he fully looks.

"He's in the dugout. He can't see you," I say.

"Right," he says, sucking in his bottom lip.

"You don't have to say his *sorrys*, by the way. I know he's not you. And you aren't responsible for him. He can say them himself, or not. That's a direct reflection on him."

Cannon nods, shuffling backward a few steps to not get caught dawdling. My dad's favorite word is *hustle.*

"How'd you get to be so smart?" He punctuates his flattering question with a crooked smile that turns into a wink.

"Lots and lots of lessons learned," I say, alluding to more than he realizes. He takes it at face value, though, and nods toward the track.

"You better hustle," he teases. I'll have my laps done in time. The one true perk to being coach's daughter is knowing not to fail to meet his expectations. I know what I'm supposed to do and when, which is why letting Zack get a hit he didn't earn yesterday irks me so much.

Apparently, it's still quite a sticking point for my dad, too. He's pulled Zack aside in the bullpen, and based on his familiar and animated hand gestures, I'd venture to guess he's putting some pressure on him.

Great. Pressure on Zack is going to translate into more hostility toward me.

I finish a little slower than my normal time. I don't check on my smartwatch, but I don't have to. I slowed down on purpose, putting off the inevitable head-to-head competition I know is coming. I was pumped for it until I caught my dad giving Zack the anti-pep talk.

I dump my gear in the corner of the dugout as they return from their chat session, and the glare Zack shoots my way is ice cold.

"Go throw," my dad says, tossing a ball with a little extra zip straight into Zack's chest. "With her," my father adds, pointing in my general direction.

"*Pssh.*" The annoyed rush of air that slips from Zack isn't meant for my dad, and he manages to keep it just quiet enough for me and me alone.

"Well? Hurry up," Zack says, not bothering to wait for me or look my direction.

I follow Zack to the outfield, where we pair up next to everyone except the pitchers. My dad paces around the duos, assessing form and how serious each player is taking something so simple. It doesn't take more than three or four throws for him to get to us and make an example of Zack.

"Is that how you throw down to second?" My dad asks the question loud enough for nearby players to hear. Zack's cheeks burn bright red, and it's not from the cold air.

"I'm still warming up, Coach," Zack replies, throwing the ball back to me with more energy under my father's watchful eyes.

"Uh huh. Well, we should always practice with the same verve we have when we play." My father's sunglasses hide his eyes enough that it's hard to tell when he's looking at you. He has a habit of never quite staring at someone head-on. It's a trick he uses to see what expressions people make when they think he's not fully paying attention.

He is *always* paying attention.

My dad spreads his legs to get comfortable in his stance, arms crossed over his chest while his head swivels to follow the ball Zack and I continue to throw. My partner's footwork is sloppy, and I notice my father's focus on the ground for several seconds, my clue that he sees it. He's memorizing it. It won't be something that comes up now, but it will come up today.

We manage to survive warm-ups without more commentary from my dad, and as much as I want Zack to get his due, I also don't want to be this close to him when he gets it. I feel a little bit like the tool being used to punish him.

I'm grateful for the distance that comes with my dad dividing up the teams. He puts Zack with Cannon, which could be for a lot of reasons, but it's definitely not because he's letting him off the hook. There are enough of us out here to have three squads, and one of the new assistant coaches takes mine. His name's Ernie Ruiz, and my dad lured him away from a school two towns over. He made the call the moment he landed this job. Ernie Ruiz has one key line on his resume that singled him out and made him my father's number-one candidate—*he was a Yankee.* Only for sixteen games in the majors, but wearing pinstripes for any amount of time is as good as blood to my dad.

For most of the guys out here, today is going to be a good time. That's what will separate the keepers from the cuts. It's a game of three outs, and the three teams keep rotating, scoring as many runs as they can until my father decides time is up. It seems like a silly game to take everyone's minds off of the pressure of warmups and tryouts just around the corner, but every coach out here is watching for the ones who truly work. All games count for something.

It doesn't take long for the first two squads to make their outs, so I do a little strategizing with my squad as we take the field. I didn't get Cannon, but I did luck out with Roland on my team, and the one thing he has in his arsenal is a really good curveball. Zack might have gotten the pitch he wanted yesterday, but today he won't be so lucky.

"Look out, DD, here comes your nemesis," Zack shouts from the dugout. I glare through my mask in time to catch him stretching out his hands as he puts on his batting gloves. His joke carries to a few of the other guys, who laugh at my expense, pitifully trying to cover their snickers with fists over their mouths.

Fools.

Any sympathy I had for Zack drains. I get the rough spot Cannon is in, but it's like I told him—*he* is not his cousin. I won't treat them the same. Zack hasn't yet earned my respect.

"Batter up, Big Z!" I say, pounding my glove as I crouch into my squat. I can tell by his swagger as he steps up to the plate that he thinks I'm complimenting him, feeding his ego.

"You like that homer yesterday? I got plenty more in here. It's gonna be a long season, babe." I'm not sure whether his voice is as snarky as I hear it, or if it's the filter I seem to wear whenever he speaks. I'm not sure I could hear him any other way.

"I bet it is, Big Z," I say, echoing the nickname.

He sniffles out a laugh and digs his toes in. Everything about his approach is so affected, so cartoon-like. His feet are so set in their position, there's no chance for him to move them at a moment's notice.

"Come on Zack, you got this," Cannon calls from the bench. His encouragement hits my gut in a curious way. I'm a little soured by it, which I know isn't fair. He is being positive, which is what he should always do. And that's his cousin, so there is that extra pressure. It's just . . . I truly want Zack to fail this time.

I signal for a fastball low and outside, just like before, knowing it will work. And like yesterday, he swings himself off balance, landing on his knee as he twists.

"Strike one," my dad says, marking it on his scoresheet from behind the backstop. My dad likes to watch scrimmages from off the field, to see how people react to him being present but not in their face.

"I got this. Come on," Zack says, sniffing again, but this time as a show of how tough he is. He digs his feet into the exact same spot and I stare at them for a beat while a wave of tightness twists my insides. He isn't learning.

"You sure you don't want to make an adjustment?" I cough out my suggestion, keeping my voice low enough for my dad not to notice. I'm not sure why I'm helping, and I know before his reaction that he won't take my advice.

"Thanks, Double D. I got this, though," he says, spitting on the plate.

My eyes fall shut for a moment as I tuck my chin, acting as though I'm thinking about what to call next. Really, I'm just dreading the ass-chewing Zack has coming his way. Spitting on the plate is disrespectful, and there's no way my dad didn't see that. No matter where Roland throws this next ball, it'll be called a strike simply because Zack just hit my dad's nerve.

My head up, I send the same sign to Roland and line him up in the same location, maybe an inch or two more outside just to be safe. At this point, Zack would swing at the ball if he rolled it in. He's too jacked and ready to show off his muscles.

Roland isn't as good at hitting his target, and he ends up throwing the ball enough inside that Zack gets his bat on a piece of it, foul-tipping it right into my chest. It hurts as much as it always does, but the sting is gone by the time Zack is done chuckling. That guilty weight in my chest is gone now too.

"Strike two," my dad says. I glance over my shoulder to catch the reflection off of his glasses. I squint at the brightness, but I give my dad a nod. I shouldn't, because it's these little communications that can get both of us into trouble, but I can't help myself. Zack is under my skin, and he's under my dad's, too.

"Alright, Big Z. Time to show up or shut up," I say. I rarely devolve into trash talk, but the guy brings out the worst of my personality.

He scoffs at me and digs in, his leg twitching with what I assume is a sense of urgency pulsing through it. He's going to look ridiculous in about six seconds.

I signal for the curve, and Roland has a hard time hiding his smirk. If Zack were paying attention, he'd see it and be prepared. But he's too far gone inside his head.

I set up dead-center of the plate, knowing that Zack will see me in his periphery and probably think that he's going to get a fat meatball to rocket over the fence again. His swing comes almost a full half-second before the ball, the bat flinging end over end toward the dugout from his failed grip.

"That's one!" I shout, counting the outs as I throw the ball around with my team.

I'm still standing on the plate when Zack leans forward and spits again, purposely targeting my cleat. The act is purposeful, spiteful, and cruel. And he is about to wish he weren't in his own shoes.

"Bad move, Big Z. I mean, Big Zero." I give in and let any hope for mercy slip away.

"Jennings!"

There's no confusion about who he's calling. My dad's glasses are off, tucked into the front of his shirt by the time I spin around. He throws the clipboard down on the metal bleacher seat behind him, the clatter echoing around the field. My dad takes long strides around the backstop, through the gate, and into the dirt behind home plate where he steps in close enough to Zack that he could literally bite his nose if he wanted to. What surprises me, though, is the level of bravado puffing up Zack's chest and drawing him just as close to my dad. This is how wild dogs get into fights.

Knowing I should, I walk out to the mound to give them some privacy. The distance doesn't matter much, because my dad can be heard clear as day.

"Do you even want to be out here?"

His hand claps against his thigh, a gesture he makes when he's truly frustrated.

"This is a team, not Zack Jennings play time!"

He turns to walk away but pivots almost immediately, pointing.

"Uncoachable. Disrespectful. Not the kind of athlete I want on my team!"

The quiet before the storm is thick, palpable, and we all taste it. Zack shuffles back a few steps, angry laughter bubbling from his chest as he glances to his side and stares in Cannon's direction. There will be regret, probably on his part, and he will think he can repair the damage he's about to do, but he can't. My father is basically the Mr. Darcy of coaches, his opinion of someone gets set in stone pretty quickly.

Zack unvelcros his batting glove, making a show of it, his tongue pushed so hard into the crook of his cheek that I can see the lump it forms from several feet away. He leans over and spits on the ground between where he and my father stand, and before it hits the dirt, my father shouts, "Get off my field!"

My dad points to the parking lot, and his stare at Zack is hard. He rarely looks people directly in the eyes, but there's no mistaking the point he makes right now. It'll take a miracle for Zack to set foot on this field tomorrow, and I have never seen such a miracle happen in all my years of watching my dad coach.

It takes Zack a good fifteen minutes to pack up and lug his gear out to the lot, making a show of everything in front of the rest of us while we all do our best to play as if my father didn't just lose his shit. To add insult, Zack peels out from the lot, fishtailing the back end of his car enough to send burnt-rubber-smoke into the air. The squeal was his ultimate F-U to my dad.

That miracle he'll need just keeps getting farther and farther away.

Despite the sudden and very present tension felt on every square inch of the field and dugouts, we all manage to get through another hour of games until my dad calls the rest of practice and makes the next day's workouts optional.

I linger, not packing up until everyone has cleared the field. I have to wait for my dad to finish talking with the other coaches anyhow, but I also want to talk with Cannon. He's been abandoned here.

"Do you all live far?" I have a vague idea where their house is, but I've never been.

"Far enough," he says, punching out a laugh. He lifts his bag up over his shoulder and breathes out heavily through his nose, his tired gaze landing on mine.

"You can't walk home," I say.

"I'll be fine—"

I don't let him bother with the lie and march over to my dad, calling him out of the circle of coaches and doing my best not to eavesdrop. I hear enough to clue me in on things perhaps getting a little messy after today. Drama tends to do that, especially in high school sports.

"Cannon's stuck here now," I explain.

My father's eyes flit from me to where Cannon stands beyond my shoulder. His shoulders slump and he glances back to the coaches waiting on him to finish their talk.

"I can't give players rides. You know that," my dad says. I understand. Especially now that he made such a public stand against Zack's attitude. I also know enough to get why Zack's father makes this messy.

"I'll take him home. I'll be back before you're done." I lean my head to the side and droop my eyes just enough to prey on his weak spot. I am just a player out here, but in all other aspects, I truly am daddy's little girl.

He sighs and drops his hands in his pockets, looking off to the side before bringing the keys out and holding them out for me to take. Before I can grab them, he clutches them in his palm.

"Come right back. And this has nothing to do with practice. This is a friend driving a friend home." He's very literal, and given everything we've gone through in the past, I understand why.

"Got it." I nod.

I take the keys and march back to Cannon. "Come on," I say as I pass him, urging him to join me.

"Thanks," he finally says when we're halfway across the field. "Think he'll be long? Should we just drop our stuff in the van then come back?"

"My dad can't drive you, so I've gotta take you then come right back to get him," I explain.

He scrunches his face as I hit the button that automatically pops open the back.

"That's kinda weird. Nobody really cares," he says.

I drop my bag inside and turn to face him as he shifts his to rest next to mine. Our eyes meet and I do my best to portray exactly how serious this is.

"Everybody cares. They always do, but only bring it up when they need to," I say.

His brow knits as I close the back hatch, and I leave him there puzzled until I get inside and he joins me.

"My dad follows rules and regulations to a T. He documents everything, and he gets witness statements. Everyone in that circle out there talking today is going to be asked to write down their account of what happened. My dad doesn't mess around." *And it's all because of me.*

Cannon gives me general directions as I pull out of the lot, and the first few minutes of the drive are spent with him alerting me where to turn and when. We're turning onto his street when he brings the subject back to the one weighing on both our minds.

"My cousin is just really wound up, and the stress comes out poorly," he says.

I put the van in park a few houses away from his and lean back with a sigh, letting my hands fall to the bottom of the wheel.

"Quit making excuses for him," I say, rolling my head along the seat back until our eyes meet.

He blinks rapidly, as if computing my words, but instead of the argument I expect, he says, "You're right."

I offer a crooked, sympathetic smile.

"I know this isn't fair for you. I'm so sorry." Zack's car isn't in the driveway up ahead, which means he's gone somewhere to blow off steam.

"He's probably with Tory or Lucas," Cannon says, pushing the lever to lean his seat back a little. He props a leg up and holds his knee, his eyes darting around the landscape beyond the van, as though searching for a way to make all of this right.

"Why does your dad play by the rules, like you said?"

I do my best to mask the sick expression I want to make. The way I feel inside can't be helped. This subject was bound to come up, and I need to learn it's simply part of the journey of a female athlete in a man's world. It doesn't make me hate it any less.

"Back in New York . . ." I pause to draw in a deep breath, to swallow down some courage. "Well, I'm sure you'll be shocked to hear this, but not *everyone* wanted me to be on the team."

He chuckles, but when he realizes it's actually a sad statement on human behavior, he lets go of the humor, his laugh lines fading with the fall of his mouth back into a straight line.

"The weird thing is, most of the guys on the team? They were fine with it. My ex—"

"Ex?" he pipes up. Of course that's the part he pays attention to.

"Yes, *ex*. Meaning, not my current boyfriend." *Are you my current boyfriend?* This sudden question tangles in my head while I sort out the details of my sophomore and junior years at Xavier to share with him.

"His name is Jordan, so let's just call him Jordan," I say.

"I don't like him."

I laugh out and grab Cannon's arm, and can't help but smile at this sudden possessiveness. Also, it's strange to reach out and touch him like this. It's both natural and terrifying, a sensation only amplified by the way he reaches over with his other hand and weaves our fingers together.

"Oh," I stammer out, staring at the way our hands look together. The story I was telling slips away, but Cannon brings it back to the forefront.

"I'm listening," he says. And he truly is. This would probably be easier if he weren't, at least not so intently.

I swallow.

"Jordan's dad, his name's Bill. He's this big donor— Xavier's a private school."

Cannon nods, understanding.

"Anyhow, he basically ran the school's sports department. He wasn't the athletic director, or an employee. He was nothing more than a guy with one vote on a board of trustees. But he was—*is*—big on tradition. And girls should be on the sidelines, and in the stands, or . . ."

I pause to snort out a laugh because the thought is so ridiculous.

"In the kitchen, learning how to be a good and proper wife. A girl playing ball was, well, in his words, 'a travesty.'" I add the air quotes to drive it home.

I can think of a lot of things that are travesties. Homelessness, hunger, a truly great person being murdered in cold blood. Me playing ball? Not even close. My presence is an inconvenience to sexist assholes who were probably never half as good as me.

"So, what did they do, like, make a rule or something against you?"

I shake my head and look out my side window, the memories still crystal clear in my head.

"Our field was about a block away from the campus, which is kinda normal for Staten Island. Our locker room was in a basement under the gym, and the coaches' offices were buried in the back, behind the showers. No matter what time of day it was, when the power went out, it got pitch black in there. We had a big game against our rival, and one of the other players' dads caught me during my walk to the field and told me my dad left his scorebook on his desk."

The self-blame weighs down my insides the way it always does. No matter how many times I rationalize what happened, the small inner voice I try to keep quiet pipes up and tells me I let it all happen.

"The locker room was clear. I made sure because I was only supposed to be on the women's side. I was just going to run in, grab the book, and go. I didn't even suspect something when the lights went out because, like I said, that stuff happened all the time."

I can tell Cannon expects something worse by the way his eyes are locked open yet slanted with disappointment. Thank God it wasn't worse. That thought repeats in my head a lot. Really, though, what I'm doing is giving them all an excuse for what they did do to me.

"I couldn't find the book."

"There was no book," he concludes.

I breathe out through my nose and look down at the place where our hands still touch, at the way his thumb is now stroking my skin in careful, slow circles. I shake my head.

"There was no book," I echo him.

His fingers twitch as his muscle tense.

"Nobody was in there," I add quickly, taking the *worse* scenarios out of his imagination. "They locked the door. It was made of thick, heavy metal and it was old. Nothing about my old campus was to code, and that was the only way out. The most important game of the year was about to happen and I was buried below ground a block away."

"Damn, Hollis." His head falls to the side in sympathy, but I also see the relief in his eyes. I understand it because I feel the same relief whenever I remember what happened. I'm coming to terms with the fact it was a truly awful thing, even though it wasn't *worse.*

"I missed the first two innings. Jordan finally came looking for me with my father's keys. There was a scout for the local community college there who never got to see me play. Maybe for a lot of players that isn't the end of the world, but for a girl who wants to play this game in college, any school open to the idea of putting me on their roster is a big deal. They took that away from me.".

"Did the guys get kicked off the team? Expelled? Suspended at least?" His questions are so full of hope. I'm about to dash his outlook on humanity.

"It was parents who locked me in there. Three in particular, including Jordan's dad, Bill."

The way Cannon's mouth hangs open isn't rehearsed or pretend. His eyes drill into me, unblinking, waiting for me to say, "*Psych!*" or, "*Just kidding.*" Oh, how I wish I could.

Cannon twists in his seat, letting go of my hand for a moment while his gaze drifts off into the place where the pavement meets the horizon.

"You deserve to play, Hollis. No, you deserve to *start.*" He's so resolute in his words, his mouth closed tight to punctuate the finality of them while he shakes his head. His eyes haze and it's almost as if he's playing out an argument with someone else in his head, preparing to defend me.

Before I can talk myself out of it, I lean over the console and press my lips to his cheek, holding his jaw with my hand. His head moves in slow motion, turning to face me, his mouth opening with a faint breath. Our eyes meet briefly, his falling lashes my only clue that his close just before mine. He palms my cheek as his mouth captures my bottom lip, and in a single heartbeat, we're kissing.

Nothing about the moment is rushed, and every pass of his lips against mine is tender and sweet. Light tastes of my tongue with his are tempered by measured suckles of my top and bottom lips. He takes his time, shifting enough in his seat to steady my head in both of his hands. The way he holds me makes me feel cherished, and this is now one more thing that's going on my list of things to really, truly adore about Cannon Jennings.

THIRTEEN

CANNON

Walking in on a conversation and having it go stone-cold silent is never a good sign. That's what just happened, and I know my uncle and Zack were talking about pushing out Coach Taylor. I heard enough before I came down the stairs to get the general idea of their discussion.

The fact they aren't bringing it up now, in front of me? That means they don't trust me to know the details. That's both good and bad. Good morally because I don't want to be a part of something I don't believe is right, and bad because I can't prepare anyone for what might be coming.

Would I warn Hollis, though? Should I now, even though what I know is really just a bunch of bitching and whining over runny eggs at the breakfast table.

I don't know what time Zack got in last night, but I know he was drunk. I heard him vomit, twice. After Hollis dropped me off, I called Tory and spent most of the night playing video games with him and his brother and Lucas. I suspect Zack was out with a few of the baseball guys, getting support for his bruised ego.

If anyone tries to take this out on Hollis, I am going to lose my shit.

"How'd practice go yesterday?" My uncle tests me with that question.

"Ask Zack," I say without meeting his gaze. I stuff a mouthful of eggs and potatoes in my mouth.

"I wouldn't know. I got *sent home*," Zack grits out, shoveling food into his own mouth to avoid talking.

Clearly, they've already talked about what happened. Everything about Zack's tone is rehearsed. The awkward silence, broken by the occasional scrape of a fork along a plate or the clunk of a full coffee mug on the table, is meant to flush me out. I don't fall for any of it.

"What do you think your dad will think, Cannon?" My uncle changes up his route.

I shrug, eyes focused on my now half-empty plate as I scoop up more food.

"You think he'll be okay with moving your family across country so you can throw to some girl?"

I drop my fork at that comment, my chest tightening into a thick ball right where my ribs meet. I push the plate away, done, and unfurl the napkin my aunt always rolls up for us at the table. I run it over my mouth and chin.

"I guess we can ask him when he gets here," I say, standing and taking my plate to the sink. I meet my aunt's eyes as I do and get the sense that she's had to suffer through this conversation all morning.

"Speaking of, he might get in tomorrow," my uncle says. His chair drags along the floor as he stands.

My buzzing nerves instantly calm at that bit of news. My dad is sensible, even if he's competitive. He and I have had long talks about what might happen if I get recruited by places where Zack doesn't have a shot. My dad's helped me realize that even though Zack and I formed this dream together, I can still forge out on my own if that's what's best for me. Uncle Joel seems to think carrying Zack is my responsibility. I finally see the difference between loyalty and being taken advantage of.

"Is he driving straight through?" I drop my rinsed plate into the washer rack and turn to keep my back to my uncle as he steps in close.

"Yep," he confirms.

Finally looking up, my gaze runs smack into my cousin's. He's leaning back in his chair, rocking it on the back two legs while balancing a steaming cup of coffee on his propped up knee. The way he's eying me pushes my guard up like an invisible wall. When we were kids and I got a better Christmas gift than he did, he made the same smug face he's making right now—as though he has secret plans to sabotage whatever I have that he doesn't. Back then, it was a bike chain breaking or a wood bat splintering after too few uses. The things he could ruin for me now are far more important.

"There's a big meeting today. Isn't there, Dad?" My cousin's eyes remain on me despite his question.

"Hopefully," my uncle responds, his answer cut short from a phone call. He walks between us and holds up a finger as if I'm supposed to stick around and see what this call is all about. My gaze follows his path down the hall and through the front door before I return my focus to Zack, who is still staring at me, his hint of a smile the kind a villain wears while he watches his victim drink down poison. I do my best to ignore his silent plea for attention, but when a quiet laugh slips from his mouth while I haul my backpack up on my shoulder, I break.

"What's your deal, dude. Just spill it. I don't have time to play the *What's Wrong with Zack* game this morning. I have a test to get ready for." I don't have a test, but there's no way I'm hanging out in the parking lot with him all morning just so he can glare at me and say cryptic shit.

"Board's not really happy with Coach Taylor's preseason, and it seems *someone* at the district found out." Zack leans forward and sets his mug on the table, then folds his hands together near it, pleased with himself, as if he did anything other than act like an asshat at practice.

"What's wrong with preseason?" I shake my head and pinch my lips tight.

"Uhm, maybe that he's not pulling the team together and building a sense of unity? Or that he's broken up the core group of players who have been incredibly successful the last three years in a row?" I can tell by how foreign these words sound coming out of his mouth that he's probably parroting talking points that my uncle already said. I'm also guessing Uncle Joel is the someone who told these same talking points to the district.

Instead of gratifying Zack with a response, I just stare at him and quirk up one side of my mouth and corresponding brow, a gesture that says "Seriously?" without having to utter the word.

"*Pfff.*" Zack rolls his eyes and stands, sliding the mug to the other end of the table. His mom takes it, and I'm upset for her that she's expected to clean up after him.

"You need a ride today or is your little girlfriend coming to get you?" His shoulder bumps into my chest with an extra thrust as he passes and asks that question. I tilt my head to the side and wait for him to turn back and look at me, but he doesn't.

That knot in my chest pulls tighter, but I stay on my path and don't give in to his passive aggressive quips. I'm not sure whether he says that because of something he suspects about me and Hollis or because of something he *saw*, but he's being a douche.

Without a word, I follow him out the door and get into the passenger side, dropping my backpack between my legs and buckling up. He pauses to stare at me for a few hard seconds, finally letting out a dismissive chuckle and buckling up himself.

"Whatever, man," he says. And thank God, we drive the rest of the way to school in total silence.

My plan to head straight to class and fake a bullshit test gets cut short the moment we pull into the lot. My gaze tracks Hollis's movement as she picks up her steps and speeds over to the last row of parking spots. Zack sees her a few seconds after me and lets out a muffled grunt when he realizes she's trying to catch up with us.

"What the fuck does she want?" he grumbles.

My stomach sinks. I've been riding a rollercoaster ever since I snuck out yesterday morning to meet Hollis at the gulch. Maybe I got on this ride at that New Year's party. It's hard to tell anymore, the line's so blurred. I've gone from being pissed off that she dares to exist in my carefully made plans to wanting to fight like hell to make sure she stays in them. Hollis, she makes me a better person.

The car stops hard and I lurch forward, slapping my palms on the dash.

"Dick!" I bark.

My cousin's arms are locked at the steering wheel, and he has yet to kill the engine. When I survey what's happening just outside his window, I spot the reason why. Hollis is making a gesture, and my cousin is going to shit all over it.

"This your idea?" Zack rolls his head to the side and hits me with lazy, annoyed eyes. I lean forward enough to read the logo on the box Hollis is holding: CUPPIES.

Shit. She brought him cupcakes.

I shake my head and cross my finger over my chest in an X.

"Swear to God, man. This is all her." *Give her credit for being nice,* I continue in my head, knowing he won't.

Cuppies is in the mall on the outskirts of town, one of those places where you can get oversized cupcakes and personalized cookies for special occasions. They're overpriced for cake, in my opinion, which makes this peace offering she's holding in her palms that much more thoughtful.

As my cousin pushes open his door, I sit with my back firmly pressed into my seat. I can't bear to watch, and maybe, if I'm lucky, he'll close the door before I have to listen.

"Awe, shucks, Double D. It's not my birthday," he says, leaving the door wide open behind him. I breathe out through my nose and close my eyes. He has to stop calling her that. It's harassment, and it doesn't help his cause. More importantly, she doesn't deserve it.

"I know, I just— I don't know why things between us are so . . . you know," she stammers. Fuck, I should get out and help her through this. I should be her wingman, make my cousin accept this gracefully. But I am still sitting here. All I've been able to muster is the strength to reopen my eyes so I can watch this disaster go down in flames.

"Well, how do you want things to be between us?" He leans into the side of the door, blocking my view. I lean forward to catch Hollis's gaze. Her eyes flit nervously to me then back to him.

"I don't know. Cordial, I guess?"

My lip ticks up with a stunted laugh. Ten bucks says Zack has no idea what the word *cordial* means.

"So you bought me cupcakes?" He steps forward, taking the box from her hands.

"Everyone says this place is good, and I wasn't sure whether you liked vanilla or chocolate, so I got both."

Goddamn, she's being so thoughtful. I'm not sure why she's trying so hard with him, but I can't help but feel this has something to do with that board meeting and the whispers at the district level about her dad and his coaching position. Not to say that Hollis isn't capable of doing something nice for Zack for no reason, but from what I know of her and from what I've seen of my cousin's behavior, I would say he sure as shit doesn't deserve it.

"Let's see," Zack says, tucking the open box in the crook of his arm, pinching it between his side and elbow while he pulls the paper from the bottom of a gooey, chocolate cake. I can tell by the movement of his head and jaw that he's taking a bite.

"Nope, don't like chocolate," he says, letting the cake fall from his hand to the ground. The thick frosting spatters. Hollis's lips part in disbelief as she blinks slowly at the wasted cake.

"Zack, knock it off," I finally say. I hate that I let it play out as far as it did. The liar inside me wants to say it's because I was giving Zack the benefit of the doubt, but really, I'm just a coward.

I get out of the car and pull my bag up on my arm as I step around to meet my cousin and the girl I'm maybe starting to like too much. Her jaw is flexed in a way that has the offended, open-mouthed smile locked in place.

"She's just trying to be nice, dude. Say thank you and take the damn cupcakes." I sigh, shaking my head and wondering how this is the conversation I'm having this morning. Hollis is still staring at the discarded cake on the ground.

"Was she, though? Being nice, I mean." My cousin tilts his head to the side and glances at me then back to Hollis again, practically daring her to stare back at him.

Lifting her chin, she closes her mouth and lets it fall into a stubborn, hardened frown.

Not wanting to see this escalate further, especially given the many places my mind is taking it, I intervene completely, taking the box into my own hands, closing the lid, and shoving it into my cousin's chest. I step into the space between him and Hollis, cutting them off from one another.

"Yes, she was. Now, say thank you and go to first hour." I hold his stare for longer than I want. His eyes swirl with something truly hateful mixed with unwarranted betrayal. He didn't give me a choice with this. I will stand by him when he's right, but I've never been about signing up to be part of the school dick squad. I've got enough of a label floating around out there from being an introvert who doesn't like parties and small talk. Just ask that girl, Abby.

Zack finally gives in and breaks our stare, but only so he can look down at the mess he made on the asphalt.

"Thanks for the shitty present, Double D," he says, and I shove his chest, crinkling the box when I do it.

"Her name is Hollis," I seethe.

His smirk is faint and cynical, and it's the only thing I'm going to get in return. My body teems with aggression, and if he were to let loose and take a swing at me, I might knock him out. Maybe he senses that, or maybe he likes the attention he's drawn from people standing nearby. Roland and a few other guys from the team have gathered on the walkway that leads to the school, and they're entertained, trying to choke off their own laughter. All I keep thinking is how disgusted Coach Taylor would be if he saw them, even if it wasn't his daughter they're targeting. The fact it is Hollis only makes it worse.

Zack steps into me, his hot breath in my face. A few more inches closer and he'll be crushing the box into my chest.

"Whatever," he grunts out, crashing his shoulder into mine again, harder than he did earlier. My shoulders swivel but my feet remain firm where I stand. I reach forward and slam his car door shut, then trail his steps with my eyes as he joins the laughing group of trolls who have picked the wrong side in this war. Without looking back once, he tosses the crumpled box of sweets into the trash as soon as he reaches the flag pole, and all I can do is laugh out loud and apologize for him.

"Hollis, I'm sor—"

She shakes her head, and I get the point before she even has to ask. I'm always apologizing for him. That needs to stop, and it stops here.

FOURTEEN

HOLLIS

I'm not the kind of girl who has, well, girl kinda problems.

I've had seven major crushes in my life, and six boyfriends to complete them. Granted, the first four were all before fifth grade, but still, they count. I mean, it's hard to resist the girl who always gets picked first in dodgeball; at least, it used to be. That's all it took for me to make Ridge Howard, Miguel Velasquez, Shawn Sutter and Logan Sutter—*that's right, both Sutter brothers*—declare their love for me in the good ole days of elementary school.

My freshman year was all about Angus Lowenstein. He was smart, and completely unlike my usual type. He was into theater, and even convinced me to try out for the high school musical with him. He got the lead. I got cut. (Newsflash: I can't sing worth a damn.) It didn't matter, though, because Angus was perfection in the boyfriend department and on the stage. He was also gay. When I told him I didn't mind, he explained that the problem was dating me kinda got in the way of him being his true self. He's studying in France now, and he's got a French boyfriend who isn't vague or grumpy or mixed up in messy family drama that involves my dad's coaching and my passion for the game. Nope, Angus is in a normal, healthy relationship where everyone knows exactly where they stand and who they are. In essence, he's still perfect.

And this brings me to my two most recent crushes. Jordan was mutual love in every single way, except for the part where his father tried to intimidate me into quitting by locking me in the basement of my school and Jordan refused to stand up to him about it. I recently stopped blaming Jordan, and I have the Cannon situation to thank for that. Going against your family isn't easy, and in many ways, it feels impossible. That's basically what I asked Jordan to do when the Dean of Students called everyone in for interviews after the basement incident. I asked Jordan to turn on his dad, and despite the broken relationship he had with his father, the thought of severing it completely was too much. His lack of testimony was enough to give the powers that be at Xavier an excuse to not do a damn thing except, of course, fire my dad.

And now I'm looking to Cannon to do something very similar, to step away from blindly supporting his cousin to stand with me instead. He seems so willing, and yet I know the damage this will do to his relationship with his cousin and probably his uncle too. Maybe even his dad. I'm not sure making out with me in a mom van is truly worth the sacrifice.

"So, let me make sure I got this straight. You brought Zack cupcakes even though he's a dickhead and he threw them away—because he's a dickhead." June takes a bite of her carrot while her eyes stare at my lunch tray as though she's reading notes to help her process the facts about my screwed up life.

"Yes, that pretty much sums it up," I agree.

"And Cannon called him out on it, but you guys aren't a thing, or maybe you are, you don't know, but you've made out twice." She snaps another bite, her eyes still focused on my tray.

"Three times, actually, if you count New Year's."

"Oh, you always count New Year's," June says through a devious laugh. She takes a deep breath and tosses what's left of her carrot into the open cup of ranch, then pushes her tray to the middle of the table, folds her arms, and sets her gaze on me.

"That's pretty much it," I say, reaching to her tray and commandeering the leftover ranch. I flick the carrot out of the cup and dip the crust of my pizza in to see if that will make this poor excuse for a slice of pie any better. She wrinkles her nose and tells me I'm gross.

It's actually better this way, but no matter what I dip this crap in, it's still not New York pizza.

"I'm not seeing the problem. Lola?" June looks to her friend, who still owes me some beachy waves.

Lola sucks up the last few drops of her smoothie while she shakes her head, her lips puckered around the straw.

"There's no problem. And you totes know I think Cannon is an asshole. But it sounds like he's actually being kind of chivalrous."

I knit my brow at Lola's odd word choice.

"She's reading *Canterbury Tales* in English. Excuse her obsession with knights in shining armor," June explains.

"*Mmm*, armor," Lola adds, swiveling side-to-side in her seat, her lips curled coyly beneath her dreamy eyes. I half expect a white horse with a knight riding on top to bust through the cafeteria doors and whisk her away.

"I know he's being a good guy, and doing the right things, but I still feel like—"

"Like the house of cards is going to collapse at any moment," June finishes for me.

I look down and consider her visual, quickly deciding she's right. And that I'm probably not being fair, but I've watched cards fall before.

"I do. His uncle is the kind of loud guy who refuses to back off quietly. And his son is an apple that did not fall far from the tree. Zack is not going to like me—ever. He's never going to think I deserve anything I earn, and Cannon is trapped right between us, fruitlessly trying to convince him otherwise. And maybe—"

June cuts me off, drawing a line over her lips like a zipper.

"Don't you dare say you aren't worth it." Her expression is serious, and it's the first time I've seen her make a stern face to put someone in their place. Weird that she's making it at me.

"It's just a lot to ask," I relent, discarding what's left of my pizza crust on the tray and flopping back into my seat. I glance down at my pegged jeans, ripped holes in both knees, and torn-up skate shoes with stick figures drawn on every square inch. It's hard not to feel inadequate sitting this close to a girl like Lola, who Cannon already snubbed, uninterested. My sweat-shirt is two-sizes too big because I like it that way. Lola's clothes are painted on, her curves made for race cars and the boys who drive them.

"He likes *you*." June interrupts my negative thoughts, leaning forward with her hands one on top of the other, resting on the tabletop right in front of me. "You are Cannon Jennings's type, based on everything you have told us. Mystery solved. That grumpy SOB has a weakness, and it's a girl who can keep up with him and put him in his place. Don't sell yourself short, Hollis. You're a hottie, and nothing like anyone else."

Well, shit. I might be in love with June just a little. I smile at her bashfully because that was a pretty big string of compliments to sit and take in all at once.

"Thanks," I eek out. I'm more accustomed to someone telling me, "Nice line drive."

Emboldened by June's killer pep talk, I walk into study hall and take the seat to Cannon's right, ignoring my usual self-imposed rules about sitting next to him. There's no reason it should be any different in here than it is in our first hour, where we talk and laugh and sometimes—*sometimes*—brush fingertips over arms or thighs when the teacher isn't looking.

"Hey," I say, reaching over and squeezing his shoulder as I sit. He stiffens and immediately shifts his posture to lose my touch and put a few more inches of distance between us. It's obvious, and his acting is bad.

"You scared me," he lies. I'm starting to recognize the differences in his laughs, and the thin ones with more breath to them are definitely forced. Like this one.

"Yeah, I'm stealthy like that." I look at him sideways, a little judgement in my squinted eyes.

"Right," he says, shutting his mouth into a tight smile. He holds up his notebook and points to it, as if it's some exhibit to prove he's hard at work on his studies. The page is blank, and I can't wait to see what he fills it with.

"Uh huh," I say, pivoting in my seat so I face him more than not. Wearing my wry smile, I rest my elbow on my desktop and hold my chin while I glare at his mundane tasks.

He writes his name at the top, then the date. He taps the point of his pen on the next line a few times, finally writing down the word Canterbury.

"You're not in Lola's class," I point out quickly. I know he's not because he and I have the same teacher, just opposite hours. And we aren't studying Canterbury right now; we're still on Shakespeare.

Cannon blinks a few times while staring at the page, finally drawing a scribble of lines through his fake essay title before laying the pen flat on the page.

"Oh, hey, Hollis. What's up?" Tory reaches over my shoulder as he walks in, holding out a fist. I pound it, already accepted into his circle. He takes the seat in front of Cannon but remains sitting to the side while the rest of the class filters in. His gaze bobs between the two of us—me staring at Cannon and Cannon pretending he sees nothing at all.

"Things weird here?" Tory wiggles his finger in the air between us, and I laugh out once, hard.

"Seems so." I shake my head and right myself in my chair, leaning the opposite way to pull out my own notebook—for *actual* homework.

"Oh, I get it. You two hooked up," Tory teases. My cheeks burn and I know without looking they're florescent pink. I cough, unable to get the words out to put up an argument, and Cannon takes care of it for me, slapping his friend on the shoulder with his notepad.

"Dude, don't be like Zack," he grumbles.

"Ah, I see. Didn't we already have this talk?" Tory waits for Cannon to lift his chin, and when he does, they spend a few seconds in a staring competition as though neither wants to give in.

"You aren't responsible for your cousin, and your life is separate from his," Tory finally says.

I draw my attention down to my notes and doodle, and wish I'd sat at least one more seat away. The smile inching into my cheeks is hard to hide. I like Tory, and I like what he said even more.

Cannon flattens his notebook again and brings both his hands to his face, rubbing his eyes then moving his fingers into his hair, kneading his scalp.

"I know that, man. I know. He's just in this super fucked up place, and I don't know what's going on. I'm sorry." He rolls his head to the side in his palm and reaches toward me with his free hand, fingers stretched out wide for me to weave mine into the empty spaces. I do and he squeezes a little, shaking our hands together in a gentle movement that's also reassuring—and very, very public.

So does this mean we are a—we?

"Well, for the record. I like you two. I like her more, but I like the two of you as a thing," Tory says, pointing to me when he makes the joke at Cannon's expense. We both breathe out a small laugh, and before our hands separate, Cannon's thumb runs along my knuckles a few times for added reassurance.

The door clicks shut behind us and we all straighten in our seats out of habit. So far, Mr. Orson has been a cool study hall monitor. In the nearly two weeks I've spent with him, I've learned that as long as you remain fairly quiet, you can do whatever you want in here. You can also walk out for restroom and water bottle-filling breaks anytime you want. A girl I know does lines in the bathroom and goes missing for the middle twenty minutes of class every single day.

Maybe it was my power lunch with June, or perhaps the little tease of Cannon's hand on mine—whatever the root of it, I decide to test the liberal in-and-out policy for people who aren't ditchers and drug-addicts. Well, not *full-time* ditchers anyhow. I would say I'm more of an extended-leaver who wants to make out with my maybe boyfriend.

The idea doesn't feel stupid when I bite my lip and glance over my shoulder while nudging Cannon, and I still feel pretty bold and confident all the way out the door. The humiliation doesn't creep in until I've been leaning against the wall just outside the culinary arts room for five full minutes and my stomach rumbles because the bread smells so freaking good.

I'm close to giving up my nefarious plan and head back into class when the door swings open at the opposite end of the hallway and Cannon steps out. I push off of the wall and tuck my hands into my back pockets. He stops in his tracks and drops his hands into his front ones, tilting his head to the side before nodding toward the building exit on his end. I nod back and we maintain eye contact while we leave the farthest building from the main office.

Our doors open in sync, but I hold on to mine for an extra second or two while I take in the view of him as he makes his way closer to me. A sly grin pushes a dimple into his right cheek. He cocks his head to the left a few feet from the exit and soon disappears behind a brick wall.

Nervously scanning the area around me, I rush to duck around the same space, freaked out that I'll get caught doing something I shouldn't. My smile is almost manic over this tiny moment of social and academic recklessness. My cheeks are pushed high and my lips stretched as wide as they'll go to accommodate my aching grin when I round the corner and run into Cannon's chest head-on.

"Oh, door locked?" I laugh out nervously. His hands grip my shoulders to spin me around, and he cages me like a defender keeping me from getting to the goal line. It only takes a second for my mind to switch gears and realize he is ushering me away from something.

"What is it?" I force my body to face him, working against his efforts to turn me around.

"It's nothing. Door locked, so let's go somewhere else."

He's a bad liar. His tone betrays him easily, the even volume and guarded choice of words indicating that something set him off. His caginess ratchets up my frustration so I push past him, flinging his hands from my waist and arms until I break free and step into the walled-off space he was hiding from me.

Someone called me a cunt.

Wow.

"That must have been a pretty fat Sharpie," I say, my arms going limp to my sides while I take in the scribbled words on the maintenance door.

HOLLIS IS A CUNT

"I mean, it isn't very original," I say, quick to pretend I'm unfazed. "He's just playing off of tropes and sensationalism. And there's a pretty big movement among women to take that word back and redefine it, make it our own."

The tears come regardless of my brave face. I shudder, and choke on the emotion that rises up my throat faster than I can push it back down. The insult burns and I hate that I let it.

"Hollis." Cannon's arms are around me before I can protest. I rock as he holds me from behind, non-stop sniffles and guarded breaths working to wipe away any proof that this affected me whatsoever.

"It's fine," I say, pulling an arm free to wipe my palm across my cheeks and eyes. "I'm fine. Whatever. It's stupid."

Trembles have set in. I'm both hurt and livid, and both fight to rule my emotions. The one thing I'm not, though, is surprised. And in a moment when all I want to do is erase this experience from existence and rush back to the safety of my desk and the walls of study hall, I can't because the distant sound of male laughter and a golf cart motor gets louder by the heartbeat.

Cannon and I both duck behind the wall, his body flush against mine as if shielding me from oncoming enemy fire. His fingers move to my chin then slide up my lips, holding my mouth closed lightly as he breathes out, "*Shh.*"

I mean, it's not like I'm going to shout, "Hey, here I am—ditching class to check out the mural smearing my character."

His touch on my face softens, but his hand stays where it is. I'm quickly more comforted by it than I am offended, especially as the voices of the two men in the cart become clearer. This part of campus is the most private. That's why it's where students go to vape, and it's why a minute ago I thought maybe I was going to make out back here with a guy I'm quickly letting every guard I've ever had down for.

For our school's athletic director, Tom Wallis, and Cannon's uncle Joel, though, this spot is the perfect spot to organize a coup.

"You think you have enough players willing to go on the record that Taylor's breaking code of conduct? This can't be some *me too* shit show."

My breathing becomes harsh, my chest quaking with fury as my hands grip the front of Cannon's sweatshirt, forming fists around the fabric.

"Yeah, it'll go way beyond him playing favorites with his girl. The man just isn't the right fit for our program, and it's a plain and simple fact. His methods aren't going to work out here, and we have to make the fix before tryouts." Joel Jennings's tone is even. Calm, in fact. He's had this plan brewing for days. For the life of me, though, I can't fathom anyone other than Zack who'd back the crazy idea that my dad isn't the kind of coach who builds great programs. He's either bluffing that he has the numbers behind him or he's paying players to take up his cause.

"He'll lawyer up, you know," our athletic director says.

A muffled voice breaks through on the radio in their cart, something about being needed at the front office.

"Let him. In the meantime, Coach Gage is ready to take over."

They drive off, finishing their conversation too far away to be heard. Those few words Cannon and I heard are enough, though. Coach Gage is a nice guy, but he's seventy-two. He's been volunteering out here for decades. My dad was talking about him at dinner the other night, joking to my mom and Ben and I about how impressive it is that he can still hit pop flies so well. The guy has no interest in leading a team, but he's also a pushover, which is probably how Zack's dad pressured him into taking over my dad's job.

"I have to tell him," I realize aloud, pushing from Cannon's cover and slipping out into the open.

The golf cart is nowhere to be seen. I bite the back of my hand, teeth gripping my knuckles while I sort out the rush of thoughts. Cannon is never more than inches away from me. I'm shaking mad.

"Hollis." He spins me and palms both of my shoulders to catch my gaze and stop the world from spinning. I'm having a panic attack.

"Breathe," he says.

So I do.

FIFTEEN

CANNON

I knew Hollis wouldn't be able to wait for the end of the day to see her dad. I'm only glad she didn't rush over to his office in the state she was in. When she skipped out on weightlifting, I figured she was probably talking to him. Now that his door is locked shut and she's out on the field throwing with Zack and a few of the other guys, I'm not sure what to think.

Today was optional. It's my cousin's fault that Coach called off the remaining organized practices for the week. Next week is the last one before tryouts. I'm not worried about myself, but I am worried about Zack. It's not that he needs the practice, as much as he needs a serious personality adjustment to make sure he doesn't get himself benched—or worse, cut.

Or course, if Coach Taylor goes away, maybe that's not an issue. I can't buy into the idea that Coach Gage will like my cousin any better, though. I guess that fact is moot, since Coach Gage will be manipulated into building the team as my uncle sees fit.

I miss my dad.

My gear bag slung over my shoulder, I pull my phone from my pocket and send my father a text while I walk out to join the others. I wonder if they bothered to run? I'm sure Hollis did.

I message my dad to see where he's at, and when he replies with *100 miles to go,* my lungs open up, taking what feels like the first full breath I've drawn in ages.

A hundred miles puts him in town tonight. It means I'll have a rational set of ears to talk to, and wise advice to help me navigate this clusterfuck of a senior season.

With a clearing breath, I tuck my phone in the side pocket of my bag and head down to the field to join the others.

"We ran already," Zack says before I drop my bag and change my shoes. He's robotic with his throwing, and equally so with his words.

I glance to Hollis for verification and she quirks a brow and nods. That fucker really did run.

I stare at her for a few extra seconds while she throws, long enough to get a read on her expression to see how things are after talking with her dad, if she even had a chance to. I'm not able to read much from her expression, but I can tell she isn't exactly happy. She doesn't look as worried as before, though, so I leave them to finish throwing while I get in my run.

My times are getting faster every time I do this. I think about the difference I've seen in myself since I met Coach Taylor—and Hollis. I'm more than faster; I do things with purpose, and that thinking is beyond the field.

I wonder how I would react to the way my cousin acts if I didn't have a personal connection to Hollis. What if I never went to that New Year's party? What if she was simply coach's daughter, no connection to me at all? Would I have bothered to form one?

I never would have liked what Zack has done, but shamefully, I'm pretty sure I would have tolerated it—more so than I already have. I would have drawn a line and made it not my problem. My dad is like that. He doesn't approve of a lot of things, including the way the CEO of his engineering firm back home treated his female coworkers. My dad never said anything to anyone who could do anything about it, though. I suppose I haven't, either. I have made my point to Zack, though. I realize that's not enough, especially after what we saw—and heard—outside the study hall rooms.

I'm pacing after my run, checking the time on my smart watch, when Hollis jogs over from the infield. My instinct is to rush back with her, to avoid giving my cousin more reason to talk about us being alone, but then it hits me.

Fuck it.

Let him hate on me too.

"Hey," I say, leaning into her and kissing her jaw. She's sweaty, but I don't give a damn.

Her eyes are wide when I pull back, and her mouth is a hard line.

"What are you doing?" she growls in a whisper.

I scrunch my shoulders and tilt my head, a little thrown that she's not game for throwing the PDA in my cousin's face. If he's part of my uncle's plans, then he can deal. In fact, he can deal no matter what.

"Zack's being weird," she adds.

I glance over her shoulder where my cousin is dragging mats out for hitting on the field. He seems super motivated, especially compared to the half-assed effort he's put into workouts so far.

"I'll give you that, yeah," I agree, picking up my gear and walking with her back to the field. She holds my mitt to justify walking with me.

"Did you talk to your dad?" I ask.

"That's the thing."

My head swivels to meet her gaze, and I can tell by the slant to her eyes that something changed.

"Yeah?" I question.

She walks close to me as we enter the dugout, constantly scanning to make sure we're alone enough for her to share details. She nods to Roland and I study him while he pulls his water jug to his mouth and chugs. He laughed at her this morning, which speaks volumes about his character. *Would I have been different? I like to think so but honestly, probably not.*

Hollis waits for him to jog out to the base path to help Zack unroll the mats. Not wasting a second of our time out of earshot, she leans over the back of the bench and looks me in the eyes.

"Coach Gage told my dad he's going to have to retire. Said he and the wife bought an RV and plan to visit the grandkids in California. He's done after tryouts."

We blink at one another while I digest the new information and form an opinion. I'm not sure what to make of it, and I can tell neither is she. One thing is certain: the school won't be able to count on Coach Gage to fill a last minute coaching vacancy this close to tryouts. It means we have time, though I'm not sure how much. My uncle works quickly, and secretly. He's good at making connections; part of his slick marketing savvy.

We make a pact to play along, to play dumb and let Zack lead out here. Giving him a little bit of authority might be a good way to reach him, but my gut says we have to play this careful.

Hollis warms up my arm and we spend the next hour and a half taking live at-bats. About a dozen players show up, and between Roland and me, we throw a good eighty pitches. The rest of the at-bats are taken off the tee or the machine, which must be about as old as the clubhouse. The metal plates are warped, which makes every fifth pitch come out a little wild. One buzzes my cousin's head, and as he collapses to his ass and tosses his bat to the center of the field, I brace myself for him to think Hollis did it on purpose, simply because she dropped a ball into the feeder.

"Damn, girl. You trying to mimic Cannon's pitches with that thing?" My cousin gets to his feet and claps the dirt from his hands, his laughter pulling up his cheeks into a huge smile. It's as if he's a pod person. Or knows his initial plan with my uncle fell through.

Maybe it's both.

"That my nephew all grown up taking hacks out there?" My dad's voice is like salve for a wound I didn't realize I was nursing. Damn, I've missed him.

"Uncle Mike!" My cousin tosses his bat to the ground and jogs around one side of the backstop while I saunter around the other.

Zack's strong enough now to pick my father up, and he does. For a moment, watching them embrace, I soak in the genuine laughter and slaps on the back with big hugs. I forget that I have a lot of shit to catch my dad up on when it comes to my uncle and cousin. I keep that pushed to the side a little longer as my dad lets go of Zack's neck and opens his arms wide to me. It's been a few long months since we've seen each other in real life. Video chats just aren't the same.

"Hey, Dad," I say through an earnest grin.

"Come here, kiddo." He tugs on the shoulder of my shirt and we fall into a warm embrace, his large hand slapping against my shoulder blade while mine does the same. He's been calling me kiddo since I could understand language. It's nice to know that some things you don't grow out of.

"I got in a few hours early and figured I'd come find you in your element." He steps back and to the side, giving me a good view of my truck. It's filthy from its trip across the country, but damn, I'm almost as glad to see my wheels as I am my pops.

"I'm guessing you're gonna need my help unloading that?" I gesture toward the full load tied down with ropes in the back of the truck.

"Well, since most of that is yours—"

"Like hell it is. That's Mom's shoes and clothes and you know it," I joke.

We both cough out a good laugh before a brief moment of awkward quiet settles in among all of us. It's in this beat, right now, that I remember how messed up everything has become, and how much worse I fear it might get.

"Mr. Jennings, it's nice to meet you," Hollis says, stepping in next to me. She reaches out her hand for my dad to take. He knows very little about

Hollis other than the big picture—we have a girl on our team, she's good, and Zack doesn't like her.

"Ah, so you're this big hitter I've been hearing about." My dad speaks through a practiced smile, maybe sensing the bitterness wafting off of my cousin like fumes.

"She hits all right," Zack pipes in, leaving our small circle and moving back toward the plate to his discarded bat. Hollis glances at his back as he walks away and lets out a short laugh.

"I hit better than he does," she whispers, cupping her hand as if she's sharing a secret with my father.

My dad chuckles.

"I bet you do," he whispers back with a wink.

I want my dad to like Hollis. Whatever this thing is between me and her has been cast under a dark cloud because of all the shit with Zack and my uncle. It'll be nice to admit out loud to someone that I really like this girl.

"We about done here?" I ask over my shoulder. My cousin scans the area. Most of the other players are gassed and already packing up. I can tell he wants to go more, probably to show off in front of my dad. But all I want is to get in my truck and talk with my father alone for the first time in way too long. I've missed him.

"Yeah, guess so," Zack says, tossing his bat on top of his equipment bag before jerking one of the Velcro straps of his batting glove loose.

"I can stay, if you want to take a few more swings?"

Hollis's offer is only within earshot of me, Zack and my dad, and I wish someone else heard so they would give in and stick around, too. As it is, I bristle at her suggestion and Zack seems poised to ignore it.

"I don't mind sticking around, watching for a while," my dad offers. He's bound to be exhausted, and since he got in early, he shouldn't have to leave for the airport for an entire day. I'm sure he wants to sleep.

"No, seriously . . . I'd like to work on a few things, too," Hollis adds. Her gaze strikes a deal with mine, and I don't like the dangerous gamble she's making. Plus, I'm not certain how she's getting home. The thought of her on this field alone with Zack, in a car—alone, with Zack—makes my stomach fold up into itself.

"I mean, I'm about done," Zack says, building up an excuse of his own when Hollis cuts him short, grabbing his wrist with her hand. His eyes zero in on the enemy threat, and mine flash protectively, a sour feeling coating my insides and pulling down the sides of my mouth.

"Just another round, two tops," she says.

The two of them stare at one another, only inches apart, and my pulse jackhammers in my chest, tempting my fist into action. But Zack doesn't do anything. Why Hollis is making this offer—*wanting* to spend time with a guy I've been ashamed to call family lately—is lost on me. Unless . . . she really is just good. Stubborn, perhaps, is more fitting.

"You want me to come back in a bit, give you a lift home?" My motives are obvious to everyone, and Zack shoots me a snarky glare that's his way of calling me pathetic.

"I can get her home." My cousin holds my gaze for a solid beat, and our eyes briefly war. While his seem to tell me to trust him, mine warn him not to push me too far.

"Great. Okay, well, I'll catch up with you later," Hollis says, ending the discussion. She squeezes my forearm, this touch more tender than the way she grabbed Zack's, and again, my cousin and I zero in on it. My body rushes with heat at getting caught, a sensation that sinks my stomach with the G-force of a roller coaster when my dad elbows my side and lifts a brow.

"See you at home, cuz," Zack says, his smile falling into an ominous, relaxed line that reads like a devious plan. He lifts the bucket of balls and heads toward the tee to join Hollis. *She's strong, and she's safe.* I keep those two thoughts on repeat until my dad and I pull out of the parking lot and head toward our temporary home.

"So, you didn't mention that Hollis is—"

"Hot," I sigh out. I punch out a laugh before my head falls back to the head rest and rolls to the side to meet my dad's waiting gaze.

"Pretty much that, yeah," he says, giving me a crooked grin that tilts his thick mustache up on the right. His familiar laughter is a welcome sound, as is the endearing, soft punch he presses into my shoulder.

"Zack hates her," I say, shaking my head.

My dad's brow knits and he chews at his lips.

"Didn't seem so bad back there." My dad got the performance of a lifetime, from both of them. There's way too much to get into for this short time we have together, so I don't dispute him outright, but I don't completely agree.

"Yeah, well, you were watching. You know how he looks up to you." I wait for my dad to glance my direction again, and his faint smile lets me know that he gets how rough life is for my cousin.

"Yeah," he agrees, moving his eyes back to the road.

My dad and I have never talked about it openly, but I think there's a silent understanding between us that Zack had it harder growing up under my uncle's rule. It's always been the little things, like the public displays of discipline when we were little, or the immediate excuses my uncle made any time my cousin failed at anything.

"Zack would have gotten more hits today, but I had him up late last night practicing," my uncle would say. Or, *"I told him to only go seventy-five percent for this game since it didn't matter as much as the championship will."*

Then, if Zack wasn't perfect for the championship, he got his ass chewed out all the way home.

It was the same for everything we did—if he got a B in school and I got an A, if we went bowling and I scored higher, if my birthday cake was bigger than his. The competition was this constant undertone, but I was never an active participant. I'm pretty sure my dad never was, either. Zack had no choice, though, and I guess that's why he is how he is, because my uncle bred him that way.

"When you and Uncle Joel played together in high school, what was that like?" I'm feeling things out with this question, and I think my dad senses it. He shifts in his seat and wrings his hands around the steering wheel a few times while his eyes haze into the distance of the road ahead. I point to the intersection coming up to let my father know where to turn.

"It was good," my dad says.

"Ha, that's a non-answer." I dip my chin and challenge him with a glare. He gives in to the heat of it and finally looks in my direction, rolling his neck and rubbing it with his palm.

"Yeah, it is. But mostly because that was so long ago. I mean, we had a good time, and our team went to state twice. We both got to college on the game, so that was pretty cool."

"Was he better?" I challenge.

"Joel?" My dad's head swivels in my direction and he blinks before gurgling out a laugh. "Uh, no. He was good, but I was—" My dad shrugs.

"Better," I finish for him.

He smiles at me with tight lips and I point to the next turn ahead.

Deep down, I've always known this was the case. None of us ever talk about it, mostly because my dad is not the kind of guy who has to keep score against others. For him, the memories of playing with my uncle are more about living life and having an experience. The greatness of the two of them together is always played up more by my uncle. Nobody, though, ever compares the two. My grandmother, before she passed last year, always gave everyone equal everything. That spirit sorta bled out into the rest of the family, because nobody ever feels the need to compete with one another or brag.

Until Zack.

Moving to Indiana did something to my cousin and his dad. It's as though this time we've been apart unleashed a kind of envy. If Hollis weren't here, I sort of wonder if all of this rage would instead point toward me. My aunt steers clear of the topic, praising Zack for doing his best. Deep down, however, my uncle never quite got over no longer being my cousin's number-one coach. He still wants to be the only voice he hears on the field. And if Zack isn't playing because someone better steals his spot, what will Uncle Joel have to do with his spring afternoons?

We pull into the driveway and my aunt and uncle are waiting in the driveway.

"Mikey!" Hearing my uncle call my dad by the little kid version of his name always makes me laugh.

My dad gets out of my truck and moves toward my uncle, both of their arms out like wings. I wonder if one day Zack and I will be like this, or if I'll resent him forever the way I do right now. I hate this feeling taking over my body, like tar seeping through my insides making it hard to breathe. Maybe Zack isn't the one who changed. Maybe I have.

I'm caught up in the reunion in front of me and lost in my thoughts when they're interrupted by the low idle of a car pulling into the space behind my truck. My immediate reaction when I see Zack and Hollis in the car together is to protect her, but after a blink I realize they are both smiling.

My face puzzles as Hollis gets out and Zack rushes from the driver's side toward my father and uncle.

"I thought you were getting in extra work?" I'm still on guard, and my face must show it because Zack calls me out.

"We catch you in the middle of something? You look surprised." he says.

"Yeah," I huff out through a suspicious laugh.

"I could tell he changed his mind and was sticking around for me, so coming here was my suggestion," Hollis answers.

I shift my focus to her, giving her my perplexed expression. She laughs silently and steps in close.

"I'm fine," she reassures. "Just trying to build a bridge, maybe stop the fire before he starts it."

Nodding slowly, I make room for her to stand next to me and be a part of the conversation unfolding in my driveway. Upon seeing her, my uncle's eyes light up in a way that makes my skin crawl. I hope Hollis doesn't notice.

"So, you're the female phenom, huh?" Uncle Joel reaches out a hand as if he doesn't already have a file on Hollis stashed somewhere, filled with nefarious plots to bump her out of his kid's way.

"I'm trying out for the team, if that's what you mean. Yeah." She shrugs off his compliment with a polite laugh, and I realize she's playing the game too; I'm proud of her for it.

"Oh, I hear you're pretty much a sure bet," my uncle says when their hands touch for the shake. He winks in that car salesman way of his.

I glance to my cousin to get his take, but his eyes are focused on the ground, his face void of giving anything away. He must know about Coach Gage retiring.

"Oh, this is my brother, by the way. Cannon's dad, Mikey," Uncle Joel continues, shaking my dad by the shoulder as he shows him off. My dad is only a year younger, but my uncle always gives the impression there's more age and wisdom between them. He only quit calling him baby brother after an awkward family fight at Thanksgiving four years ago. It's one of the few times I've seen my dad snap at my uncle, and it makes me wonder how long it bothered him before he finally broke.

"We met," my dad explains, smiling and nodding toward Hollis.

My uncle's face dims at the news, but he quickly masks it.

"Oh, right. Out on the field. Did you get to see any of the action?" my uncle asks.

"I mean, they were pretty great at putting balls in the bucket," my dad says through a chuckle.

"Ah." Uncle Joel nods, clearly hoping for a better scouting report.

"Well, Hollis. Now that you're here . . ."

I tense at my uncle's lead-in.

". . . You should stay for dinner. Meg has a roast going. We're a big meat and potatoes family. You can tell us about New York and your dad. Being coach's daughter, I mean. That must be—"

"A lot of pressure," Hollis throws in.

"Yes, right," Uncle Joel agrees.

There's clearly a game of chess in play and everyone seems acutely aware. We're all doing our best to stay off the board and just let Hollis and Uncle Joel battle it out. I refuse to leave her in this alone, though. Without giving her warning, I reach to her side and find her fisted hand pressed against her thigh. It twitches at my touch, and she turns her attention to me with a flinch.

I give her a slight nod. I'm willing to make a grander gesture than this if she refuses. Thankfully, she doesn't. Her hand unfurls and her fingers stretch out for mine. Our palms meld together as I bring her hand to my mouth and kiss the back of it in a blatant show of solidarity—and an enormous F-U—to my cousin and uncle. They mask their reactions poorly, their eyes seething in a way that shows the connection between the apple and the tree.

"You'll love my aunt's cooking. Her roast is seriously the best, like magazine cover-worthy," I brag. It's not a lie, and Aunt Meg has no part in this grudge-match. And judging by the approving smile I just got from my father, neither does he.

SIXTEEN

HOLLIS

Cannon wasn't wrong about the roast. It was the literal definition of Midwestern home-cooked amazingness. I didn't think I liked carrots, but it turns out the ingredient I've been missing to completely appreciate them is marinating them for hours in a bath of greasy beef broth.

For a little while tonight, I forgot about the weirdness. We all sat around the table laughing while Cannon's dad and uncle swapped stories about the dumb things they did in high school. Like the time they dragged their team's field in the middle of the night using their dad's old Jeep with a bunch of random yard tools tied to the back. Took them an entire weekend to repair the tire grooves and divots they left behind, but they both swear the party dare that led them to do it was worth it.

Cannon's dad is nice. And not in the way you call someone nice because you don't think you'll ever get to know them well so it doesn't matter. No, he's truly kind. And when Joel is in the environment we were all in tonight—together, with family—he seems nice, too. It brought out a better side to Zack, as well. It would have been easy to erase the last two and a half weeks and start over, but just as we were leaving, Zack's dad reminded me that none of them are to be trusted.

"Hey, tell your dad I'll be giving him a call about that town hall he needs to hold with the board. Routine thing. We'll just be asking him some questions. It's good for the public to buy in on things. Helps with fundraising." He practically whistled out the last few words like a snake.

All I did was nod and say I would. And I have spent—*no, wasted!*—my short ride home alone with Cannon in his truck thinking about all the things I should have said instead. I should have probed, asked about the last time they held one of those, or subtly hinted how it's too bad Coach Gage is retiring. Just one little hint to make him wonder if I heard his plan, if I know something.

"So, I can't tell if that was fun for you." Cannon sighs and lets his weight fall back into his seat as he shifts into park outside my house.

I texted my dad earlier to let him know I was meeting Cannon's dad for dinner, and my gut tells me my father's been waiting for me to roll up to our house ever since. When the blinds at the front window dip and spill out light from the television, I smile and nod to myself. He's waiting.

"It was *mostly* fun?" I lift one shoulder and smile on one side of my mouth.

Cannon laughs.

"Okay, fair enough."

He reaches over and takes my hand in his, turning my palm over and drawing soft lines along the ones in my palm while his mouth hangs open with indecision.

"You're thinking about apologizing for your uncle and cousin again, aren't you?" I close my hand around his thumb and jiggle it teasingly.

He laughs again and wiggles his head.

"I am," he confesses.

"They were fine tonight. I made it through the fire. I survived. And their plan we overheard—"

"Is going to move on to Plan B," he finishes.

I shrug, pretending I can't guarantee he's right, but honestly, he is.

"I liked your dad," I say, changing the subject to the positive part of the evening.

Cannon grins in response, and I can tell his relationship with his dad means a lot to him.

"You must miss him," I prompt.

"I do."

The last thing I want to do is go inside my house right now. Not because my dad will grill me with overprotective questions. He won't. He's more the "pretend my daughter doesn't date" kinda dad. I don't want to go inside because I don't want to leave this truck. It's so warm in here, and being near Cannon without pretense for once is so goddamn nice. A quick glance out my window tells me that staying out here for a few extra minutes, though, is all I'm going to get. My dad has actually fully opened the blinds, and I can make out his profile as he sits by the window fake reading a book.

"I'm a bit afraid to kiss you." Cannon laughs out nervously, leaning against his steering wheel and nodding toward my dad's figure.

I sigh.

"Is it because he's your coach? Or is it because he's my dad?"

Cannon mulls it over for a few seconds, drawing his brow in before meeting my gaze in a snap.

"Definitely both."

He takes my hand again and brings it to his mouth, pressing his lips to the inside of my wrist and lingering there just long enough to signal that in any other situation, this would lead to more. *Way* more.

"I really, *really* like you, Cannon Jennings from Indiana."

A soft smile plays at his lips as he lowers my hand, his thumb grazing along the tender skin where his kiss left coolness behind.

"I really, *really* like you, Hollis Taylor from Indiana . . . by way of *Staten Island*." His attempt to mock my accent is adorable, despite how bad he is at playing New York.

"You are so accent-less," I tease.

"Hey, I'm from the southwest." He pushes my arm playfully and I push back, my fingers raking down his arm and snagging on the material of his hoodie. I grab on and tug gently before letting go of his shirt and picking his phone up from the center console. I hold it up to his face to force it to unlock.

"Are we already at the snooping-on-each-other's-phone stage of the relationship?" He laughs off his comment, but the sound fades quickly and his eyes go wide and dart away.

Relationship.

I tuck my bottom lip under my teeth to quash my nervous grin threatening to ruin my bluff while I pretend to be unfazed by his words. Inside my chest, though, is an epic house party, complete with strobe lights and twelve-inch woofers.

"I'm giving you my number," I say, sending a text to me from his phone. I hold it up to face him when I'm done, showing that I typed the word RELATIONSHIP. The best thing about Cannon's thick eyelashes is the way they shudder like butterfly wings when he's nervous. He stares at the word without breathing for a few seconds. I hold it in the space between us to give him the opportunity to take it back. I'm not sure why I expect him to. Maybe because I know how many issues come with us having that word.

"You got a text message. You should probably answer that," he says in a low voice that's close to a whisper. His eyes flit up to mine, and I let my lip come loose so I can show him the smile I've been keeping in.

I take comfort in knowing the buzz in my back pocket is a message I sent myself but that he let me send. What's strange is that I still plan on reading it—staring at that one little word—all . . . night . . . long.

"I should get in. You know, before my dad comes out."

We both bow our heads with a nervous laugh.

"God yes, please. Don't let him come out here," Cannon says.

"I'll see you tomorrow? Maybe, you want a ride to school?" He cocks his head to the side, leaning into the steering wheel, and the party in my chest puts on another song to keep things going.

"I'd like that," I say.

No kiss. Not here where we're being watched. Honestly, it's not even that he is one of the players on my team, one of my dad's players. It's that I'm daddy's girl, and having your father catch you getting a good night kiss is mortifying and cringe-worthy for everyone involved.

"You can leave your gear in the back, then. I'll lock it up and bring it when I come get you in the morning."

We nod our good-byes and I slip out the door, pushing it closed while I stumble backward like a drunk in from a bender.

Per the norm, my dad is relaxing with his feet up and one of his favorite coaching books cracked open in his lap. I'm no longer sure if the man has ever actually read it. I'm starting to think the only time it gets pulled out is when I'm in the driveway with a boy and he's playing studious by the window.

"Have a good time?" He doesn't look up from the pages as he asks. This is part of his act, too.

"I did. We ate roast. It was oddly delicious," I say.

"Better than Meno's?" He quirks a brow with that question.

"Let's not get crazy now, Dad," I say, putting on a serious tone. Meno's was *our* pizza joint. It's the place where my dad took the team after big games, win or lose. No amount of grease-soaked carrots in the world could ever compete with that.

"Well, I'm pretty beat. See you in the morning?" He stretches with a yawn as he stands from his chair, dropping his fake-read book on the side table.

"Actually," I begin, waiting for him to pull the string on the small lamp to kill the light enough for me to tell him this. "Cannon is picking me up."

His lack of response is almost worse than any word he could have said out loud. I'm relieved with he finally utters, "Oh."

"Just tomorrow. I'm sure. Ya know, to be nice." I'm babbling, making excuses, and thankfully he lets me off the hook. It's weird to crush on a guy and want to admit it to your dad and gush with him the way you would a girlfriend. I do, though. Probably because Cannon is totally the kind of guy my dad would pick for me out of a lineup of eligible bachelors. I've seen the way he works with him, coaches him; he's grown to respect him. They respect each other.

Then there's Zack.

Folding his big flannel-covered arms around my shoulders and neck, my dad pulls me close and kisses the top of my head.

"Good night, angel," he says.

"Good night, Daddy."

With the lights out in the house, I wait in the darkness downstairs while he climbs up and shuts his bedroom door, probably to spill the beans about everything he thinks he knows to my mom.

My pocket buzzes before I hit the stairs. I hook my bag on the finial at the end of the staircase and pull my phone out to read the text message I expect to be some razzing tease from my nosy little brother, or maybe June checking in on me after our girl-chat lunch today. Deep down, I hope it's from Cannon, but hope is a lot different than expectation.

How do you feel about one block away? Surely your dad's window seat doesn't look out that far.

My lips tug up at his text. I'm out the door in three seconds, feet pounding pavement in a near sprint toward the glowing tail lights just beyond the stop sign. I climb into the passenger seat I vacated only a minute or two before, yanking the door closed behind me. Before I breathe another word, Cannon's hands are on my cheeks, fingers sliding into my hair as his mouth meets mine in a hungry kiss that we've both been holding back for far too long.

I crawl toward him on my knees, and his hands slide down my arms then over my ribs and around my waist, guiding me over the center console until I sit sideways in his lap with my head resting on his driver's side window.

"Goddamn, have I been dying to kiss you like that since our missed opportunity in study hall," he says, pulling back for air while holding my forehead against his. Our noses touch, and it makes me giggle like a girl with a crush when he playfully wiggles his against mine.

"Imagine if our New Year's kiss was like that," I say.

"What, this?" He again tickles his nose against mine and I laugh harder, chastising him with a flat palm against his chest. I leave it there, feeling the heat pour from his body, the hard beat underneath his shirt.

"No, silly. I meant like this," I say, sitting back enough to focus on his eyes. They're blue like the sea, like dusk back home. I reach to my side and turn the music up a little to fill the nervous gaps in the air, the song some alt-pop tune by one of those new female artists who sings as though she's broken. These songs are my favorites.

Propping myself up to face him, I push the button that slides his seat back enough to make room for the two of us. When his hands slip to my hips then down to my thighs, fire burns in my belly. And lower. I'm swallowed up in layers of clothes, and more than anything, all I want to do is *feel* him. I want to see if that beat in his chest matches up with mine. I want them to be close, to beat together or echo on constant repeat.

Straddling his lap as he lays back in his seat, my hands tremble as I reach down for the bottom of my sweatshirt, my tummy tightening with a rush of nerves as I peel the tattered cotton up and over my head. My hands reach behind my neck to find the thick band holding my hair together in a twisted knot. I tug it loose, but pause to laugh at myself when it gets tangled in my hair.

"You and this goddamn hair," Cannon teases, swatting my hand out of the way to help get the band out of my wild mane.

"I should just cut it." I sigh.

The band finally free from my hair, he rolls it onto his wrist, then holds my chin with his thumb, forcing our eyes to meet again.

"Don't you dare. I love your knotty-ass blonde tangles." He makes a serious face that doesn't break for almost a full five seconds, but when I see the curl tempt his lips, I squeeze his shoulders and press my forehead into his.

"You liar!" I laugh out.

His hands press into my sides, tickling me, and I squeeze my thighs around him while we wrestle in this tiny space, taunting each other like grade schoolers who haven't quite discovered puberty. Only, we aren't kids at all. We're both seventeen, almost eighteen. Our birthdays are two weeks apart in February—I checked.

Cannon's birthday is on Valentine's Day. Perhaps St. Valentine or Cupid or whatever gifted him with arrows because of it. Whatever the case, I've been shot with something, and the drug quickly fills my veins. As I rock my body forward to feel Cannon rock-hard beneath me, I can tell that he is drunk on our physical chemistry as well.

"May I?" His eyes scan down the length of my neck and chest to the bottom of the blue jersey I wore to practice today. His fingers flirt with the hem.

I love that he asked.

"You may," I say, cheeks heated and voice quiet. I'm bashful.

Cannon gathers the bottom of my jersey into his hands, lifting with his thumbs while I slowly raise my arms above my head, helping him to remove my shirt completely. I'm still scuffed with dirt on my elbows and legs from our practice, and though I haven't told him, he's worn a smudge of dirt on his right cheek the entire night. I trace it now with my thumb, wishing it were permanent because I love the tough appearance it gives him.

Dipping down, my hands weave into his hair, grabbing hold of thick waves. I wonder what his hair feels like when it's wet, like in the shower. The tension hugging my chest loosens suddenly and I tuck my chin to confirm that his thumb and index finger have tugged the zipper at the front of my sports bra down about two inches.

"Up? Or down?" His eyes haze, thick with want and clearly rooting for option number two. My body begs for that as well.

Sitting up to put a few extra inches of space between us, I wrap my hand around his to nudge it lower. Together, we lower the zipper until the sides separate, and I gasp from both the cool air and the release. I lean back until my shoulders touch the steering wheel and hook my thumbs into the band of my sweatpants, tugging them down enough to show that I am mad with want, and give him permission to touch me.

His eyes smolder in the faint light as he drags the edges of both palms up the center of my belly and chest, peeling away the unzipped bra from each of my breasts one at a time. His thumbs rub over my hard nipples as they pass and I arch and moan.

"Fucking goddess," he says, his voice deep and not shy. He sucks one of his thumbs, coating it in his saliva, then rubs it over one of my raw, pink tips while he reaches behind my back to pull me into him, covering my other breast in his mouth. His teeth grip the tender skin, and his lips wrap around my nipple and suck so hard it burns. He soothes it by blowing on the tender skin, then taking gentle swipes with his tongue.

His hands roam to my back and follow my curves, fingers dipping inside the band of my sweatpants and teasing the tight wrap of my sliding shorts still on underneath. His mouth forms a devilish smile that I can't help but dust with my curious one.

"What's so funny?" I ask, peppering his lips with teasing kisses before holding on to his upper lip with my teeth. It pulls free as his smile stretches larger.

"Most girls probably have some sexy little panties on underneath their sweats and you've got sliding shorts." He laughs lightly, but I can tell he's not laughing *at* me. Cannon sees me for who I am, and I've never wanted to be something I'm not.

"Mizuno sliding shorts are hella sexy," I boast, rolling my hips.

"*Mmm*," he hums, lifting his chin just enough to lock gazes. "That they are."

His hands run down the taut fabric around my waist until his hands cup my ass and he pulls me snug into him.

"Oh!" My breath hitches at the sudden surge of electricity that jolts my core. Wanting to touch his chest and feel its warmth against mine, I flatten my palms on his stomach and slide them up under his long-sleeved tee and sweatshirt until he helps me remove them the rest of the way.

Cannon holds me close, one hand firm on my butt, the other carving a warm line up my spine until I'm flat against him. His hand continues its path up my neck and into my hair. Hidden behind fogged windows in his pickup parked just out of the glow of a nearby streetlamp, we kiss breathlessly, our mouths finding the perfect fit against one another with each nip and every pass of the tongue.

Friction builds as I rock against him and he pulls me close—tight—my swollen center finding relief, even through the layers, against his hard erection. This could so easily transition into something more, but there's no sign from Cannon that he expects it, that he needs it. This here, feeling each other like this, it's enough. *For now.*

I gasp as he pushes up against me and I hungrily rub against him, both of us chasing a relief that's eluded us for longer than I realized. Cannon does things to me, makes me feel things, that are somehow more than anything ever before.

"Make me come," I beg, my bold words dragging a growl from his chest that spills out into a grunt against my neck. The sharp edge of his teeth pierce the skin below my ear as his hips push up into me and his hands hold me to him, anxious fists clutching my tight shorts as he rolls me back and forth in the sweetest rhythm ever.

I look up, feeling the sensation building to the cliff, and his tongue flicks against the base of my neck. He licks up to my chin, then bites at my swollen lower lip, holding me hostage between his teeth as he playfully growls. His hands have pushed inside my shorts, his warm palms melded against my bare skin, fingers moving closer and closer to my desperate center with each rock of my hips until I finally feel the tips of them brush against my soaking wet center.

I break our kiss long enough to meet his gaze and nod, begging for him to continue. "Yes!" The word comes out without my control when his hands reach around me completely, one of his fingers sinking inside of me and pressing against my swollen insides. The quivers come hard and fast, an uncontrollable rush of waves that makes my body convulse and fall into him completely.

"So fucking hot," he whispers harshly against my ear, his voice strained with his own need to find relief. I sink into him harder, still riding the swell of pleasure from where his finger presses on my insides. I ride the next wave, my own orgasm extended with every touch of Cannon against me. My body is a time bomb of sensations, ready to explode with every touch, and his is near the same. A small whimper from my lips is all it takes to push him over the edge, his eyes fluttering closed, his lips parting in a satisfied groan.

I rock and he flicks his fingers against me until our bodies are drained of feeling, numb from satisfaction, and hot from pleasure. It's freezing outside this truck but in here it's an inferno. The thought of how this must look from the outside pushes a giggle out of me, but I don't move. There are no feelings of shame or embarrassment at wearing what I wear. I don't feel inadequate or unworthy or used. I feel close to Cannon. A bond of trust and faith that has been brewing is sealed in place with our physical deed, an act that tells him as much as it tells me that I trust him.

"I really, *really* like you, Cannon Jennings from Indiana," I say, repeating my words from before. The hoarse tone of my voice carries a different vulnerability to it this time, though, and I think Cannon knows. Pushing away the sweat-strewn locks of hair from my cheek and forehead, he lifts his chin and presses a long, tender kiss against it. He's quiet, leaving his lips against my skin for several long seconds before finally replying to my raw and honest declaration.

"I like you more, Hollis. I like you a whole lot more," he whispers, and in this very moment, dare I say, I believe maybe he does.

SEVENTEEN

CANNON

I left home early, before the sun was up in fact, and drove to the same corner where Hollis and I gave in to everything last night. Well, not *everything*. I didn't need it, though, my God, did I want it. I wanted every inch of her, to touch and taste her body in all the places, and mark her as mine in every place I'd been.

I'm attracted to every trait she possesses, from her physical form to the confidence that radiates from her. Her raspy voice, her shortened words coated in her native New York roots, her feistiness.

I managed to avoid talking to Zack when I came home after dropping her off. He was locked in his room with the music up annoyingly loud. I gave my dad what's been serving as my room for the night and slept on the couch. I have to take my father to the airport after school today, and I hate letting him go, though he'll be back in a few days. I'm done being here, in this house. I'm ready for our own walls, my own rules. This constant air of suspicion I have for Zack and his motives makes my stomach hurt nonstop. There are moments it's downright hard to breathe.

I can't lie. There have been moments when begging my dad to move back home have crossed my mind. We're here for more than just me playing my senior year with my cousin, though.

My dad misses family. My grandparents are dead, and he and my uncle are all each other has. Despite how different they are, there's a bond between them that's unbreakable, forged from memories and time. One day, Zack will be all I have, at least in blood. And now that I have Hollis, well, leaving has lost its appeal.

Ready?

I send her the text then pull my truck up closer to her house, but still not directly in front of it. My hands still buzz with the feel of her, and the thought of making eye contact with her father right now is a torture I don't have the balls for. The man is intimidating, and he still holds my future in his hands.

Yes. Be right out. Also, uhm. Need a favor.

I cock my head and stare at her message for a full breath. It's that *uhm* part that's got me a little nervous. I type back *ok*, but two full minutes pass without a response.

Rolling up to her driveway, I brace myself for a lecture from her dad as the garage door rolls up. When I see her legs, tight black jeans and bright white Nikes on her feet, I grin. Then there's a matching version, only shorter and topped with a New York Islanders sweatshirt that's about two sizes too big.

I roll the window down so I can talk to her and her brother.

"So, uhm," she says, a continuation of her message. "Can we give Ben a lift to school? My dad has a meeting, and my mom is already holding office hours online."

"What's up, Cannon?" her brother says, giving me a nod but not a glance as he rolls an over-stuffed hockey bag toward the back of my truck. I've never officially met the kid, but he's immediately made us bros. I laugh and have to admire him.

"What's up, Ben?"

Shit, I hope I remembered his name right. He doesn't flinch, so I feel more certain than not that I nailed it. I hop out of the truck when the latch releases in the back. He's hoisting the bag by the time I join him, but he's struggling. I slide it the rest of the way in and pull up the tailgate, locking it in place. I'm about to jog around to the driver's side again when Ben reaches up and squeezes my bicep with his much smaller hand.

"Whoa, serious guns there. A'right, a'right. I feel ya, Cannon. I feel ya." He winks and backs away, leaving me there speechless with the dumbest smile on my face. I think I'm actually flattered by his compliment.

Ben climbs in the back seat of the full cab and Hollis slides into the passenger seat. Our eyes meet briefly and her cheeks blush, likely remembering what we did in here just a few hours ago. Awkward thought now that her baby brother is buckling up in the back.

"Sorry," she apologizes for her brother.

"Dude, no problem. Ben and I are buddies now. Aren't we, Ben?" I look into the rearview and wait for him to lift himself enough to make eye contact with me. The kid twists his lips, considering my offer, then reaches forward, patting my shoulder with three heavy slaps.

"Let's take things slow, Cannon. That's my sister, after all. I'm watching you," he says, pointing with one hand at his eyes then flipping his fingers to point at me in the mirror. *This kid is unreal!*

"Got it." I agree to his test. "Slow it is."

My gaze automatically moves to Hollis, a double meaning on that promise. She slides her hand across the console for me to take, and I do, even through her brother's remarks that we're making him vomit up his oatmeal.

I like this kid.

We get Ben to school and I help him wheel his bag up to the entrance where he leaves me with a handshake he suddenly decides to invent for just us. By the time Hollis and I get to school, the bell is ringing so we have to rush from the faraway spot where I had to park, peeling into our first hour together with laughter as we race to our seats.

Everyone's eyes are on us, and I don't care. So much so that I hook my pinky with hers to form a bridge between our two seats. Neither of us sees Dr. V approaching behind us, so when he taps our linked knuckles with the end of his ballpoint pen, we both startle.

"This is not a school dance, thank you, Mr. Jennings. Miss Taylor." His tone is more teasing than angry, so we shrink in our seats and suck in our smiles. "Though, I do find the odds of this fascinating. Have to admit, I didn't see this coming."

His joke draws a few laughs from the class, but he doesn't dwell on us after that.

The rest of the day flies by, but this new normal seems to have crawled up into my chest cavity and helps keep that pitted feeling I've been living with at bay. Hollis makes me happy. Liking Hollis so much makes me happy.

I have to take off to drive my dad soon. In fact, I'm probably a little late, but it's worth it to see her one more time in the daylight. I'll miss practice today, and even though it's optional, I let her dad know. *Coach.* That part is going to take a while to get used to. The things I did to her, *want* to do to her, need to stay on lockdown when I'm in Coach Taylor's presence. I have this unearthly fear that he can read minds. Last night, I had a nightmare that he kept piling on the laps, making me run faster and faster by shocking me with a cattle prod, all because he thought he saw us kiss. I'm all for keeping us secret from him for a little while longer.

My entire body lightens when Hollis walks around the corner. I don't even mind the way her freshman shadow, Maddy, squeals about how cute we are.

"Hey, I thought you'd be gone," Hollis says as I take her hand and pull her into my chest.

Catching her jaw with my hand, I tilt her head just enough to get kissed.

"Uh uh," I say through a smile that hasn't left for almost twenty-four hours. "Couldn't leave without one more of these."

I catch Maddy's blush over Hollis's shoulder as I go in for a deep kiss, taking her mouth over completely and walking her backward a few paces so she bends into my embrace. When I pull away, she's left breathless, and I'm beat-my-chest proud. Also, a few of the other guys who I *know* have been checking her out now know not to bother.

"Hi, Daddy," she says, looking over my shoulder and waving. I swallow my heart, feeling it lodge somewhere in my throat while I forget how to breathe. I turn to find nothing but a closed door and a long, empty sidewalk.

"That was so mean!" I poke her side where I know she's ticklish. Her laugh is loud and free, and she rushes at me for one more kiss on my cheek while she and Maddy pass to head into the locker room.

"Keeping you on your toes, Cannon Jennings from Indiana." She winks just before the door closes behind her, and I am slayed.

My grin carries me all the way to my truck, and I wear it all the way back to Uncle Joel's where my father is waiting anxiously, slapping the boarding pass he printed out in their den last night against his open palm.

"Cutting it close, aren't we?" He gets in while he gives me the mini lecture. Rather than make up an excuse, I decide to give it to him straight.

"Had to see a girl." I hold his stare while I back out the driveway, his stupid sideways grin sliding up to match mine.

"Yeah, I thought there was something more to this whole Hollis thing." He settles into his seat, smug as if he knows it all. He probably does, clever old bastard that he is.

"Your mom's gonna love her." He chuckles, unfolding his boarding pass to check the gate and time for the millionth time.

"You know you can do that all by phone now," I explain. He quirks a brow because he's old school. The man still has file folders for everything.

It's a wonder he's an engineer because I don't think he likes computers all that well. He just likes math.

"What are you going to do if they change your gate?" I glance his way in time to watch his mind work, and he finally gives in and pulls his phone from his back pocket to open the browser.

"Fine, I'll modernize," he grumbles.

I laugh and already miss him before he's gone. That feeling tugs away pieces of everything that's been so good. The moment my father is gone, I'll be left with Uncle Joel and Zack and all of their opinions. Aunt Meg won't be the voice that stands up for me; she avoids conflict. But I know it's coming. I feel it in my bones.

"Spit it out," my dad says, his sudden break in the silence jarring as I maneuver onto the freeway on ramp.

I draw in my brow as though I'm not sure what he's questioning, but after he shakes his head with a grimace, I know it's no use.

"Uncle Joel and Zack aren't big Hollis fans. And before you bring up dinner, I know, they weren't blatantly mean. At least, not there. But Uncle Joel feels threatened, and so does Zack, and I—

"Is she better?"

My dad breaks in with a succinct question. I don't have to think about my response, but I let the pregnant pause build because the minute I answer, my dad will work to convince me that all problems are solved. He sees things black and white, right and wrong. If Hollis is better, which she is, then she gets the job, and Zack has to work hard to take it away from her. But in that gray is all the stuff that makes me sick—my cousin hating me for rooting for her, him maybe improving enough to take that starting position away from her, me resenting him for it down the road. And then, Uncle Joel playing politics. *That* is perhaps the heaviest blanket of them all.

"She's amazing."

Now it's his turn to let my words linger, followed by silence. He never addresses them at all; in fact, just nods when I finally glance in his direction. I meant what I said, and it covers all things Hollis. My nagging worry over my father's relationship with my uncle finally scratches at me enough that my new worries come out as I exit the freeway.

"I'm afraid Uncle Joel will try to do something, I don't know, illegal?" I scrunch my shoulders, tucking my neck in at how foolish that sounds. It only gets worse when my dad laughs.

"He's not going to do anything illegal. Is he going to be loud? Oh, for sure. Will he complain that life isn't fair? My brother has been doing that since the first time he got in trouble for punching me in the arm. But in the end, it's all noise. If Hollis wants to walk this path, I'm sure she's gotten used to hearing a lot of noise. You just need to train your ears on when to tune it out."

My brow dents at my dad's incredibly wise advice.

"You sound like Mom," I compliment. He breathes out a laugh because we both know Mom is the one with the most level head of all.

"I learned a lot from that woman." He glances out his window and I can tell he's thinking of her, his mind on getting back to her and making this trip again with her by his side.

I've learned a lot from Hollis, too. I've known her for a month, not quite even, and when I compare the man I am right now with the one who didn't think he had much to learn, I'm kinda proud of my progress. Turns out a faster mile time isn't the only self-improvement on my resume this year.

Full breaths no longer elude me by the time I drop my dad off at his terminal, and I manage to slip back into highway traffic on the verge of rush hour, which puts me back on campus before the sun is down. There's an off chance Hollis is here still, but when I see my cousin pulling from the school lot with Roland and Jay, I know there's no way she'd let them quit workouts before her.

I pass Zack and roll down my window, figuring he'd stop to talk, but he doesn't even glance in my direction as he drives by with the guys. I spend the next few seconds, as I pull in and find a spot, convincing myself he didn't see me or that he waved and I missed it. That's not the case, though. With nobody here to witness, he decided to be a dick, and those knots I finally untangled in my chest? They're back again, and a fuck-load tighter.

Deciding this parking lot is too damn far, I pull onto the curb and drive along the wide sidewalk between the buildings and the fields, getting as close as I can to the places where Hollis could be. My chests thumps with worry, and the quiet out on the baseball field leaves my stomach unsettled.

Goddamn, Zack. What did you do?

I don't know when her dad will be here, or if she planned on walking or having her mom come. I wasn't supposed to make it back this fast, so she's not expecting me, but if something is wrong, she would have called, right? She would have called.

I'm out of my truck in one second, jogging toward the clubhouse with my phone clutched in my hand, hoping to feel it buzz with a text from her that tells my gut I'm wrong. I can make it to her faster than my call would go through. The more strides I take without feeling a vibration from a text, the more my pace picks up until I'm sprinting toward the freezing metal door that shouldn't be so easy to lock.

Gripping the handle, I pull it open hard, not mentally prepared for what might be on the other side. I don't know if he hurt her, if they all did, or something . . . worse.

Worse.

It takes my eyes a few seconds to focus on her, my next breath filled with relief that her shirt doesn't look torn, that her body doesn't look bruised. Fuck, the evil thoughts were so bad that I'm honestly glad she's clothed. I feel sick, and arrange my features before she turns and faces me, but I let everything go when I see how soaking wet she is.

"Hollis, are you okay?" I rush to her, expecting tears or rage, but when she spins to face me, her expression is nothing but even.

"Oh! Hey, I didn't think you were coming." She grips the front of her T-shirt and undershirt in her hands, twisting to wring out some of the water. It pools on the floor between her feet. Her pants, socks, everything is plastered to her body as if she jumped, fully clothed, into a swimming pool.

"I made good time. Why are you . . ?" I reach forward and tug on a soaked sleeve.

"Oh, yeah. So, just me being silly. I was in the showers, and I thought I'd rinse off some of the dirt in my hair. You know, by leaning forward?" Her laugh is suspicious and my gut tells me she's making up some bullshit right now. I say so with my face, my head cocked to one side while my eyes grill her for the truth.

"What? Oh, just me not thinking clearly. I'm fine, maybe cold, but . . ." I swear there's a slight quiver in her lips, but she stretches them into a smile before I can call her on it.

"And you're in here because?"

Her eyes flare briefly with her quick swallow. She's thinking of an excuse. This doesn't add up.

"Clothes. I thought maybe I left some in one of the cubbies, or maybe there were some shirts in storage." She wraps her arms around her body and bounces on her feet, letting her mouth shiver with the chill. She isn't making up being cold.

I glance around the space, then move to the corner where boxes from past seasons have been stacked for what looks like years. There's a layer of dust on them that is scoopable. I slide one box to the ground and it sends a cloud of shit into the air. I wave it away from my face, coughing.

"There might be some in here," I say, flipping open the cardboard flaps to reveal yellowed long-sleeve shirts. She's probably screwed in the pants department.

I toss her one from the middle of the stash and she peels her clothes away without warning, saying thanks as if this isn't a big deal.

"What? You've seen all this," she says, laughing through the words. Her hands shake as they work to pull her wet shirts away, and I swear there is more to it than just her being cold.

"Oh, I remember." I smile as I move closer to help her pull the rest of the sodden mess over her head. The wet fabric keeps rolling. I play along with her, flirting. But now that I'm close I study her bare arms, her neck, the small of her back, looking for signs that something else happened here. Her skin is blotchy in places, red spots on her arms that could either be bruises forming or a reaction to the cold and the wet fabric.

I ready the dry shirt for her to slip her arms inside while she pulls her sports bra down her arms. My damn male instincts can't help but look at her breasts, nipples puckered into tight tips that make my mouth water. She reaches her hands into the bottom of the shirt I hold up, the length gathered in my hands, and I help her work it up her arms and over her head.

"Maybe . . . two of these," she says through chattering teeth.

I breathe out a short laugh, her hard nipples practically cutting through the cotton shirt. I nod, knowing in my gut that now is not the time to respond to this physical craving I can't help but feel. She's comfortable with me, but she's not okay. Something else is going on.

I grab another shirt from the box and help her layer it over the first, then flip through the rest of the boxes in the pile, coming up with old scorebooks and helmets but nothing that will warm her.

"Alright, well." I shrug, tugging my sweatpants down so I'm in my boxer briefs and a black hoodie. I toss my sweatpants at Hollis and she catches them in one hand while holding the other against her mouth in a fist, poorly hiding laughter.

"What?" I hold my arms out, knowing how funny I probably look. Also knowing that my reaction to her naked body is very apparent. When her eyes lower to my erection, I shrug, and her cheeks redden.

"I was fine wearing these home," she says, her teeth still chattering from the cold.

"Liar," I say, kneeling in front of her to help her roll the long socks down her calves while she slides her pants down. She leaves her sliding shorts on, for modesty I'm sure, and even though they're soaking wet, I don't press the issue.

I take over pulling the wet pants down over her knees, her pale skin beading up from the instant chill, and that's when the bright red scratches along the inside of her thigh come into view. I freeze my position and stare at her skin, my mind racing through dozens of awful scenarios. The one conclusion that I know is certain—she struggled.

Hollis stops breathing and her body goes incredibly still. I lift my hand and brush my knuckles along the line of abrasions that run from the curve of her knee up to the middle of her inner thigh. I lift my gaze but she's stoic, clutching my sweats to her chest while she looks straight ahead. So much work is going into her expression to hold it at peace. She's doing her best to give nothing away, but it's her breath—or lack of—that speaks volumes. Leaning into her, I kiss the bruise forming along her knee and shut my eyes when her hand pushes my hoodie back and sinks into my hair.

"Tell me what happened." My request is soft, and I get the answer I expect.

"It's nothing. I'm fine."

I kiss the deepest red line again and blow to cool it, the goose bumps far from this part of her. With a hard swallow, I finish helping her pull her legs and feet away from the wet pants, then let her balance herself on my shoulder while she steps into my sweats. When I stand, we're inches apart and her mask is not prepared. It's only a glimpse, but her eyes are glassy. It's a different kind of emotion she's feeling; there's a simmering to it. Those aren't tears from fear or crying. No. That's from anger.

"Hollis."

"I said I'm fine. It's nothing," she snaps.

Foolishly standing in our frigid clubhouse in underwear and a hoodie, I have to take her at her word. It doesn't mean I'm not going to make people pay.

We had plans to meet up with June, Lucas, Hayden, and Tory at Eight Lanes tonight, but I'll let that be her call. I know how hard it is to hide how you *really* feel. It's exhausting, and I've never had to do it for reasons that are meaningful and real, as I suspect she is right now.

"Take you home?" I lean my head toward the door and give her a moment to take in how ridiculous I look. As her lips curve, I know she's let her guard down just a little, so to keep the bad thoughts from breaking in, I decide to dance. In the time my hands make it from the back of my head to my hips, she's laughing hard.

"What is that?" She points at my legs in a circling motion, the sleeves of her double shirt tucked over her fingers.

"It's the Macarena," I pronounce, rolling my hips like an expensive stripper. In my head, I'm totally Magic Mike. I'm guessing by the way she covers her mouth and holds her stomach, though, the actual visual is a lot less sexy.

"No . . . it's not," she busts out mid-laugh.

"Oh, I beg your pardon," I say, feeling challenged to sell it. I make my body perform every awkward stripper move I know, knowing full well this is a mess, but it makes her laugh. It keeps her warm. It makes her smile for real instead of the pretend one that was stamped on her face.

Now, I need to keep it that way until I can even the score for her. I know exactly where to start, too, but for right now, I'll drive her home.

EIGHTEEN

HOLLIS

Every girl just needs a good cry sometimes. I spend a lot of time holding mine in. Even when it's earned and I have every right to be weak and ugly, I suck it up and fake that everything is fine. I say I do it for others, to protect them from guilt, from feeling responsible or spending all their empathy on me. Honestly, though, I do it because I'm embarrassed. That thought in and of itself is shameful. It's also true. I'm embarrassed that I let something break me, even a little. I'm embarrassed by the attention. I hate when people ask if I'm okay. So, rather than cry, I shove that feeling and all that sparked it deep into the pit of my soul.

I should have known that one day, something would finally be too much.

Cannon is waiting outside in his truck, the engine running. We're going out with friends. It's like an actual real date, in front of people, and I want to feel the same on the inside that I've been pretending to be on the outside.

I didn't feel the tears coming. I ran upstairs for a quick shower and to change, because Cannon needs his pants back. And I want to look nice, to smell nice, to have goddamn beach waves in my hair!

Instead, I have been full-on wailing into my bath towel for five minutes straight, praying that the spray of the shower masks any sounds I let slip out.

It's a good cry.

An ugly cry.

A necessary cry.

It's all mine, and I'm taking it. I've sold myself short so many times, but no more. I'm tired. So fucking tired.

The hardest part is stopping myself from giving in to the same excuse I always use—*at least it wasn't worse.* Truth be told, I've been through worse. I've had guys throw fastballs at my face on purpose when I'm in the batter's box. I've had things stolen, had my name disparaged, been called insults that no guy on any of my teams would ever be called. They don't spray paint those same insults on school walls about the guys, either. In the grand scheme of things, a little hazing by three guys who have fragile egos and feel threatened should not be the thing that breaks me.

But it is.

It is. It does. And it continues to while I stand with one leg in the shower and one out.

I hate that I saw it coming. I hate that I still gave them the benefit of the doubt when Roland and Jay took opposite sides of me in the dugout while we packed up. I knew they were going to grab me. I even braced myself for it, prepared all the things I would say, practiced the face I'd make to pretend I was having as much of a good time as they were. It happened like clockwork—the two of them taking me by the arms, lifting me high enough that my feet couldn't reach the ground. It had to be them. They're the only two tall enough.

I laughed while they dragged me through the dugout, my thigh catching on the loose chain link while I kicked.

I didn't kick enough.

I kicked *just* enough.

Zack was only pretending to roll up the hose after watering the field. The water was still on. I heard the pump; the hose was taut from the pressure; the spray nozzle was leaking.

The first blast of water stung. I didn't shiver until at least twenty seconds passed. I was still laughing, still playing along and taking this rite of passage that I know no other guy on this team had to go through.

"You wanna be one of us, don't you?" Zack shouted.

Yes. yes, I do!

The words were internal, only for me. Outside, I laughed and played along.

"Don't! It's cold!"

Of course it was. They knew it was. I struggled to break free, but they held me down and Zack moved closer, the spray harder, the water colder. My skin was numb, already ripped apart as much as it could be from the blast of cold water. It hit my face next, and I coughed from the drowning sensation.

I stopped laughing. I started kicking in earnest.

"Come on, Double-D. It's just a little water!"

His cackling laughter was muffled by the water, by the rush of blood over my eardrums, by the pounding in my chest, and the screams of anger clawing their way up from where I'd buried them for far too long.

The cry was coming. They were going to see it.

I wonder if Zack's eye is black? I hit him so very hard.

"Honey, everything all right in there?" I drop the towel on the floor at the sound of my mom's voice.

"Just cleaning out a strawberry from sliding today!" She'll buy the lie. She always does.

"That boy has been sitting in his truck in the driveway for a while now, so, uh, Dad went out to talk with him." That thought actual breaks through the noise in my head. The puckered smile on my lips feels good.

"He'll survive," I shout through the heavy rain that I let hit my face. With every drop of water, my eyes free themselves. The puffiness is disappearing; the redness will go away soon. This cry has come to its end.

I'm able to pull myself together with the aid of five more minutes of hot water, and after a half-assed attempt to scrunch my own hair into beachy waves, I rush downstairs to save Cannon from my father's company.

"Sorry, I had a lot more dirt than I realized," I lie as I slip into the passenger seat. I lean over the console to meet my dad's gaze through Cannon's window.

"Hey, Daddy." I smile at my father, everything from before neatly packed away where it belongs.

"Take it easy on him," my dad jokes. He pats the open window frame twice with his heavy hand, and I stifle my laugh because that's his way of warning Cannon that he could end him if he wanted to.

"Good night, sir."

My dad's expression as Cannon rolls up the window is priceless, his brow pulled in tight and his mouth twisted in a very distinct version of, "What the hell was that?"

"He intimidates you." I snuggle into my seat, glad to be dry and warm and clean.

"Yes. Very much," Cannon agrees without flinching.

For the short drive to Eight Lanes, I get to live in this little bliss. There's no need to pretend, no threat to my pride lurking around the corner.

Only, *there is.*

Cannon doesn't know Zack's joining us tonight. I can tell by the abrupt stop that sends me forward into the dash. I plant both my palms against it to stop myself. The jarring action is too much to keep my bliss in place.

"I'm gonna kill him," Cannon seethes. It's just a thing people say, but I think perhaps he means it.

"Please, Cannon." The sound of my hard breathing is strange to my ears. I'm struggling with this. It's too big this time. I feel Cannon's eyes on me but I force myself not to look into his until I'm in complete control of myself. I don't know that I could ever be fully prepared for all I see in his eyes when I finally do.

I'm not alone in this.

It isn't about baseball, or about his season or his brotherhood—hell, his family! It's about a wrong, and doing what's right. And I'm asking him to ignore that feeling in his own chest. I don't want him to. I don't want this to be anything. I want it to go away so I can win on the field. I'll do it that way, the only way it ever should be between me and any other teammate or competitor. Equal—*even.*

"What did he do, Hollis? You can trust me," he says.

"I know," I answer without hesitation. I grab his hand and squeeze it hard. My eyes focus on my grip, the way my veins bulge with the strength of my clasp on his hand. When I loosen my hold, he tightens his, and that small gesture breaks me just a little.

"It was just hazing," I begin, knowing in my gut that I'm starting out with a lie.

I shake my head.

"Tell me, Hollis. I promise you, I won't betray you."

His words are direct, and they cut deep. My dam breaks, and those tears I worked so hard to bury, the embers I put out in the shower, they come gushing out again.

Cannon pulls into the lot and drives to the opposite end, to an area where the lights don't fully glow. We're protected by the darkness and fully alone. He kills the motor, shifts in his seat and cups my face in both his hands, erasing the tears with his thumbs as fast as they fall.

"He hurt you."

I shake my head no, because he didn't really. None of them did. Not physically, other than some scrapes and bruises. Emotionally, though, yeah, Cannon is right. The only way forward is to share what happened, but the last time I did this, committees met, parents got together and made alliances and cast votes. My dad was out and we were on our way to Indiana.

Without pause, Cannon leans forward into me, pressing his lips on mine softly, as if sucking away my struggles and making them his own.

"Promise me you won't tell my dad," I say. It can't become his battle again. He's fought for me too many times. He's lost.

"I won't do anything you don't want me to." His words come out in soft kisses against me, whispers as he closes the space between us even more, ensuring our privacy.

I breathe deeply and let the silence settle in, looking down as I sit back because I think it's easier without staring into his perfect blue eyes. No more excuses at my disposal, no more fear of judgement. Just one more abusive, sexist, small-minded moment in an unfortunately long teenaged history of such moments.

"Jay and Roland picked me up first."

I swallow before continuing, feeling the weight of his eyes on me even though I'm not looking at them. I deliver the rest of the story—an event that lasted seven minutes at the most—with very few breaths. Once the words begin to flow, they don't stop, and details I made excuses for, like the way Zack pushed his knee into my thigh and lifted the bottom of my shirt to expose my stomach so he could see if the harsh spray tickled.

Are you ticklish, Double-D?

By the time I'm done with the story, I'm no longer crying. My breathing is normal, and my rage is under control. I've given the power to someone I trust, and he's struggling with it, his hands gripping the steering wheel as if wringing someone's neck.

"You promised you wouldn't say anything," I repeat.

"I did, and I won't." His voice is hoarse, that familiar anger I've felt so often brewing in his throat.

"We don't have to go in. We can just stay here, in the truck. Or somewhere else—"

"I don't know how you could stand to see him . . . any of them? Hollis, I don't know how you can do this. I'm not strong enough." He shakes his head in disbelief of it all.

"You don't have to be strong enough. I do." It's a simple fact, something I learned young and live every time I play the game I love.

His eyes close and his nostrils flare for a few deep breaths, a move I also recognize.

"You don't have to be nice to him," I relent, a give that makes him smile slightly on one side. I figured he wouldn't be able to keep his mouth shut with Zack, but it's everyone else who I don't want involved. Mostly, I don't want this to be my dad's obligation. Not again, however wrong that is for me to think.

Cannon glances up to his rearview mirror, scanning the lot for several quiet seconds, then finally cranks the key and shifts his focus to me.

"You sure you still want to be here?"

I contemplate my choices. I can go into that bowling alley and be with my friends and have a great night with a guy I'm falling for more every second he blinks, or I could let Zack win. I could go back home and sulk about all the things I'm missing out on. I could think about what happened today and how I reacted. I could replay it and think of all the ways it's coming at me again.

"I choose to live my life, and I want to be here with you. If Zack wants to go home, he's more than welcome."

I'm committed. Clearly, so is Cannon.

His eyes harden on his rearview mirror as he shifts into reverse. We fly backward in a straight line, and I test the tautness of my seat belt just in case.

"Hold on," Cannon says, and I should probably be afraid and tell him to slow down. Those words don't leave my lips, though, because I know exactly what comes next. And though I didn't ask for it, I want to let it happen.

I'm *going to* let it happen.

It's probably wrong.

I don't care.

We're maybe going twenty-five, tops, on impact. It's enough to completely crumple Zack's trunk and tear the bumper from his car. Cannon pulls forward just as quickly as he smashed into his cousin's car and whips around the parking lot, eyes scanning for witnesses. He finally comes to a stop in a spot near the front of the alley, close to the door—dozens of spots from the scene of the crime.

Is it a crime when it's family?

"I think I can keep my mouth shut now," he says.

A slow grin creeps into my cheeks. I unbuckle and lunge at him, wrapping my arms around his neck and shoulders and kissing him so hard he laughs a little at the force of it. Within seconds, he's kissing back, cradling me over the center console and running his fingers through what in my mind are the most awesome beachy waves.

"Thank you," I say when we break away. I make the awkward crawl back to my side of the truck, but before I step out, Cannon flips up the center console into the seatback, making a smooth bridge between us for the ride home.

"Huh. So, you're saying I could have done that, like, a while ago?" I quirk a brow, my energy still buzzing with adrenaline. I feel like a justified delinquent, and it feels amazing.

"I like watching you climb over the center." He shrugs, not one bit ashamed.

I hold on to that beautiful blue gaze while I slide the rest of the way out of the truck and close the door on his stare. We meet at the front of his truck, wearing matching smirks reserved for people who share epic secrets. Cannon slings his arm around me and holds his key fob up over his other shoulder, beeping his truck locked as we make our way inside the alley.

"Don't you want to check the damage to your truck?" I ask.

"I don't give a fuck."

I believe every word.

NINETEEN

CANNON

I want to punch him. His car is barely drivable, but that's not enough. I want to rip his perfectly combed hair from the roots of his scalp and feed him the clumps. He's a disgrace to our family, to our name, and I'm not going to let him get away with this.

I won't break Hollis's trust. I won't go to her father. But I *am* going to tell someone. And if this goes down the way it should, none of this will touch any of them and justice will get served. It's going to require some faith from me, though. And the things my father told me will need to be true.

Tory's the first to see us walk in, and his arrogant grin brings me out of my angry euphoria enough to interact with humans like something other than a Neanderthal.

"Look at you heeding my advice," he says, grabbing my hand and bringing me in for a bro-hug. Hollis slips into a seat between Lola and June, who quickly checks the size of her shoes, then rushes to the counter to swap them out for larger ones.

Hollis Taylor does not walk on dainty feet.

"Are you actually going to take full credit for me and Hollis?"

I quirk a brow at Tory, testing him. A breathy laugh shakes his chest while he pops a pretzel into his mouth. After chewing for a second, he says, "I sure am," then winks before punching my arm.

"Oh, I see how this is." I chuckle, sliding into the seat across from him and slipping off my shoes. He kicks over the pair he grabbed for me when I texted him from Hollis's driveway, then tosses a pretzel about a foot in the air, leaning his head back and catching it in his mouth.

I know his weak spot, though. Tory and I have hung out a lot, and he's told me enough that I have pieced together his secret.

"So, when are we all going to see Abby again?" He kicks the plastic of the chair between my legs with enough force that it cracks. My only response is laughter because I've hit a nerve. He's dating a soon-to-be mega star, and he's keeping it on the down-low because one, they aren't in the same country right now, and two, he's still terrified that something'll mess it up.

I get it, because I'm a little worried about that too.

The month is ending soon, thirty days that I've known Hollis. We're too new for something to mess us up so soon, but it's hard not to feel the threat when our biggest obstacle is cutting lasers into my chest with his eyes across the alley.

Zack was finishing up a pool game with Lucas when we walked in. I'm not sure whether Hollis saw him, but I did, catching his glare in my periphery. He stopped lining up his shot and straightened to watch us pass like some bully who thinks he owns a biker bar. Zack doesn't own shit. In fact, he hardly owns a car now, thanks to me and my short-wick temper.

The air gets cooler somehow when my cousin joins us. I feel him before I see him, and the ice in his stare is as frosty as I expected.

"Nice shiner," I say, my quip earning me a warning glance from my girl a few seats away.

I promised not to say anything about what he did to deserve it. Doesn't mean I can't comment on the obvious.

"Hardly feel it," he says back. That means it smarts like hell.

"I bet. You don't feel much." I yawn my words out and turn my body to create a physical barrier to end our conversation. Despite my literal cold shoulder, I feel him watching.

"There's too many of us, so who wants lane seven?" June asks, tapping her fingers on the computer.

Hollis stands, volunteering, and takes June by the hand, picking her alliance and moving to the chairs that give her the most distance from my cousin.

"But I wanted to make a little wager, Hollis," Zack teases. He must know she shared everything with me, because even though his taunting is directed at her, his eyes are on me.

"She'll just embarrass you," I say, unable to stop myself from defending her.

My retort must have crossed a line in our unwritten contract, though, because before I can make it worse, Hollis steps over my lap, letting her hand drag across my chest possessively as she passes.

"Oh, we can wager, Zack. I'm not afraid of you." Arms folded over her chest, she stops right in front of him, and I realize she isn't afraid of him at all; she hates how he made her feel. That he has the power to do that, period.

"Winner buys loser's beer at the party next weekend."

I open my mouth in protest—she's Coach's daughter and that's not a cool ask—but Hollis flashes an open palm behind her back to stop me.

"Fine." She pushes her hip out with an extra flair, her exposed thigh popping through her ripped up jeans. I never got this style before, but seeing it on her gives me a new perspective.

Zack is a decent bowler, so I'm a little conflicted about this wager. With everything that's happened, my mind immediately unravels his motive. Somehow, Hollis having alcohol will turn into a scandal.

She's already locked herself into this battle, one of many in her exhausting war. My only option without being *that* boyfriend is to stand by her side, so I hold my palms up and back away. I'll let this play out fair and square, and watch from over here on good ole lane seven.

"Zack's a prick, bro. How are you two related?" Tory asks, flipping the top shut on the pizza box and carrying it to the open seat near me. June went back to join Hollis, leaving my cousin surrounded by the girls while Lucas, Tory, Hayden and I take turns daring one another to find the most embarrassing way possible to push the ball down the lane. I have it in the bag with my repeat of Magic Mike, but then Lucas actually gets down on all fours and pushes the ball with nothing more than his nose, somehow rolling that sucker dead-center with enough speed that it knocks down every freaking pin.

We slap hands and celebrate his mini-victory, but while nothing is serious on lane seven, it's intense over on lane eight.

I keep tabs on Hollis's game, glad she's up with each consecutive frame but wishing that gap between her and my cousin would widen a little more. By the time it's down to the tenth frame, I'm too invested to care about finishing my own, and let Tory throw my last two balls. He earns me a whopping seven to bring my score to a non-brag-worthy ninety-six. If I were over on the other lane, I'd be battling Lola for last place. June is clearly wiping the floor with everyone, but those two scores in the middle—they are neck and neck.

Zack holds his hand over the blower on the ball return, his eyes flitting up to the scoreboard then back to the pins lined up in front of him. I can envision his brain working the math. If he bowls a strike, he can make things pretty tough.

I might not be able to help Hollis with her tenth frame, but I can do something to tilt this environment in her favor. While my cousin brings his ball into his hands, I reach forward and hook my finger in the belt loop of Hollis's jeans. She yelps with surprise, but lets me tug her toward me until she falls into my lap. I catch Zack's glare, so I push Hollis's hair over her shoulder and kiss the curve of her neck.

Most people would chalk up the look on his face to jealousy, but I know better. He feels betrayed. I picked her over him. He never thought I would sell him out like that, but then, I never imagined he'd assault a girl and demoralize her in front of two other teammates, so I guess touché. We ain't even, though. Not by a long shot.

That little wedge I drove into Zack's head works. His shoulders scrunch while he lines up his ball, and his footwork is sloppy from the start. When he ends up only knocking down four, he lets his emotions boil over, screaming, "Fuck!" so loud that families turn to look from several lanes away.

He's already blown it; he knows he has. He doesn't even wait for his ball to return but grabs the first one available and chucks it down the lane before the pins are reset. Hollis doesn't even need her turn, but she takes it, maybe a little to make my cousin watch and suffer while she finishes with a one-sixty-three, bettering him by twenty.

Zack pretends not to care while he pulls a slice of pizza from the box, tipping his head back and biting off the end. Hollis brushes her hands together, gloating because she earned it, and she stops on the other side of the high top that Zack is sitting at, pretending as if he isn't there.

"I like the hard lemonade shit," she says, peeking in the box but scrunching her nose at the pizza inside. My cousin doesn't react to her. He takes large bites of his slice, chewing methodically, his eyes focused on some commercial playing on the TV mounted on the wall. After a full minute of being ignored, Hollis slaps her hand down on the table. That gets his attention.

"I said I like hard lemonade," she repeats.

My cousin tosses his crust on top of the box, then brushes the grease from his fingers with a crumpled napkin. I expect him to walk away without responding. He doesn't necessarily need the last word in things, he just needs to leave a mark. I've been in enough arguments with the guy to know how he fights, and sometimes it's his refusal to engage, period, that drives me to my maddest. He's doing that to Hollis.

I'm not ready for his next move. Nobody is. That's why he makes it, casually flipping the full pitcher over so the bulk of the liquid splashes on Hollis's pants and onto her feet. I want to blacken his other eye so badly that I lunge at him. The only thing stopping me is the touch of my girl's wet, sticky hand gripping my forearm.

"Ooops," Zack says, no sign of the cousin I used to make future plans with in his dead eyes. He's let this animosity take over his soul. I mourn him.

He leaves his mess for us, backing away until he turns and pushes through the double doors that lead out into the lot. In about thirty seconds, he's going to see the smashed back end of his car. About a minute after that, he'll realize he can't open that trunk. And when he drives away from this place, he's going to see a whole lot of white paint on my massive rear bumper. Thing is, though, as spontaneous as it all was, I knew what I was doing.

Between my father and me, we've backed into some pretty heinous things, including a horse trailer in Santa Fe and a cactus somewhere outside Albuquerque. There are so many colors, dents and dings on the back of my truck that it looks like a painter's palette. The hitch also gives me a solid steel buffer that I'm sure punched a hole right through his sedan.

Deep down, my cousin will know it was me who rammed his car. He won't be able to prove it, and that will make him mad. That part is almost more satisfying than the impact was itself.

No matter, though, because by the time I'm done telling Uncle Joel about the moral and ethical lines his son has crossed, a hit and run at a bowling alley is going to feel like tee ball.

I'm the first to breakfast this morning. I'm never first on Saturdays, and already that has suspicions raised. I scared my Aunt Meg when I slid the stool across the tile floor, and she ended up turning around and throwing her spatula at me. She's used to about twenty more minutes of alone time in here, something I just realized she cherishes. She always hums when she cooks, and hearing it this morning while sipping on coffee that's mostly cream leaves me at peace with my decision.

I've already finished a plate of pancakes by the time my cousin careens down the stairs. I stare at him over the steaming mug in my hands, but he doesn't give me a single glance. I know I'm not transparent. It's killing him to keep his anger bottled inside and to avoid gaslighting me in front of his mom. He'll wait for Uncle Joel to join us. I'm waiting for Uncle Joel, too.

"Have you heard from your parents yet?" Meg takes my dirty plate from in front of me and smiles. In all of the drama I forgot that my parents are already on the road, my dad's second trip across country to get here.

"Not yet, but if my dad's driving, I'm sure they'll get here ahead of schedule." We both laugh at the truth. My dad has points on his license from speeding tickets, and I'm pretty sure he's banned from ever taking traffic school again. If he hasn't learned his lessons by now, he's hopeless in the eyes of the law.

"What's on your agenda today?" She loops her arm with Zack's, squeezing his bicep while he eats his breakfast at the counter, his back strategically to me. He stiffens at her touch, and the cold shoulder leads her to sag her arms and let her hand slip away.

"Someone hit the car. Jay's dad owns a garage though, so . . ." He turns his head enough to convey he knows exactly what happened.

"Oh, no! Does your dad know? We have insurance. Did the person leave a note?" My aunt's questions barrel out, and I take a longer than normal sip of my coffee in an effort to hide my smile. I feel a little guilty because in the heat of the moment I didn't consider that my aunt and uncle would be the ones paying for the damage. My uncle does make Zack work in the summer to help pay for things, though. That's my guilt loophole, and I take it.

"No note. Fucking coward," Zack says, shoveling the last of his pancake into his mouth. He rushed through breakfast to get out of here. *Good.*

My aunt smacks him lightly on the back of the neck for his swear, and he halfheartedly apologizes while dumping his plate in the sink. My cousin won't call me out for being his hit and run in front of my aunt. The information I have is a lot more damaging. And now that I let that notion simmer in my mind, I realize I'm going about this all wrong. It isn't my uncle I need to talk to; it's my aunt.

I'm patient, waiting for Zack to guzzle down his juice and rush out the door to drag his cracked-up car to Jay's house. When my uncle comes down and joins us for breakfast, I let him tell me what he knows about tryouts, what he's heard is on the agenda for Monday and Tuesday. I play along while he makes his own predictions, noting the way he always puts Zack in the starting catcher's job, reminding him of Hollis only once.

"Yeah, she'll make the team, I'm sure. I mean she has to, right?" He easily dismisses her talent, assuming daddy's girl is only there for one reason. Fury builds in my chest because of how clearly I now see it all. Hollis lives with this, and now that I see that double standard, I realize it exists everywhere.

My aunt clears the table and does the dishes all on her own. She works as an intake specialist for high end orders at a lumber yard six days a week, yet her weekend time is somehow not as sacred as my uncle's. My mom was always the one to take off for everything when I was little—when I got sick, when I had appointments, when I needed to go somewhere for travel baseball. My dad got to show up for the big things, be there for game time. Often his chair was ready and waiting for his ass to sit in it. When my mom was finally promoted to IT director at the financial company she works for, it was a big deal that she was a woman—the *first* woman. It took her eighteen years to move up to a salary my father got to in five. My uncle, my dad—they don't live the double standard on purpose. I don't think they see it because it's routine for them, but I bet there are times when my mom and my aunt do. I bet they'd like things to be easy just once.

I wait for my uncle to leave the room before I broach the subject with my Aunt Meg.

"What do you think of Hollis?" I'm not sure why this is how I break into this subject, but I know it's the right choice by the way my aunt settles her gaze on me as she finally sits at the table to drink her own damn cup of coffee in peace.

"She seems like a pretty strong girl." She stares at me over the top of her cup while she sips. She knows more than she lets on, she just doesn't dive head first into the drama. I can learn a lot from this woman.

"Yeah," I agree, hugging my now-empty cup between my hands while I lean forward across from her. I tap my fingers against the ceramic while I ride the mental teeter-totter of what to say next. Telling my aunt about her son's behavior puts the burden on her, something else I realize about this situation.

My struggle, though, is with what's right. What Hollis is enduring isn't. That much is certain, but am I taking the power away from her by starting this chain reaction? My aunt will confront my uncle. Together, they'll confront Zack. My cousin will blame me, and the issue will get tied up in this ugly knot that never leaves this house.

But I promised her I wouldn't tell her dad.

"You know, sometimes, Cannon . . ." My aunt busts into my circling thoughts and I glance up to find her knowing smile waiting, her tongue held between her teeth as she taps her own nails against her mug. "All a person needs is someone in their corner."

I breathe in her words and lean back, letting them settle around my busy mind. She doesn't know the full breadth of what happened. She would be deeply disappointed in her husband and son. I have a feeling she's heard enough of their bitching and complaining about what is and isn't fair to form a pretty solid picture, though. She's in Hollis's corner, and perhaps she's said things to Uncle Joel and to my cousin that can only truly be understood and relayed by a woman. I am in Hollis's corner, too. She *is* strong. And if the circumstances are right, she'll expose everyone for being who they are simply by being who she is. Maybe my job is to support her the way a man should. Lead by example, and let her shine.

I give my aunt a tight-lipped smile and stand from my seat, leaning forward to check the level of her coffee. I rinse my mug out and leave it on the counter, then grab the pot and top her off, kissing the top of her head while she gives my arm a squeeze.

I put the pot back and grab my keys from the counter, grabbing the hoodie I left hanging on the hook by the door.

"I got a corner to get to," I say over my shoulder. My aunt raises her cup and I smile. I text Hollis that I'm on my way to her house, and I tell her to bundle up. We've got some ziplines to explore.

TWENTY

HOLLIS

This abandoned park is definitely a different experience during the day. Unlike our trips across the canyon at dawn, this afternoon adventure offers clear views of exactly how far the drop is. I never thought I was afraid of heights, but maybe I just needed to meet the right circumstances.

I cling to Cannon for the first trip across, and barely loosen my grip on the way back. But now, on our fifth ride, I'm able to scope out everything below, including the icy stream that trickles across some gnarly logs and rocks.

"What's on this side?" I ask while Cannon unhooks us in preparation for our climb up the eastern pedestal.

He squints from the bright sun and clouds, scanning the thick woods, then shrugs.

"Don't know. Zack and I didn't explore this stuff."

"We should check it out." I clutch the front of his hoodie with my hand. I wore my knit gloves with the fingers cut out so I could grip better when I climbed.

The trip here was easier in Cannon's truck, and I haven't seen or heard a single vehicle in the area all morning, and we've been here an hour. While the young adventurer in my heart does like the idea of wandering around the woods to explore, the seventeen-year-old who has been holding on to Cannon's tight arms and broad chest wants to explore *other* things, maybe under a little extra cover of some wintered branches.

Cannon helps me out of my harness before kicking the straps away from his own legs. We climb down from the middle platform, jumping the last few feet onto the hard ground still dotted with blotches of ice and snow.

I can see my breath, but at this very moment, I am not cold. Not in the least.

"Come on," I say, grabbing his hand in mine and heading straight ahead through the thickest cluster of trees.

"Are you trying to get us lost?"

"Yes!" I reply.

He laughs as he tags along behind me, my pace rushed because all I can think about is how I'm going to feel when his hands are on me. I keep glancing backward, testing to see whether I can still spot the poles, the lines over the gulch, and Cannon's truck. I decide we're far enough when we get a quarter mile out and I spin on my heels, letting my body collide with his.

"Whoa!" He laughs, the fog from his mouth intermingling with mine.

I practically climb onto him, holding his sweatshirt in clutched fists while pulling him tight against me. Every first move is mine, the kiss hard and swift. My hands cover his and guide them under my three layers of shirts, up my sides and against my bare skin, letting go just below my breasts. My own hands roam across the ripples and valleys of his chest and sides, teasing the V that travels from his stomach into his joggers. Emboldened and heated to my core, I dip my hands lower, finding him hard and eager for my touch.

"Oh, fuck," he breathes out the moment my hand wraps fully around his erection.

I smile against his lips, loving the way I make them quiver. I love being in charge. I also am ready for him to take over.

"Just exploring the woods, huh?" Devilish laughter gurgles from his lips as he dips his chin and holds my gaze. His eyes are as hard as he is. His hood has slid from his head, and his mussy hair is soft and calling to me. I stroke him to encourage him and let him know I want this. I do it again, and he reacts, his fingers digging in more against my back, dropping lower until they slide under my waistband and grip my ass.

I let go of him and move my arms over his shoulders, my hands sliding into his thick hair just as he lifts me up; I wrap my legs around his body. In three steps, he has my back against a tree, and we are kissing so hard my lips feel raw from the friction and the cold. I don't care if I can't speak for a week. I need this, need him.

Now.

I tug at the bottom of his sweatshirt. In one fluid movement, I drop back to my feet and he lets go to free his arms and toss his shirts to the ground. His hard chest is smooth like a marble sculpture under my touch, his skin hot.

His eyes meet mine as his hands gather my sweatshirt and the two long-sleeved tees I have layered underneath. I nod and lift my chin, giving permission, and he pulls the clothing up and over my head, taking my knit cap off with it. My hair falls around my bare shoulders, strands blowing across my face in the slight breeze. Light spills through the thick branches, dead leaves still plastered to the ground from the melted and dried snow. There's a hint of wood burning in the air, a scent from someone's cabin perhaps. The thought of being caught out here with him excites me.

Cannon pulls me to him, kissing me and letting his teeth drag against my lower lip as his thumbs slide the straps of my bra down my shoulders. I wore the only pretty undergarment I own just so he could see me in it. I unclasp the hooks at my back and let the garment fall to the ground with the rest of our clothing as he pushes his head against mine so he can take in my bare breasts. The freezing air tightens my nipples into hard buds that ache for his touch. I arch instinctively as his hand glides up my spine, lifting my tits to encourage his mouth to taste them. He takes the hint, suckling one into a raw peak, his tongue swirling around the tip while I moan and lift one of my legs to hook around his hip.

In a swift, smooth movement, Cannon lifts me against him again, supporting my legs while I steady myself with my arms around his neck. His tongue draws lines like a map around my neck and jaw as he circles us so we're positioned to fall on our pile of clothes on the ground. He lowers to one knee before breaking our kiss and resting me on my back atop our sweatshirts. I pant wildly as he stands, straddling me, his erection so strained that it peeks out of the top of his boxers and pants.

"I have condoms," I admit, biting my lip and reaching into the back pocket of my jeans. I pull out two and hold them up.

Cannon takes the packets in his hand and holds my stare with a crooked smile.

"You're the one who brought condoms. Goddamn," he says, shaking his head with a breathy laugh.

I shrug, shivering and wanting his warmth on top of me stat.

"I'm a modern woman. What can I say?"

Truth is, I have an honest relationship with my mom, and she knows I have been sexually active. I got the talk in sixth grade, even though I was a virgin until I was sixteen. Condoms are things that are just purchased along with the rest of my feminine stuff.

My body clenches as Cannon slides his pants down his hips and his very large penis springs free. While he tears the packet open and rolls on the condom, I unbutton and unzip my jeans, lifting my hips to prepare myself for sliding them down my legs. Cannon stops me before I can, parting my legs and dropping to his knees. He covers my hands with his and stares at my bare stomach with his mouth hung open, hungry.

"Please let me do this. It's part of the fantasy I have lived for the last two nights."

"Only two?" I tease.

He smirks and briefly meets my gaze.

"Fine, three," he jokes.

I bite at my lip, mostly because I'm nervous and want to look sexy. I'm not afraid of the act; I'm afraid of the change that follows sex. I more than like Cannon, and he has the power to crush me if he wants to. All of the hazing and teasing in the world wouldn't compare to a broken heart from him.

As if he can hear my thoughts and worries, he bends down and draws my lips up with a soft kiss, whispering against them as he lifts my hips and drags my jeans and panties down my thighs.

"So, so beautiful," he says.

My eyelids flutter closed, the rush of cold mixing with my hot core as he says that tiny phrase over and over until I feel him push my pants completely free from my body. We're out here in nothing but thick socks, and it's oddly hot as fuck. Sitting back between my legs, Cannon brings my knees up, then runs his hand along my thighs until his thumbs press into my swollen center, sliding over the slick skin and sending shockwaves through my body that force me to rock uncontrollable with his touch.

"Oh, my God," I cry out, already feeling the threat of an orgasm.

I arch my back but open my eyes, wanting to see his face when he enters me. I feel his tip slide against my skin and both our mouths open in awe, our breaths held until he slowly pushes in, eyes locked on mine to make sure I'm okay, that I'm all in.

I stretch to fit him, the burn of his size subsiding into silk as he rocks into me. I cling to his back, my nails digging into his skin, leaving scratches along the hard surface of his thick muscles. We find our rhythm, his gentle movements growing faster and more urgent as he bends his head down, the tips of his hair tickling against my cheeks. I raise my chin until our lips meet, and we nibble at each other between pants and half-breaths.

My chest beads with moisture and I swear steam rises from our bodies. I lift my knees to hug him against me, wrapping my legs around him to hold him to me tight while he pushes into my very core, hitting places inside that threaten to break wide open with pleasure every time his hot skin passes against mine.

I let my arms fall above my head while he cradles me between his forearms and holds up his body weight to gaze into my eyes. The ground beneath my head is damp from the recent snow, and my hair sticks to sharp twigs poking out of the ground. But my body is protected, Cannon quick to shield my skin with his hands as we move together. He swells inside me when my own body climbs, and I encourage him by biting his earlobe, gently at first, then suckling it as his breathing becomes more feral, more urgent. Each rock of his hips gets hard, and his right hand sweeps behind my back to hold me up and protect me from the sharp ground as he slides me back an inch at a time with each pummel.

My own orgasm peaks and I grip him tightly, crying into his ear with a single word—*please!* It's enough to push him over the edge with me, and he pulses in me while my insides squeeze and shudder with pleasure.

He holds me close through every shiver, the nerves rolling from my shoulders down my chest and stomach and into my toes. I want to flatten our bodies together, to hold him here against me forever, to never let him leave the places where he is inside of me. And when the word slips out, I don't even care or feel vulnerable because it's mine to say when I feel like it, and I feel like it now.

"I love you," I breathe out, the sudden confession not jarring him visibly as his breathing slows to normal and he holds me close, rolling so I'm on top and his body takes the weight and the bluntness of the ground.

The chill hits my skin, but the harshness is erotic for now, my body still feeling satiated and teeming with excitement from what we did, where we are, and how I feel right this very moment. I lift my head enough to look him in the eyes and he tucks his chin into his chest as his gaze sweeps around my face, his hand pulling a leaf from my tangled hair as he laughs. The quake in his chest is like a warm fire on a winter day.

His fingers comb through my hair a few more times until the strands are smooth enough for him to curl around his fingers. His eyes follow the movement as my hair slips through his fingers like golden ribbons and he brings one curl to the tip of his nose, drawing in the scent as if he's trying to etch it into his memory. His focus slips from his own hands to my eyes as the strand slides free and falls back to the ground beside my face. His eyes soften and I tremble lightly, the breeze breaking through our lust and finally cutting into my skin. Sensing I'm cold, Cannon draws my arms into his protection, tucking most of my body within his before peppering my shoulder with kisses.

"There is not a single thing I don't love about you, Hollis. Not one single thing."

He rests his head flat against my chest, listening to my heart, maybe waiting for it to react. I'm glad he's there, because he can make sure I'm still alive. I'm pretty sure my heart stopped with his words. Stopped, then exploded. I will walk this world as a ghost from here on out, one who feels as though she can do anything. Reborn a little stronger, moving from warrior to queen. If I can own Cannon Jennings's heart, then there is nothing I can't claim. And I want it all.

TWENTY-ONE

CANNON

Tryouts are closed to parents, but that hasn't stopped my uncle from setting up in the parking lot. Everyone sees him. He's the only truck sitting so close to the field. From the outfield, I spot him holding binoculars to his eyes as we run by for our cool down. I bet he's proud and glowing right now. Zack had a decent day. He still wasn't as solid as Hollis behind the plate, though.

A week ago I might have let my uncle's presence change my mind from what I pledged to do today. But being with Hollis is a feeling I won't trade for all the family loyalty in the world, especially when I don't believe in the ideas my cousin and uncle preach.

Zack and I haven't spoken since Friday night at the bowling alley. He was conveniently gone for the weekend, probably spending the night at Jay's house. We both needed our space. It also let my parents arrive and get settled into the room I've been sleeping in while I slept alone in Zack's. I doubt I will be welcome in there after today, but I talked things out with my dad, and we agreed that a few days on the floor in their room was worth it while my parents nailed down a rental.

My dad went through the same emotions I did when I told him everything. We both believe that Uncle Joel would draw the line at what my cousin did, but while my dad wanted me to sit down and tell my uncle everything last night when we talked, I convinced him it would be better to give the power to Hollis. This is her story to control, and I will echo and preach her gospel all damn day, but only when she says so.

Giving things a little nudge, however, might be called for. I had a teacher in junior high who used this technique with us. She called it flushing out the bad seeds, which, upon reflection, was probably a harsh way to categorize thirteen-year-olds. But we had some real assholes in my school, including the Hayworth twins who ditched their last hour to steal bikes, then put them up for sale online the same day. She flushed them out by sitting everyone down and showing a slideshow of used bikes for sale, all posted within the last month. They needed a little extra heat, so she called the number posted on one of the ads. Lo and behold, Kale Hayworth's phone lit up like a restaurant buzzer. Their mini chop shop ended real fast.

I'm not going to put the screws on like Mrs. Reed did back then. But I am going to set up a community standard that won't tolerate the kinds of things Zack and Jay and Roland did on Friday. When that standard goes up, I have a feeling they'll out themselves.

"Alright, everyone, circle up!" Coach Taylor and his assistants stand around the mound while the sixty or so of us out here for tryouts all take a knee. I should probably listen harder than I am, but I can't stop mentally rehearsing everything I plan to say.

"We saw some good stuff out there today. Keep in mind, tomorrow is scrimmage day. You'll be broken up into six squads, and we'll be using all three fields. You'll get a text with your team tonight, and that's your only notification. You're all young adults now, so no excuses if you bring the wrong color shirt, don't have your cleats, forget your glove."

There's a murmur of laughter among us because we've all done at least one of those.

"Your moms and dads are not the ones trying out. *You* are. Which brings me to point number two. Please remind your parents, no matter who they are, that our tryouts are closed." Coach Taylor folds his arms around his clipboard and holds it to his chest, scanning the crowd but pausing pointedly on my cousin. Even his sunglasses can't mask that he's calling out my Uncle Joel.

"If anyone would like personal feedback about their performances today, please see me or any of the assistant coaches. Our ultimate goal is for you to achieve growth. We want to help you get better because we all can. Except me. I'm the best coach of all time." His joke gets bigger laughs this time. I'm mostly amused by the way his daughter rolls her eyes.

"Anything else?" He leans forward and looks down the line at his coaches, and I prepare myself. I get my hand in position to raise it high and clear my throat quietly so my words come out loud and clear.

"Gentlemen, any questions?"

I maybe should wait a beat before jetting my hand up in case anyone else has something to say, but it's too late now. My arm is already in the air.

"Jennings, shoot," Coach Taylor says.

I get to my feet and remind myself not to look at anyone in particular, especially not Hollis. I'm sure both she and my cousin are on high alert, though. Only one of them should be.

"I don't actually have a question, but more something I want to say, as a senior trying out this year, and as a new member of this school." My voice breaks a little and my heart pounds behind my ribs. I can throw fastballs in front of a crowd but I'm absolutely screwed when it comes to speaking in front of people. It's freaking cold out here, yet sweat is dripping down my spine.

"Go on." Coach shifts his posture, settling in with eager ears. Here goes nothing.

"Right, okay. Well, I'm a bit of a baseball nerd, I guess. My dad is always sending me these blog links to read about baseball psychology and team dynamics and all of that, and recently he sent me this story about character. It got me thinking about how important that is, maybe even more than skill, when it comes to a team's chemistry." I look down at some of the guys kneeling near me. Most of the faces are looking at me, and I'm relieved I haven't lost people yet.

"The article was about this team in Texas that had a serious problem with hazing." I haven't looked at Zack once, yet I know just from saying that word out loud—*hazing*—that his eyes are on me. I can feel the heat from them, and I welcome it.

"It got so bad that the rumors about players being pulled into bathrooms and pink bellied or held down and sprayed with water turned students off from playing any sport at that school, period. Colleges heard the stories and revoked scholarships. Finally, some of the star pitchers were expelled from the school because, and I'm quoting the reporter who spoke to law enforcement, 'Whether you call it hazing or not, at its core, the act is assault.' Basically, what the story says is it doesn't matter why it's done or when it's done or who you do it to. If you physically or mentally harm someone intentionally, you are an assailant. At that moment, you cease to be a ballplayer and you become a criminal."

I glance around the crowd and catch one or two yawns, but for the most part, eyes are wide and mouths shut.

"I heard something the other day that I didn't like. It made me feel ashamed to be here. And maybe it's only a rumor, but that's how things started at this other school too—with rumors. I decided I'd stand up today and pledge to act honorably, respectfully, and with character. I'd like to invite the rest of you to do the same. And not like in some ceremony or whatever, but maybe after Coach dismisses us. Let's shake on it. I'll promise you individually, and you do the same."

When I practiced this speech in the shower this morning, I kinda imagined the slow clap coming in right about now. My expectations probably make the silence feel more awkward than it is, but I'm still glad I said it all, every word.

"Thanks, Cannon. That displays leadership, and it's what I hope to see from all of you, especially the seniors," Coach says, nodding at me. Before he can continue his talk, though, my cousin's fragile ego takes over the space.

"Fucking bullshit," Zack utters. Whether it's poor timing that he said those words in a quiet lull or he just couldn't contain his aggression, all eyes are now on him. He's got the stage, but he is not the one I expected to stand up in this spotlight. I thought Hollis would call him out, but not until we are dismissed. Maybe he'll call himself out. He can make things right or he can drown—here and now—in his own bad choices. I kneel, letting him have his moment. I'd like to say I am rooting for him, but I'm not. I'm so damn ashamed of what he did and the person he's become that I'm not being the bigger person. I want him to fall apart. I want him to fail.

"What was that?" Coach Taylor's glasses are off, and there is no mistaking the direction of his stare.

"Nothing," Zack says, trying to erase the last ten seconds and literally eat his words.

"No, you had something to add, clearly. We all heard it. Go on." Coach takes a few steps and the freshmen on their knees in the front crawl out of his way. Nobody wants to get caught in crossfire.

A standoff is underway between Coach and my cousin, and for an uncomfortable and full minute, I worry neither will give in. Hollis's dad is clearly fine standing in that spot all night with his arms crossed and his heavy brow leveled at my cousin's head. Young and stupid, though, are two qualities that can be toxic when mixed, and my cousin is about to turn them into a back-firing grenade.

"I said it was bullshit," my cousin finally says.

"I believe you used the words *fucking* bullshit, in response to a speech about character. Please, elaborate." A few noticeable mumbles simmer around us. A few "Oh, my God's" and "Oh shits."

"Fine. I will. That speech was all just more *fucking bullshit.* My cousin doesn't believe that crap. I've played ball with him before, for years."

"Maybe I've grown," I speak up. I'm a little surprised myself, but now that I'm in it, I realize exactly how much my speech and that made-up story about a school means to me—how much my own character means to me. I'm going to defend it.

"Ha, sure. Whatever. Or maybe you're just in love." There's a collective gasp.

"Maybe you're threatened by a girl." My heart stops at the sound of her voice. This was my end goal, but suddenly I'm surprised to hear Hollis assert herself. I turn to find her standing several feet away, her arms folded over her chest, like her father's.

"Sweetheart, I'm not—"

"Sexist? Is that what you were going to follow that up with? Or do you call everybody sweetheart?" Hollis steps over a few of the guys and brushes against my chest as she passes me and jets straight toward Zack. They're toe-to-toe, and Jay and Roland are staring at the grass, too chicken shit to look her in the eyes.

"I'll go head-to-head with you anytime and win." Nobody else would notice the slight grit to my cousin's voice, but I hear it. I also see the way his jaw is working. He knows he's lying, but he's paddling for air, frantic to save face with desperate words followed by *more* desperate words. What's worse is his father is taking long strides behind him, crossing the football field on his way to see what's going down.

"Ha! I wish that were the case, but you can't handle a fair fight with me. You're too afraid you'll lose. You're so afraid that—"

"Are you still bent over that little fun we had with the field hose on Friday?" His snarky laughter stands out in the sudden quiet. Even the breeze stops, and with darkness coming on quick, the air is cold and sound travels. My uncle is plenty close enough to hear that. Zack obviously has no idea he's there, standing with about four rows of players between them.

Hollis steps in closer, turning four feet into two, then one, and eventually pushing at Zack's chest with her finger. "You held me down," she growls. "You belittled me in front of my teammates. *You made them participate!* I'm working my ass off, trying to earn respect, and at every turn you're there, trying to strip it away. That story your cousin told isn't bullshit. It's true. Only that assault didn't happen in Texas, did it Zack?"

My cousin looks down and to the side, rolling his eyes as if she's crazy and making things up.

"Roland? Jay?" I call out their names to offer them a chance to stand up for her. They keep their eyes on the ground, but their silence is validation enough.

"Zachery!" My uncle's voice booms over everything else, and my cousin spins on his heels, coming face-to-face with the man who should have been a better role model.

My chest squeezes with guilt I haven't felt until now. What maybe should have been a private moment is now very public. I don't feel as right about any of it as I thought I would, but I don't feel wrong, either.

Hollis stands her ground, not giving my cousin a place to turn so he's forced to face his father. Her own dad calls everyone's attention back to him. I remain in this limbo where I'm paying attention to everything and nothing all at once.

"I think maybe we need to add something to our tryouts this year. An interview," he says, and as I turn to face him, our eyes meet. "One about your character."

I swallow, worried that he's questioning mine after all this. It's so hard to decide what's right, and maybe I was on a crusade. Maybe I was in more than her corner with this; maybe I took up her whole damn room, siphoning the air and taking all the credit.

"Bring it in," Coach says. Everyone scrambles to their feet and moves to form a tight circle around him. Everyone but the three of us.

Leaving Zack alone with his dad, Hollis turns until she faces me. I'm speechless, my face a blank slate, probably the same as hers. I don't know if I let her down or lifted her up, but I do know I want to be a better person. I know she's the reason. Because of her, I'm not as selfish, or I try not to be. I'm less closed off, and more open to criticism and coaching. I'm a better player for sure, but a better human too. I've still got work though.

"One, two, three—Eagles!"

"Hollis." I say her name just as the cheer breaks behind me. She blinks twice, her expression never changing, then moves her focus to the dugout where her gear sits in a pile.

"Hey." I reach out toward her as she moves toward her things. When she brings her arms in close to avoid my touch, I feel a punch to my gut. I didn't do this right. I fucked this up.

I wallow in my own self-pity until my uncle marches back to his truck, leaving my cousin to swim in his alone. There won't be any lights coming on. Tryouts are done when the sun sets, and with the gray sky looming above, that's a little earlier tonight.

"Jennings." Both Zack and I turn at the sound of our name being called. Coach's form is barely visible in the dwindling light. He's alone, most of the players well on their way to the parking lot. His daughter is in the dugout under the yellow glow of lights that barely work. She looks furious, something I can read from her posture even this far away.

"Both of you," he begins, and we move closer to him.

My heart pounds in my chest, the rush of adrenaline from everything I've done and said, and the fear of being called out for something unexpected. Stronger than my fear of Coach, though, is my crushing dread that I messed things up with Hollis. That I broke her trust and told her secret. I'll run a thousand miles if that's what Coach asks me to do, if it means I might be able to make it up to her. My intent was good. She must know that.

"Sorry, Coach," I say right out of the gate. My cousin doesn't call me a kiss-up this time, and he's probably mad that I apologized first.

"Fix this." Coach wiggles his finger between us then points over his shoulder with his thumb toward Hollis.

"And you." He shifts his position, closing me off so he's speaking only to Zack. "I want you to look deep inside tonight and assess yourself. You have decisions to make."

Zack swallows loud enough that I hear it.

"Yes, sir," he says.

His eyes shift to me briefly. I can't apologize for giving him his due. He did that all on his own.

"Come ready to throw tomorrow." Coach's eyes square with mine and I nod, uttering the same, "Yes, sir" that my cousin did.

Coach Taylor turns his back on us and heads toward the back of the gym where his office is, whistling toward the dugout to let Hollis know to follow. My cousin leaves me standing there alone, too caught up in his own drama and misplaced rage to stick this out. I take every bit of my punishment, though, from her first steps from the dugout when the lights inside go out to the point where she reaches the walkway that splits in two directions. Hollis will either head toward me or her father's office, and I can't help but feel that the direction she chooses is a commentary on who makes her feel the safest.

I'm not totally surprised when it isn't me. Still, it hurts like hell.

TWENTY-TWO

HOLLIS

I've already cried my cry. I'm not doing it again. I'm not living it again. I did it and it's done. Every time my dad asks if I have anything he needs to know, though, the damn tears threaten to show their ugly side in the corners of my eyes.

"I need to know if I have to report something." His face is stern, and it's hard not to feel attacked. It isn't fair; I'm not the person who should be getting grilled about this.

"It's handled," I say, leveling him with another blank stare. We take turns blinking at one another as if it's a contest.

I don't know why it's our method, but it is. When I was a kid and did something wrong, my father would look at me, wordlessly, and blink through a long hard stare until I broke under the pressure and admitted to everything. As I got older, I learned the same trick worked on him, only I used it when he told me no for no good reason. Throw in a "Please, Daddy," and the world was mine.

"I hate this world for you. You know that, right?" He finally gives in and doesn't force me to make this into something bigger. Maybe it should be. What Zack did isn't okay, but I don't want to be the poster child. I just want to play baseball. That's it. If my face shows up in the newspaper, I want it to be for an All-Star bid or for some college that's taking a chance on a girl who can catch.

"I'll change it. This world will be just fine when I'm done."

He laughs at my confident response, but it's a sad laugh. It breaks down some of my bravado.

"I might be a little late here, you know," he says, holding up his scoring book filled with charts and notes he made from today's tryout. He flops it down on top of the four others from his assistants.

"I'll help," I say, putting my finger on the spiral binding of one of them. He pulls them away and gives me a sideways glance.

"I know, I know. Coach's daughter can't be involved. No showing favoritism. Just . . . tell me. What did Coach Dixon think of my sixty time?"

My father smirks and a genuine laugh finally slips out from his wind-burned lips.

"I don't have to read it to tell you he said you got a slow jump and need to work on breaking faster."

I pull in my brow, scowling at him.

"*You* said that. And I know." I sigh.

I sit back in the chair on the opposite side of his desk and put a foot up on the corner, near his mug that reads World's Best Coach. I gave him that in Little League and we all signed it. Most of the signatures have worn off, but I love that he still drinks out of it every single day.

"Are you just gonna stare at me while I go through these?" He's slipped on his reading glasses and asks me while glaring over the rims. It's funny to see him old, though he'd be quick to put me in my place.

"Nah," I say, leaning to the side and pulling out my pack of gum. I unwrap a piece and pop it in my mouth, then hold the pack out for him. He shakes his head.

"Suit yourself," I say, pushing it back into my right back pocket then shifting my weight to pull my phone out of my left. I prop my device up on my knee and open the meme app that always makes me laugh. It starts off with a bang with a video of a kitten on top of a record player, spinning.

"I think I'd rather you stare at me than make that sound," my dad says.

I glance up at him and snap my gum.

"What sound?"

He flattens his pencil on his desk and drops his head into his hands, pulling his glasses away so he can pinch the bridge of his nose.

"Sorry." I shrink into my seat and turn the volume down on my phone, then spit my barely broken in gum into the wastebasket at my side.

My father continues to stare at me, and I know it's because he feels guilty that I was somebody's target again. This is exactly what I didn't want. I don't want sympathy, I want change, but that is going to be slow, and probably not fully happen in my lifetime. But if I start something, if I inspire someone—a little version of me? Maybe my great granddaughter will be able to go out for whatever sport she wants and get the respect she deserves.

"You know there's a pretty decent guy hovering outside my door waiting to take you home, right?" My mouth drops because no, I didn't.

I look over my shoulder at the closed door with nothing but a slit window that's dirty and impossible to see through.

"He's texted me twice," my dad admits. He twists his own phone around to show me, pushing it forward on his desk with one finger so I can read it. It feels a little intrusive, but it doesn't stop me.

Coach, I am sorry if I caused problems today. If Hollis is still here, can you tell her I'm outside?

Coach, I'm still outside. Does Hollis need a ride home?

I don't realize I'm grinning until my dad calls me on it, covering the screen with his palm until I look up and feel it sting my face.

"He was trying to do right by you," my father says. He shrugs, then adds, "Be part of that change you want, you know?

I look down to my hands kneading in my lap and pick at the dry corners of my nails. I know he meant well, and the position I put him in, having to hold in a secret like that, was unfair. It's just that I'm so tired of the fight. Every time, with everything—*a fight.*

"Go on. If you stay here, you're going to get on my nerves."

I meet my dad's stare and it's earnest, and he isn't lying. I will drive him nuts for the next two hours. I'll also spend the time sitting here wondering if Cannon is going to text me, if he's still outside.

"See ya at home?" I lift my bag up over my shoulder.

My dad points at me.

"Promptly home. This is a school night." He puts his glasses back on but lets his glare linger for a second. I snort out a laugh, mostly because it gets under his skin. He just looks down at his work and waves me off.

All of the sureness in my decision fades away the second I step outside. I look to my left and my right, adjusting to the stark darkness outside.

"Cannon?" I whisper his name, testing the sound. The only response is a whistle of wind against my face. I drop my bag to pull out my heavy sweatshirt and pull it on, then tug my bag up on my arm and light my pathway with my phone.

"Cannon?" I call out louder this time, my chest tightening. I'm afraid. I'm scared because I'm a woman alone in the dark. I'm so mad that I have to feel this way, that I'm looking for someone I trust while fearing those I don't. Goddamn Zack for making me feel that way!

When my phone buzzes in my hand, I jump and flatten my back against the wall. I touch my screen to read the message, my pulse skipping for a good reason this time when I see Cannon's name.

Was that you? I'm still here.

I type back *Yes* and walk faster toward the parking lot.

"Hollis?" My name is called from around the building, so I rush toward the sound and round the corner, running into his chest, his arms swallowing me up. I'm crying on impact, and let it happen. It's not a bad cry this time. It's one born from relief, from happiness that he's still here.

"I'm so sorry. I only wanted to help, and—"

I shake my head and drop my bag at our feet, holding his face between my freezing palms so I can kiss him.

"Shut up," I demand. "I know. *I know.*"

As good as his kiss feels, it's his hug that makes a world of difference. Every misfire in my chest rights itself, my breaths even out, and my eyes focus on the soft sweatshirt and hard chest in front of me, around me, holding me.

Cannon is an ally. He is a voice different than mine but up for fighting my battles along with me. He's tender and honest and fearless. He gives me hope, and that's all I ask for. Hope, and the chance to catch for a pitcher like him.

"Let me take you home, Hollis Taylor from Indiana." His soft smile shines back at me. I rub my arm across my eyes to dry the tears and make room for the smile I mean with every bit of my soul.

There will be more to face tomorrow, questions from people who were there, accusations from Cannon's uncle, and poor excuses from Zack. It'll be ugly, and I wanted to spare everyone from that. But all I did was keep the negative for myself, take the abuse, and make myself small. I'm ready to live large again.

I thread my fingers through Cannon's while he hoists my bag up on his shoulder with a heavy groan. Catcher's gear is no joke, and he's used to nothing but a glove. It's about time I let someone else carry the load.

EPILOGUE

CANNON

When we first started this journey, there was snow on the ground. Never a lot, but it was there. Today, it's unseasonably warm—a balmy eighty-five with humidity crawling up and down my ass. How Hollis survives in that gear beats me, but we're literally one out away from going to state.

One.

I'm at eighty-one pitches. That means I can throw this guy eighteen and still be under my cap. God help me if I have to throw more than four, though. My arm is beat.

I'd like more than a one-run lead in my arsenal, especially now that the Henderson team seems to know what to do with my fastball, but I'm glad to have the edge. My dad has always told me that pressure is what makes the man on the mound. Well, if I'm not man enough after throwing up my orange Gatorade behind the dugout before this inning and still climbing back up on this rubber, I don't know what a man is.

"Come on, Can. You got this."

My dad's voice cuts through everyone else's and I manage to block the rest of the noise. We started this inning in the heart of their line-up, and the guy at the plate is the only one to have gotten a hit off me tonight. It was a dinger over the right field fence.

Breathe in through the nose, out through the mouth. Repeat.

My cousin taught me that trick when we were kids. I don't know if there's any truth to it, but he said it controls the heart rate and helps you clear your head. Maybe it's all voodoo bullshit he made up, but in baseball, whatever works is never considered weird. Hell, Hollis has worn the same socks for every game in the division playoffs—unwashed. If we make it to the state championship, her dad is going to make her ride on the roof of the bus, or at least put her socks in cargo.

"Hey!" Her muffled voice carries through her mask and she punches her mitt to get me focused. I wait for her sign, praying it isn't a fastball. My ego can't take another dinger. She gives me the slider sign, and I take another one of those deep breaths before bringing my glove in to my chest and winding up. I miss my mark, but Mr. Eager Homerun Hitter swings and misses.

"That's right, Can! Go right at him!"

This time, it's Zack's voice that breaks through. After all the shit we went through, somehow, we've mended a lot of broken trust. It took an entire season to get to where we are, and we still have a ways to go, but I credit Zack for making the first move. He marched into Coach's office the morning after he sent him home to think and told him to remove him from the potential roster for the season. In the back of his mind, maybe he thought Coach Taylor would go soft and tell him to stay, but he couldn't, not after everything he did. And not after a two-week suspension from school on top of it all.

At this point, baseball isn't healthy for Zack. At least, not competing. It's something he's slowly come to realize, thanks to therapy. That was his second move, an idea of his own. Being a fierce competitor who sometimes gets carried away isn't so bad when you're eight and weigh fifty-seven pounds. When you shave and weigh two-ten? Different story. Zack's anger issues were more than festering, they were exploding, and it'll take him a while to fully scratch the surface and see what's underneath. Competition, though, is a trigger. That much he's learned. But he seems to handle it all right when he's on the coaching side.

I went to Coach Taylor in mid-April, right before playoffs started, and with Hollis's blessing, asked if he could be team manager. Zack missed the camaraderie so much, and it never seemed fair that Jay and Roland got to skate by but he didn't. Hollis didn't call them out publicly, and neither did Zack. They accepted the free pass, and that's on their consciences. Every time they ask Hollis to forgive them, though, she says, "No." They get a taste of what they deserve.

Zack's worked his way back into some good grace, though I think he will always be held at arm's length by Hollis and her dad. My Uncle Joel was also pretty rocked by the realization that his son was willing to physically intimidate a girl just to get his way on the field. There was a lot of self-reckoning at the start of the season, and my uncle has learned enough over the last few months to know that he can't be here to watch while his son sits inside the dugout with a clipboard. This was never part of the dream.

Breathe in through the nose, out through the mouth. Repeat.

Hollis sets up for another slider and I take her sign, willing my arm to listen to her this time and throw the ball exactly where she wants it. I'm closer, but I still miss my location, and the little piece of the ball that the giant in the batter's box gets goes flying into the night sky and across the road that runs behind the clubhouse, slamming into the metal roof of someone's shed. I can't fathom the dents that must exist up there.

Eighty-three pitches thrown. One more, and I can be done. One more, and this guy goes home. *We* go home. I kiss Hollis. I get that offer from Vandy that I've been holding out for before committing to Cal Tech. Hollis is in Tennessee, at a small D-two that has no idea the bargain they got when they offered her a scholarship. I need to be in Tennessee so I can witness it happen—the moment she changes the world.

I'm no longer able to block out the noise. I can't focus on only my father, or coach, or Zack. It's all chaos ringing in my ears, my mental state too zapped to do more than focus on throwing a ball ninety feet right where Hollis wants it.

I shake my arms out at my sides and lean forward for her sign. She gives me a fastball and I shake her off. She looks down then over to her dad, and I take the time for one more round of voodoo.

Breathe in through the nose, out through the mouth. No time to repeat.

Hollis punches her mitt, and I read into the force she puts behind it. She's gonna call for a fastball, and if I shake her off, she'll call time and come talk to me. I just don't know if I can throw it to this guy.

She gives me the sign and I stare at it for a solid three seconds before giving in with a nod. I don't have faith in my arm, but for some reason, she does. If I've learned anything from four months of throwing to this woman, it's that she knows her shit, and when I don't listen, I get burned.

I bring the ball in and spare a glance at the hitter's eyes. He's squinting, and I'm not sure whether he can't see me or he's so amped with adrenaline that he's narrowed his vision down to nothing but the ball.

Hollis flashes her glove at the outside corner then sets up inside in an attempt to throw him off. I feel for the threads of the ball with my fingers, search for that perfect spot. There's one thread that's a millimeter thicker than the rest. I've located it before, and I swear it gives me an extra mile per hour on release. My index finger finds it and my lip ticks up.

Okay, buddy.

I wind up, trying hard to give nothing away, but grunt when I release the ball. I swear everything gets all movie magic-like the moment the ball leaves my hand. I hear music in my head and the ball seems to travel in slow-motion from my fingertips to Hollis's glove. The rotation is perfect, and my leg rotation is enough to send me down the mound and off to the left. I keep my glove up, ready for the big guy to zip the ball right back at me, and with the swing he's loading, if he does, it will knock out my teeth.

I flinch as his bat passes through the zone. When I hear the smack of the ball against Hollis's leather, I fall to the ground in exhausted disbelief.

The rush of cheering caves in on me as I blink up at the sky, letting my glove fall off my hand and the stupid grin eat up my face. Hollis falls on top of me first, her mask tossed off somewhere along the way.

"That's what I'm talking about!" She's screaming in my ear, and it's glorious. I poke at her sides and she pokes back until more of our teammates pile on. We're suddenly children, wallowing and kicking in the dirt and grass because we won a plastic trophy that will sit in a glass case for fifty years. It's a big-ass plastic trophy, though, and that's worth it.

I finally get to my feet and rush over to my cousin, lifting him in a bear hug as he pounds on my head with excitement.

"Yeah!" He growls as I set him down and we bump chests. Having him here for this, still, despite everything, hits me hard, and I hug him a second time. Tighter.

"I'm so proud of you," he says, his mouth at my ear. "So fucking proud."

And happy tears break free.

His heavy hand pats my back as we rock, and then he hands me off to Coach who is as big a cry baby about this as I am. In fact, a quick look around the celebration and I realize Hollis is the only one of us with dry eyes. So much for stereotypes.

When the division president walks out from the dugout with our trophy in hand, we settle down, each of us taking a knee despite the fact we want to keep jumping and screaming until our voices are gone.

"Coach Travis Taylor," the man says, holding the trophy on one side while Coach holds the other. Flashes go off for the photo op while parents and students whistle and clap. "On behalf of District Twelve in the great state of Indiana, our congratulations to the Allensville Public Fighting

Eagles for winning this season's district championship tournament. Represent us well at State."

Our roar breaks through before he can finish his words. He shakes our coach's hand, and takes a step back so Coach Taylor can hold that pretty award high above his head.

"You did this! Lady, gentlemen." We all laugh because it's maybe the first time he's gotten Hollis's request right.

The moment is amazing all on its own, and would be enough if it ended here. But then something unexpected trumps everything else.

"Hol-lis. Hol-lis. Hol-lis."

Zack starts the chant, clapping with her name, encouraging others to join in. That one-run lead we had came off her bat. She drove in two, and those runs were the only ones we scored all night. I may have thrown well, but even that is thanks to her. This game? This series? It's her win as much as it is ours.

"Hol-lis! Hol-lis! Hol-lis!"

We're all doing it now, clapping loudly and turning her cheeks cherry red. Her dad walks toward her with the trophy in hand and urges her to her feet. She's bashful about it, but I know at her core, she's also eating up the moment. Inside that body lives a tiger.

As soon as she takes the trophy from her dad, our howling becomes deafening. We're on our feet in a second, and Miguel, our shortstop, and I raise Hollis up on our shoulders. I watch his hands because as proud as I am of her, I'm also a jealous boyfriend. I'll take over her full weight and run her ass out into the parking lot if he makes a move.

Miguel keeps his hands in check, though, and Hollis wears a smile that dents her cheeks with dimples so deep I think they may never get erased. Her brother begs for the trophy at her father's side, so we finally let her down and Coach Taylor takes over possession, keeping guard on the prize while everyone alternates taking pictures with it.

The only prize I care about is still in my arms.

"You know the Vandy guy came, right?" She puckers her lips into a controlled smile while I nod, swaying her in my arms while we stand apart from the crowd.

"Uh huh." I'd actually managed to keep that thought under control for that last batter, and it's a good thing I did. If I let that thought enter my domain, I probably would have sailed my first pitch into the dugout.

"I have a good feeling," she says, leaning into me until our foreheads touch.

I let my hands fall to her hips and close my eyes to protect this moment and keep this small space between only us.

"I've had a good feeling since midnight on January first," I say.

"Oh, is that right?" she asks.

"*Mmm*. It is."

"Still, though. Vandy." She lets my dream linger in the air as a wish.

"I have a good feeling, too," I finally admit. "My gut instinct has very little to do with tonight's game, though."

She pulls back enough to show me her quirked brow.

I tuck her hair behind her ear, knowing she'll tie it in a knot the first chance she gets.

"There can be no Hollis Taylor of Tennessee without a Cannon Jennings in the same area code."

My stupid joke earns a beautiful smile, and we seal it with a kiss before joining our family and teammates and friends for what promises to be a long night of celebration. That wish will have to linger a little while longer, but I'm no longer worried about it coming true.

What Hollis says goes, and if it doesn't, she'll bend it to her will.

She's a game-changer.

SERIES EPILOGUE

LUCAS FULLER

Whoever thinks being smart must equate to being good at giving speeches clearly never heard my attempts.

Writing my graduation speech was easy. I knocked that sucker out in forty minutes. It's just one big trope when you think about it. *The future is waiting. It's yours to take. We all will change, yet stay the same . . . blah . . . blah . . . blah.* Saying it in front of six hundred people, however, is a whole different ball game.

And Tory will not quit bagging on me about it.

"Don't forget to take your change, I mean make change, I mean accept change, or I'm changing. I change, you change, we all change! *Weee!*" He's really latched on to the theme, which I blundered and completely blew, forgetting two lines then going back to them later, awkwardly.

I punch his arm hard enough to make him spill a little beer in his lap.

"Hey!"

"You done now?" I glare at him and he brings his mug close to his chest, hugging it with both hands.

"Ch-ch-ch-changes." He gets out one more, but thankfully Abby made it back in time for graduation and is there to smack him on the back of the neck for me.

"Thank you," I say to her, crossing behind her and kissing the top of her head.

It's after hours at Eight Lanes. Well, technically, it's closed. But June still has a key, and her former boss pretty much thinks she walks on water, so we moved the party here. We all chipped in forty bucks to pay for the beer we plan to drink tonight because we don't want to steal. But we do aim to get lit. Hayden and Lola volunteered to play sober, so we'll make it home in decent shape.

I can't believe after tonight, half our crew will be gone. It still doesn't feel real, even though in less than twelve hours, it's happening.

Cannon and Hollis are the first to go, and I think the only reason they're partying it up tonight is because they know they have a thirty-one-hour bus ride to look forward to when they wake up. I love football, but man, there's no sport on the planet I find important enough to ride on a bus for that long. They're going to Cali for a summer baseball league before making that same awful trip back in August so Cannon can report to fall camp for Vanderbilt. It's too bad that Central Metropolitan doesn't get to play Vandy just for one exhibition. I'd love to see those two go head-to-head on the field. June and I plan to go watch a few of their games in Cali, a last-hurrah trip before we pack up and move in together in Boston.

I'm surprised her mom went for it, but when June got accepted at the last minute to Boston College, one of the best ways to cut costs was for the both of us to split a bedroom in a two-bedroom apartment. Our roommates are a gay couple who have lived in the place for two years, and after a few video chats to make sure we all gel, June and I decided they are the same exact personalities as us. Conner is June, for sure, and Dax is me, to the point he and I have already made plans to host the fantasy football draft for the league we're starting in the fall.

I have a damn good feeling about life there—*life with June in general.* But one step at a time. We both come from broken marriages, so taking the long route to forever gets us there all the same.

Lola, Hayden and Naomi are leaving next week for Europe. I guess that's what I get for opting out of my last year of Spanish. They both stuck with it and get to go on an immersion trip to Spain for three weeks. It'll also cancel their language requirement for their undergrad without having to test out of it. I'm going to have to spend my summer on a refresher crash course so I pass when I get to MIT. My brain only has room for so much, and with the math I'm looking to face, language classes are out.

At least Tory and Abby will be around for most of the summer, though I can tell they're anxious to get to Chicago permanently. They've driven there at least six times in the last month for theater auditions, registration, and freaking deep-dish.

I'm a little lost in the nostalgia when June crawls into my lap, but she has a way of bringing me back to the present. She's home, and as I look around at my group of friends, I realize in so many senses of the word, we are all home to one another.

We've taken over one of the pool tables because lighting up the lanes makes this place look way too open. Tonight is all about us, our final time together, and we don't want outsiders busting in.

"Ladies and gents! A toast!" Tory announces.

June hands me a ten spot without looking over her shoulder because I won our bet for who would be the first person to stand on the table. It's always D'Angelo—always *this* D'Angelo.

Properly beered up, we each raise a glass, holding our amber-filled mugs high and proud.

"To ups and downs, and forever friends. Allensville will never look the same without us. In fact, someone might say that this place is going to *change.*" I lean my head back and close my eyes while I groan. He is literally *never* going to stop making fun of me.

"Cheers!" June says, doing what she does best by putting the focus on the positive.

"Cheers!" The sound of our collective voices imprints in my mind and I immediately tell myself to hold on to it. To this moment.

We're scattering. It's inevitable. But we'll all still have this place in time. We'll always have *us,* and that was the point of my speech. Change happens regardless of how hard you hold on—to people, to places—and want to keep them the same. But life isn't about the place or the time—it's the friendships. And when you change together with those you love, you can always find your way back.

THE END

ACKNOWLEDGMENTS

It's always bittersweet coming to an end. I have loved every inch of this series. These characters have floated around my imagination, in some form or another, for quite a while. The series was born when I started to realize how these interesting people fit together. These are friends—lifelong-type of friends. I hope you have enjoyed spending time in their lives as much as I have.

These books have also been a wonderful escape for me. I think we can all agree that this year—the *Pandemic* one—has been a load of crap. I could not have gotten to this finish line without the help of a lot of people. This starts first and foremost with my boys. Tim and Carter, you are my air and life. I love you. Tina Scott, I love you and hit the lottery in the mom department. Mariah Dietz and Jennie Marts – thank you for the sprints! Alyson Santos, you genius with words you, thank you for being an amazing critique partner and for working with my weird-ass schedule and process this go-round. My betas, Jen, TeriLyn and Shelley, you are the masters of my weird-ass process and the fact that you are still willing to open my emails means so much to me! Thank you for every ounce of your time. I'm so grateful. Autumn – you know you complete me. Sometimes, you complete me in places I didn't even realize I was missing things lol! (Autumn keeps me from being a mess.) Michelle Lancaster, my God, woman—you are a talent behind the lens. I have wanted to use one of your photos for a cover for a long time, and I feel like this was that perfect moment. Andy Murray, you were the perfect muse for Cannon's spirit. Thank you both for being YOU!

Lastly, and not even close to least, Brenda Letendre . . . you single-handedly carried my limping self across this finish line. You are more than an editor; you are a true friend. You helped me move life's mountains out of the way to get this book to you and to readers, and I will be forever grateful.

If you liked this book and/or series, please don't be shy about it. I wanna hear. More than that, I would be so grateful if you would tell others. Reviews are life for us authors, but so are things like recommendations in person or on websites, posts on social media, mentions and tags and creative awesome-sauce that readers come up with. The Varsity Series finds the readers it's meant to because of readers like you, because you are the most amazing readers in the entire world. I can't thank you enough for your support. We've come to this finish line, but that means I'm at the starting gates again, and I can't wait to give you more.

XO
Ginger

GINGER SCOTT'S COMPLETE BACKLIST AND SERIES READING ORDER:

The Fuel Series

Shift

Wreck

Burn

The Varsity Series

Varsity Heartbreaker

Varsity Tiebreaker

Varsity Rule breaker

Varsity Captain

The Waiting Series

Waiting on the Sidelines

Going Long

The Hail Mary

Like Us Duet

A Boy Like You

A Girl Like Me

The Falling Series

This Is Falling

You And Everything After

The Girl I Was Before

In Your Dreams

The Harper Boys

Wild Reckless

Wicked Restless

Standalone Reads

Candy Colored Sky

Cowboy Villain Damsel Duel

Drummer Girl

BRED

Cry Baby

The Hard Count

Memphis

Hold My Breath

Blindness

How We Deal With Gravity

ABOUT THE AUTHOR

Ginger Scott is a *USA Today*, *Wall Street Journal* and Amazon-bestselling author from Peoria, Arizona. She has also been nominated for the Goodreads Choice and RWA Rita Awards. She is the author of several young and new adult romances, including bestsellers Cry Baby, The Hard Count, A Boy Like You, This Is Falling and Wild Reckless.

A sucker for a good romance, Ginger's other passion is sports, and she often blends the two in her stories. When she's not writing, the odds are high that she's somewhere near a baseball diamond, either watching her son swing for the fences or cheering on her favorite baseball team, the Arizona Diamondbacks. Ginger lives in Arizona and is married to her college sweetheart whom she met at ASU (fork 'em, Devils).

FIND GINGER ONLINE: www.littlemisswrite.com

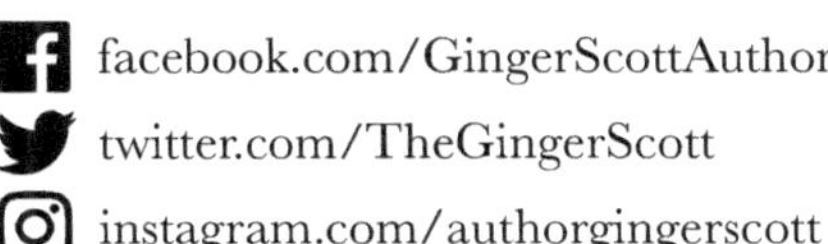

www.ingramcontent.com/pod-product-compliance
Lightning Source LLC
LaVergne TN
LVHW020052110826
845155LV00022B/71